TALES OF IAIRIA

SHARDS OF DESTINY

by

Tyler Tullis

authorHOUSE™

1663 LIBERTY DRIVE, SUITE 200
BLOOMINGTON, INDIANA 47403
(800) 839-8640
WWW.AUTHORHOUSE.COM

First published by AuthorHouse 01/16/06

ISBN: 1-4259-0042-9 (sc)

Library of Congress Control Number: 2005910258

Printed in the United States of America
Bloomington, Indiana

This book is printed on acid-free paper.

Cover art created by Ron Hausske and Danny Watkins

*For my friends who, whether they know it or not, gave me
the strength and creativity to do this*

KAP, Princess, Male-Man, Horsy, Schlitz, Britches,
T-Rev, Cinderella, Partypaloza, Hanson, Red Scare,
and everyone else

Thanks for always being there

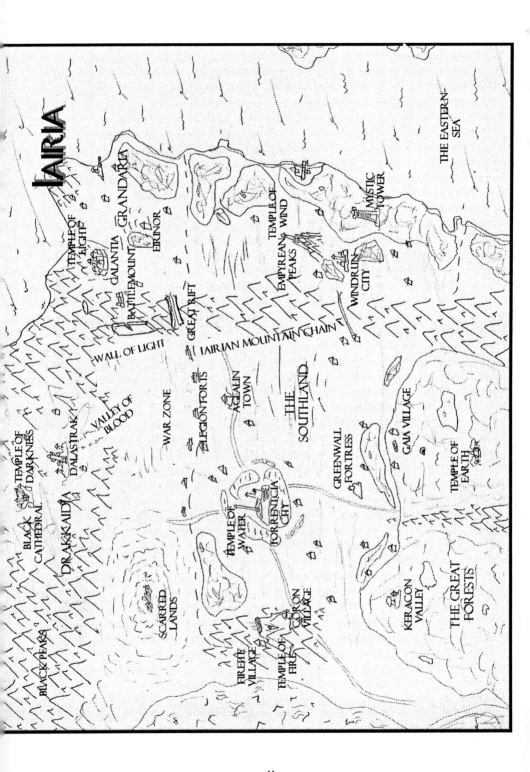

Prologue

<u>The Legend of the Holy Emerald</u>

During the ages of the old world in the land of Iairia, countless legends came to exist that shroud this period before written history. In the great Mystic Tower, these legends are catalogued in vast libraries courtesy of the Mystic Sages. Deep within the texts of the libraries, there tells of an ultimate power that can harness all six of the elemental energies found throughout all matter in the universe. This was the sacred Holy Emerald. Because this all-powerful talisman could control all the elemental power of the world together, it was capable of unleashing the one, true, raw power of all things. The legend tells that the Holy Emerald was kept in a green river valley under the protection of Granis, the righteous God of Light. There it lay dormant in an aureate shrine, its powers fueling the elements across the lands of the world.

But such power was not unnoticed by he who sought to use it for his own purposes. The God of Darkness and Granis' opposite, Drakkan, started the Battle of the Gods to seize the sacred emerald for himself. During the mass chaos that ensued in the seemingly eternal battle of good versus evil, Drakkan managed to steal the Holy Emerald. The magical stone would not avail him, however, for he was still defeated before its full power could be summoned forth. After the battle and Drakkan's banishment to the Netherworld below, Granis knew that the Holy Emerald's true ultimate strength had been brought to bear, granting any who held it the most potent power in the universe. Granis saw this power as too much of a temptation for men, so he decided to destroy the talisman. He shattered the Holy Emerald into six shards, one for each element, and spread them across the lands of Iairia. Its powers would remain intact, but not active until all the shards were reunited as one.

The prophecy tells that if the shards were ever assembled together by man, that man would be endowed with the ultimate, limitless power of the Holy Emerald. The only people aware of this legend are the few remaining Mystic Sages of the Southland, the Supreme Granisian and his priests in Grandaria, and the Black Church of Drakkan in the far northwest lands of Drakkaidia. The various shards' locations, however, have safely remained a mystery over the eons they have lain dormant, existing now as only a memory of a distant and forgotten legend.

Part One
A Time of Prophesy

Chapter 1

<u>Boys of Eirinor</u>

It was a brisk autumn morning as Tavinious Tieloc gazed out at the rolling green Hills of Eirinor in the center of Grandaria. This particular morning, however, they were not as blissfully green as usual. A battalion of armor clad Grandarian troops had been stationed there for the better part of six months training for battle. Finally, after nearly an hour of waiting and watching from the patient young Grandarian boy on the hillside, the sun at last began to creep over the hills to the east and cast its fervent light glittering across the seemingly endless rows of ornately decorated armor, sparkling gold and silver. With the intense glare off the shining attire, Tavinious was forced to squint his deep blue eyes to maintain contact with the gleaming spectacle. As he continued to look on the shimmering fields, a faint morning breeze rustled past him, waving his thick brown hair back and forth like the undulating grass before him.

Tavinious, or Tavin to his friends and family, watched in deep remorse and a profound sense of helplessness as the units of soldiers began to march over the hills and away from his village. He wished more than anything that he could be going with them; seeing action, adventure, and the chance to defend his golden land against the constant threat of its eternal enemy to the west, Drakkaidia. Tavin's father, Darein Tieloc, was a seasoned drill master in the Grandarian army- one that all new recruits trained with at one point or another. In fact, Tavin's family had always been a part of the Grandarian military or government in some way. The first fabled Warrior of Light, who commanded an enchanted sword with the essence of the God of Light, Lord Granis himself, was a Tieloc. Ages ago he had cast down the wanton Warrior of Darkness to save Grandaria and all the lands of Iairia from his wicked power and hordes of savage warriors. This legend had made the Tielocs a very important figurehead in Grandarian society, and the soldiers under Darein Tieloc held him in the highest of respect accordingly.

Every year Tavin's father would march a battalion of troops from Grandaria's gleaming capital city of Galantia in the north to the central secluded Hills of Eirinor for basic combat training, and every year for as long as he could remember, Tavin had been alongside them training at his own pace. While most soldiers were required to experience at least two years of such training to be admitted into the ranks of regular foot soldiers, Tavin had gone through about ten. Thanks to the inherent skill passed through his family, there was nothing he enjoyed more. Though only at the age of nineteen, he could easily best most soldiers with the sword, and could outsmart the bulk of them in a wide variety of combat, practically making him a living legend among the soldiers who passed through the training grounds. Tavin clenched his fists. This fact made it all the harder for him to stay behind again; knowing that he was a great deal stronger and smarter than most of them now marching into the horizon. According to Grandarian law however, the earliest a man could become a soldier was when he formally became a man, at the age of twenty-two. He was ready now, he thought.

Even back in his childhood, Tavin had always been a courageous boy with a strong sense of determination and an iron will not commonly found in such young men as he. After mere minutes of speaking with him, it was not difficult to tell he was much more than the average adolescent with aspirations for excitement and adventure. He had always been devoted to supporting his friends, family, and nation in any way he could; constantly willing to drop whatever he was doing to lend a helping hand. This unmatched purity distinctly set him apart from his peers. While he remained a calm and carefree young man in his daily demeanor, Tavin had always been prone to volatility at the sight of injustice being done unto others. Boasting such a gallant persona, it was no great wonder the boy became a well known and well liked personality all over the Hills of Eirinor and for those who knew him in the golden city of Galantia, where he frequently journeyed with his father on military business.

As Tavin sullenly watched the battalion march into the distance, the silhouette of another figure approaching from behind drew his attention. He didn't have to turn around to know who it was.

"So ends another season of training, huh?" the figure sighed dramatically. Tavin took a deep breath, exhaling slowly.

"Yeah…" he replied lamely as the figure stepped into view. It was of course Tavin's best friend, Jaren Garrinal. It had become a tradition for the two to see the troops off on that hillside every year. Though it was never a welcome feeling to be left behind, Tavin and Jaren were always there without fail.

"Sorry I'm late," Jaren began sarcastically, "but you know how much I love to get up this early in the morning." A faint smile crept across Tavin's face as he silently chuckled to himself.

"You do seem to end up here last every year. But then I don't have to sneak out of my house to get where I need to go, do I?" Tavin mentioned, shooting a quick glace at his friend from the corner of his eye. Jaren returned Tavin's glance with a full frontal glare.

"Well maybe if *some* people didn't go and get *other* people punished for things they didn't mean to do, I would have a little more freedom!" he snapped. Tavin rolled his eyes.

"Well maybe if *some* people had enough sense to take a little aim before they fired an arrow into their own house and impaled one of their own walls, they wouldn't *be* in trouble." Jaren turned and blasted his response right into Tavin's face.

"Don't even try to push that on me! You told me I was all clear!"

"How could I possibly have known you could shoot that far? Seems like your range increases every time you pick up a bow." Jaren cooled off a little in the silence that followed.

"I'll take that as a complement," he managed eventually, folding his arms. Either from all his training alongside the Tielocs or by some miraculous gift that he was born with, Jaren was one of the best shots with a bow in the Hills of Eirinor- an incredible accomplishment for one only nineteen years of age. Coupled with Tavin's prowess with the blade, the two were (and had been for some time) a powerful team that few could manage to best in any way. Having grown up with each other since they were infants, they shared remarkably similar personality traits and goals in their lives. The two

5

knew each other inside out and had for so long, that they could and would both frequently claim to know what the other was thinking. The ironic thing was that they usually did.

Despite being so close, they had always been very different as well. Compared to Tavin, Jaren was always blunt and forward. Not afraid of anything or anyone, his overly confident and often cocky attitude frequently got him into trouble. Not as patient as his friend, Jaren quickly adopted a much more headstrong personality. Because of these contrasting points, they were also each others biggest rivals.

As they watched the last units of troops march over the hills, Tavin fell back into his melancholy state.

"Someday that'll be us, Jaren. We'll be out there seeing the world, having adventure, and beating the Draks. I swear I'll be out there with them someday." The words were full of the meaning and unflagging resolve that Jaren had become accustomed to hearing from his friend. As Tavin stared out at the horizon, he gripped something in his right hand. Jaren glanced down.

"Oh for the love of Granis, Tavin. You still have that thing? I thought you'd lost it by now." Tavin broke his view off from the hills and set his eyes upon the brilliant white crystal in his hand, the lucky charm he had possessed since childhood. He smiled.

"Are you kidding me? I've had this thing forever. I'd never get rid of it." Jaren shrugged.

"Whatever. Well, I think that's enough inspirational conversation for one morning, don't you?" he joked. "Come on, let's get back to the village before I'm missed and punished for another month." Tavin nodded. As Jaren began to stroll back the way he had come, Tavin glanced back at the rolling green hills in the distance, just as the last soldier disappeared over the ridge.

With nothing left to see, he turned and sauntered back over the hill toward the small Village of Eirinor. It instantly felt deserted now that the soldiers that had been occupying it for the past months were gone. Like many small villages on the outskirts of the Grandarian nation, it was a quiet community that lay unnoticed by the rest of the world except for the frequent travelers on their way to Galantia farther north. As Tavin caught up with Jaren, they decided to head over to the inn that doubled as the town's tavern for breakfast, passing by the Tieloc household on their way. Despite their sincerest efforts to sneak by unnoticed, they caught the attention of Darein Tieloc, sitting inside munching on something with his wife. He leaned out an open window, catching them by surprise.

"Why good morning, gentlemen." The two jumped and wheeled around to find Tavin's father smiling at them. "I see we've been off to the hillside to do our yearly moping," he tantalized. The two boys did not return the senior Tieloc's smile. "Now where are you off to? Not to fire an arrow into the Garrinal household, or for that matter, mine I hope?" While Jaren could only painfully smile in aggravation, Tavin began to laugh hysterically at his friend's misfortune.

"Really funny, Tavin," said Jaren, his voice laced with scorn. A slight smile appeared on his face. "I guess we'll see how funny it is when I beat you to breakfast!" he shouted, sprinting away as fast as he could. Tavin was after him instantly with determination racing through his body, never willing to pass up a challenge from Jaren.

"You cheating Drak! You got a head start! Get back here!" Tavin yelled after him, already spinning past the corner of his house nearly out of control. Darein Tieloc simply grinned as he watched his son race after his best friend toward the inn. He turned back to take a seat next to his wife, who stared at him with a tickled look.

"Kids," he said, taking a bite of bread with a smile.

Chapter 2

<u>Man in Gray</u>

After Jaren unjustly won the race to the inn that morning, the rest of the day proceeded casually. Tavin went about his daily chores for his father, stopping only to eat and take a walk with Jaren toward noon as they frequently did to pass the time on this cheerless day of the year. As the afternoon's rolling blue skies turned heavy auburn in the settling evening air, a hush befell the small village. The first few days without the hundreds of soldiers occupying the tavern and roaming the streets of Eirinor were always especially quiet. The village was actually quite small. The only reason it was used for the training of hundreds of Grandarian troops was because of the expansive fields outside the community.

The village itself was nestled in its own private valley surrounded by thick trees around the perimeter. It was just big enough to sustain about a hundred regular occupants comfortably. The economy relied on its peoples' skills with agriculture and the logging of the small forest to the north. It was a friendly community where everyone knew everyone, though it frequently received visitors on their way to and from the capital. Tavin would spend a majority of his nights in the tavern listening to passing travelers' tales of world events. He found it particularly enjoyable to eavesdrop on conversations between hunters and merchants from the massive nation of the Southland. Though it lay just southwest of Grandaria and the expansive Iairian Mountain Chain stretching from end to end of the continent, neither he nor Jaren had never been there.

It was on this evening as well that Tavin and Jaren decided to pay a visit to the inn's tavern for dinner, anxious to hear of word from the outer world. Meeting once more outside Tavin's house, the two passed along the roads of the cozy village and arrived as a veil of darkness began to blanket the world, the last bit of the sun disappearing behind the hills to the west. Tavin and Jaren entered the inn to find a group of bounty hunters or something of the sort from the southern border sitting at the bar. Ordering meals, the boys sat and soaked up all the information they could. Apparently there was a rogue beast prowling through the lower hills and preying on innocents, though its description sounded less than animal to Tavin. Later in the evening as the two boys talked amongst themselves, the hefty innkeeper named Carfon asked Jaren to fetch wood for the fireplace. Despite his grumbling, he agreed and left his friend inside the warm inn to himself. As he made his way to the woodpile on the other side of the village, the chilly night air nipped at Jaren's face.

When he reached the chopping block he immediately set to work, not wanting to stay out in the cold and dark of the night a moment longer than absolutely necessary. He placed a hunk of wood atop the block and took hold of the axe at its side, but a faint noise from not too far behind him caught his acute attention. Jaren stopped for a moment, listening. Just as he was about to dismiss it as nothing, another sound echoed its way into his ear. Identifying it as the rustling of brush next to an oak behind the small tree line, he turned his head to try to survey the area for any other who might have been out there with him. Confident as always, Jaren wrenched forth the axe from the chopping block and slowly moved toward the source of the noises. Almost on top of the bushes, he called out.

"Anybody out there?" Jaren bellowed into the crisp evening air. Nothing. "If anyone *is* out there, they'd best show themselves. I don't care to be snuck up on," he stated with authority, mounting the axe over his shoulder. After several seconds passed with no response of any kind, Jaren was satisfied it was just his imagination acting up and nodded to prove to himself he was indeed alone. He turned then and began to make his way back to the chopping block. Just as he fully rotated his chilled body, a bundle of dark gray robes suddenly appeared with lightning speed over his axe head, jerking him back and forcing him to drop the weapon. Before he could so much as squeak a cry for help, a mysterious figure had his arms locked around his neck like a vice, leaving him struggling for breath. While he attempted to pry his own fingers through the figure's iron grasp, Jaren managed to catch a glimpse of his attacker. He was a tall man, but hidden in massive yet simple gray robes with the rest of his face also hooded and cloaked, concealing everything but a short gruff beard.

After hastily scanning his surroundings for any witnesses, the cloaked figure bent down and harshly whispered into Jaren's ear.

"If you place any value on your life at all, don't lie to me," he warned. He wheeled backward to scan the forest line again, as if expecting someone to appear behind him. After a moment he turned back and asked, "What is your name, boy?" Jaren wished he could retaliate in some way, but he and his attacker both knew he was in no position to do so while it took all the strength he could muster just to breathe. Not able to think clearly, he responded.

"Jaren Garrinal," he managed to gasp. Jaren could feel the figure wince at the answer and curse under his breath. He tightened his grip around Jaren's neck.

"Where can Tavinious Tieloc be found right now?" he grilled without pause. Jaren's mind was whirling with conflict at this question. Should he say something that might please the figure and ease him off, or should he keep quiet and his best friend's whereabouts safe? "Well?" the figure pressed impatiently, still looking about frantically. Jaren gave an answer before he knew what he was saying.

"Who?" he lied. "I don't know anyone named -"

"I told you no lies, boy!" the figure whispered irritated, tightening his grip further. "I know he lives in this village, and I know people in a village this small are familiar with their neighbors. Now where is he?" Jaren's mind raced. His attacker somehow knew Tavin. This information left the boy with few options.

"I don't know. He was out all day hunting. He might not be back for-"

"Tell me another lie and you'll find yourself missing a head! I know he's somewhere in this village right now. This is your last chance, boy. Where is the one I seek?" Jaren was at a loss. His words ahead of his brain, he started speaking.

"He's at the inn, alright? Now get the blazes off of me!" Jaren gasped. The figure loosened his grip for a moment and scanned his surroundings once more. It seemed like an eternity for Jaren before the figure finally responded.

"All right boy, this is what's going to happen now. I'm going to release you in a moment but first I'm going to tell you something. First, I am not an enemy." In spite of himself, Jaren managed a quick chuckle echoing out from deep in his throat.

"Oh really?" he gasped sarcastically. "This is one interesting way to greet a friend-"

"Enough. I talk, you listen, understand? It is imperative that I find the one I seek as soon as possible. I don't have time for greetings and pleasantries. I am here on an errand of great importance; one you could not comprehend if you tried. That is all you need know at this point, so now you are going to help me accomplish my task. The first thing I need you to do is trust me and what I have just told you. Can you do that?" Jaren rolled his eyes and mentally agreed to appease the figure for the moment. "Good. I am going to release you now. Please 'behave' when I do so." With that, the figure's iron grip around Jaren's neck gradually softened until he was free once more. Jaren collapsed to the ground, struggling to regain the oxygen he had been brutally deprived of the past few minutes. Once he had regained some composure, he glared up at his attacker with his inherently nasty temper flaring.

"All right you maniac. Before you say another word, I want to know who you are and what you want with Tavin." The figure remained stoic as he gathered his gray robes about him.

"It is enough that you know I am someone of importance on business of great importance."

"You didn't answer my question, pal. I want a real answer now!" The figure moved closer to him, anger and impatience flaring in his movements.

"I will not play this game with you, boy. We do not have time for this. The business I have here is between 'Tavin' and me alone. I can tell you that I mean no harm to him or anyone else. Now let's go. There are things abroad this night that you would not wish to encounter in open territory, or any territory for that matter. We must be on our way indoors. Lead me to this inn, and stay off the beaten path. I don't wish to draw any attention from your fellow villagers."

Jaren decided the answer was satisfactory for the moment. At the request of his attacker, he started up toward the other end of town for the inn. As the two walked, Jaren shot an occasional glance back to analyze the mysterious figure. The first thing he noticed was that he seemed even taller than before, but with the thick gray robes encasing him, his face and the rest of his body were concealed from view. His strides were long, swift, and powerful- obviously emphasizing his determined desire for haste. The massive outline of his shoulders protruded high off of his body and rhythmically rose and fell like those of a wild cat on the prowl, doing little to subtract from his ominous appearance.

The only thing that puzzled Jaren was how the stranger kept scanning his surroundings. It was as if he was afraid of something pursing him. He thought back to the statement that the figure had made earlier about the things abroad that he would not wish to encounter. Whatever was out there, it could not be any more dangerous than the figure, Jaren thought. He had made up his mind this stranger was not to be trusted, and cursed himself for helping someone he knew was obviously evil. There would be an overabundance of men present at the inn, however, and should any further conflict arise there would be ample help to deal with him.

As their destination came into view, the figure placed a massive hand on Jaren's shoulder and pulled him close.

"Listen carefully, Jaren," he said. It was perturbing to Jaren to hear the dangerous stranger call him by name. "I want you to take me around back and leave me in a remote room away from the crowds of people. You will then go and fetch Tavinious for me. Bring him and him alone, for it is only his business that I bring. Tell no one of my presence or our meeting earlier. My time here must remain very secret and very short, so it is imperative that you hurry. Do you understand?" Jaren frowned at his orders.

"What in the name of Granis do you have to say that's so secret and important? And what's with the time limit? Who's out there that's making you so-" The figure's hand shot over Jaren's mouth, silencing him instantly for fear of getting himself into another chokehold.

"I told you before; I haven't the time for these questions!" Jaren could tell the figure was growing exceedingly impatient. "No more talk! Just do as I say for both our sakes." Jaren again swallowed his willful pride and led the figure into the back storage room of the inn. Eager to leave the cloaked man, he set out to find Tavin. Walking into the back kitchen, he ran into the innkeeper washing a collection of dirtied dishes.

"Hey, Carfon. Is Tavin still here?" Jaren asked. The innkeeper cocked his head back for a moment, thinking.

"Ah, yes. I saw him up by the front mantle talking with the old men from Rafol about five, ten minutes ago," he remembered.

"Thanks, Carfon," Jaren responded.

"What's the matter, Jaren? You look like you've seen a ghost or something," questioned the innkeeper. Jaren just shrugged and lied,

"I just need his help with the firewood is all." With that, he marched into the front room. Upon entering the tavern, he was relieved to find a full house, just in case a volatile situation should arise with the figure. After scanning the room for a moment, he found Tavin by the mantle warming himself. Jaren slowly proceeded over to him in a glum state. As he approached, Tavin looked up in disbelief.

"What happened to you? How long does it take to gather a little firewood?" Tavin joked. When no smile or witty comeback was retorted, Tavin's expression grew serious. "Jaren, what's wrong? You look... beat." Jaren pulled Tavin up by his shirt from where he sat and heatedly replied,

"You've got a visitor."

Chapter 3

<u>Warning</u>

As Jaren led Tavin back to where he had left the mysterious stranger, he began to relate the story of their less than favorable meeting and all that the figure had told him. At first, Tavin was sure that his friend was playing some sort of joke on him, but when he looked into the eyes of someone he had come to know better than anyone else in the world, he could tell that Jaren was more than serious. Besides, he was a horribly bad liar; he always had been. When Jaren ended his story, Tavin wasn't sure if he was more confused or excited to meet this mysterious stranger who apparently knew him. Jaren wasn't so enthralled.

"Now look, Tavin. This guy is a lot... tougher, than he seems," Jaren explained. "Physically and verbally. You just can't argue with the guy. There's something in his voice that convinces you to listen to him before you can even think about what he's saying. We've got to be careful if we're going to do this." Tavin nodded, ready for anything. As they arrived at the back storage room, they found the door wide open and gingerly proceeded into the darkness beyond, groping for a light. The moment they had completely entered the room, the door slammed closed behind them extinguishing the last remnant of the glow from outside. A shiver shot down Tavin's back as if death itself had passed through the room claiming the life of the light. Before either of the two could turn around to even attempt an escape, the ominous silhouette of the cloaked figure rose in front of them. His daunting frame was illuminated by the pale sliver of moonlight leaking into the air from a solitary window above them. With the snap of his fingers, the smoldering sparks around one of the dulled candles in the room bounded back into flame, at last revealing to Tavin the entire cloaked form of the mysterious traveler. After a long silence, the figure let out a sigh of frustration.

"I told you, boy," he said speaking at Jaren, "this is between Tavinious and I only." Jaren's temper flared.

"Excuse me, but I think I've become involved in any business you have here since you took the liberty to attack me *and* since this is my best friend. If you don't like it, too bad." The figure was almost on top of him instantly.

"How many times must I tell you, whelp? This information is not for you to hear! It is too dangerous for anyone else to know." Before the two ended up in an all out brawl, Tavin stepped in pushing his friend backward. He raised his eyes to the dark figure.

"Look, whoever you are. Whatever you have to tell me is going to get back to him one way or another. If you don't tell him now, I'll just tell him later. I'm sure you could explain whatever you have to say better than I, so let it come from you. He's involved in this whether you like it or not." Jaren was filled with pride and power at Tavin's words while the figure stood silent and still for a moment, as if contemplating what to do next. Finally he responded.

"Very well then. I'm sure that this... *insistent* lad would never give you peace if he did not know what this is all about. But I warn you, boy, that you'll be involved in this just as much as Tavinious is should you linger here," he cautioned. Jaren nodded in defiance. Tavin was lost upon hearing all of this.

"Excuse me," he began, "but just what do you want with me anyway? And who are you exactly?"

"Yes, yes, we'll get to all that. But first have a seat." He pointed to a bench nearby. After the two boys sat, the man continued. "All right. Pay very close attention because our time is short. I must be gone soon for it is not safe for my presence to remain here long. Take heed of all that I tell you, and please trust what you hear." The figure let back his hood, revealing his face at last. He was a haggard man obviously aged, but not elderly. His short but thick black beard covered most of his face, giving him a rugged but distinguished look. "My name is Zeroan," he continued, "and I am one of the Mystic Sages of the Southland."

Upon hearing this, Tavin and Jaren were shocked almost out of their seats. Even north in Grandaria, everyone knew the rumors of Zeroan of the Mystic Sages. He was supposed to be one of the most powerful sorcerers of the age. While most of the sages were supposed to be reclusive practitioners of simple magic, it was said Zeroan was a rogue sorcerer that had magical ability instilled into his very body. The rumors even told that he was so powerful he had been ostracized from the rest of the sages for fear his power would eventually envelop the entire council under his rule.

Zeroan let a dark smile creep across his rugged face. "I see you have heard something of me. Not quite what you were expecting I can also see. But know that what you think you might know of me is almost guaranteed to be false, or at least somewhat, well... exaggerated." Zeroan took a deep breath as he considered what to say next. "I am here to deliver a warning to you, Tavinious. For now, all I can say is that you are in grave danger." Tavin's face tightened with seriousness again. Jaren was quick to interrupt.

"What do you mean, 'danger?'" he asked impatiently. Zeroan's face went rigid with frustration.

"I knew this was a mistake. Keep quiet or you will find yourself without a voice to annoy me with at all," he threatened. Jaren sank back a little. "Just listen for now. There are creatures all over Iairia hunting for you right now, Tavinious. You are sought after for two reasons. First, you carry something of great importance with you even now. That gem you have in your pocket is much more than it would seem." Tavin pulled his lucky crystal out of his pocket (baffled the figure knew of it or how it was there) and presented it to him in confusion. Zeroan's eyes widened as he saw it. "Yes... that's it... Do either of you know of the legend of the Holy Emerald?"

"The Holy what?" Jaren asked.

"I thought as much," Zeroan mumbled. "Well, I suppose that's fine. The common man should not know of such things for his own good. Well, to begin with, you both know of the six elements of power, correct?" They both nodded, aware of what he was speaking of, if not in great detail. "Very good. They are fire, water, earth, wind, light, and darkness. It is also common knowledge that the source of all elemental power comes from the Elemental Temples across the lands of Iairia. Each element's power is housed in one of the six temples. Long ago in the old world of the gods, however, this was not so. Before the age of man and the temples, all of the elemental power was housed together in one immensely powerful source. This was the Holy Emerald. With all of the six elements of power sealed within, the Holy Emerald was nothing short of all-powerful; the single greatest source of authority in the universe. It lay dormant for eons in the care of Lord Granis, who kept it safe with him in a Holy Shrine."

"And there the emerald remained until the Battle of the Gods began. Determined to have this ultimate power for himself, the evil God of Darkness, Drakkan, started a war with the divine Lord Granis. The scope of this battle was so immense that the land where they fought still remains scarred today. During their massive and long stretched conflict, Drakkan managed to gain possession of the Holy Emerald. Just before he unlocked the secrets of its power, however, Granis defeated him and his hordes of unholy minions, casting him away into the bowels of the earth under the black lands to the far north. At the end of the war, Granis decided it was far to dangerous to leave the ultimate power in the universe for any and all to claim, so he separated the six elements from each other and sent them to their own places in the world to thrive. To accomplish this, he shattered the emerald into six shards. The first shard containing the source of the element of fire was sent to the west to mold new mountains and volcanoes; water was sent to the center of Iairia to flood the lands with lakes and rivers; earth was sent to the deep south to cultivate thick forests and marshes; and wind was sent to the east to bring the sky and earth together by means of the mighty gales."

"But the other two shards were sent to the north. The element of light fell to the northeast to shine Granis' glory onto the land that would become Grandaria, and the element of darkness was cast to the northwest with its evil master Drakkan to poison the land with barren fields of ash and rock, covering the skies with black storms for eternity. Thus the Holy Emerald's one raw power was separated into the six elements we know today and the shards of the emerald have rested hidden for eons. But no longer. Some five centuries ago, we sages and other leaders of both Grandaria and Drakkaidia discovered several age old texts that tell of the all powerful Holy Emerald and a prophesy left by Lord Granis. The prophesy tells that should the shards of the Holy Emerald ever be reunited by the hands of one man, the ultimate power of the stone would return to it and be granted to the man who reunited the shards, leaving him to mold the destiny of all.

"With the help of the Supreme Granisians over the years, I have been able to locate all of the shards of the emerald. Unfortunately, the evil ruler of the Drakkaidians, Valif Montrox, is carrying on the old Drakkaidians' wishes to locate the emerald. He is searching for the shards in an attempt to achieve ultimate power, and he already has possession of one. Using it he has somehow summoned age old evils from the dark Netherworld below. If he is ever able to summon the power of the fully assembled emerald, we would be doomed. With all the power of the universe at his disposal, it is more than likely that Montrox would inadvertently open the gateway to the Netherworld. If he does that, Drakkan himself could escape from his imprisonment there." Tavin and Jaren looked at each other with mystification and deeply rooted alarm mirrored in their eyes. Zeroan sensed their fear but still continued.

"That's right. Drakkan. If his evil is reintroduced into this world, a second Battle of the Gods would surely commence, utterly destroying the entire world as we know it. For every shard Montrox collects, the evil he summons will become more and more potent, and it will bring the banished god Drakkan one step closer to his return to the world more powerful than ever. Montrox has already foolishly awoken and summoned to him a few of the weaker demons of the old world so he can hunt down the remaining shards. The first shard is already in his possession. The shards of wind and water are in our possession, hidden at the Mystic Tower to the south. But these are the only shards I have actually been able to gather, for the locations of the others are very vague. The fire shard is to the west in the proximity of Mt. Coron and the earth shard is in the deep south in the forests or swamps. And as you have no doubt gathered, Tavinious, that crystal you hold in your hand now is the sixth shard; the shard of light." A long silence followed. Tavin stared down in disbelief at his good luck charm, which he now learned was a key to the ultimate power in the universe.

"But... this just can't be, Zeroan. I found this lying in a creek outside the village when I was a just a child. There's just no way..." he trailed off. Zeroan stared at the crystal as well, letting the unison of the silence hang about them for a lingering moment.

"Whether you believe it or not, that is the sixth shard. Getting back to the reason I'm here, your possession of that shard is why you are in such peril. If you are found by the agents of the Drakkaidians, they will destroy you to gain it for their evil master. " After he was sure the sage had stopped for the moment, Tavin was quick to ask questions.

"If you and the other Mystic Sages want the shards, then why don't you take it? That would seem to solve both our problems. You have one more shard that won't get into the Draks' hands, and I stay safe," Tavin suggested. Zeroan shook his head.

"I wish it were that simple, young Grandarian, but this situation has become far more complex. For one reason, you could not give it to me at this time because the servants of Montrox would sense its power with me." Jaren jumped out of his seat at this.

"Are you saying that he can sense where it is? Does that mean he knows its here now?"

"Be calm, boy," Zeroan ordered, motioning for him to sit back down. "It's very complicated, but a simple way to say it is that those who possess magical ability can only sense a talisman of power, in this case a shard of the Holy Emerald, when another with magical ability carries it. He would sense it with me because I am using magic now even as we speak to throw pursuers off my trail, but as long as it stays here, its presence will remain masked." Jaren was still upset with worry at the mention of pursuers.

"Wait a minute! What was all that about 'things I wouldn't want to encounter' you were talking about and all that looking around you were doing earlier? If they don't know where to look, why were you concerned that they were out in the hills?" Zeroan looked grave.

"While the minions of the Drakkaidians do not know that the shard is here, they could be anywhere, and are more than likely looking here in Grandaria. There are still only a few of the weakest of them now, but more powerful demons will come if Montrox gains another shard. They are creatures spawned from the dark Netherworld that will not be spoken of, especially at this hour of night. Besides that, I believe that some may be attempting to track me. But fear not, they cannot do this. I have a great many... tricks, to keep them off my trail. In any case, our time is almost up, so listen carefully to this next part. Tavinious, for now you must keep possession of that shard, but there will come a time when, one way or another, the agents of the Drakkaidians will find you even here. If you are caught, all is lost, so-" Before he could finish, Zeroan was interrupted by a distant but shrill screech in the night. He stood up hastily and gazed out the small window to the top of the room. "Blast, they must have a Valcanor with them," Zeroan cursed. Tavin was quick to rise as well.'

"What was that? I thought you said we were safe here! And what's a 'Valcanor'?" he exclaimed. Zeroan moved back to them quickly, pulling his hood back over his face.

"They must have a creature with them that can fly. I hadn't anticipated this. I must go quickly to throw them off again. I would take you with me but it is too dangerous now, so this conversation must wait for another day. Listen well, young ones. As I said earlier, you are safe here for now, but that will not last. I would guess in no more than a month Montrox will learn of you. When he does, you must be gone. Before his agents arrive, I will give you a warning to flee. Look to the skies for the warning. When you see it, you will have until nightfall to be far away from here. Make sure you are out of the Hills of Eirinor. Make for the capital of Galantia. Take what refuge you can there. With any luck, I should be able to find you in your flight, but if not I will find you at Galantia."

Zeroan was pulling the two out the door toward the exterior of the inn now. Outside, the sage knelt before them.

"Jaren, you are now responsible for the safety of that shard the same as your friend because of what you have heard. Tavinious, guard it with your life! This piece must remain safe until it arrives in Galantia." Tavin was panicking with questions.

"Zeroan, what sign will I look for?" he managed to ask.

"Just look to the skies; you will know it when you see it, trust me. When you do, leave immediately- do not delay. Tell no one of any of this matter. Make your flight secret. Montrox has many well disguised spies that pass through Grandaria every day that would bring the demons here." Zeroan could see the slight terror in the boys' faces as he repeated the word 'demon.' "Just so you are both aware, I do not keep referring to Montrox's minions as demons to frighten you, but that is truly what they are. Creatures of unimaginable evil. When you leave, be wary and never underestimate them. Remember, they are not of this world and are not bound by the laws of physics that you and I are; they are capable of much more. Try to gather as much knowledge as you can of events and rumors in the outside world, for most will be true in this prelude to a time of darkness. Now I must go. Remember, go to Galantia and I will find you if I do not meet with you before then. Be careful, both of you. I wish you luck."

With that he stood and wheeled around for the hillside leading out of the village. Before he could get far, however, Tavin remembered something.

"Zeroan! I have one more question!" he exclaimed. The tall figure turned back to face him. "You said that there were two reasons that I am in danger. One was the shard. What was other?" Jaren had completely forgotten about the second reason. The shard was bad enough. What could the other possibly be? Zeroan exhaled sharply, slowly turned, and came back to them. There was an anxious but distant look in the sage's eyes.

"That conversation must wait for our next meeting, young Grandarian. There is no time now. It is enough that you know that the shard you carry is not the primary reason that Montrox wishes you dead. There is another that you shall learn for yourself soon. Now I must go. Safe journey, my friends. Stay indoors now and do not leave the village for any reason except to flee when the time comes. Good luck to you both." With that last statement, he leapt into the tree line and was gone, leaving two very shocked and confused boys standing out in the cold, dark night.

Chapter 4

<u>Dark Skies</u>

Tavin and Jaren spent the rest of that evening debating over their disturbing conversation with the Mystic Sage Zeroan. For hours into the night, the two boys stole away in the back of the inn trying to sort it all out. While Tavin took the position to believe what he had been told, Jaren was naturally much more skeptical.

"I can't believe you're even considering buying into this insanity! Have you lost your mind!?!" Jaren was incredulous as he started into his tirade. Tavin was still so shocked by all that had befallen them earlier in the evening he was barely listening to Jaren. "Hey! Are you even paying attention to me?" Tavin looked up with frustration in his deep blue eyes.

"You're the only insane person around here, you know," he began with fervor. "This is always the kind of view you take on things! How can you be so quick to dismiss that whole encounter as nothing? Why would some guy run into the village and go through everything he did tonight just for the fun of it? Why would he be making all this up?"

"I can think of about twenty reasons right off the top of my head!" Jaren was beside himself. "You want to know why I always take this position, huh? Gee, maybe it's because someone has to be the voice of reason around here!" Jaren exhaled loudly and pulled a chair over to Tavin, sitting down. "Tavin, you don't think this stuff through. You're so quick to get involved in any grand adventure that comes your way that you go blind to the obvious. Do you realize what this idiot wants us to believe? He says you're holding the key to the destruction of the world in you pocket right now! I mean Granis on high, Tavin! Does that look like a legendary piece of the ultimate power in the universe to you?" Tavin looked down for a moment. The words of his friend seemed to pierce him through the heart.

He knew that Jaren was right to a degree. He was always so eager for action that he often jumped into things before he knew what he was doing. Reaching into his pocket to pull forth the crystal, he stared into its glossy white surface and still rigid edges. Jaren could see the disappointment and conflict mirrored in his eyes.

"Look, I'm sorry to be so harsh, but if you slow down, step back, and look at all this, you've got to admit the whole thing is pretty farfetched." Tavin managed to bring his eyes to meet Jaren's.

"I can see what you mean, Jaren, and I know what you're saying makes sense. But... something about this is different from all those other times. You were with me for the entire thing, Jaren. Didn't you see his eyes? Didn't you see the way he moved? I've never seen an actor that good; that authentic. Have you?" Jaren couldn't find the words to respond. "And what about those shrieks in the night? Did he set those up too? And how did he know all of that history? I've heard a lot from dad and some other big shots in Galantia, and that sounded word perfect to me. I know this looks outrageous, but it just doesn't make sense to me that someone would go to all this trouble for some kind of sick joke." Tavin's sincere gaze seemed to burn through Jaren.

"All right, all right," he began to give in, letting out a monstrous huff of aggravation. "I'll make a deal with you. Since this has gotten you so worked up, I'll go along with it. Here are my terms. We go on with life as usual in the village, and wait around for the month that the "demons" are supposed to find the place. If we see any *perfectly* clear warning in the sky during that time, you will have convinced me. But it's got to be a good, evident, sign. If the month passes with no warning, though, you have to agree that it must have been some extremely bad joke, and we forget it ever happened. What do you say?" Tavin thought for moment, and decided it was a good idea. If there was a warning, they would know the message was true, and if not, Zeroan had either been mistaken or just toying with them.

So this is how it came to pass. Every day for the next few weeks, the two boys kept an ever watchful eye on the sky for the warning. Though Jaren was convinced it was not coming, he found himself packing a small bag of food and supplies with Tavin one night, just in case. As the two worked outside, even the most minute of noises or objects drifting by in the

23

wind caught their attention, and every time it did they shot each other uneasy glances. Tavin's father had noticed their strange behavior after the first few days passed, but both denied anything was wrong. All the while, Tavin kept an extra careful eye on his lucky charm, never letting it away from his person.

During the last week, Jaren was satisfied that no sign was coming, and to officially celebrate the end of his imprisonment in his own village, he dragged Tavin to the inn for lunch. They set out in a hurry, wanting to beat the inevitable storm that had been building from the west for hours. As they walked, the two were in considerably different moods. Jaren bounced along with a particularly pert smile laced across his face, while Tavin dragged onward looking somewhat defeated. Jaren attempted to raise his friend's spirits.

"Oh what in the name of Granis are you so down about? You didn't actually want to see that stupid warning did you? Why would you want to leave the place just before harvest? It's the best time to be here!" Tavin looked up and faintly smiled back.

"Yeah, you're right, Jaren. I guess this whole thing was a joke after all. Granis on high, would I love to get my hands on that "Mystic Sage." What a lunatic." They laughed together for a time, making their way to the inn. As they walked, it started to drizzle a soft rain. "Oh great," Tavin complained. "Just what we need." They hurriedly made their way inside, finding a mass assembly of men they had never seen before speaking to the tavern's usuals. Tavin shot Jaren a puzzled glance, who commented they were probably a group of merchants on their way to Galantia. They sat down at the bar looking over at the group of men speaking to the villagers. Tavin couldn't help but overhear.

"Scariest damned thing I ever seen," a worn and shaky old man said. "Before we knew it, the heavens were falling apart. Rain, hail, wind, and lightning like you can't imagine!"

"It was like hell itself was breaking loose," another man added. "I reckon it'll be here before nightfall, and I can tell you right now I don't intend to be here when it arrives." Tavin looked back at the bar to find the innkeeper, Carfon, staring at the group as well.

"Hey, Carfon?" Tavin began. "What's with all the commotion over there?" He let out a small sigh and leaned in close to the boys.

"These guys showed up early this morning. They said that last night they were caught in the worst storm of all time. You must have heard them. Gales, rain, and hail. But the strangest part is they say the whole sky was raining lightning, making weird lights in the clouds." Letting the words slowly digest into his mind, Tavin's eyes grew wide as he slowly turned to meet with Jaren, already peering at him with an apprehensive look about his face. "Anyway, they say the storm will be here by nightfall. They're advising everyone to stay indoors and patch up their houses. It's already getting pretty nasty outside." Carfon threw his hands onto the boys' shoulders. "So guess what? I'm going to pay the both of you handsomely to get on out there and cover up the windows with the planks in the back shed. I don't want any damage to my inn. What do you say?" Tavin and Jaren were too lost in thought to respond.

After they came to their senses, they agreed to patch the place up. As they gathered the planks out back, they were both on edge. Moving outside with the boards and ladders in hand, Tavin leaned over to Jaren, eyes wide.

"Jaren, is it just me, or does this strike you as some sort of a sign in the sky?" asked Tavin. Jaren shook his head and thrust a shaking finger in front of Tavin's face.

"Don't let the weather get to you. It's just a storm," he asserted convincingly, more to reassure himself than Tavin. While Jaren finished his sentence, a massive burst of wind wrenched a board out of his grasp to go flying out away from his sight. He gulped. "A really bad storm..." As Jaren trailed off, the rain stared pouring. It came so hard and so fast from the wind blasting it into them it felt like being pierced by a barrage of needles. They managed to secure the front windows in a rather makeshift manner, but as they moved onto the sides, the raging gusts grew too strong. Before Tavin could secure the boards to the windows, his ladder was blown from under him like a giants arm throwing it away. Tavin was sent straight into the ground. He landed painfully on his side and sprawled out on his back.

Giving into his fatigue and loosening his body, Tavin let his eyes drift up to the dark clouds crashing like ocean waves. From deep within the rolling black billows he noticed what appeared to be a massive swell of lightning building up. Drawing his complete attention, it was not long until he observed that the charge of light was not electricity. Eyes fixed upward, Tavin gazed on as the blackness of the clouds opened to reveal an ominous yellow light from within. Fixated on it, Tavin could not look away. He helplessly gaped up through the wind and rain as the light began to take shape. Then, as clear a day, Tavin recognized what it had formed.

Jaren leapt down off his ladder to Tavin's side, screaming out to be heard.

"Tavin! Are you all right?" He didn't respond. Jaren knelt down to his friend and tried to pull him up. "Tavin! We've got to get inside!" Too entranced and awestruck to utter a single sound, Tavin slowly raised his hand, pointing to the fearsome sky. Jaren looked upward to find what held Tavin's attention. Then, he saw it too. His eyes opened even wider than Tavin's. Spelled out as plain as day in a swell of light from inside the dark clouds were the two words, "get out."

Chapter 5

<u>Flight</u>

It did not take long after that for the two boys to be on their way out of the village. Even Jaren with all his doubts was instantly convinced that the warning had indeed come. Once they regained their senses, the two boys rapidly made their way to their homes, gathered the provisions and weapons they had packed, and silently departed from Eirinor as swiftly as their legs would carry them. Leaving only a small message with a murky explanation behind for Tavin's father, they made their way out undetected through the still raging storm. Eager to escape the village and its surrounding countryside, they moved at an enterprising pace, only briefly stopping once to catch their breath.

Racing through the trees in the small corner of an undersized forest north of the village, Tavin's mind was full of a thousand different thoughts ranging from a sense of exhilaration and excitement to his darkest fears of what might be closing in on them even as they ran. Jaren was still so shocked that the warning had actually come (and in such a grand scale) he was too stunned to know what to think. He rapidly gave up on that, however, just running after his friend trying to make some sense of this unbelievable situation he found himself in.

As the sun began to sink in the west behind the dark rolling clouds superimposed over the sky, they took the first serious break in their flight since they begun some five hours before. At the edge of the small forest, they halted and sat to rest their aching feet and munch on some bread they had taken from the inn. In the midst of all their running, the two had conversed little. It was now that they began to discuss how they would manage the remainder of their flight to the Grandarian capital. As they spoke, Tavin looked into his pouch to be sure the shard he was carrying was still secure.

When he found it laying in all its crystal clear glory just as he had left it, he sealed the pouch again and turned over to his weary friend.

"We need to make this quick, Jaren," Tavin advised looking back to the south where they had come. "I don't like just sitting around while those things Zeroan warned us about could be out here searching for us." Jaren looked up in disgust from the ground where he lay aching.

"Well *sorry*, mister run-you-to-death. Give me a break here! I've been running my Grandarian butt off for hours on end. We've been cooped up in that village for so long I thought I had forgotten how to run." He reached down to massage his legs. "I guess I remember now..." he murmured in pain.

"Look," Tavin said, "I know you're tired-" Jaren let out a disgusted huff.

"'Tired' does not scratch the surface. Try fatigued to the point of death. That's a little more accurate."

"Hey, you're not the only guy here who's out of energy!" Tavin exclaimed, repositioning his sword over his back. "I don't think I've been this exhausted in months, but we need to figure out what our next move is." Jaren sat up as a puzzled but caustic expression made its way across his face.

"What 'move'? We run to Galantia, and don't get caught by most-likely *bloodthirsty* monsters from Drakkaidia. Sounds pretty simple to me," he morbidly replied.

"I know, but there's more to it than that. We're at the edge of the woods right now. After this we'll be in the hills; wide open territory. I don't want to be out there with no cover if we run into any," Tavin hesitated to say the word, "demons..."

"There's not much else we can do, you know. If I recall correctly, we're in a hurry to get to Galantia. The fastest route is straight through the hills." Tavin sat back in dismay. Jaren was right again. The only quick route to the Valley of Galantia from the Eirinor Hills was to go straight to them in the great wide open. There was no other option.

"Fine, but lets get going then." Tavin turned back to the west to observe the sun sinking beyond view, signaling their deadline to be out of the village. "If Zeroan was right, those things could be arriving in the village any time now. If they know who they're looking for and they find us not there, I think they'll be smart enough to do a perimeter check. They might even have one of those flying things like last time." Jaren thought back to the night of Zeroan's warning and the ear piercing shriek he had heard in the distance. Though he was horribly exhausted, he didn't want to be found by whatever had made that noise. So with that, the two set out again into the open fields of the Hills of Eirinor for Galantia to the north. They kept a careful eye behind them as they traveled, moving from what cover they could find to the next.

The night passed in a similar fashion. No major resting point was taken for fear of being caught by whatever might be behind them. The following morning they were nearing the end of a downward progression of steep hills when the storm caught Tavin's attention once more. As the two made their way through the last stretch of the hillside, Tavin had begun to notice that the storm was now moving north instead of west and had caught up with them as it began to gust and rain with newly fueled intensity. On the verge of collapsing, Jaren purposefully fell to his knees to catch his breath. Tavin halted and turned back for his friend, yelling for his voice to be audible over the raging squalls of wind.

"Jaren, come on! We're almost out of these hills. From here on it's just easy rolling stuff! We have to keep going! I don't like the looks of this storm starting to rage like this so suddenly again!" Too out of breath to respond, Jaren struggled to stand. As Tavin moved back to bolster the exhausted boy up, a dark movement above them caught his attention. Through the rain and hail falling violently from the skies, a massive black silhouette of something huge made its way over the hills, surveying all that lay beneath it. Quickly noticing the threat himself, Jaren found new energy blasting its way through his body. They quickly made their way into a nearby pile of brush rolling around in the wind and pulled it over them with just enough to cover them both. As the beastly figure slipped in and out of view between the clouds above them, the pair nervously scanned the rest of the countryside for any other potential problems. Seeing none, and with the erratic monster in the skies gone from view, Jaren leaned over to Tavin.

"What was that thing!" he whispered, beside himself with alarm. Tavin sensed the fear and alarm in Jaren's voice.

"I don't know..." Tavin replied, still concerned with the possibility of the winged creature appearing again. Jaren stared at him for a moment, waiting for more to the response. When none came he rammed his fist into Tavin's arm.

29

"What in the blazing hell is 'I don't know?'" Jaren was out of control with panic. "Where's your plan, fearless leader? What are we going to do?" Tavin gave the skies another sweep with his eyes before he gave the same response in an even more monotonous tone. Jaren groaned and buried his head in his arms. After a few more minutes with no sign of the creature, Tavin finally decided to act.

"Okay, I think whatever that thing was is gone. We need to get out of these hills, *now*," he said with resolve. Jaren gave him an incredulous look.

"Let me get this straight- you want me to go... *out there* with a giant... *thing* on the loose!?!"

"Would you rather wait for it to come back or for the rest of his buddies to find us just lying here? I'm not wild about being out there with that thing either but we don't have many options. We have to get to Galantia soon, or Granis knows how many more there might be catching up to us. Besides, Zeroan said he would try to find us on the way there, remember? He might be out there looking for us right now. He won't find us hiding in this bush, will he?" Jaren had almost completely forgotten about the Mystic Sage Zeroan. He took some solace in the fact that a powerful sorcerer could be out there to help them, so he reluctantly agreed to set off with Tavin in the lead. Shortly after the two began moving once more, the storm grew even more intense. With virtually no cover at this point in the increasingly flat hills, Tavin and Jaren had no choice but to sprint as hard as they could forward, hoping that either Zeroan would locate them or the demons would not.

It was the latter that found them. As the two ran on with sweat beading on their flushed faces, a mind numbing screech suddenly sounded throughout the air stopping the very blood in Tavin's veins from flowing. The boys wheeled around to scan for the source of the shriek, immediately observing a large misshapen figure reared back on the hillside behind them to let another shriek echo out of its throat into the storm. Tavin didn't need to see any more. With an expression of determination and iron will strapped across his face like armor, he yelled at Jaren to start running again. As they took off over the hills, three more figures appeared over the ridge to the south. Letting one last screech fly into the gusts of wind seemingly tearing a rift in the air itself, the four of them shot off after the two boys. Spinning his head back to examine his pursuers, Tavin observed them trailing about 500 yards, but gaining steadily. The dark creatures ran on all fours, built like horses but with deep crimson skin and sharp claws protruding all over their scaled bodies. With still no sign of Zeroan and his mystic powers to aid them, Tavin knew things were looking bleak.

The chase would not have gone on for much longer if not for the party of rangers ahead of Tavin and Jaren. Known for their nomadic lifestyle of moving from village to village raising fine horses, they were just what the two boys needed. With their pursuers gaining quickly, they raced into the camp and into a makeshift stable to find a lone ranger tending to three horses. Tavin immediately ripped out his satchel to empty it of all the currency he could find. Already mounting one of the horses with Jaren doing the same a moment later, he thrust the money into the ranger's hands.

"Sorry, but we need these more than you can imagine," Tavin managed to say, out of breath. "Let's go, Jaren." Moving out just as the demons made their way into camp, the other rangers observed the virtual theft and started off after them until they caught sight of the boy's pursuers. Thirsty for death, the demons sidetracked to the two rangers and leapt upon them, violently ending their existence in seconds. As the two men screamed for the last time, Tavin looked back in fury.

"Damn these things!" he bellowed enraged. He spun around to Jaren and drew his sword from the sheath on his back, assuming command. "Jaren! Let's see what these godforsaken things think of a few arrows sticking out of their miserable hides!" Jaren grinned darkly, ready to stand up for himself at last and to see what the creatures were truly made of. Halting his horse, Jaren loaded his bow and took precise aim, then quickly released an arrow to be delivered straight into one of the demons' sides. Before the monster could so much as let out a shriek of pain, another of the lean missiles came careening into its forehead, dropping it with an inaudible thud. Silently applauding himself, Jaren was already stringing up another shot.

31

The three remaining demons didn't have to think twice about starting after their primary objectives after the loss of the first of their kin. Despite Tavin's order to get moving again, Jaren fired one last arrow into the advancing demons to catch one of them in its forearm, sending it plowing down into the earth, apparently crippled. With the two left advancing at an enterprising rate, both parties sped away toward the Valley of Galantia in the distance once more.

Chapter 6

<u>Standoff</u>

The chase went on for the better part of a half an hour. With the darkly empowered demons never growing tired and the two elite Grandarian horses just beginning to break a sweat, neither side showed any sign of slowing. Tavin and Jaren raced over the end of the hills as fast as their steeds could move with the ever present threat of their evil pursuers never more than forty yards behind. As Tavin, Jaren, and the demons flew through the end of the hills, the massive Valley of Galantia that contained the shining capital city came into distinct view. The largest city in all of Iairia, Galantia rested on top of a massive hillside surrounded by towering walls around the perimeter of the municipality. Its golden ramparts stretched from the main gate at the base of the hill to the mountainous cliffs behind the city, serving as a natural barrier at its rear that did not call for the safety of a wall.

Inside the heart of the city and making up the majority of the Golden Castle was the Elemental Temple of Light. Tavin's father had told him long ago that the Grandarians of the old world treasured the Temple of Light so much that they constructed their city of Galantia around it, making it a part of the castle at its core. They had even renamed the tallest peak of the temple the Tower of Granis to further glorify their lord. The tower had become the most prized and momentous piece of architecture in the city, standing high over all other towers and shining in the sun's fervent light like a beacon through the darkest storm. With the thickest and tallest walls at its perimeter, a massive population inside, and the Elemental Temple of Light built into the castle itself, Galantia was easily the single greatest location in all of Iairia, or so any Grandarian would say.

Tavin shot a glace at Jaren that signaled they were close to safety. Their pursuers behind them had other plans, however. As Tavin and Jaren moved into the start of the valley, the demons plunged forward with a burst of vitality. Tavin looked back to observe the two figures rapidly closing the gap between them. Realizing outrunning them any longer was now impossible, Tavin decided to direct the now fatigued horses into the thicket of woods to their left. With superior knowledge of the terrain, Tavin figured they would stand a better chance against them there than on horseback. He turned back over his shoulder and shouted back to Jaren still closely following.

"Jaren! When we get to that huge tree in that vale ahead of us, jump off!" he bellowed. Jaren looked at him in disgusted confusion.

"What!?!" he responded in dismay.

"Just trust me!" Tavin assured him. So as the horses made their way into the small vale in the woods, Tavin and Jaren moved them off to the left side near some brush. Tavin jumped first, the forest foliage breaking his fall. Jaren looked ahead and muttered to himself.

"I hate my life..." he complained as he leapt off of his speeding stead into the trees, uncomfortably landing in a tangle of indigenous vegetation.

As soon as the two landed they were back on their feet drawing their weapons and turning to each other.

"There's only two left. We can take 'em. I'll catch the first one when he comes in. You take the second. And make sure finish him on the first shot." Jaren was offended. He was the reason they were dealing with two of these monsters instead of four. Swallowing his pride, Jaren strung an arrow and took aim at the entrance to the vale as Tavin took position to implant his steel into the first crimson beast to appear. After several minutes passed, however, they remained alone. Tavin looked over at Jaren who returned his puzzled expression. He wondered if the demons had withdrawn because they had failed to stop their prey in the hills, or if they simply didn't wish to exit open terrain. Still at the ready position, nothing came.

Just when it seemed that they had somehow miraculously lost the two foul creatures, a massive shadow slowly rose to tower over Jaren. His eye's widened and his heart seemed to drop into his stomach. Immediately aware of what he had carelessly let happen, Jaren pulled himself back together and tightened his arrow into the bowstring. Taking one last deep breath, he wheeled around to find both demons lunging at him from the dark forest. The sudden movement caught Tavin's attention as well. Caught by surprise and locked up in terror, Jaren could barely release the arrow at all; much less finish the demon with his first shot. The arrow pierced it through its lower chest as it toppled over him, forcing it to let out one of its ear piercing screeches. The other crimson monster leapt over the first, attempting to pull out its quarry trapped under the mountain of bleeding flesh that lay helpless over Jaren.

What the creature failed to notice while it tried to uncover its prey was Tavin, who had positioned himself behind it. With a massive vertical swing of his broadsword downward, Tavin cut deeply into the creature's back, sending it reeling away screaming in pain. Now the primary target of the dark creature, Tavin brought himself into his perfected fighting stance, preparing for his enemy's charge. The determination and unwavering resolve Tavin had become known for were mirrored in his eyes as the enraged monster bounded forward screaming its war cry as it came. Just before it was upon him, Tavin swiftly rolled to his left, lifting his weapon sideways and using his attacker's own speed and momentum against it. The blade tore into the foe's side as it passed by, ripping through its tainted body. Though Tavin managed to heavily wound it, the creature's scaly skin was so tough that it wrenched the sword out of Tavin's hands, sending him tumbling backward defenseless. He quickly rolled to his feet scanning the ground for his blade. It was then that he realized it was still lodged in the demon's side.

With two heavy wounds searing into its damaged body, the crimson creature was now on the verge of death, but still paced in front of the boy not ready to let him attain victory. Desperate for an idea, Tavin surveyed his surroundings to observe just what he needed. He brought his eyes back to meet with the creature's, holding its biting gaze for what seemed like an eternity. It was then that Tavin abruptly wheeled around and sprinted for the idea he had hatched behind him. The creature came bounding after him the moment he was off. As Tavin ran for the single tree in front of him, his whispered a quick prayer to Granis.

"I could use a little help with this," he mumbled, completely out of breath. With his attacker directly behind him, Tavin gathered every last ounce of energy he could find and burst toward the tree, stepping up its trunk and then kicking backward off of it. On his way back down to the earth beneath him, he latched onto the hilt of his sword still embedded in the demon's side. Screaming at the top of his lungs to muster all his muscle, Tavin forced the sword sideways into the demon with enough force for the bloody tip of his blade to come jetting out through the opposite side. The demon, still moving at full force, lost all of its senses in this most recent blow to its fearsome frame and plunged out of control headfirst into the trunk. Coupled with the three blade wounds and its forceful impact with the tree, the evil creature finally dropped to the cold earth, lifeless.

Tavin sank next to it struggling for breath, in utter disbelief that he had just done what he had done. After a minute of lying in the misting rain that had developed around him, he finally made his way back to his feet. Slowly leaning down to the dispatched hulk of his enemy, he took hold of the hilt of his sword and wrenched it free. Suddenly he remembered there was still a second demon to contend with. He hurriedly raced through the trees back to the vale where he left his friend. When he entered, Tavin found the monster dying with Jaren still under it. As Tavin approached, he could hear his frustrated friend violently cursing underneath. Finishing the demon quickly with one swift strike to the head, he leaned over and assisted Jaren in lifting the corpse off of him. Jaren was thrilled to breathe fresh air again.

"Thank Granis! Get this sack of disgusting horseflesh off of me!" he cried with relief. He looked up at Tavin with an eyebrow raised. "What took you so long?" Tavin returned his stare for a moment, then just silently laughed at what he hoped was sarcasm.

As the two worked to free Jaren from his veritable prison, the misting rain finally stopped. Tavin and Jaren, both exhausted, stopped to just sit and gather their breath. It was refreshing to be free of their pursuers and know they were safe. The two conversed quietly about how stupid they had been to let the demons ambush them and how Tavin had brought down the second with his skill and luck alone. Jaren sat in awe as Tavin told the story.

"You have got to be kidding me," Jaren stated in disbelief. "You actually flipped off the tree and rammed the sword through that thing on the way back down?" Tavin nodded with a humble smile.

"Blade's honor," he replied, holding up the stained and chipped sword beside him. Jaren laughed.

"You never cease to amaze me, buddy."

While the Grandarian boys sat in the peace of the moment, a strange feeling washed over Tavin. For some reason, he felt inclined to look up and scan the tree line around the perimeter of the vale. Jaren noticed him looking around and asked what he was doing.

"It's nothing, I just... feel like something's wrong," he quietly said. After examining everything around them for the source of his worry, Tavin noticed something. "Jaren, is it just me or is it way too quiet all of a sudden?" Jaren stared at him confused.

"What are you worried about? The storm just died down now that the demons are gone, that's all," he offered. Tavin shook his head, standing up.

"No, that's not it. The storm is still over us; look at the clouds. But... just listen. It's not just quiet out there: it's dead silent. There's not a sound coming from anything." Jaren stood to meet his friend. At last, he nodded his head in agreement.

"You're right. I can't hear a thing out there. Wow, that's really... creepy." When Tavin was about to suggest they be on their way again, he caught a faint wisp wind audible from above. Jaren heard it too, and they both looked up at the rolling dark clouds together. The sound became perceptible again, rhythmic. "Can you hear that?" Jaren asked quietly.

"Yeah..." replied Tavin even softer. The noises grew louder, and the wind's sudden gusts transformed into the sound of flapping. Not the flapping of a birds wings, but something much bigger. A dark expression of realization spread across Tavin's face as he remembered back to the hills that morning. "Oh no..." he mouthed. Lifting his sword, he prepared for the massive black shadow descending from the clouds. Upon seeing the gargantuan shape in the sky, Jaren came to realize where the noises had come from as well and brought forth his bow.

The two stayed frozen in place as the ghastly form of the winged demon from above the hills slowly landed in the vale before them. It was a black and crimson monster with a smooth oval body, sunken and withdrawn. Its thin bent arms and legs looked out of place jutting off of it, working like mangled hydraulics with massive claws upon each. Its head sat directly on its body without any neck whatsoever, sporting two oval eyes radiating blood red light. The crowning features on the mammoth beast were its two enormous bat-like wings mounted high up on his back. The wingspan easily doubled its height, which was at least that of the trees it stood among.

Too exhausted to retaliate in any way, the two stood firm, realizing that this would be their last stand. There was no place to run and no place to hide.

"Tavin," said Jaren in a surprisingly calm tone, "I just want you to know that you're my best friend and you always have been." Tavin held his gaze on the slowly approaching demon, but responded in an equally relaxed voice.

"My dad always says that a man is only as good as his friends. That must make me the best there is. Not many guys would have stuck by me like this." After Tavin finished, the demon's hinged and gnarled legs came trudging forth, crushing and sinking in the earth around it. "So do you want to try to take a shot at his eyes or something?" Tavin asked. Jaren nodded, still fixed on the demon.

"Looks like there are arteries over his legs. Why don't you rush them and see if you can cause some damage?"

"Sounds good," Tavin said.

Just as the creature was about to strike, Tavin felt a strange vibration from under his feet. He looked down to see the ground underneath him starting to shake. At first it was just a slight tremor, but as the seconds ticked by, it grew into a low and heavy rumble. The two boys shot uneasy glances at each other while the winged nightmare came to a halt and cast its gaze downward as well. Before long, Tavin and Jaren were knocked to the ground, struggling to keep their balance in the midst of the full blown earthquake. Realizing that something was obviously wrong, the monster attempted to make itself airborne, but it was far too late. The ground began to split and rupture around it until a massive column of soil and rock came blasting out of the earth's crust to rain back down onto it, pummeling the monster with boulders. It wasn't until Tavin noticed the strange green aura of light to the right of the vale that he figured out what was going on. As the winged horror was being beaten by the earth itself, a line of horsemen came bursting forth from the entrance to the vale. The leader was a brawny man clad in forest garb and heavy Southland Legion armor, radiating with green energy. He called out to Tavin and Jaren in a hurry.

"What are you waiting for, boys!?! Mount a horse and let us be gone before the creature is airborne! I can't hold it forever!" the man exclaimed. Without a word, Tavin and Jaren sprinted to the horses, mounted, and set off away from the vale. The man engulfed in the green energy raised his hands one final time and brought forth one last mighty boulder from the earth's crust. "Chew on this, Valcanor," he cursed. With the flick of his wrist, the boulder smacked the creature with such force it was sent careening out of control through the end of the vale and into the woods. The man chuckled as the deep green energy dissipated around him and he set off after the rest of his men.

Chapter 7

<u>Golden City</u>

As the party of horsemen moved across the fields of the Valley of Galantia with Tavin and Jaren, the two boys were feeling a great deal of mixed emotion. Just minutes ago they were ready for death to claim them, and now here they were safe and riding to Galantia under the guard of what appeared to be, of all things, a Southland Legion patrol. Before Tavin could even sort out his feelings and figure out what had happened in the course of the last few minutes, he was interrupted by one of the horsemen.

"Hold on there, boys! We need to wait for Garoll," he informed them. Tavin and Jaren halted their steeds turned back to the soldiers.

"Of course," Tavin began remembering their savior in the vale. "Thank you for the rescue by the way. It would have been all over if you hadn't arrived when you did."

"You're quite welcome," he stated casually, looking over his shoulder to see the one he called Garoll riding out of the woods toward them. "It was nothing. Besides, it looked like you were going to give that thing a rough time before you went down." Tavin found himself at a loss for words until the leader arrived, trotting straight over to the boys. Getting a better look at the man, Tavin could tell he was a seasoned warrior, but he could detect an affable warmth to him as well. His rugged light brown beard suggested that he and his men had been out and riding for quite a few days.

"Well congratulations, boys," he began heartily, unstrapping his helmet to reveal the rest of his face. "You just survived an encounter with a Valcanor and two Liradds. Not many men could best one of those things, much less two boys. It's a pleasure indeed." He extended his hand in greeting toward Tavin. "I'm called Garoll Nelpia." Tavin took firm grasp of his hand.

40

"I'm Tavinious Tieloc, but please call me Tavin. I'd let Jaren over there introduce himself, but I think he's still a little shaken up." Jaren snapped up at that.

"Don't listen to him," Jaren said, shooting a scowl at Tavin. "I'm just fine. My name's Garrinal. Jaren Garrinal. Thanks for the help back there." Jaren grinned and cocked his head. "Would've been hell to kill that thing on our own." Most of the men laughed at that. Overcome by his swelling ego, Jaren just smiled to himself, convinced that he could have taken it. Tavin rolled his eyes and continued.

"The pleasure is ours, sir. Despite the opinion of my friend here, we owe you our lives. But may I pose a question?" Tavin asked with respect in the face of the obviously highly ranked man.

"Let me guess," he responded. "Who are we and how did we know to come for you?" Tavin nodded, but added something.

"Well, I'm pretty sure who you are at least. Your attire and armor sides you with the Southland and the Legion. And if I had to guess, I'd say you in particular were one of the Elemental Warriors. The Warrior of Earth, to be precise." Garoll was impressed.

"Well you do know your stuff, don't you m' boy! You're exactly correct of course. And the name is Garoll, not sir, if you don't mind." Tavin smiled in acknowledgment. Jaren was completely lost.

"Um, could you slow down a little bit there? I'm not as well schooled as Tavin here. What's an 'Elemental Warrior' again?" Garoll smiled and glanced over at the shining city of Galantia in the distance as if contemplating if he had enough time to linger for a few more moments.

"Well, as you know there are six elements in the world," he began, shifting his gaze back to Jaren. "For each element, there is an Elemental Temple somewhere in Iairia that houses the source of that element's power. Every generation, the Mystic Sages choose one person to be its warrior, or guardian you might call it. These people are transformed in the temples and the crest of the element they are destined to protect and wield appears on the back of their hand." Garoll removed the glove from his right hand and revealed the elemental crest of the earth. "I, for example, wield the power of the earth. Rocks, plants, and the very ground itself. The other five control different elements." He turned back to Tavin. "As for the other half of the question, we were sent here to aid you in your flight to Galantia." Tavin looked puzzled.

"But who in the world would send you to do that? Who would know we were making this journey except..." Tavin stopped, his brow furrowing.

"That's right!" Garoll exclaimed. "You're far more famous than even you yourself realize, young man. I'm a loyal friend and ally to the Mystic Sages of the Southland, particularly to Zeroan. He knew that there would be creatures after you in force and didn't want anything to happen to you until you reached Galantia. I'm one of the few people who know how important you are because of this quest you're on." Tavin reached into a satchel and pulled out the crystal shard, eager to tell him of its safety.

"Yes, the shard is still safe-" Tavin was cut off by Garoll instantly.

"No, no, no, that's not what I'm talking about. The shard is important yes, but not nearly as important as what you carry in your very veins, m' boy!" A look of bewilderment crossed Tavin's face. Could he be speaking of the other thing that Zeroan had told him about the night they met? Or was it something else? Just as Tavin was about to ask what Garoll was talking about, a huge crash sounded inside the forest they had just escaped from. Garoll spun around on his steed.

"Oh great," he cursed, his voice laced with disdain. He then turned to his men and shouted into them. "The Valcanor is up! We've got to get to Galantia fast if we are to get these two there safely! Let's move!" As the others started riding, Tavin had no time to ask what they were talking about. He guessed he would find out when they got there.

Shortly after the riders took off for the golden city of Galantia now directly before them, the winged demon called the Valcanor rose from the vale it had been defeated in. It savagely beat its rigid bat-like wings to gain altitude, filled with blind fury and hatred for the men who had temporarily bested it. Tavin looked back to observe that the dark clouds that had followed them all the way from Eirinor were rolling around the creature, surging with ominous light. Before Tavin knew what was happening, several more pairs of glowing crimson eyes began to emerge all over the banks of clouds. Familiar screeches filled the air and movement caught the Grandarian's eye from behind the clouds and the forest line.

As the demons mobilized behind them, Tavin looked ahead to the primary golden gates of Galantia, beginning to lower. But the foes to their backs were intent on making sure that Tavin would never reach those gates. With one massive war cry from the original Valcanor, two addition winged monsters and four of the runners Tavin and Jaren had fled from earlier all came plowing forward through the tree line. The chase again resumed, but Tavin was doubtful that a handful of tired horses could outrun three of the massive winged Valcanor and the other energized demons.

But as it turned out, they wouldn't need to outrun them. Tavin looked back to the shining capital of Galantia to see the huge golden gates gradually drop down with power to reveal several units of horsemen armed to the teeth and clad in golden cavalry armor. Tavin and Jaren couldn't help but cheer with glory as the Grandarians charged past them to meet the pursuing demons. As Tavin's convoy passed through the massive city gates, he watched as they blasted into the grounded monsters. Before he could see any more, the gates slowly began to pull back up. It was always an adventure riding into Galantia. The main entrance was the legendary Gate Yard, constructed after the First Holy War five centuries ago against Drakkaidia. The actual gate stood some fifty feet tall and nearly five feet thick. Since its construction, no force had ever come close to breaching it. Garoll and his men led the boys into the main Gate Yard where a handful of servants were waiting for them. Garoll brought his men to a stop and moved over to Tavin.

"This is where we part for now, my young friend. My men and I must join the battle to aid the Grandarians. It is your task to keep safe until you can meet with the Mystic Sage who should be here shortly. Go with these servants. They are sent by the Supreme Granisian himself, so you should be in good care. Until our next meeting, boys." With that, the Southlander brought up his blade and commanded, "To battle, men!" The Southlanders cheered and rode back to the gates. Tavin and Jaren dismounted and ran after them to get a good look at the battle. The Grandarians had beaten the few demons back into the woods, but he knew better than most their resilience to steel. As the gate slowly moved back up, Tavin and Jaren wished they could rearm themselves and help, but the servants of the Supreme Granisian were on them instantly.

"Do not let their sacrifice be in vain, young ones," one of the servants advised. "Now please come with us. Your presence is required at once in the castle." Tavin was taken aback once more. How could their presence be required if no one knew they were coming? Had Zeroan made all of these arrangements but not come to help them in person? Tavin and Jaren exchanged baffled glances as they were led to a royal coach and out of the Gate Yard to the next level of the city. As they sped out of the Gate Yard, Tavin noticed the sky growing darker and darker as the demonic storm rolled in above them.

Traveling into the city at a nearly dangerous speed on the tiled roads, Tavin and Jaren hardly had time to enjoy its beautiful scenery. Galantia was broken into four distinct levels. The first was the Gate Yard, the entrance and military base of the city. It was also the center where trade was conducted on behalf of the entire city. Next was the main city, filled with common people and all things that pertained to them. Though city life was grand even for them, a step up was the more extravagant houses for nobles and other such people of importance among the Grandarians. Last was the legendary Golden Castle that housed the Elemental Temple of Light at its core. Having been built centuries ago by the first Supreme Granisian, it was one of the oldest but most well maintained structures still standing in Iairia.

As they moved into the castle courtyard and exited the carriage, Tavin and Jaren looked around them in amazement. Even with his father, Tavin had never been in the proximity of the Golden Castle. There was another protective wall around it and inside a massive courtyard for assemblies, yet there were no gates to the structure. The entrance was a massive arching hallway known as the Grand Vestibule that branched off into the castle. Not long after they pulled into the courtyard, they were greeted by two more figures to add to the group of servants. The first was a calm and collected looking individual draped in white robes with ornate golden crests littered over them. The second was a young girl no older than the boys, covered in a simple silver cloak. Jaren looked to the man in white as he began to speak, but found it difficult to keep his eyes of the striking young girl.

"Greetings, young sirs," he said in a disarming tone. "I am Seriol, the Chief Advisor to His Holiness the Supreme Granisian, Corinicus Kolior. It is my pleasure to welcome you to the Golden Castle. My assistant and I are here to escort you both to your respective destinations. Master Garrinal, you will go with my assistant here, Mary, and Tavinious, you will need to follow me." Jaren managed to tear his eyes away from the girl just long enough to issue a complaint.

"Now wait just a minute," he interrupted with fervor. "I have no idea how you know who I am, but I guarantee you don't know what I've been through these past days, and I'm not about to leave Tavin now!" Seriol smiled at Jaren.

"I can see you are loyal to your friend, Master Garrinal. But for now, I must ask you to trust me, for a matter of great importance awaits Tavinious which he must see to alone. You will be able to see him with Mary no doubt very soon." Jaren looked to Tavin, who nodded for him to trust the man in white. "Fine..." he muttered. While he hated being separated from his friend, he didn't mind the beautiful company of the servant girl at all.

So Tavin parted with his best friend for the first time since they left their village almost over a day ago. While Jaren went with Seriol's assistant Mary and the group of servants he had met in the Gate Yard, Tavin made his way into the Golden Castle with Seriol. Still lost in current events, the boy grew somewhat frustrated that everyone seemed to know more about him than he did lately. Though hesitant to speak in the fabulous Grand Vestibule, he asked Seriol what they were doing, a pinch of irritation in his voice. The advisor smiled again.

"I must ask you to remain patient for a little while longer, young Tavinious. We will be there soon," he assured.

"Could you at least tell me where you are leading me, Seriol?" Tavin asked again.

"We are going to the Tower of Granis." Tavin was awestruck at this revelation. Being part of the Temple of Light, the Tower of Granis housed some of the most important artifacts and talismans in all of Grandaria. Not just anyone was admitted entrance.

Led by the disarming Chief Advisor of the Supreme Granisian, Tavin was taken through the most extravagant surroundings he had ever seen in the course of his life. With statues, paintings, armor, and everything else one could imagine on display in the most ornate of presentations, Tavin felt overwhelmed by the environment for royalty. They passed through extravagant halls and stairwells for what seemed like an hour to Tavin. Eventually, they came to a massive hall decorated with detailed and colorful Grandarian crests and ancient battle armor. At the end of the hall stood an outdoor balcony that overlooked the entire castle. Now high above the ground, Tavin's eyes went wide as he looked down. The Golden Castle seemed to end all of a sudden below him, creating a rounded gap between it and the even more illustrious building ahead of him.

As Tavin looked ahead to the end of the balcony, the highest peak in the city came into view; the Tower of Granis. It was enough of an honor to enter the Golden Castle, but to pass into the Elemental Temple of Light was the greatest privilege any self respecting Grandarian could ever hope to have. They entered the illustrious gate with Seriol motioning for its powerful guards to move aside so they could ascend the staircases spiraling around the floors of relics and tokens of splendor revered by the Grandarian people. The halls were lit not with flame, but with orbs of golden light just hovering over the walls illuminating their surroundings like broad daylight. After the long ascent up the seemingly endless staircases, they at last arrived at the doors to the central chamber of the tower. Seriol stopped and moved beside the doors.

"What waits inside is for you only, Tavinious," Seriol explained in a gentle tone. "Step inside please." Tavin's face was twisted with conflicting emotion ranging from excited wonder to frustrated confusion. Though he had no idea why any of this was happening, he decided not to challenge what he was being told. With reluctance, Tavin stepped toward the massive golden doors and heaved them open, taking care to treat everything around him with the utmost respect and attention. As he stepped into the room, he heard the door lock as it closed behind him. There was something about this whole thing that didn't seem quite right. The magnificent chamber he stood in stole his attention away from his suspicions, however. He treaded in slowly, admiring the various decorations, weapons, and art throughout the chamber. It was a spellbinding environment and Tavin realized he was standing in one of the most precious rooms in all of Iairia.

He was about halfway through the main hall of the first floor when he saw the greatest treasure of them all. His mouth opened and his eyes widened as he realized what he was staring at. Not more than twenty feet away from him lay the legendary Sword of Granis, the ultimate weapon of the Grandarian nation. This was the very blade that cut down the first Warrior of Darkness centuries ago, saving the world from his conquest of darkness. As Tavin grew closer, he observed the weapon was embedded in a marble stone, supposedly keeping it safe from any who tried to take it who was not the legendary Warrior of Light; the only one who could successfully wield the sword. There was not a single inhabitant in all of Iairia that had not heard the legends of the Sword of Granis. Daring to move closer to the shimmering blade, Tavin recalled the stories he had heard from this father in his childhood. This blade was said to have been blessed by Lord Granis himself, containing the very essence of his godly powers of light.

As he marveled at the blade's silver and golden hilt with its two brilliant yellow crystals implanted in the base, a movement behind him caught Tavin's attention. Not wanting to be surprised again today, Tavin spun around quickly wrenching his own sword from its sheath over his back, ready to defend against whoever, or whatever, lurked behind him. What he found when he wheeled around surprised him more than even the foulest demon he could have imagined. The figure standing before him now was none other than the Mystic Sage Zeroan.

Chapter 8

<u>Revelation</u>

Tavin stood speechless in the towering presence of Zeroan for several long moments before the shock of his appearance was finally overridden by the frustration and curiosity that had developed around all the questions he had for the sage. Tavin lowered his weapon and began to formulate his first words for Zeroan. The sage beat him to the punch.

"It is good to see you in relatively good health, young Tieloc," he stated with a stoic expression strapped onto his dark hooded face. "I was hoping the riders of the Legion would arrive sooner than they did, but alas, they apparently left the Southland too late. Judging from your current physical state however," he said, observing Tavin's bruised and fatigued but still intact body, "you can obviously take care of yourself." Tavin moved back uncomfortably, unsure of what the sage was saying. "In any case," he continued, moving closer to the boy, "you have successfully reached Galantia and now we have a task of the utmost importance to attend to that cannot wait another moment. Come with me." With that, the cloaked sage strode around Tavin and further down the hallway. Tavin was even more flabbergasted than he had previously been. He was quick to interject with anger brimming in his voice.

"Zeroan!" he shouted. "I will do nothing further until I have some answers!" As Tavin's confident statement hit the sage, he stopped and slightly turned his head back to the daring boy.

"There are matters that warrant our immediate attention. Your inquiry can wait for later on," he told him. Tavin's eyes flared at this.

"I said no. I want to know what's going on, and I want to know what's going on right now. You've kept me in the dark for too long, sage. I want to know what everyone else seems to know about me that I don't," Tavin insisted with passion. Zeroan kept silent for a moment, and then fully turned back to Tavin. His massive form towered over the boy, but Tavin held firm, not moving or cowering back a bit.

"Very well," responded Zeroan in a hushed tone. "What would you have me tell you then?" Tavin looked down for a moment, gathering all of his thoughts. His head shot up again.

"All right. I think that all of these strange things that are happening are connected to just one thing, and I think it has something to do with what you withheld from me back at the village the night me met. Zeroan, what is the second reason why I am wanted dead by Valif Montrox and the rest of Drakkaidia?" he asked, a slight quiver of fear in his voice. The sage looked down and let out a small sigh.

"I suppose some time can be made," he said with reluctance. "This conversation needs to take place anyway. Please have a seat with me," he said, pointing over to a row of chairs in front of the platform housing the Sword of Granis. As they sat, the sage began again. "First off," he said with meaning, "I must again ask you to trust everything that I relate to you. You are the one asking for the truth, and that is all that I am offering you. Do you agree?" he asked. Tavin slowly nodded his head, trying to prepare himself for the most likely hard to believe story that the cloaked man would tell. "You are brighter than I gave you credit for to have pieced together all that you have," Zeroan complemented. "You are correct, of course. You are wanted and needed for many reasons, good and evil, because of the second reason I spoke of back in your village. I suppose I should start from that night on. When we parted company, I fled quickly from your village and through the hills to the north. I had underestimated the resourcefulness of the creatures hunting for you, and those assigned to follow me. They were much closer than even I could have imagined. I managed to lead them away from the hills, however, attracting them with a little magic." Tavin looked confused.

"What do you mean, attracting them with magic?" he asked. The sage shifted in his seat.

"All creatures fueled by the use of magic, dark or light, can feel the presence of other magic when it is active nearby. Greater magic can be sensed at greater distances. I brought forth some of the mystic powers of old that I possess and they came bolting after it, curious to discover its source. They followed me to Galantia, where they have remained until the day one of them managed to locate your village. You obviously found the warning I sent you." Tavin thought back to the day the wanton storm and the words of light in the clouds came bellowing into the hills.

"How did you create something so huge? Couldn't you have just sent a messenger or something less destructive?" Tavin asked skeptically. Zeroan shook his head no.

"The storm was not of my creation. Massive storm clouds always follow packs of Valcanor with Liradds or other such creatures of dark power. They are the winged demons and ground beasts you encountered. The storm was on its way with the Valcanor, and I used it to my advantage. It would have been hard to miss a warning of that magnitude, wouldn't it? In any case, shortly after you and Jaren departed, I sent word to the south for my ally, Garoll, already on his way here for other reasons. As you no doubt have figured out, he is one of the Elemental Warriors. I knew you would need some magic of your own if you were to keep safe on the journey here. I would have come to your aid myself, but matters of equal importance held my attention here."

"So you've been here at Galantia the whole time since you left us a month ago?" Tavin asked incredulously. Zeroan paused for a moment but clearly answered afterwards.

"...Yes. I have been here preparing for your arrival, which is how the servants of the Supreme Granisian knew to expect you. You see, Tavinious, there is a great threat to Montrox and even his evil god that lies in this temple, separated into two parts. If these two parts are united as one, it could bring about the downfall of all of the Drakkaidian's evil once and for all. One part lies in front of you, incased in marble." Tavin looked over to the legendary weapon that lay before him.

"The Sword of Granis," he said emotionlessly. "What is the second part?" Zeroan met Tavin's eyes and stared into them hard.

"The second part, Tavinious, is you."

Jaren sat quietly as he and the servant appointed to him, Mary, rode back to the Gate Yard where he just came from in the regal coach of the Supreme Granisian himself. Mary had told him that his presence would be necessary in the Gate Yard in a short while, and they were to be ready there when that time came. The girl spent most of her time gazing out the window at either the tranquil landscape of Galantia, or up at the ominous storm clouds that were growing over the skies of the city. Despite the amazing view outside, Jaren found it hard to take his eyes away from his guide, the beautiful girl dressed in silver known to him only as Mary. He frequently caught himself staring helplessly at her silky chestnut hair that passed across her soft face every time she turned. In the midst of the silence that hung about the two, their eyes occasionally met, but Mary quickly looked away, flushing as red as a cherry. Feeling awkward in such an uncomfortable atmosphere, Jaren at last decided to say something.

"I don't suppose you could tell me *why* we're going back to the Gate Yard, could you?" he asked in his usually direct manner. Mary looked up at him not saying anything for a moment, as if gathering a satisfactory answer to the boy's question.

"Well, not really," she stated shyly. "I am not permitted to tell you much more than our destination." Jaren slid back in his seat, a frustrated expression coming over his face.

"It's that Seriol guy, huh?" he guessed. "Is he the head man around here?" Mary looked up in surprise.

"You should know that Seriol is second in power only to the Supreme Granisian himself. However, Seriol and I received our orders to take care of you and your friend from another person," she stated.

"And who might that be?" Jaren inquired further, his naturally cynical tone appearing.

"You know him, I believe," she said casually. "I am acting at the request of the Mystic Sage of the Southland, Zeroan." Jaren jumped out of his seat, frightening Mary nearly to death.

"Zeroan is here?" he asked in disbelief. "For how long? Why has he just been sitting here when Tavin and I were on the verge of death out there?"

"Please calm yourself, Master Garrinal!" Mary implored, motioning for him to take his seat. "The sage Zeroan has been here off and on for about two weeks now. He arrived

51

just after he left you and your friend in the Hills of Eirinor, or so I'm told. He has been here protecting something of great importance for we Grandarians. Please do not think ill of him for not coming to your aid. He wanted to, I'm sure, but his charge kept him stationed here. Besides," she said, trying to ease Jaren down, "I heard you were a great warrior anyway. Would you have really needed his help?" Jaren sat down, regaining his composure.

"Oh, I guess not. I am a pretty great warrior, now that you mention it," he said, reveling in the attention. Mary giggled, assuming he was just toying with her.

The two began to talk more easily then, as Jaren slowly brought Mary out of her shell with his humor and sly wit. They arrived back at the Gate Yards a short while later, only to find a surprisingly large unit of troops obviously preparing for battle. He turned to Mary with a puzzled look on his face.

"What's with the assembly all of a sudden?" he asked. Mary's face grew grave as she bade him to follow her through the Gate Yard and upward to the front wall.

"According to the sage Zeroan, there is going to be an attack on the city soon," she began. "There have been reports of horrible monsters roaming the outskirts of the city at night, and he has told us that they are going to appear before us today. Zeroan says that they are looking for something. He will not tell us what it is, however. We have soldiers ready as you can see, but with most of our troops at the Wall of Light to the west, we have no army here." The two scaled upward to the top of the Golden Wall. Fierce storm clouds surging with lightning blockaded the skies over the woods where Jaren and Tavin had fought the two Liradds earlier in the day. Jaren stood in awe at the sight of the enormous dark clouds choking the sky with the evil they contained. Mary turned to face Jaren. "Zeroan told me you were one of the best bowmen in the whole of Grandaria. He said you could help hold them back considerably when they break out of those clouds, Master Garrinal." Jaren stared at her in disbelief, wondering how the sage knew anything about him, or why he would make such a bold assumption. Jaren looked back out at the storm and drew his bow.

"Well then," he said with a sly grin, "let's get ready. And by the way. 'Master Garrinal' is making my skin creep. The name's Jaren." Mary blushed and nodded in acknowledgment.

Tavin stared at Zeroan trying to make sense of this revelation the sage had shared with him. Too confused to say anything, Tavin patiently waited for Zeroan to continue. When no further explanation of his forthright statement came, Tavin pressed further himself.

"What do you mean, 'I'm the other part?'" he slowly asked, almost afraid of what the sage might say. Zeroan stood up and gathered his gray flowing robes about him.

"I mean exactly what I said. As a Grandarian, you know the prophesy of the Warrior of Light. It tells us that when the Sword of Granis joins with the one with chosen blood, their dormant powers will both be unlocked to flare up with new incredible power," he explained. Tavin sat in shock, not knowing what to think.

"What are you saying, Zeroan?" he asked quietly.

"You know what I am saying, Tavinious," he responded equally quiet. "There is power flowing through your veins. You know this. You have felt it your entire life. Your ancestor, the first Tieloc, was the original Warrior of Light, savior of old Grandaria. All those in his lineage since then have possessed that same power, dormant in within their hearts, and you are no exception. The key to reactivating that power is in that sword; it is a key. Evil has resurfaced to destroy the world once more and the time has come for another Warrior of Light to rise up and wield the Sword of Granis against it."

"But, but..." Tavin was stammering over himself, "The Warrior of Light is supposed to be the most powerful being in the world! I'm not even an adult yet! What could I do with this kind of power? And how do you know that my family is connected to the first Tieloc? Do you know how common that name is here? I mean *my* family isn't even sure if we're related to him anymore." Zeroan did not flinch.

"Remember when I said that it is possible to sense the Holy Emerald shards when they are in possession of one with magical ability? Well it may be too faint for Montrox to detect, but I have felt the power of a Tieloc holding a talisman of power with him before, and it is the same with you, Tavinious.

From the first moment you picked up that shard years ago, I have felt it and known." Tavin remained skeptical.

"Fine, but if anyone in my family could be the Warrior of Light, why me? Couldn't my father do a better job with this responsibility?" Zeroan moved over to the trembling boy, towering over him again.

"Do not doubt yourself, Tavinious," he snapped. "Your father would be the one to take up the sword but he is, simply put, too old. His aged and worn body couldn't wield the full extent of the power needed to destroy the most potent evil in existence physically unscathed. You are still young and pure of heart. It must be you. Now enough of this talk. You must have faith in yourself if you are to take up the sword and unleash its power now." Tavin was standing now as well.

"What? Why would you want me to do that!?!" he questioned almost yelling.

"Because, young man," Zeroan continued frustrated with the boy's uncooperative attitude, "you and the power you possess is the only thing standing in Valif Montrox's way to gathering the remaining five shards of the Holy Emerald and resurrecting the God of Darkness to subjugate the entire land of Iairia. He is the Warrior of Darkness, just as you are the Warrior of Light, and the only power that can stand against his is yours. It is your destiny to save the world from his evil. That is why he wants you dead, not because of the shard you carry. That is the second reason I spoke of. Does all that satisfy you, Tavinious?" he asked sharply, as if the subject matter he had just imparted was nothing.

Tavin stared at him with his jaw dropped, not able to utter a single sound. Zeroan turned toward the Sword of Granis. "I told you that all I was offering was the truth. That was it. Now if that is all for the moment, we have work to do. Montrox and his demons now know that you have arrived in Galantia, and he will no doubt attempt to strike the city to stop you from activating the power buried deep inside you. Even now, his demons prepare for a final attack, and you must be there, sword in hand, to stop them. Now come." As the cloaked figure strode toward the sword, Tavin struggled to come to terms with what he had just learned. "Hurry, Tavinious," Zeroan ordered. "The battle will begin any minute, and this could take a considerable amount of time to accomplish." Tavin regained some of his senses, and slowly walked after Zeroan toward the mighty Sword of Granis.

Chapter 9

<u>Rebirth</u>

Shortly after he and Mary arrived atop the Golden Wall of Galantia bordering the Gate Yard from the outside of the city, Jaren noticed a group of horsemen riding over the southeast ridge toward the city. He set down his bow he had been restringing and walked over to Mary, leaning over the wall.

"Hey, who are those riders down there?" he asked the girl, pointing over to them. Mary breathed a sigh of relief when she caught sight of them and smiled over at Jaren.

"Those are the Southlanders and the Elemental Warrior of the Earth, I believe. You have already met him, correct?" Jaren didn't respond, but stared at her in amazement instead. Jaren thought he had been knocked unconscious when Mary smiled at him. She looked somewhat confused. "What is it?" she asked a little nervous. He shook his head and raised his eyebrows as he replied.

"Your smile is ridiculously pretty," he whispered in his usual forthright manner, completely catching the girl off guard. Mary blushed brighter than she had all day and giggled again, not really knowing how to respond.

As the band of horsemen rode into the city gates, Jaren and Mary rushed down to meet them. Garoll was the first to notice the two.

"Hey! Look who it is! How are you doing, kid?" he asked. Jaren enthusiastically shook his hand as the burly man dismounted his horse with the rest of the riders.

"I'm still in one piece, thanks to you and your men," he said graciously. He looked around at the other Southlanders moving toward him and Garoll.

"Ah! Come on over here Legionnaires," Garoll called. "I want you to meet the boy. Jaren, these are the other elite volunteers of the Southland Legion to accompany me here. Everyone, this is the young bowman I told you about! He

55

and his friend took down four Liradds without any magic and were about to take on a Valcanor!" Jaren grinned from ear to ear as the attention came flowing at him. Garoll shot his head up at the sky. "Looks like we got here just in time, too. Those clouds don't look too normal to me," he observed, staring upward.

The Warrior of Earth's eyes drifted down to meet Jaren's once more but spotted the gentle form of Mary first. "Why, Your Highness," he exclaimed taken aback. "I didn't think you would be out here now!" Jaren's eyes widened as he turned to Mary. The girl's face locked up as she rushed toward Garoll to jump up to her tiptoes and whisper something in his ear. He nodded in response, grinning. Before Jaren could ask what that was all about, his attention was taken by the sounding of several horns atop the Golden Wall. At the sound of the horns, all the military personnel around them scrambled upward in a frantic frenzy to take defensive positions around the perimeter of the wall. Garoll shot his head back to the skies. "Legionnaires, to the walls! They're coming!" he shouted.

Back in the aureate Elemental Temple of Light, Tavin and Zeroan had both moved to the large and ornate platform at the end of the tower's first hall where the Sword of Granis peacefully rested, the tip of its blade encased in a block of marble. Tavin stood in awe at its splendor, wondering how he could ever wield such a magnificent and legendary talisman. Tavin's subconscious thoughts were interrupted as the Mystic Sage Zeroan's head suddenly bolted around. He cursed under his breath and brought his eyes back to meet with the boy's. Tavin could see a sense of urgency and alarm tearing through the sage's face.

"Tavinious," he began in a hurry, "our time is shorter than I thought. The demons attack now and in greater numbers than I had anticipated. You must hurry and complete the trial." He looked down, thinking to himself, then turned back to the door. "Seriol!" he called. The massive golden doors slowly swung open revealing the form of the Chief Advisor to the Supreme Granisian, Seriol. Tavin shot a confused glance toward Zeroan. "The prophesy of the Warrior of Light tells that there must be two witnesses present for him to take possession of the sword. Now to begin." Zeroan moved over to Tavin and placed his hand on the boy's shoulder. "You are about to embark on the most important trial of your life, Tavinious. To succeed, you must be strong of body, strong of mind, and strong of heart."

Zeroan led Tavin over to where the sword rested and knelt down beside him, revealing the whole of his usually hidden face. There was an ambiguity and reservation in the boy's eyes that had never been present there before. Zeroan attempted to alter the tone of his voice to speak to him accordingly.

"Tavinious, I know you must be shrouded with uncertainty and doubt right now, but you are who you are. But do not take my word for it. If you still doubt or distrust what I have said, dispel your doubts for yourself. Go and place your hands around the hilt of the sword. If it does not react, then I will have been wrong. But should it accept you as its rightful master, it will commence your trial and you will see for yourself that you are indeed the rightful Warrior of Light." Tavin was still beside himself with disbelief that any of this was happening.

"...Zeroan, I..." he fumbled.

"Tavin, do as I have said," the sage responded, strangely tender. "What have you to lose?" Hearing that, Tavin realized he didn't have anything to lose. Though he knew he could not be who the sage claimed him to be, there would be no harm in proving him wrong. Suddenly becoming somewhat clear again, Tavin slowly nodded his head and fixed his gaze back onto the sage.

"Fine," he murmured almost inaudibly. Zeroan faintly smiled.

"Good, Tavinious. Now when the sword responds to your touch," he stated with confidence, "it will then take you to a world out of this one. When you reach it, go forth and find the sword again. You will then be tested. I do not know the nature of this test, but I am confident you will pass it." The sage placed one of his massive hands over the boy's right shoulder. "Listen to me, Tavin. You may not wish to accept this responsibility, or even this truth, but this *is* your destiny; your charge in life. You are the only one who can wield the Sword of Granis, and that is the only way your hidden powers will ever be awakened to stand against the evil of Drakkaidia.

You must believe in yourself and in your destiny. I know it is hard to take in right now, but you must have faith in yourself if you are to pass the test. Do you understand?" Tavin found it impossibly hard to listen to all of this, and even harder to respond.

"But, Zeroan," he managed quietly, "If you're right, I'm not sure if I can handle a charge like this. And even if I can, I'm not sure that I want it," he truthfully replied. Zeroan smiled.

"It is enough that you can admit that. This is your destiny, and the sword will know it. In time, you will come to know this as well." Tavin looked back at him, meeting his uncharacteristically gentle gaze. The boy felt somewhat eased at these words as a wave of new found confidence and understanding flushed through him.

"I'll try my best, Zeroan," he stated, pulling himself together. The sage smiled once more, rose, and turned back to walk down the platform.

Tavin moved over to the base where the sword lay, gazing at its vast beauty once again. A blast of determination and purpose then burst through him as he raised his hands and wrapped them firmly around the hilt of the sword. As he did, it began to slowly and faintly radiate with golden light. Tavin's eyes opened wide, realizing he had triggered the luminosity. Soon after he acknowledged the mighty blade was indeed reacting to him, its now fervent light quickly spread across the entire golden chamber, engulfing all it drew near in the shimmering rays. The piercing light then transferred from the blade itself over and onto Tavin, engulfing him in the radiating energy as well. The glow became too intense to maintain eye contact with, and Zeroan and Seriol were forced to look away.

Tavin came awake slowly, hesitating to open his eyes because of the blinding light emitting from everywhere they seemed to drift. Slowly shifting, he found himself resting on his back in the middle of a thick forest, though he quickly realized it was far from ordinary. Gazing around mesmerized, Tavin observed that every last tree or plant he saw was glowing in a fierce golden aura of light. He struggled to adjust his vision to properly examine his bright surroundings. When he opened his eyes again, he saw that the environment was not only just radiating the golden light; it was made up of it. He slowly rose to his feet, feeling the air withdrawing from his lungs from his excitement and qualms. The Sword of Granis had reacted to him and sent him to another world, just as Zeroan had said. Did this mean that he was indeed the Warrior of Light? Or was this just some universal effect of laying hands on the legendary talisman? Whatever had happened, Tavin was now faced with the prospect of getting back to his world.

Forgetting his worries over the Sword of Granis for a moment, Tavin let his gaze fall onto the tree line comprised of light. He walked over to one of the massive trunks protruding from the golden earth, his bedazzled eyes squinting from the brilliant emanating radiance. With hesitancy, he brought forth his hand and placed it on the tree. The light flared outward upon contact, sending a revitalized wave of amazement through the boy. Bewildered and awestruck at his surroundings, he walked down the path he had woke from in the middle of the forest of light. Noticing a sharp radiance beneath him, he brought his head down to observe that every step he took caused the very earth he stood on to flare with luminosity. Tavin gazed around him taking in his beautiful surroundings as best he could, a quiet smile creeping across his face. At one point a small bird also made up of the shimmering light emerged from the confines of its nest and took flight past him. It left a trail of shining particles in the wake of its flapping wings that slowly dissolved into the air after a few moments. He felt awkward being the only normally colored and solid thing in the forest made up of light, but remained captivated by the dream world he stood within.

Tavin kept walking until he came to a large platform in front of him. He stopped suddenly, sensing a strange familiarity about the glowing structure. The boy moved closer until the whole of it was in his view. He wondered what a glamorous platform like this would be doing hidden in the forest. It was not until his eyes found what the platform contained that he realized why it appeared so familiar to him. This was the same platform that resided inside the Tower of Granis from where he had just come. Sure enough, the replica came complete with the object it was designed to house: the Sword of Granis. Upon first laying his eyes on the copy of the sword, Tavin immediately noticed that, like him, it was not made up of the light that everything else in this world was. As he slowly approached it, the sword began to pulse with the same energy it had back at the tower.

When Tavin was not more than a few feet away from it, a deep voice suddenly emanated through the air.

"Welcome, Tavinious Tieloc," the deep but disarming voice sounded. Tavin was stunned that the mysterious voice knew his name. He stepped onto the platform gathering his thoughts, not sure where to direct his response.

"Where am I?" he asked. The voice was slow to answer him.

"That is not possible to answer, for you reside in two places now." Tavin struggled with the voice's response.

"What do you mean I'm in two places?" he asked with careful curiosity entangled in his own voice. The other responded simply and surely.

"Your physical self can be found inside the Elemental Temple of Light, along with the Sword of Granis. You spiritual self is here, inside the spirit of the sword. But now *I* must ask a question of *you*, young Grandarian. Why are you here?" the voice questioned. Tavin's thoughts all froze hearing this, not sure how to respond. Though he still harbored a lingering doubt that all this could be real, he now came to the realization that the Mystic Sage back in the Temple of Light could be right. Tavin was related to the first Tieloc, the original Warrior of Light centuries ago. The Sword of Granis had indeed reacted to him and sent him to another world as had been said. And most importantly of all, Tavin could feel something inside him now; something that he had always subconsciously known was there, but had never been able to identify. There was a feeling of some untold strength boiling inside of his very veins, calling to him to be activated; awoken from its state of dormancy. Tavin nodded his head to prove to himself that this was all true, and slowly brought his gaze back onto the weapon.

"I am here to claim the Sword of Granis to become the Warrior of Light," he stated, stunning but stimulating himself at the same time.

"You truly believe that you are the Warrior of Light?" the voice inquired. As the sword's energy radiated when the voice sounded, Tavin realized that it was the weapon itself speaking to him. Now focused on this new all important goal before him, his confidence finally reached its peak and he responded with assurance.

"Yes," he replied, locking his eyes on the weapon.

"And do you possess the strength to wield me?" the blade asked in a challenging manner, aware that Tavin had discovered it was the source of the voice. Tavin didn't miss a beat.

"Yes," Tavin said with assertion that astonished even himself.

"Then if you possess the strength," the sword finished almost arrogantly, "come and take possession of me." Accepting the blade's apparent challenge, Tavin gradually moved forward toward the golden stone of light where the blade lay entrapped. Staring the radiant weapon down for a moment, he at last made his move. For the second time, he thrust his grip onto the hilt of the blade. This time, the reaction was even more spectacular than in the tower. The once barely glowing light of the sword burst forth in an explosion of golden rays searing into Tavin's body with a tidal wave of force and pain, wrenching him free of the hilt and blowing him backward to the far side of the platform. Tavin landed forcefully on his back in pain. The voice from the sword let out a huff of disgust. "You possess the strength indeed. You are nothing more than a common weakling." The words from the blade tore at Tavin even harder and more painfully than the erupting energy had.

Not willing to have gone through all that he had the past few days only to meet with failure now, Tavin locked his face into battle position and stood up, raw determination to succeed pulsing through his veins. He strode back over to the hilt of the sword and threw the full force of his body into it with a scream of the unwavering resolve that had taken possession of him. As soon as he met with the sword, the explosion of energy tore into him again. As Tavin desperately struggled to keep his hands around the hilt, the pain tore through his body with the force of it threatening to crush his very bones to dust. But through the onslaught of the ripping energy, Tavin held firm.

Right at the end of the struggle, he could feel the power radiating from the sword increase dramatically. Such force came blasting into him it was as if it was incinerating every last cell in his body. He could feel his grip loosening around the hilt and his strength draining away. With his hopes dwindling, a flash of memories came hurdling into his mind, covering all that had befallen him and Jaren in the past two days. After all they had endured and all those who had helped them so Tavin could reach this sword, there was no way he could let so many people who were depending on him down. Through the pain and agony he was enduring, Tavin offered a final charge of resistance against that of the sword.

"I'm not giving up!" he bellowed. "I will have you, Sword of Granis!"

Right then, deep in the core of his soul, Tavin could feel something happen; something change. Some long hidden previously invisible barrier was smashed to pieces and a rush of feeling came pouring out. The feeling was not as though he was experiencing it for the first time, however. It felt as if it had always been with him, but now simply appeared to him more clearly. With the incredible feeling of power ready and available to him, Tavin pulled every ounce of it outward, steadily rising and countering the effects of the sword's power. After a few moments of this power rising throughout his body, any and all traces of force or pain against him disappeared. Then, as if the Sword of Granis knew right then and there that it was beaten; that it knew this boy was indeed the one destined to wield it, the force of its power shifted.

Instead of working its power against him, it fused with Tavin's and flowed. The Grandarian boy then felt power as he had never dreamt possible engulfing him. Caught up in the rush of strength surging through his body, Tavin barely noticed that his surroundings had changed. He was reunited with his physical body back in the Tower of Granis, with Zeroan and Seriol standing not more than fifteen feet away. As he stood there on the platform radiating in his newly found power, Tavin realized that the sword was no longer resisting him in any way. With barely any effort at all, he heaved the mighty blade upward, jetting it out of its marble prison to be free once more.

As the Sword of Granis came bursting forth, a magnificent ringing of steel cut through the air, echoing through the golden halls of the tower with power surging through every wave of sound. Tavin could not help but grin as the incredible strength continued to swarm around him leaving his once aching body with new strength in every cell. He had never felt so energized or ready for anything in his life. The power from the Sword of Granis flowing with his own in perfect harmony, he felt a new bond with it, as if the sword itself was now a part of his being that he could not physically be without.

As Tavin began to realize the connection he had made with the Sword of Granis, he raised its shimmering hilt to his eyes, mesmerized by its craftsmanship and beauty. The hilt was long, allowing for plenty of room for both of its wielder's hands to be placed over it when drawn. Shining with a metallic silver body and ornately decorated with gold gilded where the hilt met the blade, it was by far the most radiant object that he had ever dreamed of. As Tavin ran his eyes up the razor sharp blade of the weapon, he found the words "Sword of Granis" engraved into the lower segment. Two golden crystals lay embedded near the hilt of the weapon; one mounted where the blade met it and shining with light, and the other directly below it, dormant.

As Tavin stood there engulfed in the radiating field of golden light, Zeroan let a slight smile spread across his face.

Well done, Tavinious, he thought. Well done.

Chapter 10

<u>New Light</u>

As the aura of golden energy radiating from Tavin and the Sword of Granis slowly began to fade, the Mystic Sage Zeroan gathered his gray robes about him and started forward. He could see the empowered look in the boy's eyes. Though Tavin was exhausted from his ordeal in the spirit of the sword, Zeroan could tell he was bristling with his newfound power that provided him with a level of energy he never knew he possessed. These mixed emotions were cut short for Tavin as Zeroan came striding up to the platform. The boy turned to meet him, his breathing returning to normal. Zeroan stopped in front of him and patted Tavin on the shoulder.

"Congratulations, Tavinious," he quietly praised. "You are the first since your eldest ancestor to take up the Sword of Granis and become the legendary Warrior of Light. There are few who have ever lived or who will ever live who posses the strength and determination required to overcome the trial of the sword. You have passed with flying colors, my young Grandarian." Still struggling to think over all that had befallen him with the sword, it was all Tavin could do to nod and squeeze a tight smile back in acknowledgment. Zeroan's face morphed back to its usually stern expression as he began his next statement. "While I wish you could have some time to rest yourself and recover all of your natural energy, there is one last urgent task we must see to before you can." Tavin's jaw nearly dropped to the floor along with the tip of the sword.

"What?" he shouted in disbelief. "I just passed through the biggest challenge in my life, and now you want me do something else? What is it with you, Zeroan!?!" yelled Tavin in aggravation.

"I assure you this is very important. If you would be so good as to recall, there is a host of demons from the bowels of the Netherworld attacking the Gate Yard as we speak, threatening the entire populace as well as your friends on the wall. Them seeing your power is the only thing that will drive them away," he explained. "Now hurry, Tavinious. We have lingered too long as it is. We must be off." As Zeroan turned back for the door, Seriol approached Tavin carrying something in his hands.

"This is for you, Tavinious," he said as he brought forth an ornate sheath obviously intended for the Sword of Granis. "Congratulations on your success with the sword. If there is anything I can ever do for you, please just ask."

"Well thank you, Seriol," Tavin said flattered. "And there is something you can do for me, actually. This goes for you as well, Zeroan." The sage turned his head to face him.

"What is it, Tavinious?" he asked. Tavin raised the glamorous Sword of Granis before him, his eyes passing over its incredible surface one last time before he slowly sheathed its blade. The Warrior of Light smiled and said,

"Call me Tavin."

Meanwhile in the Gate Yard, Jaren, Mary, the Grandarian troops, and Garoll with his Southlanders were scrambling to get to the top of the wall to meet the advancing demons that had just emerged from the line of storm clouds beyond the city. Upon reaching the top, Jaren could make out several of the Liradd amongst a few other dark creatures, some scaly and horned, some more hairy and mammal like. He also counted at least four of the winged monsters know as Valcanor sweeping across the skies down onto the helpless soldiers.

As the Grandarians and Legionnaires from the south lined the walls with bows and swords, Jaren and the Elemental Warrior of Earth had spread across the wall to aid the overwhelmed and frightened soldiers with their various skills and abilities where they could. The Valcanor were the primary threat, but they were far too large and powerful to be harmed by simple arrows even from Jaren's deadly accurate bow. He instead took aim at the Liradds and other such ground based beasts attempting to scale the walls with their sharp claws. With Mary behind him constantly replenishing his ammunition, Jaren was able to fire arrow after arrow in rapid succession, keeping the beasts back from the top of the wall. As he battled over the side of the wall, Garoll and his guard contended with some of the nastier demons who had already invaded the wall or the airspace above it. Garoll and his powers over the earth lifted enormous boulders that came ripping out of the ground and into the skies to pummel the four airborne monsters.

The defense was weakening as the demons grew closer to the wall, for Jaren could not hold all of them by himself. As one of the clawed monsters fell under his hail of missiles, a mammoth black creature covered in wild tangled hair came catapulting over Jaren, landing just behind him and the now terrified Mary. Jaren immediately spun around and fired his arrow into the creature's face, buzzing straight past Mary's with a jet of wind. Landing in its eye, the demon immediately set to work screaming and pawing at the protruding source of its pain with its razor covered claws. Prying it loose, it flung back its head in rage and charged wildly at the frozen and trembling girl in front of it.

Already moving to keep his self-appointed charge safe, Jaren leapt as hard and fast as he could, catching the girl and pulling her out of the demon's way just before it could latch onto her. Not quick enough to escape completely unscathed, Jaren felt a sudden burst of excruciating pain rush from his leg up to his brain. He clamped down his jaws to keep himself from screaming out. The demon had clawed into Jaren's lower leg before he cleared out of range, and then bounded back at him. Not stopping for anything Jaren scooped up his bow and snatched the three arrows that Mary still held in her grasp as if clinging onto life itself. Before the monster could turn back and get to them, he strung all three and let them fly right into the demon's gnarled skull with one obviously penetrating too far in as it quickly fell to the ground to meet with a quick death.

Watching his foe fell to the cold surface of the wall, Jaren dropped his bow in relief and slid back against the barrier behind him. Breathing hard, his head turned over to find the still frozen and shaking form of Mary cowering beside him. He slowly reached out to her and gently placed his hand over her shoulder. She jumped and wheeled around violently.

"Hey, it's okay," Jaren said with assurance poured into his voice as if he were comforting a crying child missing its mother. "We're fine now." Jaren wrapped his arm around the trembling girl, still frightened out of her mind. As Jaren held her in his steady arms, Mary relaxed some. She glanced down for a moment and noticed that Jaren was hurt.

"Jaren, your leg is bleeding," she managed to say. He nodded in a no big deal kind of way.

"You don't think I know that?" he told her with a smile. "It's nothing I haven't had before at one time or another. But listen. I think its time for you to get out of here. It's starting to get nasty and even with Garoll's power, I don't think that we can do much more by ourselves..." Jaren suddenly stopped short. As he stared upward, Mary could see fear mirrored in his eyes.

Jaren pulled the girl close as the beat of a familiar pair of massive wings echoed in his ears. Plummeting down from the skies came the same massive Valcanor that Jaren and Tavin and encountered in the vale that morning. It was damaged from the boulder that Garoll had hurled into it, but it was still plenty strong to finish a wounded boy and a trembling, helpless girl. Jaren grinned in spite of himself, realizing the irony that fate had dealt him.

"I got away from you once when you were about to finish me," he quietly said to the mighty Valcanor. "Looks like your gonna' finish the job after all."

As the winged nightmare advanced toward the two helpless figures, a familiar war cry followed by the strident ringing of steel sounded through the clamor of the battle behind the Valcanor. Noting the piercing cry of metal from behind it as well, the Valcanor began to turn its ravaged head back. Before it could so much as turn to face whatever was behind it however, it abruptly let out an ear piercing shriek and jerked forward in terrible pain. Baffled at what could have damaged the gargantuan creature that had before been seemingly immune to any physical attack, Jaren observed a fervent golden aura of shimmering light emerge from behind the demon's hulking figure. As the light from behind it intensified, another slash of a blade ripping into its savage form caused the Valcanor to scream out in pain once more and spread its massive wings in retreat, immediately lifting it off the wall.

As the Valcanor sped away over him, Jaren could make out its gnarled arms covering two deep slashes in its side. Bringing his head back in amazement to the light before him, Jaren finally realized it was a person with a shimmering blade in his hands that was emanating the light. It was hard for him to make out the face of the person before him, but as the light began to slightly dim, Jaren saw who had just somehow saved their lives. Tavin stood there, a magnificent sword in hand, radiating golden energy from his very body and smiling down at him. Jaren's eyes spread as wide as they could get as Tavin started walking toward him, the shimmering energy surrounding his body. He knelt down to the two.

"Hey, I'm back," he said with a grin. Jaren nodded, and let out a laugh, almost hyperventilating.

"Took you long enough," he joked, too stunned to do anything else.

"Obviously. I leave you for a few minutes and you go and get yourself nearly killed. What *would* you do without me?" Tavin smiled wider as his eyes fell down to the quaking form of Mary, pressing herself tightly against Jaren and staring up at Tavin in confusion. "I see you replaced me as your best friend, too." Mary let out a smile herself for the first time in quite awhile, though she was far too worked up to say anything. Tavin was about to help his friend up when a bundle of flying robes came bolting upward over the inside of the wall. The appearance of the Mystic Sage Zeroan nearly shocked Jaren even more than the arrival of his best friend with his mysterious new power. Before the sage could say anything, two Liradds plowing over a group of Grandarian archers descended on the four. Quick to respond, the sage sealed his eyes and silently began muttering a collection in a strange dialect. Then as his eyes burst open, he threw his right hand back sending his robes flying out with it. He clenched his open hand into a fist, locking a telekinetic grip onto the few remaining arrows scattered around Jaren, and quickly threw his arm forward toward the advancing Liradds. Following the powerful command of the Mystic Sage, the arrows flew off the ground whizzing past Zeroan's flailing robes and into the Liradds' wicked faces, casting their instantly lifeless corpses into the ground. Zeroan shouted over to Tavin.

"Tavin! You must use your power! Focus now and let it flow. Hold up the Sword of Granis and shine its light outward! The demons have not seen it for centuries and cannot yet bear its mere presence. Hurry! I cannot hold them for long!" Tavin looked uncertain.

"I'll try," he responded.

"There isn't any time to try!" Zeroan shouted back. "Do it!" he commanded, firing another flurry of lose arrows into an approaching demon.

Ready to help in anyway he could, Tavin closed his eyes and brought up the sword, holding it tight and close to his torso. Jaren watched in awe as the golden aura of light flared up anew around him, then surged into the blade of his new ornate sword. Tavin's eyes shot open, determination mirrored in them. With both hands wrapped around the hilt of the legendary weapon, he thrust the tip of its blade into the air above him to pour out the radiant energy of its light into the atmosphere. The glow was so intense that even the commanding Zeroan was forced to tightly close his eyes. The demons still on the wall fared far worse as the righteous light fell upon their tainted flesh. Burning into them with searing pain that they had not felt the likes of for centuries, every last one of the dark creatures backed away in terror. Observing the effects of the omnipotent light from his blade, Tavin lowered it from above his head and thrust it outward into the remaining demons on the wall. Crying out in untold pain, whatever was left of their forces backed away and sped into full retreat.

Watching the monsters withdrawing from the wall and back across the hill below the city, Tavin could not help but grin at the blow he had just dealt to the previously near invincible creatures of darkness. His mind at ease, the brilliant aura of light shimmering from his form began to slowly fade. While Jaren sat speechless, the defenders of Galantia found the wall free of demons and began cheering with fervor, calling out praise for the Warrior of Light. Garoll Nelpia looked over the wall at the fields below and yelled out to the Grandarians in triumph.

"The Warrior of Light has done it! They are retreating!" he bellowed with elation.

As Tavin received his plaudits from the soldiers, the dark cloaked figure of Zeroan strode over to the golden warrior.

"Impressive, Tavin," the sage said. "I didn't think you would be able to harness the will of the sword so quickly." Tavin smiled casually as the last shroud of light dissipated around him.

"Thanks, Zeroan. But I really hope there are no other 'tasks' we have to see to," he pleaded. Zeroan chuckled darkly in spite of himself.

"No my young friend, it is over for now. You can finally get your rest." Tavin let out a massive sigh of relief. As he did, he caught Jaren out of the corner of his eye and turned to meet his friend. Jaren stared wide eyed with his jaw dropped. They both just stared at each other, one too shocked and the other too tired to say anything, until Jaren finally broke the silence.

"Okay," he started awestruck, "what did I miss?"

Chapter 11

<u>Recuperation</u>

After the battle atop the Golden Wall of the city of Galantia just before dusk, the two boys from Eirinor were rushed back to the Golden Castle. While Jaren was ready to bask in all his glory as the lone bowman that held back waves of unholy minions, the Mystic Sage Zeroan insisted that he and especially Tavin remain anonymous for their own good. Disappointed, Jaren was sent to the castle's infirmary for immediate medical attention at the request of Mary, still by his side. Meanwhile, the regal form of Seriol appeared again to inform Tavin he was invited into the castle as well, promising him all the rest he could ever need. He accepted without a second thought. After entering the grand citadel, Tavin and Jaren reluctantly split paths once more. Though they both wished to hear of each other's exploits since their previous parting, Zeroan promised that they would have all the time they wanted later the next day.

After the boys parted, Jaren found himself living life as if he was the Supreme Granisian himself. In the infirmary, he quickly discovered that being a war hero wasn't so bad. All he had to do was snap his fingers to have a flock of the finest medical professionals available, the servants of the royal family, and Mary, practically begging to assist him in any way possible. As they patched him up through the night, the young hero continually boasted that 'it was nothing and he would be fine.'

Meanwhile in the royal guest room of the castle, Tavin quickly dismissed the veritable legion of servants and leapt straight for the massive bed, falling fast asleep with the Sword of Granis still latched onto his back. Zeroan appeared outside from time to time, coming and going between his numerous errands throughout the castle to check on him. As the next morning arrived, Tavin awoke feeling revitalized like never before. He sprung out of bed to find the horde of servants returned, waiting to be of any help they could. Tavin respectfully sent them on their way once more, explaining he was partial to doing things himself. Realizing he hadn't eaten in over a day, he did see fit to order enough food for three boys his size.

Tavin bathed himself and then dressed in the regal attire that had been laid out for him. Not feeling too comfortable wearing the various pieces of armor and the blue and gold flowing cape, he strapped on an ornately decorated blue tunic complete with an equally elaborate pair of white and golden pants instead. He completed his new outfit with matching blue boots and cutoff gloves, and swung the Sword of Granis back over his shoulder, not wanting to part with it for more than a few seconds, knowing what an incredible duo they made.

Soon after he was dressed the feast he ordered arrived, catered in by rows of servants. Before he began, he managed to flag down one of them and ask if someone could contact his parents back in Eirinor Village to at least them know that he was alright. The servant agreed to deliver the message personally and as soon as possible. Tavin knew his mother would be in hysterics by now and felt some small measure of relief to know his no doubt worried sick parents would be notified he was safe. After the servants left, he sat straight down and began shoveling food into his mouth as if it was his last meal.

As Tavin sat feasting, another figure entered the room. Easily startled in times of late, Tavin jerked his head upward and yanked the Sword of Granis free of its sheath, sending a deafening metallic ring slicing through the air. The mirror and other glass in the room seemed to vibrate. The figure winced slightly at the ringing noise from the sword but put up his hands in a disarming gesture. The robed man turned out to be Seriol, smiling as always. A wave of relief and slight embarrassment washed over Tavin as he lowered his blade and swallowed the food still in his mouth.

"A little on edge, I see," Seriol said smiling. Tavin tried a quick smile in return and shrugged.

"I don't know what to expect anymore," the boy admitted. "Every time I hear a knock I assume it to be some creature here to kill me or a sage here to get me to save the world." Seriol laughed at that, taking a seat in front of Tavin and folding his regal attire over his lap.

"I can assure you that you won't be seeing anything of Zeroan until later on today," he promised.

"Where is he now?" Tavin wondered out loud. Seriol crossed his leg over the other.

"I suspect Zeroan is out in the Gate Yard greeting the other three Elemental Warriors from the Southland." Tavin's head bolted upright upon hearing this.

"You mean to tell me all four of the Elemental Warriors are assembled here in Galantia right now? Has that ever happened before?"

"No," Seriol simply replied. "But then a great many things are happening now that have never happened before, and if we are to be ready for them, we must all unite in advance. And by the way, there are five Elemental Warriors here, not four." Seriol pointed to the Sword of Granis slung over Tavin's back. The boy had almost failed to realize that he was now an Elemental Warrior himself, and potentially more powerful than all the others at that. "But as I was saying, there will most likely be a council called tonight in the grand chambers above us."

"Why must there be a council, Seriol?" The figure in white gave him a peculiar look.

"You know better than most the reasons for the need of a council, Tavin. But all I can say to you now is that it is imperative that we find and collect the other shards of the Holy Emerald before the forces of darkness in Drakkaidia can do so. Great evil has been thrust upon the lands of Iairia and it must be dealt with swiftly before it grows beyond our power to halt. The council will address how we will mobilize against the dark forces to the north and how we will go about preventing Valif Montrox from finding the other shards of the emerald of legend." When Seriol mentioned the shards, Tavin remembered that he had not looked to make sure his shard was safe since the previous night. He hastily gathered up his affects to make sure it was safe. When he emptied all of his satchels and found the shard not in his possession, Tavin

73

was beside himself. Seriol could see the dilemma in Tavin's face and quickly intervened.

"Looking for the shard?" he asked. Tavin wheeled backward to face Seriol.

"Have you taken it?" he asked worriedly. Seriol smiled.

"Well *I* haven't," he said, "but I do believe that Zeroan took it from you as you slept last night. It is a burden that you do not need to be saddled with while so many other important matters warrant your attention." Though he was relived the shard was in good hands, Tavin was sad to loose his lucky charm that he had kept with him since he was just a little boy. Seriol shifted in his seat, observing the hurt in Tavin's eyes. "Oh don't worry about the shard. There is no one in the world that I would trust more to keep the shard safe than Zeroan," he assured. Tavin looked up, wanting to ask a question that had been on his mind for over a month now.

"Seriol," he began, "may I ask you a question?"

"If it is within my ability to answer, I promise you I will," he responded. Tavin's eyes shifted around in his head, trying to formulate the question he wanted to ask.

"Seriol, I want to know about Zeroan," he said at last. "I've been living under his order for the last month now, but I don't know much about him except rumors of his... journeys over the years. Can you tell me about him?" Seriol nodded, sitting in his chair to think.

"Tell you about Zeroan, eh?" he said, contemplating a suitable answer. "Well, as you know, Zeroan is one of the few Mystic Sages left in the world. Over the long years since their creation, their number has been steadily declining, but Zeroan has been here for some time. He has lived much longer than the average man. Some say he has survived over five centuries, even during the time of the first Holy War, but most find it hard to believe he has existed for quite that long." Seriol looked up at the ceiling, as if having a difficult time trying to find the word to describe the sage. "From my experiences with him and the stories I have heard of him, I can tell you that he is a very untraditional Mystic Sage. He has always been something of a recluse from the rest of the order.

"As you must have observed when you first met him, he cuts straight to business and tells you only what you absolutely must know. He is very selective about what information he reveals. He moves quietly and secretly, preferring not to attract any unnecessary attention. He is a firm believer in stealth." Seriol stopped for a moment, staring into space. "He leaves nothing to chance, always taking special care to everything that needs his attention." He looked back at Tavin as he continued. "You see Tavin, the Mystic Sages have become far more isolated from the world of Iairia in the last hundred years or so. They prefer to stay locked in their tower to the south, and leave the world on its own against the wishes and customs of their founders.

"Zeroan is considered to be somewhat of an outcast because he is very concerned with the events and business of Iairia. He is the world's self appointed guardian against the dark powers to the north or anywhere else. He knows everything about nearly anything you can imagine, and even more about what you can't. His powers, as you saw on the wall, are also not to be toyed with. The Mystic Sages use an ancient power that combines all forms of elemental power but uses them only on a submissive level, allowing them to seize and manipulate matter and magic in a variety of ways. They have a deep understanding of the nature of how the universe works. The Master Sage is able to work his power beyond that of the others, but that is not Zeroan. The order as a whole, however, has lost its magical edge over the years as they lost interest in their original objective and mission. Zeroan is an excessive traditionalist of the old sages, though extreme even by their standards I'm sure. He's more of a rogue sorcerer, not living by the same code as others in the current order. He has studied the arts of very unique mystic magics and elemental powers for many years, and is without a doubt one of the most powerful men alive, despite the fact that he is not the Master Sage."

Seeing the amazement in Tavin's eyes, Seriol stopped there.

"I can see you did not expect our friend to be quite so intricate a character, did you?" Tavin shook his head no.

"I guess all the rumors about him are true then..." he said trailing off. Seriol nodded.

"Most are, even if he does not agree with their accuracy. But do not think on this too hard, m' boy. You have other things to focus on this day." Tavin looked puzzled.

"What other things?" he questioned.

"Well for starters, you and your friend Master Garrinal are to be honored at a private awards ceremony around noon time. You will both be commended for your courage at the wall yesterday, and you, Tavin, will receive the Supreme Granisian's blessing as the new Warrior of Light. Corinicus Kolior wanted to hold a public ceremony to honor you, but as per Zeroan's request to keep your identify as secret as possible, it will be before tonight's council members only." Tavin was curious at that statement.

"Why must my identity be kept secret?" he asked.

"As I stated earlier, it is best that your face not be recognizable throughout Iairia at the moment. There are a great many agents of the Drakkaidians who would seek to do you harm, Tavin," Seriol explained.

"I guess that makes sense," Tavin agreed. "Who will be at the council tonight?" Seriol cocked his head in thought.

"Well of course, the Supreme Granisian will be present with the rest of the royal family, along with the other high Granisians and governors of Galantia. As their Chief Advisor, I will be there as well. General Taroct, as you must know from your father, is the commander of the Grandarian military, so he will be present. The five Elemental Warriors will be there, including you. Oh, and don't let me forget that because of his heroics yesterday, someone has petitioned for Jaren to be present at the meeting for saving Mary's life, but you would have seen to it that he was there anyway, wouldn't you? A representative form the Southland Legion should be present as well. I believe he arrived with the other three warriors this morning. And last but not least, Zeroan will head up the council since he was the one to organize this meeting in the first place. And that should be everyone." Tavin was reminded of how honoring it was to be the Warrior of Light as thoughts of meeting the most important people in all of Iairia entered his mind.

Seriol stood up then, adjusting his white robe about him. He smiled as he looked over at Tavin's attire.

"You look very good in those colors," he complemented Tavin as he looked down at his clothing, observing it for himself. "I'm afraid that you must dress to your fullest, though. You are about to be honored by the Supreme Granisian himself after all. There is a set of small armor over there on the bed. There should be two gold shoulder plates, a blue and gold torso plate, and some knee plates to go above your boots." Tavin looked back at the decorative armor on the bed with a frown. Tavin wasn't accustomed to dressing so extravagantly.

But as Seriol advised, he strapped on the armor all over his body. When he was done, Tavin was surprised at how light the armor was. He turned back to Seriol so he could examine him. "Very nice," he said with a smile, "but there is one last piece to your attire there on the chair behind you." Tavin turned back to find the blue cape with the ornate gold lining lying on the chair where he had thrown it earlier. A look of depression came over his face.

"Seriol, do I really have to wear the cape? I look so dumb in them," he complained. Seriol insisted.

"Come now, Tavin. The least you can do is try it on. You can hang the Sword of Granis from your belt as it should be."

So with a silent groan, Tavin removed his powerful talisman and the shoulder armor from his back and replaced it with the elaborately decorated cape. He then placed the shoulder armor back on top of the cape and hung the sword from his side. Seriol told him to go over to the mirror by his bed and take a look for himself, which he did to find a surprisingly well dressed young man starring back at him. Though it felt a bit awkward, the cape didn't look as bad as he thought it might.

"Wow..." Tavin muttered quietly, raising his eyebrows in surprise. Seriol smiled again.

"You see? You look like a true Warrior of Light now," he complemented. "Well if you're done, Tavin, we must be on our way. If you want to meet Jaren and the others before the ceremony that is." That was all he needed to say. Tavin came bursting away from the mirror ready to go, eager to see his best friend. Seriol happily led Tavin out of the room, into the great halls of the castle.

Chapter 12

<u>Iron Fist</u>

"What!?! I'm not going in there! He'll butcher me!" objected the High Priest Zalignt of the Black Church of Drakkan.

"Well I don't intend on going in there either!" stated the Dark Mage speaking with him. "I accepted the responsibility for not finding him at the deadline! There is no way he'd let me live after a failure like this. And besides, he thinks more of you anyway." Zalignt let his head drop as he motioned for the Dark Mage to leave him, which he did in a hurry, sprinting as far away from the throne room as possible. Zalignt looked out a nearby window at the dark, oppressive city far below him. With the return of what was left of the defeated demons from the battle at Galantia the previous day, the skies over the Drakkaidian capital of Dalastrak were darker and more threatening than usual, overrun with the black storm clouds that followed the packs of Valcanor everywhere they flew. The first of the demons arrived just hours previous, speaking through ancient black magics to one of the Dark Mages. They related the ill news of their defeat at the hands of the newly reborn Warrior of Light.

When the High Priest Zalignt first heard the news of their most powerful enemy's reemergence, he was instantly distraught with worry. It had been his charge from the king himself to be sure that this possible threat to his plans was not allowed to come into being. Now that he heard from the Dark Mages that the demons had failed, it was also his charge to accept responsibility for the failure and apologize to his master. He knew that his dark lord would be furious, so he immediately tired to heap the task onto one of the mages. Now it seemed he was left with no choice but to explain the failure himself.

Zalignt rubbed his eyes in frustration as a bolt of lightning stuck the mountainside outside the black castle where he stood high above the rest of the city. He unhurriedly set off down the black and lifeless halls, wishing only to postpone his inevitable encounter with Valif Montrox, the dictator of Drakkaidia. Montrox was a man of supreme power. With the exception of his great-grandfather long gone, never before had the nation of Drakkaidia seen such an iron fisted and tyrannical ruler. Many who went into his throne room for even the most trivial issues did not come out alive. Zalignt was sure he would be one of the many to die at the hands of his master. Mercy and forgiveness were not qualities that Montrox was familiar with.

When the High Priest Zalignt finally reached the doors to the chamber where Montrox was waiting for him, the four black armored sentries standing guard at the door stared at him as if not expecting to see him again. They pushed the massive wooden doors open and announced his presence. Upon entering the chamber, Zalignt saw rows of servants, advisors, and even the powerful Dark Mages, but could not find his master himself. His savage throne stood on the platform of stairs at the far end of the chamber, flanked by two shorter seats on either side that always remained empty. Just when Zalignt was about to hastily exit the chamber to postpone his report (and death) until later, a voice from across the room echoed into his ears.

"Welcome, High Priest," came the low and menacing voice. "I hope you are not too eager to escape from me, are you?" Zalignt took a deep breath, gathered his rigid black robes about him, and proceeded over to the window where Valif Montrox stood staring out on his ravaged capital city. The High Priest kneeled before his master trembling in the darkness, threatening to close in about him and steal the very air from his lungs.

"My lord," he greeted sheepishly. Montrox did not bother turning around. The savagely spiked black and silver armor that covered his body was still new and quite cumbersome to move in, not that it would have been a problem for one as physically powerful as Montrox. As the tyrant breathed deeply out of the window, his scarred face was illuminated by the repetitive strikes of lightning outside. The breeze that filtered in through the room blew his crimson hair from side to side. Before he began his words again, he exhaled sharply, bringing his eyes wide open.

"Why have you come?" Montrox asked with a false hint of gentleness in his voice.

"I bring word of the demons' progress at Galantia, my lord," he answered, well aware that he was signing his own death warrant speaking these words. Montrox kept his gaze fixed out onto the city.

"Really?" he continued, interest and concern present in his words. "What news then?" Zalignt swallowed hard and lowered his head as far as he could.

"I am afraid that the demons could not stop our enemies from achieving their goals, my lord. They were too slow in their attack," he said in a slightly accusing tone, trying to shift some of the blame toward the demons. Montrox finally turned from the window and brought his piercing blood red eyes down onto the High Priest. Just the sight of the Drakkaidian ruler's emotionless face was enough to send a jolting wave of terror down his spine.

"So what you're saying is, *my* idiotic rabble of brainless demons failed to prevent the one threat to me and my plans from entering back into the world. Is that what you are trying to tell me?" he asked in a low unaffected tone. The High Priest nodded his tremulous head and replied yes. Montrox stood silent for a moment, hands behind his back. The assembly of guards and servants shot each other uneasy glances in the silence. After a time of leaving Zalignt to cower at his feet, Montrox at last responded and did something no one expected: he smiled. "Well, it is of no concern," he said in a dismissive tone, nearly knocking the men in the room off their feet with surprise. Zalignt looked up in amazement, wondering why he wasn't dead yet. Montrox motioned for him to rise and went on. "Oh come now, High Priest. It is of little consequence if one boy has acquired a small amount of insignificant power, isn't it?" Zalignt nodded his head, confused but not daring to speak. Montrox continued and even patted the High Priest on the back with his overbearing armor.

"Yes. He is only a boy." But then, a sudden look of overly dramatic confusion crossed Montrox's face. "But wait. Isn't this boy the grandson of the same person who defeated my grandfather so many years ago? And isn't the power he has acquired the same that managed to best the power I carry now?" The intensity in the tyrant's voice began to escalate. "And doesn't it say in the prophesies that the one true threat to my plan is the Warrior of Light, no matter how small or weak he appears? Maybe this 'boy' is more of a threat than you thought, since you saw fit not to send enough demons to find him before the Grandarians did and finish the job when you had the chance!" Montrox was shouting now. "Your lack of brainpower has just released the one and only thing in the world that could have ever challenged me! That makes me very upset! And when I am upset, ignorant fools like you meet Drakkan!"

The enraged Warrior of Darkness shot his arm forward, lifted the violently quivering figure of the High Priest off the ground and heaved him out of the window he had been staring out of the past few moments. As the flailing man plummeted from the tower window, he screamed madly until his fragile body eventually made contact with the cold, hard ground stories downward where he landed, silencing him forever. Back in the throne room, Montrox raised his arm again and sent it careening down into a nearby table, snapping it in two. He shouted dark curses in fury and then turned to the mages cowering away from him on the other side of the room. As he stood enraged, a small level of raw energy generated by his blind fury began to softly pulsate off of his armor-covered body.

"I *do* not and *will* not tolerate failure when I am this close to achieving my goals!" he howled into them. "Now I will have to contend with this power out there looking for the other shards as well! This does not please me at all!" Montrox shouted again and kicked the broken half of the table, shattering it instantly and sending its wooden fragments jetting into several nearby advisors impaling them like shrapnel. Montrox stood there for a few minutes, slowly cooling off. After his rage had subsided some, he made his way back onto his throne at the end of the black chamber and exhaled sharply again as he sat. "It is of no concern, though. We are already in possession of one of the shards, and the other five grow closer every day." Montrox called over one of the secondary Dark Mages to report the details of the defeat at Galantia. After he finished, Montrox remembered the status of the shard in the Grandarian capital.

"Have we received any word from the insider in Galantia?" asked Montrox. The mage nodded his head yes.

"We have, my lord. He contacted... the late High Priest this morning very early. He claims that the shard is safe in the confines of the Tower of Granis, not beyond his reach. He also informed us that it will remain there until the Mystic Sage returns for it after he has found the two lying undiscovered in the Southland." Montrox sat back and crossed his hands, nodding his head.

"Very good. With our insider within striking range of the Grandarian officials and our "special forces" in preparation to secretly penetrate the borders to the south, we will take the shards from the hands of our enemies by force. As for the other two, we will summon another group of demons to add to those we just lost. We will not be able to facilitate their use as hunters of the Warrior of Light much longer, seeing as they will soon be needed for more important matters. So I want those shards found, and I want them found soon. Is that perfectly clear, High Priest?" The mage nodded quickly and raised his hand to speak.

"Are you really making me the new High Priest, my lord?" he asked in nervous anticipation. Montrox frowned.

"That is what I just said, isn't it? Now get out my sight, all of you."

With that, the mages and guards hastily exited the chambers, leaving Valif Montrox to himself in the darkness of his black throne room. As he sat drumming his fingers on the arm rests of his savage throne, he smiled as the lightning outside struck again, illuminating the spacious chamber. Though he did not tolerate failure, he was not really upset that the Warrior of Light had returned. He had expected it; wanted it. Now he had the chance to avenge his great grandfather's defeat eons ago at the hands of his enemy. And besides, his insider had already taken steps to destroy the Warrior of Light before his power could mature, so it was of little consequence.

"Go, Warrior of Light. Lead me to the other shards. For every one you find, I will be there to take it from you. And once I have all six, not even you will be able to stop me. Not even Granis himself will be able to stop me." Montrox let a twisted and purely evil grin overtake his dangerous face. "Oh, what an end I have arranged for you and Grandaria," he chuckled. Montrox laughed ominously as he thought of how everything was going as planned. His maniacal laughter echoed throughout the halls of his entire castle as the fearsome storm raged outside.

Chapter 13

<u>Awards</u>

As Seriol calmly strolled through the beautiful halls and chambers of the Golden Castle in Galantia, Tavin bounded behind him full of energy and vitality, stopping to examine every little detail that caught his attention. Not under such grave circumstances as the last time he was led through these halls, he was able to fully appreciate his gorgeous surroundings.

"Seriol!" he would call, as the white robed figured turned his head back to answer him. "Where did this come from?" he asked with curiosity, pointing up at a towering representation of Lord Granis holding his mighty sword that now resided at Tavin's side. Seriol responded smiling as he continued walking down the halls to the audience chamber of the castle.

"That was constructed from a massive block of sea stone at the request of the second Supreme Granisian centuries ago." A grin passed across Tavin's face as he gazed up at the brilliantly detailed statue. Just as he was about to examine other statues across from him in the hall, an archway composed of singing angels caught Tavin's attention. He shot down the hall eager to analyze the archway from a closer distance. As he was passing Seriol, the tail of the boy's cape somehow found its way under his foot, sending him on a collision course for the decorative carpets. After the shock from tripping like a child left his mind, Tavin looked up at Seriol in disbelief that he had just embarrassed himself this way. Seriol just kept walking past him, smiling as he opened his mouth to speak.

"Do be careful in these halls. We wouldn't want you damaging anything valuable, such as your attire," he commented with sarcasm lacing his voice. Tavin gave him a look of irritation as he picked himself up off the floor, smoothing out the wrinkles in shirt.

"I was just breaking in the clothes," he lied poorly. "I'm fine by the way." Seriol grinned again before he continued speaking.

"Well if you're quite through thrashing around in the halls," he said halting in front of a large golden door, "we have arrived at the audience chamber preparation room. Shall we?" Seriol motioned for the two brightly colored royal guards to open the doors, revealing a petite room with two massive doors on its far side. To its left side stood a collection of familiar faces including Zeroan, wrapped in his signature gray robes, Garoll Nelpia, loaded to the max with Legionnaire armor and green garb from the deep south of Iairia, and his best friend Jaren, covered in silver; the color to honor Grandarian soldiers who had done a special service for the nation and its people. As soon as Tavin came through the doorway after Seriol, Jaren's eyes grew wide. Both comrades met each other grinning and laughing at how impressive they both looked.

Tavin was ecstatic to hear everything his friend had to tell him about the royal treatment he had received from the army of servants during his trip to the infirmary.

"I'm not joking, Tavin!" Jaren exclaimed him as they moved to the side of the room by the others. "It would have been worth losing a leg to get that kind of treatment." Tavin laughed happily as his eyes drifted down to the wound his friend had sustained the previous day. There was no sign of any permanent damage or for that matter, any temporary damage.

"They sure fixed you up in a hurry. From the look of that gash you had, I thought you'd be out of action for days!" he stated in disbelief. Jaren just grinned.

"Yeah, they take care of you like you were the king of the *world* up there!" he exclaimed. "Not that I like getting hacked to pieces, though." Jaren's eyes caught sight of the Sword of Granis hanging from Tavin's side in all its glory. The crystal mounted on its hilt where the blade came jutting out glowed with golden light as Tavin discovered it always did while in his possession. The second crystal below it, however, always remained dormant. Jaren's eyes went wide as he pointed down to the sword.

"There is no way that is what I think that is..." he managed, so dwarfed by the object in front of him he began to stagger back. Tavin looked down, observing the sword as the source of Jaren's amazement. Tavin struggled for the words to explain the radical transformation he had just undergone. As if sensing the boy's dilemma, Zeroan stepped in to aid him.

"It is, Jaren," the sage spoke quietly in his reserved tone. "I thought you would have put this together by now. Just as his great grandfather was centuries before him, Tavinious is now the Warrior of Light, guardian of the entire world against the evils of Drakkaidia. The blade you so observantly pointed out is the mighty Sword of Granis, which Tavin claimed as his own. You should be proud of your friend, Jaren," Zeroan stated, shooting a quick glance at Tavin, to which he returned a coy smile. As Jaren stood wide eyed with his jaw dropped to the floor, Tavin could only shrug at all the sage had told Jaren.

"What do you know?" he said modestly. "I never knew I had it in me."

As Jaren slowly recovered from the shock that his best friend was now the single most powerful person he had ever heard of, Seriol approached them to let them both know that the Supreme Granisian had just arrived inside the audience room and the ceremony was about to be under way. Zeroan and the others with him stepped into the room to receive applause for their parts in recent events from the small but important crowd assembled inside. Tavin, Jaren, and Seriol remained in the hallway.

"Listen carefully boys," Seriol began. "It is quite an honor to be recognized by the Supreme Granisian, so please present yourselves as professionally and appropriately as possible inside. Jaren, you will come in and be honored first. After you receive your medal from the Princess, you will move to the right side of the stairs in front of the Supreme Granisian's throne." Jaren turned from Seriol to make eye contact with Tavin, raising his eyebrows at the mention of a Princess. Tavin rolled his eyes. "Tavin, you will be announced by the captain of the royal guard as you enter. When the doors open, come in. The Supreme Granisian will then recognize and award you with a medal of your own. From there, you will know what to do. That is all. Good luck to the both of you. Jaren, come in whenever you are ready."

With that, Seriol winked at the two and proceeded into the chamber to join the Supreme Granisian. Jaren let out a sigh of nervousness. Tavin smiled and gently punched his friend on the forearm.

"Hey relax, will you? What's the problem? Are you lonely without your new best friend latching onto your manly chest?" Tavin teased. Jaren fixed his gaze on his friend flaring his eyes.

"You, Tavinious Tieloc, are just jealous. She's somewhere in there right now, I bet." he stated with confidence, letting out one more hearty sigh. "Here goes nothing," he stated, proceeding into the chamber leaving Tavin to himself in the little preparation room.

As Jaren entered the massive chamber, its audience of Grandarian officials such as priests, royal guards, advisors like Seriol, and other important figures came to attention on the left side of the room. On the right side, the Elemental Warriors and other friends and allies from the Southland including Zeroan, mobilized to respect Jaren as he passed by on his way to the Supreme Granisian at the end of the chamber. It was a gorgeously decorated room with bright stain glassed windows open to let in as much sunlight as possible. Long flowing banners and crests of the Grandarian people hung waving in the breeze as he passed them by.

As Jaren approached the head of the room, he found himself nearing the Supreme Granisian and nervously swallowed hard. The Grandarian ruler was a kind but nevertheless imposing figure, wrapped in flowing white and golden robes mounted with beautiful crystals and gems all over the outline of his attire. To his right was Seriol and the Queen. She had a very gentle figure and a very kind look about her face. But the primary individual to absorb his attention was the person standing to the left of the extravagantly dressed Supreme Granisian.

Holding a medal in her delicately white gloved hands, was the beautiful form of Mary. Wearing a soft pink and white dress with golden jewelry all over her slender body, Jaren felt like nothing made sense anymore. First his best friend had turned into the legendary Warrior of Light, and now the simple servant to the Supreme Granisian, Mary, had turned out to be the Princess of the whole kingdom of Grandaria. Jaren could not take his eyes off of her gorgeous appearance as he drew nearer to the end of the chamber. As he approached the foot of the stairs, she flashed her ravishing smile, nearly knocking Jaren off his feet once more. The only thing that broke his gaze was when the Supreme Granisian began his speech.

"My friends and allies from here in Grandaria and from our neighbor to the south, I would like to take this opportunity to welcome you all to our grand capital of Galantia," he began in a collected tone that instantly displayed the ultimate professionalism his title required of him. "As you are all aware, a time of prophesy is upon us. We now find ourselves facing a great and evil enemy of which we have not seen the likes of in centuries. Though we no doubt face a difficult road to tread upon in the coming days, weeks, and months ahead, we will endure. Why?" he asked, gazing around the room, and then placing his eyes on the humbled figure of Jaren. "It is because of the courage of brave young men like this lad standing before me." The Supreme Granisian smiled at Jaren and then motioned for Mary to come forward. She did so, lifting the silver and golden medal she carried forward.

"Jaren Garrinal of Eirinor," he continued. "In the face of great danger you have proven yourself a cunning and resourceful warrior, as well as a true hero of the Grandarian people. On a more personal note, the Queen as well as I myself are indebted to you more than you could ever know. Your bravery and quick thinking on the Golden Wall managed to save our daughter's life. We are all forever grateful to you. Princess Maréttiny?" The Supreme Granisian then moved over to his left to allow the Princess access to Jaren's body, nearly quivering with anticipation.

As the beautiful girl came directly in front of him, Jaren grinned and inquisitively mouthed the word 'Princess.' Mary returned his grin and instructed him to lower his head. The Princess regained her royal composure before she placed the medal around his neck and thanked him personally for his bravery on the wall. As Jaren brought up his head, Mary came one step nearer and leaned in close, causing her flowing chestnut hair to come tumbling down and spill over his shoulders. She quietly thanked him one more time before she leaned closer still, and softly kissed him on the cheek. Jaren felt the feeling in his legs draining away as the girl led him over to the left side of the steps.

The only thing that kept him from fainting with unparalleled elation was the rows of trumpets that sounded at the end of the hallway. The assembly in the room all turned back to the massive golden doors to face the Captain of the Royal Guard, who stood with attention as he began to introduce the second boy to be honored.

"Ladies and gentlemen, the Warrior of Light!" he exclaimed as the doors came swinging open. From out of the darkness of the small preparation room stepped Tavin, the light glistening off of his armor and the hilt of the Sword of Granis like the radiating energy of his power had the day before. He managed a quick smile, overwhelmed again, and deeply inhaled once more before starting down the aisle. The crowd, ordered to maintain silence until the proceedings had ended, exchanged hushed whispers as the sight of the Warrior of Light came strolling down the hallway.

As Tavin drew closer to the stairs at the end of the chamber where the Supreme Granisian stood waiting, he was keenly interested to observe the select few present. The Grandarian officials and priests made up the majority of the crowd, but there were four in the ranks of Legionnaires that stood out like the sun in Drakkaidia. They were of course the Elemental Warriors. The first he noticed was Garoll Nelpia, who gave him a complementary salute as he walked by. Tavin smiled in response. Next he encountered an aged woman in purple flowing robes. Tavin guessed that she would have to be the Warrior of Wind, though somewhat surprised at her age. The third was an older boy incased in layers of thin blue armor. Tavin assumed him to be the Warrior of Water. And last but not least, he came to a group of three figures dressed in fervent reds and yellows. In their ranks stood two strong robed men and a girl who did not appear to be any older than Tavin. He guessed one of the men was the Warrior of Fire.

As Tavin passed by the fiery red haired girl, her unusual but striking deep red eyes locked onto him. He suddenly felt uneasy as he realized how attractive he found this girl who was staring straight at him, penetrating. It was hard to look away when he passed her by, but he found a new figure for his gaze to fix on as he found himself at the base of the dais where the Supreme Granisian stood. Tavin proceeded up the stairs and turned to observe his best friend standing beside the Princess. His eyes widened and his mouth opened as he recognized the royal Princess and the servant girl Mary to be one in the same. As he pointed to her in confusion, Jaren and Mary both silently giggled. Tavin then brought his attention back to the Supreme Granisian in front of him, embarrassed. The extravagantly robed figure gave a quick chuckle as he turned to his daughter as well.

"It would seem that neither of these boys knew that the Princess was indeed a Princess before just now," he chuckled once more, causing the whole crowd to echo a quick laugh as well. "I believe that will be the last time that I allow my daughter to go incognito when she assists Seriol." Tavin and Jaren both flushed red. The Supreme Granisian brought his gaze back down onto the Warrior of Light and beamed. "Welcome, Tavinious Tieloc. It is an esteemed honor to meet the man of prophesy at last. Within just minutes of acquiring your legendary power, you used it to save a great many of our soldiers, as well as protect the safety of thousands within the walls of this city. We already owe you our deepest respect and gratitude. I can only imagine the good you will do in the future, my young friend," the Supreme Granisian concluded his words, heaping a great deal of pressure onto Tavin. He then motioned for Mary to come forward with another medal.

Tavin bowed his head as the beautiful Princess placed the golden medal around his neck smiling at him with reverence. At the request of the Supreme Granisian, the two boys then turned about and received their applause from the small audience present. Tavin and Jaren turned to each other and grinned, enjoying the moment. Zeroan, already striding away for the door, rolled his eyes as a small smile crept across his worn face.

Chapter 14

<u>Fire of the West</u>

It was several hours after the awards ceremony hailing Tavin and Jaren that Arilia Embrin came strolling down the halls of the Golden Castle in an attempt to find a moment to relax from the day's veritably endless activities. Since her arrival in the Grandarian capital that morning, it seemed as though she had been introduced to virtually every last Grandarian official alive and taken through every nook and cranny in the city. Not used to the splendor of such elaborate and enormous surroundings as these, she was eager to find a simpler, more peaceful location for some time to herself. Before she could get far, however, she heard her name being called from the end of the ornate hallway from which she was trying to escape. Arilia rolled her deep red eyes and turned around slowly, observing her two fearless guardians, Pyre and Spillo, swiftly on their way down the hallway to meet her.

As they arrived out of breath, the girl placed her hands on her hips and raised an eyebrow at the two.

"What is it now, boys?" she mocked, brushing locks of her fiery red hair from her face. Pyre was the first to begin.

"Ril, you know that you are not permitted to leave on your own without consulting us first," he began. "We are here to protect you. Do you know what your father would do to us if something ever happened to you while you were out alone?" She released a small groan as she rolled her eyes again.

"Pyre, my father isn't here right now, is he?" she stated observantly. "And you two should know above anyone that I can take care of myself just fine. I am an Elemental Warrior after all. I think the world of you both, but you're only here because daddy is so paranoid of everything. I'm only going for a walk through a guard infested castle. There is nothing to worry about!" Pyre looked over at Spillo with a nervous look on his face. He nodded and brought his face to meet the girl's.

"All right," he gave in. "You can have a little time to yourself, but make sure you're careful. You may be in a seemingly safe place, but *you* should know above anyone that it's not safe anywhere." Arilia beamed at the two and leaned forward to give them both a colossal hug.

"Ah, you two are so cute when you get protective," she said in an overly dramatic tone, giggling. The scarlet robed guardians only frowned and motioned for her to be on her way.

So with that, Arilia turned with her flowing hair whirling around her as she continued down the halls. As she left the sight of her two guardians, she shook her head thinking back to the day they were assigned to her. They were both two of the finest warriors that could be found in Coron Village or anywhere in the west. Being the Warrior of Fire, Arilia (or Ril to her friends) was a very important figure to her people back in the west. Her father, an equally important man of political power at the base of Mt. Coron, had always been reluctant to let his baby girl become an Elemental Warrior, not wanting her to be saddled with so much responsibly so early in life. Ril smiled and peered down at the locket around her neck as thoughts of her cautious but sweet father entered her mind. She had never met her biological parents; her mother died giving birth to her and her father disappeared shortly before. The only thing she had of them was a strange crimson locket they left around her neck. Alone and defenseless in a western village beyond even Mt. Coron, the man who would become her father found her and adopted her as his own. Though he never married, no one could argue he had done a remarkable job raising her.

Having just turned eighteen, Ril was the youngest Elemental Warrior the Southland had ever seen. Most of the warriors were not anointed until adults, but for unknown reasons, she had been chosen as a child, making her a very special young lady. This was her father's motive to provide her with extra protection in her journeys and errands as one of the magically endowed warriors. To meet this need, two guardians were assigned to protect her at her father's request shortly after she was officially declared an Elemental Warrior by the Mystic Sages. Though Ril did have to admit they came in handy on occasion, they would both have to admit she could take care of herself just fine on her own with all of her power and personality. Ril had grown to love her two protectors over time, but it was bothersome to have them constantly watching her, never giving her a moment's peace.

Though Ril was very popular amongst her family, friends, and especially her fellow Elemental Warriors, they all seemed to treat her as if she was not their equal even though she clearly was. This was the root of her developing into an unusually strong and independent girl, never getting too close to anyone besides her two guardians and her family. She was friendly enough, but rarely accepted help from anyone unless absolutely necessary.

Enthralled to finally have some time to herself away from Pyre and Spillo, she set out at a faster pace through the halls. As she passed through the immense corridors of the Golden Castle, she noticed a large opening into the refreshing autumn afternoon outside. Eager to get some fresh air pumping into her body, Ril set out for the aperture at the end of the illustrious hallway. As she exited the halls, she found herself in the center of the most beautiful and well maintained garden she had ever seen, even more elaborate than her own luscious landscapes back west. With a vast assortment of the most exotic flowers and trees she had ever seen littering the grounds, Ril was quick to venture into them. She stood upon a mighty stone walkway that stretched high above the garden floor, connecting the northern and southern segments of the castle. A quick shiver ran down her spine as the crisp autumn air nipped at her skin. Wearing only a special Coron tunic and her traditional red and white garments, Ril wished she had brought some sort of coat.

Focusing back on her surroundings, Ril continued to gaze amazed at all the colorful plants around her, but one particularly caught her attention. There was a gargantuan tree at the base of the gardens below her whose thick branches stretched all the way up to where Ril stood floors higher. Its thick leaves shimmered deep crimson in the waning sunlight, and she wanted so badly to touch one that she reached out over the balcony to try and pluck one off of its branch. Ril stretched her tongue out of her mouth and squinted with determination to grab one as she stepped up on the tips of her toes and over the balcony. To her surprise, however, Ril suddenly heard a crack from below her. She nervously looked down to observe a huge gash in the stone railing that had been supporting her. Before she could react in any way, the railing gave way, letting Ril down with it.

Just as she was about to totally lose her balance and plummet to the ground far below her, an arm from behind her quickly shot forward wrapping around her waist and pulling her back onto the walkway she had been separated from. Still struggling for balance, Ril collapsed onto her savior, sending them both tumbling backward onto the ground. As the fear of nearly dying from her own curiosity and stupidity began to dissipate, Ril slowly turned her head upward to view the face of her rescuer still clutching on to her, obviously shaken himself. It was the second time she had gazed into this individual's eyes today. Staring back down at her was the face of Tavinious Tieloc, the boy she had seen at the awards assembly earlier in the day.

As the two sat holding each others' gazes still breathing hard from the traumatic incident seconds ago, Tavin eventually let a small smile materialize across his face, not sure what else to do in the awkwardness of the position he now found himself in. Ril was nearly hypnotized by the boy's warm smile. Then as if suddenly realizing that he was still nearly squeezing this girl he had never met before to death, Tavin instinctively let go, blushing, and proceeded to help her back to her feet. Though still shocked at what had just happened, she finally found her senses as the boy was about to ask her if she was all right.

"Hey! What do you think you're doing?" she started almost offended. Tavin looked at her strangely for a long moment, raising an eyebrow.

"Is that how you thank someone who just saved your life?" he asked, brushing himself off.

"You didn't save my life," she informed him, crossing her arms. "I was about to rebound back. You just snagged me first- that's all." As Tavin looked at her incredulously, he recognized her as the attractive girl from the crowd at the ceremony earlier in the day. He straightened himself out, readjusting the Sword of Granis around his belt, and at last responded.

"Well, your welcome. So what were you doing over there, anyway?" he asked her with a puzzled look about his face. Ril blushed a little but held her head high.

"I was just admiring the tree," she informed him. "What about you? Were you just patrolling the garden for someone who might need saving?" Tavin just shrugged.

"I came out to get a little thinking done, but I was starting to feel a little lonely by myself," Tavin admitted. "I saw you out here alone and thought you might like some company. Unless you'd prefer to be by yourself, why don't you walk with me for a while?" Though Ril came out here with the idea of being alone, she decided that some company might be nice after all. Besides that, she did feel like she owed her savior at least a few moments of her plentiful time. As Tavin began to readjust his belt, Ril observed that he was still dressed in the same brightly ornate attire from earlier in the day, though he had removed his medal.

She nodded slowly, lowering her defenses, and told him that would be fine. After they both collected themselves again, they started off down the ramp way to the ground level where Ril was eager to stay at that point. As she began to regain all of her senses she had lost in the incident on the walkway, Ril quickly remembered she had yet to introduce herself to the boy.

"My name is Arilia Embrin," she began, turning to shake the boy's hand. Tavin accepted it and gently shook it. "I already know who you are. Tavinious, right?" she stated with assurance. Tavin nodded his head, at first confused at how she knew him. She could see the puzzled look in his eyes. "I was at the award ceremony today, remember? I heard your name there." Tavin smiled, remembering that fact now. He nodded.

"Tavinious Tieloc, at your service," he said taking a playful bow. "But please call me Tavin. 'Tavinious' is a traditional family name, but it can drive you crazy after a while." Ril nodded in agreement.

"I know what you mean. My nickname is Ril. Only my father and superiors back where I'm from call me Arilia." Tavin looked at her with curiosity.

"Where are you from, Ril?" he asked with sincere interest in his voice. Ril looked over to him a little taken aback, intrigued at how polite and kind this boy that she had just shunned was treating her. Though she had assumed to be a just another Grandarian publicity stunt, his geniality penetrated the girl's hard exterior and took hold. Ashamed to think he was a fraud, she now found herself at a loss at what to make of him. Ril was compelled to stay a little longer and answer his questions.

"Well, I was born in Fireite Village by Mt. Coron in the far west Southland. I never knew my true parents, but the man who became my father took me in when I was a baby. After I was chosen by the sages, we moved to Coron Village and I was taken to be placed in our Source," she explained. Something caught Tavin that didn't make sense.

"Your 'Source'?" he repeated perplexed. Ril shot him a puzzled glance at his question.

"But you're an Elemental Warrior too. You should know that every warrior goes to their temple to be placed in its Source. That's how we get our power instilled into us," she explained confused. Tavin froze in his tracks and looked at her in disbelief.

"Wait a minute- you're an Elemental Warrior?" he asked incredulously. Ril raised her eyebrows.

"Why so surprised?" she asked defensively, raising her right hand to show him the crest of fire imprinted onto her skin just as Garoll had the crest of earth. Tavin was eager to correct himself.

"Well, it's just that when I saw you and those other two men in red in the audience chamber today, I figured that one of them was the Elemental Warrior of Fire." Upon hearing this, Ril stopped and pointed down to a large leaf lying on the ground.

"See that?" she asked curtly. Ril snapped her fingers and the leaf instantly burst into flames, disintegrating. Tavin shot her an apologetic glance.

"Wow," he said in amazement. "Sorry. I just didn't think that Elemental Warriors were as young as you." Ril kept walking forward looking him over.

"There's no way you could be much older than me, and you're supposed to be the greatest of us all," the girl pointed out. Tavin looked away uneasily and shrugged again.

"I'm a little different than the ones from the Southland," he returned in a somewhat distant tone.

"How so?" she grilled. Tavin looked at her and smiled.

"You'd be surprised," was all he could say.

The two continued strolling through the gardens for the better part of an hour as Tavin related his entire adventure from the appearance of Zeroan in the Eirinor Hills to his battle on the Golden Wall against the demons. When he was finished, Ril could only stare at him with amazement mirrored in her eyes.

"I can't believe that's how you were given your powers over your element..." she stated amazed. "I always thought the Sword of Granis was just a Grandarian myth." Tavin was quick to add a little more information to help her understand.

"Well it's not as simple as just picking up the sword and getting all these powers along with it," he began. "I wasn't chosen by the Mystic Sages like you; my power was already in my blood. No one can wield the Sword of Granis except people in my family because my great grandfather was the first Warrior of Light centuries ago. From that point on, all the Tielocs after him have possessed those powers deep down inside them, hidden away from our reach. The trial of the Sword of Granis I told you about is the only thing that can awaken them. I've always had these powers dormant in me, I guess, and I just never realized it. But now that I have them, I can feel them there as if they've always been with me..." Tavin trailed off, shrugged, then smiled over at her. "But then, if you would have told me three or four days ago that I was destined to become the legendary Warrior of Light-the only person who could stand up against the evils from Drakkaidia- I'd have said you were nuts." Ril giggled at this.

Just as the two were about to make another lap around the lower gardens, a strange movement from behind them caught Tavin's attention. Sensing trouble already, he decided to not leave anything to chance and whirled around to send the metallic ringing of the Sword of Granis bursting through the air as he drew it forth, nearly causing Ril to jump out of her skin. Tavin was again mistaken in his worries, however, as the figure behind them turned out only to be the cloaked form of the Mystic Sage Zeroan. Tavin exhaled hard, bringing the Sword of Granis down slowly. The sage came striding up to them from the shadows under the stairs to the upper levels in his usually ominous manner. Tavin was the first to speak.

"You nearly scared me to death, Zeroan," he breathed, sheathing the Sword of Granis. Zeroan remained stoic as usual.

"You two have wasted enough time out here for one day," he told them abruptly at last, earning a scowl from Ril. "It's time that you both went indoors to prepare for tonight." A shock of remembrance hit Tavin as the council that Seriol had informed him of came to mind. "Yes, Tavin. You need to come with me so I can prepare you for the council. And I would suggest that you go and make yourself ready as well, Arilia Embrin." Ril glared at him.

"I'll have you know that I am already very well prepared for anything you have to say, sage," she commented in a cold tone.

"How nice for you to think so, but I highly doubt that, Arilia," the sage responded with an equally icy voice. "The fact remains, however, that I still need Tavinious here. So if you will finish your business quickly please, I will be waiting on the bridge that you saw fit to damage on the higher levels of the garden." With that, Zeroan turned quickly with his simple gray robes flying up behind him and disappeared up the massive staircase. Tavin looked back at Ril with an apologetic expression on his face again.

"Sorry about him," the boy began. "He's always like that I guess." Ril nodded.

"I know Zeroan all too well, and it's nothing I haven't heard before. There are quite a few people who don't think much about me because of my position and my age," she admitted, letting her body sulk back a bit. He felt the need to say something to raise her spirits that the seemingly heartless sage had just crushed.

"Well I can't see why anyone would think that. I think you're just as capable as anyone else in the world, if not more so, to be an Elemental Warrior. I'm glad to have met you, Ril Embrin." Ril looked into his sincere eyes with curiosity, as if this boy had been sent to her from Granis himself to enjoy for the past hour. Someone this kind and respectful from Grandaria seemed to be too good to be true.

"And I'm glad to have met you, Tavin Tieloc," she stated truthfully with a mystified blankness over her face. "It's nice to have someone to talk to who thinks of me as a person instead of a child." They stood silent for a moment before Tavin at last told her that he would speak to her again at the council later that evening and finally took his leave for the staircase waving goodbye one last time. As he left her alone in the sprawling gardens, Arilia Embrin reflected on all that had befallen her the last hour between her near death experience and the appearance of the Mystic Sage. As she stood in the gardens contemplating, she found herself happy that she did not get her original wish to be alone.

Chapter 15

<u>Council</u>

After Tavin met back with Zeroan on the top level of the Galantian gardens, they swiftly made their way to the Supreme Granisian's grand meeting chamber where the sovereign was briefed on current events in his kingdom from his elite group of advisors. This night, however, a far different council was to take place in the royal chambers. As the two walked, Zeroan began to discretely inform Tavin of the nature of the council they were going to attend.

"This is sure to be a very high-tension and controversial evening," the Mystic Sage began. "The information that I am going to impart to the council's attendees is sure to frustrate and confuse them, so they are all going be cumbersome with which to deal." The sage looked down at Tavin as they walked. "I understand you have already been informed who will be present tonight." Tavin nodded his head as Zeroan brought his back forward. "Then you know you are going to be surrounded by some of the most important and influential leaders in the entirety of Iairia. Though you are not the one I need to tell this to," he said thinking of the rambunctious Jaren, "please behave accordingly." Tavin nodded again, as the rows of guards in front of him opened the massive door coming into view. "We have arrived," Zeroan announced.

The sentries posted at the door greeted them both, but paid extra attention to the ornately dressed Warrior of Light they had heard so much about. Not sure whether to salute or bow down before him, they both assailed him with questions as soon as he came into view. After Zeroan pulled Tavin into the chamber away from the star-struck sentries, the quiet form of Seriol rose at the far end of a long cedar table that stretched from one side of the assembly room to the other.

Accompanying him were Jaren and Mary who sat talking at the end of the table until they caught sight of Tavin and rushed over to meet him. Zeroan passed them by, making his way to Seriol.

"Are we still on schedule?" he asked with calm anticipation. Seriol nodded and told him all was as it should be. The sage then turned back to the three chatting adolescents and called them to the end of the table to be seated. They did so as Zeroan stood towering before them preparing to speak.

"All right. You three will sit here for the rest of the evening. Remember that this is a very serious council, so do treat it like one," he said with eyes locked onto Jaren, who merely shrugged causing Mary to giggle under her breath. "I do not expect you will have to address the council, but if the need should arise, do so professionally and to the best of your ability. The select few attending should be here before the end of the hour. Until then, I will be out to take care of other matters. Stay here with Seriol."

With that, the foreboding gray cloaked figure drew away, retreating from the chamber as fast as he had appeared. It was not long after that the first members of the council began to arrive. First came Grandarian advisors and the minor Granisians, each eager to meet the Warrior of Light for themselves. As Tavin received the droves of attention, Jaren sat resting his head on his arm, rolling his eyes. Mary leaned down to his ear and whispered in.

"Jealous?" she asked. He turned his head and raised an eyebrow.

"Of Tavin? Please," he said rotating his head back to his friend. "He may have the fancy title, but I could still kick his butt any day of the week." Tavin released the hand of the Captain of the Royal Guard and sat back down.

"I heard that," he said smiling at Mary.

"Good," Jaren retorted, leaning back in his chair and folding his arms.

The next groups to enter were the representatives and the Elemental Warriors of the Southland. As they began to seat themselves at the far end of the table, Tavin kept vigil for the fiery haired girl he had met earlier. She entered at last, flanked by her two guardians she had told him about; Pyre and Spillo. As she found her seat, she managed to catch Tavin smiling in her direction and casually waving at her at the far side of the table. She returned his smile with a coy grin of her own and gingerly waved back, sitting down. Catching sight of this exchange of smiles, Jaren was instantly tugging hard on Tavin's cape. He turned to find Jaren staring him down with eyebrows raised. Tavin squinted and punched his friend over the shoulder. Jaren just sat back silently laughing.

Just as Tavin was about to continue speaking with the Granisians around him, Seriol stood to introduce the approaching figure from the back of the room. The assembly all stood as the Supreme Granisian came walking forth with his Queen to find his chair at the end of the table where Tavin stood. Upon his arrival, the assembly sat once more. The Supreme Granisian shifted his gaze over to Seriol.

"Are we ready to begin?" he asked softly. Seriol shook his head no.

"We are still waiting for the Mystic Sage Zeroan, Your Eminence," he informed. "He should be here in a matter of moments." The Supreme Granisian nodded and brought his gaze to his daughter along with the two boys he had honored earlier in the day.

"I see you three are ready," he stated with a smile. "I am glad to see you present tonight, boys." Tavin was the first to respond.

"We are both very honored to be here, Your Highness," Tavin responded with respect, still overwhelmed he was speaking to the sovereign of Grandaria.

As the crowd began to fall silent, expecting to begin soon, the front doors of the chamber burst open one last time to reveal the gray figure of Zeroan, striding in with robes drifting after him and his hood up to conceal his face as always. After he had arrived at the end of the table, the door was sealed securely shut by the multitude of sentries outside.

"The room is secure, Seriol?" he asked to the white robed Chief Advisor before beginning. When Seriol nodded confidently, the sage breathed deeply and cleared his throat to address the entire assembly. "Welcome, goods friends and allies to the lands of Iairia," he greeted as stoic and serious as ever. Tavin was surprised once more to hear the sage's usually hushed voice boom when it had to. "I thank you all, especially you from the Southland, for possessing the intelligence and responsibility to accept my invitation to attend tonight's council. As you are all no doubt aware, we face a great danger and a difficult time approaching us. We must be prepared and organized if we are to survive it."

Zeroan paused for a moment, looking over to Tavin at the far side of the table, and then continued. "I suppose I should start from the very beginning. As you all know, long ago when the Elemental Warriors first came into creation, there were two of the six who possessed powers and control over their respective elements on a very different scale than the other four. They were of course the Elemental Warriors of Light and Darkness. Naturally opposing one another, the two first clashed hundreds of years ago in the first Holy War. The Warrior of Light was the victor, casting the Warrior of Darkness back into the pits of the northern lands. There that dark power has stayed dormant in the veins of the Warrior of Darkness's lineage, but no longer."

"After centuries of waiting, the Warrior of Darkness has reemerged into the world in the form of Drakkaidia's current ruler, Valif Montrox." The assembly shot uneasy glances around the table at this revelation. Though most had discovered before now that a new Warrior of Darkness had indeed returned, no one knew it was the leader of the enemy himself. Zeroan continued after the council members had gotten the initial shock out of their systems. "Fortunately for us," he continued looking over to Tavin, "we have managed to find a new Warrior of Light to stand against Montrox and his evil. As you all witnessed earlier today, Tavinious Tieloc of Eirinor is now the second Warrior of Light. He is the only one who can fulfill this position because his ancestor, the first Tieloc, was the first Warrior of Light as well. It is in his blood to wield the Sword of Granis against the evil of Drakkaidia and defeat it once and for all." As Zeroan brought his gaze away from Tavin and back to the rest of the assembly, his expression grew even graver than it had been, chilling most of them to the bone.

"Though it is bad enough that Drakkaidia is stirring to life with new evil in the form of the Warrior of Darkness, we have a far more serious problem apart from that," Zeroan warned, making the council very nervous. "In recent times, we Mystic Sages and other such leaders with access to the ancient texts and prophecies of old have discovered a great power lying dormant across the lands of Iairia. All of the magic and elemental power in the world does not even come close to matching the power I speak of. In the old world of the two gods, Lord Granis kept watch over the ultimate power in the universe, know as the Holy Emerald. This sacred emerald was so powerful because it stored all of the elemental powers of the world inside it at once. Coveting this power, Drakkan began the Battle of the Gods to take it for himself. Before the end, he managed to seize it, but could not use it in time to save himself. Granis defeated him before he could use it, banishing him to the abyss of the Netherworld below."

"Knowing that such power as the Holy Emerald would always be a temptation for the men across the lands, Granis shattered the Holy Emerald and sent its six shards with their power intact across the lands where the Elemental Temples were built around them by the ancients. After the power of the six Sources seeped out of the shards, however, they were discarded and lost. Now, to a degree at least, we have found them. The first two shards are in our possession in the Mystic Tower to the south. The third piece is here in this very castle, found by none other than our new Warrior of Light when he was just an unsuspecting child. Fate is an ironic force, it would seem. The fourth and fifth pieces have been taken by forces unknown to us out in the world. One is in the deep south somewhere in the forests of the Grailen, and the other is hidden in the west around Mt. Coron. The last piece is lost to us; Montrox found it in the Black Peaks of Drakkaidia." Zeroan stiffened and lifted his arms in warning.

"Legend tells us that should the shards of the Holy Emerald ever be assembled together at the hand of man, that man would be endowed with all of the power in the universe with control over all elements for himself. That is what Montrox seeks to accomplish. If he locates and collects all of the shards before we do, he will be unstoppable even to the Warrior of Light. As if this is not bad enough, Montrox will unknowingly use his new ultimate power to resurrect the God of Darkness, Drakkan, more powerful than ever from where he has been gathering strength in the Netherworld for thousands upon thousands of years. If this happens, the world will be thrust into a second Battle of the Gods that would surely destroy anything and everything in its wake. None will survive if that happens."

Upon hearing all of this, the groups of leaders from across Iairia were so stunned they could not find the words to respond to the sage. Ril's eyes were wide as she turned back to Pyre and Spillo, equally shocked. The only person collected enough to speak was the Supreme Granisian.

"Zeroan," he began, "I would first wish to thank you on behalf of us all for bringing these most urgent matters to our attention. I know that among all of the Mystic Sages, you are by far the most valuable to the rest of the world." He stopped for a moment, looking up at Zeroan almost helplessly. "What is it that you would have us do?" he asked with a pinch of fear in his voice. Zeroan remained stoic in his response.

"The only thing we can do is separate our forces to counter Drakkaidia. Valif Montrox has gone to far more trouble and created a far more intricate plan than you know, Supreme Granisian. He has been preparing for this war, this personal vendetta against Grandaria, for his entire life. As we speak, he is using his black power coupled with his shard of the Holy Emerald to summon creatures from the Netherworld to add to his ever growing patrols of demons. Once he has amassed enough, he will loose them onto the world to kill, ravage, and destroy at will until he has possession of all six shards of the Holy Emerald. He is already looking for the missing shards and is preparing to take our shards from us by force." A look of offense passed through General Taroct's face, the commander of the Grandarian Army. He sat forward and frowned at the sage.

"Take them by force?" he asked with disbelief. "Are you suggesting that Drakkaidian forces are planning to assault Grandaria?" This disturbing suggestion forced a brief round of whispers exchanged around the table. Zeroan shifted his gaze to the disgruntled general.

"I do not suggest anything. I am telling you that the Drakkaidian Army with the aid of the demon horde being assembled even now is going to assault Grandaria with energy and a craving for your blood that you have never seen the likes of before, even in the old days of the first Holy Wars. You have held them at your mighty barrier the Wall of Light in the wars zones for over five centuries now, but with their newly empowered armies, they will eventually penetrate it if we do not act to stop them." General Taroct laughed at this.

"I have no idea where you are getting this information, sage, but I assure you that the Wall of Light cannot and will not ever be 'penetrated,'" he said in disgust. Zeroan glared at him again, making the general very uneasy.

"For all our sakes, let us hope you are right. But that is not all. Montrox and his subordinates have also devised a plan to invade the Southland." Half of the assembly came bounding forward in their chairs at this. Amongst those yelling out at the sage that he was out of his mind, the representative from the Southland Legion was the loudest in his complaint.

"You've lost your mind, sage!" he exclaimed. "Whatever new strength the Drakkaidians have acquired, it will never be enough to get past the Southland Legion. Not one Drakkaidia soldier has ever managed to set foot on Southland soil. It is impossible," he argued.

After Seriol regained order, Zeroan simply turned over to Taroct again.

"General," he asked. "According to your latest intelligence from the Wall of Light, what are the numbers of Drakkaidian soldiers in the war zone?" Taroct frowned at him uneasy.

"That isn't a fair question..." he said before Zeroan cut him off.

"Answer it, nonetheless," the sage commanded. Taroct swallowed and finally responded.

"Latest intelligence reports Drakkaidian forces at battalion strength emerging from the Valley of Blood. There are thousands in the war zone. More come by the day." The assembly went quiet again until Zeroan added to the statement.

"I can also assure you that that figure's strength will triple in the next few months as the demon horde joins with it. With some of the monsters they have on their side, that is more than enough to storm the border at its weak points, and more than enough to keep the Grandarians occupied at their wall until the Southland is no more." The Southlander in command was still skeptical.

"You must be wrong," he said. "There is no such force in Drakkaidia."

"As I said," the sage continued, "Montrox has been planning and preparing for this attack for decades. He has done nothing but breed an army for his entire life. Every able bodied man in Drakkaidia is a soldier to him, and he will send them to fight accordingly. There is an infinite force of demons in the Netherworld for him to muster. Though I am confident the Grandarians can hold their Wall of Light for a greater longevity, I do not believe the border to the Southland will last as long if you are merely pitting armies against each other. You cannot win open war against the Drakkaidians at this point in time. The Southland Legion is gargantuan to be sure, but with the aid of demons like the Valcanor, your lines will crumble before their might. And most importantly, the Legion is still scattered and unorganized in the wake of the Second Holy War a century ago. There is no Legion to speak of anymore.

"Aside from the threat of direct combat, there is also some great plan to take the Southland that Montrox has concocted and I have not been able to discover. I would guess however, that this plan has already been set into motion even now and the dark lord is going to work at disassembling the Legion as much as he can before his attack. We must be ready for anything."

The room stayed quiet for a time after the sage's response. Tavin could see the confusion and frustration he had been warned about as he looked about the room. It was again the Supreme Granisian who broke the silence.

"Mystic Sage Zeroan," he quietly called, "you still have not answered my question. What is it you would have us do to avoid this doom?" Zeroan gazed around the room again.

"We will divide and stop him," he said with confidence.

Chapter 16

<u>Plan of Action</u>

As Zeroan's forthright statement fell onto the council's ears, Taroct was the first to respond with the frustration most were feeling.

"What in the name of Granis on high does that mean?" he asked irritably. Zeroan responded with self-assurance again.

"It means exactly what it sounds like, General," he stated. "Montrox has several different objectives he will seek to complete. Though his forces are vast, they will be stretched thin to be everywhere at once. And until he has gathered more shards, he cannot have more than a handful of relatively weak demons in our world at one time, so we will divide up our strongest forces and place them in defensive positions around central Iairia. First of all, we will need to dispatch the Elemental Warriors to defend the critical points that will most certainly fall under attack.

"We will need one to stay here at Galantia to protect the city from further raids from the demons in the area and to protect the Holy Emerald shard that will be left here. Another must go to the Mystic Tower in the South to guard the shards in the vaults there. We must also have a warrior sent to the Southland border as soon as possible to prepare and assist the Legion with its inevitable battle with the Drakkaidians when Montrox has fully assembled his power. This will be exceptionally difficult to do considering the Legion is spread all across the Southland in a state of dormancy."

"And last but not least, one of the four warriors from the south will accompany the Elemental Warrior of Light to locate and collect the two missing shards in the Southland. This will be the most important task of all, for everything depends on us securing the other shards to stop Montrox from awakening greater evil to stand against us. With every shard he collects, his power over the demons from the Netherworld will increase drastically. If Montrox does not find any more shards, he will not be able to summon his demon horde and send out his armies to fully engage Grandaria and the Southland. That is why we must assemble a party of our greatest warriors to find the missing shards to the south." The various Elemental Warriors shot each other puzzled glances as if trying to decide who should go where. "Which of you will do what?" asked Zeroan, obviously giving them the choice. It was the younger Warrior of Water who spoke up first.

"Well, if it's up to us," he began to the other Elemental Warriors, "I think that I would like to stand at the border to assist the Legion. My power over the water would do the most good there close to the central wetlands, and I am close to the Temple of Water should I need it." The other warriors agreed as they sat contemplating where their powers would do the most good. As Ril thought about where she would volunteer to go, she suddenly thought of Tavin at the far end of the table. If she was to go on the most important mission of them all, perhaps she would finally get the respect she deserved as an Elemental Warrior. As she looked up at the young Warrior of Light, she thought back to their encounter in the garden earlier, remembering how kind he had been to her and how he had saved her life despite her claiming otherwise. If she was going to be with someone on this adventure, it might as well be Tavin, one of the few people she knew who treated her as an equal.

Before she could say anything, however, the Elemental Warrior of Wind sat forward to speak. Ril could only pray she would not volunteer to journey with Tavin.

"I believe that I would do the most good at the Mystic Valley," the older woman said, sending a wave of relief washing through Ril. "With the high gusts of wind constantly blowing atop that high tower, my power would do considerable good there. The other sages would listen to me over some of their *other* peers since they see me out of Windrun so often." Zeroan nodded to her in silent approval, ignoring her comment about the others. Ril was quick to chime in next to be sure she went where she wanted to go.

"I would like to assist the Warrior of Light on his journey to collect the two missing shards of the Holy Emerald," she stated quickly, causing Tavin to wheel his head in her direction somewhat surprised. Upon hearing this, Zeroan let out a small sigh of dissatisfaction.

"Just wonderful…" he muttered under his breath. The sage brought his gaze back to her. "I was hoping that you would remain here to defend Galantia," he told her. "This will not be an easy journey for one as young as you, and there will be no breaks or rest stops on this quest." Ril was so offended she stood up out of her chair and nearly yelled at the sage.

"What kind of talk is that?" she asked angrily, surprising the others, especially Tavin. "I am so tired of you and everyone else treating me different from the other warriors just because I'm younger! I'm just as capable as anyone of the others, if not more so. And as far as my age goes, Tavin and I are both the same!" Zeroan was quick to forcefully jump back in her face.

"Listen carefully, Warrior of Fire. No one here downgrades you due to your age, least of all me. I know how capable you are. But I don't know if you would be ready for something like this; it will not be a simple journey to just pick up the shards. We are sure to encounter danger and evil that you cannot even begin to fathom. And as far as your age goes," he repeated, "I would not take Tavin if I could help it, but seeing as he is the only Warrior of Light, I am left with little choice. This will not be easy for him either." Ril was still standing with anger.

"I don't care what obstacles or dangers you face, sage, I promise I will not slow you down. My power would be of far more use to you than that of earth!" she argued. Garoll decided to assist her at this point.

"She's right about that, Zeroan," the Warrior of Earth added. "She is the only one amongst us who can manifest her element out of thin air, not just manipulate one already there like we do. That would be a valuable asset to you on your journey. I would be better off here at Galantia with the rocky earth around it anyway." Ril agreed and looked back at the sage for his ruling. Zeroan exhaled sharply, returning Ril's gaze. At last, he responded.

"Fine. You may come with us on the search for the other shards," he gave in. Ril let a small smile spread across her face as she thanked him. Tavin could only stare at her, wondering why she would go to so much trouble just to come on a dangerous quest when she had seemed to be only annoyed with him that afternoon. As Ril took her seat, however, Zeroan gave her an ominous warning. "You may come, girl, but if you get in my way or slow me down just once, I promise we will be leaving you at the nearest village we can find." Ril gave him a look of disbelief.

"You're going as well?" she asked.

"That is correct," he said with authority. "I am the only one who knows where to look for the shards, and believe me when I say that even the Warrior of Light will need my help until he learns to control his power. Now then," he said looking over the other members of the council, "we will need a few more than that on this quest if are to be successful." Ril's two guardians were both up and standing at once. Zeroan cut them off before they could utter a single word. "If Miss Embrin thinks she is strong enough to go on this quest and defend herself, you two will not be necessary. I will have no further argument, because I will take only who we need. Now sit, both of you," the sage commanded in a powerful tone. They reluctantly did so, realizing argument with Zeroan was pointless. "Who else?"

Instantly, Jaren's hand was in the air volunteering.

"If Tavin is going on this little adventure deal, then so am I. I know what you're going to say, Zeroan," he said with raising his hand to cut the sage off, "but I haven't been through as much as I have with Tavin just to leave him now. I'm going and that's that. Besides, who was it that said I was the best bowman in Grandaria?" Zeroan frowned at him.

"There was obviously a failure of communication there," he snapped as he motioned for the boy to quiet. "I know full well that I could not separate you and Tavin if I tried, and because of your skill with a bow, I will allow you to go as well. But the same warning I gave to the Warrior of Fire applies to you." Jaren smiled in triumph toward Tavin while the Princess next to him leaned in closer.

"Do you think I could go?" she asked sincerely. Jaren was quick to shake his head.

"Sorry, kiddo," he started, "but after that little scene with the Warrior of Fire, there is no way that guy would even consider it. Don't waste your breath." Mary looked hurt at this, though she knew Jaren was right. He leaned over to her and tried to cheer her up by telling her what she could do here while they were gone.

"Are there any others?" Zeroan asked. The first to volunteer this time were two men at the far side of the table. One was a large and rugged man with a massive double bladed axe mounted on his back.

"I am Parnox Guilldon, here to represent the Grailen and Greenwall Fortress in the plains. I know the Great Forests that you have been speaking of well, and I can also handle this fairly well," he said in a deep voice, patting his ridiculously huge axe.

"And I am Kohlin Marraea from Aggiest Village, just outside of Windrun City to the south," the other thin and clean cut young man offered. "I am a trained tracker and I can defend myself," he said, repositioning the duel sabers mounted at his sides. "I would be most honored to offer what help I can to this cause," the blonde young man said with purpose. Zeroan nodded and motioned for them to sit. Garoll Nelpia chimed in to aid them.

"I can vouch for both of these men, Zeroan," he said with confidence. "I know from experience that Parnox is one of the finest warriors and navigators of the Grailen there is, and I have heard a great deal of Kohlin Marraea, the man who found the Sky Sprite lair, as well." Zeroan nodded at Garoll, acknowledging their credentials.

"The Southland has sent a fine assemblage of warriors to aid us," the sage said quietly. "I was hoping you would volunteer to go with us. I have heard of you both as well, Parnox Guilldon of the Grailen and Kohlin Marraea of Windrun. You are both most welcome." As they took their seats, Zeroan began to speak again.

"That will be enough for the quest to collect the shards of the Holy Emerald. Six is a good number to travel with. We will be small enough to move fast and draw little attention, but large enough to protect ourselves from anything we might encounter. Now we must put our attention elsewhere. If we are to keep Grandaria and the majority of the Southland safe, we must prepare our defensive forces. General Taroct, I would advise preparing your army to mobilize at the Wall of Light immediately. Believe me when I say they will be needed there. I cannot predict what Montrox is planning, but he may come at you with everything he has. I would also put out a warning at the Battlemount villages should the worst happen at the wall." Taroct was growing very impatient with the sage's obvious lack of faith in his army.

"Look," he said cocking his head, "I'll strengthen our defenses on the wall, but there is no need for a warning of any kind. Even if the impossible happened and we lost the wall, we would still have our mountain base at the Battlemount to hold them back. There is no way in hell the Drakkaidians have become as powerful as you seem to give them credit for. You underestimate the Grandarian Army." Zeroan's ice cold gaze beamed through this hood and into the general's eyes.

"Even if I do, be *sure* that you do not underestimate the Drakkaidian Army. In my travels to the far north, I have seen first hand its ferocity, and it is aided by demons that cannot be harmed with steel from swords or arrowheads. As for the Southland Legion, muster what strength you have at the borderline and prepare yourselves for the worst battle you have ever seen there. You will have the Warrior of Water to aid you and summon the Legion, but that will not be enough to stop the full force of their armies from breaking through your lines. Representatives of the four lands, be sure you raise the alarm in all of your cities and villages. There will be things out in the open now even in the daylight that would do you and your people harm." Zeroan turned his head down to the other end of the table toward Seriol and the Supreme Granisian.

"Now for the last part of our plan. We must be sure that we are guarding the shards that we possess very carefully if the worst should happen and they are put at risk. I leave the first shard here to be kept safe in the Tower of Granis. Seriol, I trust you to see that it is kept safe." Seriol nodded at the end of the table. "As for the shards at the Mystic Tower, I want someone who attended this council to be with them. My few fellow sages will not watch over them as they need to. As you have undoubtedly heard, I have indeed been 'banished' from the Order of Alberic. The others have become blind to the movement of Drakkaidia and do not trouble with what little they do see. I cannot trust them. Just to be sure the shards stay where they need to be, I need someone to volunteer to keep watch over them should the other sages seek to do anything foolish. My voice must be present there."

At first, no response came. Then at the end of the table, a small hand was raised next to Jaren. Zeroan looked at its owner, curious.

"You wish for this responsibility, Princess Maréttiny?" As he heard the sound of their daughter's name, the Supreme Granisian and the Queen turned to her in disbelief.

"Mary, what are you doing?" her mother asked questioningly. "It is your duty to stay here in your kingdom and keep watch over the shard here. You just went out with Seriol against my wishes into the heat of a battle. I will not allow you to risk your life further!" Mary shook her head.

"No mother," she replied. "I am always kept here inside this city, never doing much of anything. I want to be of help for once; to do something that has meaning. I would feel horribly guilty to let everyone else help this cause while I just sit here." The Queen was about to argue further, but Corinicus Kolior raised his hand for silence. He looked at his daughter, as if he didn't know she possessed such bravery. "Please, father," Mary said. "I want to help." He gazed down at her for one more moment, and then smiled at her as he placed his hand over both of hers.

"It would seem I underestimated my own daughter's strength," he said. He then nodded his approval as he spoke. "With Zeroan's consent, you may go to the Mystic Tower if you wish it." Mary beamed at him, and then at Jaren, who sat staring eyes wide.

"I would like to go to the Mystic Tower, Zeroan," she stated. Zeroan's eyes found the Supreme Granisian's one last time, where he found the answer he had previously decreed. Zeroan brought his gaze back upon the Princess.

"Very well, Princess. You will go with the Warrior of Wind to the Mystic Tower and keep watch over the shard stored there with the Mystic Sages." Mary beamed again and excessively thanked him.

Zeroan stood silent for a moment then, nodding his head with satisfaction.

"Very good," he said at last. "It would seem that we are ready to counter Drakkaidia. Unless there are any further questions, I think that we are done here." When no response came, the sage thanked the council one last time and ended the meeting. As the attendees began to filter out of the room, Tavin quickly rose out of his seat and made his way over to the red haired girl on the other side of the table. When she caught sight of him coming over, she rose as well, a greeting smile covering her face. Tavin returned it as he arrived.

"Ril," he started, "that was incredible back there. I've never seen anyone challenge Zeroan like that before." Ril shrugged and brushed some of her crimson hair out of her face.

"Well, I thought someone needed to remind him he's not Granis," she grinned. Tavin laughed at that.

"Well I'm glad you're coming with me," he told her. "It's always good to have another friend with you." Ril smiled again, just nodding.

As the two began to talk a little more, the familiar voice of Zeroan called from behind them.

"Tavin, Arilia, come over here please," he beckoned. They shot each other nervous glances then turned to approach. As they came closer to Zeroan, Tavin noticed the entire party that they would be taking on the quest to find the missing shards had assembled around the Supreme Granisian, the Queen, Seriol, and Mary. As Zeroan observed the whole group around him, he began to speak one last time for the evening.

"Thank you all for volunteering to join Tavinious on his quest," the sage started. "As I said earlier, finding the missing emerald shards before Montrox is the most effective way to preclude his plans from being put into effect. But because we are hard pressed to find them before Drakkaidia and its dark agents and time is stacked against us, we must leave as soon as humanly possible." Jaren raised an eyebrow at this.

"How early are we talking, here?" he asked nervously.

"We leave tomorrow at dawn," he stated. Jaren's jaw dropped down to the floor. "Make yourself ready by then. Get a good night's sleep, and I will meet you all in the Gate Yard in the morning. Be sure you are not late. I will not be available for the rest of the evening, so if anyone has anything they wish to ask or say, do so now." Tavin stood thinking for a moment before he remembered what he wanted to ask some time ago.

"Zeroan," he asked the sage, "I was wondering if we could talk before you go." Zeroan looked down at him and nodded.

"Yes, I know, Tavin. There will be time tomorrow. Until then, keep your questions in the back of your mind and do not dwell on them. Enjoy your last night here," the sage advised. With that, the Mystic Sage turned his back on the crowd and made his way to the doorway.

"I will see you at dawn in the Gate Yard. Until then," he called striding out of the room, leaving the party to themselves. The young man from Windrun was the next to speak.

"Well, it was a pleasure to meet all of you," he said with respect. "I suppose we'll see you tomorrow, then." Tavin smiled and shook his hand.

"I look forward to it, Kohlin Marraea," responded Tavin, minding his manners to never forget a name. As the rest of the party bade each other goodbye, Tavin introduced Ril to Jaren.

"Ril, this is my best friend Jaren Garrinal. Jaren, this is the Warrior of Fire, Arilia Embrin." The two shook hands as they greeted each other. Jaren immediately raised his eyebrows and seized the girl's hand once more upon closer inspection of her beautiful figure.

"Hello indeed, miss," Jaren greeted, turning up the charm. Tavin rolled his eyes so far around his head they nearly stuck their permanently. Jaren gently bowed his head down to her hand and gingerly kissed it. Ril flashed the boy a caustic smile as she quickly ignited a small flame in her hand, causing Jaren to recoil back in a burst of pain. Tavin had to bite his tongue to keep from laughing hysterically at his friend's harsh rejection.

Tavin wanted to talk longer, but Ril's guardians were eager to get her back to her room to get some well deserved rest from such a busy day. Ril waved goodbye as she walked away and out into the halls. As Mary and her parents left after Ril, Jaren stood beside Tavin, sucking on his stinging hand and scowling. Tavin struggled to suppress his laughter.

"Tavin…" Jaren began glaring, "mark my words: that girl is going to be the death of us. You keep her away from me, or I'm liable to get angry and teach her some manners."

"Like you did just now?" Tavin asked sarcastically, walking away and out of the doorway to the end of the room. Glaring once more, Jaren ran to catch up with his friend out in the golden halls of the castle.

Part Two
The Quest Begins

Chapter 17

<u>Departure</u>

The next morning came sooner than any in the party wished. Tavin and Jaren were awakened with a start by Seriol, some time before dawn. After the council the previous night, Seriol had advised them to get to sleep immediately, for they would rise very early. Obviously he was not kidding. While Tavin was eager to get up and prepare himself for the first day of his quest, Jaren had to be pulled out of bed by his feet to even come awake. After they both bathed, they entered the massive guest room to find a surplus of supplies and rations packed for them both at Seriol's request. The Chief Advisor of Grandaria had also seen fit to lay out both of their attire for the long journey. Tavin found clothes much like the ones he wore yesterday: a blue and gold tunic, thick white pants, blue boots and gloves, and a flowing blue cape with a fervent red lining. Thought he didn't have to wear the ornately decorated golden armor from the day before, he did strap on some simple blue armor that covered his torso, upper back, and shoulders, and threw his warm cape on over that. Jaren found a similar set of armor, but green instead to match the rest of his Grandarian hunting garb.

As the two dressed and loaded their backpacks with the essentials they would need, Seriol personally brought their weapons to them. Tavin strapped the Sword of Granis to his side, its top golden crystal bursting with light as it fell into his grasp. Jaren was given a custom built bow carried only by the Royal Guard. After they gathered everything they could think of for the journey, Seriol opened the door to their chamber and led them away. As the group passed through the massive torch-lit halls, Tavin looked out one of the massive windows to observe a ray of the sun beginning to ascend over the hills to the east.

After making their way through the Golden Castle's beautiful corridors and the Grand Vestibule one final time, the trio exited into the courtyard to find three regal carriages waiting for them. Tavin guessed that the others in his party had not yet arrived. As Seriol beckoned the boys to enter the first of the three carriages, Tavin heard the faint sound of footsteps behind him. Entering the carriage, he turned his head back to find both the Southlanders Parnox Guilldon from the forestland and Kohlin Marraea from the hills of the Windrun emerging out of the castle. Before he could so much as raise an arm to wave, however, the carriage was already away for the Gate Yard. Seriol sat Tavin down as they hastily drove through the streets.

"We must get to the Gate Yard quickly, Tavin. We have no time for any pleasantries this morning," he explained in a hushed tone. Tavin and Jaren stared at him curiously, about to ask him why before he saved them the trouble. "I know what you would ask. As you know about our friend Zeroan, secrecy and stealth are assets he values very much. He wishes to attract as little attention as possible when you leave to keep this journey a secret. He wants you to be off before the sun rises, so it is imperative we get there as soon as possible."

Tavin looked over to his friend with exhilaration present in his face from the importance of the mission they were about to embark upon. Jaren was slightly more reserved in his opinion of this whole matter, still thinking that the sage Zeroan was more insane than wise. Speeding through the separate districts of Galantia, the occupants of the carriage could now detect similar patterns of wheels racing down the stone pathways behind them. The boys looked back to find the other two carriages coming swiftly behind.

At the enterprising pace the carriages traveled, it did not take the convoy long to reach the Gate Yards. Tavin and Jaren arrived first, halting in front of the smaller gates to the side of the yard. They exited quickly, expecting to find the towering figure of Zeroan close by. When they observed he was nowhere to be found, they quickly turned back to Seriol, who merely pointed over to the smallest gate next to the military garrisons. As Tavin squinted his eyes through the shadows, he could barely make out the silhouette of a robed figure waiting for them. Tavin turned his head to look at Seriol questioningly.

"Zeroan instructed me to inform you that you will depart once the entire group has assembled," Seriol explained to them. Tavin nodded at this, shifting his gaze to the other two carriages pulling into the Gate Yard beside theirs. The door of the first opened quickly, revealing the brisk young figure of Kohlin Marraea, followed by the burly Parnox Guilldon mounting his forbidding axe to his back. As the two proceeded toward Tavin and Jaren, they quietly greeted each other with hardy handshakes. Jaren thought that he would be sent careening into the ground from the force Parnox exerted on his comparatively weak limb. The boy winced but smiled broadly, casting a quick glance of helplessness at Tavin who stood grinning back at him.

The opening of the final carriage's door caught Tavin's attention as he turned his head over to see the two crimson cloaked men appearing to form around the door like sentries. Tavin felt his pulse quicken as the slender form of Arilia Embrin came slowly stepping out of the carriage to the ground, her cherry hair flowing about her face like a tepid summer breeze. Tavin could not help but stare as she turned to her two guardians and gave them a warm but sad smile. She latched onto them, obviously saying a very hard goodbye to them both. Even Jaren with all his pride could feel something touch his heart as a small tear ran down the girl's delicate cheek. Pyre was quick to gently wipe it away as he beckoned her to join the rest of her party. Raising her head to meet his eyes, she gradually pulled away and reached up to her chest to tuck her dark scarlet locket dangling around her neck beneath the layers of clothes.

As the Warrior of Fire said her final goodbye, she at last turned around and strode toward the party. She was dressed in the same vibrantly colored attire that Tavin had met her in the day before; a fiery red and orange tunic fit tightly around her top half with the ends concealing the top of her tight red and white trousers along with her traveling pack. While the mere sight of the girl caused Tavin's blood to boil, her attire also gave off the appearance of an obvious tomboy- something Tavin could easily classify her as. Not many women, much less girls her age, would ever wish to undergo a journey like this.

Tavin could see the hurt mirrored in Ril's eyes as she arrived next to them. He tried a quick smile and a warm welcome.

"Morning, Ril," he spoke empathetically. Ril brought her eyes up to meet with the boy's, remembering how kind he had been to her the previous day. Grateful for his sensitivity, she managed to flash him a healthy smile in response.

"Good morning," she replied wiping the last residue of a tear from her eyes. "Are we ready to go?" Tavin nodded his head.

"We are now," he said as the other three members of their group began to venture over to the dark form of Zeroan. Tavin motioned for Ril to proceed ahead of him, eager to get the expedition under way. As they arrived at the opening of the small gate in the wall, the sage seemed to materialize before them in the shadows.

"Good morning to you all," he greeted in his usual stoic tone. "I thank you all for being punctual. Are you all prepared to leave?" The party members all nodded yes in response, ready to begin as well. "Excellent. Now before we depart, I wish to remind you of a few simple things. As you already know, the quest that we are about to embark on is of the utmost importance to the survival of the world. If we are to succeed in locating the two missing shards of the Holy Emerald before the agents of the Drakkaidians, we must move quickly and quietly. We will travel on foot for now, as horses will be too cumbersome to deal with on the route we will be taking through the mountains. Wherever we go, we will not stay in the same place for long. The outside world is not safe any longer. Demons now roam freely across the face of the Iairia and destruction is left in their wake. Valif Montrox is sure to be aware that we will try to find the missing shards now that the Warrior of Light has come, and he will be on the lookout for us across the lands." The sage rustled under his robes.

"The overall rule that you need to be aware of on this quest, however, is that my voice is the one you must trust and follow in times of hardship and danger. I have extensive knowledge of all possible perils we may face, so you must rely on my judgment though your own may dictate otherwise. If you can comply with that, we should be able to complete this journey safely. Are there any questions regarding what I have just told you?" None were asked. "Very good. Now just for your own personal reference, I will provide you a brief overview of our destinations. As long as our presence is kept secret as we move, we will travel on foot southwest across Grandaria and into the Iairian Mountain Chain. The Great Rift that connects Grandaria with the top of the Southland should be open to us, so we will pass through the mountains there. If not, the Windrun Road further south will be an option."

"Once we have entered the Southland," he continued, "we will head south into the Grailen Plains and the Great Forests. The first shard we are looking for is somewhere in that vicinity. After we acquire it, we will make our way northwest to the volcanic regions around Mt. Coron." Ril's expression brightened at the mention of her homeland. "The second shard lies there somewhere in the fire seeping mountains. Once we have both the shards, we will find a faster mode of transportation and make our way to the Mystic Tower. I will leave you for a moment to return to Galantia and gather the shard that rests here." Tavin was confused with this part of the plan.

"Zeroan," he asked puzzled, "why not just take the shard with us so we don't have to come back for it?" Zeroan shook his head no.

"No, Tavin, I will not carry three shards at once," he stated with authority. "If something should happen to our party, Montrox would have all three. It is risky enough to travel with the two we will find. In any case, once we have the five shards in our possession, I will attempt to destroy them permanently with the forbidden magic of old, something that should never be used for anything else. Should that fail, I can at least cast them out of anyone's reach at the Mystic Tower where I can access the peak of my power. From that point, it will be Montrox's move. With no other shards to summon further dark powers and increase his own, he will have only his armies of mortal men and his own powers as the Warrior of Darkness. With only those two forces in his favor, we will be able to repel Drakkaidia as in the first Holy War." As Zeroan finished his speech, the members of the small group looked at each other with approval. It would be a risky and difficult journey to be sure, but they all knew it had to be made.

Zeroan nodded his head in satisfaction. With that, he instructed them to keep their conversation limited to a whisper as they made their way away from Galantia to the south and out of the valley. As Zeroan led the party out the secretive gateway of the Gate Yard, Seriol tapped Jaren on his shoulder and presented him with a letter. Jaren accepted it with reluctance, not sure who would be sending him a letter in Galantia. Seriol smiled.

"Princess Maréttiny instructed me to give you this before you left," he stated. "She apologies for not being here to see you off personally, but previous engagements held her attention. Being an official letter from the Princess herself, the contents are highly confidential." Jaren glanced down at the letter as a sly grin crept over his face. He extended his arm to grasp onto Seriol's, shaking it firmly. With that, the boy stowed the letter in his tunic pocket and made his way out of the closing gate.

As the small doorway tightly closed behind the boy, Seriol stood in the darkness of the Gate Yard for several long minutes, contemplating, before he at last turned and began striding back to the castle on foot. A murky smile crept onto his face. As he causally made his way back through the Gate Yard, he emitted a soft but ominous laugh that echoed throughout the fresh morning air into the darkness.

Chapter 18

<u>One Small Spark</u>

It was a good hour after the party departed from Galantia that the golden city began to slip out of their vision. The last remnant of the capital still visible was the mighty Tower of Granis now guarding the first of the Holy Emerald shards. They marched forward with purpose and high spirits coursing through their bodies, driving them onward toward the Great Rift in the Iairian Mountain Chain to the southwest. They immediately established a basic formation while they marched. The Mystic Sage Zeroan remained in front leading them forward at a demanding pace with the nimble Kohlin Marraea following closely, occasionally scouting ahead to keep watch for anything out of the ordinary with his keen senses and superb tracking ability. The other Southlander, Parnox Guilldon, strode steadily at the rear of the group, guarding their back with his fearsome strength and hulking figure.

Arilia Embrin trailed after Kohlin, with Tavin and Jaren following close behind. Though the party maintained complete silence as they exited the Valley of Galantia, these three companions began to come together afterwards to converse about anything they could. Coming from very different places in Iairia, both Ril and the boys were eager to hear about each other and what their lifestyles were like. Ril pleasured them with stories of her exciting duties as the Warrior of Fire, telling exotic tales of her various trips and tasks to maintain what was refereed to as 'elemental order' all over the Southland. Tavin and Jaren were nothing short of amazed of what she had done and seen at such a young age, but they were just as interested in her calm daily life at home. Though Ril enjoyed having the company of such energetic boys who gave her all the attention she could ever want, she eventually remembered that they were just boys, and Grandarian

125

boys at that, causing her to grow uninterested with their discussions after the day had elapsed. Jaren just shrugged at her frustrations and continued his usually senseless and immature conversation. By the time they fell asleep in camp that night, the three youths had already grown to know each other fairly well.

The party traveled on like this for the next four days, passing through the Valley of Galantia, the Northern Hills of Eirinor, and the green mounts of the west until they had reached the more rugged terrain in the base lands of the Iairian Mountain Chain. On the fourth nightfall, Zeroan called for the team to halt early. Pleased with the amount of distance they had traveled for the time being, he ordered camp be made for the night in a small thicket of bushes at the western end of the rocky hillside they had traversed. As the other five members of the party prepared a small fire to warm their food, the Mystic Sage disappeared, leaving Tavin to assume he was out scouting for any danger before they turned in. When he failed to return after over an hour, the group decided to get some rest while they could, taking turns to keep watch for the sage's return or anything unfavorable the night might have been harboring.

Zeroan returned, hurriedly waking them once again, at the first light of dawn. While Jaren found it particularly hard to comprehend the sage's reasoning for departing so early, they all reluctantly gathered up their supplies and were off once again. The party traveled in the darkness of the early morning until the sun began to spread its warming light over the hills to the east revealing their current position to the rest of the group. Moving at the near grueling pace they had discovered was the norm for Zeroan, the small company had covered considerable ground in a surprisingly short period of time. Tavin could now observe that they had passed out of the last remnant of the western hillsides and were now into the craggy forestland northwest of the mountains.

As the group passed through the luscious scenery in the cool morning air, Ril felt a quick shiver run down her spine as the biting winds of the north came assailing into her. Not used to such a cold climate being born in the proximity of an active volcano and one of the warmest habitats in the Southland, the shivering girl made an attempt to warm herself. She slowly brought her arms close to her face where a small burst of flame sparked to life in the palm of her hands, spreading its warmth across her smooth skin. Not more than a few moments after Ril birthed the tiny flame, Zeroan's head jerked upward a few yards ahead of her and wheeled around, catching them all by surprise. The Mystic Sage fixed a sharp glare down on the form of the shivering Warrior of Fire, violently cursing under his breath as he leapt over to her across the rugged terrain. Unsure of the cause of his apparent alarm, Ril's eye shot open with nervous curiosity. Before she could inquire as to the problem, however, Zeroan thrust his hands toward hers, clasping them together to smother the fire. His face was hard and angry as he locked his eyes onto the girl.

"What do you think you are doing?" he scolded harshly. Ril could only stare back at him helplessly still unaware of any fault she had committed. The others in the party were equally confused as they all gazed at him. "You know better than to use magic when we are being sought after by creatures that can sense even the smallest bit of it leagues away! Was I not clear enough when I said that there are sure to be Drakkaidian spies on the lookout for us? If any of them were in Grandaria or the Great Rift right now, they would have sensed that little display of yours and come to kill us!" Zeroan's face tightened further as his irate eyes locked onto hers. "If you *wish* to attract our enemies, next time set yourself on fire and relieve me of your bumbling idiocy!" Upset and humiliated by his ruthless upbraiding, Ril struggled to find the words to repel him.

"What are you so worried about?" she questioned defensively, violently recoiling back. "It was just a spark! There is no way anything could have sensed that!" The animosity that flared in the sage's eyes then frightened the girl so much she took a step back.

"Don't be a fool!" he yelled. "You know nothing of the predators that are sure to be searching for us. If they cannot sense 'just a spark' how was I able to- because I don't even possess half the heightened senses they do!" Realizing that this was going to turn into a fully fledged war before it was done, Tavin decided to step in between them in an effort to restore the peace.

"Zeroan," he interrupted with inflection in his voice, "that should be enough. What's done is done, and she knows now not to use any magic again unless it's safe. It was an honest mistake, and you don't need to be so harsh with your words." Ril uncertainly shifted her gaze over to Tavin, who stood beside her with conviction mirrored in his eyes. Zeroan locked his glare over to the boy ready to say something, but instead chose to contain himself and remain silent. At last he responded.

"Do not interfere with my affairs, young man," he quietly advised. "There are foes out there that can easily destroy us right now, even with your power to aid us. I do not want the safety or secrecy of this group compromised." Zeroan nodded then and brought his eyes back to Ril. "But there is no use dwelling on this blunder now. We must evacuate this position quickly before-"

The sage did not have the time to finish his statement, as the sound of a familiar ear piercing shriek suddenly echoed through the thin mountain air from the southwest in the mountains. Zeroan wheeled around, instantly scanning the rugged land where the cry had originated. After no immediate threat presented itself, the sage quickly gathered up the others in the group and pushed them into a nearby thicket of shrubs.

"All right, pay very close attention. As you just heard, there is at least one demon out there that has locked on to our position, and if there is one, there could be more not too far off. Go out and finish him quickly, but do not use any further magic or we'll have the entire horde on top of us before we so much as unsheathe a blade. I'll stay here and mask our presence to any other creatures that may have detected us. Now go!" That was all the burly form of Parnox Guilldon needed to hear. Leaping up, he grabbed hold of Jaren and Kohlin.

"You two come with me," he commanded, taking charge. "Tavin and Ril, stay here and protect Zeroan. Do not use your magic." With that, he wrenched Jaren and Kohlin up once more, ripping out into the open clearing to attract the advancing demon. "Jaren!" he shouted. "Lets see if you're as good with that bow as you claim. Take it down now!" Jaren reluctantly pulled forth his bow, not sure if even he could nail a demon as agile as the one sprinting down through the jagged base of the mountains. The creature resembled a Liradd from the vale, but it was much thinner and more aerodynamic in appearance as it jetted through the rocky terrain. Jaren quickly strung an arrow and tried to take aim as fast as he could. The creature's movements were erratic; too unpredictable to take precise aim.

Not wanting to waste any more time planning his shot, Jaren let his arrow fly. As it cut through the thin air, the demon must have had the reflexes to see it coming, because it suddenly reared back and shot skywards right over it. Jaren took advantage of this fatal error at once. Before the demon could even reach the peak of its jump, he had another arrow strung and zipping over to it to catch it on its way back down. The arrow planted itself in its upper back and forced it back to its feet with a thud. This monster proved to possess far greater stamina than the Liradds, however; instantly back on the charge toward the young archer who had wounded it.

While Jaren was about to restring and try his luck again, both of the Southlanders bellowed for him to withdraw and cover them from the bushes with Tavin and Ril. Cursing under his breath, Jaren sped backward. Not missing a beat, the massive Parnox came blasting forward like a hurricane bringing his colossal double bladed axe over his head. At the exact moment the demon leapt up to meet him, the axe came plummeting down onto it, tearing into its side. While this agonizing blow would have most certainly made short work of the Liradds from before, this demon would not stop. As if reveling in the pain, the monster wheeled around and charged forward again, catching the burly Southlander off guard. Before he could send his axe into his foe again, the monster was upon him with the momentum of a rolling boulder. Pinned and helpless under the weight of the demon, its rows of bloodstained teeth shown brightly in the sunlight signaling the end for the stouthearted Southlander.

If not for Kohlin Marraea, it certainly would have been. With speed and agility almost matching that of his foe, the young Southlander came soaring downward onto the back of the creature the moment it stopped. In the same movement, his slender duel blades ran the beast through the sides like bolts of lightning, instantly cutting its seemingly endless stamina in two. Summoning the last of its strength, it brandished its claws and raised them above its pinned quarry. Before either the demon or the Southlanders could react, however, a final arrow came jetting directly past Kohlin's face and embedded itself in the ailing creatures head. Life drained from the creature's body as fast as the missile had come. As the defeated hulk of flesh collapsed onto the earth, Parnox felt his chest collapsing with it as the heavy corpse with Kohlin still sitting upon it came down onto his torso. The burly Southlander struggled for breath as Jaren once had beneath the Liradd in the vale.

"Off!" he managed to wheeze. Kohlin came bounding downward to help him push the lifeless demon off of him with Tavin, Ril, and Jaren running out of the trees to assist them. After they had dispatched of the corpse and Parnox was up and breathing regularly again, the party shook hands and celebrated in their first success against the Drakkaidian monsters. Before they had much time to congratulate themselves, Zeroan came striding out of the bushes looming over them all, voraciously collecting his robes about him as he began to speak.

"This is not the time for any festivity or commemoration," he admonished angrily. "I have managed to mask our presence from any who would seek it once more, but it is still far from safe to remain here when there could be more of these Arnosmn in the area." As usual, the Mystic Sage's reprimands considerably lowered the company's moral, even though they knew he was probably right. The sage then broke his gaze from the party and brought up one of his rough hands to massage his forehead, thinking. "This changes things," he muttered shaking his head. "Montrox would not have placed his agents here and now by chance. He must somehow be specifically aware of us. Now we will have to avoid the Great Rift to be sure." The others in the party shot frightful glances at each other, remembering the second option of passing through the mountains Zeroan had mentioned.

"Are you telling us that we are going to have to pass through the Windrun Road, Zeroan?" Kohlin asked. The sage dropped his hand back into his robes as he shook his head no.

"No, Southlander," he breathed. "Our movements are now confined by the possible presence of the creatures of the Netherworld, and we cannot risk travel all the way down to the road. We will simply have to attempt the Pass of Sycoth above the Great Rift. We should be able to avoid detection there..." he trailed off. After a moment of collecting his thoughts, the sage wheeled around and set back to the front of the group.

"Let me worry about such things for now, though. We press on. And remember," he said, glaring at Ril, "no magic."

With that, the sage turned toward the mountains and started off once more. The rest of the group exchanged uneasy glances and decided to push on before they lost the sage completely. As Jaren bounded behind his new comrades in arms to receive plaudits for his skill with the bow, Tavin turned back to the flustered and aggravated form of Arilia Embrin. Though he was about to break the silence with an apology on behalf of Zeroan, she turned her head to lock onto his eyes and cut him off.

"Listen to me for a minute, Tavin," she began with a hint of resentment present in her words, "I told you that I don't like to be treated like a child. I'm glad you're strong enough to stand up to that... sage, but I don't need you to fight my battles for me. I can do that myself," she concluded vigorously, turning her eyes away from him. Though Tavin was not expecting the discontented barrage from the girl, he was quick to realize that despite his good intentions he had done to her the very thing she was aggravated by all too often. He stood beside her motionless form for another few moments before noticing that, after that entire ordeal, she was still shivering in the wake of the biting winds. Though not wanting to upset her further by apologizing, he was struck with an idea. He brought his hands up to the cape around his neck and quickly unfastened it. Pulling it off over his head, he turned back to the freezing Warrior of Fire and wordlessly wrapped it around her shoulders. Taken aback, Ril looked up at the boy as he gently pulled the flowing cape down over her head.

"I look terrible in these things anyway," he said as he fastened it around her. Not sure what to do in response, it was all Ril could do to stare back at him in silence. As Tavin finished securing the garment, he extended his arm to help her back up to the rocks where he stood. Ril still only stared, not sure what the boy's motives for being so kind in the face of her aggression could be. Tavin held her gaze, growing a little uncomfortable himself. At last the Warrior of Fire shook off her uncertainty and managed a quick thank you. Tavin smiled back in response.

Chapter 19

<u>Outpost</u>

After Tavin and Ril hastily joined back up with the group, Zeroan quickened their pace even further as they began to enter into the steep hillsides leading toward the Great Rift. The widest gap in the Iairian Mountain Chain, it signaled the beginning of the Border Mountains that kept Grandaria safe from Drakkaidian invasion along with the Wall of Light. The Great Rift had become the most well known and frequently used mountain pass in the whole of Iairia, large enough to march a small army through. With a small community of isolated homes and businesses spreading throughout its interior, it had become the quickest, safest, and most convenient way to pass through the mountains to or from Grandaria or the northeast Southland.

For the remainder of that day, Zeroan marched the company deeper and deeper into the mountains, eager to be well on their way to the rift by nightfall. As it turned out, the group would penetrate all the way to the outskirts of the first scattered settlement by that time. Even the Mystic Sage himself was somewhat surprised at the incredible time they had made in just five short days. As he turned to meet his group, however, he quickly realized how much the grueling pace he had been driving them at had worn them down. With the entrance to the Great Rift not more than a half of a mile away, Zeroan singled for the company to halt. Happy to comply, the group nearly fell to their feet with exhaustion.

"As you should be able to see if you look over this ridge," the sage began, "we are drawing near to the entrance to the Great Rift. From here we turn to the south another mile or two and will be able to find the entrance to the narrow Pass of Sycoth. If we hurry, we should be able to reach it before the sun is totally lost to us." Jaren jerked his head up and groaned.

"And I thought the trip to Galantia was bad," he mumbled. "I don't think I'll ever be able walk again." Zeroan placed his gaze on the fatigued Grandarian.

"If we reach the outpost in the pass tonight, Jaren, you will have the pleasure of staying indoors and a real breakfast in the morning," he bribed. That was all it took.

"Done deal," Jaren exclaimed for the whole group, revitalized. "Come on, people!" he encouraged, lifting Tavin back to his feet from the rock where he sat regaining his breath. "We've got to move!" Zeroan could not help but to smirk as the energetic young man pushed the team onward toward the outpost.

As the group began their final stretch onward for the evening, Tavin left Jaren and casually strode up to the cloaked figure of Zeroan. The sage did not have to look at the boy to know why he was there.

"You have a question, don't you?" he asked monotonously.

"Yes, actually," Tavin responded, not at all surprised the sage had guessed correctly. "I was thinking back to our fight with the demon earlier today..."

"The Arnosmn," the sage corrected.

"Yes, that. Why was it so much stronger than the other creatures that Jaren and I ran into back in the Hills of Eirinor? It was at least twice as strong and fast." Zeroan sighed knowing he was in for a long walk to the mountain pass.

"It's fairly simple to understand," he said plainly. "There is a vast assortment of demons in the Netherworld. Because Montrox only holds one shard, he is only able to muster the weakest into our world. But as his power grows, he will be able to unleash creatures with more strength and stamina, greater speed, and overall more power. However, we measure the strength of a demon not by its physical strength, but by its resistance to withstand your power, Tavin. The easier it is for the elemental power of light to dispatch it, the weaker it is. But should Montrox summon creatures with the power of multiple emerald shards, you would be hard pressed to defeat them even with the depths of your abilities mastered." Tavin nodded his head but sustained his inquiry.

"I see. Could I ask you something else?" he continued. Zeroan nodded and told him he might as well get it out of his system. "I also don't understand how your magic worked today to hide our presence. You said that anything that uses magic can sense other magic when it's close and in use." The sage did not bother to let him complete his thought.

"But if that's so, why didn't the demons detect the magic I used to mask us with?" Zeroan finished for him. Tavin nodded his head. "You're thinking of things a little too black and white, young Grandarian," the sage stated. "There are many different kinds of magics, used for many different kinds of things. The only type you are familiar with is the simple yet powerful elemental magics. What you don't know is there is another world beyond that, and the kind I possess is beyond even that. Its source does not originate from any one elemental power, and therefore it is much more... complicated in nature. The power of the Order of Alberic comes from a universal energy field the first sage discovered that connects with all the elemental energies in matter wrapped together. We harness the elements at a passive level to manipulate material, living and not, already present in the world. It can twist or reverse the laws of physics and magics. The purpose of the particular magic I used today is to keep a veil over our location. It is "designed" to be so subtle that it cannot be sensed. The mystic magics of old are hard to detect, which is why I can often get away with using them in dangerous situations when I would like to remain unknown to others." Tavin still looked somewhat baffled.

"I'm still not sure I understand that," he confessed. "I always just thought magic was magic." The sage nodded.

"Do not dwell on it, Tavinious. You will come to understand the nature of magic and power in time when you have been sufficiently exposed to it. Until then, just accept things for the way they are." Tavin reluctantly decided to trust the sage's words, but still felt the need to persist with his inquiry.

"Zeroan, there is something else I wanted to speak with you about," Tavin swiftly transitioned. Zeroan looked down at him with a look that responded he already knew. "I wanted to ask about my own power in particular."

"I was wondering when you would," the sage said. He exhaled sharply and motioned for him to continue. Tavin readjusted the Sword of Granis over his shoulder as he did.

"Well, first of all I was wondering why I'm so different from the others."

"Others?"

"You know, the other Elemental Warriors. Ril told me that she and the other warriors from the Southland get their powers from Sources in the temples. Why am I so different?" Zeroan eyed him skeptically.

"You are different, Tavin," he began, "but only from the Southland warriors. Remember, there are six elements, but two are more prevailing than the other four."

"Light and darkness," Tavin continued for him. Zeroan nodded.

"For this reason, the Warriors of Light and Darkness have been inherently different since the birth of the Elemental Warriors. There is always a warrior of the four neutral elements, chosen by we Mystic Sages every generation when someone has proven him or herself truly great. But the Warriors of Light and Darkness only appear once in a great while. You and Montrox are only the second Iairia has ever seen. This is because you are decedents of the originals. Everyone in your family has the potential to be the Warrior of Light, but your power must be activated by the Sword of Granis as it was with you. The same goes with Montrox. He must be blessed by the Black Church and its High Priest to be endowed with his power. After the first Holy War centuries ago, the first Montrox was defeated and his line scattered. Your ancestor simply chose to lay down his power, but it has been a part of your lineage ever since. You are different from the others because you are more powerful. Unlike the neutral elements, the powers of light and darkness are limitless; they transcend all." Tavin remained confused.

"If I'm so strong, why can't I summon my power when I want? When I first pulled the Sword of Granis out of the tower, I could feel an incredibly intense feeling... circulating all through my body. I used it at the battle on the Golden Wall, but ever since it disappeared afterwards, I haven't been able to bring it back no matter how hard I try."

"Of course not," the Mystic Sage replied to the dumbfounded boy. "You must understand, Tavin, that the power you possess is one of the most potent and 'incredibly intense' in the whole of the world. It will take you a great deal of time to develop it and even longer to truly master it. Your great grandfather Tieloc never did in his entire life. Until you learn to control your power over time with a great deal of training and experience, you will not be able to call it forth at will. It is still very spontaneous at present; it only appears when it is needed. It came to you on the wall because you knew in your heart that if you did not stop that Valcanor, your friends would have perished. Your power responded to that need." A look of doubt and frustration overcame the boy's face.

"But what if I need it someday and it doesn't come? What if I can't control it when I need to the most?" Tavin asked with doubt laced in his voice. Zeroan brought his gaze down to the boy one last time.

"It will have to come, Tavin," he stated with confidence. Tavin was still doubtful.

"Why?"

"Because it is your destiny to control it. It is your destiny to master it. And it is your destiny to call it forth when you need it most and vanquish the darkness with its light." Tavin was speechless at that. Zeroan let a long silence hang between them before he at last closed the matter. "All you need to do is believe in yourself, Tavin; believe in your destiny. If you can do that, you will learn to control the power and do amazing things with it that the world has never seen before." Zeroan shifted in his gray robes again as the last remnant of sunlight faded from the dark sky. "Now go and see to the others. We are almost upon the outpost and we need to be ready for whatever might lie in wait for us there."

Deciding against pursuing the matter further, Tavin deemed Zeroan's explanation acceptable for the time being and obeyed his order to return to the others. As the party approached the entrance to the pass, Zeroan leapt up a small incline in the terrain to scope the outpost at a better angle. After the sage scanned the small collection of rundown buildings in the outpost and its surroundings, he dropped back down to the eagerly awaiting group.

"Listen carefully, all of you," he ordered quietly. "This is not the Great Rift some of you have seen before. It is a small, trashy, dangerous outpost filled with corresponding occupants. We will be looked upon with suspicion for being such a 'colorful' group. Stay close to me, and keep to yourself." He cast a sharp glance down at Jaren as he finished that last statement. The boy raised his arms with an affronted expression. "Let's go then, and keep your guard up."

Zeroan spun around and led the company into the clearing of the outpost. The group looked up to observe the massive walls of the steep cliffs rising all about them. The Great Rift aside from them really did look artificial at first glace; like a canyon carved right in the middle of the depression in the mountains. Nearly a quarter of a mile wide, it was large enough to contain a mountain village for travelers passing from one entrance to the other. Here upon the more jagged and inhospitable Pass of Sycoth, however, a far less appealing scenario waited ahead. The few buildings that Tavin could make out consisted of the ratty inn they were headed for, a stable next to it, and two apparently private homes not much larger than a shed back in his home of Eirinor Village.

As the group entered the light of the inn, several rugged and considerably unfriendly looking men gathered around the exterior of the various buildings. More lay sleeping or drunk on the muddy road, bottles of anything and everything lying in their grasp. Obviously wishing to avoid any possible conflict, Zeroan turned and ordered his fellow travelers to remain behind by the side of the inn and await his return. The sage then set out for the doorway alone. As he disappeared from view, the burly Southlander Parnox grit his teeth.

"I don't like this," he worried out loud. "I've been through the Great Rift on more than one occasion, and a pass as major as this one is usually brimming with healthy activity; not swimming with filth like this." Ril agreed as she nodded her head in disgust.

"That's right. Even on the way over here to Grandaria it appeared a little friendlier than it seems now..." She trailed off as two of the men across the outpost began to curse at each other and brawl. Tavin shook his head.

"You all heard Zeroan," he reminded them. "This isn't the actual rift. It's a small and dangerous pathway around the main roads, so it wouldn't be as hospitable, now would it? And besides, there aren't many people crossing the mountains during harvest season when they should be at their own home villages." The group nodded in agreement as they watched two drunken men pummel each other into the ground to litter it with their presence moments later.

It seemed like an eternity in the dark and dreary surroundings of the outpost before Zeroan at last reappeared from behind them, causing them all to jump with a fright.

"Where did you come from?" Jaren gasped, his startled heart beating rapidly. The sage remained stoic as always as he responded.

"Follow me quickly," he ordered. "I found us a place to stay for the night, but I would like our presence here to stay as unnoticed as possible. Quickly now."

As the Mystic Sage turned to disappear behind the back end of the inn, the group hurriedly followed. The party's moral quickly dropped as Zeroan stopped in front of their lodging for the night: the stable he had pointed out earlier.

"This is the smartest place for us to be overnight," he explained in a hushed tone, observing the disappointment in their eyes. "Inside quickly, and I'll explain further." As the group made their way inside, Zeroan motioned for Parnox to assist him in closing the massive doors of the stable for their privacy. The sage then sat them all down and began to explain the situation. "Something does not fit right here," he began mordantly. "I overheard troubling news inside the inn that preludes me from risking a stay there for the night. There have been sightings of strange parties of what sounds to be mercenaries passing through the Great Rift not but a day ago, looking for something near the Grandarian entrance. This presence in addition to the demon we encountered earlier provokes my curiosity. It is not probable that we would be plagued by so many hindrances when we have barely even started our journey. I fear Montrox may somehow have learned of us and our plans specifically. I'm not sure how, but we seem to have been marked and targeted." He began to trail off again, as if lost in thought. "Get some rest, all of you. We must be away from here and into the Southland as soon as possible. It is not beyond the realm of possibility that there are more demons in the area, and I don't trust our current company in the outpost as far as I could throw all of them combined. Sleep now. I will be back by morning." With that, the sage stood and quietly made his way out of the stable to the surprise of the rest of the group.

"Does he ever sleep?" asked Jaren questioningly.

"He is a durable man," answered Kohlin, preparing to lay himself down. "I have heard that he never sleeps, for he does not need it with his mystic powers always keeping him energized." Jaren rolled his eyes and fell into a pile of hay beneath him. Ril got up from the crate she rested upon and found herself a place to sleep as well.

"It's no bed," she announced disgruntled, "but will work for tonight I guess." As she began to lay herself down, her eyes shot open as she realized Tavin's cape was still draped over her. She quickly pulled it over her head to hand it back to him, but the Grandarian extended his arms and gently pushed it back.

"You need it a lot more than I do," he stated with a tired smile crossing his face. Ril shook her head almost violently.

"I insist," she stated. "I've had this for far to long as it is..." Tavin cut her off.

"No I insist. I'm plenty warm in all this garb I'm wearing, and I'm used to this kind of temperature. Hold onto it for the night at least." Ril looked into his eyes then, immediately noticing the familiar sincerity she had observed before. At last Ril gave in, in her heart happy to keep herself concealed in its warmth. Still feeling guilty to keep taking from the boy, her brow furrowed as she formulated her next words.

"...How can you be so kind when I haven't given you any reason to be?" she asked softly as if deeply confused. Tavin gave her a peculiar look, to which she continued. "You treat me better than I deserve and what have I given you in return?" He just yawned back at her, laying his head near Jaren's.

"Friendship is the most valuable thing you can ever get from someone," he stated as if this profound avowal was nothing more than a bit of random common knowledge. Ril again found herself at a loss for words as she stared helplessly into Tavin's deep blue eyes. After a long moment she at last broke the silence.

"You have my friendship, Tavin Tieloc," she responded with a smile faintly gracing her soft face.

"I'm glad..." he trailed off. As Tavin's head hit the hay beneath him, he nodded once more and sleepily smiled back at her as his eyes closed and sealed him into his sleep. Ril almost giggled at how tired he obviously was. She continued to gaze at his gentle figure sleeping for the rest of the night until she finally fell into sleep of her own. Ril smiled one last time as her eyes closed shut.

Chapter 20

Ambush

As the group had now become accustomed, the Mystic Sage Zeroan was stirring them to wake as soon as the first ray of light slipped into the sky to the east. Wiping the stagnant residue of their slumber off them, the party watched Zeroan quickly hustling about the stable gathering loose supplies and preparing to leave. After Tavin managed to yank Jaren out of the confines of his makeshift bed, he was quick to turn to the turbulent sage to ask what was going on. Zeroan merely heaped a bundle of supplies into his arms and ordered him to distribute them to the group.

"I will explain as we depart, but we must be away now," he informed. Tavin complied with the command and proceeded to hand out small supplies of food and new clothing to the group. When he arrived to Ril, still struggling to wash the sleep out of her eyes, he handed her the thickest robe he could find in exchange for his cape. Ril thanked him kindly as she rose to secure the garment back around his neck. Tavin shook his head hard to fasten it down into a comfortable position as he dispersed the remainder of the supplies to the group.

Without so much as a moment to collect themselves or prepare for the coming day, Zeroan directed them out into the crisp morning air as quickly as possible. Jaren frowned hard as he realized that his hopes for his promised breakfast had just been launched out the window. Herding the party through the shadows of the small outpost, they quickly exited to arrive inside the actual cavernous road of the pass. Zeroan turned back to them as he continued to move forward and offer an explanation as to the hasty retreat from their lodgings.

"I am sorry to propel us forward so quickly with no notice, but I acquired information last night that threatens our safety here," the sage began. "I was informed by a passing party of Grandarian merchants that there is a group of marauders looking for a party with a cloaked figure, a large woodsman, a Windrun Warrior, and three youths headed through the rift. Obviously, this would be us." Tavin shot his head around the group to observe their reactions of nervousness and frustration. Jaren was quick to object to the retreat.

"Um, maybe it's just me but I don't really think we need to worry about a ragtag rabble of brainless thugs. We do seem to have some of the finest and most powerful warriors in the whole world with us," he reminded sarcastically. Zeroan looked down on him with annoyance.

"I am well aware that any group of mercenaries is no threat. However, if you would have the common decency to listen a little further without venturing out your idiotic thoughts, I would have told you that thugs are not my reason for worry. This confirms beyond a shadow of a doubt that Montrox is indeed aware of us and somehow our position as well, and if he is trying to rid himself of us, he will be soliciting the use of more than just hired swords. Should we encounter this enemy party, it is likely there will be one or more demons nearby. We would be forced to give away our position with the use of magic, and that is not something we can afford to do. We must make our way out of the mountains and into the northeast plains of the Southland before the spies of the Drakkaidians manage to locate us."

The sage then turned back to face the path ahead of him as he marched on.

"If we are to avoid detection from opposing parties that wish us harm, we must stay off the beaten path. There are several smaller roads through the pass, but they are very treacherous. Stay close and do not speak. Follow quickly now." With that, the sage led on at his grueling pace, nearly leaving the worn band of adventurers behind. As they marched on in the shadows of the ravine above the Great Rift, the sun began to rise into plain view. It was not a very friendly sky that met them, however. A thick blanket of clouds had moved in over the night, blocking off the celestial orb's warming rays.

Zeroan continued to lead the group toward the steep side of the pass until they eventually came upon a narrow and rigid walkway of stone that led up the hillsides of the pass away from the sight of the common traveler. Tavin and the others were hard pressed to navigate their way through the sharp and confined surroundings of earth and rock, but plowed onward as hard as they could after the sage. It was not too far into the dark morning before the group encountered their greatest fear. Zeroan suddenly froze in front of Kohlin trailing quickly behind, almost causing the Southlander to crash into him. The sage hurriedly motioned for them all to squat down as he brought his head upward. Noticing the sudden appearance of storm clouds himself earlier in the morning, Zeroan had kept an uneasy gaze on the sky.

As the billows above him began to roll heavier and darker by the minute, the sudden rush of a wingtip in the air caught the entire group's attention. Tavin and Jaren were quick to exchange worried glances as the memory of the winged nightmare from the vale in Grandaria came hurling into their minds. Zeroan tightened his face and turned back to the others to whisper,

"Where there is one Valcanor, there are more. I will use my power to hide our presence, so as long as we stay silent and hidden in the shadows, we will be invisible to the naked eye of even the demons. Stay quiet and close now." The Mystic Sage rose then, folding his arms and remaining perfectly still. As he stood, Tavin could see a faint blue aura encase the members of the party. "Quickly now," the sage quietly said as he began to move forward again, quickly scanning the skies.

The group continued on through the intricate and narrow passages above the primary ravine for the better part of an hour after the Mystic Sage wrapped his invisible cloak of magic around them. All the while, Tavin kept his eyes on the dark clouds above, nervously waiting for one of the winged demons to see through Zeroan's barrier of stealth and launch down at them. But as they moved on, no attack came. They continued hiking through the pass for hours to come, still silent and secretive as they went. It was the late afternoon before the silence around the valley was finally compromised.

As they came around a corner of rock, an expansive downward slope appeared to their left, straight down to the Great Rift's primary pathways. Before they could start around the corner, however, the Mystic Sage suddenly called for the group to come to a halt and motioned for the Kohlin to come forward. Tavin could make out the two exchanging words before the Southlander hurriedly bounded away for the hillside below them. The rest of the group waited anxiously for his return, wondering why the sage had sent him ahead alone. After a short and uneasy silence, Kohlin came creeping back over the hillside motioning for them to proceed, but put his finger to his lips to signal the need for supreme silence. Tavin and the others made their way down to where Kohlin bent hiding behind a large boulder. Down in the main roads of the Great Rift, a party of unfavorable looking men were lined up from one side of the path to the other, blocking all traffic that might have passed through.

Zeroan frowned as he gingerly let his cloaking magic fade away.

"A blockade," he muttered to no one in particular. "This is worse than I thought. We should continue to move around them, so as not to attract any attention. If they spot us, we will have the patrolling Valcanor to contend with as well. Not to mention the possibility of..." Zeroan trailed off suddenly, as if his power to speak had been withdrawn. The other members of the party glanced over at the sage waiting for him to finish his statement. Zeroan shot his eyes over to them now and began to speak so quietly his voice was nearly lost. "There is something behind us right now as I speak not more than a few yards away. Everyone ready your weapons, for as soon as we move at all, it will be on us." Tavin's face tightened, the enormity of the sage's dire words unbelievable at first. "Tavin and Ril: hold nothing back. Summon as much of your power as you are able as we make our escape." The sage shot his eyes back and forth at the bottom of the pass.

"I will deal with whatever lies behind us. The rest of you make straight for the primary pass below. Run as hard and fast as you can straight down until you meet the ends of the rift and enter the Southland side of the mountains. It should not be far now. I will be right behind you, so do not stop for anything. If we are lucky, we will be able to evacuate the Great Rift and be on our way out of the mountains before the pack of Valcanor-" The sage would not have time to finish. He was interrupted by the sudden war cry that sounded directly behind them coupled with the sound of something very large tearing into the earth. At nearly the same instant, Zeroan wheeled around hard and extended his arms forward in one fluent motion. A hard and sharp burst of widespread throbbing force came blasting forward from the palms of his hands to hammer into the airborne figure of an Arnosmn, forcing the beast backward over twice the distance it had jumped.

Zeroan jerked his head toward them as he rose, screaming at the top of his lungs.

"Get moving! *Now*!!!" he bellowed, another wave of invisible force careening forth from his hands into the earth beneath the demon, surging up to pelt the creature with rock. That was all that the battle hardened Parnox needed to hear as he hoisted Tavin, Jaren, and Ril to their feet.

"Blast it all, you heard the man! Make for the roads!" he commanded, sprinting forward himself. Jaren was already stringing an arrow in his bow as he jumped forward after the haggard Southlander. Kohlin came after him, drawing his duel blades as well. As Ril struggled to her feet, however, she turned back to the sage fighting off the savage monster. Cupping her hands into a bowl, her face ignited with resolve as a small flame burst to life in her hands. Before Tavin could grab her to get her moving with the others, she thrust out her hands, transforming the minuscule ember into a raging inferno blasting outward.

Tavin and even Zeroan looked to her in surprise as the wave of fire violently collided with the Arnosmn, forcing it back to avoid the intense heat. As the beam of fire died around her hands, Tavin came back to his senses and wheeled the girl around by the shoulder.

"We have to move!" he shouted. Ril nodded quickly and joined him in running down the hillside. With all the commotion erupting so quickly, the band of mercenaries were just now coming aware of the group they hunted flying down the hill to their right. Seeing his enemies come to attention, Jaren took up aim with his bow as he fled down the slope and let an arrow fly downward into them. The young archer was shocked, however, to watch as the first of the mercenaries brought up the face of an axe head to deflect the jetting arrow away from him as fast as it came.

"Okay..." Jaren muttered in surprise, "maybe these guys are a little better than I thought." As Jaren, Parnox, and Kohlin reached the main pathway through the Great Rift, Tavin and Ril came bounding down the hill as well, leaving the Mystic Sage to do battle with the fearsome Arnosmn alone. The hillside was so steep that the two could only ski down its side, their capes and robes flying back into the wind. Tavin counted out thirteen of the mercenaries at the base of the hill in total, realizing how severely outnumbered they were with the demons in the sky still out there somewhere. Instinctively, he wrenched free the Sword of Granis hanging at his side, sending its metallic ringing searing into the air.

With Tavin and Ril landing down at the surface of the hill, the party amassed themselves together to engage the mercenaries as one force. One of their foes clad in the deep purple hued cloaks stepped forward with an arrogant grin on his scarred face.

"This is the mighty party from Grandaria?" he asked with a chuckle. "Two weakling Southlanders and three children? I thought we were promised a challenge, boys!" The other men laughed after their leader. As Jaren gritted his teeth with ire at the moronic men before him, several distant screeches from the apparently approaching pack of Valcanor came echoing through the walls of the ravine. Ril then stepped forward with her own anger flaring, raising her arms to form a fervent fire burning around each.

"We don't have time for this," she declared coldly, her eyes locked onto her foe. As the mercenaries began to laugh once more, Tavin felt himself shrinking back from fear of the girl's temper igniting again. Charging her elemental power, the Warrior of Fire brought her arms downward to the men's feet to ignite a spiral of wheeling flame bursting around them, catching them in a ring of the raging fire. The men reeled back in shock and fear, trapped in the burning walls. The rest of the group stood daunted and gazing at Ril, breathing hard from the energy required to launch her fiery assault. "Is this child a little too much for you, boys?" she exclaimed vengefully. Jaren raised his eyebrows and leaned over to Tavin.

"Remind me not to get her angry again..." he said quietly. Tavin rolled his eyes as Parnox gathered the group back up.

"Come on!" he yelled, starting off down the path. "We need to get out of here now! There is still a pack of Valcanor airborne somewhere. I would rather not face them even with the obvious power this group possesses. Let's go!" With that, the rest of the party came running after the rugged Southlander, eager to escape before the winged demons found them as well.

Chapter 21

Lighting the Way

The five members of the group from Grandaria ran on down the pathways of the wide open Great Rift as hard as they could for hours to come. With the view of the northeast hills of the Southland in sight, all five felt a surge of new vitality coursing through them. Though Tavin looked back frequently for the lost member of their group, the Mystic Sage Zeroan did not appear. Confident that the powerful sage could handle himself, Tavin did not dwell on his safety, preferring to worry about that of his remaining comrades. Almost out of the Great Rift and into the opposite side of the mountains, Tavin's fear of the demons behind him was overridden by his excitement to finally reach the Southland he had always dreamed of visiting.

The party kept up its strenuous pace out of the rift led by their temporary leader Parnox Guilldon. Though they covered a great distance down the mountains in the next hour or so, the dark rolling storm clouds above them seemed to grow darker and closer with every step. With the faint screeches from the distant skies behind them more audible than ever, the band sought what cover they could every time they pierced the air. It was in the final stretch of the mountains that the pack of Valcanor finally found the group and attacked.

Heeding the reverberations of massive wings amidst the clouded air, Tavin drew the Sword of Granis, preparing to face the inevitable threat of the aerial foes. As the ringing of silver steel from the blade rang through the company's ears, they all stopped together realizing they had been found and escape was no longer an option. Parnox gritted his thick teeth and wrenched his massive axe from his shoulder with a loud grunt while Kohlin pulled forth his duel blades from his sides. Jaren cursed at his misfortune yet again and prepared to string an arrow into his bow, thrusting it upward. One last screech tore through the seemingly frantic air around them. Aware that their position had already been discovered, Ril summoned up her elemental power to send waves of flame flowing around her arms and clenched fists. As the band stood at the ready to face whatever lurked inside the banks of clouds, a final hush befell the scene around them.

The eerie silence was shattered by the first of the Valcanor as it came bursting out from the rows of clouds directly above, plummeting downward at terminal velocity. The monster made a horizontal sweep over the group, slashing its mangled arm out to catch Parnox and Tavin and hurl them away from their companions. Ril immediately brought up her arms to launch an arching ball of flame toward the creature, but beating its massive wings it strafed away with agility enough to evade any fire based attack. Jaren knew better that to waste his arrows when they would do no damage against the beast, but tried one shot into the head of the dark creature anyway. The Valcanor swiped the missile away with the mere flap of its wing, forcing Jaren back as well. Having separated the band from each other, the Valcanor was joined by five more, materializing out of the clouds to make violent landings around the perimeter of Ril, Jaren, and Kohlin, splitting the earth from the force of impact.

Tavin and Parnox were instantly back on their feet and on a collision course to aid their overwhelmed comrades. Remembering how his new power over the element of light had made quick work of the Valcanor at the Golden Wall, Tavin took a massive running hack at one of the creature's legs, desperately wishing the sword to react to him. As he feared, not so much as a flash of golden energy appeared. Feeling the equivalent of a pinprick on its leg, the Valcanor raised its gnarled limb and stomped its oversized foot over Tavin, forcing him to the ground. The air rushing out of his compressed chest, it was all he could to struggle for dear life under the weight of the massive demon.

Raising her arms in the Warrior of Light's defense, Ril sent a wave of fervent flame bursting forward to smash into the Valcanor's sunken head, sending it reeling back in pain. The other demons responded to Ril swiftly, recognizing her as the only serious threat to their defenses. The Valcanor behind her threw an arm downward, seizing the fighting girl in its mangled fingers. Ril's body surged with fire defensively, but not caring of the pain, the demon did not let go and began squeezing. Ril screamed in fear and agony as the bones in her chest began to compress. With the remainder of the party being snatched where they stood in a similar manner, Tavin could see their end was at hand. He fiercely squirmed, but nothing could free him from the demon's prodigious weight.

With all hope fading, Tavin could do nothing but watch the Valcanor breaking his party to pieces and listen to their screams. His rage and fury began to rise and swell inside of him. Not willing to let it end this way for him and his friends, the deep power dormant in him suddenly revealed itself all over again as it had in the Tower of Granis, responding to the absolute need that Zeroan had spoken of. Sensing its master's power awakening, the small golden crystal mounted on the blade began to pulsate brighter by the second, signaling the inevitable explosion of righteous power about to erupt. With resolve and unbreakable will that would not allow anything to stop him, he could feel raw energy surging inside threatening to consume him if it was not freed. Tavin bellowed with passion as his power ignited outward, sending a familiar shimmering golden light ripping in every direction.

The pack of Valcanor all wheeled around to face the boy, bringing their twisted and maimed arms over their faces to shield themselves from the righteous light. When Tavin found himself still trapped under the foot of the heavy demon, his power began escalating at an incredible velocity until it became so intense the light from the boy began burning into the demon's flesh, slowly incinerating its tainted legs into black ash. The other Valcanor instantly dropped the other members of the party and nervously stepped back. His fury still not satisfied, Tavin lunged upward from the ground, landing squarely on his feet to charge forward toward the other demons, engulfed in the shimmering light.

Moving with speed and dexterity that he never knew he possessed, Tavin screamed again as he brought the mighty Sword of Granis ringing downward straight through one of the demon's arms with no resistance whatsoever; completely severing it. Tavin leapt backward, hacking through the side of the beast behind him. Though any normal blade would have barely managed to penetrate the Valcanor's skin, Tavin and the Sword of Granis slashed straight through its mighty frame like a knife through butter. Not needing to see any more to know they were bested, the four remaining demons immediately began to beat their tattered wings and move skyward while still intact. Though Tavin inflicted heavy damage as they lifted off, the tainted creatures managed to escape with their lives.

As the Valcanor reemerged with the banks of clouds in full retreat, Tavin stood watching engulfed in his golden power and lowered the Sword of Granis to his side. The radiating energy ruffled his cape and clothing to and fro as if caught in a gust of wind. The others in the group rose from where they had dropped in awe at the display of beautiful power shrouding Tavin. As the light gradually began to dissipate, the memory of Ril shrieking in pain raced back into his mind. He turned to find the girl still lying on the ground struggling for breath, staring up at him with an amazed expression over her flushed face. Tavin quickly sheathed the glowing Sword of Granis as he rushed over and knelt to her level.

"Are you alright?" he asked, realizing how out of breath he was as well. Ril stared at him a moment longer, surprised at how fast he had changed from the supreme Warrior of Light of legend back into the casual and courteous boy she had come to know. Ril smiled softly and nodded her head as she gingerly rubbed her sides.

"I'll be fine," she told him. "I'm just a little sore around the sides is all." Tavin smiled and tilted his head as he started to speak.

"I know you don't want me to carry you around, but can I at least help you up?" he asked almost facetiously through his sporadic breathing. Ril managed a quick laugh despite herself before she nodded and shot him a smug look. Tavin was quick to gently lift her and bolster her on his shoulder. The others crowded around the two.

"I think that was the most awesome display of power that I had ever thought possible, young man," Parnox told him, still taken aback. Jaren nodded in agreement.

"I don't know how you kept all that inside you all these years, but *good Granis* you've got it now!" exclaimed Jaren. "That was even more amazing than at the wall in Galantia. What a fighter you are with that power!" Tavin shrugged and tried a quick smile, not sure how to deal with all of the attention. Ril smiled up at his modesty as she leaned away to stand on her own. It was Kohlin who spoke next.

"That was very impressive, Tavin," he congratulated, "but I think it would be best if we moved on now." The young Southlander shifted his gaze back up to the clouds. "I would wait for Zeroan, but I still think we should follow his orders and keep moving for the Southland as fast as we can. Knowing him, he will surely find us sooner or later." Parnox nodded.

"Yes, we should go. Though I doubt that party will return, there are still other foes our there who have most likely sensed that display," he reminded. The group then set off once more, destined for the northeast Southland fields, now within view. By nightfall, the party from Grandaria finally made their way out of the mountains and into the fields. Tavin and Jaren stood side by side as they gazed out at the green lands with a smile. As their eyes met, they didn't need to say anything. They both knew what the other was thinking. They had finally arrived in the Southland; where their real quest would now begin.

Chapter 22

Dark Hunter

Dalastrak was in the grip of yet another fearsome and unnatural storm. High above the escalating levels of the city on the jagged peaks of the mountains, the savage royal castle stood shrouded by darkness only occasionally illuminated by the sporadic lightning strikes tearing through the air. Through the ominous shadows of the night, a lone figure marched up the steep rows of cracked and barren steps that led to the citadel's massive entrance. The ferocious wind bit at his bare, clearly unhappy face while he climbed upward through the savage weather. The figure appeared to be in his late teenage years, but harbored a staid and aloof demeanor of seriousness about him that masked his youth. His tattered gray and battle-scarred coat flailed about behind him in the grip of the monstrous gusts making the dark and rigid glyphs exhibited over it distorted and mangled. Along with his dark attire, the boy's constantly cold and emotionless face and blood red hair did little to make him look any friendlier.

As the figure finally arrived at the main gate to the massive castle, two black armor clad guards brought their spiked spears into a cross in front of him. His face quickly tightened with irritation. Seeing the emotion flare up in his unusual red eyes, the guards fumbled to explain their orders.

"My apologies, Your Highness, but His Supreme Highness has ordered none to enter the castle for any reason whatsoever. I have my orders," he carefully explained, a hint of fear intertwined in his shaking voice. The boy's brow furrowed at this. He stood there for a moment, letting an uneasy silence hang. Before either of the guards knew what hit them, the boy pulled a broadsword out of seemingly thin air to rest in front of one of their thick helmets.

"You must know I will kill you both if I have to," he quietly informed them with malice in his eyes, causing both

151

guards to swallow hard. "I must have an audience with 'His Supreme Highness' at once." When the guards still failed to move their spears out of the boy's path, he struck with lighting reflexes. All in one fluid motion, he brought his blade arching downward into the cross point of the spears forcing them both down. He then leapt over them and forward into the gate, kicking it open with strength not found in even the most powerful of men much less an adolescent boy, just long enough to squeeze through. Landing behind the gates before they closed once more, he wheeled around and sent his boot into the torso plates of both guards in one swift arching movement. The two lost their balance in the heavy suits of armor and found themselves careening down the steep stairway back to the first gate of the citadel at its base.

As the two defeated guards tumbled downward outside, the lean boy rose and made his way into the dark halls of the castle, his flat broadsword instantly dematerialized in a foam of deem red mist dissipating with the weapon. The dim torchlight glowed through the corridors of the castle halls, sending waves of shadows dancing across the boy's hard face and deep red hair. Any who found themselves unlucky enough to run into him quickly cowered back to the dark stone walls or immediately turned around for an alternate path. He continued on at an enterprising pace ascending the many levels of the castle to the top where his objective was sure to be.

After the long trek through the abysmal corridors of the citadel's top level, the boy at last reached the throne room of the Warrior of Darkness, Valif Montrox. When he found the thick doors locked again, he grit his teeth in frustration and kicked them open as he had the main gate earlier, forcing them rushing open to smash against the walls. He entered in a fit of fury, scanning the room for the ruthless dictator of Drakkaidia. Valif Montrox stood alone gazing out of his favorite window to the left of the three empty thrones. He was the first to speak.

"I locked the door for a reason," he stated, seemingly aloof from reality. The boy still harbored expressions of anger about his face as he promptly changed the subject.

"I understand you have sent a group of the demons to hunt the Warrior of Light yet again," he said harshly, swiftly making his way to the foreboding figure. Montrox nodded his head.

"What if I have?" he responded, not missing a beat. The boy was just as quick to respond as he continued moving closer with new rage exploding from his mouth with every word.

"You of all people know how fragile the veil between this world and the Netherworld is, Highness," he began. "For every new demon that you summon out of that accursed pit, the veil tears and weakens further. If it fails completely, every last creature in all of hell will be upon you faster than you can deal with. It is too dangerous to keep using them until you have acquired all the shards of the Holy Emerald." Montrox turned to him, remaining calm in the face of these harsh criticisms that he was not accustomed to hearing from anyone.

"I can control them now without the shards," he said with self-righteous confidence. "Besides, I only trust my most powerful minions to finish the Warrior of Light and his party before they are able to do any damage to my plans. In fact, they should be arriving here anytime to report their success in his destruction. Rest assured I have sent enough to get the job done right this time."

"Then it is my pleasure to disappoint you in this matter, Sire," the boy told him then. Montrox locked his eyes on him looking confused as he asked what he was talking about. The boy darkly smiled in spite of himself as he continued. "Your 'most powerful minions,' the Valcanor, have utterly failed you again, my lord. What is left of them just arrived and I have heard from the Dark Mages that the Warrior of Light and his party defeated them with ease." Montrox stood silently staring at the boy for a moment, a quiet rage now building in his blood red eyes.

"You are sure of this?" he asked.

"That is what I said, lord," he replied acidly. Montrox tightened his face as he angrily strode past the boy to his throne. "More damage to the veil and nothing to show for it, it would seem. I hope you will now gain the intelligence to stop putting our people and lands in danger with the threat of renegade creatures of the underworld and send something capable of stopping this threat." Montrox wheeled sharply and thrust his arm forward at the boy, lifting him off the ground with his power.

"Damn you, Verix! How many times must I tell you that you will not speak to your master in this tone!" he bellowed at the boy, propelling him into the air struggling for breath in the grasp of the mighty tyrant. "I tell you again, I am in control of the demons and the power of the Netherworld! You have much to learn of power before you can judge or criticize me!" With that, the ferocious man threw the boy downward onto the floor with such force the stone tiling of the ground cracked and split around him. Montrox turned sharply and marched up to his savage looking throne. Verix slowly raised himself from the ground and spat the fresh blood out of his mouth. He picked himself up and followed Montrox over to where he now sat, kneeling before him.

"My lord," he started in a much more humble voice, "I wish for our country's providence just as much as you, but I tell you that you send an uncontrollable force to do your work. If you truly want this warrior dead, send me and only me. I will do this myself." Montrox gazed down at the boy and drummed his fingers on the armrests of his throne. At last, he nodded his head and sat forward in his chair.

"Very well, Verix," he agreed. "You will leave immediately after the Warrior of Light, apparently now in the northeast Southland. Next to me, you are the strongest living thing in this world. You will finish this threat to my plans, my son." The Drakkaidian Prince bowed further and began to rise as Montrox continued. "You will, however, take the remaining demons in Dalastrak. There should be a few Liradds left. They will assist you with the others." Upon hearing this, Verix cringed sharply, but reluctantly agreed.

"Very well, father," he said. "I will be off as soon as possible." Verix met his father's gaze head on with unwavering eyes. "But please, my lord. Do not summon any further unholy powers from the Netherworld until we have secured the other shards to control them." With that, the boy turned sharply and left the room in a hurry. Montrox sat pondering the words of his powerful son. What does he know, the Warrior of Darkness thought? He had enough power now. The dictator rose and turned for the door to his left to begin the unholy ceremony to summon replacements for the demons destroyed at the hand of his eternal enemy. Montrox gritted his teeth in hatred as he exited the room.

Chapter 23

<u>Sudden Sickness</u>

In the aftermath of the battle with the Valcanor in the last stretch of the mountains, the party that set out from Grandaria was now to the point of exhaustion they had only dreamed possible. Jaren, asleep the moment Parnox pointed out their camp for the night, lay peacefully away from the group in his makeshift bed of foliage. The others quickly made a small fire courtesy of Ril and her powers to warm themselves in cooler Southland temperatures. Though even the strong willed Warrior of Fire was uneasy to use her power after they had just battled a group of demons, Tavin assured her that Zeroan told him they would have to go back to Drakkaidia and Montrox before they would be after them again. This gave them at least this night without worry of being discovered by the demons. After they all settled in around the fire for the night, Parnox called their attention to him.

"I think I should tell you all something," he began to say. "The morning we departed from Galantia, Zeroan pulled me aside and gave me a very specific set of instructions." Ril puzzled at this statement as she edged closer to her fire.

"What are you talking about, Parnox?" she questioned. The brawny Southlander shifted on the earth.

"It's just something that I think we may need to acknowledge for the time being. Zeroan instructed me that if something should draw him away from the group for more than a day, I was to assume command of the party and move us onto the next major destination."

"And that would be..." Ril asked questioningly.

"We are headed toward the wetlands and Torrentcia City. Since Zeroan has been gone for near a day now and since he instructed us back at the Great Rift to continue on without him until he caught up, I think we should keep moving

155

on without him and wait for him to reunite with us in the Torrentcia territories somewhere." When no other voice came after that, Parnox nodded to himself, taking the unison of the silence as agreement. "Very well. If there are no other thoughts on the matter, we will be off for Torrentcia City in the morning. It's a few weeks away if we move like we have been so far. And we should be able to stop at either Agealin Town or another smaller village if we need to refresh our supplies or what not."

Ril nodded, accepting this new plan. She was about to ask for Tavin's opinion on the whereabouts of the Mystic Sage when she noticed he was no longer present around the fire. Looking around worriedly, she was quick to alert the others to the boy's absence.

"Hey, where did Tavin go?" she asked them. Kohlin looked over to the spot where he should have been sitting, observing for himself he was missing.

"He was just there a moment ago," offered Kohlin. Ril was on her feet now, scanning her surroundings.

"Well he's not there now, is he?" she stated flustered. Ril brought her hands up to her mouth and called out. "Tavin! Where are you?" she shouted. When no response came, Ril lifted her right arm summoning a burst of flame around it serving as a torch in the night's dark veil. Before she could begin searching however, a faint murmur from behind her echoed into her ears. She turned sharply to find the lost Grandarian boy leaning up against the trunk of a tree, clutching his chest. Extinguishing the flames around her arm, she rushed over to the boy to support him. "Tavin! What's going on? What's wrong?" Tavin breathed hard as he continued to grasp at his chest.

"It's nothing," he stated, his voice low and hurt. "I just feel a little woozy, that's all." As the boy winced in pain, the two other members of the party came rushing over to help Ril bolster him upright. "No, I'm fine. I don't need any..." Trailing off, Tavin suddenly lost his balance as his knees buckled from underneath him. The mighty Parnox was there to catch him, bringing the boy gently down near the fire. Ril was by his side, anxious to discover what was causing him pain.

"Nothing indeed," she commented obviously upset. "You look like you're dying. Tell me what's wrong." Tavin shook his head.

"It's just that..." he stopped. Ril encouraged him on, placing her warm hand over his.

"It's just what?" Tavin felt he should answer her, though he would have preferred not to.

"Well, ever since my power started to fade after the battle in the mountains, I've been feeling a little strange inside. I had the same feeling when the power left me at Galantia the first time I used it, but it wasn't anywhere near as bad as this."

"What does it feel like, Tavin?" He managed to shrug before he cringed at a sharp shooting pain once more.

"...It's like there's some sort of residue from the power exploding inside of me." He winced again as he tightened his grip over his chest. "Whatever it is, it feels like the exact opposite of the power. It hurts me; it's like there's a dozen arrows all shot into my heart at once. It's been getting worse since the battle was over until now. I can barely talk without this pain searing into my-" Tavin grimaced hard from another sharp stab inside. Ril put a reassuring hand over his chest, apparently the source of his pain. She looked over to the other two Southlanders, not sure what to do. When they returned her confused and helpless glance, she brought her gaze back to Tavin.

"I'm not sure what to tell you, Tavin," she confessed, a look of defeat in her eyes. The Grandarian boy managed a tight smile.

"I wouldn't worry about it," he told her in a calming tone. "Last time I just got some sleep and I felt like a new man in the morning. Maybe that's all I need this time." Ril gazed down at him amazed as always at how the boy dealt with such serious situations as easily and courageously as he did.

"Is there anything we can do for you? Some water or anything?" she offered him sincerely. Tavin just shook his head.

"I just need to rest a little; that should do the trick," he told her.

With that, Ril smiled down at him again and pulled away. Kohlin and Parnox reluctantly retired to their own resting spots for the night, keeping a close eye on the boy until they had fallen into their dreams. After they had all turned in and doused the fire, Ril silently moved back over to Tavin in the darkness to tuck an extra blanket over him. He looked back up at her, nearly asleep. Ril softly smiled back down at him, whispering.

"I wish I was as brave as you," she told him. Too tired to respond, Tavin lost himself in his sleep. Feeling extremely comfortable beside him, Ril lay down snuggling next to the warmth of the fire as she closed her own eyes. "Sweet dreams," the girl whispered.

Jaren Garrinal woke the next morning to find the rest of his party in an interesting state. Kohlin stood over by the thicket to his right, obviously scouting out their surroundings in the first light. Parnox was by himself on a log close to the small fire munching on a biscuit from Galantia, still looking half asleep. On the opposite side of the burly Southlander, Tavin lay still completely asleep with Ril wrapped around him like a winter cloak. And to top it all off, there was still no sign of the cloaked figure of Zeroan. Jaren shook his head in disgust.

"I fall asleep for one night and the whole place goes to hell," he stated sardonically to himself. "What would you guys do without me?" After Jaren and Kohlin came back over to the camp site, the two Southlanders informed Jaren of the scare from Tavin the previous night. Jaren listened in disbelief as he wondered if he even really knew his best friend at all, with all these undiscovered things happening to him that had never seen fit to surface before. Jaren strapped on his green shoulder and chest armor as he moved over to the still slumbering forms of Tavin and Ril. Nudging them both, they began to stir awake almost instantly. Jaren leaned over to Tavin, stiff and rigid from the previous night.

"I hear you got an ouchy, mister big, tough, Warrior of Light," Jaren joked in an overly dramatic voice. Tavin reached up to wipe the sleep away from his face as he turned his head to respond.

"Shut up, Jaren," he mumbled groggily. When Ril began to stir with life, Jaren moved in close and whispered into Tavin's ear.

"Got some new armor, huh? Looks nice, but I don't know what good it will do in battle," the cocky boy remarked. Tavin turned his head again and repeated himself.

"Shut up, Jaren," he mumbled, reaching out to punch his friend in the chest, sending him toppling down. Jaren just laughed. As Ril sat up, she realized all four of her companions were staring at her latched onto Tavin as if holding on to dear life itself. She immediately shot up, her face flushing with color.

"Tavin, I, um..." she stuttered at once, unable to say anything else. He smiled back at her, a little confused, but sensitive enough to change the subject.

"I guess I was right about the sleep last night," he said. "I feel just like new." Ril smiled and blushed even more as she lowered her head with a look of supreme embarrassment stuck on her delicate face.

"I'm glad," she managed to say, regaining some of her composure. "You had us all sick with worry when the most powerful warrior in the world couldn't even stand. Don't scare us like that again." Jaren sprawled over on his back, laughing out loud at the morning's events. Ril shot up her head with a fresh scowl on her face. She extended her hand to him, sending a wave of flame combusting over his chest. Jaren immediately ceased his laughter and rolled around on the dirt to extinguish the fire. It was Tavin's turn to laugh then.

While the group got on with their chores for the morning, Tavin stood up on his own with only a faint trace of discomfort present in his chest. As per Parnox's request, the group was off once more into the knolls of the northeast Southland, eager to arrive in the Torrentcia wetlands as soon as possible. Parnox led them onward with Kohlin still checking ahead and behind to scout out any possible danger as they traveled. Tavin, Ril, and Jaren now walked together all of the time, exchanging stories from their pasts and wondering out loud what they thought would be awaiting them on the next stages of their quest. Even with the temporary loss of their leader Zeroan, the party from Grandaria still pressed onward in their quest with unwavering resolve.

Chapter 24

<u>Marauders</u>

The bulking Southlander Parnox Guilldon shook his head as he leaned over the boulder he stood upon in the morning's light. He brought his gaze down to meet the lean form of Kohlin Marraea, staring up at him with confusion about his eyes.

"Sorry," the Windrun Warrior began questioningly, "but I think I missed the source of your apparent worry." Parnox grunted softly to clear his thick throat.

"I don't know if it's just me," he stated staring out to the empty field in front of them, "but it seems a little too quiet around here for troublesome times like these." Kohlin continued to wear his confused expression.

"My apologies, but I still don't follow you," he confessed. Parnox kept his gaze on the fields.

"Kohlin," he began again, "how long has it been since we left the mountains and entered the Southland?" he inquired. Kohlin drifted for a moment as he gathered his thoughts.

"Almost two weeks," he remembered.

"And how many units of Legionnaires have you seen in that time?" There was a silence from Kohlin as he realized he had not observed any. "Have you noticed any Legion Patrols then?" Parnox pressed further. "Have you seen any Legionnaires at all?"

"Not even one," Kohlin admitted, beginning to see where this was going.

"Not even one," the massive Southlander repeated. "Don't you find the absence of any and all Southland military forces this close to the border a little odd considering the inevitable aggression from Drakkaidia is looming over us like a pine's shadow at dusk? I would have guessed there'd be units marching all over these hills patrolling the border in these times of tension."

160

"So what does all this mean?" Kohlin inquired. Parnox shrugged and turned back from his position.

"Who knows?" he said vaguely, leaving Kohlin feeling a bit ripped off until he continued again. "Could be a combination of any number of things. Perhaps all of the troops we can muster have been summoned to the capital to mobilize. Or maybe we haven't been able to muster enough Legionnaires to get up here yet." Parnox laughed and threw his hand down onto Kohlin's shoulder. "Hell, maybe we're too late and everybody's already dead! Who knows?" Kohlin brought his eyes onto the chortling man above him, raising an eyebrow.

"I fail to see the humor, Master Guilldon," he stated coldly. Parnox just chuckled and kept walking.

The two continued back until they reached the other three members in their party resting by a small creek. Parnox took a seat beside them on a granite rock deeply rooted into the earth.

"How are we doing, children?" he asked, repositioning his mighty axe over his shoulder. Jaren's brow furrowed at that remark.

"Children?" he repeated. Tavin rolled his eyes.

"You tell us, Parnox," he responded, getting back on topic. "How *are* we doing?" Parnox shrugged again.

"Can't really say, but I know we're getting close to the northernmost village in the area. Once we reach it, it's just a hop skip and a jump into the Torrentcia wetlands in the central Southland. Despite the lack of any and all travelers or soldiers in the fields, we should be able to get there safely and relatively quickly if we get moving again."

"How long is relatively quickly?" Ril asked standing up.

"I'd say about noon if we hurry," he guessed.

That was all it took to get the group moving again. With the possibility of a real meal ahead of them, they were eager to be off once more. Continuing on through the hilly area just northeast of the Torrentcia Territories, the party bore witness to several of nature's beautiful simplicities littering the surrounding country. Creeks and ponds seemed to flow across the plains like veins through a body, obviously signaling their approach to the wetlands. Massive willow trees lined the riverbank sheltering the various wildlife gathering for a drink alongside the water. It seemed like not long after the group set forth that Jaren suddenly let out a shout and pointed over a hillside.

"Look!" he exclaimed. "I can see smoke over the hills! The village must be just over that ridge! What in the name of Granis on high are you all waiting for? Here I am starving to death from all this 'questing' and you just keep walking like you're just fine to keep going past our lunch! Let's get a move on, people!" Jaren went bounding back to them to hustle them along. He positioned himself behind Parnox and began to shove with what little might he had left. The massive Southlander just chuckled, not being moved even an inch faster than he was already traveling.

As Jaren attempted to hurry the group along, Kohlin's sharp eyes caught a sign of a potential problem ahead. He turned back quickly from his spot at the head of the party and swiftly made his way back to Parnox, still toying with Jaren.

"I think we may have a situation ahead of us," he stated collecting himself. The burly Southlander immediately grew serious and stiff.

"What did you see, Kohlin?" he asked, instinctively, scanning their surroundings more carefully as well. The nimble Southlander bade Parnox to follow him, who did the same to the three other party members, confused and frustrated at this latest development to disturb their plans. Kohlin brought the others over behind a large series of boulders that lined the hillside overlooking the village.

"That smoke that Jaren observed earlier is far too thick and plentiful to be coming from any chimney," he stated worriedly. "Take a closer look over the hillside." Still confused but willing to do as they were instructed, the rest of the party slowly peered over the boulder they hid behind to find a small village occupied by a familiar looking group of men concealed in deep purple garb that covered every inch of their body, including their faces. Appearing to be more of the mercenaries they had encountered in the Great Rift, no one had to guess hard that they were up to no good. Upon closer inspection of the town, the group observed they were burning several larger buildings at the southern end. Parnox leaned back and cursed under his breath the moment he laid eyes on them.

"Of all the people, of all the times," he mumbled. Tavin was the first to speak up with questions.

"Parnox, are those men the same band we found in the Great Rift?" he grilled. Parnox shifted where he sat as he silently gathered the words to respond.

"That village you see down there is called Agealin Town. Those men surrounding it are known as the Purging Flame. They are an infamous band of marauders that have been preying on villages in the Southland for decades now. They completely loot towns then burn them to the ground, hence their twisted name. They never leave any survivors..." Tavin and Jaren exchanged nervous glances at the thought of this kind of activity normal in the Southland. Parnox continued after a moment to further examine the town.

"They rarely come out during the day. They must know that there are no Legionnaire patrols anywhere around this area and struck while the defenses were weak," Parnox explained. "Still, I'm surprised to see so many in broad daylight..." The massive Southlander was interrupted as the sudden sound of screaming from the town broke through the air.

The group looked down onto the village to observe several of the marauders appearing form one of the burning buildings with a trembling group of townspeople in their custody. One of the women in chains screamed again as a member of the Purging Flame brutally ripped the child she was carrying away from her. The Warrior of Fire in particular was horrified to witness the woman's attempt to run after the child only to be fiercely slapped to the ground by the marauder who possessed it. Ril grit her teeth in rage.

"What are those animals doing down there!?!" she bellowed with anger. Kohlin was quick to gently but firmly place his hand over the furious girl's mouth. He leaned in carefully to whisper into her ear.

"We are vastly outnumbered by the marauders, Arilia," he reminded her. "It would be most unwise to attract any unwanted attention and give away our position." As Kohlin gingerly released her, Ril lowered the tone of her voice but not that of her emotion.

"Well what do you want me to do?" she asked staring him straight in the eyes. Kohlin returned her hard gaze.

"For now, we wait," he said collectively. "Parnox? You are the leader for the time being. What would you advise that we do?" Parnox gave Kohlin a somewhat uneasy look, as if he did not want to be the one to make this decision. He then turned his head to gaze back down onto Agealin Town smoldering in the fires set by the Purging Flame. He slowly brought his head back to his party to find Ril's deep eyes staring into his with earnest.

"Don't look at me like that, miss," he started. "I know this is a terrible thing but we're outnumbered fifty to five at best and we just don't have time to get involved right now. We have far more pressing matters to attend to-" Ril was beside herself with rage.

"More pressing matters to attend to!?!" she repeated aghast. "All we are currently doing is traveling to the central Southland! How could you sleep at night knowing that we left these innocent people here to die when we just passed on to wait around for Zeroan! I took an oath as an Elemental Warrior to help those in need. I think this qualifies!" Ril took a moment to collect herself and place her hand over the worn Southlander's. "Please, Parnox. We have to do something to help these people," she begged. The burly woodsman exhaled sharply and shook his head.

"Very well," he gave in reluctantly. Ril's face eased as she shot forward to give Parnox a quick hug. "But we make it quick and cautious if we are serious about doing this, understand?" He pointed over to Kohlin. "Kohlin and I will move around to the other side of the village and try to find our way into the manors of the nobles. If I know the Purging Flame, the leader of this group will be stationed there 'negotiating' with the richest man of the town. We'll take him out and get away before anyone knows what happened." Jaren's brow furrowed at this.

"And how to you plan to do that?" he asked curiously. "There are sure to be guards lining the walls of that place."

"I've dealt with this kind of scum before, Jaren," he reminded. "I know what to expect and what to do to get the job done. Now while Kohlin and I are busy with that task, Tavin and Ril will move in from the front of the town." Parnox pointed over to a barn of some kind and motioned for Tavin and Ril to look over behind it.

"When the Purging Flame is done interrogating and looting their prisoners, the monsters set them all in one building and burn them alive. They've been herding people in that barn down there, so that should be the place. You should have time to get in there and lead them out before the fire overtakes the barn. The number one rule is, don't get caught. Number two is don't use magic. There are sure to be fresh demons back on our trail after our last encounter and I don't want any of them showing up right now, thank you very much. We have plenty of enemies down there to worry about without more showing up. The marauders travel in heavy numbers; around forty to fifty, so I don't want any fighting unless an opportune moment presents itself." Jaren sarcastically raised his hand to speak.

"And where do you want me, great leader?" he asked. Parnox pointed over to another boulder on the west end of the village.

"You head over there behind those rocks and get in a good position to cover us with your bow. We'll see if you are as good a shot as you seem to think you are if the plan goes bad. If we have to make a run for it, empty that quiver of yours." Parnox stopped for a moment to get another look around the village. "Now we don't want to get in a war here. Fifty against five aren't exactly great odds in my book, so once again, don't get caught. Once the leader is dead and the people are safely over the hill, we will lead them into the Torrentcia territories for the nearest Legion outpost to deliver them there."

Parnox looked around at the others to read their faces. They were all nodding with confidence, ready to go.

"All right then," he stated, "let's go." He pointed to Tavin and Ril and raised his eyebrows. "And you two, remember the two most important rules."

Chapter 25

<u>True Motives</u>

With the two important rules in mind, Tavinious Tieloc and Arilia Embrin crept down the hillside of Agealin Town with the utmost discretion and stealth. Looking over the ridge that they had just descended, Tavin observed his two companions Parnox Guilldon and Kohlin Marraea slipping over the hillside to reach the opposite end of the town. Jaren had disappeared from sight, but he had most likely found his covering position somewhere in the rocks to the upper slopes of the town. Satisfied all was going according to plan thus far, Tavin turned back to motion for Ril to continue following him down into the town. He quickly discovered, however, that she was the one leading him; his usual determination dwarfed by her own.

The two quietly moved over the long grass between them and the first row of buildings that led down to the barn in which the townspeople were condemned to die. As silent as shadows in the black of night, the two moved on into the buildings taking care to map out their surroundings as they went for their escape route. Agealin Town was not so different from Tavin's own home village of Eirinor. Concealed in a depression in the lands surrounded by boulders and trees, the rows of small buildings were concentrated along the perimeter of the village with a large grassy yard at the heart of the town. Tavin observed the tallest building at the opposite end of the town with its ornately decorated walls and roofing. This would have to be the lord of the town's manor that had most likely been commandeered by the leader of the Purging Flame.

As the two crept through the city, they found the town virtually devoid of any and all activity. All the citizens of the town had been locked away in the barn and the depraved marauders had apparently finished their looting and were now patrolling for intruders. Intruders such as the party from Galantia. As Ril voraciously pulled Tavin along from cover to cover in the shadows of the buildings deeper into the town, footsteps and conversations between the marauders became audible. Tavin stiffened his back against the wall of a house and motioned for Ril to do the same with a movement of his eyes.

He slowly turned and hesitantly poked his head out from the cover of the wall to better grasp a feeling for his surroundings. Scanning the environment, Tavin memorized everything before him and gingerly withdrew his head from the wall. Ril was eager to hear his report.

"Well?" she anxiously whispered, "what are we looking at?" Tavin knelt down and shook his head.

"This isn't going to be easy," he responded immediately. "There's a street in front of us. On the other side is the barn, packed to the gunnels with people. But there are two members of the Purging Flame standing just left of the street. They'll see us for sure if we try to sneak straight across." Ril was displeased with the report.

"Well we can't just stay here, can we?" she solicited sharply. "There must be another way around."

"There is," Tavin responded a little impatiently. "There are sure to be guards surrounding the perimeter of the barn, but if we can manage to jump across a gap in some bushes to its north wall, we can get into an exposed area that should take us inside. We'll figure out what's next when we have a better perspective on the barn." Satisfied with the plan, Ril nodded her head in agreement.

With her approval, Tavin nodded as well and they silently resumed their trek around the houses keeping to the shadows. As they turned the corner to get to the house adjacent to the row of bushes, Tavin was suddenly halted by a sharp tug on his cape. He turned quickly to find Ril pointing over to the far side of the bushes where two more of the marauders were patrolling. Waiting for them to pass, Tavin glanced back to Ril to give her a quick look of thanks. She smiled coyly in return.

After the two patrols had passed, the two Elemental Warriors knelt down to their hands and feet and began to slowly trudge alongside the opposite side of the bushes, keeping them hidden from the first two marauders' view. As they passed along the line of shrubbery, Tavin was looking ahead of himself at the barn when he carelessly let his cape get underneath his hand to bring him fumbling down to the earth with a faint thud. Ril bit her lip and froze to listen for the sounds of approaching guards that she knew would be coming. When a long silence passed over the two with no sign of detection from any of the surrounding guards, the very relieved girl let out a deep but quiet sigh.

Observing Tavin had still not moved since his blunder, she crawled over to him as he was beginning to pick himself up. Ril could see his frustration from his mistake. She leaned in close and whispered in his ear.

"Do you just want me to stand up and sing them a song? If you want to get caught that bad, I can do it no problem," she whispered with sarcasm laced in her voice. Feeling he probably deserved that, Tavin took the hit and rose back to his hands and knees once more to carefully tuck his cape back into his belt as best he could. When he had situated himself once more, the two continued crawling onward until they reached the gap between the bushes and the barn. They halted at the end of the bushes to gauge how long they would need to jump to clear the small opening in their cover. Just as they were ready to make a go for it, the sound of a group of men's footsteps again froze them where they crouched. Tavin motioned for Ril to move back slightly so as not to be too close to the proximity of the barn.

In the following moments, a group of several of the dark purple cloaked members of the Purging Flame appeared from the west side of the building with torches in hand. Tavin and Ril exchanged nervous glances, already aware of what they were up to. The men with the torches performed some sort of movement with their hands, apparently condemning the innocents they were about to slaughter. Then without missing a beat, they heaved the torches onto the rickety old building, igniting it nearly the moment they landed. Ril grit her teeth in disgust once more as she watched the men locking the doors of the barn, laughing heartlessly. Ril tugged at Tavin once more as she whispered to him.

"Tavin, I can extinguish the fire," she suggested. He was quick to shake his head no.

"Ril, remember what happened the last time you used your powers when the Draks were looking for us?" Tavin reminded her. "If there are any demons out there that sense you, our position will be revealed to them all, and I really don't feel up to going into 'Warrior of Light' mode right now. We have to follow the plan and lead them out through this exposed area in the wall. We're just going to have to hurry." Ril reluctantly nodded her head in agreement and prepared to jump over to the side of the wall with the hole in its side. As soon as the band of marauders retreated away from the old burning building, Tavin and Ril jumped across the gap in the bushes, desperate to get the townspeople out of the barn before it was too late.

While the Elemental Warriors moved into the burning barn, Parnox and Kohlin had managed to sneak past the much more secure perimeter on the opposite end of Agealin Town using a few tricks from their respective experiences. They continued onward through the buildings until they reached the perimeter of the lord's manor, surrounded by the Purging Flame. Kohlin looked up at his brawny companion with anxiety in his eyes.

"I guess we found the right building..." he stated. "Now how do you propose we get in there?" Parnox returned Kohlin's dumbfounded expression and pressed his back onto the wall to think. As he turned his head to reposition his axe again, the mighty woodsman caught sight of an opportunity too good to pass up. Parnox gestured Kohlin to look back at the inn behind the row of homes they hid from. A lone marauder sat drinking inside near the window of the inn. Parnox shifted his gaze back down onto his younger friend.

"Are you thinking what I am?" Kohlin smiled in acknowledgement as they both carefully rushed back over to the front of the inn. Getting positioned on both sides of the window where the lone marauder sat, the two Southlanders exchanged nods that they were ready. Kohlin leapt in front of the window and called out to the man.

"Excuse me, but you need to get out of this town right now," he stated simply. The marauder was instantly on his feet running for the doorway. As he collected his robes about him, Kohlin ran across the entryway as if to escape. The moment the unfortunate man exited the doorway, he was greeted by the oversized fist of Parnox Guilldon careening into his face, sending him clear off his feet and back into the inn unconscious. The two quickly entered after him, aware that someone would have heard that. As the sound of footsteps from the manor became audible, Kohlin quickly removed the cloak from the downed marauder and draped himself in it as Parnox hid the body in a dark corner.

Moments later, several other cloaked members of the Purging Flame came bursting in the doorway to the inn to find one of their own holding a massive man with his hands bound behind him.

"Found this one hiding in here," Kohlin lied to them, attempting to disguise his voice. The other marauders looked somewhat surprised for a moment.

"You handled this big guy all by yourself?" one of them asked with doubt.

"He's not as strong as he looks," Kohlin lied. They laughed.

"All right then, take him over to the barn. There's plenty of room for one more!" the man joked. Kohlin shook his head.

"Actually, I was told the boss wanted to see this man." The others' laughter died in a split second.

"What?" one of them asked cautiously. "What did this guy do to get the Drakkaidian sore at him?" Kohlin went rigid upon hearing this.

"Drakkaidian?" Kohlin pressed, fishing for information.

"What, you don't know? Are you new or something?" the other asked curiously.

"Uh, yeah. I just joined up a few weeks ago," Kohlin lied. The marauder shrugged.

"That's about the same time he showed up. But if you're new, I can tell you the story." The marauder motioned for his companions to sit down at the tables while he really tied Parnox to a post by the stairs. When they had all been seated, the man continued in a hushed voice. "One night about three weeks ago, we were raiding a party of rangers in the plains just south of here. While we were finishing with them, a strange thing appeared off to the northern horizon. Before any one knew what to think, this huge winged monster, the size of a house, come busting down from the skies right in front of us. Now, we're all so scared stiff we can barely move. A few moments passed before we finally caught a glimpse of him." The marauder stopped for a moment and shuddered as if these were not memories he wished to remember.

"A glimpse of who?" Kohlin pressed.

"It was a dark one from the far north. You know, high in the northern parts of Drakkaidia. And this wasn't just any Drakkaidian. This guy was a mage from the Black Church itself. Too bad we didn't know that at the time…" The man trailed off for a moment, looking at his companions with what appeared to be remorse. "Anyway, he was riding on this evil looking bat thing's back and hops off, drenched in these black and red robes with all sorts of bizarre marks over them. We could tell right off there was something really off about the guy when he spoke for the first time. He greeted us kindly, but we knew he was full of hot air. Said he had been sent from his master to hire the whole lot of us to work for him and to let us disguise a small force of Drakkaidian soldiers as Purging Flame so they could get past the border. At first, we thought the guy was out of his mind, so one of our guys fires a crossbow right at his face. But before it could get to him, it was deflected right back at the man who fired it with some weird energy field from around the guy. He wasn't so friendly after that. He killed three more of us by lifting his hand to choke the life out of three more. Ever since that night, the entire Purging Flame has been Drakkaidia's secret muscle." Kohlin was still confused with the story.

"Well what has he got us doing for him that someone that powerful couldn't do himself?" Kohlin asked puzzled. Before the marauder could answer, however, Kohlin noticed an ominous shadow had appeared over his face. The marauder suddenly locked up with fear as the realization of what was happening washed over him. He slowly began to levitate into the air until he hovered over the table he had just been leaning on. Then, as if some terrible unseen force collided into his entire body, the man was sent flying back into the wall of the inn and clear through it. As Kohlin stared horrified at the limp form of the man lying dead in the rubble, a distant but audible voice sounded through the room from the doorway. Kohlin looked back to find the cloaked form of the Dark Mage that had just been described to him, cloaked in black and red ragged robes with a dangerous face behind his hood.

"To answer your question, boy," the dark figure said, "my master is using their number to attack the Southland border from the inside and make sure the Legion is not assembled." Kohlin was in utter shock to learn that the Dark Mage had somehow discovered who he was. "Don't be so surprised," he continued. "You and your band are known to all of my master's forces. And orders are," he said stepping forward and lifting Kohlin out of his seat and into the air with a gesture of his hand alone, "to terminate you on sight."

Chapter 26

<u>Defenders</u>

After crawling through the small hole in the wall, the two Elemental Warriors entered an already smoke filled room with what was left of the town's populace overtaken by chaos and panic. Tavin rose back to his feet and leapt up to a row of crates to better announce his presence to the people.

"People of Agealin Town!" Tavin yelled loud enough to get their attention. While still in a panic, most of the people turned to face the voice. Tavin began once again and pulled Ril up to stand next to him. "We are here to help you, but you've got to stay calm!" Tavin continued, trying to soothe the frantic masses. "There is a small passage behind me, but you can only pass through it one at a time..."

The Grandarian was cut short by an overhead beam from the loft above him suddenly giving way from the fire to come crashing down. With Tavin preoccupied with the frantic crowd, Ril was the only one to react in time to save them. Hearing the charred wood snap above them, she grabbed hold of Tavin's arm and hurriedly leapt off the crate she stood on with the Grandarian boy in her wake. They landed on their backs over the heated ground just as the fire engulfed beam smashed through the crate. Bringing his head up to observe the damage that could have been done to him, he quickly shot a glance over to Ril, staring back with eyes wide and frazzled breaths.

"Thanks," he managed struggling back to his feet. She could not help but smile back and tell him they were even. Despite their dangerous circumstances, he helped her up with a grin of his own. It quickly disappeared however, realizing that they were now just as trapped in the burning barn as the rest of the townspeople, now even more frantic with fear.

"Tavin!" she shouted over the noise. "Tavin, you have to let me use my powers! If I don't extinguish the flames we'll

173

all die in the fire!" As resolute as ever, Tavin still shook his head violently.

"No!" he shouted back to her. "I can get us out of here without magic!" Ril's protest was cut off by the Sword of Granis ringing through the air, gaining the attention of the entire room. "I'd rather fight off a party of marauders than another pack of Valcanor! No magic! Now come on!" Tavin's commanding tone took Ril by surprise. She had never seen him so determined and ready to take charge than he was now.

With that, Tavin wheeled around toward the crowd of people and made his way through them to the front end of the now fully burning barn. Stopping at the central entrance, Tavin readied the Sword of Granis and gauged where he would strike. Mentally targeting the position of the lock on the outside, Tavin heaved the sword downward in a vertical slash clean through the door as easily as through empty air. Hearing the lock drop in pieces outside the doorway, Tavin reared back and kicked forward to blast the door open, smashing what was left of the wooden walls outside. He turned back to Ril, gaping and astonished the boy's crude ingenuity had worked so well.

"Ril!" he called to her. "Get them out of here! Someone will have seen that so lead them as far away from here as you can before you're caught!" Ril was becoming as frantic as the townspeople themselves.

"What about you?" she yelled back to him.

"I'll stay behind to get them out until we've got everyone! Now get moving! We have *no* time!" With that, Tavin ran back to the other end of the blazing barn once more leaving Ril at the head with a mass of screaming villagers. Quickly coming back to her senses, Ril made for the door and called out for them to follow her out of the burning passage. Emerging from the barn, Ril found a yard full of marauders coming to attention to her right. Not in any better position as they had been moments before, Ril bellowed her already strained voice for the townspeople to run after her the way she and Tavin had come.

Inside the burning barn, the isolated fires had now fused to become one raging inferno engulfing the whole building. With dozens of townspeople still trapped inside, Tavin had grown overwhelmed with the chores of keeping them calm, aiding the wounded out, and keeping the small doorway he had created safe enough to pass through. As he struggled to keep the panicked crowds steadily flowing, the environment grew even more savage with burning debris now freely raining on top of them from the singed ceiling above. As the last rush of townspeople came surging forward to pass through the doorway, Tavin was preparing to exit himself when a faint cry from behind him found its way to his ears. Turning back to the heart of the fire, a young girl sat crying on the floor next to the body of a dead woman, what he assumed to be her mother. Cursing his bad luck, Tavin made one final burst back through the debris into the center of the flames.

With embers and sparks soaring all around him, the path to his target was nearly impossible to navigate. Rows of downed beams from the ceiling lay smoldering as he bounded over them, more barely missing him with every step he took. Pressing on, the boy's reflexes proved to be far too strained to avoid some damage to his person. Leaping over a burning post from the charred walls, a fireball from the ceiling plummeted onto his extended right arm, causing Tavin to stumble forth grimacing in searing pain from the burn. Forcing himself on through the hurt, he at last reached the child crying hysterically on the floor. Picking her up and securing her in his good arm, Tavin mustered every last ounce of strength and speed left in his fatigued body as he maneuvered through the flaming obstacles on his final charge out of the barn. As he came up on the doorway, its last intact framework came collapsing down. Pressing the child tight against him, Tavin grit his teeth with determination and leapt straight through the wall of fire, out into the open, clear air again.

With a hard landing on his back to keep the child tucked safe and tight in his arm, the Warrior of Light lay taut on the grassy earth breathing so hard he thought that he would surely suck in all the oxygen in the atmosphere before he would be able to move again. But upon the sound of men yelling and rushing in his direction, Tavin was forced to pick himself up once more, running on strength that he no longer had. Rising with fierce determination to save himself and the others, he sprinted onward into the yard where Ril had been cut off in her escape route by several of the cloaked marauders sprinting directly toward her with rusty cutlasses in hand. Knowing the girl possessed no means of defense but the magic he had forbidden her to use, there was nothing to protect the fleeing people who had no chance of outrunning the marauders with women and children among them. With the child he had rescued in one hand and the Sword of Granis in the other, Tavin plowed forward to reach them first. As he ran, the golden crystal on the hilt of the sword began to shimmer with light responding to the dire circumstances he found himself in.

Rushing past the chaotic masses, Tavin at last reached Ril herding the slower people away from the approaching marauders. He startled her as he heaped the crying child into her arms.

"Take her!" he commanded, already grasping his legendary weapon back into both hands. Ril was quick to notice the horrible burn on his right arm as she gathered the child into her grasp.

"You're hurt! You can't fight them!" she cried seeing his silver blade rising into the air. Tavin was already on his way to intercept their oncoming assailants.

"Don't worry about me!" he bellowed, clashing with and breaking the first of the marauder's blades with the mighty Sword of Granis. "I'll be right behind you! Now get out of here!" he commanded as he caught another of his enemies through the abdomen with the edge of his blade. Watching as Tavin engaged the waves of the Purging Flame with nothing but his legendary sword and iron will, Ril could not bring herself to move until the cries of the child she held returned her to her senses. Overcoming her emotion, Ril spun around and ran after the townspeople.

Kohlin Marraea found himself lying in the dusty street outside the inn, surrounded by the debris of the window he had just been blasted out of. He was already bruised and bleeding from the sheer force of the blow dealt to him by his attacker. Not missing a beat, the shadowy form of the Dark Mage came looming back outside to face his prey once again. Realizing the chances of defeating a foe such as this were slim to none, Kohlin staggered to get back to his feet devising a plan to escape. Not allowing him that time however, the Dark Mage again raised his gloved hand upward, raising Kohlin with it. As the Windrun Warrior hung suspended in midair struggling for breath in the clutches of the mage's deadly grip, his enemy began to utter a faint and distant laugh from behind his concealing hood.

"What chance do you believe you have, boy?" the figure questioned. "A Southlander against a Dark Mage of Drakkan? Those do not sound like favorable odds to me-" To Kohlin's surprise, the evil mage was suddenly interrupted by the bulky figure of Parnox Guilldon bursting out of the inn's doorway and crashing into him, flattening the foe into the dust instantly. Though his hands were still bound, Parnox continued with haste over the mage to reach his downed companion. With the threatening resonance of the marauders that had been inside the inn drawing swords after them, Kohlin was instantly back on his feet and unsheathing his twin sabers to cut his rescuer's bonds.

"I certainly owe you one now," Kohlin said with thanks poured into his voice as he finished sawing through the thick rope.

"Let's just focus on getting the hell out of this town with our lives for now," Parnox replied hastily, taking hold of his mighty axe from his back ready to fend off the oncoming attackers. As the two met blades and axes with the Purging Flame, the temporarily humiliated Dark Mage was springing back to his feet in rage. In a burst of blind fury, the black and crimson cloaked figure thrust both of his arms forth with a fierce cry to blast a wave of surging red energy from the palms of his hands to send the entire group of marauders and both Southlanders off their feet onto the dusty street.

"Fools!" he bellowed mad with enmity. "You cannot harm me! I am beyond any of your pitiful weaponry or your cowardly physical attacks! *Now die!*" Consumed by his rage and humiliation, the Dark Mage once more grabbed hold of both of his enemies with his dark power and suspended them into the air. Both Kohlin and Parnox could instantly feel the very air in their lungs suddenly compressed outward in one swift blow. Their chests crushing with force, the two companions hovered just above the ground with life steadily draining away.

Just as Kohlin could feel himself falling into darkness, a different sensation suddenly whizzed directly past his head, leaving a wake of sharp wind grazing across his skin. Moments after the bizarre jet of air passed him, the crushing force holding his near broken body immediately vanished, dropping both he and Parnox onto the hard earth beneath them with the other downed marauders. As new life and air found its way into his lungs, Kohlin sat on the road panting hard, grateful to still be alive.

It was not until now that the Windrun Warrior remembered the source of his pain moments ago and shifted his bewildered gaze onto the Dark Mage lying not ten feet away from them on the ground with an arrow protruding from his hood. Kohlin shot a confused glance at Parnox, but before he could utter a single word he was cut off by another voice from behind.

"Hey!" it called, seemingly irritated. Kohlin and Parnox both spun their heads around to find a familiar face staring back at them with a look of disgust mounted on it. "Sorry 'bout that," Jaren told them not very apologetically. "Couldn't get the shot from up there. Had to get a little closer. From the looks of it I was just in time." The two stunned Southlanders could only sit in sheer amazement at the boy's incredible timing. Jaren did not return their emotionless gazes however; already turning back and waving for them to follow.

"Jaren... what about the noble?" Parnox asked. Jaren impatiently turned back and shook his head.

"Dead. I already looked. The only survivors are at the other side of the village. In case you forgot, Tavin and the girl are still out there trying to move a pack of frantic villagers out of here with about forty marauders on them and another hundred coming in from the east side of the town we didn't see. They're armed to the teeth, too. You just gonna' sit there all day?" At the mention of their other young companions horribly outnumbered seventy to one, Kohlin and Parnox were up like a shot after Jaren. They sprinted as hard as they could for the other end of the town, praying they would arrive in time to help Tavin and Ril.

Chapter 27

<u>Cavalry</u>

Unfortunately for Tavin and Ril, they had not made it quite as far as Jaren had predicted. By now, Ril had managed to lead the populace to the last row of buildings and was beginning to herd them up the hillside to the cover of the rocks above town. From there, however, she had no idea what she would do. Leading them into the open fields with only one exhausted boy as their sole defense was not a good plan at all.

As Ril debated what to do with the people, Tavin continued to hold the line at the rear of the group with unflagging ferocity toward the onslaught of the Purging Flame. His pattern of movement from the grassy yard where his struggle began to his current position consisted of a wave of marauders eventually catching up to the fleeing townspeople, forcing him to engage and defeat them, then rushing back to the people to hurry them along before the next wave caught up. As Tavin battled with the Purging Flame, he began to notice that even without the magical power of the Sword of Granis invoked, the weapon's sheer physical strength gave him additional power enough to hold his ground. With the Purging Flame relying on rusty old cutlasses, the indestructible blade of the sword often shattered them to pieces.

Upon reaching the end of the town and the hillside, Tavin found that even with the legendary Sword of Granis in his possession he could not keep so many of the marauders' impossible numbers at bay. As the last of the people began their ascent up the ridge, the waves of the Purging Flame had begun to pile up and Tavin now found himself facing over twenty marauders at once with more arriving by the second. With every moment that passed, he could feel himself dipping into the very life-force maintaining his heartbeat just to keep him upright on his feet. He knew he couldn't carry on like this much longer.

As the front line of the marauders came charging into Tavin, he savagely swung the Sword of Granis in a 360 degree spin, cutting down several of the careless foes in one powerful laceration. More quickly replaced the ones he felled, however, and as he parried a cutlass thrust toward his torso, another of the marauders drove forward to further damage Tavin's already burnt right arm. He let out a shout and grimaced in biting pain. Now not even capable of defending himself from the overbearing numbers of his foes, Tavin was quickly grounded and at last overtaken.

Herding the townspeople along, Ril looked back in horror to the base of the hillside to observe her courageous protector down and surrounded by the barbaric marauders. Feeling the air withdraw from her lungs in horror, the Warrior of Fire could no longer contain herself. Convinced the only way to save Tavin was with her power, she prepared to rush back down the hillside with fire blazing. Before she could start her charge to his rescue, she noticed a group of the marauders by the first row of buildings being cut down. Realizing the identities the trio battling the Purging Flame, she frantically called down to them for help.

"Kohlin! Parnox! Jaren!" she shrieked hysterically pointing at the mob around Tavin. "He's trapped! Hurry!" As the three hacked, slashed, and shot their way through the vast numbers of the Purging Flame, Parnox called for cover.

"Follow me boys!" he ordered, raising the broad side of his axe out in front of him. "Hold on to your asses!" With these crude words, the massive Southlander began to plow his way forward under the cover of Jaren's precise arrow cover and Kohlin's deadly duel blades. As Parnox trampled over the Purging Flame, he at last reached the mound of men over the downed Warrior of Light and released his mighty axe from in front of him to send it slicing through the lines of marauders with near inhuman strength.

Just as the mob around Tavin collapsed, one of the marauders to escape the reach of Parnox's blade quickly pressed his cutlass to Tavin's throat, obviously unaware of Jaren's bow.

"One more move from any of you and he-" The marauder was cut off as an arrow embedded itself into his chest.

"Dies?" Jaren caustically finished. Kohlin quickly rushed forth to help Tavin off the ground while the others continued to fend off the Purging Flame until outnumbered so badly that they were forced to make a run for it. As the four warriors made their way to the top of the hillside while the marauders regrouped, Ril bounded over to Tavin and latched onto him so hard he could feel what breath he had left fleeing him. After the embrace, Ril stepped back and stared him straight in the eye with a very serious expression spread full length on her face.

"You are the most reckless, headstrong, and just plain stupid person that I have ever seen..." she told him suddenly, somewhat catching him off guard once more. Her face softened then as she drew close to squeeze him tight, her flowing red hair draping over his shoulders as she pulled him close. "But you have got to be the bravest too." As the emotional girl kept firm hold over Tavin who had not even had the chance to lower his sword, the young Grandarian felt more flattered than he had ever dreamed possible, as evident by his face being as red as Ril's crimson hair. Jaren quickly turned his attention to them.

"Um, pardon me for interrupting people," the boy began as he tapped Tavin on the shoulder, "but there is still a very large group of madmen with lots of swords who want to kill us just over the ridge. It might be wise to leave right about now." Parnox agreed as he struck down an advancing marauder with his axe.

"The boy is quite right! We need to move!" he bellowed. With that audacious command, Ril quickly came back to reality and released Tavin, allowing oxygen back into his lungs. As the reunited party was about to set off after the townspeople, an ominous shadow appeared over the group causing them all to halt and observe the enormous thing that had cut off their sunlight. As the group turned back to the skies above them, the view of a familiar winged monstrosity crushed their hopes of escape. The Dark Mage from before was somehow alive again standing atop a Valcanor. Every jaw in the group dropped. A baffled and offended look overcame Jaren's face, having thought he had already disposed of this adversary.

"W-What do we do now?" Ril quietly quivered.

"Running for our lives strikes me as an excellent idea," Jaren remarked equally hushed. Tavin was quick to shake his head no, not letting his eyes off the winged terror.

"Why bother?" he replied brutally honest. "We can't outrun it, or the Purging Flame. We have to make a stand." Tavin turned to Ril as he raised the Sword of Granis once more, its ornate blade glistening in the lone pocket of sunlight. "Ril, there's no sense in holding back your power now. There's a Valcanor right above us, so I'd say our cover is blown. Bring it on." Ril almost grinned with glee at this.

"Finally," she responded, already clenching her fists with fire spouting around them. "I've been waiting forever to unleash some justice onto these animals." With that, Ril prepared for her assault onto the marauders while Tavin raised his blade to the Dark Mage in the skies, ready try to summon his own hidden powers of light to drive the creature off.

As it turned out, he wouldn't have to. Just as Ril was about to flare her powers onto the seemingly endless number of marauders, a strange sensation of a familiar presence rippled through her and Tavin. With their ability to sense the use of nearby magical power, they both began to detect something building up behind them. Turning around quickly, the two felt a throbbing surge of invisible force tearing through the air above them to soar into the unsuspecting Dark Mage, who barely managed to deflect the bulk of it with his own counter spell of dark power at the last moment. The Valcanor staggered to regain the rhythm of its flapping wings from the force of impact. As the blast of invisible energy temporarily stunned the wicked figure and his mount, the entire party and the remaining forces of the Purging Flame all stopped cold in their tracks, staring behind them. An entire battalion of Southland Legionnaires was forming up on the far side of the ridge behind Agealin Town, safely gathering the townspeople behind them.

Nearly forgetting the presence of his overbearing enemy behind him, Tavin's eyes were immediately fixated on the gray cloaked figure at the head of the battalion, arms raised to summon his troops to him. That was all it took for Tavin to realize who this mysterious cloaked figure was.

"Zeroan!" he shouted as loudly as his tattered voice allowed. Not to be frightened, the infuriated Dark Mage boomed his own voice once more to his cowardly troops.

"He is only one man! Stand your ground and destroy those pitiful Legionnaires! Leave the other to me!" the mage commanded, kicking his demonic Valcanor forward toward the Mystic Sage and his forces. Not daring to disobey their frightful master, the still heavy numbers of the Purging Flame poured forward with wavering vitality, forcing the five warriors still holding their number back to retreat for help once more.

On the opposite side of the ridge, the gray cloaked figure was quick to respond. Turning to face them, the rows of Legionnaires came to swift attention. Standing tall with their green and white armor shining in the rays of the sun, their leader called out to them.

"Southland Legion!" his powerful voice boomed. "The marauders of the Purging Flame have destroyed your towns and terrorized your people for too long! This day let you end their reign of terror!" he commanded. Raising their broad shields and tall lances, the battalion of the Legion did so, heavily outnumbering even the great forces of the faction of the Purging Flame. As the troops of the Southland came charging ahead, Parnox quickly stopped his retreating allies and called out for their attention.

"I don't know about the rest of you," he yelled to them, "but I'll not leave my countrymen to fight and die protecting me from my own fight!" Firing an arrow into one of his advancing enemies, Jaren's face was aghast.

"What!?!" he screamed, releasing another arrow backward. "We've held them off long enough! Let these guys finish them now! They have more than enough to take them!"

"Exactly!" Parnox replied back. "We can't lose now. Why not join in?" Jaren glanced at him as though he was out of what little mind he had for a long moment, but eventually rolled his eyes and silently nodded, stringing another arrow into his bow. Smiling and winking at the Grandarian boy, Tavin could not help but do the same. Forming a miniature line of their own, the five stood waiting for the charge to reach them. When it did, their number increased from about five to five hundred strong. Tavin and the others burst forward with weapons and magic in hand for one final stand against the barbaric marauders of the Purging Flame. Leaping into them with weapons thrusting forward, the party hammered into the Purging Flame with a new sense of vitality coursing through their veins, sending a wave of trepidation ripping through the marauders like no arrow or sword point could do.

Chapter 28

<u>Culmination</u>

With the indestructible Sword of Granis, deadly accurate arrows, twin Windrun sabers, bursts of singing flame, and an oversized axe adding into the fray of the Legionnaire charge, the fearful marauders of the Purging Flame did not choose to fight for long. Realizing how hopelessly outnumbered they had become, even fear of their ruthless leader was not enough to keep them on a battlefield where they would surely perish. As the first lines of both forces clashed, nearly all of the marauders had moved into full retreat with the Legion in full pursuit. Those that did choose to fight, however, were willingly met by the tips of hundreds of Southland swords cutting into them with unflagging determination. With the help of his companions and his last pocket of strength fueling him on, Tavin slashed through the lines of marauders with unparalleled swordsmanship and dexterity.

The young Warrior of Light, however, suddenly froze as the sight of the Dark Mage and his Valcanor passed over him and was moving toward the stationary figure of Zeroan back at the other side of the ridge. Tavin quickly turned to grab one of his companions and found Jaren closest to him.

"Jaren!" he called out to him through the mass of charging Legionnaires. Jaren quickly wheeled around to his friend, already running back to the aid of Zeroan.

As Tavin ran onward toward the Mystic Sage, the Dark Mage and his winged mount had already reached him. Knowing the Drakkaidian mage possessed powers that could challenge his own, Zeroan quickly thrust his hands forward into a cup to prepare for the bleeding crimson light building in his foe's hands. With a detonation of surging power, the mage leapt from the Valcanor's back and released the energy surging in his hands toward Zeroan. The Mystic Sage powerfully accepted it in his outstretched hands and carefully wrapped his fingers around it. Zeroan quickly closed his hands around the energy and shrunk it out of existence. Concentrating on striking out at the Dark Mage sailing down to him, Zeroan temporarily forgot about the Valcanor that had swooped in from behind and latched onto him with its mighty gnarled fingers, forcing the Mystic Sage to the ground. Seeing this, Tavin clutched the Sword of Granis tighter in his still functioning left arm and attempted to increase his speed to aid the sage.

Finally landing from the leap off his winged steed, the Dark Mage met with the earth about ten yards in front of Zeroan, held tight under the weight of the mighty Valcanor. Gathering his black and crimson robes about him, the mage began to echo a faint laugh as he had before with Kohlin.

"So I finally meet the legendary Mystic Sage Zeroan..." he began almost proudly. "I have heard much of your exploits over the long years of your life, sage," he continued raising his arms to form a surge of pulsating red power growing larger by the minute above him. Zeroan lay before the mage ever calm and collected in the face of immanent danger.

"Then you must have heard how many of your kind I have had the pleasure of dispatching from this world over the much longer than you know years of my life," he responded with an ominously quiet tone intertwined in his voice. The Dark Mage only laughed further at this.

"Oh yes, but I can assure you that you will not survive me," the mage promised, raising the now gargantuan sphere of erupting energy above his cloaked head. "If you would be so kind as to allow me to show you." With a powerful downward movement of his arms, the prodigious ball of energy came revving forward from its resting place above the mage's head, jetting toward the helpless form of Zeroan.

While the sage might have been able to perform some sort of incredible escape and save himself, Tavin Tieloc would not take that chance. Bounding forward at top speed, the audacious Warrior of Light arrived to aid the sage just in time. As the blast of evil energy came plowing forward, Tavin grabbed hold of the Sword of Granis with both hands, brought it back over his right shoulder, and swung with every last pocket of strength in his body to impact dark power. That moment, responding to the need to save his friend, Tavin's hidden powers came bursting forth from the deaths of his heart to engulf him in the radiant shimmering light once more. Finally meeting with the fully empowered Warrior of Light, the weak dark matter was not able to withstand the power of its advisory. It shattered the moment it touched the tip of the blade, spreading the deep red energy forth in every direction, including into the body of the massive Valcanor, already frightened by Tavin's burning power. It fell backward over itself, releasing Zeroan from its grasp.

Standing alone on a boulder in the savage mountains of the Valley of Blood connecting southern Drakkaidia to the war zone, Verix Montrox lifted his head as he sensed a unique flash of Grandarian power come to life far to the southeast of his current position. His dark eyes narrowed as he brushed a lock of his short red hair away from his hard face. Evaluating what he had sensed for another long moment, he leapt down from the boulder.

As soon as he was freed from the demon's fingers, Zeroan was instantly back on his feet and summoning another charge of mystic power from his body. While the sage prepared to deal with the Dark Mage, Tavin was quick to contend with the Valcanor. Slashing at the downed demon's body with the Sword of Granis gleaming in all its glory, the tainted creature could barely stand up much less become airborne to escape. But before the end of the struggle, the monster offered one last fierce attack in the form of smashing downward with its mighty hydraulic arms. Tavin nimbly dodged the blow and rolled out of the way, but falling victim to his fatigue he lost his grip on the sword. Wrenched away by the Valcanor, it spiraled sporadically through the air until at last plunging in to the earth behind the demon.

With the Sword of Granis lost to him and his debt from the excess use of energy finally catching up to him, Tavin could not find the strength to raise himself from the ground as his gargantuan advisory took flight, hovering just above him. Thankfully, however, the Mystic Sage Zeroan had not forgotten his savior. Recoiling from the weakened Dark Mage, Zeroan bounded backward, this time seizing the tips of the Valcanor's wings with his telekinetic grip, forcing them together and pushing it to the earth. Careening down and struggling for balance, the creature at last seemed to acknowledge defeat and gained enough altitude to escape the sage's might.

It was a particularly painful moment for the Dark Mage of Drakkaidia then as he looked around the hillside. With his "army" of marauders scattered and in full retreat, the entire party he sought to destroy surging forward to aid the two already in front of him, and his wounded Valcanor evacuating the scene of battle without him, he at last realized how pointless further resistance was in his weakened state. He had failed his master miserably. Cursing in some form of an ancient Drakkaidian dialect, the Dark Mage gathered himself in his black and crimson robes, knelt upon the ground where he stood, and began to violently shake as a dim aura of blackness began to develop around him.

Turning back to face his opponent, Zeroan instantly knew what he was attempting to do. Standing fast to prepare for the immanent blast, Zeroan overheard one final threat from his enemy.

"I promise you, sage," he sneered with his voice shaking along with his body, "you may have bested one Dark Mage, but even your Warrior of Light will not fair as well against the Black Seven. In time, Lord Montrox will have them at his side. Then you will know the true power of the Dark Mages!" Laughing his haunting laugh one last time, the wanton figure suddenly exploded, his very skin erupting apart in a wave of black light, knocking Zeroan off his feet back onto the ground alongside Tavin. Dematerializing as it spread, the explosion and the Dark Mage faded into oblivion with only his shredded black and crimson robes falling to the ground after.

With his primary foe gone and the now leaderless Purging Flame dispersing into the distance in fear, Zeroan sat himself up to just rest for a moment, breathing hard. Taking a very well deserved moment of rest himself, Tavin looked up at the wheezing Mystic Sage curiously.

187

"What's wrong Zeroan?" he asked even more winded, propping himself up with his left arm. "I never thought someone with your caliber of power could be out of breath." Zeroan sat silent for a moment as if not hearing the boy's question, then finally began to chuckle from beneath his hood.

"My caliber of power?" he repeated amused. "Tavinious, as you well know by now, it is no easy task to summon heavy portions of magic all at one time." The sage turned his head to make eye contact with the young boy, giving him an unexpected surprise. Zeroan's face had turned haggard and worn beyond anything he had ever looked like before. Tavin looked upon him bewildered. Observing the confusion, Zeroan quietly smiled and tried to explain. "While my power is quite potent against enemy powers, it is that very nature of it that heaps somewhat negative consequences on my body the more I employ it. Even I have my limitations, my young friend." Not quite sure what that meant, Tavin decided he was far too tired to care at the moment.

The loud cheers from behind them on the first side of the ridge drew Tavin and Zeroan's attention as they lay there upon the clawed and blasted earth. Shifting their gaze to the rows of cheering Legionnaires, it was obvious the battle had been won. With their enemies crushed, the other four of Tavin's company had quickly noticed he was missing and shot off toward him through the crowds of soldiers. Observing their speedy approach, Zeroan quickly turned his head back to Tavin holding his gaze behind the mask of his hood for a long moment before he at last reached out and placed his hand over the boy's shoulder.

"I was careless in the battle today, young Grandarian. I would not have been able to escape from the demon in time to save myself. You have saved my life, and I am grateful to you," the Mystic Sage told him sincerely. Tavin could only stare back at the sage's suddenly disarming face, so surprised to hear such positive words from his mouth he could not find the words to reply. "I am glad I found you, Tavin. You indeed possess the courage to be the Warrior of Light, as you have certainly proved here today." Thinking back on all the day's strenuous events that had pushed his body to the limit and beyond, Tavin fell back on the cold ground with a grunt, this time with exactly the right words to respond.

"Zeroan," he began with a look of veteran experience over his face, "you have no idea." The sage could only quietly chuckle once more as he patted Tavin on the shoulder and rose.

"I'm sure you will tell me someday," he smiled, stepping back from the boy as his four other companions at last rushed in and over to him. The first to come sliding down next to him were Jaren and Ril, practically fighting each other to reach the boy's side first. Tavin began to laugh out loud at his friends' antics, causing them both to look down at him surprised and a little embarrassed. Jaren raised his eyebrows and began to speak.

"If I was as beat up as you," he began, "the last thing I would be doing is laughing." Tavin did not stop as he brought his eyes to meet with his best friend's.

"Jaren, if you were as beat up as me, you'd be dead," he responded, not taking anything from his cocky friend this day. In spite of all her mixed emotions, Ril could not contain a giggle. Jaren shot him a caustic glance and gently punched his friend in the arm, unaware of Tavin's painful injury. Recoiling in hurt and grasping his singed and charred right arm, Ril was taken aback when she saw the damage the fire in the barn had inflicted onto his skin. She immediately slapped Jaren out of the way, scolding him for his insensitivity even though he had no idea his friend was wounded.

As Ril reached down to properly examine Tavin's burns, her hand quickly shot over her mouth as view of his raw, singed skin came into view. Tavin let a depressed expression overtake his face.

"That bad, huh?" he asked quickly to the obviously appalled girl. Regretting she had done that, Ril quickly composed herself and shook her head.

"No, no," she lied. Tavin gave her a look that told her he saw past her bad acting. "Okay, it is pretty bad," she at last admitted, looking the burns over again. "But it's nothing I can't fix," she said with confidence, reaching out for his arm. Tavin was quick to withdraw it, a fearful expression passing over his face.

"What's that supposed to mean?" he asked guarding his damaged limb. Ril slumped in frustration.

"It means just what it sounds like. I'm the Elemental Warrior of Fire, if you recall. Those wounds were caused by fire, and I can heal them by reversing the effects of the burn if you'd let me see your arm," she told him. Tavin remained reluctant. "Or would you rather have it cut off because it has been infected and turned gangrene by the time we reach a healer?" That was all Tavin needed to hear to give up his hesitation. He surrendered his incapacitated limb to the girl who gingerly accepted it into both of hers and rested it across her lap. Carefully rolling his charred sleeve up to expose the whole of his wounds, Ril took a deep breath and began to summon her power. Slowly closing her eyes and placing her hands directly over the burned area, a fervent flame burst outward from the girl's hands onto Tavin's arm swirling around it, making him dreadfully uneasy and Jaren ready to jump out of his skin.

"What in Granis' name are you doing, girl?" Jaren yelled, ready to shove her away to protect his friend. Not able to ignore his ignorant remarks any longer, Ril's eyes opened with frustration and shot back to glare at Jaren.

"If you don't shut up and let me do this, I'm going to transfer his burns to your mouth to keep it closed! Now be quiet!" she yelled back threateningly, sending Jaren several steps back to join Parnox and Kohlin. As Ril turned back to her work, Jaren discreetly leaned over to Parnox and whispered in his ear nervously.

"Can she do that?" he whispered out of the corner of his mouth. Parnox gazed hard for a moment and turned to the young Grandarian boy.

"I don't know," he remarked, not making him feel any better. As the others stood apart from her, Ril once again set to work applying the passionate flames around Tavin's burns giving him a strange tingling sensation of numbness from the tips of his fingers to his shoulder. Moments later, he lay in amazement as Ril announced she was finished. Lifting his arm in front of his face, not so much as a trace of a scar was present, and all the pain from the burn had completely disappeared. Looking past his arm into his miracle worker's face, Tavin could not find the words to thank her. Ril just smiled back into his deep blue eyes, grateful to be of help.

That was when Tavin's last remnant of strength finally abandoned him. Basking in the warmth of the crimson haired girl's radiant smile, he felt the world around him blurring as his eyes slowly closed shut, at last granting him the peace of sleep he had needed since he arrived in the village that morning. When Ril at last decided to say something, it was already too late. Tavin was completely and totally lost to his dreams, and she merely smiled on the courageous youth who had saved the day. Unfortunately, the peace of the moment was disrupted by Jaren's ignorance yet again.

"You killed him!!!" he bellowed aghast at the top of his lungs, pointing an accusing finger at Ril. That was the comment that broke her back. Her eyes reflecting her vehemence, the Warrior of Fire rose from her place on the ground to ignite her entire body with erupting flame. Kohlin quickly leaned over to Jaren.

"He's just fallen asleep, Jaren," the Southlander corrected. "And if I were you, I'd start running right about now." Jaren gave him a peculiar glance, and then shifted his eyes to the girl engulfed in the inferno slowly making her way toward him. Jaren tried a small, quirky smile.

"Oh..." he said, pacing backward himself. "Well in that case, no hard feelings..." his worthless apology was cut short by a charging fireball from Ril's fist, just missing his head. Off like a shot, Ril began pursuing her target. Kohlin turned to Parnox.

"Should we break that up?" he questioned, eyes still on the retreating Grandarian archer. Parnox furrowed his brow and shook his head.

"Nah. Let her crisp him up a bit. She can always heal him later, right?"

"Would you trust her to do that?" Parnox shifted his gaze to his companion.

"Maybe you're right," he admitted. "Let's hurry." With that, the two Southlanders set off after the Warrior of Fire before she charred Jaren beyond recognition.

As the four companions chased after each other, the Mystic Sage Zeroan reappeared over the sleeping figure of Tavin with the temporarily lost Sword of Granis in hand. Silently plunging its razor sharp blade into the earth beside him, Zeroan smiled once more.

"Rest well, Tavinious Tieloc. Your adventure is still only beginning..."

Chapter 29

<u>Crippled</u>

The bright sunlight of the following morning was what gently woke the rested Warrior of Light from his makeshift bed in a small thicket of flowers overlooking the hillside of Agealin Town. As the luminous rays from the celestial orb in the skies came shining down onto the sleepy Grandarian boy, his eyes slowly began to open, flickering from the intensity of the glaring light. Turning his body over to prop himself up, Tavin reached up to his eyes with his fully healed right arm to wipe the sleep away. Sitting up on the thick blankets around him, he immediately surveyed his surroundings to try and find his companions. When he noticed he was alone in the center of a collection of empty blankets, however, he turned his attention up the grassy hill above him where a faint clamor echoed into his ears. At the top of the hill not more than twenty yards away he found groups of Legionnaires camped out around several small fires and beginning to gather themselves together, most likely to be off back to the outpost they had been marching for before their gallant rescue of the town.

Not too far away from the last row of Legionnaires, Tavin caught sight of a few of his party members sitting around a fire of their own, apparently eating breakfast. His best friend Jaren was of course stuffing his face with as much food as he could shovel into it, causing Tavin to silently laugh as he watched from a distance. Across from him and several other Legionnaires sat the fervently dressed Warrior of Fire, Arilia Embrin. While the other two Southlanders Parnox and Kohlin and the Mystic Sage Zeroan were nowhere to be found, Tavin assumed they were not far off.

Though he was eager to join his companions again and indulge himself with as much food as he could find, he decided that his personal hygiene should take priority. Tavin rose and gathered his few belongings, fitting his light shoulder and chest armor and cape back over his head. Picking up the Sword of Granis resting by his side, the still sleepy Grandarian boy started away from the campsite of Legionnaires toward the small creek hidden in a thicket of trees faintly audible in the distance. Passing into the few groups of towering trees, Tavin looked down a small ridge beneath him to reveal the small creek lying just beyond.

Eager to swiftly reach the fresh water and wash away the remnant of sleep still lingering about his face, he slid down the fairly steep incline to the creek. He reached the basin quickly and sprinted over to the flowing water, kneeling down to cup his soiled hands into the cool liquid. He quickly brought his hands full of sparkling water upward to splash into his face, waking every last cell in his body with its frigid touch.

As Tavin sat there washing the sleep away from his eyes in peace, a flicker of light from beside him disrupted the boy's blissful day dreaming. Bringing his dripping wet face down to investigate its source, he noticed that the luminous little crystal on the Sword of Granis had begun to shine brighter than usual. Confused, he reached down to further examine the weapon. Slowly unsheathing the blade to quiet its customary metallic ring, he locked his eyes onto the small but glorious crystal now flashing with light, almost as if trying to communicate.

It was at this moment that the first wave of it hit him yet again. As the Warrior of Light sat examining his weapon, an all too familiar sensation suddenly burst awake from inside his chest. As if his entire body was suddenly clamped together within a giant vice, the very air in his lungs withdrew as an explosion of rushing pain came to life inside. Releasing his grip on the Sword of Granis, he thrust his hands away from its glamorous hilt to his ailing torso containing the epicenter of his pain. Tavin sprawled onto the ground on his back, not able to think or do anything at all while the force of the pain tore through his body. The power of this attack had come much faster and harder than even the last, not even leaving him with the strength to call out for help. As the boy lay convulsing erratically on the damp earth, he could feel the attack killing him this time, leaving him more frightened than he had ever felt in his life.

"What the heck are you doing?" Jaren Garrinal asked curtly as he stared at Arilia Embrin with a questioning look on his face. Ril was quick to fire a scowl at the rude Grandarian boy from across the campfire. She sat with some bread in one hand and a small flame of her creation resting just under it in the palm of her other.

"What does it look like I'm doing?" she replied in an equally harsh tone of voice. "I'm toasting this cold bread so I can eat it. Despite what your mommy must have told you as a child, Jaren, there is such thing as a stupid question." The group of Legionnaires around the two consuming their own makeshift breakfasts (courtesy of the grateful citizens of Agealin Town) began to chuckle under their breath at the veritable war of words that raged on between the two. Jaren took a bite of his own bread before he responded with his mouth overflowing, purposefully disrespecting her.

"What, are you too good to use the fire in front of you? Do you need your own private flame to warm your food?" he asked mordantly. Ril dramatically sighed out loud and rose, extinguishing the enchanted flame in her palm. She squinted her fiery eyes at the obnoxious boy.

"I don't need this from you," she told him with ice hanging from her words. "Now if you'll excuse me, I'm leaving to check on a *kind* Grandarian boy. But you wouldn't know anything about that, would you?" Jaren threw his arms into the air and shook his head violently as an overly theatrical expression took form on his face.

"Nope. Not at all. I mean, he's only my best friend, for Granis' sake," Jaren retorted, rolling his eyes. Ril glared at him as she gathered some food to take to Tavin.

"How he can stomach you is beyond me," the girl snapped. "Do you think he's awake yet?" Jaren cocked his head and raised an eyebrow.

"Unfortunately, I've been sitting here with you all morning," he informed her brusquely. "How would I know? There is such thing as a stupid question, your highness." Ril's glare was upgraded to a look of deathly revulsion as she snatched up her food and spun around in a huff. Jaren shook his head as she marched off toward their provisional bedding.

"Women..." he managed, taking another bite of his breakfast.

After the Warrior of Fire stormed off from where she had consumed her breakfast, she made her way down the hill where they had left Tavin sleeping soundly earlier in the morning. As the party's bedding came into view, however, the girl noticed that his blankets were sprawled over the ground missing the person they had kept warm the previous night. Wondering where Tavin had gotten to if he had not come over to their campfire when he woke, Ril began to worry. Even if he had chosen to sit at another fire than hers, she or Jaren would have spotted him. It was then that she noticed a series of indentations in the tall grass that led away from their bedding in the opposite direction of the camps.

Though Ril was no tracker, she immediately set off following the steps in the deep grass that led into the small thicket of trees on the ridge of Agealin Town. As she grew closer to the entrance of the thicket, the sound of flowing water from the creek she had observed earlier echoed into her ears. Guessing Tavin had just went down to get a quick drink or wash himself, Ril relaxed but pressed onward into the thicket of trees at an enterprising pace.

As she stumbled through the dense foliage listening to the now very audible flowing creek sounding into the morning air, she at last came upon a steep incline at the edge of the trees to reveal the water she had heard. Ril quickly scanned her surroundings in search of Tavin, but he was nowhere to be found by the creek. When she was about to conclude that Tavin had moved further downstream or that she had just plain missed him on the way there, the reflection of a light at the base of the stream found its way to her eyes. Squinting to get a better view, she suddenly realized that the light was being reflected off the legendary Sword of Granis, just lying in the mud unsheathed and unattended.

Seeing Tavin's treasured sword lying in the mud told Ril something was definitely awry. Dropping the bundle of foods she held in her hands, the Warrior of Fire frantically jumped over the edge of the ridge and ran down the incline to its base that met with the small creek. Ril leaned down and hesitantly picked up the mighty sword from its disgraceful position on the ground and lifted it back into the air. To Ril's surprise, it was heavier than it had appeared seeing Tavin wield it with relative ease. Grasping the hilt, Ril noticed that the upper golden crystal on the blade was flickering; something that she thought it only did while Tavin held it. As she stared almost mesmerized, it suddenly flared outward and shot forth a beam of light from the deaths of its shining core. Still clutching the sword, Ril stared after the small ray of light that seemed to be pointing out away from her.

Following the beam to her left, she found what she was looking for. The sword's owner lay violently shaking and grasping at his chest huddled around a thick tree trunk. Ril gasped out loud as she recognized this attack on the Grandarian boy as the same from the night two weeks ago when they had first entered the Southland. Running over to him and calling out as she went, the light from the crystal dimmed in her grasp as if it knew she had found Tavin. Ril dropped the sword as she slid down to his level, putting her hands over his muddied chest apparently the source of his pain as it had been the last time.

"Tavin!" she called, getting no response other than painful wincing noises. Realizing that this attack was far worse than the one previous, she could only watch the boy struggle for breath and contort as if in the grip of a seizure. Remembering how powerless she had been last time, Ril felt a wave of helplessness overcoming her. Knowing she could do nothing to aid Tavin herself, she rose and lifted her hand to the skies. Summoning the most potent level of energy she could in the palm of her hand, a massive raging fireball quickly formed above her. When the inferno of flame was as large as she could make it in such a short timeframe, Ril brought forth her other arm to send the blast of fire shooting skyward at a raging velocity.

As it passed through the trees singeing their branches as it went, it finally rose above them and into the clear atmosphere. Upon reaching the pinnacle of its rise skyward, Ril's already energy pulsating fist clenched tight, signaling for the fireball to detonate in midair and scatter streaking embers in all directions. Satisfied the entire camp must have noticed her call for help, Ril brought her attention back to the weakening form of the Warrior of Light huddled against the tree trunk. Sitting beside him and letting Tavin grab at her hand as he convulsed uncontrollably, the girl tried a weak smile through her overworked emotions.

"It's going to be alright, Tavin," she spoke out to him uncertain but comforting all the same. "Zeroan is here this time. He'll know what to do. Just hold on until he gets here, Tavin. Just hold on."

As Ril sat trying her best to soothe Tavin, the camp above the thicket had instantly come to new life as the spectacle above the trees came into view. As Ril had hoped, the Mystic Sage Zeroan was the first to be on his way to the source of the gigantic display of fire. Running through the rows of Legionnaires, his gray hooded face tightened with worry at what might have caused Ril to do something as drastic as this to get his attention. He reached the far end of the camp quickly and found Jaren standing in awe with the rest of the men until he turned to see the approaching sage dashing by.

"Zeroan!" he yelled. "Was that Ril?"

"Of course it was!" he yelled back to the boy as he sprinted on. "She must be in some sort of trouble to do something like that. Are you just going to stand there?" Even though the fervent Elemental Warrior from the west was not his favorite person in the world, Jaren's good heart and thrill for adventure thrust him forward, slinging his bow and arrows over his back.

The two ran on through the group's bedding from the night before causing Jaren to notice Tavin was missing from his bed. Realizing his best friend could be in danger as well, the Grandarian archer sped forward all the faster. At top speed, Jaren and Zeroan made good time into the thicket of the trees and over the ridge where view of the creek appeared. Maneuvering through the trees, Jaren could just follow the rapid sage's flying cloak and hope he knew where they were going. As the two ran along the ridge, Zeroan suddenly halted and spun around at the faint sound of a small voice behind him. Jaren stopped as well, turning back to find Zeroan already leaping over an incline leading down to the flowing water at its base. Confused but trusting the sage's judgment, he did the same to meet with Zeroan listening carefully for where the calls for help were originating.

"Zeroan!" came the emotional cry to their left in a dense patch of trees. Both the sage and Jaren spun around to find Tavin sprawled on the ground in the grip of what appeared to be some sort of a seizure with Ril hovering just over him with worry embedded into her delicate face. Jaren slumped back in anguish to see Tavin in the same condition he had been in weeks ago when this sickness first struck.

"Oh no, not again..." Jaren managed rushing over to Tavin. Zeroan quickly turned back to him with a frustrated and questioning look on his haggard face.

"What do you mean, 'not again?'" he asked fearfully. Jaren only pointed to Ril as they both arrived and knelt down to Tavin's level.

"You're the one who saw this last time," Jaren reminded Ril. "You better tell him what's going on." Ril nodded, fumbling over her words as she struggled to explain.

"Zeroan, this is the second time I've found him like this," she told him motioning down to the convulsing boy in a sweat. "Last time he managed to tell us there was a piercing pain tearing at his chest. He fell asleep and the next morning it was nearly completely gone. But this time he can't even respond when I talk to him..." Ril trailed off as Tavin gripped her hand even tighter through his wild movements. Zeroan was quick to inquire for more information as he set to work examining the boy for the source of his pain.

"Arilia, do you have any idea what could be causing this?" he asked her reaching down to remove Tavin's cape and armor to get a better look at his chest. Ril did not respond but instead held her gaze on Tavin. "Ril?" he pressed hurriedly, needing an answer. Just as she was about to respond no, she remembered something that Tavin had told her the first time the sickness struck.

"When I was tending to him last time, he told me that he thought it might be related to his power as the Warrior of Light. He said that every time his elemental power had come out since that battle at Galantia this pain had hit him worse and worse but every time it eventually faded away." Zeroan looked at her skeptically hearing this.

"That doesn't make any sense," he returned with aggravation. "The power of the Warrior of Light does not leave any side affects on the body when he is finished using it. As long as he bears the Sword of Granis while using the power, this should not happen. He's had it with him since the moment he first laid eyes on it in the Tower of Granis." Ril shot her free hand out to point down at Tavin and yelled at the sage.

"Then what is this all about!" she snapped at him, caught up in distress. Despite all of his vast knowledge, the sage could not find an answer. He knew a great deal about illnesses and healing from his long experience, but he had never seen anything this powerful strike someone unprovoked. Though he didn't believe it to be possible, there did not seem to be any other reason why Tavin would have been subjugated to this kind of illness unless it did somehow relate to his newfound power sealing incorrectly. As the boy continued to grasp at his chest, he was now beginning to scream out loud, causing Ril to nearly totally lose control of her emotions. "Zeroan," she called to him helplessly, "you have an arsenal of mystic powers and magics at your disposal! Do something!" Returning her gaze almost as helplessly, Zeroan finally acted and reached down for the convulsing Warrior of Light heaving him over his massive shoulder and standing up. The sage motioned with his head for the two to stand.

"Jaren, retrieve the Sword of Granis from the creek. Follow me quickly, Ril," he ordered them, already turning back over the steep incline back to the camp. Ril gathered herself up after the sage crying out to him for an answer.

"Zeroan, what are you going to do?" she asked him frantically. The sage just kept on running over the hillside with Tavin over his shoulder, not having the heart to tell her that he didn't know.

Chapter 30

<u>Road to Torrentcia</u>

It was not long after Tavin's mysterious illness suddenly reappeared that the party from Galantia and the entire camp of Legionnaires were off and moving back to the capital city of the Southland, Torrentcia City. The Mystic Sage Zeroan had told the members of his party the night before that after they were separated at the Great Rift, he was cut off in his escape by a wall of marauders from the Purging Flame, and had to take another even more secret and dangerous route around them, costing him a great deal of time. Discovering that the Purging Flame had been empowered by Drakkaidian soldiers that had somehow slipped over the border and were now controlling the marauders, he knew they would surely find his party sooner or later across the expansive fields of the northeast Southland.

After penetrating through the mountains and into the Southland, the sage encountered a Legion battalion marching north to Torrentcia City. Utilizing his renowned authority and persuasive skill, he managed to commandeer them for a brief time to march back east and destroy the corrupted Purging Flame ravaging local villages on the outskirts of the Torrentcia territories, hoping to find his party before his enemy did. Marching the battalion to the largest town in the northeast plains, Zeroan arrived just in time to find his comrades fending off nearly two hundred of the marauders. After the battle was won, Zeroan informed his company that they would now be moving west across the plains as originally planned to Torrentcia City, though his motives for going there had now changed with the discovery of Drakkaidians already across the border.

Saying their goodbyes to the grateful people of Agealin Town, the party and Legionnaires began marching westward into the Torrentcia territories at the grueling pace that Zeroan had become infamous for. As the enormous band roamed across the fields of the northern Southland, they encountered a wide variety of visual wonders that the Grandarian boy Jaren had never seen the likes of before. The wetlands of the Torrentcia territories boasted creeks, streams, and rivers everywhere over the landscape; almost covering the surface more than the land. Much like the luscious scenery around Agealin Town only bordering on the territories, groups of towering willow trees full of wildlife were littered across the earth, raining their gently falling leaves as the faint breeze wafted through the air.

Zeroan, however, was not as concerned with the surrounding milieu as he was with the young Warrior of Light still hanging onto life behind him. As they traveled, Tavin remained in a perpetual seizure-like state. The only thing keeping him from falling down from the horse he sat on was the Warrior of Fire along side him, repositioning him by the minute. With Tavin's condition only growing worse with every passing day, Ril's own well being had begun to seriously deteriorate as she helplessly watched him sit in agony, most likely dying from the attack that would not fade away. As they rode on, Jaren had fastened the Sword of Granis back at Tavin's side, hoping that its power might do something to aid him. Unfortunately, the sword lay inactive but for the top golden crystal on its hilt that continued to flicker with light.

It was the better part of a week later when they arrived at the Southland capital in the afternoon. As sight of a massive plateau of sorts came into Jaren's enthralled view, he found a mighty citadel over it that's beauty and craftsmanship nearly equaled that of his own nation's capital of Galantia. With sharp towers glistening skywards in the afternoon sunlight, the silvery fortresses stood like the Southland's own personal guardian, overseeing all that rested before it. Behind the castle lying peacefully in the heart of the plateau was the most expansive body of water Jaren had ever laid eyes on.

The excited Grandarian boy quickly turned back to make his way to the gray cloaked figure of Zeroan marching on in his usual staid manner, letting out a faint sigh sighting Jaren approach.

"What is it this time?" he asked sardonically. Jaren squinted at the sage, but ignored his curt comment to point up at the massive fortress on the plateau in front of them.

"So that's Torrentcia City?" he asked in disbelief. Zeroan nodded his head and began to offer some background to appease the boy's curiosity.

"It is. And unlike Grandaria's capital of Galantia, this city is relatively new. It was only completed about the time you were born, I would guess. There used to be a smaller fortress where the Legion would gather, but after it was taken by a small force of Drakkaidians that managed to penetrate the border about a century ago in the second Holy War, the a council decided to relocate the capital. It was moved to what was left of a stronghold here on top of this naturally protected plateau surrounded by steep cliffs and the massive Lake Torrent just to its west.

"But that was not the only reason the city was built here," Zeroan stated, leaving Jaren curious. The sage turned his hooded face down to meet with Jaren's. "Don't you find it a little odd that a lake the size of the one in front of us has formed there when there is no mountain water of any kind flowing into it? In fact, the lake itself in on top of the plateau. Water cannot flow uphill, so how did that lake come into being?" Jaren frowned up at the sage for making him feel particularly dumb in this matter. All he could do was shrug clueless.

Zeroan merely chuckled seeing how badly he had puzzled the boy.

"Don't worry yourself over that, young Grandarian," he told him. "The cause of Lake Torrent's formation is most unnatural. Do you see that blue stoned peak high above all the other silver ones in the city?" Jaren shifted his gaze up to the towering walled citadel to locate the single blue tower that the sage had spoken of. "That is not a part of the city. That is the tower jetting out of the Elemental Temple of Water. Because the Source of all water in the world is found right on top of that plateau, this area has been drastically altered. Before the temple's existence, it used to be a barren wasteland, dead and devoid of any life from the Battle of the Gods eons ago. But when Granis separated the six elements apart from each other and the ancients encased them in the elemental temples, the lands where they rested took on characteristics of that element. This area, for example, has been transformed from a desolate wasteland into the fruitful wetland streaming with water as it is today.

202

"A constant river is continuously pouring out of the Elemental Temple up there, keeping Lake Torrent overflowing, which in turn keeps the various rivers and streams flowing." Jaren stood amazed at this revelation, never believing the elemental temples could affect the lands this much. It was at this point that Zeroan stopped and turned back for a moment, beckoning Jaren to do the same. Obeying the Mystic Sage, Zeroan led him back to the horse that carried the still ailing Warrior of Light. Ril remained standing beside him keeping the boy as comfortable as possible. In the excitement of seeing these new lands, Jaren had nearly forgotten about his best friend.

When Zeroan met back up with Ril, he whistled out loud into the groups of Legionnaires behind him. Not long after, the two Southlanders Parnox and Kohlin came bustling forward to meet with their leader. Upon their arrival, Zeroan began to address them all.

"All right, everyone," he began. "One stage of our journey is over. We have successfully made it into the Southland and temporarily away from the forces of Drakkaidia, but that will not last for long. We will rest here at Torrentcia City for tonight for two reasons, neither of which I had anticipated. First of all, our young Warrior of Light is in bad condition, and I regretfully do not know how to treat him for I do not know the nature of the sickness that has seen fit to attack him. To be perfectly honest with all of you, I believe that Tavin is slowly dying as we speak." These words tore into the group, especially at Jaren and Ril.

"Unfortunately, there is most likely little time now. If I cannot find a solution to this problem in the next few days, we may very well lose him. While it was merely a night of rest that saved him last time, I do not believe this will be the case now. These erratic convulsions are only growing worse." Zeroan gathered his robes about him once more as he lifted his head and changed the tone of his gruff voice to move on to another topic. "The other reason we must stop here is the Sarton." At the mention of this name, Ril and the other two Southlanders in the group suddenly let out a sighs of frustration and looks of disgruntlement cross their faces. Jaren remained puzzled.

"So this guy isn't all that popular, huh?" he asked them. Parnox grunted at that statement.

"Damned fool," he muttered under his breath. Kohlin and Ril both nodded at this. Zeroan motioned for them to calm themselves with a downward movement of his hand. He turned to Jaren and began to explain.

"While his servants around him think the world of the current Sarton, you can plainly see that there are others that do not think as much of him. For over a century now, the Southland Legion and the entire Southland has been under the command of one man during times of emergency that the various lands elect every so often. This position is known as the Sarton of the Legion. The current Sarton, Ecriate Bon Othan, has not proven himself to be the greatest leader we have ever seen. During his command over the Legion, he has completely turned a deaf ear to its generals' voices and only followed his own foolish mind in making more that his fair share of less than wise decisions.

"His weak control over the Legion is going to cost the entire Southland more than they can afford if its full strength is not mustered and mobilized at the border soon. The Legion has not been needed since the last Holy War, so it has fallen into disorganization over time. The general of this battalion has also informed me the Sarton has what is left of the Legion divided and spread all over the Southland after the demon sightings. This is exactly what Montrox is sure to be hoping for when he eventually storms the border. There will be minimal resistance to oppose him. The Sarton must be convinced to order his troops to the border and quit wasting their time investigating the reports of activity that they can do nothing about. Ril was quick to interject hearing this.

"Zeroan, you know he won't listen to you," she stated, tucking Tavin back onto the saddle of the horse. "Othan can't stand the sages, much less you in particular. After my anointment, there is no way he'll see you." Jaren looked at her curiously.

"What happened there?" he asked. Zeroan stepped in to answer that.

"The Sarton has never been a supporter of anything magical in nature: the sages, the Grandarians and their few remaining powers, or even the Elemental Warriors of his own nation. When he heard Arilia, a young girl, was to be the new Warrior of Fire years ago in her early childhood, he personally set off to the Elemental Temple of Fire to try and stop it. I was there to 'remind' him that it was not his place to deny the anointment of a chosen Elemental Warrior. He has had the utmost hatred for me since that day when I humiliated him and overrode his power." Zeroan once more changed the subject as the enormous ramp that led over a river and up to the top of the plateau came into view.

"But enough of this," he said to them. "The Sarton is sure to be furious to learn that I had commandeered a battalion he specifically ordered directly to Torrentcia City, so our presence will not be welcome in the citadel. We will secure a room in a local inn I have stayed at before. The innkeeper is a good man and will take care of Tavin while the rest of you get some well deserved rest of your own. Go out and have a good meal tonight. I will venture into the citadel and face the Sarton. Hopefully, I can convince him to summon the full Legion from its state of dormancy.

"From there, I will be in the libraries. While they are not as complete as the ones at Galantia or the Mystic Tower to the east, some sort of answer to Tavin's problem might be found there. I will meet with you at the inn later. For now, just follow my lead. And you," he said pointing to Jaren with an untold fury ready to encompass his entire face, "don't do or say *anything* without me or my permission." Jaren just squinted at the sage as the group began their accent up the roundabout pass to the glorious city above them.

As they walked, Jaren noticed Ril eyeing Zeroan strangely. Perplexed, he turned and whispered to Parnox.

"What's her deal with Zeroan, Parnox? I can understand why she isn't a big fan of the guy, but she really doesn't like him." The burly Southlander brought his gaze down to him, a knowing look in his eyes.

"You couldn't have known this, Jaren," he said quietly, "but they have a bit of a history. You see, while most every sage anoints Elemental Warriors several times in his life, Zeroan has never, and I mean never, done it before that day almost twenty years ago. Ril was the first person he had ever anointed, and he did it when she was a baby; not even old enough to speak. That's why the Sarton and the other sages hate him. Elemental Warriors are supposed to be chosen because they have proven themselves in life. But no one could stop him, because he is a sage and it is his right. No one knows why he did it, and to this day Ril is still...

frustrated with him for it." Jaren looked back to the Warrior of Fire, then to Zeroan, once more unsure of what was truly behind him.

Chapter 31

<u>Silver City</u>

As the two Grandarians and the gargantuan party of Southlanders made their way up the rounding hillside path that led to the uppermost level of the plateau, Jaren could at last begin to see the base of the mighty Southland capital. The city itself was concealed inside a barricade of walls that surrounded the perimeter of the small plateau, only opening at the massive gate that he and the others were now approaching. As the groups of Legionnaires massing around the walls of the archway called downward to the guards at the base of the gate, it slowly lurched with an enormous grinding noise, causing Jaren to almost jump out of his skin.

As the thick wooden gates began to slowly open, Jaren's eyes grew wide as view of the silver city began to reveal itself in all its glory. Catching the amazement mirrored in the young Grandarian's eyes, Zeroan spoke.

"You look surprised," he said. "This city is nothing much compared to your own nation's capital." Jaren looked back and shrugged.

"Maybe, but I've seen Galantia a hundred times. This is something new for a change, and it's a heck of a lot more modern looking." Zeroan smiled and silently chuckled.

As the party from Galantia passed through the massive wooden gates in front of the Legionnaires, Zeroan instructed them to wait by the entrance to the city ahead while he thanked the general once more. Jaren nodded as he moved forward, admiring his surroundings.

"Yeah, this place isn't half bad," he stated to no one in particular, getting a laugh out of the burly Parnox, bringing his arm down to pat the boy on the back.

"No it's not," he confirmed with a smile. "It's not much compared to your big city in Grandaria, but it works just fine for us Southlanders." As Parnox gave Jaren a little more history of the city, Zeroan finally bid farewell to the battalion of Legionnaires and made his way back over to his companions, pulling his thick gray cloak taut around his body. Parnox gave him a strange look. "Cold?" he asked. The sage merely concealed himself tighter before responding.

"There are more than a few eyes and ears of the Sarton that would not be pleased to find me walking abroad in these streets," he informed them. "I do not wish to be seen by any of his lapdog spies wandering the city." The sage shifted his gaze to the exhausted redhead still beside Tavin. "How is he doing, Arilia?" Ril swiftly finished checking the boy's burning fever and turned harshly, impatience in her eyes.

"How does it look like?" she replied bitterly, not able to keep her aggravation of what was happening to Tavin at bay. "He's dying, and if we don't do something quick there's no telling how long he will last." Zeroan remained still for a moment noting the girl's aggravation, then nodded silently and began again in a hushed tone.

"Very well, then," he continued. "Sitting on top of that horse is not doing him any good. The inn that I spoke of is not to far away from here." The sage motioned up past the garrisons where an opening of buildings caught the group's attention. "It is father up that hill, in the heart of the city's marketplace. Follow me and do not stray. The last thing we need is someone getting lost," Zeroan said, glaring down at Jaren who just stared back defensively.

After Parnox gently lifted the ailing Warrior of Light from the steed and situated him in his muscular arms, the party of six set off through the busy city streets toward the inn farther up the plateau. Moving into the bustling marketplace, Jaren found himself surrounded by swarms of townspeople jostling through each other. While the plateau was quite large in appearance from the outside, the majority of its space was reserved for the citadel and Lake Torrent higher up, leaving the actual city feeling a bit more congested than it needed to be. The people obviously made do, however. Vibrant decorations and loud activity jauntily cluttered across the streets displayed the exciting splendor and spirit that easily matched the golden city of Galantia.

Being the diverse area it was, the marketplace attracted all sorts of people, some obviously less fortunate than others, and the city seemed somehow poorer because of it. Compared to the proud Galantia where even plebeians and common folk were fairly well off, dirtied faces wrought with strain from life's hardships made up a major portion of the populace here. This stood out to Jaren as the perfect example why Grandaria remained a generally more successful nation than its neighbor to the south. With its unflagging unity under Lord Granis and the presence of the strong central government, it had always been able to take care of its entire populace. The Southland, in contrast, was established ages later as a massive, completely open land that would have no primary government to rule. Though this essentially made the Southland a freer place to live than Grandaria, it suffered from its diversity more than it gained when it needed to come together. People who lived here were independent by nature, and those who were less fortunate seemed to stay that way.

Pressing onward through the marketplace, the group exited the cluttered streets and entered a massive courtyard. Jaren marveled at the sudden beauty of the city that now lay before him free from the clamor of the streets behind. The courtyard was surrounded by homes and businesses along its perimeter, with two roads on its opposite ends. The road behind them lead back down to the lower city and the marketplace, while the high road in front of them opened up to the higher class sector of the city, leading up to the citadel and Lake Torrent. In the center of the courtyard, an ornate and colorful fountain powered by the nearby Elemental Temple sat spewing crystal clean water from its numerous apertures, delivering a constant wave of mist washing over Jaren's face.

Though Zeroan had told him to stay close, the boy could not help but scurry over to the other end of the courtyard to get a better view of the higher city. Rushing to an opening between two of the buildings to a ledge over the courtyard, Jaren stood in awe as his eyes fell onto the resplendent pinnacle of the plateau. The silver citadel of the Southland sat basking in all its glory as if carefully watching the entire country beneath it to keep it safe with its protective gaze. Below and beyond the fortress lay the massive Lake Torrent, and resting at its center was the towering Temple of Water, jetting its single blue peak far up into the sky above the clouds. From its tallest peak Jaren could make out a brilliant azure light shining forth. Though he could not see the temple's base, he could see it was not built into a castle like the Temple of Light in Galantia. In fact, the structure looked more like a massive lighthouse than a temple. Though not as elaborate as the Temple of Light, it was still a glamorous sight to behold.

As Jaren stood wondering how a structure so massive could have ever been erected, a shadow appeared behind him covering his entire body. He quickly sped around to find Zeroan standing behind him once more. Jaren breathed deeply in relief it was only the sage.

"Has anyone ever told you have a bad habit of sneaking up on people?" Jaren asked. The Mystic Sage smiled darkly at the boy.

"At least I didn't have to incapacitate you like last time," he reminded, citing the first time they had met back in Eirinor Village. Jaren scowled at the sage.

"Don't remind me," he curtly replied. Zeroan chuckled darkly again as he pulled the boy back away from the ledge and toward the courtyard once again.

"I told you not to go running off, didn't I?" he asked. Jaren gave him an incredulous look.

"How am I not supposed to notice that?" he stated pointing back to the Elemental Temple. Zeroan nodded indicating he understood.

"Yes, it is quite a spectacle. While not as overall impressive as the Temple of Light, it is fantastic in its own unique way. All of the water in the Southland flows from the Source of Water at the pinnacle of the temple's tower." Jaren held his gaze confused as they passed across the courtyard and its aqueous fountain.

"I don't get that," he stated puzzled. "Where does it all come from?"

"I just told you. The water is manifested in the temple's Source. Every temple has at its core, a Source, where all of its elemental power exists in raw, energetic form, creating the physical nature of the element that we see every day. Just like this Source gives us water, the Source in the east in the Temple of Wind creates the air that we breathe. You see, we are dependent on the various Elemental Temples to survive. They are responsible for creating, maintaining, and empowering all the elemental power that correspond with them and provide life." Jaren still harbored a deep level of bemusement, but tried to make the best sense out of it as he could. Zeroan shook his head seeing he was still not satisfied. "Perhaps it's best if you just accept things for the way they are and don't dwell on them too hard. I wouldn't want you to hurt yourself thinking before this journey is over."

As Jaren searched for an appropriate retort for the condescending statement, they finally arrived at the inn Zeroan spoke of. It was a small but quaint building nestled into the rows of the others, almost unnoticeable to a passing traveler. Zeroan pushed the door open and entered, moving past the empty innkeeper's desk. Proceeding past it, the sage led Jaren up a small staircase to a hall on the upper level with rooms along its sides. The door at the far end of the hall was open, revealing the familiar sound of a young girl's voice calling out to the Mystic Sage from inside. Zeroan made his way down the hallway and into the room to find Parnox, Kohlin and Ril all sitting around a bed containing Tavin in anguish from his condition.

"He's getting worse, Zeroan," Ril called out with a worried expression latched onto her fatigued face. Zeroan nodded as he strode over to the end of the bed with Jaren moving over to the two Southlanders on the other side.

"Yes, I know," he told her shaking his head. "But as you well know, there is nothing further we can do for him at this time. For now, I suggest that you all, and you especially Arilia, take some time to rest yourselves. You need it." Ril was on her feet with anger hearing this.

"And leave him here by himself if he should need us? Don't tell me what I need, sage. Go if you wish, but I'm staying here," she declared with passion. Parnox was the first to respond to the girl's outburst. He gently laid his hand over Ril's shoulder and stared straight into her eyes.

"Ril, I know you're concerned about the boy; we all are. But Zeroan is right. You can't see it but you're working and worrying yourself into the ground. You need to take a breather." Zeroan chimed back in to put her worries to rest.

"The innkeeper here has a wife who has volunteered to look after Tavin for a short while. There is a tavern of sorts across the courtyard. You can eat something and be back here before an hour has passed if you wish." Ril brought her head down to Tavin, realizing just how tired she was after tending to him for so many days. She was physically and emotionally drained to the point where even the smallest break sounded like a lifelong vacation. Though still reluctant, she at last gave in and agreed to take her leave for dinner as she rubbed the fatigue from her eyes with her wrists.

"Fine. But I'm not going to be gone long. The sun is setting right now. I want to be back here well before it's gone," Ril said, stating her terms. The others gladly accepted, retreating to their own rooms and unpacked their belongings to be ready for dinner. Jaren was about to set out his own things in Tavin's room when Ril grabbed hold of his pack and thrust it onto his back once more. "You can have my room down the hall for the night," she told him. Jaren brought his head forward in disbelief.

"*What*?" he asked sharply. Ril raised her eyebrows and pointed for him to proceed out the door as she continued.

"You heard me," she responded. "I'm not entrusting Tavin's health to you all night long. Though you claim to be his best friend, I don't recall you helping him at all since this happened. You've been at the front marveling at the land and city instead." Jaren stumbled back unable to comprehend the girl's logic.

"That's because every time I got near him you threatened to kill me like a dog protecting its meat!" he shouted angrily. Ril did not change her mind.

"You might as well stop wasting your breath. I'm staying here tonight and that's all there is to it. Now you can either get to your room right now," she told him raising her fist with a ball of fire igniting around it, "or I can help you out. Which will it be?" Jaren stared at the stubborn tomboy incredulously, nearly ready to lose it himself.

"That's it!" he yelled at the top of his lungs, causing the whole inn to stir awake wondering what was going on in the room. "I've taken orders from you for too long! You may be an Elemental Warrior, but I still outrank you on the friendship scale for that guy over there!" Jaren's face warped with antagonism. "Now you better get off my back or I'm liable to get angry and teach you some manners you nasty little-" Jaren was immediately cut off by an incredibly tight grip suddenly clamping down around his neck. Summoning what strength he could, Jaren stared up to find a *very* unhappy looking Zeroan with enraged eyes burning into his own. For the second time, he had the Grandarian boy in a chokehold completely restricting his airflow.

"Enough!" he hissed at them both, looking up at Ril as well. "You two children are going to get us thrown out if you don't close your mouths! Since you are both obviously too immature to settle a simple matter like this, I will take the liberty for you." Zeroan released his iron grip on Jaren and powerfully threw him aside onto the twin bed next to Tavin's as if light as a feather. "Jaren will stay in this room with Tavin," he suddenly ordered, causing Ril to rise with fury again. Her anger was instantly dwarfed by the sage's, however, as he quickly rose to meet her, towering over her comparatively small form. "No more, girl," he spoke with supreme authority, putting her rebuttal to silence with his furious eyes alone. "I understand you wish to remain at Tavin's side, but the whelp over there is right in his argument. You have forgotten your place in this matter. Jaren is Tavin's best friend and he will tend to his health accordingly. Should he require your assistance during the night, he is more than welcome to call for it." Jaren let out a huff rising from the bed.

"Fat chance," he mumbled coldly. Zeroan wheeled on him and threw him back onto the bed to stare him down irately.

"And you, Jaren Garrinal, will not address the Warrior of Fire and a lady in such a manner. I told you both in Galantia that I would not stand for this kind of behavior on this quest. Furthermore, boy, if you don't drop this cocky, flippant, belligerent, impudent, pig headed, and overall worthless attitude toward your fellow companions right here and now and forever after, I *promise* that I will make it so you will never be able plague us with your senseless babble again! Is that *perfectly* understood!?!" Jaren was now paralyzed with fear on the bed, cowering back from the sage's vehemence. "I said is that understood!?!" he pressed in rage. Jaren quickly nodded up and down in a delirious manner, causing even Ril to take a little pity on him. Zeroan grit his teeth at the two once more as he rose back up and gathered his dark gray robes about him and turned to face Parnox and Kohlin standing at the doorway, eyes wide open surprised at the sage's outburst.

The Mystic Sage calmed himself and began to address them all.

"That is the end of that," he stated. "Now it is time for us to depart. If I can still get the innkeepers wife to watch Tavin, you all need to be off to get some relaxation for the night. I will be off to see the Sarton this evening, so I will not be back until long after dark. If anyone needs to say anything, do so now." No questions came, the entire group still a little terrified of the sage right then. Zeroan nodded and moved toward the doorway turning back once more to Ril and Jaren with malice in his eyes. "Now you two make up. And I mean now. If I hear even one report of the slightest hostility between you two, I swear there will be hell to pay that you will never see the likes of in the Netherworld itself." After the sage finished, he immediately set out through the doorway, the tails of his robes whipping along after him as he strode away mumbling under his breath. Parnox was the first to speak after the very long silence that followed.

"So..." he began, "shall we get going, Kohlin?" The Windrun Warrior nodded in response and quickly bolted along after Parnox, leaving Ril and Jaren to themselves. Jaren slowly rose from the bed, straightening his wrinkled clothing and bringing his flustered eyes to meet with the equally uncomfortable Warrior of Fire. He slowly dusted himself off to postpone the apology that he had been ordered to offer. After the longest awkward silence either of the two had ever experienced, Jaren at last cleared his throat and spoke.

"Sorry," he managed to choke out. Ril nodded in response.

"Me too," she seconded. Jaren cocked his head in wonder as he collected himself again.

"If Tavin could have just heard that, I'd never hear the end of it," he stated, causing Ril to actually smile. It was not long after the two finally made peace that the kind innkeeper's wife arrived in the room to watch after Tavin. Though he had apparently fallen asleep at last, neither his erratic movements nor his irregular breathing had ceased. When both Jaren and Ril were satisfied that Tavin was in good hands for the moment, they reluctantly made their way out of the room after the two Southlanders headed for the tavern.

Chapter 32

<u>Politics</u>

In the aftermath of the battle at Agealin Town, the remaining populace had been quick to organize a clean up crew to properly dispose of the dead bodies of the Purging Flame littering the ridge where their number had been cut down by the battalion of Legionnaires. As the following night had descended upon them, however, the townspeople had retreated back into their homes for the evening, leaving a multitude of dead marauders still rotting out on the fields. Amidst the dead, one man in the middle of the field remained alive, having somehow clung to life this long despite his severe wound to the chest from the day before and his lack of food and water. Lying crippled in his bloodstained robes, he stared up at the placid stars waiting for death to eventually take him.

Just before he was about to let his ravaged body drift into what might have been its final sleep, however, a perceptible sound caught the attention of his dulled senses not to far behind him. As the dying marauder looked back, a looming figure gingerly appeared just over his head, blocking off the faintly moonlit sky above him. The figure slowly knelt before him with no expression on his dark face whatsoever. Several uncomfortable moments passed before the now delirious man spoke out to the figure.

"Are you the spirit of death?" the shivering marauder asked. The figure did not respond, simply holding the dying man's gaze with an unmoving shadowed face. Eventually, the dark figure drew a savage broadsword from behind his back and lowered it to the man's level, resting its blade upon his blood dampened chest.

"Verix will do," the figure at last replied in a concealing tone. "Before I ease your pain, I have a question to ask of you." The shaking man silently nodded, seeing no reason not to answer with his final moments upon him. "Good. Now who was it who did this to your band of marauders? Besides the Legion, I mean." The man tried hard to think back to the battle the day before, trying to remember what had befallen him to lead him to this fate. His glazed eyes opened suddenly, revealing the answer.

"I was struck down by naught but a boy," the man responded. The figure remained stoic as he turned the blade of his savage sword to its edge upon the man's chest.

"Did this boy possess magic?" the figure pressed on. The man again thought for a moment and nodded his head yes.

"A sword," he said. "A glowing sword that cut me down." The figure was satisfied with this answer. He rose then, his gray tattered and battle-scarred coat shifting as a quiet breeze ruffled through the dank evening air. "Very well. Thank you for your assistance." With that, the dark figure began walking away, his savage broadsword dematerializing into a shroud of foaming crimson light. As he made his way over the hillside past the dying marauder, he quickly snapped his fingers into the night air. Not long after the self-appointed spirit of death had passed him by, another set of footsteps sounded into the man's ears. Struggling to bring his head up to see past his bloody chest, a fearsome shadowy form stood on all fours just in front of him. Frozen with fear, the marauder never even had time to scream before the gruesome Liradd was upon him. Verix Montrox was catching up to his prey.

In the main chambers of the citadel in Torrentcia City, Sarton Ecriate Bon Othan was furious.

"I will not have my halls defiled with his presence!" the Sarton boomed, rising from his elegant throne to send his commanding voice echoing through his illustrious silver chambers. "That man is not welcome here. He is not to be allowed entrance. That is an order, Captain Morrol." With this order perfectly clear, the young captain of the Southland Legion respectfully bowed his head and withdrew from his leader's throne room. Passing through the doorway back to the hallway outside, he came face to face with the other upset man he was trying to deal with. The captain raised his arms and shrugged in defeat.

"I'm sorry," he began, "but the Sarton has ordered me to-"

"-deny me entrance," the heavily cloaked figure before him finished. "Yes, I heard the Sarton's tirade for myself. But I tell you again, this matter is of the utmost importance. Believe me when I say that the Sarton needs to hear my council for the sake of the entire Southland. I must be allowed an audience." The captain shook his head, mentally cursing his bad luck to be forced into such problems.

"What would you have me do, sage?" he asked almost helplessly, surprising both sentries around the door. "The Sarton has denied you entrance, and I cannot do anything about it. I have already pled your case before him twice now. He will not change his mind. You know that, so why do you persist?" Though frustrated with the captain's hopeless attitude, he knew he was right. Othan was a stubborn fool and would not allow him inside. It was then that Zeroan was struck with an idea.

"Very well," he stated suddenly, turning back for the hall behind him. The unexpected retreat astounded the captain, amazed he had given up so easily. Upon reaching the end of the hallway, however, Zeroan stopped and looked around at the three different hallways before him, turning back with a puzzled look about his shadowed face. "Pardon me, Captain, but I seem to have lost my bearings in this large castle again. Do you suppose you could help me find my way out?" Captain Morrol let out a huff of air but feigned a smile. Walking down to guide him out, he disappeared down the hallway to the left with Zeroan following after him.

It was not more than a few minutes later when the captain reappeared, smiling and rolling his eyes to the sentries around the door.

"For a sage, he's not all that wise," he chuckled, getting a smile out of the sentries as well. "If you'll excuse me, gentlemen, I wish to report to the Sarton in private. If you would be so kind as to move down to the far end of the hallway until I am finished." Following orders, the two guards moved down to the far end of the hallway to reassume their duties there. With the guards gone, the young captain opened the doorway to the Sarton's throne room once more. Upon his entrance, the Sarton rose from his table where he stood drinking alone, eager to hear his captain's report.

"Thank you for ridding me of the pest, Morrol," Othan said turning his back on the captain to pour himself another glass of ale. "It's simply amazing how even the most worthless of people are allowed to assume positions of power in this world."

"I couldn't agree more, Othan," a deep voice sounded through the chamber. Realizing the voice did not belong to his captain, the Sarton turned back in dismay to find the man suddenly morphing into a taller figure cloaked in gray, merely standing before him after the transformation was complete. A deeply rooted frown made its way onto the Sarton's face as he quickly shot down his ale and slammed the glass back to the table.

"How clever of you, sage," Othan said spitefully. "Haven't I seen you do that before?" The Mystic Sage Zeroan shifted in his robes and answered coldly.

"I used the same technique to infiltrate your guard the last time we met, Sarton," he reminded. "A simple mystic magic to shortly copy the appearance of someone as long as they remain peacefully asleep, as your captain safely is just down the hallway." Othan nodded and moved back to his throne atop the steps behind him.

"Well as long as you're here," Othan continued, apparently giving in to the sage's presence, "what is it that you want?"

"Just for you to hear me out," Zeroan stated coolly. "Since you chose not to send one of your representatives to me at Galantia when I called for them there, I am bringing my council to you."

"I chose not to send a representative because I do not desire your council on any matter," Othan coldly replied. Zeroan continued to step forward with frustration building in his eyes.

"You need it more than you know, Sarton. On my way here I encountered four of your outlaying villages to the northeast looted, burned, and completely destroyed by marauders." Othan disrespectfully rested his head on his fist as he responded.

"So you took the liberty to commandeer an entire battalion of my Legionnaires to do my job for me, is that it? I do not need your help in defending my own country from the marauders of the Purging Flame or other such mercenary factions."

"Not to defend your country from marauders, but you do need my help to defend your country from Drakkaidians already inside your borders." The Sarton went silent for a moment before he let out a huff of vexation.

"You have lost your mind sage," the Sarton replied. "Not one Drak soldier has set foot in the Southland for over a century. They cannot and will not ever get past the Legion." Zeroan was quick to jump at him at this.

"What Legion?" he asked in disbelief. "Your defenses at the border are pitiful. There are only a few patrols stationed along miles and miles of open territory ready to be stormed. What is left of the old Legion is spread all over the Southland scattered and leaderless." The Sarton sat forward with a quiet rage now present in his eyes as well.

"What are you suggesting, sage?" he asked bitterly.

"I am suggesting that unless you gather your forces from the senseless errands you have them on across the Southland, you will be leaving yourself open to invasion very soon. Your scouts from the front line must be telling you that the Grandarians are trapped at the Wall of Light by the Drakkaidian Army mobilizing in the war zone. There is nothing stopping them from attacking your borders. With the Legion absent to defend it and covert Drakkaidian forces already inside the border, it will not hold for more than a day should it fall under siege. The entire Drakkaidian army will be here at your doorstep before you can muster any kind of defense at all, and neither the Grandarians nor the Alerrians will come to your aid when you call for it." The Sarton stared at Zeroan incredulously, starting to chuckle.

"Well that's quite the theory you have there, sage," he laughed in spite of himself. Zeroan did not return Othan's smile as he frowned back under his hood. "Do you have a power that lets you see into the future now as well? Drakkaidians storming the border indeed..." he trailed off with his gloomy expression making its way back across his face. "You speak of matters you know nothing about, sage," the Sarton informed him. "My forces are dispersed throughout the Southland responding to the reports of strange elemental disturbances you seem to be oblivious to. To the south there is talk of Golthrouts in the Great Forests, and reports of other creatures have been coming in from everywhere. The troops are needed there, not at an impenetrable border that the Drakkaidians would never even attempt to come near if they valued their miserable lives."

"You are wrong, Othan," Zeroan simply replied. "The disturbances you speak of are Valif Montrox of Drakkaidia's doing and are meant to keep the Legion immobile so he can take it with ease. The Legion is not meant to serve as a friendly security force for the Southland, it is an army meant to defend it against enemies from the north. You need to use it accordingly." Othan was brimming with rage now.

"The last time I looked, I was still the Sarton of the Southland!" he yelled. "Do not instruct me on how to use my own Legion." Zeroan was just as quick to respond with anger lacing into his voice.

"It would seem I need to remind you when Drakkaidian troops disguised as the Purging Flame have already penetrated your border and are moving across your lands destroying at will. You must form the full Legion along the border, and you must do it quickly before it is too late."

"The Purging Flame is being dealt with by my troops as we speak, and even if a few Drakkaidians are amongst their ranks, they are still only a leaderless band of brigands."

"Wrong, Othan!" Zeroan fumed. "The marauders are acting under the direct rule of the Dark Mages of the Black Church themselves. I just destroyed one leading them at Agealin Town myself. Your battalions would have marched right passed them if not for my intervention."

"I tell you, I have control of my lands, sage!" Othan was on his feet now, lashing out at the sage with every word. "You have forgotten your place once again, Zeroan. Now I want you out of my citadel or I will have your head for your malcontent!"

"Perhaps I should let you have it," Zeroan began infuriated, "at least then you would have the brain that goes with it!" The Sarton was screaming at the top of his lungs.

"You cannot speak to me this way! I am the Sarton-"

"You are a fool!" Zeroan bellowed indignantly. Seeing it pointless to continue speaking to one deaf to his words any further, the Mystic Sage furiously spun around and made his way for the door, his gray robes trailing behind him. As he opened the doorway to leave, Zeroan exhaled slowly and turned his head back to the irate Sarton one last time. "I know you do not credit my words, Othan, but you should heed these nonetheless. Drakkaidia is mobilizing against you as we speak. Whether you are prepared for him or not, Montrox will attack you sooner or later. It is already begun as the Purging Flame under his control build their numbers inside your borders. I have not told you that Montrox has far more than his human armies at his disposal. There are demons now aiding him you cannot fathom. Even with the full Legion assembled, you will still be hard pressed to hold them for long. It is time to start thinking of your people and act in their favor instead of in your own. I leave you now, but heed my words; war is coming, and as it stands now, you are doomed to failure and death."

With that, the Mystic Sage Zeroan opened the doorway further and exited the grand throne room, leaving a very confused and angry Sarton standing alone in the chamber.

Chapter 33

<u>Sabotage</u>

Arilia Embrin ran her fingers through her long flowing hair as she sat alone in the corner of her group's table in the tavern. While the other three members of her company were off talking to anybody who would listen to them to get the boredom out of their systems, Ril was far too weary from her emotional state to seek out such trivial conversation. She drummed her free hand over the table staring down into space. From the moment her party arrived in the Southland, this quest had become much more than Ril had expected it to be. Though she had been well aware of and expecting a host of dangerous adversaries and the most hazardous terrain in the Southland to navigate, she had not predicted the mental and emotional toll that this adventure was going to cost.

Letting her thoughts drift between how she would survive the remainder of this journey to how the group was going to save Tavin from his mysterious sickness, Ril let out a deep sigh and brought her slender legs up to the chair where she sat to warm herself with her own body heat.

"Perturbed?" came the gentle voice from behind her. Ril quickly turned her head back to find Kohlin Marraea taking a seat beside her. She tried a faint smile as she opened her mouth to respond.

"Just tired," she said nestling her head over her knees tightly pressed against her body. The Windrun Warrior slightly cocked his head and returned her distant smile.

"They say talking while you travel is healthy," the Southlander remarked informatively. "It looks you've quite a bit on your mind. Anything you want to talk about?" Deciding that she could use some friendly company, Ril nodded bringing her head back up revealing the whole of her delicate face to the young man.

"Oh I don't know," she began searching for the words to express her thoughts. "I guess I'm just feeling a little overwhelmed by everything all of the sudden. This whole quest has been different from how I had expected it to be since day one. We're only just starting the real part of it now, and I'm already not sure if I'll be able to finish it out." As she proceeded, the glazed-over look from when Kohlin had first found her began to subtly form back over her deep red eyes. "This was supposed to be my perfect opportunity to prove myself as a real Elemental Warrior once and for all, but so far I feel like I've just been getting in the way. Zeroan hardly ever let's me use my power, so I don't know what real good I'm doing. And on top of everything, I can't stop worrying about..." Ril trailed off then, realizing she had said too much in pouring out her emotions.

"Tavin," Kohlin filled in after she left her sentence hanging. Ril's eyes came back awake and shot over to Kohlin's not sure whether to be more surprised or embarrassed he knew what she was thinking. With the Southlander still just staring into her eyes and smiling in his usual gentle manner, Ril at last nodded her head yes in response, breaking their eye contact. Noticing out of the corner of his eye that Jaren was drifting a little too far into the other unfavorable groups in the opposite side of the tavern, Kohlin rose and stood parallel to the blushing girl to put a hand over her shoulder. "Zeroan will find a way to save him, Ril," he stated with confidence. "Zeroan will find a way."

It was not long after Kohlin and Ril's conversation that the sun had sunk over the illustrious capital city of the Southland, covering its once busy and bustling streets with a veil of darkness that silenced the clamoring marketplace soon after. As the narrow winding streets emptied for the night, the large courtyard where the group's inn rested fell devoid of activity as well. The peaceful silence lingered through the crisp air for nearly another hour before one solitary figure at last emerged from the streets leading down from the citadel high atop the plateau.

Cloaked in his signature gray robes as always, the Mystic Sage Zeroan slowly slipped through the night shadows of the courtyard unseen and unheard. With only the pale silver moonlight illuminating his dark path, he made his way further along the stone walkway until reaching the concealed inn. Slightly turning his hooded face backward as he opened the doorway, Zeroan observed the faint lights still shining across the courtyard where his party remained. As a distant cry of impossibly loud laughter from what sounded like Jaren found its way into his sharp ears, Zeroan rolled his eyes and he mumbled to himself as entered the inn.

Closing the door behind him, the sage once again found the innkeeper's desk empty, presuming he had retired for the evening. Zeroan silently proceeded to make his way up the small staircase to his left then, reaching the hallway above him. At the end of the corridor, the door to Tavin's room was slightly cracked open, revealing another form sitting beside him reading something to herself. Zeroan quietly cracked the door open further, startling the other with his towering frame. He quietly motioned for her to remain quiet as he whispered across the room.

"Rest easy, it is only me," he spoke softly. The innkeeper's wife let a slight smile cross over her face as she rose to greet him.

"Zeroan, you scared me nearly to death," she responded equally quiet.

"My apologies, Anen," the sage smiled at her. His gaze then moved over to the still quivering form of Tavin, beads of sweat dripping off of his tightly shaking head. Though his condition had improved in terms of the violent and erratic convulsions from earlier in the day, his overall appearance had worsened greatly. The boy's entire body was now flushing with color and sweating uncontrollably, apparently in the grip of another heat flash. He projected a perpetual series of faint moans as if caught in the middle of a nightmare he could not awaken from. Zeroan turned back to the innkeeper's wife and whispered again.

"Thank you for looking after the boy, Anen. My group very much needed a break from tending to him, for as you can see, he is a very time demanding charge." Anen nodded her head as she bent down to the ailing boy's bedside to pull the sheets over his chest like a caring mother tucking her child in for the night.

"It was no trouble at all," she assured him, moving to the doorway. "He looks like a fine lad. I do hope he recovers well." Zeroan nodded in the darkness of the room once more.

"As do I," he responded quietly. "Thank you again." With that, the innkeeper's wife bowed goodbye and made her way down the hallway leaving Zeroan alone with the indisposed Warrior of Light. Watching once more as Tavin struggled for air through his irregular repertory patterns, the sage silently cursed himself for still not being able to aid him in even the smallest way despite his expansive knowledge of healing and his vast mystic powers.

"I'm sorry I cannot be of help to you, Tavinious," he quietly told the boy though he knew he could not hear the words. "I can't determine what is causing this problem, but until I do, you must keep fighting. You have strength in you, Warrior of Light. You must hold on." Then as if to physically reinforce his words, Zeroan reached inside of his deep robes and pulled forth the sheathed Sword of Granis that he had taken for safe keeping while its master lay incapacitated and laid the mighty talisman over his body. The miniature golden crystal at the top of the hilt came swelling to life as it touched him, faintly illuminating the small room.

With the sword touching its master once more, Zeroan turned behind him to find the chair the innkeeper's wife had occupied. As his back was turned to gather his seat, Zeroan observed a disturbance in the luminous yellow light filling the room. Slowly turning back to the Sword of Granis, the sage noticed for the first time that the crystal was flickering. He gave it a puzzled look and leaned down to more closely inspect it.

"What's this?" he asked himself out loud. "The light from the Sword of Granis does not wane in the possession of its master..." As the Mystic Sage scanned his eyes over the sword, he noticed something he had not before. Staring incredulously at the hilt, Zeroan found himself looking at another golden crystal identical to the first lower on the hilt. Bearing his gaze down onto the mysterious other, he curiously reached down to examine it. The moment his rough fingers met with it, a sudden jolt of pain seared into his arm. Pulling it back to him in surprise, he ogled disbelievingly as the lower crystal's golden hue suddenly flared with a potent wave of darkness swirling through its core. Zeroan's eyes burst wide open. Quickly reaching down to snatch the sword from Tavin, the light from the top crystal instantly faded. Zeroan grit his teeth at his own stupidity for not having observed this weeks ago.

Finally aware of the problem, Zeroan immediately set to resolve it. Fully extending his left arm that held the sword firmly in its grasp, he held his right in front of him to begin charging it with flaring energy from an ancient mystic spell. Within moments, his hand was shining with brilliant white energy. Once completely engulfed in the piercing light, the sage thrust his hand forward and wrapped it around the lower crystal on the hilt of the sword. The moment it made contact, the same dark power from before surged to life, sending its potent jolts of pain lashing into its attacker. While this pain and force emitting from the crystal would have easily knocked a normal man to the ground buckling him over with pain, the powerful Mystic Sage stood firm with resilience.

It was several long moments later when the lower crystal smothered in Zeroan's magical grasp began to palpitate with a visible power of its own; emanating black light through his very flesh in a desperate effort to remain intact. Sensing this was the gem's last measure of defense should it be threatened, Zeroan blasted his mystic power onward rushing through his arm and bombarding out of his hand.

It was under this immense pressure that the dark crystal was never intended to endure that its last pocket of stamina deserted it. Through his barrage of power blasting into the crystal, Zeroan's sensitive ears detected the sudden cracking and shattering of what sounded like glass underneath the palm of his energized hand. Cutting off the flow of his mystic energy from the depths of his body and letting the pulsating white light around his hand fade, the sage slowly released his immeasurably powerful grip over the hilt of the sword. As he removed his hand, the fragments of the shattered dark crystal planted on the hilt of the sword broke from the rest of the physically unscathed Sword of Granis.

The devastated pieces of the crystal plummeted to the floor, dissolving into the room's quiet atmosphere before the towering sage. With the dark mist hovering just in front of him, Zeroan raised the blade of the Sword of Granis in the heart of it, quickly dissipating it into oblivion. With his task complete, Zeroan lowered the mighty sword and hunched over to breathe deeply, fatigued from the full exertion of such power. It was a faint noise behind him that drew his attention soon after. Turning to face the opposite side of the room, he laid eyes upon a most welcome sight. Tavinious Tieloc was lying quietly and breathing deeply over the bed he rested on with the sweat and color covering his body completely vanished.

Letting a slim smile overcome his worn bearded face, Zeroan sighed with relief. Picking himself up and striding over to the soundly sleeping form of Tavin, the sage once again rested the legendary Sword of Granis over the boy's chest, its one true golden crystal igniting with newly revitalized shimmering light the moment it touched his young form. Basking in the now fervent glow illuminating the small room, Zeroan gazed down with anticipation as Tavin's head began to stir with new life from the freely flowing energy of the sword. As the burning intensity of the light at last began to subside, Zeroan uncharacteristically beamed seeing Tavin's eyelids gingerly slide open to reveal his deep blue eyes for the first time since the sickness had struck.

As the young boy's head slowly tilted to face Zeroan's, he looked up questioningly at the sage.

"...Zeroan?" he asked sleepily. "Where am I?" Enthralled to hear the Warrior of Light speaking again, Zeroan was eager to respond.

"You are safe now, Tavin," the sage imparted to him. "We are currently at the capital of the Southland, Torrentcia City. We have been here since late this afternoon." Tavin looked confused hearing this at first, not remembering any journey to Torrentcia City. Beginning to sit up with his quickly recovering strength, Tavin turned his head downward observing the Sword of Granis resting down the length of his body, its lustrous crystal shining brightly as if happy to see him awake again. Suddenly remembering the events of his last conscience morning, Tavin shot up to Zeroan.

"Zeroan! I think there is something wrong with-"

"Yes I know, Tavin," the sage interrupted him, raising a hand for him to calm down. "I know all about the mysterious sickness that has been attacking you, and I have dealt with it. I promise you that it will never be coming back." Even further confused at how Zeroan could have known that and apparently cured him during his sleep, Tavin shot the sage a lost gaze. Zeroan only chuckled dryly. "Perhaps I should give you a quick summary to bring you up to speed on recent events," he started, taking the seat he had moved to get in the first place when he entered the room.

In the following minutes, Zeroan related all that had befallen him from the time that they were separated in the Great Rift, how Ril had found the boy incapacitated, the group's arrival in Torrentcia City in the afternoon, and how he had identified his sickness. At the end of the sage's explanation, Tavin sat in awe and confusion staring at him incredulously.

"Zeroan, I don't understand how the sword was responsible for making me sick," he stated. "If you just used it to revive me, how could it have been the problem?" Zeroan stood up from his seat then and gathered his gray robes about him.

"That is a question best answered later, my young friend," he said. "There are a few others who will want to know that you are revived and to hear the cause of your ailment as well." Tavin's eyes opened wide remembering the others of his party were not present.

"Hey, that's right! Where is everyone?" he asked curiously.

"Across the street from this inn, taking a well deserved rest from the exhausting task of caring for you," he stated, making Tavin feel a little burdensome. Zeroan nodded then as he walked to the doorway picking up the rest of the boy's attire, tossing it to him still sitting on the bed. "Why don't we go get them?" he asked. "I'll go on ahead while you dress yourself. Make haste." Tavin jumped up eagerly at the mention of his friends. As Zeroan turned to make his way out of the doorway and into the hallway outside, Tavin set to work dressing himself with his shirt, armor and cape, following with strapping the gleaming Sword of Granis back to his side. As he did so, Tavin noticed something peculiarly different about the legendary blade. As Zeroan disappeared out of the doorway, he called out curiously.

"Zeroan, weren't there two of these golden crystals on the hilt of the sword?" he asked carefully observing the ornate hilt again. The Mystic Sage Zeroan let out a huff of arid laughter as he descended down the stairway, leaving Tavin pondering why behind.

Chapter 34

<u>Tears</u>

"I'm going to be closing up here in a few minutes, you know," the bartender of the courtyard tavern called out. Temporarily turning away from his three companions on the opposite side of their table by the window, Parnox Guilldon smiled and raised his muscular arm in acknowledgement as the innkeeper nodded and walked into the back room behind the bar. Completely alone at last, Parnox shifted back to his companions and grabbed hold of his mug once more.

"Well, I don't know about you all," he started, interrupting his speech by taking one last swig of ale from his mug, "but I think we ought to be getting back to the inn about now." He concluded by slamming his cup down on the table and releasing an impossibly loud belch. A torrent of disgust echoed through everyone's faces.

"Is that the kind of table etiquette you woodsmen practice around ladies?" Kohlin asked sarcastically. Jaren was quick to speak himself as wind of the fowl smell found its way into his nostrils.

"For Granis' sake, man," Jaren began repulsed, waving the tainted air in front of him away. "You really need to see a doctor about that." Parnox just shrugged, getting a quiet chortle out of Ril before she began to speak.

"While Parnox's atrocious manners do need some serious tending too," she began with a distant smile, "we do need to get back to the inn. Even though Tavin's had the innkeeper's wife looking after him, we haven't checked on him for hours now, and I doubt that Zeroan is back from whatever it is that he's been doing at the citadel."

"What makes you think that?" a rough voice quietly sounded from the doorway. Ril's eyes immediately shot up to the opening of the tavern to find the towering form of Zeroan standing halfway through, casting his prodigious shadow onto the floor below. The others immediately spun around to greet the sage, taken off guard by another of his discrete entrances.

"How long has it been since you returned from the citadel?" Kohlin asked.

"I have been back from my visit to the upper city for some time now," he commented, "most of which I have spent with our young Warrior of Light back at the inn." Wondering if the sage had anything new to report, Ril was quick to lean forward in her seat to assail him with questions.

"Is there any change, Zeroan? Were you able to learn anything of his sickness at the citadel? How is he?" she asked hopefully, bombarding Zeroan with her inquiries. He signaled for the excited girl to calm down with a slow motion of his hands downward. He slowly stepped into the light, revealing a strangely warm expression over his usually grave face. The others looked at him curiously as he suddenly lifted his hand to point into the courtyard.

"Why don't you look out that window and see for yourself?" he advised softly. The puzzled girl twisted her head to the window. Staring out to the moonlit courtyard, a small movement across the street instantly caught her attention. Realizing the door to the group's inn was opening, her eyes widened in disbelief as they found a caped figure stepping out of it. Ril's mouth dropped open in shock then exploded upward beaming with relief. Literally leaping out of her chair, the Warrior of Fire bounded past the table of her companions and burst out the doorway, rushing into the courtyard.

Confused at what the wild girl could have seen, the others around the table jumped out of their seats for the doorway she had ran out of. Peering out, they too observed what Ril had. Tavin stood closing the door to inn he had just emerged from fully rejuvenated from the negative effects of his illness viciously attacking him just minutes before. Though Jaren was about to burst out of the tavern after Ril to meet his best friend, he felt the sudden presence of a hand resting over his shoulder. He looked back to find Kohlin holding his gaze with a coy expression on his face.

"Why don't you give her a moment, Jaren," he asked respectfully. "You will see him soon enough." Returning the Southlander's gaze, Jaren let out a small huff of frustration as he folded his arms and leaned up against the frame of the doorway beside him.

As the group of four watched from the tavern across the courtyard, Tavin gently pushed the door to the inn shut behind him, not wanting to wake anyone with its creaking noise. Turning back to face the moonlit courtyard before him, he was startled by the view of someone racing across the street straight at him. Not able to determine the identity of the mysterious figure in the night's darkness with only a moonlit sky to see, it wasn't until she was within a few meters of him that a smile of recognition passed over Tavin's surprised face.

"Ril?" he asked incredulously as her form drew closer still. Before he could say another word, however, the already stunned boy was completely caught off guard as the young Warrior of Fire leapt off the ground and latched her arms around his shoulders like a vice. Nothing short of awestruck, Tavin didn't quite know how to respond to the girl's emotional greeting. It was not until the barely audible sound of Ril beginning to weep that he at last surrounded her with his arms to return her strong embrace, astounded but flattered at her behavior. With Ril only tightening her hold on him and crying harder in the moments that passed, he began to rub her back in small circular motions to attempt to calm her down. Back across the street, Jaren stood in awe himself that Ril was making such a scene with her whole party watching.

It was several emotional minutes later when Ril at last managed to release her grip on the boy and pull away. Her face was flush with color, and as their eyes met it was all Tavin could do to drive the shock from his face and smile uncertainly. Though obviously embarrassed, Ril grinned through her tears as well. Letting the unexpectedly comfortable silence hang between them for another few moments, Tavin formulated what he would say.

"Well," he started with his smile only growing, "if I get a welcome back like that every time, I think I'll try to get sick more often." With a torrent of emotions ranging from the deepest embarrassment to the highest pinnacle of joy she experienced in days, Ril could only giggle, just happy to have the kindhearted boy back and safe again. She beamed and nodded.

"You'd better not," she managed to squeak through her emotions. "I missed you too much to have you gone like that again."

"You don't have to worry about that anymore," he told her calmly. "It sounds like Zeroan fixed whatever the problem was permanently." Ril breathed deeply as his words echoed into her ears, relieved. His smile broadened again. "Not to hurry you, but I think he's getting a little anxious over there." As Tavin pointed with his eyes at the band of their companions (particularly Jaren) staring out of the doorway, Ril's face blushed anew realizing everyone had just seen her unusually reckless display of emotion. Tavin just kept smiling.

It was not more than a few moments later when the Mystic Sage Zeroan at last stepped out of the tavern doorway, immediately followed by an excessively impatient Jaren and the others. Swiftly making their way across the quiet courtyard, the group at last reached Tavin and Ril near the inn, separating from each other as the others approached. For the second time in the past few minutes, another sprinting body leapt out at Tavin, though this time he was far from surprised. Respectfully allowing the two best friends their moment together, Ril brought her forearm to her misty face to rub the tears away with the sleeve of her shirt, embarrassed. As the Southlanders rushed forward giving the Warrior of Light quick embraces, Zeroan halted next to Ril and shuffled in his robes.

"We need to be getting back indoors," the sage informed them, morphing back into his usually staid and serious manner. "There are matters that warrant our immediate attention, including how I was able to heal Tavin. Now quickly, inside and up to the last room of the hallway." As Tavin and Jaren finally managed to quiet their laughter and pleasure to be back together for the first time in nearly a week, the group reassembled and began silently trailing back through the inn's doorway. Turning back for Ril, Tavin caught her motioning for him to continue on without her for a moment. Respectfully complying, Tavin moved out of the doorway inside after the others.

With only Ril and Zeroan still standing outside, she turned to face him. Before he could instruct her to be on her way inside after the others, the girl spoke with a thankful and apologetic look in her eyes.

"Whatever you did, Zeroan," she began quietly, "thank you." The sage nodded underneath his concealing hood at this, his face hidden in the darkness of the night. Ril smiled again and turned back to make her way after Tavin and the others to their room. Zeroan remained standing there in the darkness for a moment, contemplating the actions of the young Warrior of Fire. Not accustomed to any manner of thanks or warmth directed at him from anyone, particularly Ril, he could not help but smile again. Quietly passing through and closing the doorway to the inn, he left the empty courtyard in the silence and solitude of the night once more.

Chapter 35

<u>Disturbing Possibility</u>

As Zeroan slowly trailed behind his party up the stairs of the inn, the others in the group hovered around Tavin, ecstatically inquiring how he had recuperated. When he replied he was just as in the dark as the rest of them and that only Zeroan had the answer, they were quick to make their way back to Tavin and Jaren's room to hear what the sage had to say. Filtering in one by one, Kohlin took it upon himself to light a small lantern and illuminate their otherwise black surroundings. As the warm light spread across the room, the Mystic Sage finally appeared at the door concealed beneath his flowing gray robes, taking care to securely close it behind him. While Parnox took a seat in the lone chair and Kohlin lowered himself onto the left bed, Tavin, flanked by Ril and Jaren, found his way to the right bed where he had laid in anguish less than half an hour before.

Turning to face his seated companions, Zeroan was immediately assailed with a salvo of questions. Far too weary from the day's strenuous events, the impatient sage let a quick burst of light burst from his fist inside his robes, sending a timid but noticeably present wave of energy passing through the members of his group scattered across the room. Silencing them instantly, the sage grit his teeth to prevent his impatience from getting the best of him.

"Just because I am a Mystic Sage," he began with tired irritation bleeding from his voice, "does not mean that I am immune to fatigue and its unfavorable effects unlike the rest of you. And as you all know by this point, frustration and anger are no strangers to me. I have a great deal to relate to you, so please keep the questions that you will most likely have until I am finished." Pausing for a moment to observe his companions nodding in accord, the sage made his way over to the windowsill at the end of the room and slowly sat, relaxing his legs.

"Very well, then," he began again. "Let's keep this quiet. There is no measure of security we should be overlooking anymore." Zeroan motioned for Tavin to rise and move toward him with a waving movement from his right arm, which he cooperatively obeyed. "Unsheathe the Sword of Granis, Tavin. And do it quietly, please." Minding once again, the boy reached down to the hilt of his illustrious weapon and gingerly drew it out, careful to mask its customary metallic ringing. Once unsheathed, the sage took hold of the sword's hilt along with Tavin and pointed to the fervently glowing crystal.

"Do you all see this crystal embedded here where the blade meets with the hilt?" he asked, receiving an immediate response of nodded heads. "This is a unique feature built into the Sword of Granis by the ancient Grandarians that forged it. It is called the Granic Crystal, and it is the heart of the sword's power. Any time the Warrior of Light is in physical possession of the sword, the Granic Crystal shines brightly. But as Tavin pointed out earlier, there used to be an exactly identical crystal situated a little lower on the hilt."

"Hey, yeah," Jaren mumbled questioningly on the bed where he sat across from the sage. "That's what I was thinking was wrong. Where did that other one get to?" Zeroan's face was hard and stoic.

"I just destroyed it," he said with ruthless efficiency. Tavin looked at the sage incredulously upon hearing this.

"What does that mean?" he asked in dismay.

"It means just what it sounds like it means," Zeroan responded, motioning for the boy to take a seat once more. "It turns out that that other crystal was the sole source of the problem. Nothing else." Ril looked at the sage with an impossible look set into her face.

"I don't understand, Zeroan," she stated making room on the bed for Tavin to sit back down. "Are you saying that the Sword of Granis was responsible for Tavin's sickness?" Zeroan shook his head no, frustration reappearing in his eyes.

"If you would be so kind as to let me finish like I asked you when we began, I am getting to that," he reminded intolerantly. The girl immediately sealed her mouth, shrinking back from the sage as he continued. "But to answer your question, no.

That crystal was not a part of the Sword of Granis at all. It was nothing but a clever Drakkaidian deception used to sabotage us from within." Everyone leaned closer, stunned. "But before we delve into that, let me explain the nature of the other crystal." Zeroan paused once more to formulate a simple way to translate the complicated language of magic into a common explanation that the group could understand. "This is difficult to explain, but I will try to keep it as basic as possible.

"Until Tavin has fully acquired his abilities as the Warrior of Light, he must use the Sword of Granis to activate random portions of it each time through a desperate, spontaneous need. Every time he does this, a channel is established between his body and the sword. When he is finished using the power and it begins to dissipate, the power inside his body- inside his blood- begins to seal itself. The sword needs to do this as well in order to close the channel that had been created between the two. Should one of the two parts of the power not properly close, however, Tavin would have a serious problem. With one part of his power sealed but the other still flaring out of sequence, it would feed internally off of the other part to keep itself alive. In this case, the power inside his body was sealing as it should, but the Sword of Granis was not closing the circuit. Its power was not allowed to fade because of external intervention. This was the imposter crystal mounted on the hilt of the sword.

"Acting as a blockade of sorts, the crystal contained inside it a dark magic designed to keep the flow of magic alive, even when it naturally wants to fade. Every time Tavin activated his power, the crystal forced the sword to remain active long after it was needed. With the sword's power not on par with that of Tavin's body, it had no choice but to draw power from its master to keep its own energy level at optimum efficiency. And every time the sword took from him, it took more and more. If this went on unchecked for much longer, it would have eventually taken too much and killed him." A dead silent hush befell the room for a moment until the sage collected himself once more. Ril seemed to shrink back at this revelation, as if deeply disturbed on another level.

"Fortunately, I was able to discover the problem in time. I noticed that the light from the Granic Crystal was beginning to wane. That should never be so in the grasp of its master unless there is something seriously amiss with either it or the holder. In this case, the Sword of Granis was trying to say that it needed energy, and there was not enough from its master to keep its power alive. We were very close to permanently losing Tavin." The others all let out a frightened but grateful sigh of relief that he was still with them, if only just barely. Tavin himself was by far the most unnerved at this revelation, swallowing hard and contemplating just how close he had come to yet again meeting an untimely demise. "In any case, I noticed the dark crystal on the hilt of the blade and destroyed it so the sword could finally lay its power to rest.

"With the Sword of Granis and the Warrior of Light finally back in sync with each other's power levels, the free sword instantly recuperated its master as I lay it upon him. And that is how I was able to rid Tavin of his mysterious sickness." Leaving his words hanging, Tavin glanced down onto the Sword of Granis once more vexed at how this had happened in the first place.

"Thank you again for saving me, Zeroan," Tavin started, shifting his gaze back onto the sage, "but I'm still unsure of one thing." Zeroan nodded as he repositioned himself on the windowsill where he sat.

"How did the dark crystal get on the Sword of Granis in the first place?" he inquired for the boy. Tavin nodded, not at all surprised the sage had known what he was wondering. "That, Tavin, is a very disturbing possibility. Though it may be difficult to accept this, we most likely have a traitor in our midst back in Galantia." Tavin was awestruck at that statement.

"Aren't you jumping to conclusions like that a little soon, Zeroan? Couldn't some minion of the Draks have gotten into the Tower of Granis and put the imposter crystal on the sword?" Tavin inquired. The sage shook his head confidently as he justified himself.

"I will admit that it is not beyond the realm of possibility, but it is highly unlikely," he stated with assurance. "You must keep in mind that no unholy creature of the Netherworld could possibly penetrate into the sacred Temple of Light. They would not be able to survive there. Besides, there is no way in except through the front gate high in the cityscape of Galantia guarded by more elite soldiers than outside the throne room itself. The possibility of unseen penetration is non existent. Only one with access to the temple could have entered and placed the imposter crystal on the Sword of Granis. This is an even more troubling likelihood. Those with access to the Elemental Temple of Light are only those high in the Grandarian political and religious fields. This corruption in the golden city may be very high in the chain."

"Now hold on just a moment," the burly Southlander Parnox stated feeling a bit overwhelmed by all of this. "Who would possibly want to sell themselves out to the Draks? No one has anything to gain from something like that. And besides, I'm more concerned about where someone was able to find one of those dark crystals than how they got into the temple. Wouldn't they need a great understanding of magic plant that fake on the blade?" Zeroan quietly nodded in agreement.

"Quite right, Parnox," Zeroan continued. "Whoever our traitorous foe is, he must have the magical talent to activate the dark crystal. I'm sure it came from Montrox and his agents; magic like that only exists in Drakkaidia and the Black Church in these times. But enough of this talk." Zeroan stood once more, towering above the group as he changed the subject. "There is no point in dwelling on this now. If there is indeed a turncoat in Galantia, there is nothing we can do about it now. We must proceed onward with our own quest, which we can now do with our Warrior of Light returned to us. What I have just related to you is only a part of what you still need to hear this night.

"As you know, I was up in the higher city this afternoon in the grand citadel. While there, I encountered my fellow Mystic Sage Cornonathan here on business relating to the well being of the Temple of Water. Though he was not enthralled to see me, I did manage to learn from him news from the south, where our quest now takes us. Apparently, the source of the majority of the reported elemental disturbances have originated in those various regions. Greenwall Fortress in the heart of the Grailen Plains has recently been under strict lockdown due to rumors of demonic activity. There is also increased threat from the Markonian bandits and the marauders of the Purging Flame severely acting up across the countryside. Though I learned that there are Legion patrols roaming across the plains, they are in no position to combat them in their current scattered and leaderless state. The Grailen will not be a very hospitable place once we reach it. After I parted with the Mystic Sage, I set out to meet with the Sarton." Frustration was already finding its way into his voice. Parnox smiled in spite of himself.

"I can just imagine how well that must have gone," he stated sarcastically. Zeroan rolled his eyes under his hood while Tavin peered over to the hulking man, confused. Ril took it upon herself to fill him in on the negative relationship between the Sarton and sage while Zeroan proceeded.

"The meeting was not as 'productive' as I had hoped it might have been," he started irritated, "but you cannot expect much from those missing a mind of their own. Despite my hard warnings, the Sarton will not heed them and build back his defenses at the border. He feels that the Legion is needed assisting the south and other such areas with the idiotic errands he has sent them on. Montrox will seize on his stupidity. The Legion is wasting its time down there, and Othan will realize this soon enough when the first Drakkaidian assault on his border begins. The defenses will not hold for long. We are short of time in every possible way right now, which is why we must resume our journey as soon as possible." Jaren let out a moan hearing this.

"Please don't tell me we're-"

"Leaving tomorrow morning, as soon as we can get out of here," the sage completed for him, leaving Jaren ready to cry. Zeroan snapped at the Grandarian to get his attention again. "Compose yourself, boy. I can promise you for certain that you will have a full night's rest in these beds tonight, and you can have all the food you want at the tavern in the morning. I trust that isn't too harsh." While Jaren was still upset, he cocked his head slightly and gave the sage a look that told him his terms were acceptable. "Very good then. I suggest we all get some sleep now. Though we won't be up at the crack of dawn, we need to be away fairly early. I will explain to you the various details of our journey to come once we are away from this accursed city. Good night to you all."

Without another word, the sage gathered up his gray robes and strode quickly for the doorway, disappearing from view. Parnox and Kohlin rose soon after his departure.

"This accursed city?" Parnox repeated. "He sure does hate Othan, doesn't he?" Kohlin and Parnox chuckled as they said their goodnights and filtered out of the room to their own across the hall. Trailing after them was Ril, standing next to Tavin from the bed. Staring up at him, a familiar quiet hung in the air between them as they smiled, neither one quite sure what to do or say. It was after a few more passing moments that the fiery girl at last broke her gaze and spoke uncertainly.

"I'm glad you're back, Tavin," she said quickly, moving toward the doorway. As she began to step through it, it was all Tavin could do to helplessly stare back at the ravishing girl, his heart curiously pounding. As she disappeared into the darkness of the night, he stood there for what felt like forever. At last, he remembered there was still another person left in the room. Spinning his head toward Jaren, most likely ready to bombard him with sarcastic mockery, he was surprised to find his best friend already in a deep sleep spread over his bed on the far side of the room.

Part Three
Different Paths

Chapter 36

<u>A Proper Meal</u>

Fully recuperated from the effects of the dark sabotage inflicted on his body, Tavin came awake with a start the next morning and leapt out of bed to meet with the new day. As usual, Jaren was not as enthusiastic about this hour of the morning and burrowed into his bed sheets the moment his friend opened the window at the end of the room. The sun's fulgent rays saturated the small room instantly, bathing the young Grandarians in their radiant warmth. Gathering a deep breath of the crisp morning air into his lungs, Tavin spun around with a grin on his face as he called out to his friend still buried in the depths of his bed.

"Garrinal, how can you lie there wasting even a single moment of a day like this?" he beamed, turning back to gaze out the window. Jaren just groaned and dug deeper into his bedding. As Tavin propped himself up on the windowsill, his eyes met with the capital of the Southland for the first time, gaping out in awe at the incredible city that rivaled even Galantia in terms of scale and beauty. Leaning out the window, the boy's thin nightshirt whipped in the sharp wind blowing down from the cool blue skies. Both enthralled and mesmerized as he stared into the tight twisting rows of the lower city, the bustling and bright courtyard beneath him, and the incredible citadel atop the plateau, energy and vitality coursed through Tavin's veins like never before, ready for anything and everything coming his way. It was all he could do to keep himself from shouting out at the world from his window with the joy of just being alive and mobile again.

Returning him to his senses, Tavin heard his name being called out from down in the courtyard streets below. His head jerking downward to locate where it had originated, he instantaneously found the two Southlanders Parnox Guilldon and Kohlin Marraea standing out by a spectacularly crafted fountain spewing a solid stream of flowing mist over the courtyard, glistening like a storm of minuscule diamonds in the fervent morning sunlight. Making eye contact with the two, Tavin grinned back and waved. Parnox responded by raising his thick gruff hands over his mouth and shouting out through the busy streets again.

"Hey!" he bellowed at the height of his voice, causing several passing townspeople to shoot perplexed and irritated glances in his direction. "You're looking better!" he pointed out, a little surprised to see the boy so full of energy so soon. "Why don't you wake the others and get them ready to go? We'll be pulling out within the hour I guess, and only the two of us plus the sage are up!" Tavin smiled back summoning an equally loud response.

"I'm ready to move any time!" he informed them both proudly. "But I'm not so sure about my partner in here! He's still lying in his bed!" Parnox chuckled across from the courtyard, not at all surprised.

"Well, I'm sure he might be convinced to get up for a little breakfast! All he can eat at the tavern!" Tavin nodded at that, turning to inform Jaren of the enormous meal to be gained if he could pry himself from his bed. By the time he managed to fully turn around however, Jaren was already blasting out from the confines of his sheets and heading for the end of the room where his clothing and affects hang. Tavin grinned again, turning back to Parnox.

"I think you persuaded him to join us!" Tavin called out. "Now all we need is the redhead and we're all set!"

"Don't worry about me. I'm here," came a muffled voice from outside the inn two stories high. Surprised, the Grandarian boy shot his head out the window to find the shutters over the one to his left opening to reveal the crimson haired Warrior of Fire leaning out to smile in his direction. She was draped in a simple white nightgown obviously borrowed from the inn. "Good morning," she said with her usual glittering smile spreading wide. Tavin beamed back at her as he threw his arms into the air.

"Great morning!" he corrected almost lost in enthusiasm.

"It'll be better once I've gotten something to eat," came another eager voice from Tavin's room. "Tell her to get ready so we can get going!" Hearing that for herself, Ril smiled once more and quickly nodded.

"I'm on my way," she stated. "I just want to take a quick bath. No offense or anything, but I suggest that you two do the same. It's been a while since we cleaned ourselves up. I'll see you two when we're done." Tavin nodded in response as he watched her pull back from the window and close the shutters once more. Disappearing from view, Tavin at last broke his gaze from Ril's window as his blue shirt suddenly landed over his head.

"You can stare at the girl all day long if you want," Jaren began, sprinting for the bathroom, "I can only eat my breakfast once. Get ready first, stare later." Tavin could only laugh as he nodded his head and gathered up his own blue and white attire from the chair by his bed and began to remove his night clothing to make for the opposite tub of hot water in their bathroom prepared by the innkeeper's wife earlier that morning. Sinking into the steaming tubs and fully submerging their heads beneath the surface, both of the young Grandarians found it tempting to just sit in the warmth of the relaxing waters for the rest of the day. Any such thoughts were quickly overridden by the anticipation of helping themselves to an endless banquet of food, however. Quickly bathing, Tavin burst from his tub and raced to dry so he could force his Grandarian garb back over him along with his cape and light armor.

Jaren was hard pressed to keep up with his energetic friend as he donned his unique green Grandarian hunting attire. As usual, Jaren found Tavin's high spirits contagious and was soon bouncing around as pert and jaunty as the Warrior of Light. To finish their respective outfits, Jaren gathered up his bow and restocked quiver, slung them both over his back, and then took up the Sword of Granis from the bench it rested on.

"I do believe this is yours," he said with a sharp grin on his face, outstretching his arm to hand the mighty sword to his friend. Tavin took it by the sheath under the hilt, the one true Granic Crystal surging with new life and light. Tavin smiled to see the weapon respond to him.

After the Warrior of Light strapped his legendary blade back on his belt, Jaren was practically pulling him out the door to get moving. Upon entering the hallway however, Tavin forced him to wait with him outside Ril's room, rhythmically rapping on her door.

"Hey! Come on in there!" he called merrily. "We've got places to go, things to do, bad guys to stop-"

"Food to eat," Jaren chimed in impatiently. The two could hear another muffled giggle behind the door as the person inside scrambled to gather her few belongings. At last, the doorway burst open revealing Ril dressed in her usual fiery tunic with exotic reds, oranges, and yellows pressed tightly against her slim frame. Her flowing hair had been pulled back and casually gathered into a ponytail to keep it out of her face, still somewhat damp from her bath. Smiling at the two boys once more, even Jaren found it difficult to tear his eyes off of her ravishing beauty. Observing his eyes fixated upon her, Ril slightly cocked her head and raised her eyebrows to him.

"And here I thought you didn't like me at all," she stated in an overly dramatic voice. Jaren quickly blinked away to gain his senses back to him as he responded in an equally sarcastic tone.

"If anything, it's a recent development. But don't look too much into it, highness," he stated forcing a coy smile out of the girl. "Now can we please get to the tavern? I swear to Granis himself I'm not going to make it on this grand expedition much longer if I don't get a real meal today."

Submitting to Jaren's dire request, the reunited trio set out from the inn and into the city courtyard for the tavern and their breakfast. The group immediately entered the fray of the bustling streets full of amiable civilians trekking to or from the marketplace in the lower city. Making his way through the pulsing crowds, Tavin gazed back up to the higher city boasting the mighty citadel of the Southland and the single azure peak of the Elemental Temple soaring into the vast open skies seeming to touch the white banks of clouds with its power. His fixated gaze was disrupted by the subtle wave of mist from the beautiful fountain in the center of the courtyard, gracefully spewing shimmering jets of liquid into the air. As the distance between them lessened, a gentle layer of soft moisture settled onto his clothing and skin, releasing a relaxing sensation throughout his tense body.

The three at last penetrated through the diversely colored courtyard to reach the tavern with a familiar face standing in wait for them. Gleefully greeting Kohlin at the door, the growing party moved into the tavern to the same corner table they had sat at the previous night once again occupied by Parnox Guilldon, gulping down another mug of ale. This time, however, all three of the younger companions of the group were frozen in their tracks as their ravenous eyes met with the banquet of food already littered across the table. Jaren's eyes widened to the size of the massive plates of fruit and breads before him.

"Praise be to Granis," he mumbled faintly, slowly approaching the table. He reached down to a plate of some local bird cooked and browned to perfection and ran his tingling fingers over one of the legs as if to make sure it was real. Tavin couldn't help but chuckle as he and Ril moved past him to take their seats with Parnox.

"No drooling at the table, boy," Tavin mocked. Already into the cuisine like a wild animal, however, Jaren didn't care to offer anything in his defense.

It was an enjoyable and satisfying half of an hour later that the group had stuffed themselves to the point of internal explosion and they at last reemerged into the busy courtyard. Jaren turned to face his party and pat his belly contently.

"It doesn't get any better than that," he stated in a very matter of fact way. "We should really do that more often on this little adventure." Parnox laughed and threw his massive hand down onto the boy's shoulder.

"I don't think there's enough Seir in the world to pay for another meal like that," he responded. A sudden look of horror passed over Tavin's face at the mention of the bill.

"I had completely forgotten about that!" he exclaimed in shock. "Parnox, how did we manage to pay for all that?" The burly Southlander motioned for the boy to calm down as he reached into a near empty pouch of currency.

"Don't have the faintest idea where he got it all," Parnox began, fingering through the bag at the last few coins of Seir present, "but when I woke this morning, Zeroan gave me an entire satchel full of Seir. He said to be sure you three got a proper meal before we set out again. And I trust you all did." Jaren belched under his arm to confirm he had indeed gotten his fill.

"Speaking of our Mystic Sage," Ril began looking around them, "where is he this morning?" Kohlin was the one to answer her question as he pointed downward into the streets of the lower city.

"Zeroan went out to scout the lower city and the outsides of the walls for one thing or another after he gave us the

Seir. We've been instructed to gather our belongings and proceed to the city gates. He said he would meet us there." Ril nodded at that satisfactory answer and turned to the rest of the group.

"Well I know I've got everything I need, but we're going to need to restock our supplies if we're going to continue today."

"Zeroan has taken care of that as well," Kohlin chimed in. "He said that he would have fresh supplies and bags waiting for us when we arrived, so I suppose everything's taken care of. Are you all ready to depart?" Taking the time to go back and think things through, Tavin remembered one thing remained to be done before he departed the Southland capital.

"Actually, I still need to thank the innkeeper and his wife back at the inn for taking care of me yesterday," Tavin informed them. Parnox winked in response.

"Good thinking. Why don't you go take care of that right now and be done with it," he suggested. Tavin nodded and turned from the group, quickly making his way back to the inn to finish his business with its owners. As his blue and white form disappeared through the rows of passing townspeople, Jaren rolled his eyes as he picked his teeth from the meal he had just consumed.

"How thoughtful," he mumbled sarcastically, just loud enough for the others to hear. Ril wheeled on him, scorn and disdain mirrored in her fiery eyes. As did the others in the group, Jaren instantly knew he had made a mistake and braced himself for the incoming verbal assault from the girl.

"As if you would ever even consider taking the time to thank someone for something," she accused. "Compared to Tavin, you don't have a sensitive or caring bone in your body." Jaren threw his arms out in frustration with a disgusted look overtaking his face.

"Would you lighten up!" he nearly yelled back. "If you had one bone of common sense in your body you'd realize I'm only joking!" Obviously failing to see the humor, Ril turned her back on the boy folding her arms and refusing to say another word about it. Parnox and Kohlin could only silently chortle to themselves as Jaren rolled his eyes so far back into his head they nearly stuck there permanently.

Across the street a few moments later, Tavin re-emerged from the small inn one last time after gratefully thanking the gracious innkeeper and his kindhearted wife. Closing the door behind him, Tavin shot his head back in the bustling crowds to try and relocate his party. After scanning through the mobs, he at last locked onto their position and began weaving through the churning waves of Southlanders. In his haste, he accidentally bumped into a passing figure and knocked a small satchel full of food from his hand. Embarrassed of his impatient behavior, Tavin quickly turned back to face the man he had run into.

"My apologies, sir," he spit out quickly, his eyes shifting to the figure. Upon further inspection, however, Tavin noticed the figure was no older than he, despite his mature and impassive face. He was clothed in solid black and draped in a tattered gray coat with columns of strange dark glyphs exhibited over its back. As the figure wiped some of his red hair away from his eyes and opened his mouth to speak, his emotionless expression did not change.

"It was nothing," he said like it really wasn't. Bending down with Tavin to gather what food he had back into his satchel, however, his face suddenly burst awake with surprise. As Tavin looked back up, he noticed the figure was staring at him with some newfound curiosity and excitement shown in his face and movements, as apparent when he started to breath heavier.

"Is something wrong?" Tavin asked a little confused, offering the satchel back to him. The figure instantly recollected himself and forced the expression from his face once more, slowly accepting the satchel.

"Oh, I was just admiring that sword you have there," he stated casually. Tavin's face was a little taken aback hearing this. Zeroan had told him time and time again to be sure no one besides his party ever discovered the Sword of Granis. "Grandarian, if I'm not mistaken. And a fine one at that. One of the most beautiful weapons I've ever seen." Tavin nodded quickly as he rose with the other.

"Yes, it's Grandarian," Tavin said, not wishing to discuss the matter further. The other pressed on, however.

"How does it make that little light on the hilt?" he questioned pointing at the golden crystal.

"Oh, it's just a little trick that reflects sunlight is all," Tavin lied through his teeth, covering the sword with his cape. "Well if you'll excuse me, I really have to be going." The other nodded at once, letting a disturbing little smile form on the corner of his lips.

"Of course," he acknowledged smoothly, as Tavin nervously smiled once more and turned to be on his way through the crowds. The figure just stood there in the center of the passing people, not moving a muscle with the smile on his face. "Found you."

Chapter 37

<u>The Grailen</u>

The Mystic Sage Zeroan was anything but happy when he met with his party just outside the city gates. Though his anger was apparently provoked by the younger companions of the group, he saw fit to distribute it to the adult in charge.

"I told you to get them up early and feed them quickly," he began in his tirade, "not let them loaf in bed for half the morning and gorge themselves for the better part of an hour!" Parnox took responsibility for his actions, justifying that they deserved at least one low paced morning and relaxing meal every once and awhile. Zeroan was inclined to disagree, reminding them that time was ticking away at a faster rate than they could afford and they did not need to waste any of it "lounging around while the world is at risk." He was quick to forgive, however, eager to make up for lost time as he hustled the group back to the road to resume their journey.

After Zeroan cooled and assumed his typical solemn demeanor, he hastily drove them away from the proximity of the city, descending around the downward spiraling road back to the bottom of the plateau. The refreshed band of companions followed their leader in high spirits, with Tavin and Jaren directly behind him and the two Southlanders at either the front or rear of the convoy on alert for anything and everything as usual. The big change in the group, however, was the jaunty Warrior of Fire attached to the hips of the Grandarians. After the events of the past strenuously packed days, Ril had come to open herself up to the others considerably, feeling her companions had truly become invaluable friends. Upon reaching the base of the plateau, Zeroan eased the grueling pace he had set on the way down. Safely back on their way once more, he gathered the reenergized party to him for the further details about the next stage of their adventure he had promised to explain.

"Well, now that we are at last back on our way," he began with the last bit of irritation from their delayed departure dissolving, "I think I should inform you all of what is in store for us in the coming future." Jaren sunk his head down to his chest in anticipation for the most likely near impossible road before them about to be revealed. Zeroan quickly continued speaking to preclude any chance of a smug remark from the flippant Grandarian. "As I told you last evening, we are now beginning the real segment of our quest. We have successfully entered the Southland, but that was the easy stage of our journey." The sage could never have been quick enough to stop Jaren from challenging that statement.

"If that's what you call easy," he began thinking back over all that had befallen him in the past weeks, "hard must be something along the lines of taking over the entire world in a split second with nothing but your bare hands." Though Zeroan did not appreciate Jaren's facetious attitude toward his charge to save the world, he had by now come to accept that was the way he was and there wasn't much he could do about it. Breathing deeply in hopeless frustration, the sage responded.

"Funny you should mention that," Zeroan rejoined, "because that is exactly what our enemy is going to be able to do soon if we do not complete our task, and it would be much easier to do so without your trap in perpetual motion when I am trying to speak." Dwarfed once again by the sage's response, Jaren sealed his mouth and threw up his arms in defeat. Seeing the young Grandarian yield, Zeroan began again. "Very good. Now as you all know, the first of the two missing shards that we are after is somewhere within the deep south of Iairia, most likely hidden deep in the Great Forests of the Grailen." It was the other of the two Grandarian boys that interrupted this time.

"Zeroan, you keep talking about the Grailen Plains and forests, but I don't really know much about them," Tavin confessed to the sage. Zeroan stopped there, a bit taken aback at this revelation. Maintaining what patience he had left, he continued.

"What do you wish to know, Tavin?" he asked. The boy's face went blank, not exactly sure what to ask. Seeing his loss for words as she strode beside him, Ril chimed in to assist him with his inquiry.

"Maybe if you just gave them a brief background on the Grailen regions, our two Grandarians can get a general idea about them," she offered, leaving Tavin feeling a little humbled in her wake yet again. Zeroan nodded under his hood and gathered his thoughts.

"Very well," he began, recognizing this as an excellent learning opportunity for the entire group. "You should know that it is one of the six lands present in central Iairia."

"Six lands?" Tavin repeated fumbling for what the familiar term had in relation to the Grailen. Ril brought her hand up to cover her mouth and hide her smile, unable to suppress her giggles from the boy's confusion. Her pert laughter contagious, a curious smile overtook Tavin's face as he shifted his gaze at the smirking girl.

"Is something funny?" he asked. Still chuckling under her breath, Ril quickly shook her head no as she responded.

"Its just that for being the most powerful of all six Elemental Warriors, you don't know very much about the things that give us power, do you? First you tell me you don't know about the Sources, and now you don't even know about the six different elemental lands?"

"Well excuse me, all knowing Warrior of Fire," Tavin sarcastically apologized with a smile. "If you recall, I'm still kind of new at this. It hasn't even been a month yet." Having been interrupted long enough, Zeroan stepped in to resume his explanation. Summarizing what he had told Jaren about the six elements and the Sources that held their power, he elucidated everything from how they had altered the geography of Iairia to how they gave the Southland's Elemental Warriors power.

"That is how the Sources function, Tavin. Do you understand?" At the end of the sage's speech, Tavin found his curiosity racing and decided to inquire further.

"So just hypothetically speaking," he began, still forming his question, "if all of the Sources all came together at one point in the world, the landscape of Iairia would balance out?" Zeroan sighed at the question.

"Well it isn't that simple, Tavin," the sage stated. "The Sources have made the lands what they are now, and even if they were united as one once again, it would not immediately change the landscape of Iairia as you must be thinking they would. Over a period of several hundred years, yes, there would be a fair change. But it would take great longevity before the surface of the land would balance out completely. The only thing that could drastically change the way the world looks would be if all of the Sources disappeared, or were stolen away." Tavin's expression became more serious as he realized what Zeroan was saying.

"You mean if Montrox succeeds and gathers all the shards of the Hold Emerald," Tavin stated with understanding. Zeroan nodded quietly as the rest of the group also went silent.

"Exactly," the sage confirmed. "If you recall, the Holy Emerald was what housed the one, true, master Source of all the elements combined; the one ultimate power in the universe. If the emerald is assembled by the Drakkaidian lord, he will have the power to summon the Sources to him and use their power for destruction instead of creation as they currently provide. With no power to endow life to the lands, they would slowly wither and die; become black and barren like the tainted lands to the far north. All life would cease to exist." The sage stopped, looking back at Tavin. "That is one of the Three Fates that has been foretold." The entire group was overtaken by confusion at that statement.

"What are the Three Fates, Zeroan?" Tavin asked on the group's behalf. Zeroan spun his head around and mumbled something under his breath then, seeming angry at himself for something he must have said.

"That will not be discussed today," he stated with authority after contemplating how to answer that question. "But since I know how curious this group and you in particular are, Tavin," he began looking back to him, "I promise you will know another time. Until then, try not to dwell on it. To the task at hand, we are now on our way into the south and the Grailen. If we maintain a steady pace, we should arrive in the plains the day after tomorrow, and will be to the borderlands of the Great Forests within two weeks after that. From there we will head to Greenwall, the vast fortress of the south on the direct border of the Great Forests. Whether we stop there or not remains to be determined. From there, I will seek out a contact in one of the border villages who might have some information to help us. I am guessing the shard is somewhere in the Great Forests, so it will not be easy to locate. We will be relying on your expert knowledge of the area, Parnox." The brawny Southlander at the rear of the group nodded in response.

"Very good. That is all I can tell you for now, because I do not know what we will do after that," the sage confessed, though he did so with a steady voice. Jaren raised an eyebrow hearing this.

"Don't know what we will do after that?" he repeated a little frightened. "Your words don't provide much assurance that you know what you are doing, sage." Zeroan's eyes narrowed underneath his hood as he snapped back at him.

"A solution will present itself, as one always does," he boldly said. "All you need do until then is trust in my ability and judgment. Now for the bad news."

"That was the good news?" Ril asked skeptically.

"I'm afraid so. Unfortunately, there has been a recent development in Drakkaidia that could prove to be a very dangerous threat to us," Zeroan said morbidly. "Though I would not have expected either of you two to have felt it," he said addressing Tavin and Ril, "there has been a lone dark power trailing us for the better part of a day now. Though the limits of this power are somehow masked from me, I can sense it possesses great potential. I did not expect Montrox to respond to our defeating his Dark Mage so quickly with his still limited power over the dark magics, but he did. As when we left Galantia, we must keep our presence masked to our enemies at all times. With a Drakkaidian possessing the power to mask his energy signature behind us, marauders influenced by Montrox ahead, and demons hunting for us everywhere, we are once more at great risk using any magic power or making any unnecessary scenes.

"So the same rules apply now as they did when we left Grandaria. No magic whatsoever unless there is no other option and we all maintain a low profile moving across the lands. We avoid being seen by anyone when possible, and we do not stop in a settlement unless absolutely necessary. I would have liked to have acquired horses for us, but with the Sarton's spies watching us we would not have had them for long. Unless we managed to locate some elsewhere, we will have to make do on foot as before. I ask you to continue to trust my knowledge and judgment and do as I say. That is all." As the greyly cloaked sage finally ended his speech, the others in the group were left at a loss for words. They walked on for several long moments before Tavin at last opened his mouth to speak.

"Whatever lies in wait for us," he began, surprising the others with his determined and serious tone, "I'll be ready for it. I trust you, Zeroan." Following Tavin's lead, Ril concurred soon after, followed by the rest of the group. Zeroan nodded his head in acknowledgement and turned back ahead of him to continue marching into the horizon of the Grailen Plains.

The party went on like this for the remainder of the day, rejuvenated by purpose and determination coursing through them all. By the time the sun began to sink into the distant mountains to the west the day after, the group had made the gradual transition from the dense waterways of the Torrentcia territories to the point where only a few trickling creeks and gaunt looking willow tress could be seen. Ahead, only the endless rolling silhouette of the Grailen Plains was visible in the dim twilight. As night came, the party rested alongside a cool pond of still water where they immediately fell victim to their sleep. The next morning, Zeroan was waking them at the first light and moving them onward at full speed. Though he said nothing of it, Tavin could tell that whatever was behind them had not stopped to rest during the night and was too close for comfort.

The march through the now dwindling wetlands of the central Southland proceeded similar to the day before. The terrain had softened and smoothed out considerably as the group found themselves marching into plains, though the transition was subtle. The only thing that alerted Tavin upon his entrance to the Grailen was a tattered old sign that read, "Fields and Forests: Welcome to the Grailen. Greenwall Fortress ahead." Despite the sign's words, it was actually quite far off for the band of adventurers on foot. For nearly two more weeks, the team pressed onward through the seemingly endless fields and meadows of green. It was on the thirteenth day since the group had left Torrentcia City that they began to approach the borderlands of the Great Forests. Only stopping for a brief lunch, Zeroan kept them trudging along until the sun began to dip yet again into the far away west, casting the shadows of night around them. At Kohlin's suggestion, they rested for the night under the last willow tree they could find beside a thin brook breathing life into the last remnant of the wetlands, now all but forgotten in the party's mind.

As always, Zeroan disappeared into the night as soon as the team began to bed down, and Kohlin volunteered to take the first watch; as alert in the night as in the day. In the confines of the draping branches of the old willow, Parnox rested his back against the thick trunk and drifted off the moment he closed his eyes, being a heavy sleeper when he had the opportunity. Feeling the need to be different as always, Jaren took his place in the lower branches of the willow, somehow finding a comfortable position to sleep. At the base of the tree, Ril had curled up by the brook, comforted by the sounds of the trickling but ever-steady flow of the passing water. Staring into the now black road ahead of him into the plains, Tavin breathed deeply as he ran the past weeks of travel through his mind. The group's journey south had been a seemingly quick one, as he now found them within a visual range of the tops of the Great Forest borderlands. They were in quiet spirits now, the mysterious new threat of a lone Drakkaidian ever encroaching on their position keeping them on edge. Ril had transitioned the most, somehow going from excessively happy to unusually silent.

Tavin took another deep breath and lowered his arms to his sides to brush away his cape covering the Sword of Granis, revealing the gently beaming light from the Granic Crystal. Finding comfort in its silent but assuring glow, he regained his senses and began to prepare for bed himself. As he took a place further away from the tree, he turned to lay his blanket down and found Ril staring at him, bundled up in her blanket by the brook. Tavin was so surprised and mesmerized by her solemn face fixated upon him, his eyes immediately locked upon her, holding her gaze tightly. Finding it impossible to break his stare from her beautiful but emotionless face, he curiously rose through the darkness and, before he knew it, was over to where she lay; drawn like a magnet. Bending down to his knees beside her, Tavin watched as the girl gently massaged her scarlet locket in the palm of her quivering hand. As she swallowed hard, a lock of her crimson hair silently tumbled down her face. All the while, she kept her eyes focused on Tavin, not blinking once.

"We don't get much time for rest, much less sleep anymore," Tavin whispered to her, at last breaking the silence. "You should take advantage of this while you can." Though clearly hearing his words, Ril did not look away or change at all, still fixated on the boy's face. When no response came in the somewhat awkward moments that followed, Tavin noticed a

257

nameless emotion present in her eyes. Mesmerized by them, he felt a steadily growing urge to stay there beside her. As he held her gaze, Tavin could not identify what it was Ril was saying in her eyes, though he could tell they exuded some masked emotion crying to be set free. It was when Ril was overcome with this mysterious sensation ready to explode inside her that her delicate mouth slowly opened, almost trembling as it did.

"...Tavin," was all that came out, in a near inaudible whisper.

"What is it, Ril?" he managed to whisper back, eager to hear what she would say. Through her spiraling thoughts and feelings, no words could find their way out of her mouth. She just kept staring. For long moments more, the two held each others gazes until a single tear that had developed in the corner of Ril's eye fell streaming across her smooth cheek. Surprised and puzzled, he leaned closer ready to offer any support he could.

"Don't go," she softly cried, another tear falling from her closed eye. More confused than he could ever remember, Tavin slowly outstretched his legs on the ground and knelt next to her. The moment he fell to her level, Ril scooted her shaking body close to him, nestling her head below his. As she came together with him, Ril's singular tears began to roll freely down her face and she began to faintly weep with quiet, heartfelt sorrow, leaving Tavin at a complete loss. Not daring to speak, he just let her cry into the night, putting an arm gently over her in comfort. Not having the faintest idea what had provoked these tears, Tavin lay feeling as if he didn't know anything anymore.

Chapter 38

Evacuation

An overcast sky of heavy fog enveloped the following morning. So thick were the hazy vapors that even the ever alert Kohlin Marraea's precisely observant eyes could not detect the lone figure sitting atop a series of boulders to the northeast of his party's current position. The figure sat motionless but for his dilapidated coattails waving their frayed ends in the northern breeze and the rustling of his red hair. He silently watched the group of diverse adventurers preparing to be back on their way after their night's rest. Because of the wind and low patches of fog sinking into the damp morning air, it was not long before the figure lost visual contact with his quarry. About to rise and start out after them once more, a slight vibration in his coat pocket drew his attention away from his prey.

The figure let out a huff of irritation and slowly reached into his tattered coat pocket to pull forth a disfigured burgundy stone no larger than the clenched fist around it. As he opened his hand to reveal the vibrating stone, its inner core pulsated with deep, crimson, electrical surges allowing a faint murmur of sound radiating out. The inner light quickly rushed forward to focus the faint noise from an inaudible hum to perceptible speech.

"Verix," came the dark voice from the stone. "Verix, what is happening?" The figure sighed deeply with frustration as he clutched the glowing stone tightly in his palm.

"How good of you to check up on me, father," the annoyed boy stated, "but I am quite busy at the moment so if you would be so kind as to let me proceed with my task, I can-"

"Verix, what is happening?" the voice repeated, monotone anger present in the words. "I can still feel the enemy that you promised to be dead by now alive. Why does he yet draw breath?" Verix placed his free hand over his forehead, vexation wearing into his face.

"I am in pursuit of the Warrior of Light and his party now," the boy reported tediously.

"Your task is not to pursue him, your task is to destroy him," the stone's voice sounded.

"The Warrior of Light is currently on his way to locate the first of the missing shards," Verix reminded. "I will let him find the shard for me, and then I will take it from him and his pitiful band."

"Do not make the mistake of presuming to alter my orders without consulting me first, boy," the stone sounded powerfully. "I have ordered you to annihilate the Warrior of Light now, not allow him to complete his little treasure hunt and then finish him. I have just taken care of finding the missing shards. You will not bother with-" Verix's face abruptly burst awake and furiously cut the voice off.

"What do you mean you've taken care of finding them?" he asked anxiously. "Don't tell me you have summoned more of the demons, father! You know that the veil between our world and the Netherworld is damaged enough without you tearing it further!" It was the voice from the stone's turn to interrupt this time.

"I have told you time and again, boy, I know what I am doing," it confirmed with unwavering authority. "If I wanted your advice, I would ask for it. Don't concern yourself with the shards. Destroy the Warrior of Light. That is all." With that, the deep red light from the core of the stone began to fade until completely gone. Verix was on his feet now, trying to reestablish the link to Dalastrak.

"Father! You cannot control them!" the boy screamed down at the stone. It did not respond. Realizing trying to communicate any further was pointless, the Dark Prince's face twisted with untold rage. Letting out a scream in his fury, he lifted the stone over his head and threw it downward into the rugged boulder, shattering it instantly. It was several long moments later before the figure leapt off the boulder and was off again into the cloudy morning upon the Grailen Plains.

Plagued by the painful lack of knowledge as to why Ril had become so upset the previous evening, Tavin walked quietly beside her not saying much of anything the next day, deciding it best to let her tell him on her own what was wrong, if she wanted to at all. He could tell that she wanted to say something every time their eyes met, but she would always quickly look away, plainly illustrating something was holding her back. She remained conservative with her movements, just focusing on propelling herself forward. As had her personality, her bright clothes had lost some of their fire since their departure from Torrentcia; her red tunic and tight trousers were frayed and worn. The confusion was nothing short of agonizing for the Grandarian boy. He had to admit that he found himself attracted to her and thought that she felt the same to him, but this unpredictable event and apparent secret had made him unsure. Moving on in the comfortably awkward silence for the duration of the morning, the Mystic Sage at the head of the group at last halted them as they started over a ridge in the grassy plains. Returning from his scouting that he had embarked upon earlier in the morning, Kohlin Marraea appeared bounding over the ridge to address the group now gathered around Zeroan.

"You were right, Zeroan," he stated obviously a little out of breath. "I was fairly far away, but something has definitely happened. I've never seen it so packed full of people." Zeroan nodded at the report, then turned back to Parnox running his thick fingers through his dense brown beard.

"What do you make of it, Parnox?" the sage asked quietly. Parnox squinted his eyes and lowered his hand.

"Not really sure..." he mouthed vaguely. Zeroan did not let his gaze off of the Southlander, as if not satisfied with his answer. Tavin, Jaren, and Ril shot bewildered glances at each other as they stood waiting for someone to say something more. It was Parnox who again broke the silence, letting out a sigh as he did. "I just can't think of any other reason, Zeroan. Unless one of those renegade demons from Drakkaidia was out causing trouble, it had to have been a Golthrout attack. It's soon, but they've been getting more aggressive over the past few decades." Letting the impatience of his confusion over Ril spread to the matter at hand, Tavin threw his hands in the air and indignantly interrupted.

"Would everyone please hold on for a minute?" he asked resentfully. "Sorry for my apparent ignorance in this matter

261

too, but what in the name of Granis on high are you two talking about?" The others turned to him surprised to see the usually patient and understanding Warrior of Light so hostile. Parnox was the one to elaborate for him.

"Here in the Great Forests, Tavin, we have a group of predators that live deep in the caverns under the trees but appear every decade or so to prey on the outlying villages along the edges of the forests. They are monsters made of rock about twice the size of humans, but a hundred times stronger. They are called the Golthrouts- cave dwellers. Why they appear to take what humans they can captive, we don't really know, because no one has ever returned from their lair- wherever it is. Whenever they appear at the surface to prey on us though, the villages all evacuate to the fortress of Greenwall for protection. The Golthrouts never come that far out of the woods."

"And it is packed to the gunnels," Kohlin affirmed. "I even overheard a group of rangers say that they are refusing entrance to anyone except border village refugees."

"I suppose that means we won't be stopping there then," Zeroan stated from behind his robes. "That settles that. We will pass outside the fortress to gather information and supplies if necessary, and then be on our way to the border villages."

"Wait a minute," Jaren interjected. "I thought you just said the villages have been evacuated. Won't whoever you're looking for be bottled up in Greenwall?" Zeroan shook his head no.

"No, my friend in Gaia Village would not abandon his home even because of Golthrouts. I have not seen him in years, but Marcell and his family will still be there," the sage assured them. Jaren was still skeptical.

"Okay, that's all fine then, but that still leaves the matter of us marching into a rock-monster infested forest," Jaren reminded him. "How do you plan for us to defend ourselves against a gang of rock men if we can't use any magic?"

"Leave such matters for me to deal with, Jaren," the sage advised. "Now let us be off. Greenwall Fortress and the borders of the Great Forests will become visible to us once we pass over this ridge, and from there it will be in close reach. We will be at the fortress by midday. Quickly now." With that, they were off again. As Zeroan said, the mighty fortress of the forests and plains came into sharp view the moment the company passed over the ridge in the plain. Remembering what the sage had told him earlier, Tavin recalled that this fortress was once the capital of the whole Southland because of its naturally protected and well built walls to keep it safe from invasion, along with its monstrous size.

As he grew closer to the aged fortress, Tavin could tell just how old it was. It had been built into the lone rocky peak that extruded from the flat fields, serving as an extension to the fortress. Most of the manmade walls around the fortress had been overgrown with sprawling vines and thick moss-like ferns sprouting from the damp walls, obviously the reason Greenwall possessed the name it did.

He guessed that the rock-strewn protrusion had been hollowed out to fit more people or provisions inside. Despite its enormous size, it was obviously not large enough to properly house all of the people of the forest border villages, as proven evident by the masses resting in tents and makeshift shelters outside.

Hours later, the party at last arrived at the mighty fortress where the groups of evacuated villagers had set up camps. As Zeroan led his companions around the masses, he began to quietly curse under his breath. Tavin was quick to notice the sage's obvious vexation as he marched behind him.

"What's wrong, Zeroan?" he asked staring up at the greyly cloaked Mystic Sage. Zeroan turned his masked face down to the boy.

"It's Othan," he said with enmity. "The fool told me that there should be a battalion of Legionnaires here, but I have yet to see even one. What idiocy he really has them doing, Granis only knows..." Trailing off there, the sage once again left Tavin in the dark. It was Parnox again who informed him of the negative relationship between the Sage and the Sarton. As the party moved on through the crowds, Zeroan at last stopped in front of a passing refugee.

"Pardon me, sir," the sage began, "but I was hoping you could be so good as to inform me why the border villages have been evacuated." From his rushed bodily movements and the flustered look upon his dirtied face, the man seemed irritated to have to explain his business to an outsider, but he apparently choked back impatience and did so anyway.

"There's been a Golthrout attack on Marain and Gaia Village," the man imparted abrasively. "Both were completely smashed to bits and all of the villagers were taken- not a single survivor. On top of that, the local band of various brigands and outlaws has somehow turned into a veritable army and is moving across the Grailen like a virus." The man's already bitter tone of voice escaladed into an all-out tirade. "We were promised a battalion of Legionnaires from Torrentcia City weeks ago, but still we are alone. Without any help from the north, even the mighty Greenwall with be helpless before their sheer numbers.

"In any case, the border villages were ordered to be emptied at the first word of the Golthrouts, but as you can see, Greenwall is too small to fit the entire populace inside, so the rest of us refugees who took a longer time to get here have to live outside for the time being. Now if you'll excuse me, I have to attend to my family while I can." As the man set off past the group, Tavin could still feel his overwhelmed and acidic words searing. It was not just this man who felt this way, either. The other disheartened and defeated faces of the refugees from the border villages who had been denied sanctuary inside Greenwall seemed to reflect the same mood.

Thinking back over what the man had related to them, Tavin remembered that the source they were looking for lived in Gaia Village, apparently the same one wiped out by the Golthrouts. Looking up to Zeroan once more, Tavin noticed he was not moving. After an uncomfortably long time passed just standing amongst the hordes of villagers, Tavin at last spoke.

"I don't mean to hustle you, Zeroan," he began as sensitively as possible, "but I think we should be getting out of the crowds. You said yourself we should not be seen for too long." Zeroan nodded under his hood once, and without a word set off darting through the rows of people to get away from the encampments. Straining themselves to keep up with the near sprinting sage, the group emerged from the makeshift shelters. Making their way into a grove of bushes and short trees away from the proximity of Greenwall, Zeroan at last halted. Though he did not speak right away, the sage eventually turned back to his party.

"This is not good for our cause," he mumbled slowly, "not good at all." When the sage went into silence one again, the others felt it appropriate to attempt to console him.

"I'm sorry you lost your friend, Zeroan," was the sympathetic statement from Ril. Zeroan met her gaze.

"I would not be too concerned about Marcell if I were you," he stated. "He is an old friend of the sages and me. He and his family know how to evade Golthrouts." Ril found it hard to accept the sage could be so sure in his friend's abilities when everyone had supposedly been killed. "In any case, we are still going to Gaia Village. Even if Marcell is gone, we may find the clues we need in the wreckage of his home."

"Now just slow yourself down, buddy," came Jaren's voice from the back of the group moving forward. "That entire village was just wiped off the face of the map by rock monsters. I for one do not think it to be a grand idea to be waltzing in there like its no big deal." Zeroan's head shot up at the Grandarian boy.

"I have had quite enough of you and your doubts, boy," he snapped harshly. "If you have any better ideas, do feel free to share them with the rest of us." Jaren's mouth could not formulate any words to respond. "No? Then I suggest you leave such matters to those who know what they are speaking of. We have nothing to fear from a gaggle of walking rocks as long as we avoid them, which I intend to do. But we need to be on our way again. The Drakkaidian that has been trailing us has just disappeared from my senses. He has either broken off the chase, masked his power further, or is within a visual range of us. Unfortunately, it's probably the latter, so I suggest that we skip lunch and keep moving. Gaia Village is still days away from here through the first patches of the Great Forests, and I fear that we are losing time."

Zeroan gathered himself and began walking forward again.

"Come," was the last thing he said, beckoning for the others to follow. They did so with reluctance, but continuing to trust the mysterious Mystic Sage.

Chapter 39

<u>The Three Fates</u>

Hiking through the ends of the southern Grailen Plains for the remainder of the day, the party from Galantia at last came upon the first of the Great Forests. With twilight right behind them, Zeroan informed the group that they did not have the time to travel around the borders of the forests to reach the hidden village of Gaia, so they would be cutting straight through. Deciding it too dangerous to proceed into the most likely Golthrout infested forest at night, however, the sage ordered camp be made until first light. With the threat of the lone Drakkaidian exceedingly close behind them now, he also instructed camp to be made in the first row of trees to hide their position from any who would expect them to be out in the open.

With the dangers of their pursuer behind them and the monstrous Golthrouts in front, the group was on constant alert for the entire night. With two keeping watch at once and everyone's nerves at their end, little sleep was gained. For the first shift of watches, Parnox and Tavin took up the perimeter of the camp site, alert for movement of any kind. As Tavin made his way to the forest side of the camp, he passed Ril preparing to get what rest she could. Though he was tempted to approach her and try to ask what was bothering her, she quickly turned away to nestle up against the trunk of a tree the moment she laid eyes on him, sending Tavin the message she still did not desire to say anything. Concerned for her but respecting her apparent wish for privacy, he passed by, taking up his post to keep watch. As the minutes began to pass into hours, Tavin found himself staring more at Ril than at the forest, finding himself going insane with why she was suddenly sinking into this depression.

Contemplating what could have caused the girl's sullen condition, a faint movement out of the corner of Tavin's eye drew his attention away from the sleeping Warrior of Fire. Spinning his head around just in time, Tavin saw Zeroan leaving the group once again, leaping into the forest outside the camp without a sound. Having been plagued by this mystery long enough, Tavin decided that it was time he discovered for himself just why the sage left the party every night. As quietly as he could, the Warrior of Light temporarily abandoned his watch and stealthily followed after him. Having to creep through the trees to avoid detection, he was hard pressed to keep up. In fact, it was not long before Tavin lost all visual contact of Zeroan, finding himself running through the woods after him blindly.

Just when he was about to give up on the chase completely, a weak light slowly materialized to the boy's left, drawing his attention yet again. Deciding it must be Zeroan, Tavin covered up the Sword of Granis with his cape to hide the light from the Granic Crystal on the hilt and slowly crept over to the source of the luminosity. Tiptoeing as discreetly as possible, he at last came upon a lone stump amidst the thick trees where the cloaked figure of Zeroan sat hunched over holding a faint vial of a white glowing liquid. Fascinated by the mysterious substance that the sage had managed to conceal from the group this far into the journey, Tavin stepped closer to try and get a better look than the oblique one he was stuck with now.

As he inched closer, a lone branch jetting out from the foliage snagged Tavin's cape, revealing the shining light of the Granic Crystal. Though he immediately tried to smother it with his hands in a frantic thrusting movement downward, Zeroan caught sight of it the moment it shown out to him. Instantly on his feet with a surge of white energy bursting to life in his outstretched hand, Tavin fell back on the ground in surprise and fear. Seeing that the intruder was only the Warrior of Light, however, the sage quickly cut off his display of power and tucked his glowing vial away in the deep layers of his flowing gray robes. Though Tavin was relieved to see he had been recognized, Zeroan was not as happy as he instantly came towering over the Grandarian boy.

"What do you think you are doing!?!" the sage fiercely whispered through the night air. Tavin's momentary feeling of relief vanished as he fumbled to respond without upsetting the irate sage more than he already was.

"I- I was just curious why you leave every night, so I decided to find out where you always go," he weakly explained. Zeroan grit his teeth in anger, mostly at himself for allowing someone to have seen him.

"I leave *privately* every night to have my *privacy*," Zeroan angrily put in plain words. "It is none of your businesses why I leave you as long as I am back every morning. That should be enough." Unfortunately, that was not enough for Tavin, his own dormant anger ignited.

"Now wait just a minute, Zeroan," he stated challengingly, rising back to his feet to face the sage. "I don't appreciate that remark one bit. I have been as patient as humanly possible on this quest of yours, believing, supporting, and trusting you every step of the way. That's not something you can ask from most people these days, or any others for that matter. Now I've been kept in the dark about more things than I care to remember so far, and to be perfectly candid with you, I'm starting to get a little tired of the run around. I've accepted things the way they are for plenty long enough, and I think I'm entitled to a few answers about a few things right about now, and if I don't get them, I'm going to start getting very unpleasant very soon." Caught up in the heat of the moment, even Tavin himself was surprised at what he said by the end of his tirade.

Caught completely off guard by the boy's strong remarks, Zeroan stood quietly before him for the next few moments, waiting for anything else that might be coming his way. When nothing else was said, he began to respond.

"Threats do not become of one with your character, Tavin," said Zeroan ominously quiet. "But, nevertheless, you are right. I think I have been keeping you out of the loop about one too many things that you should most likely be informed of. So tell me what you want to know, Tavin, and I will try to explain as best I can, if I can." Nothing short of amazed at the sage's response to his demands, Tavin decided to take full advantage of this rare and truly golden opportunity.

"All right then," he began satisfied, "what was that glowing vial of liquid you just had out?" Zeroan let out a deep sigh.

"Yes, that would be the first question, wouldn't it," he began reluctantly. "Very well. If I tell this to you, you must swear an oath to me that you will tell no one in our party, or anyone else, about what I will relate. Agreed?" Tavin silently nodded his head. "Excellent. Now I would show it to you again, but it would have a very negative affect on your body. You probably just cut a few days off of your life just looking at it for as long as you did."

"What?" Tavin asked astounded and aghast. Zeroan nodded, once again taking a seat upon the solitary stump amidst the heavy tree trunks of the woods.

"It is true, Tavin. The potion that I just had out has been dubbed the Sage's Draught by most of us. It is an ancient substance consumed by the Mystic Sages to keep us constantly energized and awake, so we never require rest. But more importantly, every time I use it, I also perpetuate my life."

"Wait, are you saying drinking this makes you immortal?" Tavin asked in disbelief.

"Not even close," Zeroan responded quickly. "The draught can only be consumed by one well educated in the mystic arts, and he must also have a great understanding and appreciation of the effects it will take on one's body. To answer your question, it is more accurate to say that it temporarily keeps me from aging naturally. Instead, I age when I use great quantities of my other magics and powers. That is why I appear so exhausted after any battle or endeavor that requires the use of magics and mystic powers." Hearing this, Tavin found a new understanding and appreciation of the sacrifice Zeroan made in his life being a sage. "I leave you every night because it is best to keep this fact a secret so no one ever discovers there is a substance that delays old age. I must drink it every night for it to take full effect on my body. Only a drop is necessary. Any more would kill me."

"What happens when you run out of the draught, Zeroan? Surely you have consumed that vial three times over by now," Tavin pointed out.

"Conveniently, the vial I posses is the key to the draught. It is an enchanted vial that refills itself with the draught from the Mystic Tower whenever it is emptied. There is a reservoir of it there, but in that form it is not the draught, but a power; the essence of the Order of Alberic. This liquid was created by Alberic, founder of the Mystic Sages, and it contains the secret to our power and abilities," Zeroan explained. "As you know, mystic power is far more complicated than standard elemental, so I suggest we leave it at that, young Grandarian. I have already told you too much." Though Tavin's mind was bouncing around with 'what if' questions about the Sage's

Draught, he decided it best to accept that as a suitable answer and move on, seeing as how Zeroan was compromising his own code by even mentioning this to him.

"Thank you for telling me, Zeroan," he said gratefully. "You have my word I will never say anything of this. But I have another question."

"I expected you would," the sage answered. "Let's have it then."

"You said something about the Three Fates months ago when we first met and again last week, and you said they related to me," Tavin recalled. "But you never want to talk about them. What are the Three Fates?" Zeroan sighed at that question, obviously knowing he was in for a long discussion.

"The Three Fates," he repeated. "Well, I suggest you brace yourself for this. It is another prophesy foretold to us that coincides with prophesy of the Warrior of Light and Darkness. They are three possible destinies that will befall the world after the Holy Emerald is reconstructed." Tavin shot his head forward in awestruck confusion.

"What?" he exclaimed. "What do you mean *is* constructed? I thought that was what we are trying to prevent!" Zeroan shook his head no.

"Not so," he said calmly. "We are trying to prevent Montrox and his disciples from reconstructing the emerald and using its power for evil. The prophesy of the Three Fates tells us, however, that for one of them to come to pass, the Holy Emerald must be reconstructed."

"Zeroan, this doesn't make sense," Tavin declared in supreme bewilderment. "You told us that you were going to destroy the emerald shards when we set out."

"I said that," Zeroan admitted, "but I never intended to. There is a reason that few know of the Three Fates, Tavin. When one of them comes to pass, there is going to be major change all over the world; change that many would not desire. It is best that people do not know what is to become of the world after the Final Battle of Destiny." Zeroan raised his hands to stop Tavin from speaking, already fully aware what the next question would be. "Yes, I know. What is the Final Battle of Destiny, right?" Tavin nodded, not saying a word. "Of course. Well you should already be able to guess what that is, I hope. The Final Battle of Destiny will be between the Warrior of Light and Darkness and will decide the Three Fates. It is your destiny to face off against Montrox, Tavin. As you know, he is the Warrior of Darkness; your eternal enemy. You will face him at the pinnacle of your power someday in the not too distant future, and if you do not stop him once and for all right then and there, there will be no tomorrow for Iairia." Tavin didn't know what to say in response.

"That's pretty heavy," he managed to mumble, caught a little off guard by the gravity of the answer. Zeroan shrugged slightly.

"It is, but that is the truth of things. Even if we somehow manage to overcome and overpower Drakkaidia's hordes of soldiers and endless waves of demons, it will be a meaningless victory if you fail in your task. Montrox will be nothing short of a god if he is allowed to win, and if he becomes that, it will result in the true God of Darkness returning from the black side of the afterlife as well. That is one of the Three Fates."

"What are the other two, then?" Tavin pressed.

"The first of the three is what could happen if you are victorious, Tavin," Zeroan explained. "You could assemble the Holy Emerald and invoke its holy powers for good across the lands, bringing a new golden age full of righteous magic for all to use and benefit from. Iairia would become nothing short of heaven on earth. Perfect; constant; sublime; a true paradise. The second fate is what happens if Montrox wins. And the third fate is... more or less, a neutral future. If either of you two wins and assembles the emerald but then does nothing with it, or decides it best if no new magic be introduced to the lands, the world will continue on as it is now leaving humanity to face its destiny without magic to aid them. While this may seem pointless, it might end up being better for the world." Tavin was confused to no end hearing that.

"How could that possibility be a better fate for the world?" he inquired. "If we could achieve a perfect life for everyone; to create paradise, how would that not be better?" Zeroan shrugged again.

"You tell me," he stated simply. "With no one to work through or experience life's natural hardships and to have everything handed to everyone, you are essentially deciding humanity's destiny for them. What would happen to culture? What would happen to art? What would happen to progress and the future? There would be no future. Just the same, perfect, paradise for everyone forever." The look on Tavin's face seemed to suggest he did not see what Zeroan was trying to say.

"Sounds pretty good to me," Tavin remarked. Zeroan only remained still and emotionless as he spoke.

"Then that's good enough for me," he said. "You are the one that will have to make that decision, not me, so it's not for me to say. That is why I kept the Three Fates to myself. Few leaders of the world would be enthralled to know a boy is destined to decide its fate. But you have some time on your hands before you have to make that decision, don't you? Though you may believe it unnecessary now, think it over. You may be surprised at what time and experiences can do to change you." After the words sunk in, Tavin cocked his head in further confusion.

"Zeroan, suppose I did want to choose the neutral fate with the Holy Emerald," he began, "why would I bother assembling the emerald at all if nothing was to change? Couldn't I just let it remain in shards? What would be the difference?" Zeroan's head shifted under his hood.

"What would be the difference, Tavin?" he repeated as if awestruck. "We *must* reconstruct the Holy Emerald to complete the prophesy. If we do not do that, well..." Zeroan trailed off as if not knowing what to say.

"What, Zeroan?" Tavin pressed, intrigued. Zeroan exhaled sharply at Tavin.

"No one knows, actually," he admitted, to which Tavin's brow furrowed. "But it would most likely result in the eventual end of the world as we know it. Remember Tavin, that the Holy Emerald is the source of all power for everything in existence, living or no, in the entire universe. Think for a moment. If its power remains dormant forever, the world could decay and die. The emerald might be needed to regenerate the world's energies." Tavin gave the sage an incredulous look.

"'Might?' With all due respect Zeroan, it sounds like you're making this up as you go," Tavin said with a smile on his face, though Zeroan only frowned.

"Well as I said Tavin, no one knows for certain. But without the Holy Emerald, there is no telling what could happen to nature and magic. The only thing for certain would be death. And I for one, am not willing to take that chance by defying the prophesy that Granis gave us," he stated assertively. "But none of this matters anymore, does it? If we don't reconstruct it, the forces of darkness will, so we are left with little choice.

Don't dwell on it." With that, the Zeroan rose from his place on the stump. "Well then, I think you've gotten all the answers you need now, don't you?" the sage said hopefully, already moving back toward camp. As he walked past Tavin, the young Grandarian boy was struck with one last issue he wished to inquire about.

"Wait, Zeroan," he called quietly. The sage halted then, and turned his head back toward the boy.

"If this is another 'what if' question-"

"I promise its not," Tavin laughed, cutting him off.

"What is it then?" he responded sounding fatigued. Tavin bought up a hand to scratch his head as he plopped on the stump where Zeroan had sat a few moments ago.

"Well, I doubt you'd be able to help, but..."

"What is it?" the sage repeated. Tavin shrugged again, a little more embarrassed than he thought he would be speaking about this.

"Well, it's Ril," he stated. "She's been acting strange the past couple of days, but I don't know why. At first she was almost too happy, but now she's been depressed like nothing else." Zeroan nodded as he slowly turned his body back one last time.

"Yes, you're right," he replied.

"So you've noticed something's wrong?" he asked hopefully. Zeroan shook his head.

"No, I meant you were right when you said I wouldn't be able to help," he responded darkly, leaving Tavin feeling more than a little ripped off. Zeroan shook his head and ran his left hand over his face and through his short dark beard. "I am a Mystic Sage, not a personality analyst. This sounds like a problem you should deal with on your own." Tavin frowned at the towering figure.

"Oh come on, Zeroan," he said directly. "You must have noticed she seems troubled. She cried on me for nearly two hours the other night. Don't tell me you think she's fine."

"Well, now that you mention it, she has been a little distant," Zeroan admitted, lowering his arm back down to his side and withdrawing it back into the confines of his robes. "But I still can't help you. The only person she would ever talk to about something like this in our group would be you, so I suggest *you* find out what the problem is. Press for an answer, and she'll talk to you. Now come on. You need to get back to camp and get some sleep. I'll be out here doing you-know-what. Be on your way, young man." Still contemplating Zeroan's advice in regard to Ril, Tavin took his time getting back up, dusting off his cape. As he began to walk past the sage, however, he stopped and looked up to meet his gaze.

"Thank you, Zeroan," Tavin said simply with a smile on his face. "You're quite the man, no matter what anyone else says about you." Having said that, Tavin turned started back through the trees, leaving Zeroan feeling as confident as ever that he had indeed found the right Warrior of Light.

Chapter 40

<u>Midnight Surprise</u>

Leaving the Mystic Sage Zeroan to himself in the darkness of the thick woods, Tavin strode back to camp through the path he had made chasing after him. Difficult to see where he was going with only a thin blanket of faintly luminescent moonlight upon the forest floor, Tavin decided to uncover his cape over the glowing Granic Crystal to avoid walking into tree trunks and foliage. As he maneuvered through the dark forests' organic obstacles, his mind drifted on how he would approach Ril the following day. Whatever was bothering her, she was reluctant to say anything about it, as proven evident by her unwillingness to speak with him at all. But as Zeroan had suggested, the only way to get her to say anything would be to ask her. She would respond to him, or at least he hoped so.

Pondering over his inevitable talk with the Southland girl, Tavin almost completely missed the other figure entering his field of view from the right. Surprised and alarmed to find another out in the forest, Tavin's hand was instantly wrapping around the hilt of the Sword of Granis by his side. Upon closer inspection of the figure, however, Tavin observed that he was of equal size and shape to himself, leading him to conclude it was only Jaren, most likely out to look for his missing friend. Letting his tight muscles loosen as the silhouette of his best friend approached, Tavin softly called out through the night air.

"Jaren," he whispered, "I thought you were asleep." Though the figure must have heard him, he did not respond other than to continue moving forward toward him. "Jaren, come on. Let's get back to camp. I don't feel good about leaving the others there all alone with so many things out to get us tonight."

"I wouldn't feel good about it either," was the startlingly loud response from the other. Having known his best friend for his entire life, Tavin knew his voice better than anyone, and the one that came from the figure striding toward him was not his. His nerves stiffening once more, Tavin reaffirmed his grip over the hilt of the Sword of Granis. As the other grew closer still, the thin moonlight cutting through the openings in the trees revealed that he looked nothing like Jaren.

"Hold on right there," Tavin firmly started again. "Who are you?" While he heard the command, the figure did not stop until he was mere feet in front of Tavin, to the point in fact, that the Warrior of Light was about to draw his blade to show that he was dead serious. As the faint light from the Sword of Granis found its way onto the frame of the figure, a wave of remembrance washed over Tavin. "Wait," he stated curiously. "I know you. You're the guy I ran into in Torrentcia City..." As Tavin trailed off a little taken aback by this familiar person's presence, the mysterious stranger smiled a chilling and dark smile that told Tavin there was something very wrong about him the moment it spread across his face. "What do you want?" was all that Tavin could utter. He silently chuckled to himself as an enormous and savage looking broadsword materialized out of a cloud of burgundy mist from behind him.

"For the legendary Warrior of Light, you're not very bright are you?" he asked cynically, completely shocking Tavin at how he knew of his title. "Surprised? Don't be. I've been following you for weeks now. And though you might be potentially more powerful than I if you were to reach the pinnacle of your true power, you are nothing to me now. What do I want?" The figure reached behind him and took hold of his oversized weapon with one hand, and raised his free hand in front of Tavin. As he began speaking, three fingers rose from his clenched fist, the smile on his face completely dissolving. "I'm here for the sage, that sword, and your head." Then, not leaving Tavin with enough time to shift the expression on his face from the forthright and threatening statement, he lunged his gigantic blade over his head and down onto Tavin as though it's gargantuan size was nothing for him to wield.

Thanks to his years of training and now supernaturally empowered reflexes, Tavin was able to just barley leap aside of his foe's blade, though only doing so by a fraction of a hair. With the force the mysterious attacker had put into the overhead swing downward, his blade lodged itself into the hard earth upon impact, giving Tavin the vital extra seconds he needed to draw his own weapon. With his hand already over the hilt, Tavin grit his teeth as he wrenched free his legendary sword faster and harder than ever before. With such force extracting it out, the savage metallic ringing of the blade was sent careening into the fragile night air, seemingly ripping a whole in time and space as it did. Surprised by the impossibly loud clash of metal on metal, the figure let out a powerful grunt from deep in his throat, summoning a sudden burst of crimson light that formed around his struggling body, allowing him newfound strength with which to pull his own sword from the ground it was embedded in.

As his enemy's power flared, Tavin could feel it like a sixth sense in the back of his mind, just as Zeroan described he would be able to. Though surprised and amazed by the perfectly clear presence of the increase in the dark boy's power, he was left with no time to contemplate it; the broadsword sailing toward him once more. Swiftly raising the Sword of Granis in his defense, Tavin was surprised to be swatted backward upon impact, pushed several feet away and onto his back from the force. Though the Sword of Granis remained unscathed as always, Tavin was awestruck at his enemy's sheer physical strength. Nearly the exact same size as Tavin, there was no possible way that he could have been that powerful. Again not leaving Tavin any time to think, the dark assassin leapt off of the ground with equally unreal dexterity, literally landing on top of Tavin. With one foot he pinned the Grandarian boy down by his chest and with the other smothered the Sword of Granis into the dirt.

As Tavin lay struggling for breath under his foe's seemingly gargantuan weight, the darkly clad figure slowly bent down to Tavin's level, resting the tip of his blade over his throat.

"And here I was expecting you would be a challenge," he muttered disgusted. "Is this really the best the fabled Warrior of Light can do?" As if to respond, Tavin exerted all his strength upward in one last desperate attempt to work his way free. The harder he resisted, though, the harder the force of his enemy's foot drove into his chest. "A pity," the dark one finished. "Well, I still have to destroy you, so... die well." It was here in this instant when all hope had faded and all possible ways to escape evaded him that Tavin's locked away powers of light suddenly revealed themselves to him in one explosive internal burst. Although remembering that Zeroan had forbid him from summoning his powers at this time and place, Tavin found it safe to assume that the dark assassin hovering above him was the lone Drakkaidian that had been following them.

Just as the powerful boy was about to plunge his blade downward, Tavin opened the internal doorway to the core of his power and released it, sending a familiar shockwave of golden energy blasting forth from his pinned body and throwing his attacker backward. Freed, Tavin leapt back to his feet from on the ground, the now standard golden aura engulfing his body. With his attacker subdued for the moment, Tavin at last readied himself with his newfound strength beating through his veins and the gleaming Sword of Granis brandished straight before him. Stepping back to face the radiating warrior, Tavin's assassin let a faint smile reemerge on his face.

"Yes..." he murmured, letting the blade of his own dark sword pass under his tattered coat and back in front of him. "This is more of what I like to see." As Tavin waited for another strike however, the newly enthusiastic face of his attacker began to regress back into its disappointed setting. "What are you waiting for? You'll need more than that if you're serious about taking me on." Though not sure at what the figure was speaking of, Tavin was further disgusted by the obvious arrogance present in his voice.

"What are you talking about?" he questioned argumentatively. A similar look of confusion passed over the dark boy's shadowed face.

"I warn you, Grandarian," he said threateningly, "don't toy with me. I assure you you're going to need every last bit of power in you if you wish it to stand up to mine." As the moments passed by after that statement, Tavin's face remained perplexed at the figure's words. Seeing this true confusion mirrored in Tavin's eyes, the Drakkaidian's face twisted as in deeply rooted pain. "Wait. ...Don't tell me that's it." There was still no response from Tavin. "Oh, Drakkan below. That is it. This is your full strength right now, isn't it? In fact, you don't even know what I'm talking about right now, do you? You think this is the limit to your power." The dark figure rolled his crimson eyes and let out a groan of aggravation. "I can't believe this. You're still so weak it's almost as painful as your ignorance." Tavin lost his already loose patience hearing this.

"Look, whoever you are," he began caustically. "I don't know what hole you just crawled out of, but if you think you're any match for me and my friends just because you can swing a big sword and jump a fair distance, you're obviously mistaken. I possess a legendary power you can't even begin to understand." The Drakkaidian let a look of abhorrence overcome his face.

"Oh this is sad," he said painfully. "Sorry to disappoint you, oh great Warrior of Light, but your maximum power level is so low right now there are probably insects in these trees that could destroy you. Killing you isn't even worth the effort it took to catch up to you." The figure sighed once more. "But I did tell father I would finish you, weakling or no. So I suppose I'll just keep my power to myself and dispatch you-" The Drakkaidian was suddenly interrupted by the ends of his coat flying up behind him as if in the grasp of two hands pulling him back. Though surprised, Tavin knew instantly the Mystic Sage Zeroan had responded to his surge of power moments ago. As the force of the grip on the Drakkaidian's coattails increased, his balance was lost and he went soaring back against the trunk of a tree. It was not a moment later when Zeroan came bounding out of the tree line, his gray robes flying through the darkness after him.

"Tavin!" he yelled at the top of his lungs. "Get out of here! This is the Drakkaidian that has been following us! His power is far beyond yours right now! You must retreat for the moment and gather the others to escape!" With Tavin's noble but willful determination present as always, he did not move a muscle as the sage passed by him.

"I'm not leaving you to deal with him alone," Tavin decreed boldly. "There's no way this guy is any stronger than me." Zeroan wheeled his head around and lashed out at him.

"You are as inexperienced as you are naïve, boy!" he harshly blasted back. "You know nothing of the varying levels of power yet, and now is not the time to learn! He is too much for you. Now do as I say and flee! *Now!*" Despite Tavin's heart dictating otherwise, he decided that Zeroan was most likely correct in this matter, and began to fall back in response. Turning away, Tavin called out once more.

"Zeroan, what about you?" he cried out.

"I can take care of myself!" the sage bellowed back. "Just get the others and hide! Follow Parnox to our destination; I will find you. Now go!" Still hesitant to abandon the sage this way, Tavin slowly turned back with his own power fading to start back down the path to his camp. Sprinting through the brush and foliage as fast as he could, Tavin cursed himself for not aiding Zeroan. If the mysterious Drakkaidian was really so powerful, he thought, even Zeroan with all his mystical strength would not stand much of a chance. But following the sage's wisdom, he retreated, sealing off his apparently obsolete power with the Sword of Granis in hand. Running on through the trees, Tavin heard, and more importantly felt, the sounds of powers and magics flaring behind him. Though most appeared to be originating from Zeroan, an ever increasing power from the other was building to new heights as well.

Forgetting the battle behind him for a moment, Tavin noticed a familiar group of trees and brush as he ran on, signaling his approach to the camp ground. Before he even managed to enter, all four of his other companions came rushing up to him befuddled, assailing him with questions. Parnox and Kohlin brandishing their weapons and Jaren and Ril rushing to Tavin's side, they didn't give him a chance to speak. Out of breath from the running and the demanding use of energy from the quick skirmish he found himself in, Tavin was quick to scream for silence in his group.

"Quiet!" he exploded on them, gaining their attention instantly. "Listen," he began winded. "The Drakkaidian that has been following us just found me, and Zeroan stepped in to hold him off for us so we can get away." Already with his gargantuan axe in hand, Parnox growled at the chance his friend might need help in battle.

"I'll do no such thing!" he responded bravely, if a little headstrong for his age. "No one will be fighting any Drakkaidian alone in this group." Hearing this, Tavin raised his arm and the gleaming blade of the Sword of Granis in front of the Southlander to cut off his advance.

"You're not going anywhere, Parnox," he declared with authority. The woodsman was at a loss for words as he heard the order coming from one half his age and size. "I already tried to help Zeroan, but apparently this Drak is too strong for any of us to engage. Our orders are to move to Gaia Village and Zeroan will meet back with us when he can. I don't like this either, but I've learned to trust his judgment and not to argue by now." As Tavin finished, the new sense in his mind felt a sudden explosion of power behind him, causing he and Ril to turn back astounded. The others looked on them befuddled.

"What is it?" Kohlin inquired first, gazing in the direction the Elemental Warriors seemed to be drawn to. Ril was the first to respond, awestruck.

"There's a huge power rising over there!" she cried. "And it's not Zeroan's!" Tavin turned back to Ril, almost forgetting she could sense the powers of magic as he could.

"Is it normal for someone to be that strong?" he asked worried, hearing an explosive blast of energy impacting the earth. Ril could only shake her head bedazzled.

"I've never felt anything that strong coming from one person's body," she responded unbelieving in what she was sensing. As she trailed off, Tavin remembered his task at hand.

"Well forget it for now," he advised, turning her and the others forward into the opposite side of the forest. "We have to get moving. And no magic Ril. If the Drak gets away from Zeroan, I don't want him to be able to sense us like we can sense him. He didn't look it when I saw him, but this guy is obviously a little tougher than I gave him credit for. Can you get to where we're going from here Parnox?" Still focused on the sounds of battle close by, Parnox was hesitant to respond.

"Gaia Village, right? Yes, I can get us there. But I-" Parnox was cut short by a rapidly approaching blast of dark crimson energy surging with black electricity abruptly smashing through the nearby tree line to violently explode on impact, sending earth and waves of flame flying all about them. Shielding his eyes with his fist still latched onto the Sword of Granis, Tavin sensed the shifting in the dark power once more as it drastically rose yet again, giving Tavin a true understanding for just how weak his current power had become. It was in this moment of uncertainty and self doubt that what was left of the tree line beside the group immediately bowed over with the other uprooted trees as the lone Drakkaidian warrior came soaring over them engulfed in a dark aura of crimson light to land just in front of the mesmerized group. As he impacted the earth, the ground around him began to break and sink beneath his feet from his emanating power. Standing there engulfed in his dark field of swirling dark energy, the grimacing Drakkaidian watched his prey cower unconfidently.

"How incredibly pathetic," he stated with the dark scowl over his face. "But now that the sage has been settled down, I can resume my business with the Warrior of Light." Hearing the other speak of Zeroan, Tavin was filled with new anger to lash out with.

"What have you done to Zeroan?" he questioned fiercely. The Drakkaidian only frowned wider.

"Please, you didn't honestly think one pathetic Mystic Sage could stand up to a Montrox, did you?" he asked caustically. The group went rigid hearing the figure announced himself.

"You're... Montrox?" Jaren asked going pale. The figure remained still with an emotionless face.

"Not the one you're thinking of, no doubt, but yes. You see, my name is Verix Montrox. My father is Valif Montrox, the ruler of Drakkaidia and Warrior of Darkness," he said with a strange lack of enthusiasm in his voice that suggested he was somewhat less than proud to announce that. Upon learning the lone Drakkaidian's identity, the party could feel the air withdrawing from their lungs. Tavin didn't know whether to be more flabbergasted or angry at this revelation of power. If this was only the son of the Warrior of Darkness and he couldn't even stand up to him, how would he ever be able to destroy the Drakkaidian king himself? Verix Montrox fed upon the fear on their faces.

"Weren't quite expecting that, were you?" he asked darkly. "Well then, I suppose I should get this show on the road. Who will be first then?" As he scanned through the terrified but strong faces before him, the expression on his own face suddenly altered, laying eyes on something. "...What in the..." he murmured, taking a long hard stare into the center of the group. Curious as to what was delaying him, Tavin curiously looked to his side to glance at what he was fixed upon. Following the figure's cold eyes, it was not long before Tavin realized he was staring at Ril, returning his gaze and shaking with fear. He appeared to be staring at the scarlet locket hanging around her neck over her frayed clothes. Verix's mouth opened then, silently wording something to himself before he spoke. "Arilia?" he murmured quietly.

Staggered to learn the evil Prince knew who she was, Ril's eyes and mouth widened with trepidation. Equally surprised and disturbed to hear Verix even speak her name, Tavin sternly grit his teeth and tightened his already white knuckle hands around his sword. Just as he was about to step forward to at least attempt to buy the rest of his party time to get away, another new sensation of power presented itself to him. Obviously sensing it as well, Verix returned to his senses and shifted his gaze downward to the ground separating him from the group of five.

"Blast," was all he could say as a sudden quake in the earth rippled through all of them. Seemingly out of nowhere, a massive fissure blasted open as a mighty limb of solid stone came clawing out, followed by a thick rocky torso attached to it. When the entire body of living earth had emerged with soil pouring off of it, two slits of piercing yellow light slid open on its compact head, fixed onto the group of overworlders standing before it.

Chapter 41

<u>Separated</u>

As the single towering creature rose from the rift in the earth it had just torn open, the group of humans standing before it were speedily knocked off their feet from the potent force of its emergence. Rising full length upon the surface, the monster stood over fifteen feet in height and appeared to be completely composed of tightly-fit rock from deep underground. As Tavin lay shaking from its even most minute movement, he could feel the massive air of power it was exuding. Though the creature was not any celestial being, it did not give off the same dark waves as did the demons of Drakkaidia or Verix Montrox, now lying before the creature just as helpless as any of them. This was obviously one of the Golthrouts, the subterranean rock predators of the Great Forests that Parnox had informed him about before.

While Tavin sat contemplating the best course of action given the extremely volatile and dangerous situation he now found himself in, another of the towering Golthrouts appeared behind the row of trees that Verix had uprooted minutes ago. Realizing the already horrible circumstances were deteriorating even further, Tavin was quick to roll back to his feet with the Sword of Granis still in hand. With one of the stone based creatures now hovering above him, Verix also regained his senses and flipped back up to his feet with his dark power flaring up once more. Taking his mighty broadsword in hand, he leapt up off the ground clear over the Golthrout, letting his blade slash into its head on the way over. Unfortunately for the Dark Prince, however, the creature was not so easily bested. Only feeling the equivalent of a pinprick on its near impenetrable cranium, the Golthrout threw one of its enormous arms back into Verix where he had just landed, sending him flying back through the downed tree branches with his weapon lost.

Seizing this opportunity to escape, Tavin set to work rousing the others from where they struggled to rise in the wake of all the seismic activity. As he lifted Ril to her feet, he was interrupted by another of the rock-strewn arms swiping downward into them, blasting Kohlin and Jaren over to the far side of the encampment. Tavin turned his head toward the tree line to find three more of the gargantuan monsters thrashing forward. Overwhelmed by the dangerously increasing numbers of Golthrouts, Tavin found himself back on the ground spinning and rolling to avoid being trampled by the pillars of earth beating down upon them. In the distance he could feel Verix's power surging and firing blasts of energy into the hoards of giants. Remembering his own power, Tavin let what was left of it blast out, giving him the revitalized strength and dexterity to stand once more.

It was during this chaos that the Golthrout next to the downed Warrior of Fire swung out its right arm and plucked the struggling girl right off the ground, uncomfortably placing her under its limb. Squeezed between the layers of dense rock, Ril could barely open her lungs enough to breath. Desperate to be free, she summoned her powers over the element of flame and ignited her entire body in a raging inferno, illuminating the dark forest around her. Made up of stone, however, Ril's fire did little more than heat the creature and inflame the forest foliage they passed. His attention drawn by the firestorm behind him, Tavin wheeled around in dismay to find Ril being carried away screaming for help. His power exploding in response, he shot the Sword of Granis in front of him to send a blast of pure golden energy rocketing off of the glistening blade and careening toward Ril's captor.

Unfortunately, another of the rock-strewn monsters found its way into the line of fire, catching the blast in its back. Though not destroyed, the Golthrout's gravely skin was blasted apart by the shot, nearly crippling it. Either afraid of the shining aura of light engulfing Tavin or sensing the superior power of Verix somewhere off in the distance, the horde of creatures pulled into a full scale retreat into the forests and the pits they had crawled from. Though Tavin vigorously hacked into the retreating swarm of Golthrouts, they evacuated almost as quickly as they had appeared. They were gone before anyone could do anything. Left blinded by the darkness and chaos of the night, Tavin and the others had little chance to get a bearing on which direction the bulk of their number had departed to.

As the last remnant of rumbling in the earth began to fade, the Warrior of Light halted his ceaseless bursts of energy into the forest line, overwhelmed with what had just happened and how powerless he had been to stop it. Ril was now gone and he had no idea where she had disappeared to. Lowering his blade and unwillingly letting his fatigue catch up with him, Tavin stood breathing hard from the expulsion of so much of his magical power as his still flaring aura of light shown through the destroyed campsite. Looking around him, he saw for the first time the devastation they had caused. Between he, Verix and the Golthrouts, every tree in a radius of thirty feet had been uprooted and the surface of the earth had been torn open and mangled.

Gazing at the destruction, he couldn't let himself believe this was all really happening. In the past five minutes, he had been attacked by the Prince of Drakkaidia, the powerful Zeroan had possibly fallen, he had been ready to sacrifice himself so his party could escape, and now Ril had been taken captive by the monstrous Golthrouts for reasons he could only imagine. Caught up in his swirling emotions, the only thing that stopped Tavin from falling to his knees and crying was the emergence of his best friend from behind a mess of butchered shrubbery, looking just as defeated and overwhelmed as Tavin. Following the light from his body, Jaren laid eyes on Tavin and walked up to him slowly, placing his hand through his field of golden power over his shoulder.

"Tavin," he almost whispered seeing the lost expression over his friend's face. The Warrior of Light glanced up at Jaren too weighted down to even respond. At last, he spoke.

"What do we do now?" he asked uncharacteristically hopeless and distant. Surprised and torn by his friend's unusually low spirits even in the face of such disaster, Jaren placed his hand over the hilt of the Sword of Granis to lower it.

"First, I think you should close off your power so old prince-of-the-underworld can't find us if he's still out there," Jaren wisely suggested. "Just calm down for a minute so we can figure this out." Heeding the words of his friend, Tavin slowly nodded and closed his eyes to release the blazing field of light surrounding him. It slowly diffused and dissipated throughout the night air, darkening their ravaged surroundings. Jaren smiled in spite of himself then, adjusting his eyes back to the darkened scenery as he looked around. "What do we do now, you ask? Well I don't know, but I'd just like to advise right here and now that we avoid those things from here on out." Still breathing heavily through the unsettled night air, Tavin shifted his gaze over to Jaren to give him a look like he appreciated the gesture, but was not in the mood for any humor at the moment.

"Right," Tavin agreed easing his nerves a little. "Where are the others?" Jaren straightened his back as he shrugged he didn't know.

"I think we've been split apart pretty bad this time," he responded eventually. "Kohlin and I were thrown back in the trees to the south at the beginning, but I lost him when I ducked under the brush. The last I saw Parnox was with you, and Ril..." Jaren stopped himself from saying anything else, seeing Tavin's face regress back to its devastated state once again.

"They took Ril," he finished for him, lowering his head. Jaren nodded quietly in response while Tavin began slowly cursing and tightening with anger. "This is starting to drive me insane, Jaren." There was an obvious resentment and dissatisfaction with himself present in his voice as he began, escalating while he continued. "I thought I was supposed to be the most powerful Elemental Warrior of them all, and here I couldn't even stop a few piles of walking rock. I'm beginning to wonder if I can really do anything significant at all. I mean I faced off with the son of the guy I'm supposed to destroy to save the world tonight, and I couldn't even keep up with his movements. What possible good could come from me continuing on with this quest? My powers, and this stupid sword," he fumed, pulling the sheathed Sword of Granis off his belt and casting to the ground in the dirt, "are completely worthless!"

Jaren remained soundless at the end of his friend's tirade, ending with him kicking the Sword of Granis away and into the roots of a splintered tree trunk beside them. It was several long moments later when Jaren at last opened his mouth and began to quietly speak at no one in particular, his eyes staring into space.

"I remember that time when I was eight years old and I was playing out by the giant oak behind the village. I had lost my mom's favorite tablecloth that I was using as a cape or something like that," Jaren began, sending a wave of remembrance washing through Tavin who postponed his worries to listen. "It fell into the hole with those wild dogs in it and I was too scared to go down and get it. I was about to give up on it when you passed by and ended up going in after it with me. It took us almost an hour to find where the pups had dragged it off to, but we found it and you wrestled it away from them." Tavin let a single huff of a dry laugh echo from his emotionless face, not impressed by the story.

"It was ripped to shreds, and you were in trouble for a month," Tavin finished negatively. Jaren brought his eyes up to meet with his friend's.

"Maybe, but you made sure we got it back to her no matter what. You would have stayed out there brawling with every last one of those dogs for the entire night if you had to, when I would have given up in the first five minutes. You're always like that, Tavin. Never giving up is what's made you who you are. We all hit our lows like right now, but if there's one person in existence who can rise above it and pull this thing together until we find our way again, it's you. So come on, Tavin. Put aside all the destiny crap and focus on what we have to do now: find the others. What do you say?" By this time Tavin had his eyes locked onto Jaren's, finding a reaffirming strength to be taken from them. Seeing that his friend was right, Tavin thrust himself forward and locked his arms tightly around him.

As the two Grandarians stood reunited in friendship in the ruined campsite, an abrupt tapping on Tavin's right shoulder absorbed his immediate attention. Instinctively whirling around to meet the potential threat behind him, Tavin's eyes surprisingly locked onto a much taller cloaked figure through the thick darkness. The only thing that stopped him from striking out at the figure was the hilt of the Sword of Granis now resting on his shoulder. Shooting his head upward to peer into a gray hood, the depleted and haggard face of Zeroan stared back at him. Before Tavin could so much as mouth the words bundled up in his mouth, the sage followed up Jaren's speech.

"Jaren is correct in his council," he affirmed with a tired but true tone. "Your current power level means nothing to the quest's success or failure as it stands now. That will all come in due time as you gain further training and experience. For now, the only thing that matters is your character, and in terms of that, you are the most powerful entity I could have ever found. Do not fall to your despair now when we are so close to our goals and you are needed most. Now here, this belongs to you." With the Sword of Granis outstretched to him, Tavin stared down at its illustrious hilt and seized it, the golden Granic Crystal flaring to life as he did. In the new light from the sword, Tavin and Jaren were both taken aback by how devastated the sage appeared. His formerly pristine robes were now tattered and frayed, and his face was cut and lightly bleeding from several minor wounds. Having never seen the outwardly invincible sage this damaged, the two were quick to inquire about his health and how he escaped from Verix.

Zeroan motioned for the two to calm themselves with a downward gesture of his arms.

"Quiet down, please," he told them softly. "If you recall, there are quite a few things abroad tonight that wish us harm." Zeroan gathered his damaged and dirty robes together about him as he continued. "When I sensed the rise in the Drakkaidian Prince's power level, the mask he had kept over his presence was broken and his identity was revealed. There is no other that the senior Montrox has access to who could mask his power like that. In any case, I have sensed the maximum power level from the Drakkaidian Prince before, and there was and is no way that even Tavin with his righteous power could stand up to him yet." Having said that, Zeroan moved his eyes down to meet with Tavin's. "I know all this talk of power levels must be confusing to you Tavin, but that is the nature of it. It is true what I said to you about having the ultimate power running in your veins, but it will do you little good in its present state.

"You see, for those who posses an inner magical power like you and the Dark Prince, it functions much like the condition of your body. If you exercise and train it physically on a regular basis, your muscles will grow and your strength will increase. The same applies to your inner power. You have it at its bare minimum level now, but the more your use it and train with it, the stronger it will become and the greater your power will be. Once you have increased it enough, it will ascend to a higher milestone and you will be able to control it. I am sorry to have not explained this to you earlier, but it is such a common and self explanatory concept for me that

I thought you somehow already knew." Tavin looked on the sage as if understanding the major idea of what he was saying, but missing some collection of detail. Zeroan recognized the remaining puzzlement in Tavin's eyes, but chose to move on for the sake of time.

"We will continue this conversation another time, Tavin," Zeroan promised turning away from the two with his robes flying up to their chest level. "The Drakkaidia Prince was carried off into the deeper regions of the forest in his battle with the swarm of Golthrouts that were drawn to his power, but he will have destroyed any of them that remain by now and will be back on his way here soon. Where are the others?" Tavin and Jaren shot disheartening glances at each other as they began to explain what had happened during the raid and what had become of the three missing Southlanders. At the end of their explanation, Zeroan was left cursing under his breath as he frequently did when he preferred his worries remain to himself. Realizing this was the case now, Tavin was quick to inquire further.

"Zeroan, I can tell you know something that you don't want to tell us," Tavin informed him punctually. "I think you know why the Golthrouts took Ril. If you do, I want to know as well." Zeroan tilted his head back to Tavin, not surprised the intelligent boy had already learned the idiosyncrasies of his character. It was a long passing moment before Zeroan answered him.

"I have never been into the Golthrout's lair before, so I cannot say for certain why they prey upon humans," he stated before his true answer, "but the... rumor is that they use the bodies of humans for some sort of extremely primitive ritual of some kind..." It was obvious to Tavin that Zeroan still withheld something.

"What kind of ritual, Zeroan?" Tavin pressed, bracing for the worst. Zeroan sighed realizing nothing but the truth would appease the boy's mind.

"I once read from the ancient texts in the Mystic Tower that Golthrouts are only the minions of another enormous creature that dwells in the deepest and darkest of the underground caverns. Every decade or so it needs to absorb fresh life-force from the world above. The Golthrouts go out to find that energy, in the form of the humans they capture. If we do not get to her soon, the Golthrouts will offer Arilia and her power to the King of the Golthrouts. It is imperative that we reach her soon if we are to save her." Tavin breathed deeply as he mentally blamed himself for losing her in the first place. Seeing Tavin doing this to himself again, Jaren stepped in once more.

"Well then let's get going Zeroan," he suggested. "Let's find Parnox and Kohlin, and we can-"

"Parnox and Kohlin will have been captured along with Ril," Zeroan interrupted. "The only reason you two were not taken was because they couldn't find Jaren and they were frightened of your superior power, so unless they are either dead or separated from us in another region of the forest, they will have been taken. Any way you take it, they are lost to us for now. So I suggest we go in after them." Jaren looked at him curiously.

"What do you mean, go in?" he asked. The sage outstretched one of his arms under his dusty robes and pointed over and into the savage fissure that the Golthrouts had carved into he earth. Jaren gulped. "We're going inside their... tunnels?"

"As I mentioned, their lair is deep underground," Zeroan reminded him. "There are many colonies, but there would be only one primary hall where they gather for their master."

"And as you also mentioned," Jaren interjected, "you've never been down there before. How will you know where to go?" Zeroan turned then and strode over to the sides of the giant rift in the ground.

"We will trust our senses," he said jumping in with his robes flying up behind him. Surprising the two Grandarian boys, the sage's voice echoed back though the hole a moment later, finishing his statement. "And our luck." Not very comforted by the sage's words, the only thing that kept Jaren from holding his position right there was Tavin sprinting off after him and leaping in as well, new determination and purpose pumping through his veins. Cursing his bad fortune, Jaren closed his eyes and jumped in as well, immediately enveloped in the darkness of the inner earth.

Chapter 42

<u>Abyss</u>

Meeting with Zeroan in the pit of blackness they had blindly bounded into, Tavin and Jaren groped for a sense of where they stood in the consuming darkness. It was not long before Jaren began petitioning for some assistance from the Mystic Sage.

"Zeroan," he whispered, "do you think you could provide a little light?"

"I would suggest that you ask Tavin for that convenience," was the reply from a ways in front of them. Tavin remembered he had the small but ever-steady light from the Sword of Granis shinning underneath the cover of his cape. He unwrapped it, instantly illuminating their surroundings with a golden glow. As the light spread about them, Tavin and Jaren were awestruck at what it revealed. Inside the fissure they had leapt into was an enormous crossroads of several branching tunnels. The two looked down to find themselves standing on a rocky bridge; all that separated them from an apparently never ending fissure of darkness in the pits below. Realizing what fate awaited him if he would have somehow fallen, Jaren's eyes widened as he pulled closer to Tavin.

"Long way down..." he observed in a distant tone. Tavin nodded, losing himself in the enormity of the void beneath him. The two might have stood there ogling all night were it not for Zeroan calling out to them by the entrance to one of the larger rugged tunnels.

"You can stare at the pits of oblivion later; right now we need to be on our way," he reminded them quietly. Coming back to their senses at last, the two Grandarian boys broke eye contact with the caverns of nothingness and began to tiptoe along the bridge in the earth above the pits over to an alcove attached to a cliff over them. Meeting up with the sage, Zeroan began once again. "Its bigger than it looks, too," he pointed out, looking down at the endless caverns himself. Tavin was again more concerned about what they were going to do next.

"What's the plan now, Zeroan?" he asked trying to change the subject back to the rescue at hand.

"Right. We will track the Golthrouts through these freshly traveled tunnels to their primary cavern," he stated.

"And just how do you know where you're going again?" Jaren asked doubtfully. Zeroan pointed over to the wall of a tunnel in response.

"The walls, to begin with," he said simply. "These edges have been torn at recently by something very big. The Golthrouts were just through this tunnel. And we can also follow the faint signal of Ril's power occasionally flaring up to the point where we can detect it. The last time she evoked her magic, I sensed it this way, so this is the way we go. If we follow the maze of tunnels long enough, we will eventually come upon the primary cavern where the creature in control dwells. From there, we will see what happens. Quickly now, and stay close, both of you. One wrong step and you could find yourself on a one way trip into an endless fissure." Nervously gulping as he began to walk after the sage, Jaren gently grabbed hold of the ends of Tavin's cape.

The next few hours proceeded on in this nervous, silent, and secretive way. Zeroan slowly led Tavin and Jaren through the ravaged abysmal tunnels, enveloped in darkness but for the small, steady light from the Sword of Granis. The ground was unstable and dangerous to traverse, obviously not meant for the use of creatures as small and fragile as humans. Myriad rifts and crevices in the ground frequently snared Tavin and Jaren's footing, slowing the trio until they could free themselves without making any noise for fear of attracting any of their enemies prematurely. Zeroan would occasionally halt when they arrived at one of the many forks in the road, painstakingly studying the different paths before them with only the faint light from the Granic Crystal to see what he was doing. At last he would motion for the two Grandarian boys to quietly follow him onward through the tunnel he decided was the most recently used.

As Tavin held up his shining sword to elucidate the darkness before them in the new passage they had just entered, he immediately noticed that they were no longer standing enclosed in a tunnel, but rather in the entrance to a massive ravine in the earth similar to the one they had encountered upon first entering the caverns. Recognizing this slow but drastic change in scenery as well, Zeroan called for the boys to stop.

"Hold on for a moment, you two," was the whisper from his concealing hood. "We have navigated to somewhere near the primary cavern of the Golthrouts. As you can see, this is not a place where you would wish to lose your footing." Both Tavin and Jaren swallowed hard as they peered down into the endless blackness below them on the other side of the cliff. "Tavin, shine the Granic Crystal out ahead of us as far as you are able." Obeying, Tavin lifted his sword higher and let its light reach out as far as it could, stretching all the way over to the opposite side of the cliffs above them nearly fifty feet away. Zeroan nodded as if silently confirming to himself they had indeed found what they were after. He knelt down to the boys' level and pointed his long arm upward to the end of the cliffs where the light from the Sword of Granis shown.

"Do you both see that small opening up the path of the cliff?" he asked them. They both nodded, focusing in on it. Tavin was the first to notice that the light from the golden crystal was not the only luminosity present there.

"Zeroan, there's another light coming out of that opening!" he quietly exclaimed.

"Quite right," the sage confirmed, standing up full length once more. "I would guess that the main gathering place of the Golthrouts is not far off from that position. We must hurry up this cliffside and into that passage." Zeroan's words paused for a moment, obviously perturbed by something. "I can sense a slight... well, something coming from somewhere, and it is an unfavorable presence. Let's get moving again." Tavin and Jaren found it hard to believe that Zeroan wanted them to take their time up the pathway when he practically pushed them up it at his usual grueling pace. The three companions hugged the wall to their left tightly, keeping their eyes on the next footing in front of them and unavoidably on the black rift to their right. After slowly ascending up and around the long dark road to the top level of the cliffs, the pathway opened up and widened to the point where the trio could walk freely without worry of getting too close to the ends of it.

Moving down the last leg of the pathway, the light from the Sword of Granis began to blend into the emergent glow diffusing out of the passage they had finally reached. Getting a better view of the opening in the cliff wall than at the base, Tavin observed it was the entrance to another tunnel. Zeroan quickly drove them into it, working them into the light they had spotted earlier. It was a faint scarlet hue seeping from the cracks in the floor.

As the boys peered at each other in nervous wonder, Zeroan's face tightened uncomfortably and stopped them once again. "The Golthrouts must be evoking the power of some ritual of theirs. There is a stirring of a dark presence far beneath us. I fear they are summoning the creature they answer to." Zeroan let his mind wander for a moment as he quickly went over the details of some plan he must have had already concocted in the confines of his mind. "All right. The end of this tunnel must lead us to the primary cavern we are looking for. When we get inside, do not speak. And Tavin," he said letting his dark eyes lock onto the boy's, "control your emotions no matter what you see in there. I don't want your spontaneous power exploding and blowing our cover. Do you understand?" Tavin nodded growing even more worried at what might be happening to Ril and the others. Determined to get to them before anything did, Tavin quickly nodded again and pressed on as fast as he could while maintaining silence through the tunnel.

Pushing through the ominous crimson channel, it was not long before they came to a dark patch the light did not reach. Enveloped in the darkness, Tavin could not clearly make out the path before him but impulsively charged ahead anyway. It was this lapse of judgment that landed him in a naturally hidden decline in the pathway. With his mind on Ril and the others, he never saw it coming. The ground suddenly disappeared from beneath him, sending Tavin sliding down the steep road beneath him. Alarmed to see the boy instantly disappear from view, Zeroan once again jerked back on the collar of Jaren's shirt, forcing out the air from his lungs. Falling back against the powerful sage, Jaren shot his head up furiously.

"Would you stop yanking me like I'm a dog on a leash!" he whispered harshly.

"What happened to Tavin?" was the apprehensive reply from Zeroan. Looking back in front of him, Jaren too noticed his friend had suddenly vanished.

"What *did* happen to Tavin?" he repeated just as uneasy. Releasing Jaren and slowly inching his way forward and pressing against the tunnel wall to secure his footing, Zeroan caught sight of the abrupt depression in the pathway and the steep road under it with Tavin just rolling out of view at its end. Cursing under his breath, Zeroan wheeled around and latched onto Jaren once more, completely lifting his struggling form off of the ground.

"Sorry again," the sage managed to Jaren before jumping into to the decline in the earth after Tavin with the boy on top of him. Sliding down the polished rock past the dangerously close stalactite ceiling above them, the two figures met its flat bumpy base with a crash. Upon impact on the hard horizontal ground, Zeroan once again took the air out of Jaren's lungs when he landed uncontrollably on top of his squirming form. The only thing that precluded the compressed Grandarian boy from screaming out at the abusive Mystic Sage in fury was the sight of Tavin hunched over behind a small wall of rock that he was peering down from just feet in front of him. Instantly off of Jaren as quickly as he could rise, Zeroan tried to help him up but was quickly pushed away.

"I'd feel safer if you just kept your distance," he uttered, motioning for Zeroan to just stand aside. "I'll be fine." Zeroan silently chuckled in spite of himself as he nodded in response and cautiously crept over to where Tavin sat staring. Getting up and crawling over to the others, obviously in hiding for a reason, Jaren slowly poked his head over the rocky wall to see for himself what they were gazing at. As soon as his eyes climbed over the rock he hid beneath they went wide with astonishment. Before them in all its dark but still impressive glory was the most enormous cavern any of the three, even Zeroan in all his travels, had ever seen. From what the trio could see from their high vantage point, they rested upon the top of another cliff high above the eternal darkness of the fissure beneath them. On either side of their current position were thin trails similar to the tunnel they had just dropped out of. The two trails led down and around the unending pit in front of them to a large and expansive rock platform that stretched from a another cliff wall to their left over a hundred feet to their right.

The center of the mighty platform was what drew the group's attention, however. Shining like a ray directly from the sun itself was a colossal beam of dark scarlet light that illuminated the otherwise shadowy cave with its heavy glow. The giant beam emerged from a large circular portal in the platform's floor, and stretched upward until it met with the stalactite endowed ceiling looming overhead of the entire cavern.

"Granis on high..." Jaren muttered to himself in disbelief. "Zeroan, what... what is that?" Zeroan didn't have to look at the awestruck boy to know what he was referring to.

"I'm not quite sure," he stated not taking his eyes off the column of light, "but it must have something to do with the evidently quite powerful creature stirring below us in this cavern. I would guess that is either the place where the Golthrouts place their captives into or a means to absorb the energies of others for the creature..." Zeroan was interrupted by a massive series of crashes to their left that caught all of them off guard. Emerging from a large opening in the cave wall came a sudden swarm of the monstrous Golthrouts, stomping over each other to exit the tunnel from which they had emerged. Shooting nervous glances at each other, Tavin and Jaren looked back to observe the pack of nearly fifty Golthrouts stampeding across the platform past the mammoth beam of light and over to the far right edge of the platform of earth. Upon arrival, they immediately began to make a series of strange but powerful moaning sounds that echoed from somewhere behind their non existent mouths.

Looking on the seemingly maddened Golthrouts for several long minutes trying to decipher what they were up to, Zeroan and Jaren's attention was finally pulled away from them when Tavin suddenly gasped with his muscles tightening to the point where his grip might have shattered the stone wall he gripped. Trying to find the source of the Warrior of Light's sudden burst of emotion, Zeroan followed his frantic eyes to a narrow walkway on the left side of the cavern that led up to smaller platform protruding out of the cliff opposite them. Lying on the small platform of rock in a mangled bunch was Ril, still and pale.

Chapter 43

<u>Rescue</u>

It took all the lightning quick reflexes and supernatural strength that Zeroan had left to keep the Warrior of Light from leaping up and sprinting to Ril right then. Thrusting forward to latch onto the boy's right arm and jerk him back to the earth, the sage plunged a hand over his chest and drew close, his face twisting with frustration.

"Blast it all boy, don't you ever listen?" he whispered harshly at Tavin, already struggling to rise despite the sage's hold over him. Zeroan powered him back down, his wrath building. "Tavin, calm yourself! Your power is rising with your rage and it will alert the veritable *army* of Golthrouts below us of our presence if you don't collect yourself! Now calm down!" Still a mess of raw emotion, Tavin found that easier said than done. Taking heed of the sage's words, however, the Grandarian boy exhaled deeply and tried to focus himself once again. Once all traces of his power signature were suppressed once more, Zeroan began to breath easy as well. "I told you before we can't afford to be discovered in here with that many Golthrouts and Granis knows what else lurking just below us. You can't help Ril by charging in there blindly. We need a plan." Tavin wasn't satisfied with that. Hearing the Warrior of Fire's name mentioned, Jaren turned back to where Tavin had been staring to observe her silent form lying on the platform for himself. Before he could utter a word of consolation to his friend, however, Tavin was nearly lashing out at the sage.

"Zeroan, she's lying there like she's, she's..." Tavin trailed off, unable to bring himself to say what he knew might be true. Zeroan shook his head once more.

"She's fine, Tavin," he stated with assurance. "If you would stop and concentrate, you would sense that her inner power is still present, so she is obviously still alive." Zeroan turned his head to gaze past the beam of light rising from the cavern floor to the small platform jetting out of the opposite cliff with the muddied and pale girl strewn across the flat rock. "She does look unconscious, though. We'd best get to her and the others fast before the Golthrouts complete whatever they are doing and summon the creature that rules them." Zeroan let go of Tavin's shirt so he could move freely once more and then gazed back over the wall to assess the current situation and decide on a plan of action. The boys restlessly waited for his orders with only the eerie moans of the Golthrouts echoing through the cave to be heard. After what seemed like an eternity to Tavin, still abrasively on the ready to charge to Ril's side with the Sword of Granis gleaming, Zeroan motioned for the two Grandarians to come forward and gaze out at the terrain more carefully.

"All right, this is what will be done," he said with confidence. "The Golthrouts should be occupied with their ritual just long enough for us to gather our companions and be out of this place. We will move down this pathway alongside the cliff to our left and then sneak into the hopefully empty tunnel from where the Golthrouts just emerged. I'm betting that Kohlin and Parnox are being held in there until Ril has been... drained. We must proceed to the lower platform with the utmost stealth and discrepancy. If we are discovered prematurely, no one in our party will be leaving these caverns ever again." Eager to get Zeroan thinking on the positive side again, Jaren quickly changed the subject away from the possibility of their impending doom.

"Why makes you think Kohlin and Parnox are inside that tunnel?" he questioned. The sage let a tight sigh escape from his lips as he rolled his eyes in response.

"I don't see them anywhere else, Jaren; do you?" he asked bluntly. Jaren shook his head no, surprised by the simple answer from the usually impossibly complex sage. "No, if they are here they will be somewhere in those tunnels. Once we find them, we will come back out to collect Ril." Tavin once again interrupted the sage with a gritty and resolute look in his eyes.

"Are you out of your mind, Zeroan?" Tavin criticized harshly. "We should go to her now! I'm not leaving her there one minute longer than I have to." Zeroan held his ground.

"I wish we could save her now, Tavin, but she must be collected last. The Golthrouts will be focusing on her energy in their chant. If we take her from that platform, the Golthrouts are sure to feel her presence disappear and they will be on us. We can't escape them if we still have to find Kohlin and Parnox in the tunnels. She must be last." This plan was becoming more difficult for Tavin to comply with by the second. He had finally found Ril, but now he learned he could do nothing for her until they had located the other two Southlanders and had began their retreat. "Now listen carefully, both of you. This must be quick and quiet. If our luck holds, we will not be discovered until we collect Ril. But even then we will be hard pressed to escape with our lives. Just one of the rock monsters is nothing for Tavin and I to handle, but we will be quickly overwhelmed by them all when we retreat. Stay quiet as you move and stick close to me. Do as I say and don't argue. Now let's go."

With that, the Mystic Sage rose from behind the wall of rock and began to tiptoe across the cliffside toward the ragged trail leading down to the expansive platform of rock with Tavin and Jaren behind. As the trio crept down the face of the cliff and onto the narrow trail, they acquired a better view of the Golthrouts on the opposite side of the platform. The bulk of them were throwing their chunky limbs into the air in a strangely organized pattern, while the rest paced around the beam moaning their strange chants into the abysmal darkness below. Zeroan tensely watched as one of the creatures danced their way, just barely missing view of the trio stealthily creeping toward them. At the base end of the trail, they also received a new perspective of the gargantuan column of light steadily shinning out of the platform. Previously hidden from their view at the top of the cliff, a thin but perfectly cut fissure in the rock split the earth from the base of the scarlet beam, along the platform, and up the vertical cliff all the way up to Ril, making Tavin even more uneasy than before.

As the Warrior of Light exhaled uncomfortably in the grip of his fear of what could be happening to her even now, they at last came to the end of the curving pathway to the base of the platform. Still slowly pressing up against the wall as he led them creeping onward, Zeroan turned his head back to the two Grandarians apprehensively staring up toward Ril.

"She'll be alright," he whispered just audible enough to be heard, seizing the two boys' attention. "But keep your minds focused. We don't know what we are going to find in this tunnel." Having inched their way across the platform's side for the better part of five minutes now, they had at last reached the tunnel. Still concealed in the protective veil of darkness, Zeroan halted beside the opening to his left and after confirming one last time that he was all clear to proceed without the Golthrouts on the other side of the platform noticing, he let out a quick breath and slowly turned his hooded top around the corner of the opening, peering in. After an agonizingly long period of time for Tavin and Jaren to wait as he analyzed every last bit of the terrain inside, the sage at last withdrew and pressed himself back against the shadows of the wall.

"Well?" Jaren asked anxiously. Zeroan gave a quick nod to signify the all clear.

"Things are looking better than I had hoped. I had assumed there would be tunnels to be searched if we were to locate our companions, but they are both locked up in a primitive sort of rock cage in the wall not more than thirty yards beyond us now. It will take time to work them out of their prison, but we can do it. Now hurry behind me, and stay in the darkness." Zeroan once again slipped his robed form to the edge of the opening in the cavern wall and began inching his way in, still taking care to continue observing his environment for any hidden pitfalls that he may have originally missed. Following the sage's lead, Tavin and Jaren both exchanged one last nervous glance before moving off of the wall and into the corner that led into the opening.

It was in this moment when Zeroan and Jaren had completely disappeared from his view around the corner of the opening that Tavin's wandering eyes picked up on a slight flicker of familiar light from beside him. Freezing in place, his head turned back to the right to find the fissure in the platform that led from the beam of light to the platform where Ril lay beginning to steadily pulsate with distant scarlet light from beneath the ground. Following the glow up to Ril, he was awestruck to find the entire platform of stone beneath her begin to softly radiate with the light trailing up to it. At this new development, Tavin could feel himself tearing. There was no one who's words he trusted more than the sage Zeroan's, but staring at the motionless body strewn across the ominously glowing rock she rested upon, Tavin knew deep within the confines of his heart that, despite the sage's reassurances, this moment right then and there was his only chance to save Ril before it was too late. As this certainty fell over his overloaded and confused mind, all other thoughts seemed to instantly vanish. If he did not act to save Ril now, she would die. These words silently echoed through his now clear mind. His decision was made. All of his other senses, thoughts, or judgments were overridden beyond the point of return. Everything now perfectly lucid to him, the Warrior of Light's face tightened with determination that he had never felt the likes of before.

Save Ril. That was all; that was the only thing that mattered then.

Resolutely nodding his head for his own clearance to move forward, Tavin at last lifted his right foot off the ground and placed it in front of him in the direction of the steep ramp way to Ril's platform, not after Zeroan and Jaren. For the first time since their meeting nearly two months ago, he purposefully disobeyed Zeroan and his sage wisdom. Taking care to proceed with the utmost secrecy and stealth, he passed by the opening that his companions had disappeared into and continued on along the rock wall of the cavern with purpose and fortitude boiling the blood in his veins. Focused only on his goal, Tavin did not look back when the sound of robes flying up and around the air behind him found its way into his ears. In the opening to the cavern entrance, Zeroan stood furious enough for his own boiling blood to explode inside of his body. Turning back for the sage, Jaren too caught sight of his best friend creeping along the shadows of the small incline leading up to Ril's now glowing platform. He gulped as Zeroan's robes began to shutter from his fists clenching with rage.

Though he had anticipated the sage to bound after Tavin and throw him off his feet, the sage merely spun around once more with his robes flying up behind him and continued on to the cell where Parnox and Kohlin lay waiting. Jaren couldn't contain his bewilderment.

"What are you doing?" he asked before he even knew what he was saying. Zeroan's irate gaze remained fixed in front of him.

"Saving my friends, just as Tavin is doing back on that slope," was the obviously angered but surprisingly controlled reply. Baffled beyond belief but complying anyway, Jaren assumed Zeroan knew what he was doing and had let Tavin go for a reason. Quickly letting his thoughts pass in favor of keeping his stressful mind on the moment, he continued following behind the cloaked figure until they arrived at the battered Southlanders' prison. Both were ecstatic to see their believed to be dead comrades, but were obviously weakened from the brutal trip from the surface to their current position. Upon first laying eyes on the concealed Mystic Sage suddenly towering over his cell's narrow window, Parnox could barely make out the identity of the figure; much less formulate the words to address him. He was obviously beaten the worst of the two, lying in a bruised and bodied heap over the cold earth. Kohlin was much quicker to pick himself up.

"...Z- Zeroan?" he whispered in utter disbelief. "Zeroan is that you?" The stoic figure descended down to the shallow cell's level to peer out of his dense hood and reply.

"It is I, Kohlin," he responded promptly, placing a finger over his lips to signal the need for supreme silence. Though Kohlin was just as pleased to find Jaren alive and well, his face twisted with worry when only one Grandarian boy stood before him.

"Tavin?" he mouthed inaudibly to Zeroan, already setting to work analyzing how he would free the two Southlanders from their cell. The sage made a quick thrust of his head backward as he worked on and whispered to answer.

"He is out in the cavern getting Ril. He will have her soon and once he does, the Golthrouts will know it, so we have to move as lightning here. The wall around you is thick and I will need to use my power if I am to break through it, but I cannot risk revealing too much until our presence here has been discovered beyond a shadow of a doubt." Zeroan then squatted down to the thinnest side of the cell he could find and quickly thrust out his hand, laying the palm of it down along its gritty surface. Jaren could see a faint throbbing force form around the sage's hand. "This will take time, so keep quiet and still. If Tavin blows our cover, I will hold nothing back so be ready to help Parnox up and out of here. That goes double for you, Jaren."

Before the boy could so much as nod his head in response, Zeroan sealed his eyes shut and began focusing all his energies into freeing Kohlin and Parnox. With the sage virtually shut off from the rest of the world, Jaren's brow furrowed as he found himself purposeless for the moment.

"You look like you've been swimming in Golthrout fodder, Grandarian," Kohlin managed to jokingly whisper through his cell to the crusted over and dirtied boy. Snapping back to his senses, Jaren shot the imprisoned Southlander a blank look, too worried about his friend and the girl he was trying to save back outside to respond.

While Jaren stood worried in the far reaches of the small tunnel adjacent to the primary cavern, Tavin was well on his way up the dangerously steep and unstable pathway for the small glowing platform where the incapacitated Warrior of Fire lay unconscious. Though driven to reach her speedily, making his way up the cliff while maintaining his stealth was proving to be an arduous task. With every step he took, the pathway he walked became more and more illuminated by the heavy scarlet light from the colossal beam of energy jetting from the enormous platform of earth now well beneath him. He was often forced to crawl along the thin path because of the constant eyes of the massive Golthrouts on the far side of the platform falling around his position. The most unhelpful hindrance, however, were the regular earthquakes shaking the cavern from the bowels beneath him, working to destroy his balance and stealth.

Crawling along the constricting pathway to avoid detection by the rock-strewn monsters below, Tavin tightly clutched to what holds in the road he could find to keep himself steady in the wake of a substantial quake. This underground eruption was so violent that it managed to break free one of the myriad stalactites protruding from the cavern's ceiling and send it plummeting downward just past Tavin's position. His eyes burst open and his heart began to beat as fast as a galloping horse, nearly terrified out of his skin to feel the rushing wake of wind from the falling missile of rock. Turning over on his back as he gasped for the breath that had just been scared out of him, he violently shook his head back and forth. This was taking too long. At this rate, the entire cave would be shaken apart before he could even reach Ril's platform, much less get her and the others in the group out of here in one piece. He had to get moving faster no matter what the risk.

Releasing his clutch over his still pounding heart, Tavin forced himself up amidst the last remnant of the rumbling earthquake. Back on his feet, he realized just how exposed he had made himself to anything that looked his way. With no shadows to hide in, he was left with little option but to make a light-footed dash up the cliffside to and pray to Granis that he would not be spotted. Setting off once more, he felt another quake rip into the expansive cavern. As it shuddered through him, however, he felt it was somehow different from the others. The previous vibrations had all originated from deep in the abyss below, but the shockwaves from this latest tremor felt as though they had been generated from the opposite cliff; from where he, Jaren, and Zeroan had come from in the first place.

It was then that he sensed something else. Unlike the tremors in the earth, this sensation came from the sixth sense in the back of Tavin's subconscious thoughts. There was a potent and all too familiar presence that had abruptly burst to life beyond the cliff. Though he recognized it immediately, he was not able to identify it with a specific name or source; he only knew that he had felt it before. Running along the shuttering cliff pathway with a befuddled expression drawn across his face, Tavin searched his memory banks for a possible source for the rapidly approaching power beyond him. Sensing the steadily nearing presence as well, the power sensitive Golthrouts begun to gradually cease their chanting ritual. With only the faint rumbling of the mysterious force sounding through the dank cave air, Tavin suddenly lit up with remembrance, rapidly assaulted by a wave of memories flushing into his mind from just hours earlier in the night.

Realizing that the worst had come to pass and his group's position had now been compromised for certain, Tavin grit his teeth with new determination and shot off at full speed along the narrow walkway to Ril. Turning his head to the quaking cliff as he ran, the boy watched as the familiar glow of deep crimson energy began to crack through its rocky vertical surface. In seconds, the cracks ripped into fissures and half of the entire cliff was blasted away by the force of exploding power behind it, emitting an impossibly loud discharge of noise through the typically dormant cave. Then, standing on the edge of a once concealed tunnel inside the cliff, the power enveloped form of Verix Montrox emerged from the dust filled

305

wall. As the sight of the boy sent to kill him came into plain view, Tavin cursed under his breath and ran on, spinning his head back to the trail before him. Fate, it seemed, was not on his side today.

Chapter 44

<u>Emergence</u>

Examining the opening he had just made for himself, the darkly clad figure radiating with crimson power waves and surging with black electricity instantly caught sight of his target running full speed up the cliff opposite him. Verix gnarled his face together as he blast out his voice.

"Warrior of Light!" he boomed through the rumbling cave. "You cannot hide from me! You cannot escape me! Stop your running and fight me like a man!" When Tavin did not even shift his gaze as he continued running along the cliffside to Ril, Verix grit his teeth in fury. "You do not even acknowledge one who would challenge you when he speaks?" There was still no sign that Tavin even heard him. Verix's honor was insulted. "Fine! If you will not come to me that I am coming to you!" With that, the Dark Prince grimaced and leapt down along the face of the cliff, clear over the endless fissure below him, and onto the base of the platform before the gargantuan beam of scarlet light jetting out of the earth. The very ground around him cracked from the force of the power emitting from his body.

Before Verix could make his way across the expansive cavern floor to get to the beginning of the incline that Tavin was racing up, a true quake in the earth began to roar through the cavern floor, nearly knocking even the supernaturally empowered Prince to his feet. Wheeling his head to the right, he suddenly found himself faced with a veritable army of enraged Golthrouts madly crashing toward him to crush the potential threat to their ceremony. Forced to engage them once more if he wanted to get to Tavin, Verix rotated his body to the mob and thrust his right arm forward, making a fist. A small sphere of flickering dark energy began to form and build before it, and when the enraged Golthrouts were a mere arm's length away, the Dark Prince opened his fist with a

307

scream and released a solid beam of black electrified energy careening forth.

Atop the ledge leading to Ril, Tavin could not help but stare down at the incredibly powerful figure as his frightening beam of unfeasibly powerful magic made impact with the first of the monsters, burning into their gravelly exterior and blasting them off their feet. He could only shake his head incredulously as he felt the young Montrox's power skyrocket beyond what he had ever thought possible and watch him charge into the mass of opponents with his savage broadsword ablaze with energy. Realizing that this situation could actually work in his favor, Tavin broke his gaze from Verix and fixed it back on Ril. While he collected her, his enemies would destroy or at least weaken each other without his intervention, allowing him the time to escape with the others unharmed. While he looked on this as the best cased scenario, Tavin realized this would most likely not be the case and wrapped his hand over the hilt of the Sword of Granis as he ran up the final ledge of the cliffside.

"What's going on out there!?!" Kohlin Marraea yelled over the chaos erupting in the primary cavern to anyone and everyone around him. Like the cavern outside, the tunnel with the two imprisoned Southlanders and their rescuers was being shaken apart as well, and Zeroan had now completely given up on secrecy or stealth to free Kohlin and Parnox from their prison. Cursing the deteriorating situation, he stood full length over his comrades' cell to muster his full mystic strength. Focusing and reaching into the element comprising the cell wall, he took hold and smashed it apart with his mind. With the barrier between them shattered, the sage grasped the loose rubble and cast it aside with a sweeping gesture of his arms.

"Verix Montrox has found us," Zeroan declared bitterly, kicking away the last debris from the opening he had just made. "He is most likely trying to get to Tavin, but he is 'preoccupied' with the Golthrouts. If we are smart about it, we can use this to our advantage. Jaren," he called to the besieged Grandarian boy staring out at the battle between the Prince of Drakkaidia and the mass of Golthrouts. "Jaren, I want you to lead Kohlin and Parnox back to the opening we found on the first cliff and get them out of here now! I will go and assist Tavin and Ril. With any luck, we will be right behind you so don't wait for us. Tavin is sure to be confused right now and he may do something foolish if I don't intervene. Now try-"

"Zeroan!" was the cry from Kohlin Marraea as he and Parnox emerged from their cell. "Zeroan, I tried to tell you earlier, but we've picked up another member to add to our party." Not caring for the sound of that at all, Zeroan skeptically watched as the two Southlanders pulled forth a small, bearded, midget-sized man out of the hole in the cell. Jaren squinted his eyes in amazement at the appearance of the strange little man.

"Greetings, powerful Graystorm," the gnome-like creature managed to say in a foreign accented voice. "My name is Yucono, and I am-" It was Zeroan's turn to interrupt this time.

"A cronom," finished Zeroan almost darkly, frustrated to have another body to be responsible for. "A bit far from home, aren't you?" The obviously exhausted and worn little man struggled for the words to respond to the sage, also obviously humbled in his presence.

"Myself and two of my companions were taken by the rock beasts and-"

"Yes, yes, never mind," Zeroan interjected again. "We don't have time for this. Jaren, lead all three of them out to the opening and stay clear of the battle outside. If you get caught up in the fray it will be over. Now hurry, all of you! We have *no* time!" As the sage was about to turn for the entrance to the primary cavern, he was shaken by another massive earthquake thundering around them to discharge a hail of the jagged stalactites from the ceiling above, crashing down into their number. Leaping to his left by the wall of the tunnel just in time, the sage nimbly dodged a segment of the stone missile falling to where he previously stood, snagging his already tattered robes. Ripping them free as he rose once more, Zeroan spun around to his group with a rare frantic look mirrored in his dark eyes. "The Golthrouts have summoned their master! We must get clear of here, *now*!!!"

Sprinting as fast as his tired out legs would carry him, the iron willed Warrior of Light finally reached the radiating platform where Ril lay incapacitated. Sliding down to her side, he was distraught but relieved at what he found. The girl was not unconscious but looked as if she just plain couldn't stay awake for some reason. Her delicate face had grown as pale as the dim moonlight from earlier in the night and her body was colder than a Drakkaidian snow bank in the dead of winter; obviously not healthy for anyone, much less the Elemental Warrior of Fire. Torn apart to find her in such a weakened state and not quite sure what he should do now that he had reached her, the only thing that Tavin could immediately think to do was get her off of the platform that was surely sucking the life from her fatigued body.

Bearing Ril's motionless form off of the glowing rock and back onto the pathway he had just raced up, he pulled close against the back of the cliff wall to steady them against the violently shaking caverns. Once off the platform, Tavin gathered her up in his arms and rested her freezing body over his lap. Wanting desperately to warm her so she might recover some of her strength, he began fiercely rubbing her arms and exhaling his warm breath onto her frigid skin. As he continued almost violently massaging her through the chaos erupting around them, the girl's eyes began to slowly slip open and closed, struggling to wake from whatever held her inside her sleep. Hopeful that she was trying to respond, Tavin began swiftly speaking to her as if she were awake.

"Hey, Ril, wake up and talk to me," he would encourage her. "I want you to talk to me- tell me about the west again. What's it like Ril? Come on, Ril, talk to me..." Anything that she might respond to would come out, coaching her to return to her senses. Whether responding to the sound of his voice, the warmth of his body, or a combination of the two, Ril at last began to fall out of her sleepy state and open her eyes wider and wider until she at last opened her mouth to weakly utter his name. Hearing her speak back to him even that one word gave Tavin the confidence he needed to continue on as he fought back his relieved emotions and concentrate on what he was doing.

"That's right, Ril, it's me, Tavin," he confirmed with a grin. "We've got to get out of here now, Ril, so can you try to stand for me?" Ril's vacant eyes wandered around the boy's face until he was finished speaking.

"Tavin..." she began quietly, almost too inaudible to be heard over the havoc of battle below them. "I... feel so... cold." He nodded and tried a quick smile as he rubbed her frigid sides again.

"I know, Ril, I know," he comforted her. "But we're going to get you out of here to a fire and the sun. So just hold on for a while longer here, and I'll get us out. Do you hear me, Ril? Just hold on..." Tavin trailed off as she mouthed his name again and struggled to stay awake. He didn't want to waste a second just sitting there. Swiftly but gently gathering her in his arms, Tavin rose and turned back for the narrow path down the cliffside. His body tightened with grit as he looked on through the near collapsing cavern. They were going to get out of here. No matter what the cost or what sacrifice he had to make, they were going to make it out. It was his fault that Ril was taken in the first place, and he was not going to let her go again. He clenched his teeth and tightly pressed her body against him as a loose patch of earth fell over them. Though hope was slim, he would not give up.

Just before he was about to start off again, one last incredibly powerful tremor in the earth tore through the cave. Feeling already that this was the largest of the earthquakes so far, Tavin's attention was taken off of his path and drawn to another phenomenon of light back on the platform where he had just collected Ril. Since he had removed her, the light had slowly faded and the thin fissure that led from it to the massive beam of light below had gradually disappeared. When the last bit of light from the fissure was gone, something happened to the beam in the center of the massive platform below, as if responding to the sudden lack of power draining into it. Astounded, Tavin incredulously watched as the colossal scarlet beam abruptly ceased to be. With the light vanished, the enormous cavern was now completely black but for the aura of crimson light from Verix Montrox below and the small but ever steady glow from the Granic Crystal.

Caught off guard by this newest hindrance to his already near impossible escape, Tavin found himself at a loss for what he should do next. There was no way he could hope to navigate down the narrow and crumbling pathway in the darkness, and he could not find the others of his party Granis-knew-where. Searching his overwhelmed head for any semblance of an idea, the light in the cavern was suddenly renewed. A distant but rapidly rising glow of the heavy scarlet light from the hole in the main platform where the beam had once been was steadily increasing. As Tavin's eyes found their way to the growing light from beneath him, what was left of the horde of Golthrouts battling Verix abruptly pulled into full retreat, leaving the Dark Prince with nothing standing between him and his target. He too, however, stood almost mesmerized by the growing light from beneath the ground and the surprisingly large power signature that had begun to rise with it.

Then, just as suddenly as the beam of energy had vanished, it reappeared. From both sides of the hole in the platform below him, Tavin and Verix watched from their respective positions as two massive horns came crashing through the rock floor, followed by a massive boulder head uplifting and shattering the once solid surface it had emerged from. Following after the steadily rising head was a tough and rock based body identical to the Golthrouts. From the body were two massive arms that grasped onto the cliff wall where Tavin stood, working to pull the remainder of its beastly form out of the earth. As it clawed its way out of the enormous entrance it had just made shaking the very foundations of the cavern, the creature from the bowels of the earth gradually raised full length before Tavin and Ril.

Tavin was left in utter disbelief. It was built exactly like a Golthrout, but unlike the smaller foes the deep scarlet light once towering from the massive beam shown forth from in between the cracks of its thick "skin" and fiercely out the two small openings in its bull shaped head where its eyes would be. The beast had two towering horns of much smoother rock jetting off of either side of its head. All pieces put together, Tavin surmised that the foreboding creature was the beast Zeroan had warned them about: a minotaur King of the Golthrouts.

Though its terrifying appearance would have been enough to scare the life out of most, Tavin was more preoccupied with the intensity of power that the beast was emitting to be bothered by its physical exterior. Blaring out directly in front of the overwhelmed Warrior of Light, it dwarfed even the Prince of Darkness. The sheer magnitude of it burned into the back of his mind as he groped for a new plan of action to escape with the glaring eyes of his enemy locked onto him and the near lifeless girl in his arms.

Chapter 45

<u>Control</u>

The sweat on Tavinious Tieloc's face began to bead into bullets as the monstrous master of the Golthrouts abruptly made its first move. Having identified Tavin as the one who stole Ril from it, the creature took a colossal step forward on its massive rock-strewn limb, releasing seismic waves in every direction. Though still standing indomitable in his roll to protect Ril, Tavin found himself incapacitated by fear and shock of the situation before him. Before he could think of what to do next, the towering King of the Golthrouts did something he could have never expected. It spoke.

"Put her back," came the godlike rumbling voice from behind the creature's mouth. So stunned at the revelation that the seemingly demonic beast was intelligent enough to speak, Tavin wasn't sure whether to take off running or try to communicate back. Analyzing what the minotaur had said, he knew it must have been referring to Ril. Tavin was right. It had been siphoning Ril's elemental power from her on the platform and rose from the depths in response to him taking her away from it. Seeing the boy before it not responding, a powerful growl from the back of the minotaur's throat came rumbling out to transform into another outburst of its deep voice. "Put her back. Now." This time the Warrior of Light was surprised to hear a touch of anger present in the creature's menacing voice.

Before he knew what he was doing, he had opened his mouth to respond to the creature.

"*No!*" he yelled out in defiance, tucking Ril even closer into him protectively. Hearing the rebellious reaction from the insignificant boy, the minotaur's eyes flared up with intensified gleaming light, forcing Tavin to squint to maintain contact. In all its obvious fury, the minotaur challengingly thrust its head forward until mere feet from the two humans and opened its mouth full length to send a cave shaking roar blasting out of its passionately lit core. As the amazingly powerful howl from the beast bellowed through the cavern, the sheer force that came blasting outward with it was almost enough to lift Tavin off his feet. With his thick hair and clothing flying back behind him and his footing weakening, Tavin's legs at last began to cooperate with his brain.

Realizing he was no match against a beast so powerful, especially while burdened with Ril, the boy spun to his right and started sprinting for the narrow, unsteady pathway along the cliffside back down to the primary platform. Observing the hasty retreat, the heated minotaur responded by powerfully swinging its glowing right arm above its head. Then, nearly finishing the withdrawing Elemental Warriors right there, it drove its gargantuan arm downward, tearing its clenched fist through the cliffside.

Realizing what the King of the Golthrouts was going to do the moment before he did, Tavin planted his feet to come to a sliding halt just before the pathway not three feet in front of him disappeared into the darkness below. The Grandarian boy watched in horror as the last chance of their escape slowly crumbled off the cliffside in rubble, leaving a gap of over fifteen feet between his side of the path and the other. His eyes opened wide, but reflected only a void of nothingness. All hope seemed to have faded from view. He stood there for what seemed like forever, unable to look back at the impending doom looming over them. What finally brought him back to reality was the sound of the ominous minotaur's voice once again repeating its previous command.

"Put her back," the beast's subterranean voice demanded. Tavin remained motionless as the words echoed into his ears. The scenario he found himself in seemed impossible; unreal. There was always a way out of any situation, or so he had always been told by his strategic father. But if there was one now, he could not see it. There was nothing he could do. No way to escape. Tavin let his eyes fall down to Ril's shuddering form in his arms, her half open eyes placid and distant. He found it hard to look at her now; now that he had failed her. Zeroan was not here to save them this time. It was over.

As this profound sense of supreme failure filtered through his mind, Tavin's defeated eyes were drawn away from Ril onto the shining Sword of Granis. The small Granic Crystal embedded on the hilt had begun to slightly brighten. It was barely detectable at first, but as his eyes lingered there, the light it was emanating substantially increased. Inexorably fixated on the hilt of his legendary sword, Tavin could feel his mind beginning to drift. The raging tremors from the minotaur to his left gradually blurred away, and all the mad chaos in the caverns vanished. With all other cares or worries somehow temporarily erased from his mind, Tavin could faintly detect a familiar ambience sounding through his head.

"What is the matter, Tavinious Tieloc?" a soft and indistinct voice asked him. It was then that Tavin realized that while the rest of world had become a nebulous cloud of haze, the Sword of Granis below him remained crystal clear. Remembering his first experience with the sword in the world of light, he hastily concluded that it was the sword that was speaking to him. He listened carefully as the weapon continued. "Well, Tavin? What is it that holds you back?" He was unsure of how to answer.

"What are you talking about?" Tavin mentally responded. The voice echoing through the confines of his mind became clearer as it sustained its inquiry.

"I asked you why you have yet to summon the true levels of our power," the voice stated simply. Tavin remained bemused but attempted to answer as best he could, remembering the words of the Mystic Sage Zeroan.

"I need more time and training before..." he started uncertainly, trailing off. The voice let out a huff of breath as it responded.

"I know you don't need any more training, and looking around you," it stated while projecting the image of the mammoth minotaur into his otherwise blank mind, "it would seem that time is an indulgence that you don't have time for." Tavin was still unable to decipher what the sword was telling him.

"Then what should I do?" he asked with helpless frustration poured into his words. "How can I save us?" The voice responded one last time, gradually fading back into the world beyond.

"Do what you always do, Tavin," it said as his surroundings became clear once more. "Exactly what you have to." As these last words reverberated through his mind, time and reality were restored to him and he was left standing with Ril in his arms and the monstrous master of the Golthrouts looming over his left once again. He remained still for several long moments, running the sword's advice through his mind again and again with the foreboding eyes of the minotaur on him the entire time. His gaze fell back upon the shining weapon on his belt. However vague the words seemed, Tavin realized that he somehow knew their meaning.

"Yes..." he murmured inaudibly to himself, slowly nodding. It was all perfectly clear then. He knew what had to be done. And he knew he could do it. He shifted his eyes back to Ril, confirming what he knew he had to do. He was not going to fail her, he thought. He was going to save her. Save them both. Letting a small smile diffuse across his face for the first time in what seemed like eternity, Tavin at last moved. Shuffling Ril over to the far side of the cliffside he gently set her down and tucked her tightly against the wall, then rose to gradually turn back and face the now very impatient minotaur bursting with primal rage. The smile on Tavin's face vanished, replaced with a determined glare- challenging the creature. The minotaur seemed to be able to read his face as it opened his bull like mouth to repeat its command to Tavin once again.

"Put her back!" the beast boomed into him, again blowing Tavin's hair and clothing back with the force of eastern gales. He stood firm, completely unflinching, and reached down with his right hand to wrap his fingers around the hilt of the lustrous weapon strapped to his waist. Accompanied by the deafening metallic ringing of metal and metal, the Sword of Granis was ripped free and brought before the boy's chest. Both hands around its illustrious hilt brandished before him, Tavin opened his mouth to whisper his response.

"I said no," he breathed with authority that would not be denied. Then, clenching his iron grip over the sword further still, the elemental power of light began to rapidly flare up around his body. The golden aura exploded to life as it never had before, radiating from his every cell. As his power rose and engulfed him in the customary field of brilliant energy, the Granic Crystal awakened with new life, dispelling the shadows in the dank Golthrout cavern with its shimmering light.

Tavin grit his teeth with purpose and connected with himself to flex the circulating field of power as he would the muscles in his body, sending golden light burning forth. So great was his unflagging will to stand his ground that Tavin didn't even realized he had just summoned his power virtually at will; gaining a measure of control over it. The monstrous minotaur before him seemed to flinch at this revelation of power, displeased to see such an awesome display of light in its shadowy domain. The beast was far from frightened, however, tired of this game it was playing with the boy. Throwing its rocky body forward once more with another roaring blast from his mouth, it extended its arm past him, reaching for the motionless girl behind.

Realizing the creature was trying to bypass him, Tavin at last ended his stare down and swung his weapon back over his left shoulder, focusing his radiant energy around the already shimmering blade. As his power concentrated around the Sword of Granis, he let out a cry of resolve and slashed the sword downward into the minotaur's passing wrist, instantly slicing through its thick rocky exterior. Shocked and terrified of the detriment to its body from what it thought to be an insignificant threat, the minotaur reeled back its limb in what appeared to Tavin as pain. He watched in amazement as the beast carefully wrapped its fingers around the cut in its breached skin to seal off the scarlet energy pouring out. Underneath the creature's hard exterior was the apparently precious scarlet light flowing through it like blood.

Infuriated at what a hindrance the boy had become, the minotaur bellowed another roar into the caverns and released its ailing wound to prepare for something new. Throwing its head back as if readying for another howl of power, Tavin could see, and more importantly feel, a strange display of the scarlet light charging inside its mouth. Its power only continuing to rise as the moments passed, Tavin's rock solid determination began to slightly fade. His eyes widened as the continuous energy signature of the creature refused to stop growing.

The Warrior of Light could not help but let his own mouth fall open as the now massive blast of energy growing in the monsters jaws at last reached its peak, sending a new wave of quakes rumbling through the cavern. Then, aware of what was the minotaur was about to do and what was going to happen to him if he didn't do something to stop it, Tavin's hidden inner strength reacted. He could feel a new core of power suddenly awakening within him: and it felt bottomless. Aware of this new reservoir of strength available to him if only for this moment, Tavin tightened his body and mind to prepare for the King of the Golthrout's inevitable assault. His white knuckle grip on the Sword of Granis stiffened further.

Then it came. Throwing its massive rock-strewn head forward at the lone Grandarian boy, the enormous core of energy charged and ready in the minotaur's mouth exploded out, releasing a wave of scarlet energy detonating forward. Gaping at the incoming beam of volatile power speeding at him, Tavin's face hardened with purpose like never before. As if the final moment of his life, a thousand different images assailed his mind, ranging from his home in the Hills of Eirinor to the helpless form of Arilia Embrin behind him, all somehow screaming out for his help. He was the last line of defense. If he could not survive the minotaur and the caverns of the Golthrouts, how would he be able to stop Valif Montrox in the Final Battle of Destiny? He had to survive this. He had to win.

Letting these thoughts embed themselves into his mind, Tavin let his fierce determination overtake his body. Unwavering in his stance against the minotaur's attack, his need to live triggered the new core of power. It came exploding out in such a grand scale it nearly dwarfed even the gargantuan beam of energy before him. Tavin's usual field of golden power exploded to new life, easily quadrupling in size. Streaking golden light beamed throughout the cavern, now lit up like the sun. Multiplying and expanding by the second, the very ground beneath Tavin's feet began to split and fracture under the pressure of his power.

Just as he had felt in the Tower of Granis, this new power raging to life in his defense felt completely natural; like it had been with him all his life. With this new strength summoned out and his elemental powers under control at last, Tavin was ready to counter the minotaur's attack. With his commanding power focused ahead of him, Tavin slashed the supercharged Sword of Granis forward with its luminous blade shimmering in pure golden light. As the tip of the sword touched the beam of scarlet energy, its path of destruction was stopped short. Even the colossal wave of the minotaur's potent energy could not pass. The two stood in deadlock, holding each other's powers at bay.

Tavin quickly realized that despite his recent increase in power, he was still hard pressed to hold back a beam of deadly explosive energy over twice his size, and it was all he could do to keep his grip over the Sword of Granis in the face of the incoming shaft of scarlet light plowing into him with force he had never imagined the likes of before. But he was not going to let the minotaur through him. Locking his eyes onto his enemy then, Tavin noticed something lodged into between the two boulders by his eyes. There was a singular shining stone in between them, giving off all kinds of strange light.

By this time, the mighty minotaur had grown insatiably impatient. Having summoned its full inner power and still not penetrated the boy's defenses, its fury was building. Still blasting the wave of deadly energy from its gaping mouth, the master of the Golthrouts raised both of its enormous arms from its sides to and smashed them downward into the cliff, instantly shattering the ground on which the Warrior of Light stood.

Not able to see past the blade of the Sword of Granis in the explosion of intense light from the minotaur's blast hammering into him, Tavin never saw his enemy's movement until it was too late. Feeling the ground under his feet suddenly give way, the all important concentration of exerting his power forward was shattered like the earth around him, downing his defenses instantly. The look on Tavin's face morphed into one of deathly dread. He knew the possibly fatal mistake he had just made. With his grip on the Sword of Granis lost, the force of the scarlet beam still plowing forward impacted Tavin head on, blasting him off his feet into the cliff wall. Being blown through the cliffside felt just like what it was: colliding into solid rock and smashing it to pieces. If not for his still burning field of power engulfing and empowering his body he would have surely been killed.

Sensing the sudden decrease in his enemy's power, the monstrous lord of the Golthrouts finally concluded his attack. With his power at last subdued, the minotaur slowly scanned the ravaged surroundings before it. The platform it had once used to absorb the energies of his victims had been utterly incinerated by the exploding powers and there was now a gargantuan crater in the cliff wall, enveloped in a haze of soil and dust. From inside, a faint golden light shown through the dusty debris, obviously belonging to the battered Warrior of Light. The minotaur paid it little attention though, for its owner's energy level had been cut to pieces and was now not even worthy of its notice.

Watching carefully as the patches of dust cleared over the hole in the cliffside, the last remnant of the once shimmering light began to fade away into the darkness of the cave. Under a pile of rubble, one of the dirtied and torn pant legs of Tavinious Tieloc emerged. His entire form was bloodied and bruised; he felt truly broken. Opening his squinted eyes just enough to see through the faint cloud of dust before him, Tavin could vaguely make out the glowing master of the Golthrouts taking a step closer to the rock wall, and Ril.

Chapter 46

<u>Aid</u>

The malevolent King of the Golthrouts towered over the motionless Warrior of Fire, carefully studying her near lifeless form. Tavin could see what it was doing, but lying in a bloody heap underneath layers of heavy rubble, he was hard pressed just to continue breathing, much less rise to defend her. While he knew the new pinnacle of his power was lost to him, his unwavering resolve would not allow his body to remain still, and he attempted to slowly shift away what debris he could. The minotaur could hear Tavin's faint movement from inside the crater, but still disregarded the boy as any threat. Bringing its gaze back down to Ril, the minotaur let out a grunt, as if disappointed, and began unhurriedly backing away.

Tavin looked on the King of the Golthrouts with suspicion. Why had it stopped? What had caused the sudden disinterest in Ril? Then, shifting his gaze back down to the still girl, he sensed the problem. Her life energy was nearly absolutely depleted. She was still alive, but only just barely. The minotaur obviously had no interest in finishing with her now. Though momentarily relieved to see her safe, Tavin's feeling did not last long. Likely because it was angered by the loss of such a prime power source, the massive minotaur decided to dispose of the now useless girl. Tavin watched in horror as it began lifting its beastly head back into the air again and charging another colossal blast of energy between its gaping jaws.

Instantly aware of what the minotaur was going to do, Tavin's eyes became frantic. He struggled to rise once more as he hysterically managed to raise his left arm out of the rubble spread over him. He lifted his right arm and noticed that there was something missing from his grasp. The Sword of Granis had been lost to him when he was blasted into the cliff, and it was nowhere in sight. Tavin's face twisted with worry. Without the sword, he could do nothing even if he did manage to free himself, and with every passing second the King of the Golthrouts grew that much more ready to attack. The boy plunged his right arm down as far as he could through the rocky debris, scouring his surroundings for his weapon.

Once he could feel the minotaur's new blast of energy at the peak of its power, his fingers at last fell upon the smooth hilt of the sword. Clenching his grasp around it, Tavin frantically delved into the confines of his inner being and tried to gather back his new power. Though he had done this before, he had only done it once before and summoning such awesome power all at once proved to be a daunting task for the near crippled Grandarian boy. As the minotaur outside his crater took a step forward to launch his attack at him and Ril, Tavin managed to muster a portion of his golden aura of power, flaring around him to lodge the smaller rocks and rubble away.

As he struggled to work the larger boulders off the top of where he still lay, the minotaur thrust its oversized bull head forward and once again released what Tavin soon realized was an even more potent beam of energy than before. Not able to free himself, Tavin watched in horror as Ril's impending doom careened onward. Despite all of his newfound strength and his valiant efforts to repel the beast's evil power, he had still failed. They were both going to die.

Something happened then that Tavin could not have imagined possible even in his wildest and most distant dreams. From out of the shadows of the broken pathway below where Ril lay, a lone figure swallowed in a field of circulating crimson energy came bounding over the massive fifteen foot gap between the far side of the pathway and Ril, tattered gray coattails and bleeding energy trailing after him. The figure landed with a crash on what was left of the small platform where Ril lay motionless and planted his feet in front of her, just as the beam of energy reached her position. It was only then, as the figure threw his arms forward to stop the beam with his own bare hands, that Tavin realized Ril's savior was none other than Verix Montrox. His jaw felt as though it had been disconnected from the rest of his head as it dropped full length.

As the Grandarian boy stared awestruck at the climactic scene before him, the Prince of Drakkaidia let out a fierce scream as the minotaur's attack smashed into his arms. At that moment, Verix's power level exploded out and released an electrified blast of his own crimson energy forward to explode into the beam. Tavin was forced to look away and seal his eyes shut as the two red energies collided, exploding in a flurry of light that blew Verix off his feet and back against the wall over Ril where he screamed out in anguish. However badly Verix was damaged, the King of the Golthrouts at the other end of the explosion fared twice as badly. As the flurry of lights and smoke cleared enough for Tavin to see through, he found the rocky exterior over its chest and most of its face completely blown away, exposing it's fragile and tender inner core of power deeply glowing. Fragments of its skin were scattered and falling everywhere.

Realizing what had been done to it, the minotaur threw its terrified head back and roared one last burning cry of agony through the unstable and decomposing caverns. As its precious life force flowed freely, the monstrous creature at last elected to forget about the intruders from above and retreat back into its endless catacombs while it was still able. Painfully wheeling its damaged frame dropping off of the crumbling foundations of the primary platform at the base of the cavern, the minotaur's last emissions of scarlet light began to disappear through the dank cavern air as it plummeted back down into the endless fissures of the earth.

With the Golthrout's monstrous master at last gone, the exhausted Warrior of Light was left with a not much improved situation. The primary cavern, or what was left of it at least, was in ruins, with no way out anywhere. All the passageways, platforms, tunnels, and cliffsides had been utterly destroyed, and the earthquakes were only growing worse. There was no way to escape anymore. Not wanting to die in a pile of rubble, however, Tavin groaned through his pain and shifted through the rocks and gravel around him. After allowing his elemental powers to at last dissipate back into the depths of his body and the Sword of Granis, he breathed deeply and resumed making his way out of the puncture in the cliff. Slowly sheathing the Sword of Granis, he rose to his feet with the help of the wall, amazed he had not broken every last bone in his body. Struggling to stand, Tavin rubbed the fresh trickle of blood from the side of his mouth away with the frayed ends of his soiled sleeve and spat out what he could.

He staggered over to the ends of his crater and slowly worked his way off the edge until he could place his feet on the floor of the annihilated platform where he had first found Ril. As his feet touched down with its surface, however, the boy found that he had even less strength than he had anticipated. After just a few steps toward Ril and the Dark Prince no more than ten feet away, he could feel life parting with him as if it had been he who the minotaur had just drained of energy. Stumbling on, Tavin's surroundings grew blurry and dim.

Within a few feet of Ril, the violent earthquakes grew too much for him to resist and the strength in his legs gave way, sending him tumbling down to the hard earth once more. Barely able to move, it took all the remaining willpower and fortitude that he could muster to press on. Crawling his way through the dirt and rubble on the fragmented ground, Tavin reached out to Ril and grabbed hold of her left arm. He pulled himself toward her and slowly turned her over so he could see her face. She was still trembling from the cold and just as pale as before, but her eyes were at least halfway open again. The Grandarian boy could not help but let a faint smile spread across his soiled face as he wiped away the dirt from her delicate cheeks. As if responding to his touch, Ril's glazed eyes fell to meet with his. Though she did not speak, Tavin could tell she knew he was there with her.

As Ril's eyes fell away once more, Tavin's drifted to his right toward the equally devastated and drained Dark Prince, Verix Montrox. Tavin could still not believe he had just done what he had done. It didn't make any sense. Why would Verix risk and, looking at him now, possibly give up his life for Ril? Tavin's eyes remained hard as they stared at the nearly dead figure, but he had to admit if not for his intervention they would both be dead. Not that it did them any good now.

It was a group of falling stalactites from the collapsing ceiling above them that stole his attention away from Verix. Watching as they fell into the abyss, Tavin's vision clouded over once more, reducing the image of the pale Warrior of Fire next to him to a nebulous blur of red and white. The last thing that he remembered before losing consciousness were the hazy movements of two strange gnome-like creatures above him, muttering something in a strange foreign dialect.

On the opposite cliff wall of the Golthrout's primary cavern, the damage sustained was just as bad, and what was left was now caving in for good. As the last segment of the base platform of rock crumbled into the endless rift where the King of the Golthrouts just disappeared, the worn Mystic Sage Zeroan stood distraught with worry and hopeless anger at himself for allowing what had just transpired to do so. He had felt Tavin's power climb to heights it never had before just minutes ago, but now it had all but completely vanished. He was not able to tell if it he was even still alive. The sage's face tightened with fury.

Zeroan let out a scream of enraged anguish amidst the falling stalactites and rumbling earthquakes tearing the cavern apart. He had failed to protect Tavin when he needed him most, and now he could be dead. If that had happened, there was no point in even continuing the quest for the shards. As he struggled to view the highest platform of the failing cavern one last time, he was forced back by the remainder of the passageway he stood on shattering under his feet. Leaping back to the highest level of the cliffside where he and the two Grandarian boys had first arrived, the sage was left with no choice but to retreat and trust the words of his newest companion that his two allies had found Tavin and Ril before it was too late. He turned from the cavern and started down the tunnel after the rest of his party.

Chapter 47

<u>Mercy</u>

It was an exotic and indistinct field of blurred watercolors that appeared before the slowly waking Warrior of Light's heavy eyes as they began to gradually open. Among the vague but bright images sloshing back and forth above him was a fervent mass of a deep red something; continually sweeping and swaying like a bird's feather caught in the wind. It was not until it lightly brushed over his face that the rousing boy realized it was the gentle and soft touch of hair. Remembrance flooded his senses, recalling the feel of Arilia Embrin's flowing tresses. As the fiery Southland girl entered his mind, a thousand different images of the past weeks flashed into it, immediately waking him with a start. His eyes wide open, he thrust his upper body off the soft cushion he was nestled on and found a half scared to death Warrior of Fire recoiling back with a gasp from his abrupt jolt upward. She sat on the edge of the small bed he found himself lying upon in a small wooden hut.

Breathing heavily and fixing his gaze upon the startled girl, Tavin recalled the last time he had seen her was in the Golthrout's caverns; practically dead. Observing that they rested in some kind of a foreign room with morning sunlight pouring in through its multiple windows, he could only surmise they had somehow managed to escape. Between his blind confusion of how they had come to be in this strange new place and his joy to see Ril in what looked to be full health once more, he found it hard to believe all of it was real. When the stunned girl only sat before him with a hand over her mouth and eyes wide, it was all the sweating and heavily breathing Warrior of Light could do to mumble a single word in bewilderment.

"...Ril?" he murmured in a lost tone of voice. Hearing the boy speak her name, she at last recovered from her surprise at his sudden awakening and lowered the hand covering her face, revealing a soft smile that had formed behind it, growing as the silent moments passed. Before long she let a slight giggle escape from behind her mouth that soon turned into full fledged laughter. Watching the beautiful girl release her delight, Tavin could not help but grin and let a shy laugh of his own echo out with hers. Hearing the boy start as well, Ril quickly stopped and gently slapped his arm that propped his torso upright. He raised an eyebrow at her. "What was that for?" he asked puzzled, though still smiling. Ril pointed a finger at his face accusingly, but she could not hide her smile anymore that Tavin could his.

"What in the name of Granis are *you* laughing about?" she asked, trying to be serious through her giggles. "You leave me here worrying sick about you just lying there for days, like you never intended to get up again, and then all of the sudden you're bounding up like an eruption from Mt. Coron. Are you trying to give me a heart attack?" Through the girl's scolding, Tavin was so surprised and excited to see her smiling face that he could only start laughing all over again in response. Not able to contain her elation or sustain her false anger with him any longer, Ril let her feelings overtake her and she laughed freely.

Tavin would have been content to just continue laughing with the spirited girl forever, but as his eyes fell onto her exotic new green stitched clothing, he remembered his immense confusion from when he had first awoken and his face grew serious.

"Ril," he began, taking a look around at their colorful but strange new environment, "...what happened? How did we get out of the caverns to... here? And where is here? What is this place?" Ril put a hand out over his mouth to quiet him for a moment, letting her laughter fade so she could answer.

"Just calm down, Tavin," she begged him, lowering her hand. "I know how confused you must be. I know I was when I first woke up. But just listen for right now, and I'll try to explain things the best I can from what I've been told." The last remnant of her ravishing smile dissipated as she paused for a moment to collect her thoughts, not sure where to begin. She repositioned herself on the bed and brushed a lock of crimson hair out of her face and behind her ear as she began. "Well, I guess I should start back when we were separated that night in the forest by the Golthrouts. That's where I first

328

started losing my strength." Tavin could see a quiet hurt already enveloping in Ril's deep red eyes as she remembered. He could tell she did not want to recall whatever she had to say as she softly started again. "I was trying to make my way over to you and Parnox, but one of the Golthrouts plucked me off the ground and started running away from you. I tried to burn the thing, but in the end I only hurt myself. The Golthrout must have at least been aggravated by the fire, because by the time we were away from you and the others he was gripping me so hard that I started to black out. From about then on, I don't remember much myself; just bits and pieces. I can remember being carried through black tunnels for hours, and then being placed on a floor of rock in a lit chamber. ...That was..." Ril stopped for a minute and cringed. He could see a small tear swelling in the corner of her eye.

"Ril, you don't have to-"

"No," she interjected, shaking her head. "I want to tell you. Tavin, it was the... the worst feeling I've ever had in my life. I was paralyzed on a cold rock; held down by my own weakness. I could feel the life flowing out of my body like a river. Every minute felt like dying, and they all felt like an eternity. But just before all of my senses blurred away and the last bit of my energy left me, I felt something else: a warmth, shaking off the cold." Ril brought her blank gaze back up to meet with Tavin's wondering eyes, and faintly smiled. "It was you, Tavin. I... I was colder than I had ever thought possible, but something started to warm me again, and I could see your face over me. I think I might have faded away completely if you didn't show up when you did. When I heard your voice and felt your arms carrying me, I could feel a little life come through me again. After that, they told me I fell asleep." Tavin was flattered that she thought so much of his actions in the caverns, but her last statement baffled him.

"Ril, who are 'they'?" he asked bemused. Ril raised her arm to wipe away the tears formulating in her eyes before she attempted to respond.

"The cronoms," she stated with a renewed measure of cheerfulness in her voice. "There were two cronoms that were captured by the Golthrouts and brought to the cavern as well. They saw everything that happened from start to finish." Tavin had to stop her there.

"Wait a minute, Ril," he interrupted. "Who, or what, are cronoms?" Ril let a little giggle out as she dispelled the last of her earlier emotion.

"Oh that's right," she remembered. "You're a Grandarian. You wouldn't know the stories about the cronoms. Mothers in the Grailen and even some in the northern parts of the Southland tell their children about a mystical race of miniature people less than half of any human's size. They are a well-known tale, but that's all most people think they are. It's what I always thought too." She took a deep breath and repositioned herself on the edge of Tavin's bed, cocking her head with a smile. "Well, I was wrong. There is an entire village full of cronoms here in the western Great Forests, and we're in it right now." Tavin gazed at her in disbelief. She saw it in his eyes, but shook her head to stop him from saying anything. "Keracon Valley, Tavin. That's the name of this little hidden vale they've brought us to."

"Sorry, but you've completely lost me now," the boy interrupted confused. "If these little cronom things are so small, how did just two of them drag us all the way out of the destroyed caverns, through the eastern forests, over the divide, and into the west?" Ril was the one to grow impatient now.

"If you'd let me finish, I would explain," she said jokingly curt. "They said I was out for the entire journey here and days after, but I guess one of the two cronoms that dragged us out of the cavern went out to some sort of outpost in the eastern forests to send for help while the other one stayed with us waiting. When the others got to us, they took us through some secret tunnel system they have that the Golthrouts don't know about. I'm not sure how they can move so fast, but they got us here in less than two days. Considering how large the deep forests are, that should be impossible. Once we got here, they put us in this... guest hollow, and they've been nursing us back to health ever since. I woke up two days ago and met with the High Elder who granted us sanctuary here." Ril's face lit up like the sun as she began to describe the valley. "Oh Tavin, you can't believe how incredible this place is! Cronoms are primitive because they only use what they find in nature in their daily life, but they have things here that I've only seen in my wildest dreams." Laughing at the girl's liveliness, Tavin was forced to interrupt again.

"I'm glad to see you have your energy back," he chortled with a grin, "but you're still moving too fast. I don't understand why these creatures helped us. What do they have to gain from all this?" Ril eyed him skeptically.

"Did you ever stop to think they might just be trying to do the right thing by helping others?" she grilled dryly. "The two cronoms from the caverns said that you saved all of us, including them. They feel they owe us something for that. The High Elder said we are welcome to stay here as long as it takes for all three of us to recuperate. And I think that-" Tavin practically threw a hand up in front of Ril's face, his expression growing deadly serious.

"Wait a minute," he said in a tone of voice that stole the very warmth out of Ril's blood. "What do you mean, 'the three of us?'" Ril closed her eyes for a moment and exhaled sharply, realizing she had just made a mistake. She had avoided mention of the other for this exact reason. "Ril? Answer me." She looked at him hard, but responded softly.

"I mean all three of us, Tavin," she stated simply. "You, me, and... Verix." Tavin threw up the sheets over his body and dropped his legs to the floor.

"What!?!" he nearly shouted. Ril stood up and moved over him to prevent him from doing the same.

"Tavin, you shouldn't get out of bed. You're still not completely recuper-" He interrupted by quickly standing and looking the girl dead in the eyes.

"Ril, don't tell me that these cronom things brought *Verix Montrox* to this place!" he stated, shaking his head with tense alarm. Frustration found its way into the girl's eyes as she began to respond.

"Tavin, these are good natured, caring creatures. What would you have had them do? Leave him there?" she asked. Tavin was beside himself hearing this.

"That's exactly what I would have had them do!" he yelled at her, his anger soaring out of control. "I'd have had them throw him into the pits with the Golthrouts! Ril, have you forgotten why he was following us? That filthy Drak is trying to kill us!" Ril's eyes reflected the same anger as his.

"Is he, Tavin?" she responded, the tone of her voice escalating as well. Tavin gave her a look that said he thought she had lost her mind.

"What in the name of Granis are you talking about?"

331

"Think about it, Tavin. Why did he save my life then? That's right, the cronoms told me about that too. They said if he hadn't jumped in and taken the force of the giant Golthrout's attack that I would have been incinerated. Why would he do something like that if he was just going to kill me later?" Tavin threw his arms in the air and bitterly continued.

"Ril, I don't have the first damn clue," he shouted. "All I know is that the guy was on top of me ready to cut my head off with his tremendously large broadsword that night in the forest, and it sounded like he wanted to try again when he showed up in the cavern. That doesn't sound like something a friend would do to me, what about you Ril?" The Warrior of Fire did not know how to respond to that, but she still held her ground. Before she could say another word, however, the door in the right side of the room suddenly slid open, revealing a strange bearded man not even half the size of either Tavin or Ril. He had a friendly expression across his bulky little face as he spoke. Tavin could only assume that the creature before him was one of the cronoms.

"I am sorry to interrupt," he started respectfully, addressing Ril, "but you are so loud you might wake him. If you could lower your voices just a small bit, he should-" Tavin was the one to interrupt once again.

"Stop right there," he ordered coldly. "Who is...?" He did not even have to finish his question to realize about whom the miniature cronom was speaking. As the door the gnome-like creature had just emerged from creaked open further, Tavin could make out the end of another bed in the room beyond his with a savage broadsword leaning against one of the posts and a tattered gray coat hanging on the other. The Warrior of Light's expression turned indomitably cold. Turning backward to reach down and take hold of the sheathed Sword of Granis that he had earlier noticed resting beside his bed, he quickly sent its metallic ringing slicing through the air and started for the doorway to his right. It did not take long for Ril to realize what the boy was doing.

"Tavin!" she screamed, running after him. "Wait!" As the girl raced after him, Tavin moved past the small cronom by the doorway and kicked it all the way open, completely revealing the full form of the Prince of Drakkaidia, Verix Montrox, laying fast asleep in his black garbs on a small bed like Tavin's. As he lifted the Sword of Granis behind him in preparation to thrust downward, Ril went rushing by him and in front of the Drakkaidian boy, spreading her arms wide. There was determination just as resolute as Tavin's embedded in her eyes. He was the first to speak.

"Ril, get out of the way," he ordered with quiet ferocity. She did not budge a muscle.

"No," she returned, not missing a beat. "I won't let you kill him." Resentment flared in Tavin's eyes.

"Ril, this is a murderous, mindless, killing machine that you are trying to protect. He's the son of the most evil man alive; the one I'm destined to destroy. That makes him the second greatest enemy we have." When Ril's body remained still as stone before him, Tavin's rage inflated again. "Ril, he would sooner kill us both than look at us, and I will not let him get that chance! I'm ending this now, so get out of my way!" She still did not move an inch.

"Tavin, I know who he is, but he saved my life," she reminded him fervently. "You may be right about him, but I can't just let you kill him in cold blood when he nearly sacrificed himself to save me. I could never live with myself. And I don't think you could either. You're just as curious to know why he did what he did as I am. You're better than this, and I won't let you do it." Tavin found it hard to keep looking and listening to her. His lifelong hatred for Drakkaidians told him to be smart and finish Verix now, but Ril's words reached deep inside him. They made him sick with anger and frustration, but in their wake he felt an immense unworthiness overcome him.

He slowly broke his rock hard gaze from Ril and shifted it to the rigid but, at the moment, vulnerable looking face of his enemy. She was right about how the Drakkaidian had aroused his curiosity. Tavin still couldn't believe he had done what he had done; it didn't make any sense. If he was sent to kill Tavin, why would he have saved the life of his companion? And how did he recognize her in the woods earlier that night? He sighed deeply. Ignoring the training and instincts that his father had instilled into him over the years, he lowered the Sword of Granis and rested it by his side with his gaze still locked onto Verix. It was a long moment that passed before he at last murmured something to himself.

"I can't believe any of this..." he muttered, slowly inserting the Sword of Granis back into its ornate sheath. "I can't believe I'm... doing this." At this, Ril exhaled as well, a wave of relief washing over her.

"I can," she said quietly, dropping her arms. She let a soft expression pass over her face as she slowly approached the boy, still fixated on the Dark Prince. "You have too good of a heart to kill out of hatred." Tavin at last placed his gaze back onto the girl in front of him, resting his eyes on hers.

"I wish I was half the person you make me out to be, Ril," he told her, struggling for the words to impart his humanity to the girl. "But I'm not. I'm just human like all of us, and you can't expect me not to be prejudice here. He'll live for now, but I haven't changed my mind about him. He is a murdering Drak, and if he so much as looks at me wrong when he wakes up, I swear it will be the last thing that he ever does." Confusion and hurt were the elements that made up Ril's expression then, having never seen Tavin rise to anger and hatred like this. He could tell that she was unsure of him by the way she stared, and he felt a new sense of failure and shame as a result. He could not look her in the eyes as he groped for something to say. The enormity of trying to live up to what Ril thought him to be was too much to bear. Staring into space and speaking near inaudibly, he at last broke the silence hanging between them.

"...You don't know me as well as you think, Ril. I try to be the best person I can be to my friends, but..." he paused, trying to find another way to explain what he had to say without saying it, but failed. "You can't understand, Ril. You're not a Grandarian. You don't appreciate the history. We've been at war with them since before we can remember, and we're taught to hate them as babies. Its part of being a Grandarian. I'm grateful for what you're saying, but I don't feel worthy to have you think of me the way you do, and honestly, I don't want you to. You can't think of me as perfect, Ril. I'm... not." Though she was caught off guard by the Grandarian boy's words, she was quick to reinforce her own.

"I know that, Tavin, and I don't expect you to be," she stated just as quietly. "But whether you know it or not, you are so much more of a person than others. I don't want you to try to live up to an impossible standard, I just want you to... to be you. That's all I want." Tavin broke his gaze with the nothingness before him and shifted it back to her. As their eyes met again, he could not help but let a small smile overtake his face.

"Okay," he murmured looking down and nodding his head. "I can do that."

334

Chapter 48

<u>Picking Up the Pieces</u>

"What *is* this!?!" exclaimed a disgusted Jaren Garrinal, spitting out a mouthful of fruit onto the grassy earth below him. "You actually consume this, this, *poison*?" Kohlin Marraea looked over to the opposite side of their morning campsite and readied himself for another headache. He lifted an eyebrow as he replied.

"I already told you," he stated with impatience already mounting in his voice. "It's Dethan Fruit." Jaren's face cringed, revolted.

"Dethan Fruit?" he repeated in an excessively aghast tone of voice. "They ought to just call it *Death* Fruit. If I take another bite, I swear that'll be the end. How can you eat this?" Kohlin rolled his eyes, picking a fruit off of the tree branch behind him.

"I also told you that it's meant only for times of hardship," he stated flatly. "And since we've been out of food since yesterday morning, I'd say this qualifies. If you'd rather starve, so be it." Jaren shot him a loathsome glance as he dropped the tasteless fruit beside the log where he sat to join the rest of the corroded produce that had fallen out of the trees in the diminutive meadow they rested in.

"I'd rather have my stomach start feeding on itself," he murmured, exhaling sharply. Jaren brushed the juices from the sickening fruit off of his green Grandarian hunting attire, now quite worn since they had departed from Galantia nearly two months ago. Attempting to change the subject to get his mind off of food, his eyes fell onto the slumbering form of Parnox behind the boulder where Kohlin sat. "How's he doing?" Kohlin's eyes fell off of one of his twin blades he was sharpening and onto his brawny friend, snoozing. He tilted his head to the side and shrugged.

"Considering we've been moving at Zeroan's usual demanding tempo since we made it out of the caverns, not all that bad. He's a strong man, so he'll be fine once he gets a chance to catch up on all the rest he's missed."

"Speaking of which," Jaren remarked, noticing Zeroan had still not returned from the night before, "our merry little band here is still short one Mystic Sage and one pint-sized gnome. He's usually back from his nightly... whatever, by now." Kohlin merely shrugged again.

"I'd have thought that by now you would have learned not to use the words "Zeroan" and "usual" in the same sentence," he pointed out. "Zeroan will return when he returns, just like always."

"I'd have thought that by now you would have learned not to use the words "Zeroan" and "always" in the same sentence," Jaren retorted. "There isn't one consistent thing about that guy, except that he's always..." the Grandarian boy's mouth froze there, noticing a familiar black silhouette appearing out of the tree line on the opposite side of the meadow. Kohlin turned around from the rock where he sat, having heard someone marching through the brush and foliage for some time. Jaren's heart sank in his chest as the worn and jagged robes concealing Zeroan emerged from the brush.

"Yes?" was the menacing question that came from under the sage's frayed gray hood. The boy swallowed hard before feebly uttering a reply.

"Punctual," he said as his heart meshed with his intestines at the bottom of his gut.

"Perceptive boy," Zeroan said darkly, to which Kohlin began to silently chuckle. The sage shifted his gaze downward to Parnox. "You'd best wake him," he said to either of them, "we need to be off now." Jaren moaned at that, not caring if he upset the cloaked figure before him or not.

"How did I know you were going to say that," he murmured, slumping back where he sat. Zeroan ignored the boy's griping, though Jaren was not the only one upset by his order.

"You must have some patience with him, Zeroan," Kohlin tried, sheathing his blade and rising to address the sage to his face. Zeroan turned back to Kohlin and locked his eyes onto the other's; penetrating. Kohlin was unnerved, but proceeded with what he had to say. "Zeroan, you know I never question you," he began easily, "but we have had no rest since well before the caverns. We've been marching all day and most of the night for a week. We've no food, Parnox is in desperate need of sleep, and unless you're not telling us something, no one is chasing us. Perhaps you could lend us a little patience now that the situation is not as dire-" There was a dark flash that gleamed across the sage's narrowing eyes.

"Not as dire?" he repeated threateningly calm, his eyes burning into Kohlin's. "The 'situation' could not *be* any more dire. Every moment that we sit here resting, Valif Montrox is that much closer to finding the two missing shards and giving us a truly dire situation with which to deal. Patience, Southlander? That is something that I do not possess. Just like time." Kohlin exhaled in defeat, knowing that the sage was completely right.

"All right then, Zeroan," he conceded. "I still follow and trust you, but if we do continue on at this pace, would you at least do us the courtesy of explaining where we are traveling to? All you have said in the brief time you have been with us the past week is that we are traveling north. What is our destination?" His eyes still locked hard upon Kohlin's, Zeroan nodded softly.

"I'm not sure yet," he admitted in a collected tone of voice. Jaren's eyes grew wide, a mixture of fear and torment within them.

"What does that mean?" he asked incredulously. The sage's head quickly pivoted to his left toward the Grandarian boy.

"I would say that it is a fairly self-explanatory statement, wouldn't you?" he caustically replied. Zeroan turned his body away from Kohlin to take a seat by the felled oak along the tree line of the meadow, wrapping his dilapidated gray robes about his solid frame. He breathed deeply as he sat, raising his head back up to Jaren. "I have not told you of our exact destination yet because I am not sure where our presence is needed with the most urgency at the moment. I can tell you for certain, however, that you four will eventually be going back up to Torrentcia City, while I will need to pay a visit to the Mystic Tower. We may, however, need to take one or more detours along that master road first. We'll know shortly."

"How will we know that sitting out in the middle of nowhere?" Jaren asked curtly, fully aware that he was most likely inviting Zeroan's wrath. "Is some mystical creature going to stumble onto us and tell us where we need to go?"

"Yes," replied the sage simply, throwing the boy's sarcasm back into his face. "In fact, here he comes now." Jaren's brow furrowed as his head tilted to one side, assuming the sage was toying with him. Before he could ask, however, a small crash of leaves and the crackling of twigs from the east side of the meadow drew his attention away. Zeroan chuckled to himself at the noise. It was not more than a few moments later that a dirtied and out of breath cronom came practically falling through the brush of the tree line. Suddenly it all made sense. Jaren had all but forgotten about the newest addition to their party, the cronom named Yucono. He was the one who had led them out of the caverns through his peoples' intricate hidden passages along the Golthrout's principal tunnels. Soon after that, Zeroan had sent him away one night on some sort of errand which he, not surprisingly, had not revealed to the rest of them. Apparently, he had completed it. The sage smirked at the little man desperately panting for breath while attempting to brush his forest garb off and pull the foliage out of his short white beard.

"For a cronom tracker, stealth does not seem to be one of your defining attributes, Yucono," was the dry humor from the Mystic Sage. The miniature man merely looked up at him through his irregular breathing patterns and shook his head.

"You travel too fast for me, Graystorm," he managed to spout. "I had no trouble following you, but it was not as easy to catch up." Zeroan chuckled again as he rose from his seat on the tree toward the exhausted little cronom.

"I apologize, my friend, but I told you when you left that we must move with all speed to get out of the Great Forests. Did you have enough food?" Yucono nodded his head yes, still gasping for breath.

"I ran out this morning," he said, looking up to examine the faces of Jaren and Kohlin. "From the looks of it, so have all of you."

"Depending on what you have to tell me," Zeroan began, getting straight to the point as always, "we may only be a day away from refreshing our supplies and rations. What have you learned?" Jaren stared at the little man and the sage curiously, not sure what he was talking about. The cronom brought his head up to meet with the Mystic Sage's, towering over him.

"It is as we hoped, Graystorm," he began, forcing himself to control his breathing so he could speak. "Only one of the four guards remained, but he told me that someone from the caverns required help moving wounded humans to the valley. That was before we even managed to escape the caverns ourselves. They should have arrived at least two days ago." Zeroan let a soft huff of relief escape from his mouth as he patted the cronom gently on the back.

"Thank you, my friend," he said gratefully. "Our hope is restored." Putting the pieces together, it was not long after Zeroan's last statement that Jaren's eyes shot open and smile creased his face from ear to ear.

"Zeroan! Is he talking about-"

"Tavin and Ril," the sage finished for him, lighting up Jaren's face. "The cronoms on guard at their eastern outpost have graciously pulled both of our lost comrades out of the caverns and have taken them to their home over the central divide of the Great Forests on the western side. They will be safe there for the time being. Now I can answer your question." Zeroan turned back to Kohlin. "We are headed for the border village of Miystridal at the edge of the Llillial Woods. We emerged from the caverns of the Golthrouts a week ago today and have been moving north every day since, so we should not be more than a day's march away now."

"Now that gets me curious," was the deep remark from behind Kohlin. All four turned back to the massive boulder embedded in the earth with the burly Southlander waking behind it. His thick bearded head came rising upward, yawning as it did. Smacking his lips and scratching his back, he gave Zeroan a peculiar look. "Miystridal is close to Gaia; the village decimated by Golthrouts. Surely there will be no one and nothing left." Zeroan smiled once more.

"Glad to see you have not lost your touch, woodsman," was his reply. "I assure you, however, that it is now necessary to get to Miystridal as soon as possible. It is our only chance to communicate with the two elemental Warriors on the other side of the Great Forests." All of them gave him a bedazzled look upon hearing that.

"What's in Miystridal Village that would allow us to communicate with Tavin and Ril?" Jaren asked hopefully yet bewildered.

"Let me worry about that," was the traditional response from Zeroan, to which all three of them sighed. It was the cronom Yucono who cracked Zeroan's secrecy.

"You intend to somehow utilize the Sapphire Pool in this Miystridal Village, Graystorm?" he asked perplexed. The sage lowered his head down to burn the little man with his glare.

"What's the Sapphire Pool?" was the inevitable question from Jaren. It was Zeroan's turn to roll his eyes.

"Like clockwork," he mumbled. "The Sapphire Pool is an enchanted pond in the cronoms' village. I should be able to contact Tavin using its power with my own if I can get near a fairly large body of water." Parnox nodded his head, the sage's motives now clear to him.

"And the only place you'll find something like that this far away from the Torrentcia territories is by Lake Miystrinia just outside of Miystridal Village." Zeroan nodded.

"Exactly," he confirmed. "And while I am conferring with Tavin, you can all salvage whatever supplies you can from the village and get a good night's rest. I will be back by the morning."

"If you're going to talk to Tavin through this pool thing, I want to go too," Jaren chimed in from behind.

"That won't be possible," Zeroan rejected. "You need to catch up on your rest and eat, not burden me with your-"

"Zeroan, I won't be a burden and I don't need the rest," he assured, interrupting the sage. "I want to see Tavin. I'm coming with y..." It was Zeroan's turn to cut the boy off now, immediately moving and towering over him with his foreboding quiet ferocity.

"I will not suffer your insolence in this matter, boy," he started in with rage building in his shadowed eyes. "You are starving right now, in need of sleep, and you would be a thorn in my side in every possible way. More importantly, it will be difficult enough to maintain communication through the Sapphire Pool on my own. It would be impossible to try and patch you through as well. The answer is no, and if you say another word to the contrary, I swear I will do what I have been wanting to do since the first night we met and sever your voice box from your body. Am I perfectly understood?" Knowing from experience when Zeroan had reached the limits of his practically non-existent patience, Jaren swallowed his wishes to see Tavin and silently nodded yes. Pleased to have the insistently stubborn boy's cooperation at last, Zeroan closed his eyes and deeply exhaled, letting his body loosen. "Good. I promise I will send him your regards, though."

Satisfied, Zeroan moved aside to allow Jaren his breathing room once more.

"Very good, then," he began again. "It is time that we get moving if we are to reach the village by tonight. Clean up the area and meet me over the ridge ahead of us when you are ready." With that, the sage wheeled around and strode past Jaren to the end of the meadow, disappearing into the tree line with the ends of his ragged robes soaring up behind him. When he had completely disappeared, the Grandarian boy turned back to the two Southlanders and the cronom.

"I think he would have killed me right there if I had even said 'okay,'" he muttered still a little terrified. Kohlin shot him a disapproving glance as he leaned over to help the burly woodsman to his feet.

"You can't expect him not to be tense, Jaren," he said. "He's the world's only chance at surviving Montrox, and he knows it. Zeroan has the weight of the world on his shoulders, and you can bet he can feel it." Kohlin's words torn at Jaren, not quite sure what to think of the Mystic Sage at times.

After they prepared themselves for the day's march to Miystridal Village and cleaned up the meadow, the group of four followed after Zeroan. While Kohlin stayed next to Parnox to help him keep up, Jaren waited for the cronom, obviously still fatigued from his trek through the forest the past days.

"Are you going to make it, big guy?" he called back to his other companion struggling to get up the ridge they found themselves on. Yucono looked up with a smile.

"My dear boy, I am a tracker and traveler by trade," he reminded him through his arduous breathing. "Despite Graystorm's unnecessary speed, I will be fine." Jaren shot him a puzzled glance, thinking, before he remembered that was his name for Zeroan.

"I hope you don't mind me asking, but why do you call Zeroan 'Graystorm?'"

"Ah, yes," Yucono nodded. "I was wondering when someone would ask me this. Well, my people have known of Graystorm for a great deal of time. He never gave a name for himself in the beginning, so we named him ourselves." Jaren raised an eyebrow.

"I could probably guess without racking my brain too hard," he began sardonically, "but where did *Graystorm* come from?" The little cronom chortled.

"As you must know, the gray one tends to bring stormy news when he reveals himself. It may not be the most respectful name we could have fashioned, but it fits quite well. He only appears to us when a serious problem exists that only we can aid him with. He has called on me personally before to help him with matters in the Great Forests, but never before with anything of this caliber. I usually just stay around the valley, not out here in the east." The mention of the cronom's valley aroused Jaren's curiosity.

"Is that where the rest of your people live?" he asked as the little man finally caught up to him. Yucono nodded.

"All of us but the few out here at the eastern outpost," he replied.

"How big is this valley?" Jaren pressed, fishing for anything that might give him an idea of what his best friend was presently living with.

"Keracon Valley," Yucono clarified, "is the typical size of most human villages I have seen in my days. But then I have only seen a few along the borders of the Great Forests like the one we are traveling to now. But we don't live on the forest floor, so that might make it a little smaller."

"What do you mean you don't live on the forest floor? Do you live underground like the Golthrouts?" Yucono almost laughed at that.

"Don't get us wrong, my lad," he chuckled. "We are nothing like the Golthrouts. The only reason we go underground at all is for times of emergency when we have been caught there by predators like the Golthrouts and need a means to evade them, or for emergency passage between long distances. That would be how your friends got across the Great Forests and the divide so quickly. Secret, compact, and well-hidden tunnels; undetectable to Golthrouts."

"Well if you don't live underground or on the surface, where do you live?" Yucono smiled and pointed a single finger upward.

"The trees of course. There we can be safe from Golthrouts and passing humans who would do us harm. From underneath, you would not be able to tell, but we actually have a very complex and elaborate village up in the high branches." Yucono broke his eye contact with Jaren to stare off into the space in front of him, remembering his home. "We only take what we need from nature so we might seem primitive to you with your incredible stone and metal castles to the north, but our home is a beautiful place. Winding rope bridges connect our hand carved hollows nestled against the trunks of the strongest trees, stretching from one end of the valley to the other. I'm sure you would enjoy paying us a visit someday." Jaren smiled down, nodding his head.

"I'm sure I would," he agreed. For now though, only his best friend would enjoy that privilege. Jaren silently laughed in spite of himself. Even under the seemingly worst of circumstances, Tavin seemed to have all the luck.

Chapter 49

<u>Blonde Haired Girl</u>

A crisp wind blew down through the canopy of treetops over Keracon Valley as the day began to shift into evening, chilling Tavinious Tieloc's face and gently rustling his thick brown hair. He stood over a small but sturdy balcony outside the hollow he and Ril had been given to rest in, staring out into the seemingly endless treetops jutting up from the earth too far below to see. He had emerged from the hollow for the first time in days after catching a glimpse of the rest of the treetop village outside his small window that morning. Instantly mesmerized by the vastness of the sprawling, intricately connected community (and the fact that it rested hundreds of feet above the forest floor,) Tavin had wanted to step outside as quickly as possible. Ril would have nothing of the sort, however, as she quickly proved by practically wrestling him back into his bed until *she* deemed his health completely recovered.

Though she had ordered for him to remain in bed until she returned, Ril had made the mistake of leaving him unattended almost an hour ago when she ventured out into the village herself to find the chieftain of the cronoms that she had met the day before. The moment she disappeared from view, Tavin leapt out of bed to dress. His Grandarian attire was nowhere to be found, so he remained in the tight, yet strangely comfortable green cronom garb Ril had given him, pulling on his boots over them. He strapped the Sword of Granis over his back, shooting an uneasy glace toward the door to the right of his bed with a distrustful frown quickly flashing across his face. After he had collected his few belongings that remained in his possession, he turned to the slightly undersized doorway to his room and stepped outside onto a thin balcony, connected to a rope bridge leading to another structure amidst the trees. Making his way to the edge of the catwalk around his hollow to the wood railing, the young Grandarian's eyes opened wide.

His hollow was but one of the dozens spread about the branches of the tallest trees he had ever laid eyes on. The entire cronom village of Keracon Valley was nestled high in the treetops. Even though they were this high off the ground, the trunks were at least six feet in diameter to better sustain the numerous primitive but durable looking hollows built tightly against them. Every one was different from the other, structurally and decoratively. Turning back to closer inspect his own shelter from the outside, he observed that the framing and the walls all appeared to be hand carved. His brow furrowed in disbelief. It must have taken ages to carve blocks of wood into entire houses and fit them safely into the branches of these trees. From the intricate catwalks and ropeways connecting the hollows and primary pathways through the trees to the hand craftsmanship of what appeared to be each and every dwelling that could be seen, the entire village was truly an architectural masterpiece.

Turning back to the rest of the valley and scanning into the distance, Tavin could make out several small figures treading across the slender walkways between the trees. They looked to be lighting rows of short torches along the main catwalks as the evening set in around them and the rays of light from the tips of the tallest trees began to wane. Tavin watched the collection of cronoms moving from torch to torch along the bridges for nearly half of an hour before the wind began to pick up, gently swaying the ropes and suspended walkways of the village to and fro in their placid wake. Pulling his thin garments around him to better guard against the biting air, Tavin turned from the railing to face his cozy hollow once more.

Stretching his stiff body out, his mind began to wander to thoughts of Ril. Though they had come close to a veritable battle that morning, Tavin's feelings for her had only increased afterwards. She was a better person than he to stand up to him and defend the Drakkaidian Prince like she had. He felt a pang of infatuation tugging at him every time the fiery girl entered his mind, as she frequently did. He had experienced his fair share of crushes on various girls in his village and in Galantia over the years, but had never quite experienced what he did with Ril before. Though he couldn't deny his attraction to her, he was as comfortable around her as he was with Jaren. Second only to the Grandarian archer, she had quickly become his best friend.

Leaning against the walls, Tavin unslung the Sword of Granis from his back to sprawl out comfortably. As he took hold of its scabbard and hilt to lower it to his side, he felt a rush of quiet but excited energy ripple through his hand and body. He froze, the sensation feeling foreign at first. But as the moments passed with his hand nestled around the talisman, a warmth and familiarity began to emanate from it that forced Tavin to smile. Touching the sword made him realize that not only had he recovered his previous strength, but he felt an overall power within himself that had not been present before.

"That's a beautiful thing," was the soft but cheerful comment from beside him. Tavin sprang off the wall, surprised he had let someone sneak up on him, and wheeled his head around to find a petite girl, a little younger than he, staring him straight in the eyes with a cheery smile set into her bright face. The boy stared at her with a raised eyebrow for a moment longer than he should have, simply puzzled by her presence. Sensing his confusion, the jovial girl let out a slight giggle. "Sorry if I surprised you, but I've been looking for you for a while now." Struggling between his confusion and remembering his manners, Tavin tried to force a smile.

"Looking for me...?" he repeated confused. The girl giggled again and brushed a lock of her long blonde hair that had fallen across her face behind her ear.

"That's right," she said beaming. "Yerbacht and your friend want to see you at the Grand Hall." She stopped suddenly, blushing with embarrassment and putting a hand over her mouth. "Oh, but I'm sorry! Here I am summoning you and I haven't even introduced myself." The girl energetically stretched out her right arm and put her hand out in front of Tavin. "I'm Kira." His curiosity stirred to no end, Tavin slowly took her hand and shook it. She had an uncommonly strong grip for someone her age. Upon closer inspection of the girl, Tavin observed Kira was not quite as tall as Ril and looked to be several years younger than either of them. She wore clothing similar to the few female cronoms he had noticed earlier in the evening: a simple green and brown tunic with a wavy skirt that just made it to the tops of her knees. Unlike the others he had seen, however, she had a vibrant yellow lining stitched into her garb and an oversized ribbon of the same hue streaming down from her brilliant blonde hair, neatly collected into a ponytail behind her. She had bright green eyes, full of life and energy. She smiled even wider as they shook. "It is a great pleasure to meet you, Sir Light." Tavin could not help but smile and cock his head in perplexity as he heard this.

"Sir Light?" he repeated chuckling, "where in Iairia did you hear that?" The girl released his hand and raised her eyebrows, suddenly embarrassed again.

"That is your name, is it not?" she asked carefully. Tavin laughed out loud.

"Actually, I'm called Tavin," he corrected with a smile, "Tavin Tieloc. Why did you think my name was Sir Light?" The girl's face turned beet red as she coyly placed her hands behind her back.

"Oh, I'm terribly sorry," she began regretfully, fidgeting with her skirt and rolling to and fro between the front and back of her feet tightly pressed together. "I was not entirely sure, but I had thought that Miss Embrin told me you were Sir Warrior Light." Tavin eyed her with renewed curiosity at the mention of the name Embrin.

"You know Ril?" he asked in astonishment. The girl nodded quickly.

"If you mean Miss Arilia Embrin, yes. I was introduced to her yesterday," she said.

"Where is she now?" Tavin asked, a little uncertainly. Kira smiled again.

"She is currently with High Elder Yerbacht in the Grand Hall, Tavin Tieloc," she stated. "That is why I am here, you see. To summon you there." Hearing Ril was safe and accounted for, Tavin relaxed a little. Seeing the girl was still more than a little jumpy herself, Tavin tried to change the subject as he slung the Sword of Granis back over his shoulder.

"I see. And it's just Tavin, if you don't mind," he smiled again. "So who are you exactly, Kira?" he asked respectfully. "You aren't a..." he trailed off, pointing at the last few cronoms lighting the torches along the rope bridges and catwalks of the village. Kira spun her head to where the boy was pointing to observe the pint sized cronoms busy at work. She giggled again.

"A cronom?" she finished with a smile. "I may not be fully grown, but I hope I look a little taller than that." It was Tavin's turn to blush this time.

"I'm sorry, I didn't mean to..."

"Oh, don't worry, please," she stopped him. "I must admit that a single human living in a village of age old fairy creatures would get me thinking too. But I promise you I am one hundred percent human." Tavin smiled and nodded.

"All right," he stated embarrassed, though delighted with how pleasant the girl spoke. "Do you mind if I ask you how you came to be living up here with the cronoms?" Kira beamed and nodded.

"Of course not!" she replied grinning. "But if you're ready, why don't we start on our way to the Grand Hall while we talk." Tavin almost forgot why the cheery girl was here in the first place and quickly nodded.

"I'm about as ready as I'll ever be," he said, despite the fact he wished that he had his own clothes on. "Please lead the way." With that, Kira beamed once more and proceeded to turn around and step onto the closer of the two rope bridges attached to the balcony. She motioned for Tavin to follow.

"Then please walk this way," she bid him. Starting off after her, Tavin gripped the low ropes of the bridge and stepped on, a bit nervous that his weight might be a little too much for such a small ropeway to handle. "I hope you're not scared of heights," Kira called back as they moved past the beginning of the bridge.

"Oh, don't worry about that," he assured her. "I'd be more concerned about keeping my balance on this thing. It's a little... cozy." Kira giggled again as she turned her head back to face him.

"Yes, I'm sorry about that. Everything here in Keracon is a little smaller than I'm sure you're used to. But you do get used to it when you've been here as long as I have." Tavin shot her a curious look.

"How long is that, Kira?" he asked. The girl's grin dimmed a little at that, her eyes glazing over with a faint distance.

"Five years, three months, and seventeen days," she stated like a machine. After giving herself a moment to gather her thoughts, she began again on her own. "You asked me why I'm here, so let me tell you. A little over five years ago when I was eight years old, I lived with my family in a place called Gaia Village. My mother was a healer who traveled between communities helping where she could, while my father was a special kind of tracker who guided people through the woods. We were very happy together all of the time. But one day, my father found something in the woods when he was helping a lost merchant home. It was a very pretty diamond. I was too small to remember exactly why it was important, but daddy said he was going to give it to Graystorm, one of his oldest friends who knew about magic. As we were about to leave to find him, they came."

Kira paused for a moment, obviously struggling with a painful memory. "Even though we were in the middle of a calm time when they should have been underground, a whole bunch of Golthrouts attacked us on our way out of the village. They took the special diamond that we found, and... killed mommy and daddy." Noticing a tear forming in her eye, Tavin put a hand on her shoulder.

"I'm sorry, Kira," he said solemnly. "I know for myself what monsters they can be. I'm sorry I made you remember."

"No, it's the past now," she nodded, wiping her moist eyes with a shirt sleeve. "But please, let me keep going. I got away because daddy put me on our horse and sent her off. I fell off after we were away and fled into the forests. I was scared and lost; hungry and cold. I wouldn't have survived long, but one night after I had fallen asleep I found myself here. You see, cronoms usually don't have anything to do with humans but they took pity on me because I was so small and helpless. They rescued me." They stepped off one of the rope bridges and onto a balcony around another hollow similar to Tavin's. "When I told them my story, they said that they knew Graystorm very well and someday he would come to get me. I was welcome to stay until he did or I grew old enough to leave on my own.

"I wanted to leave that day, but the more I saw of the village, the more I fell in love with it and the cronoms. I stayed for four years learning from the cronoms before I finally decided to go."

"But you said you had been here for over five years," Tavin remembered as they stepped across another rope bridge. Kira nodded.

"Well, I was ready to go over a year ago, but then the Golthrouts came out of their caves. Early, too. As you can probably guess, the cronoms are very frightened of them, so I have not been allowed to leave until they have descended back into the ground again."

"So that would make you thirteen years old then?" Tavin asked, quickly running numbers through his head. She grinned broadly and nodded.

"Yep. I do miss the outside world I once knew, but I really love the valley, too. I would regret never seeing another human again, but I could probably live here for the rest of my life and be just as happy. The cronoms are such a kind and caring people. I love them so much." Tavin nodded as they passed across another balcony and across another catwalk.

"I can see why," he agreed. "They were generous enough to rescue me and my friend. We would have been in serious trouble without them." At the mention of Ril, Kira turned her head back to him.

"Is Miss Embrin your love, Tavin?" she asked honestly. Tavin's face locked up for a moment, feeling an embarrassing rush of color overcoming it. Though shocked to hear the girl ask him this, her expression remained truly curious.

"...Kira, why would you think that?" he asked awestruck. She held his gaze, growing confused.

"The cronoms told me that when a young man and a young woman are together, it is because they are in love. Is this not true?" Blushing bright red, he was not sure how to answer.

"No," he managed to utter, the words choked up in this throat.

"Then you do not love Miss Embrin, Tavin?" she asked.

"Yes, er, no... I mean..." he had to stop and exhale to collect his thoughts. Kira still stared at him curious. "Look, Kira. Just because a man is with a woman, that doesn't mean they're in love. Ril and I are just traveling together, that's all."

"So you do not love her?" she repeated, stepping off the walkway they strode on to another branching off from it. Tavin exhaled heavily again.

"She's my friend, Kira, but I'm not in love with her." Though he spoke honestly, he couldn't help feeling like he was lying to some extent.

"I see," she stated impassively turning her head back in front of her as if not aware of what she had just put him through. Though the blonde haired girl was still young, she was exceptionally naïve.

The two walked on through the intricate weaving rope bridges and balconies of the tree tops of the village for another five minutes not saying much else. Tavin found himself preoccupied with something Kira had said.

"Kira, he began again, "you said that your father found a special diamond. Can you remember anything else about it?" The girl shrugged her arms and furrowed her brow.

"Well," she started, racking her brain, "I can remember it was very shiny and white, but every time I tried to play with it my mother took it away because it was so sharp. Why do you ask?" The Grandaria boy paused, not sure what to reply with. A shiny, white, sharp, crystal that her father had found in the woods? That he was trying to get to someone with magic ability but was taken by the Golthrouts? It all pointed to one explanation; one incredibly farfetched explanation, but the only one that made sense.

"Kira, do you mind my asking if you have a last name?" he pressed, his heart suddenly beating faster. She turned back with apologetic eyes.

"Oh, I'm sorry! I forgot to tell you. It's Marcell." Tavin's pulse quickened once again. That was the name of the man Zeroan was looking for in Gaia Village, where she was from. That diamond that the Golthrouts stole had to have been a missing shard of the Holy Emerald. They had just been in the lair of the Golthrouts, most likely within an arms length of the talisman, and didn't even know it! Tavin couldn't believe it.

"Why are you so curious, Tavin?" the blonde haired girl asked puzzled. Deciding it best not to explain his entire quest to the little girl, he chose to forget until he found Ril.

Telling Kira he was just a curious person, she giggled and continued to lead him through the valley. As he wondered if this Graystorm had any relation to Zeroan or the sages, he pretended to be taken by the exotic hollows nestled tightly against the trees along the way. As he had noticed earlier, they were all different in design in one way or another. As they passed by the various structures, one of its occupants occasionally came out to say hello. If nothing else, Tavin thought, the cronoms were an excessively kind people. It took little imagination to guess where Kira had developed into the sweet girl she was. The sun had nearly completely disappeared from view when Kira at last stopped before the thickest tree trunk Tavin had ever seen.

"Here we are," the girl stated cheerfully, extending her arm up to the massive structure situated twenty feet higher in the tree's branches. Following her hand upward, Tavin's eyes opened wide. The edifice he found in the trees above him was easily ten times the size of his own miniature hut and was decorated unlike anything he had ever seen. Its walls were amazingly hand carved like the rest of the village's hollows, but were infinitely more detailed and elaborate. Strange emblems and designs obviously inspired by nature covered the thick walls and ribbons like the one in Kira's hair flew in the breeze along the roofing. The structure itself was also far superior to the others in the valley. There was one immense hollow resting in the center of several large branches, with several other huts and balconies like his own adjacent to it. Kira grinned as she watched Tavin's jaw gape open. "Impressive, isn't it?" she smiled. Coming back to his senses, the awestruck Grandarian shook off his amazement and returned her smile.

"It reminds me of my childhood tree house outside Eirinor Village," he stated, remembering the hours he and Jaren had spent there years ago. "Of course, ours was just big enough to fit the two of us. Uncomfortably, at that. This looks like it could easily hold our entire village." Kira nodded as she shifted her gaze up to the mammoth cronom construction.

"Well, it can easily fit all of the cronoms. That is why they call it the Grand Hall, after all," she chimed merrily. "In fact, just about all of them should be up there for dinner right now. You see, the Grand Hall is the central hollow of the village. All the most important places are found here. As you can see, it is broken up into several different structures called hollows. The largest one in the center is where the entire village gathers for assemblies and meals. But please, I'm sure that you are eager to see the inside for yourself. Follow me." With that, Kira turned away and up to a rope ladder stretching from the large balcony on which Tavin stood to the entrance of the Grand Hall. He eagerly followed her, his curiosity peaked with the amazing cronom construction before him. Making it up to the top of the ladder, Tavin stood and repositioned the Sword of Granis over his back. The view was incredible. He could see nearly the entire village below, and from above it looked even more complex and beautiful than before. His guide did not wait, however, so he had little time to enjoy the sights. Turning back to Kira, she bid him to ascend the staircase that led up to the doorway to the hollow. He could easily take three or four of the stairs in a single step.

After they had made their way up the staircase and the standard sized cronom doorway, Kira turned and smiled.

"Just to give you a fair warning," the girl stated putting a hand on the door's handle, "it is dinner time, and cronoms only eat once a day, so do forgive their manners while they finish. They can be a bit greedy when they eat!" Grinning back that he was quite the eater himself, the girl pushed open the surprisingly heavy double doors of the Grand Hall. Stepping inside, Tavin could see it was packed to the gunnels with what he guessed to be nearly a hundred of the miniature fairy creatures all seated around several long tables that stretched from one end of the hollow to the other. As he followed Kira inside, he was greeted by numerous slowly turning heads all chewing on a diverse assortment of exotic foods Tavin had never seen the likes of before. Though they smiled broadly as they caught a glimpse of him, they seemed much too busy to say hello.

The cronoms were like the hollows they had built throughout the village: each one different and unique from the rest. They tended to dress similarly, but that was about their only resemblance other than their height. As he and Kira made their way down the central aisle of the hollow, the blonde haired girl abruptly stopped catching sight of a childlike cronom waving and grinning at her. Another cheery smile overcame her face.

"Hello, Ureiy," she greeted merrily, bending her legs to lower herself to the cronom's level.

"Kira!" was the only word of response from the little cronom. From the babyish tone of his voice, Tavin inferred it must have still been an infant, though it was hard to tell when the tallest of these creatures stood only two feet shorter than he at most. Kira brought her bubbly face up to meet with Tavin's.

"Tavin, this is my little friend Ureiy. His parents are at the eastern outpost, so I look after him from time to time in their absence. He's still just a baby as you can see." Turning her head back to the young cronom, she grinned and stretched out her right hand to tickle him under his chin. The little cronom snickered and shook his head.

"Kira!" he repeated again with a grin. Just as Tavin was about to bend down with her to greet the little cronom, a familiar voice sounded through the hollow.

"Tavin!" was the excited call from across the room. Turning his head in surprise, he looked across the rows of tables seated with cronoms to a shorter one on a small platform at the end of the hall. Seated around it were three cronoms and a red haired girl twice their size, jumping out of her seat. Tavin grinned as she came hopping off the platform and jogging down the aisle. Though feeling a little embarrassed for her, having disturbed all the dining cronoms with her outburst, he was happier to see her than anything. Approaching with a relieved and easy smile over her soft face, Tavin's own expression reflected her sense of contentment, and this time he was not surprised when she quickly embraced him upon arrival. Tavin clasped her in his arms as her body came together with his, glad to have the old Ril back. After sharing each other's embrace for several moments, Ril looked up, her eyes questioning.

"You feel cold, Grandarian," she said with an accusing look about her face. "You've been outside since I left you an hour ago, haven't you?" Tavin held his breath, not quite sure how he was going to avoid her inevitable sermon.

"Well, I-"

"I don't even want to hear it," she cut him off quickly, though still wearing a friendly smile. Tavin shrugged as he let her fade out of his grip.

"But I had Kira here to guide me, so not long." At the mention of her name Kira was back up to their level, beaming. Ril turned and smiled back.

"Did you find him outside, Kira?" she asked the blonde haired girl, to which she glanced uncertainly at Tavin who was desperately shaking his head no from behind Ril. Seeing the girl's dilemma, Ril giggled. "Don't worry, Kira. I'm just glad you didn't have to wake him up. It wasn't pretty last time." Tavin raised an eyebrow at this, but his response was cut off by the approach of the three cronoms he had noticed sitting with Ril at the head table. They were all three dressed in more elaborately decorative clothing with simplistic crests embroidered into their attire, and all three had beards that stretched from their aged faces to their feet. Tavin had to bite his tongue to keep from laughing at their bizarre appearance. Also observing the appearance of the three cronoms, Kira quickly changed the subject.

"Tavin, I would like to introduce the three Elders of the Keracon Valley," she began extending her hand down to their level. The old cronom in the center of the three was the first of them to speak.

"Greetings, my human friend," he coughed in an ancient voice. "I am called Yerbacht. It is a great honor to meet you."

"The honor is mine, sir," Tavin respectfully acknowledged, bowing his upper body. "I have not yet had the opportunity to thank someone for saving the lives me and my friend. We are in debited to you and your people." The wrinkled cronom cackled at that.

"Oh think nothing of it, young human," he said waving his hand and grinning. "If anything, it was our payment to you for what you have done for us. I have been told that you and your magical power have saved two of my children here, so it is you that we are indebted to. You are welcome to stay and recover your strength for as long as you are inclined to do so." Tavin nodded and smiled back to Ril. "Is there anything I can do for you now, my human friend?" Tavin brought his gaze back down to the elder cronom as he quickly responded.

"Actually, I'm pretty hungry," he confessed smiling. "I don't suppose I could join you for dinner?" Ril rolled her eyes, aware that the bottomless-pit had just consumed his lunch before she left. Kira giggled as the girl stared at him accusingly.

Chapter 50

The Secret

After Tavin had been introduced to Yerbacht and the other cronom elders, he immediately took Ril aside for a moment and told her what he had just learned from Kira. Though the Warrior of Fire was skeptical, she agreed in the end, unable to believe they might have had the chance to recover the lost shard of earth and missed it. Letting the matter pass, however, they found their way to the table at the end of the hollow. Tavin quickly set to work gorging himself with all the exotic cronom food he could manage to pack into his mouth at one time.

Throughout the entire meal, he was stared at with wonder and curiosity by Kira, the elders, and everyone of the miniature cronoms in the hollow, embarrassing Ril to no end. Though fully aware that he had abandoned his manners and was eating worse than Jaren, after days of nothing but water and strange soups that Ril had been feeding him, he was hungry enough not to care. Yerbacht and the others were far from offended, however, seemingly entertained by his ravenous behavior. Ril was not as amused, and Kira continued to giggle throughout the entire meal as she continually shot him irate glances and quietly kicked him under the table. Tavin was aware he was inviting her wrath upon him, but it was far more important to him to get his fill than to avoid her vehemence after they left.

They did so after nearly an hour when the sun had completely sank into the west and the starry night sky had fully emerged over the dense treetops above Keracon Valley. Yerbacht told Tavin and Ril they could remain at their guest hollow until they chose to leave, which they in turn told him would be within the next couple of days at absolute most. Tavin noticed Kira sulk back into her chair at this, guessing she was obviously happy to see fellow humans after five years of no contact with anyone of her race. It could not be helped though, he thought, knowing they had to be out of the forests as soon as they could to try and find what had become of Jaren, Zeroan, and the others. The only thing that could delay them would be the unexpected variable he had left asleep at their hollow.

Having lingered at the Grand Hall long enough, Tavin and Ril pushed back from the table stuffed. They waited for the majority of the other cronoms around the long tables to leave for their own hollows and then rose after saying their goodbyes for the night. Kira had volunteered to show them back to the opposite side of the village, but having made her way back and forth between the Grand Hall and their hollow several times now, Ril felt confident they could manage and thankfully declined. Tavin would have allowed her to tag along anyway if not for Yerbacht, who asked her to retire for the evening herself. They exited the Grand Hall to find an incredible view below. Seemingly transformed by the night, the sun seeped valley Tavin had marveled at earlier in the day was replaced by a collection of distant but bright torch-lit walkways stretching from one end of the village to the other. Superimposed over the empty blackness of the forest beneath it, the village stood out like the night sky with the countless torches mimicking the infinite sea of stars. Though so simple compared to something as beautiful as Galantia or even Torrentcia City, it was one of the most gorgeous and captivating sights either of the two Elemental Warriors had ever seen.

After gazing down upon the endless rows of symmetric weaving torches for several long minutes, they at last turned to make their way down the rope ladder to the primary base of the village and proceeded back to their hollow on the other side. As they began to casually pass along the complex bridges and catwalks, Tavin turned to Ril, her face lowered and her eyes familiarly glazed over like they had been in the days before the caverns of the Golthrouts. They walked on in this silence for minutes until they were almost back to the last bridge leading to their hollow. Disappointed to see this strange depression returned after being so energetic earlier, Tavin tried a quick smile through the darkness and began to speak.

"Kira sure is a sweet little girl," he began, fishing for what kind of mood she had drifted into. As if lost in thought, Ril barely even responded.

"Yes. She was the first person I met when I came awake the other day," she stated somewhat monotonously. Tavin nodded his head.

"She's a little naïve, being sheltered up here for so long, but she's one of the most cheerful people I've ever met," he continued watchfully. This time, Ril merely nodded and didn't say anything at all. After another long moment of silence, Tavin looked down himself and exhaled slowly, remembering the Mystic Sage Zeroan's words from their late night talk. He knew what he had to do. Not looking up as he began, his voice was encased in a soft and careful tone. "Ril," he started slowly to get her attention, "I've had the feeling that something is... wrong for weeks now. I don't know what it is, but it seems like you've been kind of distant at certain times lately." The words sinking in, she slowly brought her gaze to his shadowed face, also coming up to look at hers. As their eyes met, he continued. "You don't have to tell me what it is, but I just wanted you to know that I'm here. If something's bothering you, I'd like to help." As Ril let his offer digest, her already sluggish walk slowed to a crawl until she was barely moving at all. Matching her speed to stay beside her, Tavin stopped on the balcony surrounding their hollow.

Her eyes seemed to soften and even moisten then, and her mouth quivered a little as if ready to say something but couldn't quite get the words out. Seeing the dilemma, Tavin spoke again to encourage her.

"What is it, Ril?" he whispered. She still held his gaze, but he could tell she was struggling to do so.

"I..." she trailed off, again unable to continue. Tavin took a step closer.

"Please tell me, Ril," he pushed. This was as far as Ril could maintain herself. Abruptly spinning her head around to face the railway of the balcony, Tavin could hear her faintly weeping like she had the night by the willow in the Grailen. Feeling it inappropriate to grill her when she was obviously so sensitive, he moved beside her facing the railway and looked down into the blackness of the forest below him, waiting. After several long moments passed, Ril at last opened her mouth again.

"Tavin," she choked softly. He was quick to respond.

"I'm listening, Ril. What is it?" She let her eyelids slip open and shut before she raised an arm to wipe the forming tears away with the tight sleeves of her cronom garb.

"Tavin, you're my friend, aren't you?" she asked almost painfully. His brow furrowed, confused.

"What kind of question is that? Of course I'm your friend." There was another moderate silence before she summoned the words to continue, though they were very soft.

"Tavin, I want to tell you something, but I'm afraid you would hate me if I did," she whispered, an obvious fear pouring from her voice. He shook his head in bewilderment again.

"Ril, nothing you could tell me would ever make me hate you," he assured her calmly. "I promise that whatever you have to say, I'll understand." She stood silent then as if not sure if that was a promise he could keep. Not able to contain her secret any longer, however, she had to continue.

"...Tavin," she said almost inaudible. He leaned closer, his eyes searching. "It was me, Tavin. It... it was me. I'm the one who almost... who almost killed you." He didn't know what she was saying.

"Ril, what are you talking about?" he asked bemused. She shook her head and let the fully formed tears swelling in the corners of her eyes flow down her delicate cheeks as she repeated her words.

"I'm telling you I'm the one, Tavin," she said again, this time much louder. "I was the one who put those Drakkaidian crystals on the Sword of Granis. I was the one who almost killed you, Tavin! It was me!" She was crying out loud now, tears flowing freely. Tavin was left in utter shock. He had no idea what she was saying. He had no idea what he was supposed to think; supposed to do. And now she was practically hysterical.

"Ril," he stammered in mass confusion, "what in the name of Granis are you talking about?"

"I told you, Tavin," she said crying. "I'm the one who put the crystals on the Sword of Granis. I almost killed you, and I couldn't keep it to myself any longer. Every day the guilt gets worse, and now when we're alone I can't even look you in the eyes without wanting to cry. I'm the one, Tavin, I'm..." she couldn't finish. Too overcome by her emotions and shame to even face him, she turned away from the railing and sank to her knees on the balcony, sobbing. Tavin stood frozen, not sure what to say. After standing there long enough to fully realize what she had just told him, he at last moved. Slowly sinking down to his knees as well, his incredulous eyes scanned her colored face.

"Why, Ril?" he asked softly. "Why would you do that?" His words were easy and quiet, but they stabbed at her nonetheless. She tried to focus enough to respond.

"I had to," she managed through her tears.

"What do you mean you had to?"

"I had to. I thought I was helping you. He said I'd be helping you..." she trailed off, not able to complete her thought. Tavin's expression tightened at this.

"Wait a minute, Ril. Who is 'he'?" he asked. She looked up at him again, struggling to get a single word out.

"...S, Seriol," she said trembling. Tavin's eyes exploded open at this revelation.

"Ril, please, I need you to calm down and talk to me. I'm not mad, Ril. I just need you to talk to me." Though she felt no better, she tried to sever her emotions at his request. "Ril, what does Seriol have to do with this?" She stared at him for a long moment, collecting her thoughts and remembering.

"Do you remember the day we first met?" she asked then, catching him off guard. Tavin nodded his head yes. "After I left you and Jaren that night at the council, I went back to my room with Pyre and Spillo. When they fell asleep, I went back outside for a walk around the castle. As I was walking, the Chief Advisor to the Supreme Granisian came to me. He told me he had a secret task for me now that I was going with you on the journey. He told me that there was something wrong with the Sword of Granis because it had been sitting in the Temple of Light for so many years and that its power needed to be revived. He said that no one could know about it except him and me because if you found out it could destroy your link to the sword when you needed its power." She sniffled and struggled to continue. "After he swore me to secrecy, he gave me this." Ril slowly sat back on her legs and reached into a pocket of her tunic. She slowly brought forward a small satchel used to carry Seir and handed it to Tavin. He took it with confusion.

"What is this?" he asked quietly. She just stared at it and motioned for him to open it with her soaked eyes. He did so slowly, untying and opening its top. Bringing the bag under one of the torches to properly view its contents and peering in, his eyes went wide. Inside the bag were over twenty of the golden imposter crystals that had been planted on the Sword of Granis. His eyes were filled with deep confusion and disturbance as he brought them back onto Ril's, simply filled with shame. "Seriol told you to put these on the sword?" Ril slowly nodded, wiping her tears away once again.

"He told me he had put the first one on before you even arrived in Galantia, but that I would need to put a new one on every three or four days after their effect wore off. I put seven on from the time we set out of Galantia and the battle at Agealin Town." She broke her gaze with him again, fresh tears formulating. "I even put one on the night before you woke in the fields outside the town. But once I found out it was the crystals that were responsible for your sickness and almost killing you, I stopped no matter what Seriol told me. I was going to tell you that night, but you were all so angry at the mention of a traitor that I was too scared." She shook her head as her voice began to swim with tearing emotion again. "I know you must hate me now, but I'm just... I am *so* sorry, Tavin. I'm so, so, sorry... You're always so kind to me and treat me so much better than everyone else, and I almost killed you. I don't deserve... I'm so sorry..." That was all she could bring herself to say, losing herself in her tears again.

As the broken Warrior of Fire cried before him, Tavin was lost in emotion of his own. He had not expected something like this to be the source of her depression, and he was still shocked beyond belief that Ril had been the one planting the crystals on his blade. Looking down at the satchel full of the dark gems, he remembered however that it was not Ril who had wanted him dead- it was Seriol. His head shot back up. Now he was the one to be ashamed. Ril had poured her soul out to him and he had just sat here questioning her. He immediately dropped the bag of crystals to the wooden floor beneath them and reached out for the girl's quaking shoulders, pulling her closer. She brought her soaked face back up to his.

"Ril, I don't hate you," he said more ashamed than her that she could even think that. "I told you I could never hate you, and I meant it. I am *not* angry at you. The only thing I'm angry about is that you would blame yourself for this." He brought a hand up to wipe a streaming tear away from her face. "Ril, this was not your fault. You were tricked into doing this by Seriol. You thought you were helping me. If anything, I owe you that much more for caring all that time." The girl's eyes blinked then, unable to comprehend how the Grandarian boy could say such things after knowing what she had done to him.

"Tavin, I almost killed you," she whimpered helplessly. "How can you just forgive me like this?" He held her gaze unblinking.

"Ril, listen to me now. Seriol tricked you. This was *not* your fault. I forgive you completely. If anyone should be apologizing here, it should be me for not telling you that from the beginning." She looked at him incredulously again, letting his word's digest. She couldn't believe it. He could see the confusion and lingering guilt in her eyes, and squeezed her tighter. "I don't want you to worry about this anymore. You're the only one who's blaming you; I won't ever." He looked at her softly, inching forward with a soft smile. "You're one of the best friends I have, Ril. After all we've been through you should know that. So please, forget about all this and give me back the Ril I know. The strong, free, smart, funny, even tomboyish Ril. That's the girl I want. What do you say?" She stared at him, now inches away, her moist eyes quietly tearing up again. After all the Grandarian boy had just said, though, they were now tears of happiness.

Ril had never experienced such kindness and understanding from anyone and was so joyful to still hear him call her his friend, she found that she could only laugh. It was silent at first, but she was soon audibly giggling through the night air right through her tears. Tavin beamed back at her as she did, guessing that whatever he said had worked. Though there were so many things she could think of saying right then, the first thing that came out was,

"What do you mean, tomboy?" she asked through all the emotion, to which Tavin slowly shook his head and joined in her laughter.

Chapter 51

<u>A Proposal</u>

Tavin and Ril probably could have stayed on the balcony around the hollow for the rest of the night just sitting there on their knees laughing, if not for the faint noise that sounded from the entrance to the dwelling moments later. So engaged with Ril and her confession, Tavin had completely failed to notice the appearance of the black silhouette leaning against the doorway, staring at them with dark eyes illuminated by the dancing torchlight. At last detecting the presence behind them, Tavin was instantly on his feet wrapping his fingers around the hilt of the Sword of Granis, scaring the still emotional Ril half to death where she sat. Tavin's face locked up defensively, not having to think twice to realize who the figure was. As Ril wheeled around to discover the source of Tavin's apparent alarm, the dark frame's red eyes shifted to her vulnerable figure, lingering there too long for Tavin's taste as he made known by taking a step forward and gritting his teeth. The figure's eyes set themselves back in alignment with Tavin's.

"Don't let me interrupt," was the soft but darkly painted remark from behind his shadowed lips, to which Tavin only narrowed his eyes and reaffirmed his grip over the Sword of Granis. Upon hearing the voice from the dark figure, Ril was quick to realize his identity as well and rise to her feet alongside Tavin. The figure silently chuckled. "Comrades in arms and the best of friends. Touching." Tavin was quickly losing his temper with every word the figure spoke, and Ril realized it as his already white knuckle grip on the hilt of his weapon began shaking. The figure noticed it as well. "There will be no need for that, Grandarian."

"What do you want, Drak?" Tavin immediately countered, his voice drenched in acid. Verix Montrox thrust himself off of the door he leaned on and into the torchlight so his entire face was illuminated by the swaying flame, emotionless. He had returned his tattered gray coat about his body and his bright red hair was still a mess from days of sleep, but he remained forbidding all the same.

"To talk," he stated in a strangely reserved tone that sounded nothing like what Tavin thought the malevolent Prince of Drakkaidia should. The Warrior of Light did not flinch.

"About what? How you want to kill us?" he questioned fiercely. Verix responded to the Grandarian boy's verbal assaults with indifference.

"To the contrary," he said, "I need you alive." Tavin's face remained hard, but his temper temporarily declined upon hearing this. No one said anything for a moment, Tavin waiting for the Dark Prince to elaborate, Verix waiting for the Warrior of Light to ask him to, and Ril waiting to get in between the two before one of them lost their patience and attacked. After several more long moments of silence however, it was she that picked up where Verix left off.

"Is that why you saved me?" she asked suddenly, catching them both off guard. Verix broke his gaze from Tavin and placed it onto the girl. As his eyes fell upon her, they seemed to acquire a new layer of quietness; their intensity subsiding, making Ril feel a little uncomfortable but glad she had lowered the tension. Verix kept his gaze upon her not saying anything, so once again, Ril did. "Why did you do that, Verix Montrox?" Once again, the Drakkaidian Prince's eyes changed; this time softening to the point where it almost looked like he wanted to say something kind. But as the long moments passed, he shook off whatever it was he was feeling and hardened them again.

"Because I have changed my mind about something," he said at last, turning his eyes back to Tavin afterwards. "Something very big. Something very important. And I find that I no longer wish you dead. I need you alive." Though his words were spoken with powerful conviction, it seemed to Ril that they were summoned at the last minute to mask something else behind them. She did not have long to dwell on it, however, as Tavin shook his head with building ferocity.

"I'm already tired of this, Montrox," he said biting with enmity. "I don't know what you're up to, but whatever it is, I'm not falling for it. Whatever you have to say, we're not interested." Verix remained still but continued, ignoring Tavin's rejection.

"What if I was to tell you that I am interested in defecting from my father to aid you on your quest?" Between the gravity of that statement and the impossibly loud ringing of steel from the drawing of the Sword of Granis that immediately followed it, Ril was ready to jump out of her skin.

"I would tell you to go to hell and rot there, you evil, deceiving, murdering, Drakkaidian piece of garbage," Tavin said with scorn dripping from his irate voice, pointing the unsheathed Sword of Granis out to Verix's neck. Anticipating an explosion like this from the passionate Warrior of Light, Ril was quick to leap in front of Verix like she had that morning. Verix didn't move a muscle. With his sword point suddenly inches away from Ril, Tavin was quick to pull it back in aggravation. "Ril, don't do this again. He's not asleep or helpless now, so get out of the way." Ril shook her head again, not moving.

"I thought we agreed that we would at least hear him out, remember?" she argued fiercely. Tavin inhaled loudly and grit his teeth, knowing he had promised her that. After another moment of warily staring her down, Tavin at last threw the Sword of Granis back into its sheath and reached out to pull her away from Verix.

"All right, Drak. I'm giving you a chance to say whatever you have to, but don't think for a minute that this changes anything. I don't know what your agenda is, but if I get so much as a hunch you're just playing with me, so help me Granis I'll-"

"Talk, Verix," Ril interrupted, precluding Tavin from saying something that might further increase the tension. Once again responding with a lack of concern for Tavin's attitude, he did as he was bid.

"I am not 'playing' with anyone," he picked up from where he left off. "This is no more a game to me than it is to you. I have just as much at stake here, if not more." He moved then for the first time in minutes, slowly striding over to the wooden railing around the balcony and taking a seat upon it. He took a deep breath then, realizing there would be no turning back after this. "Simply put," he began closing his eyes for a moment, "my father is out of his mind." Tavin and Ril both raised an eyebrow in uncertainty at this. What could he be trying to do to say such a thing, thought Tavin as he braced himself for whatever was coming next. Verix shifted his gaze onto the ground beneath him, talking out into space. "I went along with this at first hoping he would overcome it, but no more. As you know, there is great evil coming to life in my home. There is a portal to the Netherworld in Drakkaidia, and my father is foolishly putting it to use. He has crossed a threshold and pulled demons out of the Netherworld itself to do his bidding. I'm sure you've met more than you would wish already.

"But there is more happening in Dalastrak than you know. Every time my father summons a demon out of that accursed pit, the fragile veil that separates it from this world is torn. Little by little, it is shredded as each demon comes forth. If my father continues summoning these unholy creatures with only the incomplete Holy Emerald to control them, he will eventually lose that control. The day that happens, the demons will shatter the veil between the worlds and will overrun Drakkaidian and the rest of Iairia with their endless numbers and unquenchable thirst for blood. I warn him of such things, but he is blinded by his pride and power." The once emotionless Prince's words suddenly increased in fervor; his face twisting with annoyance. "He is so caught up in fulfilling his self appointed destiny to take revenge on Grandaria and Elemental Warrior of Light for his grandfather's defeat eons ago that he cannot see five minutes in front of his face. I thought that I could stop him from summoning any more demons if I completed their task of destroying you first, but I see now that his hunger for power and his need for an army of soldiers more powerful than men will never be appeased, and even if I was to kill you now it would make no difference in his plans. My father is insane, and I cannot stop him." Verix brought his gaze back up to Tavin.

"So he must be stopped another way. I cannot defeat him myself, but there is someone who can." Verix stopped and looked Tavin hard in the eyes. "You, Warrior of Light, are the only person who can stand up to his power. I must help *you*." Letting the words sink in for a few moments, Tavin slowly responded.

"I don't want your help," he said coldly. Verix Montrox held his gaze.

"You may not want it, but you need it more than you know," he returned. "Look at your situation, Grandarian.

Here you are with an emotionally unstable girl sitting lost and confused in the middle of a village occupied by pint sized fairy creatures on the opposite side of the continent from where you need to be. You have three of the six Holy Emerald shards in your possession, and as you just heard, the one in Grandaria is at risk. The girl speaks the truth. Your 'Seriol' has been working for my father for years now, and can take the shard anytime he sees fit. The two shards the sage has hidden in his tower to the east are also not safe, with more powerful demons soon to be sent there to take them. And what of the two missing shards? You still have no idea where either of them are except for which of the four lands of the Southland they are hidden in. It's like searching for a needle in a haystack but with far worse odds. To make matters better," he continued with sarcasm laced into his voice, "you are now separated from your only chance at finding them and the only one of you who has any idea what he is doing on your little quest. You don't know where the sage is, and you won't be able to find him in time to stop my father from destroying the Southland.

"After he finds the missing shards, which he will be able to easily do with his demons rising from the Netherworld and tearing the veil as they come, he will take the ones you have and be invincible. But long before then he will have his army of demons to utterly annihilate the Southland and then crush the Grandarians at the Wall of Light." Verix practically stood up and shouted at Tavin. "You don't need my help, Warrior of Light? I am your last and only chance!" In the wake of the once quiet Drakkaidian Prince's sudden verbal assault, Tavin and Ril were both left speechless. Though Tavin harbored more than his reservations of why the Drakkaidian could not be trusted, everything he said seemed to be spot on, and it impacted him right between the eyes. Not sure whether to be more humiliated or angry at everything that was unfolding before him, Tavin cut straight to the point.

"What do you want?" he asked again, this time nearly emotionless. Verix stood off the railing once more and brushed a lock of his fervent red hair away from his eyes.

"Trust," he said passionately. He could see the anger and reluctance to even continue listening to him mirrored in the Grandarian's eyes, but he continued anyway. "I am aware that you have no reason to trust me. I wouldn't trust me if I were you, but I'm asking you to nonetheless. Why? First of all, all that I just said to you is *exactly* correct, and it will all unfold *exactly* the way I said it will; that you can believe without a fraction of doubt. Second, if you step back and look at your circumstances at the moment, you will see you need help badly and are left with little choice but to solicit it from me. Third and most importantly, I can deliver. I know what my father has done, I know what he is doing now, and I know what he will do when things change. I can lead you where you need to go, I can teach you things that your sage has not told you, and I can help you avoid more trouble looking for you than you can ever fathom. Last, why not? If you are now powerful enough to best me as you seem to think you are, you would have nothing to lose, right? But for now, all I want is trust. Think it over, Grandarian."

With that, the Drakkaidian Prince strode past Tavin and Ril, making his way onto the torch-lit ropeway. Left in astonishment that he was just leaving like this, Tavin called out to him in disbelief.

"Where are you going?" he called. Verix stopped and turned his head back.

"I'm giving you time to think this over, Warrior of Light," he called. "Do so. I won't be far off." Tavin was out of his mind with incredulity.

"What do think this is, Montrox?" he called out throwing his hands into the night air. Verix stared at him. "Do you think that the Prince of Drakkaidia can just switch sides and come join Grandaria and everybody will welcome you in with open arms? It doesn't work like that! You of all people should know that what you're proposing is unthinkable. I mean, you and I are probably the first Grandarian and Drakkaidian who have ever met like this that haven't tied to kill each other instantly." Verix looked at him for a moment on the bridge, then suddenly moved back toward him. He stopped inches away from Tavin's face, his deep red eyes locked onto his. Ril was afraid one of them was going to let his ego explode and attack, but Tavin stared back just as determined, unmoving. At last, Verix moved even closer and spoke as soft as the wind humming through the night air.

"I am a Drakkaidian until the day I die, boy, and I will be long after that," he said threateningly. "I do not seek to defect to Grandaria, only to stop my father. You are a means to an end; nothing more. I don't like you any more than you like me, but right now we need each other, so I'm putting my enmity for Grandaria aside for the moment. I can do that. If you can't do the same for me, which of us is truly the 'evil' one?" They stared each other down for a long moment after that, though it seemed longest for Ril, ready to jump between the two if need be. Her worries were laid to rest as Verix suddenly pulled back and began walking away onto the rope bridge once more, calling out that he would be seeing them soon as he disappeared into the darkness of the trees and the night. As his silhouette faded, Tavin was left with so many mixed emotions he couldn't think straight. Between his lingering feelings from his discussion with Ril minutes ago, all he had taken in from Dark Prince, his Grandarian pride and instincts telling him not to trust a single word of it, and that final comment, it was all he could do to slowly turn to Ril who's delicate cheeks were still stained with the salty tears from her confession, and gape into her searching eyes.

They stared at each other for an enduring moment before eventually moving to the doorway of their hollow and closing it shut behind them, more than ready for some well deserved sleep. Letting Ril use the bed he had awoken from that morning so she could have her privacy, he took the bed that Verix Montrox had occupied until no less than an hour ago, thinking for a long time about what the Prince had asked him. The words would not leave his head. Which one was evil?

Chapter 52

<u>The Sapphire Pool</u>

The question remained buzzing in Tavin's head for the rest of the night and was there to greet him when he woke the next morning. His eyes came open slowly, adjusting to the fervent rays of light beaming in from the multitude of windows in the compact hollow, but reluctantly roused himself from beneath the comforting sheets of his bed, knowing that another long day rife with events was most likely in store for him. Sitting up and raising a hand to massage his tired face still riddled with lingering sleep, his wandering eyes fell onto the doorway separating his room from Ril's. Able to hear the faint movement of what he assumed to be the girl dressing and preparing her flowing red hair for the coming day, Tavin couldn't help but smile. There hadn't been a day that passed since the start of their journey that she hadn't beaten him up.

Tavin's wandering thoughts of the fiery Southland girl quickly vanished as an abrupt knock at the doorway of his hollow across the room sounded through the air like drums.

"Tavin!" was the blurred but shrill call from behind the wooden barrier. "Tavin, it's me, Kira! I have something for you, Tavin!" Nervously spinning his head around in the direction of the doorway, he quickly remembered he was only dressed in a pair of the cronom's shorts that fit uncomfortably tight from his waist to the tops of his thighs. "Are you awake yet, Tavin?" Her question was followed by the sudden jiggling of the doorknob, to which he leapt off his bed to preclude her from opening the door. As Kira began to push it open, he rushed across the room to catch it just before she could begin to step inside. Tavin leaned his head past the edge of the door to hide the rest of his practically bare body.

"Hi, Kira," he hastily breathed with a forced smile. The girl beamed at him.

"Good morning, Tavin," she giggled, amused at his strange behavior. "Why are you hiding behind the door?" Tavin swallowed hard and let a tiny laugh echo from the depths of his throat.

"I was just waking up and you sort of startled me is all," he sputtered quickly. "I kind of need to dress, Kira. Why don't you go talk to Ril for a minute while I get ready in here-"

"But that's why I'm here, Tavin!" she cut him short smiling. She extended her arms upward holding something. As Tavin peered down from the door's edge, he saw his familiar old clothes from the day he had left Galantia folded neatly in her arms. The girl could see the relief in his eyes. "I've been washing and mending them since you arrived. I've never seen such pretty and colorful clothes like you and Ril wear. I was happy to tend to them." She lengthened the stretch of her arms so Tavin could take hold of them, which he did with a curious look overtaking his face.

"...You washed them?" he asked peculiarly. The girl nodded her head and grinned again.

"And repaired them where they needed it," she replied modestly. "You had a lot of rips and tears in the shirt and pants, and the ends of your cape were pretty frayed so I patched them up a little. I hope you don't mind." Tavin returned her warm smile and thanked her kindly, to which she heartily blushed.

After he asked her to wait with Ril until he had prepared, he set to work ridding himself of the tight cronom garb from the day before and donned his refreshed Grandarian attire. As he pulled up the long white pants and pulled down his blue shirt, the golden embroidering and markings along their edges seemed to shine with life anew; even more so than they had at Galantia when he had first received them. Everything somehow felt softer as well; as if the material had been fused with silk since he last wore it. After pulling his sturdy blue boots over his pants and properly buttoning his shirt, Tavin reached for his blue shoulder and chest armor, polished and shimmering in the rays of sunlight. Lastly, he pulled his blue cape back over his head. It was here that he found the first of Kira's special repairs. The red interior of the cape had been separating from the blue when the golden seaming was caught in the brush of the Grailen Plains weeks ago, but she had sown the edges back with the same brilliant yellow lining that he had noticed stitched into her own clothing the day before.

Examining the rest of his attire more carefully, he found a number of other small yellow patches with elaborate weavings over former cuts on his shoulders and pant legs, and another long patch stretching across his right arm where the injury he had sustained at Agealin Town had burned. The one patch that particularly drew Tavin's attention, however, was a small pink design that appeared just under his armor. Raising his eyebrows with curiosity and lifting the front of his cape and light chest armor up, Tavin peered down to find the design of a heart where it would be located in his chest, covering the area Zeroan had ripped away when examining him the day his mysterious sickness had appeared for the third and final time. Though not sure what the pink emblem was supposed to symbolize, he gently passed his fingers along the edges of the heart on his chest and smiled.

After he had finished dressing himself in his improved Grandarian attire and completing his personal grooming, faint laughter from outside the hollow on the balcony echoed into the room, causing Tavin to turn from his bed where he stood attaching the Sword of Granis to his belt, the golden Granic Crystal immediately bursting awake with steadily radiating light. He smiled as he gathered his few loose items around the room and made his way for the door, exiting to find Kira standing and giggling with Ril, dressed in her fiery crimsons and yellows as usual. She turned to him with her flowing hair casually wrapped into a ponytail like Kira's twirling around behind her, her deep and beautiful eyes meeting with his. Tavin smiled back to her, once again amazed at her beauty with her bright clothes back to complement her red hair and eyes. Kira beamed at him as well.

"Tavin!" she shouted with glee. "Do your clothes fit comfortably?" He managed to shift his gaze off of Ril and onto the little girl beside her as he strode over to them.

"Better than new," he answered honestly. "In fact, they look better too." Tavin pulled up his hand from where it rested on the hilt of the Sword of Granis to gently pat his chest where his favorite patch had been sown in. "Thank you for all your work, Kira. I love the new look and all the other changes." The blonde haired girl blushed cherry red and coyly brought her hands behind her back to fidget with her green skirt. Ril eyes' passed down to the timid girl.

"She's quite the tailor," the Warrior of Fire agreed, motioning for Tavin to look over at her outfit. As he followed Ril's sweeping hands over her body, he noticed that her formfitting red and white pants from before had been replaced by a skirt much like Kira's, just making it down to the tops of her knees. It was of course fiery scarlet like everything else present on the girl's slender figure, complementing the locket around her neck as always. "Well?" she asked watching the boy's eyes passing along her body, to which he immediately blushed, embarrassed to be staring. He grinned broadly and brought his right arm up to scratch his head.

"You need to start your own fashion line, Kira!" he stammered quickly, not sure of the appropriate thing to say with the little girl present. Kira beamed once more while Ril coyly gazed his way, smiling at his embarrassment. After Tavin had shaken off the discomfiture, he quickly changed the subject. "So what's the plan now? I don't know about you two, but I'm ready for a little breakfast about now." Kira giggled once more, remembering his voracious appetite from the previous evening. Ril quickly shook her head, however.

"Your bottomless-pit stomach will have to wait for a while longer," she stated shooting him a disgruntled glance. "We have something else to do right now." Tavin shot her a curious look, wondering if she was referring to the third figure the cronoms had brought to the valley with them. Before he could ask, however, Kira was finishing Ril's statement.

"That's right," she chimed in. "I'm sorry to keep you from your breakfast, but Yerbacht has summoned you to the Chamber of Elders at once. He said it was an emergency." Tavin's expression morphed with dread, smelling the Drakkaidian Prince already.

"Do you know what what's wrong, Kira?" he asked hurriedly, taking a step forward. A look of uncertainty came over the little girl's face; her eyes going wide.

"I'm not positive," she began almost in a whisper, "but I overheard the name Graystorm from the elders." The Grandarian boy's dread of Verix Montrox faded some, but it was quickly replaced with further curiosity. Both he and Ril recognized it as the name of the man from Kira's story.

"Why would the man your parent's knew be here?" The girl's eyes remained wide as she waved her hand, motioning for them to follow her along the rope bridge connecting their hollow to the rest of the village.

"Come on and I'll tell you!" she called. "We're late as it is." After Tavin and Ril both took off after the jovial girl, she began to explain. She hurriedly made her way across the rope bridge and across a catwalk as she continued.

"He isn't here, or we would know it," she told them mystified. "I have never seen him myself, but the cronoms say he is the most powerful sorcerer in the world. I am not sure what Graystorm would have to do with you, but it must mean something." As Kira continued to tell the two of the legends of the mysterious Graystorm, they swiftly tread across the narrow suspended walkways of Keracon Valley until they at last reached the Grand Hall. Until they had climbed up the ladder to the higher platform of the massive hollow and were about to pass through its doorway, Tavin and Ril kept a vigilant watch around them for the still missing Verix Montrox, knowing with an absolute certainty that he would appear to them before the day was over.

The two Elemental Warriors had little time to dwell on the Dark Prince, however, as Kira led them into the Grand Hall with Yerbacht and the other two elders waiting for them at the far end. Tavin could see that the pert little faces that had giggled at his antics the night before had been replaced by serious and solemn ones as they drew near. Tavin instinctively bowed before them as Kira stopped. Yerbacht lowered his own head before speaking.

"Greetings once again, my young human friends," he started with gravity etched into his tone. "I am sorry to bother you again so soon, but a matter of great importance has just revealed itself to us, and it is come about because of your presence. Please follow me." With that, all three of the elders turned and began to stride across the end of the hollow to a small doorway on the left side. A miniature sentry armed with only a short stick opened it for them, revealing another of the compact stairways in the hollow. As Tavin and Ril began to ascend it after the elders, Kira suddenly stopped at its entrance, a look of defeat overcoming her usually cheery face. Sensing one less set of feet shuffling behind him, Tavin turned and raised an eyebrow at the blonde haired girl.

"Aren't you coming, Kira?" he asked perplexed. She lowered her head as she began to shake it.

"You are entering the Chamber of the Elders, and I am not allowed to-"

"Oh nonsense, Kira," Yerbacht interrupted her from up the staircase. "You may not be allowed up here all the time, but I want you with our guests at all times, remember? Please come with us." The girl's face lit up like the sun and came bounding up the stairs behind them. Ril turned back to her with a suddenly nervous expression about her face.

"Why are you not normally allowed to go this place?" she whispered.

"This is the Chamber of Elders, Ril," the younger girl murmured back. "No one is ever allowed entrance up here except the elders themselves. It is where they keep the Sapphire Pool." Though Ril was about to inquire as to what this pool was she was cut short by another door above them opening to reveal a balcony above the Grand Hall with no walls or ceiling to encase it. Exiting the stairway, Tavin and Ril's eyes shot open, instantly mesmerized by the cauldron-like object in the center of the balcony. The floor had been carved out to allow a hollowed out tree trunk nearly ten feet in diameter to rise three feet from the floor, taking up much of the space on the balcony. The contents of the trunk were what drew the group's attention, however. Lying in the center of the trunk was a pool of strange blue liquid. Tavin might have taken it for water at first, but upon closer inspection, it possessed a hue not found in even the most tropical of ocean waters. It was so blue it seemed to glow the color.

"This is we cronom's most sacred possession, young humans," Yerbacht suddenly spoke in a soft and taken voice. "It is the last external magic that we possess, and it is precious to us. It is the Sapphire Pool; an ancient artifact of the forest that we saved from the Golthrouts ages ago when we moved our village into the trees. We have not used it for some time, but now it radiates with life anew." Tavin stared at its impossibly blue liquid a moment longer before turning his gaze down to the elder cronom.

"What purpose does this pool serve, Yerbacht?" he asked in an equally hushed tone. The little cronom only shot him a knowing glance and moved forward pulling a small satchel from his pocket.

"See for yourself, Warrior of Light," he said lifting the satchel above the pool and letting a glittering dust fall from its opening. The moment the dust fell into the pool, its contents immediately began to stir, sloshing around and fiercely radiating the blue light from beneath its surface. Not sure what to expect, Tavin took a small step back and shot an uncertain glance to Ril and Kira, who both just stared at him unknowingly in return. As the liquid began to circulate in a consistent vortex, the elder cronom turned from the trunk and fell back into line with the other two. Closing his eyes, Yerbacht extended his hand toward the pool and made a tiny fist. Staring in amazement, Tavin watched as the pool's azure fluid began to slowly rise with the cronoms fist until it formed a column of rotating liquid, now radiating enough of the blue inner light to paint the entire wall of the Grand Hall and the thick trees around them in a deep cobalt hue.

Then, Yerbacht limply dropped his arm and opened his eyes, letting a smile overtake his worn elderly face.

"We are here, Graystorm," he managed to say with what sounded like relief. The name of the mysterious sorcerer that Kira had mentioned once again surfacing, Tavin questioningly turned back to the column of liquid swirling in the air. Then as if to respond, the column abruptly exploded in the immediate atmosphere around it and raised another four feet, almost touching the branches of the trees above them. Tavin and the others watched in astonishment as some of the liquid began to casually fall from the churning column, giving it shape. It was not more than a few seconds later before it at last stopped swirling and almost solidified into the form of a familiar figure, draping robes of blue liquid concealing its body and a thick hood positioned over its head. It was not long after that the young Grandarian boy, staring with jaw dropped and eyes wide, realized what the liquid had morphed into. He took a step forward, too amazed to say anything. When he could not, however, the figure made up of azure liquid did.

"Hello, Tavinious," an all too familiar voice echoed from beneath the transparent blue hood. Tavin's muscles tightened; his mind not able to comprehend with what his ears were telling him.

"...Zeroan?" he uttered in a whisper. Barely hearing what the boy had said, Ril brought a hand up to cover her gaping mouth, slowly shaking her head.

"It is I," the liquid figure stated, shifting his transparent sloshing robes about him. "Or at least my voice. I am physically on the eastern side of the Great Forests." Tavin, Ril, and

Kira all stared incredulously, not sure what to think. Tavin was the most taken aback of them all, so many thoughts and emotions burning into his head that he could not sort them out in time to respond. "I know you are feeling lost and confused at the moment, Tavin, but I don't have the time to explain the nature of the Sapphire Pool you stand before. I must be brief because I cannot sustain my link with it for long, so pay exceptionally close attention to what I am about to tell you. All right?" The Warrior of Light managed a quick nod. "Good." The sage lifted a hand over his face to rub his forehead as he often did when besieged by thought. "I'm not really sure where to start, so I just will. As you may or may not have learned from the cronoms that have so graciously rescued you and Ril," he paused momentarily to bow his head to the Warrior of Fire staring at him in disbelief, "I am a long time friend and ally of theirs." Tavin still just stared putting everything in his mind together.

"You're Graystorm, Zeroan?" he mused. The sage gave a single nod.

"This is the name many inhabitants of the forest know me by," he confirmed. "But to business. Are you and Ril both alright, Tavin?" The still awestruck Warrior of Light quickly nodded again and turned back to Ril, motioning for her to come up beside him. She slowly did, uneasy of the towering form of the Mystic Sage.

"We're both fine, Zeroan," he uttered quickly. "The cronoms have taken very good care of us and we're both recuperated. In fact, I feel even better than before." He broke his gaze form the sage and down to the Sword of Granis by his side, pulling it off of his belt. "I can feel a new power bursting inside me every time I even touch the sword, Zeroan. I feel like..."

"You can control your power," the sage finished for him, smiling from behind his hood. "That's right, Tavin. I could sense it that night in the caverns after we were parted. You have gained control over your elemental powers, and you are now that much closer to mastering them. I am very proud of you, my young Grandarian." Tavin could not help but slowly grin at the azure figure, silently nodding in response. Zeroan's expression quickly morphed back to one of absolute seriousness. "But despite this achievement, we are in direst of circumstances. I am currently at a lake by the first row of border villages along the eastern Great Forests, and the rest of the group is safely at a village not more than a mile away from me. They are all perfectly fine, including the cronom tracker with us." While Tavin and Ril deeply exhaled with immeasurable relief circulating through their apprehensive bodies, Yerbacht bowed to the figure of the sage.

"Thank you for taking care of him, Graystorm," the elder said graciously. The sage shook his head.

"It is I who should be thanking you for looking after the children," he returned. "But to the point, my young friends, while our party is still all alive and well, we are now divided. This and several other factors now force us to drastically alter out plans. Thanks to the Golthrouts, we were unsuccessful in locating the shard of the Holy Emerald here in the Grailen, and we are now in no condition to attempt to find the other shard in the west. We are going to have to-"

"Zeroan," Tavin interrupted, raising a hand to speak. "Before you say another word, Zeroan, Ril and I have to tell you about a few other things that have recently... come to our attention. I'd bet they will probably change things as well." Ril nervously swallowed hard and slowly shifted her gaze back over to Tavin, who turned his head to meet with her obviously frightened eyes. He took hold of her suddenly chilled hand behind his cape as he continued. Zeroan frowned.

"What is it, Tavin?" he asked quickly. Tavin slowly turned his head from Ril back to the liquid form of the sage.

"We know who the traitor in Galantia is," he said softly. Zeroan leaned forward where he stood. After he curiously asked how they learned this, Tavin began to relate to him what Ril had told him the previous night, beginning with her encounter with Seriol in the Golden Castle to showing him the satchel full of the dark imposter crystals. When he had finished, Zeroan's eyes were wide and his body was quaking.

"I can't believe it..." he trailed off with quiet fury in his voice. "Ril, are you sure beyond a shadow of a doubt that it was the Chief Advisor to the Supreme Granisian who told you to do this?" She guiltily nodded her head, softly replying yes. Zeroan thrust from where he stood, slamming his fist into his opposite hand. "If this is true, the shard in Grandaria might as well already be in Montrox's lap." He cursed for another few moments before recomposing himself and trying to continue. "All right, this changes things even further. I can't risk leaving you two alone with Golthrouts, demons, and the Dark Prince still hovering around your position, but-"

"Actually Zeroan, that's the other thing we need to tell you about," the Warrior of Light interjected once again. The sage froze, staring Tavin dead in the eyes.

"What do you mean?" he asked rapidly. Before Tavin or Ril had a chance to say anything further, a third voice from above them caught the group's attention.

"They mean, me," was the distant but very audible statement from the branches above them. Everyone shot their heads up to find the dark form of Verix Montrox sitting in the thick tree branches above them, staring down with a familiar quiet intensity mirrored in his crimson eyes.

Chapter 53

<u>Uneasy Allies</u>

"Hello sage," Verix said, leaping off the branch were he sat to plummet down onto the small balcony between Tavin and the frightened cronoms behind him. Despite his knowledge of Verix's wish for a truce between them, Tavin instinctively wrenched the Sword of Granis from its sheath, shattering the peace of the morning air with its deafening metallic ringing. Ril, Kira, the cronoms, and even Zeroan jumped at the potential scene about to explode before them, but Verix remained impassive. His emotionless eyes slowly shifted to meet the Warrior of Light's that were full of fierce determination and impatience. "Good morning to you too, Grandarian," he spoke sarcastically. While Ril pulled back on Tavin's shoulder to stop him from doing anything rash, Zeroan, wildly twisting underneath his robes, blasted out in confusion.

"What is this!?!" he boomed out of control, to which Verix turned his gaze back to the liquid form of the Mystic Sage. Though Tavin was ready to utter a spiteful remark to explain, the Drakkaidian Prince's question from the previous night ripped back into his mind, precluding him from attacking Verix until he did something to warrant it.

"Don't worry, sage," the Prince's voice eased, coming slowly and tactfully. "As I told your two Elemental Warriors last evening, you no longer have anything to fear from me. I no longer wish any of you harm, only to talk." Zeroan maliciously shifted and shouted back to Tavin.

"Tavin, what is this all about? What has he told you?" he pressed fiercely, to which Tavin only kept his eyes and blade on Verix. The Drakkaidian's view fell back in line with Tavin's, who could see the odd sincerity that he had identified there the previous night. After a moment more of distrustfully

380

staring him down, Tavin at last lowered the Sword of Granis took a step back beside Ril.

"Verix Montrox says he wants to help us, Zeroan," he stated soullessly. After that, he began to retell what Verix had related to him and Ril the previous night, with the Dark Prince stepping in to help him where he left gaps in the narrative. When the two had completely explained to the sage his entire proposal, Zeroan was just as uneasy and distrustful as Tavin had been. He raised his hand once more to massage his forehead, silently mouthing something to himself. After another moment of quiet, he at last placed his hard gaze onto Verix.

"What possible reason do we have to trust a single word that you are saying, Drakkaidian Prince?" the sage quietly blasted. Verix shrugged with indifference.

"I have already told the Warrior of Light that he has no reason to trust me, but as you of all people know given our circumstances, you are left with little choice, aren't you? These two are cut off from you now, and you cannot help them. My father is going to acquire multiple shards of the emerald very soon now, and they are going to need my help if they are to survive long enough to be of any help to your plans in the future. You need me, sage, and I think that you know that I am not lying. If I wanted these two dead, they would be by now." A long silence occurred with everyone waiting for Zeroan to make a decision. Seeing the conflict in the sage's eyes and movements, Verix took a step closer. "Not sure? Why not ask these two? They are the ones who would be traveling with me. Why not ask them if they trust me?" Letting the words sink in, Zeroan stood silent for a moment, keeping his narrow eyes locked onto Verix. "What's there to lose?"

After a long pause once again, the sage turned to Tavin and Ril standing awestruck at the Dark Prince's suggestion. Zeroan slowly opened his mouth to speak devoid of emotion.

"Well, Tavin?" he asked quietly. "What of it? What do you two think of all this?" Tavin's expression lost some of its hating bite for Verix, shocked the unassailable sage would be interested in his opinion for a decision of this magnitude. He turned back to face Ril, already staring at him with sincere eyes. He knew what she was thinking and what she would say if he asked her, so it was now up to him. Turning back to Verix, he remembered what the Prince had said to him as he left the previous night. Could he set aside his lifelong hatred for Drakkaidia and allow one of its people to help him? Did he have the tolerance? Though not sure what it meant that he was thinking of putting his hatred for his greatest enemy away, he suddenly took a step forward and started over to Verix. When he had arrived inches away from his face the way that the Dark Prince had the last time they met, he spoke with calm but hard conviction.

"I don't like you, Verix Montrox," he started coldly. "I don't like you, I don't like your father, I don't like your country, I don't like your people, I don't like your way of doing things, I don't like your attitude, and I don't like what you're proposing. I don't like anything about you, but... I believe you." A long pause followed Tavin's statement. Ril and the others of the group opened their eyes with surprise while Zeroan's liquid blue form shifted uncertainly. Verix blinked and raised an eyebrow. "I can't believe it," Tavin continued. "I don't know why I trust you, because I probably shouldn't and I really don't want to, but I do. I'm willing to let go of my feelings for Drakkaidia and you for now, because your father is my primary enemy at the moment, and with the grim situation I find myself in, I don't have any other option. So yes, Verix Montrox. I'll trust you and accept your help. But listen to me now." Tavin inched forward until he was practically touching Verix's face. "If you are lying to me, or if you do try to mislead us, it will be the last thing you ever do in this world. The second that I so much as feel something is wrong with you, it will be my esteemed pleasure to run you through. Do you perfectly understand?"

Then for the first time, Verix smiled. It was dark, but he was smiling nonetheless.

"It looks we have an agreement, Tavinious Tieloc," the red haired boy replied, nodding. The transparent figure of Zeroan deeply exhaled, obviously disturbed with the Warrior of Light's decision. With that, Tavin withdrew from Verix, inching back until he stood beside Ril once more. Aligning himself beside her, she gently tugged on his shirt sleeve. He didn't look into her eyes, but knew what he would have found there. It was Verix who broke the silence then, tightly maintaining his smile and reaching into the recesses of his tattered gray coat. "Well, I'm glad that's settled, because now I can show you this." Then, to the entire group's shock, the Drakkaidian Prince pulled forth a brilliantly shining object from his right coat pocket where he had once kept his communication stone to his father. Tavin's jaw nearly dropped to the floor of the balcony.

"...That looks like a..." he could not finish, his voice failing him in the wake of his amazement. Verix smiled again as he hoisted a brilliantly white shard of the Holy Emerald out in plain view for Zeroan to see.

"I trust this will ease your mind some, sage," he smirked almost flippantly. Zeroan shook his head bewildered.

"I can sense it really is..." he trailed off like Tavin. His eyes jumped off of the crystal and onto Verix. "Where did that come from?"

"I should think that would be obvious to you, sage," the boy commented, throwing his head back to removed a lock of his fervent hair from his face. "The only shard I could have possession of would be the missing one here in the south. I thought you would have put two and two together to realize that Golthrouts had found it, as sensitive to magic as they are. There isn't much to sense coming from it in this state, but it's enough for creatures like them. I managed to snag this little gem from their ruler as his "skin" where it was lodged exploded. It looks like our luck doesn't seem to be completely bad, does it?" Thinking back to his battle in the caverns across the forests, Tavin suddenly remembered that he had indeed seen something shimmering amidst the King of Golthrout's stony exterior. It must have been the shard. His theory had been right. Kira's father had found the earth shard but lost it to the Golthrouts, who had given it to their master.

"Let me see it, Verix," Tavin asked cautiously then, extending his arm out. The Dark Prince shot his eyes to the Grandarian boy, obviously reluctant to comply.

"I think it would be best if I continued to look after it for now," he said, his smile dispersing. Zeroan was the next to enter the conversation.

"That's not how this works, Prince," he shook his head. "We have gone out to the end of the limb to trust you. The least you can do to return our trust is let Tavin take the shard now." Verix's expression remained doubtful, but decided it best to show a little good will toward the Grandarian who had taken the first step to accept him a moment ago.

"Very well," he agreed, "the Warrior of Light can take the shard- as a token of my allegiance and trust." His words did nothing to bolster Tavin's confidence in his new ally, but he stepped forward to take hold of the shard. As his fingers ran along its still sharp and defined edges, a wave of remembrance washed through him. It was identical to his old lucky charm that he had carried for years, dispelling any lingering doubts as to its authenticity. Observing his satisfaction, Verix faintly allowed a smile to pass over his face once more and at last shifted his position. "All right then, would you like to continue with what you needed to say, sage? Or are things self explanatory enough for you to leave us be now?" The liquid model of the Mystic Sage Zeroan's eyes narrowed stridently, his body language stiffening.

"I would advise caution to you at the moment, Drakkaidian Prince," he breathed sharply. "Be mindful of your words to me. Tavinious may give you some semblance of trust, but I reserve my doubts. As such, I will keep this simple and clear. While you may now be the Elemental Warriors' guide, you are *not* their leader in any way. Though I'm sure you will see fit to input your own voice frequently, the Warrior of Light is the head of this trio." He stopped then to exhale and collect his thoughts, shifting his gaze to Tavin. "This is what we will do. Tavin, Verix will lead you and Ril to Torrentcia City where I will meet you with the rest of our divided party as soon as possible. We are closer to that location, and you will most likely not move as fluently as you would with me, so we should arrive first. Once we reassemble there, we will gather the Legion and prepare for whatever the senior Montrox has planned in regard to the Southland." Ril was the one to interrupt.

"But Zeroan, what of the shard to the west?" she asked skeptically. Zeroan shook his head.

"Without my aid, you would not be able to locate or retrieve it, Arilia," he spoke softly. "And by the time we reach the west, Drakkaidia will have gotten to it first. We must unfortunately relinquish that shard to Montrox." Though Ril was disappointed to suffer a defeat before they even tried to succeed, she was even more let down to have any chance of seeing her homeland precluded. "In any case, if what Verix has told us is accurate, Montrox will be headed to defeat the Southland and the Legion first. With the shards he has access to now, this is well within his power. Hopefully I can retrieve the two shards at the Mystic Tower before..." Zeroan stopped suddenly, some of the perfectly molded liquid comprising his figure beginning to swell and fall. "Blast, my link to the pool is nearly gone. Listen carefully, all of you. With what I already knew combined with this new information from Verix, I can surmise that there are sure to be new and fearsome creatures soon to be scouring the world looking for you and the shards. Be wary, and be off as soon as you can, for as you know, time is of the essence."

As Zeroan paused to focus his failing link to the pool, Verix silently nodded and shifted his gaze to Tavin.

"Then I think we are done here," he stated factually. "While the sage composes himself, I will take my leave." Tavin and Ril eyed him down distrustfully.

"What do you mean?" he asked glaring. The Drakkaidian Prince spun around and walked to the edge of the balcony past the three cronom elders. He placed a leg on the railing and turned his head back to face the rest of the group.

"The plan has been made, so my presence here is no longer needed. I'm sure the sage would like to have a few moments of privacy with you anyway, so I will give him what he needs. As before, I won't be far off. I will see you both soon, I'm sure." Rotating his head back to face forward again, he stood up on the railing with both legs. He remained there for a long moment, perfectly still. "And Tieloc," he spoke almost inaudible with his back still turned to them, "you have made the right choice today. For what it may be worth, thank you."

And with that, the Drakkaidian Prince leapt off the balcony down to the lower levels of the village. Tavin and Ril stood in silence with Kira and the cronoms, slowly exchanging hesitant and unknowing looks. Though Tavin could tell the fiery western girl approved of his decisions with her disarming eyes and easy smile, his own face remained plagued with a vague doubt and disbelief he had just done what he had done. After the long silence of meditation to maintain his connection with the Sapphire Pool, Zeroan at last began to speak once more, noticing Verix's absence.

"I see our newest party member has deserted us," he murmured with a frown, turning his eyes to Tavin. "I'm not sure why you have made this decision, Tavin, but you had better be prepared to deal with it now. This is not going to be easy. You and he are both leaders; in different respects, but leaders nonetheless. It will be difficult for a proud Grandarian like you to deal with a Drakkaidian and his advice; you know that better than I. Are you sure you will be able to cope with him guiding you?" Not sure how else to respond, Tavin's uncertainty turned to resentment.

"I wouldn't have accepted his offer otherwise," he returned aggravated. "I don't want to, but I feel like I trust him. But most importantly, there is no other choice, Zeroan." He stopped for a moment, staring into space. "There is still something else behind this, though. There has to be. I don't know what it is, but..." he brought his vision up to Ril, staring at him attentively. "Why did he save you?" Tavin whispered the question, to which Ril only looked even more helplessly lost. Zeroan stepped back in, rushing to finish his conversation.

"Well, it's decided now," he affirmed. "Be wary of him, Tavin. I know you have to trust him to a degree, but be cautious of what he says or does. Don't forget who he is." As Tavin silently nodded in response, Zeroan loudly exhaled. "Very good, then. Our plans are made. We are in desperate times now, but with your new power developed and at least one shard in our possession for certain, hope is not lost. We must move fast to counter Montrox, but we can do it." He paused for a moment, gazing at the two Elemental Warriors side by side staring back at him. "Tavin, would you please escort the other young lady off of the balcony with the cronoms as I fade my connection to the pool?" The Grandarian boy's brow furrowed, realizing he was asking to be left alone with Ril. She knew it as well and shot him an unsure glance. Though not wishing to leave her or the sage, he did as he was bid and turned to Kira and the three cronom elders already moving toward the door to the hollow. As he left, Tavin turned back to face Zeroan's waning liquid form once more.

"It's good to see you again, Zeroan," he said with a true smile appearing. "I promise we won't let you down." The sage could not help but smile back at the boy's honest determination, nodding.

"I have no doubt about it, Tavin," he returned softly as the group made their way to the stairway of the hollow. Once Tavin and the others had disappeared behind the now closed doorway, Ril nervously turned back to face the sage's transparent figure and swallowed hard, anticipating some sort of punishment for her actions with the dark crystals.

"Zeroan, I'm sorry that I didn't tell you that night but-"

"Settle down, Arilia," he cut her off, raising a hand for silence. "I am not going to scold you for being tricked by our traitorous "friend" in Galantia. I merely have some advice for you." The Warrior of Fire stopped then, composing herself once more. Though not sure what he could be talking about, she listened further with curiosity in her expression. "Actually, it's more of an order." He stared her hard in the eyes then, a quiet expression that she could not identify behind them. "Ril, I don't want you getting romantically caught up with Tavin." The words blasted into her like cannon fire, hit completely off guard. As they sank in, however, she slowly began to comprehend what he had said. A look of painful confusion and uncomfortable embarrassment overcame her then, in disbelief she had just heard this. Zeroan could see the tearing feelings emerging across her delicate face and quickly proceeded to cut off any possible outburst.

"I know this seems out of the blue, but hear me, Arilia," he began again gradually. "I had been wary of this from the first time I found you together in Galantia, but I now see that this has become a quandary that needs to be dealt with before it matures into a liability later on." The extremity of the sage's words stabbed at her, and her baffled expression was overridden by anger.

"A liability?" she repeated vexed. "I can't believe I'm hearing this, Zeroan! No one is getting 'caught up' here, but even so, what right do you have to-"

"Enough," the sage spoke with his quiet ferocity emerging as his dark eyes flared, cutting her short. "I will not suffer an argument from you on this, Warrior of Fire. I may be constantly preoccupied with matters of worldly importance to draw my attention, but I am not so blind to not see the way that you look at Tavin and the way he looks at you. I cannot allow this to proceed any further. An emotional entanglement is the last thing that either of you two needs right now when the direst of circumstances require your complete attention at all times. I am sorry to have to intercede into your personal feelings, but I am telling you now that I forbid a relationship beyond what it is now." Ril's flustered face flushed red with emotion, a jumble of raw unprocessed thoughts and feeling tearing at her with each passing second. The proud and independent tomboy inside her was practically screaming out to reject the sage's accusations that she was attracted to the Warrior of Light, but deeper still, another feeling she had never identified before held her back. She didn't understand what was happening. She wanted to lash out at the sage and tell him to mind his own business, but the words caught in her throat.

Zeroan exhaled again as the luminescent cobalt liquid making up his form began to slowly disperse and rain off his body. His now sloshing face eased.

"That is all, Arilia Embrin," he said, his voice now distant. "By the way, tell Tavin that Jaren sends his regards." After that, his form began to fully dump the liquid off of his body until the perfectly accurate mold of the Mystic Sage had lost all form and fallen back into the pool. Before the remainder of the light had faded, Zeroan's remote voice sounded one last time. "Remember my words, but take care of him, Ril. Take care of them both." With that, the last of the dimming light gradually disappeared from the Sapphire Pool, the link between it and the sage gone. Alone, Ril was left staring into the center of the pool with a contorted expression of bewildered pain on her red face. She stood there trying to determine what had just happened to her for several long moments until she at last loosened her taut muscles and let her arms hang. It was difficult to come to terms with it, but she had identified what was holding her back. Staring into space, she realized that despite her own policies of independence from anything like the sage had suggested, she had indeed developed a deep rooted emotion for the young Grandarian boy that she had never felt the likes of before. Though she stood in silence trying to give it a name for long moments afterwards, the only one she could come up with was love.

Chapter 54

Torn

Lightning was not an uncommon thing to see on the black peaks of the savage mountains above Dalastrak that held the towering royal Drakkaidian castle, but as Valif Montrox flew over the jagged crests with a trio of Valcanor as his transportation and his shard of the Holy Emerald in his right armored hand, the sky had seemed to respond to his dark presence with a barrage of erratic bolts of electricity ripping through the deathly air as if threatening to destroy all of Drakkaidia. The Warrior of Darkness was impassive to the challenging storm, with far more pressing matters to warrant his attention. Growing impatient with his son, who seemed to have disappeared over the past week, he had given up on the possibility that he had completed his mission and was returning home. Though it seemed highly unlikely, he must have somehow been bested and was either still trailing the Warrior of Light in wait to assassinate him stealthily or had just plain given up.

Valif Montrox grit his teeth. For his son's sake, it had better had been the former, he thought vengefully. In any case, Verix had not completed his task after over a month now, and he was not waiting any longer to do something he had wanted to do more than anything for years now. As the Valcanor steadily ascended through the fierce air above Dalastrak, Montrox's spiked towering castle rapidly came into view. He had left it that morning to see to the final preparations in the ancient graveyards of the Black Cathedral further north; the final resting place of all the Dark Mages that had passed over the years, including the most infamous of them all, the Black Seven.

The Dégamar.

Valif Montrox let a twisted wicked smile spread across his hard face as the Valcanor swept across the peaks of the mountains and moved up the savage castle walls to a balcony high at its peak, adjacent to his throne room. As they touched down, the armored Warrior of Darkness leapt off the winged creature's back onto the black flooring. Landing and picking himself up, he quickly called out for his High Priest, ordered to be waiting for him inside. He came forth quickly.

"Yes, my lord?" he quivered, nervous of what mood the Drakkaidian dictator was in. Montrox extended his arm as he approached and handed him the shard.

"Are the mage's I asked for assembled?" he asked monotonously.

"They await by the portal, Highness," he reported sheepishly, accepting the shard.

"Seven?"

"Seven, as you requested, Highness."

"Very well. Take this to the chamber and tell them to wait. I will be with you momentarily." The High Priest bowed and turned, quickly making his way to his destination with the shard. Alone once again, Montrox turned back to face the three massive Valcanor peering down at him with glowing crimson eyes tucked into their sunken heads. Montrox smiled as he approached them. "You have work to do, my minions. I'll be needing four more of you in a few moments, so go and find the others still over the Valley of Blood..." The Warrior of Darkness stopped suddenly, observing the winged nightmare on the far left of the balcony turning its head away from him and opening its bat-like wings from behind its back. Montrox was quick to let his temper slip, gritting his teeth and sharply extending his left arm to fire an abrupt charge of thin black energy beaming out from his fingertip to the creature's right eye and through the back of its head. Though it screeched in agony for a brief moment, it quickly went silent and fell backward from the force of the blow, tumbling off the balcony to the ground far beneath. The other two Valcanor mutely listened as their kin plummeted down the castle, smashing its gigantic mass on the sharp walls and steeples as it went. They both shifted their gazes back at Montrox, now staring at them with his arm pointed at their heads.

"I will *not* be ignored," he decreed with ice hanging from his words and a heated malice in his crimson eyes. They both held his gaze, motionless, to which Montrox lowered his arm. "Now go and find me *five* more of your kind. I will not wait long." With that, the Drakkaidian ruler spun around and walked off of the balcony into his throne room, leaving the demonic creatures to exchange glances with one another before extending their massive wings to propel them into the air and away to the Valley of Blood.

With the demons gone, Valif Montrox passed through his empty throne room to a door on the other side, adjusting his thick black armor over his body as he strode. There were two black armored guards stationed at the doors, which he quickly ordered away. Though this was to be a glorious moment for him, he could not help but frown as his son's warning that he could not control the occupants of the Netherworld echoed through his mind. It was just one demon with wandering eyes, he thought. The other two were quick to obey him after reminding them of his authority. And besides, he would not have to worry about the dark spirits he was about to awake questioning him given the fact they were once men that served his family. Any lingering negative feelings dissipated from the Drakkaidian ruler's face then, opening the massive double doorway to the dark chamber off of his throne room. As he strode in with a powerful look about him, Montrox found seven Dark Mages and his High Priest standing around a circular crevice in the floor that stretched down for eternity.

It was the Netherworld Portal.

Much like the ancient Grandarians had constructed Galantia around the Temple of Light, the Drakkaidians of old had built Dalastrak and the royal castle over the mountain where they had found the gateway to the underworld. This was the reason for the castle's tower-like appearance with its small but myriad levels. The portal was high on a lone peak so the castle was built around it; thin but tall. The actual portal was a captivating sight. It was a circular depression in the floor nearly fifty feet in diameter with a levitating stone platform half of that measure over its entrance, decorated in ancient glyphs from the days of the ancient Drakkaidians to symbolize its incredible importance. Valif Montrox appreciated it for what it was, but he was about to use it like the ancients had never thought possible.

Upon entering the towering cylindrical chamber, the Drakkaidian ruler turned his attention to the seven Dark Mages nervously holding his gaze on the opposite side of the portal.

"You seven have been selected by the High Priest as the strongest mages in Drakkaidia," he started vigorously. "Are you?" A few of them shot each other uncertain glances, not sure how to respond. The one at the right end was the first to speak.

"We are, my lord," he answered confidently on behalf of them all. Montrox let a sinister grin appear on his face.

"Excellent," he confirmed, motioning with the flick of his wrist for the High Priest to come to his side. "Then I will reward you with more power. Step onto the platform." Even the mage at the end of the line froze at this.

"You mean over the... portal, Sire?" one in the middle timidly asked. Montrox locked his dark eyes onto the one who spoke, his brow furrowing.

"Is there another platform that you see in this chamber, mage?" he asked scornfully. The mage quickly shook his head no and motioned for the others to follow him out to the hovering dais. Gathering their black and crimson robes about them, they proceeded to leap over the ten foot gap between the outskirts of the portal and the platform. Once all seven had arrived and situated themselves evenly over the surface, Valif Montrox grinned darkly once again, almost giddy with anticipation. "Yes... The day has arrived. Thank you all for your sacrifice. Do send Drakkan my regards as you meet him." Upon hearing this, the seven Dark Mages suddenly turned to each other stricken with worry. Before any of them could petition to be excused from whatever Montrox truly had planned for them or try to make an escape, the platform suddenly began to rapidly sink into the endless darkness of the portal. Montrox stared down with amusement as they realized what was happening to them and screamed out from the portal for mercy.

It was of course too late. By the time any of the seven mages knew what was happening to them, they were already at least twenty feet into the portal and had disappeared into its eternal darkness. As the last remnant of their screams echoed throughout the cylindrical chamber, Valif Montrox gave a nod to the frightened High Priest to raise the shard of the Holy Emerald into the air and engulf it in dark magic. The quaking man only stared his at his master in disbelief he had just sentenced his own men to hell. Montrox's smile was replaced with an intolerant frown.

"Unless you wish to join them, I suggest you do as I command, High Priest," he ordered with a wanton impatience on display in his tense body language. Realizing he was left with little choice but to do as he was ordered, the High Priest broke his gaze from the Warrior of Darkness and lifted the shard into the air. He spread his hands apart but the shard remained levitating where it was, a sudden flaring sphere of black light bursting to life around it. As the shard was enveloped in the dark magic, Valif Montrox shifted his gaze to the Netherworld Portal, its deep recess of blackness flickering with the same light. With the connection made, he slowly closed his eyes and stood silent for a moment. The High Priest looked to him uncertainly, unaware of what was happening. Then, nearly frightening the man to death, Montrox's eye lids slid open revealing both of his eyeballs emanating the same black magic that had formed around the shard. He raised his clenched fists and inhaled a mighty gasp of air before blasting his voice into the chamber.

"By the blood of the House of Montrox of Drakkaidia and the Elemental Warrior of Darkness, I command the Dégamar to take the flesh I offer them and to return to this world!" His words were like thunder, threatening to shake the entire chamber. Then, as if the portal was a sentient being that was just as afraid of disobeying the Drakkaidian dictator as the shaking High Priest beside him, a low menacing rumble began to echo out of its dark eternity and into the chamber, followed by sudden rush of the flickering dark energy. It was not long before the flicker evolved into a full blown beam of black light blasting its negative hues into the already shadowy room. "I summon the Black Seven! Come to me, Dégamar!" Valif Montrox thrust his body in the dark light now engulfing the entire chamber, increasing the distant rumbling to a full blown earthquake threatening to swallow all of Dalastrak.

The quake left the earth then, leaping into the atmosphere itself to vehemently tear through the air in the room like hurricane wind. Though Montrox stood unmovable with his electrified elemental power of darkness now emanating from his body, the High Priest was sent careening off of his feet and into the wall of the chamber, knocking him immediately unconscious. With its keeper down, Montrox extended his arm to take hold of the levitating Holy Emerald shard with a disgruntled frown. The shard let one final burst of the black light surge from its core and in turn the entire chamber.

Almost instantly after, the sphere of light around the shard dissipated and dispersed, signaling the end of the rite. With the shard now calm, the portal itself began to quiet; the black light fading back into the endless abyss and the deep rumbling subsiding into the earth and air alike.

Valif Montrox stood there with the shard in his right hand, as still and quiet as the air in the room. It was the distant humming of the levitating platform from deep in the portal that finally broke the silence. Slowly ascending back to the surface of the portal, Montrox's now smiling face watched as the Dark Mages reemerged. As the dais slowed to a stop at the entrance to the portal, he gazed at the seven figures staring back at him. They wore the exact attire as the men that had descended into the portal moments ago but were perfectly at rest. He broadly smiled his sinister grin once more; he had done it. The ultimate summoning from the Netherworld. The Black Seven were his to command.

"The Dégamar," he breathed with elation. Upon hearing him speak that last word, all seven of the hooded and cloaked figures' heads jerked up to face him, revealing their faces to the Drakkaidian ruler. The moment he laid eyes on them, however, even the malevolent Warrior of Darkness was stricken with a sudden qualm in his gut. His eyes going wide, he slowly took a step back. The strong and youthful men's faces from before had been replaced by a mess of torn, slashed, decaying flesh oozing blood and festering with rot. Many of their bones shown through their decomposing skin, giving them a skeletal appearance. The most intriguing detail of all was their eyes- or rather, the lack thereof. The only thing that could be found in their eye sockets was an empty space drenched in blood, black with age.

"They don't treat you very well down there, do they?" Montrox stated quietly. The Dégamar kept their disturbingly gory gaze on him, silent and still. Montrox still only smiled. "Well, I believe introductions are required-"

"*What do you wish of us, Valif Montrox?*" the demonic Dark Mage at the group's center asked him in a disturbingly distant and raspy voice, cutting him short. Montrox nodded, his smile dispersing.

"Straight to business, I see," he murmured, not expecting anything but silence from one dead for centuries. "Fine. Let's go over what you need to know then shall we? I am your absolute master now, and you will address me as such.

Master. Understand?" All seven nodded unanimously and silent. He let his dark grin appear again. "Excellent. Now-"

"*What do you wish of us, Valif Montrox?*" It was the same mage who spoke last. The Warrior of Darkness once again lost his pleased expression the moment after he attained it, his patience gone. He threw his arm at the mage in the center and took hold of it with his power, lifting it off the ground and pulling it toward him until within an inch of his face. When close enough to smell the decay off of the demon's body, his face twisted with quiet rage.

"I wish you to speak when spoken to, you sack of rotting filth," he commanded with ferocity. He then rapidly threw his arm back in front of him, sending the mage flying back to the others to land on its back. The six left on their feet remained staring at the impatient king, unmoving. "But since you are so eager to get to work, I will put you to it. Follow me." Turning his back then, the Warrior of Darkness began to stride toward the exit of the cylindrical chamber and his throne room. As he pushed the doors open with his left hand, he took his right and sent it careening into the head of the unconscious High Priest laying by the door to permanently put him to rest. "I lose more High Priests that way..." he breathed icily. The Black Seven leapt off the hovering platform over the portal and steadily trailed after him.

As the party passed through the throne room and onto the balcony, Valif Montrox turned and looked up at the massive steeple above him, with seven Valcanor situated about it, their massive wings wrapped around their oval bodies and their crimson eyes now locked onto him.

"That was fast," he murmured, scanning them over. He turned his attention back to the Dégamar before him. "I'm sure you are familiar with these," he said pointed up to the winged monsters above them. "They will be your transportation. One for each of you. Now this is what you are going to do. In light of my son's failure to complete his task and with your presence, I am accelerating my plans. You three," he said pointing out three of the demonic mages on the left side of their line, "are going to find me the flame shard somewhere in the west. It will be near the mountain of fire. Tear apart every inch of countryside and village until you find it. You three," this time pointing at the three to the right of the group, "are going to the east. I would have you find the shard to the south, but it is only one whereas there are two to be found at the sages' tower. Therefore we will dismiss it for the moment and acquire the two shards that we know the location of. There are men of magic there, but they will be of no threat to you. After I have those shards you can find the other in the south.

"And you," he said pointing to the lone Dégamar in the center of the group, "will be going south now. My son, Verix, has disappeared. Find him. If he is ready to kill the Warrior of Light, leave him, but if he is doing anything else, bring him back here." Montrox looked the entire group of demonically possessed spirits over before speaking again. "Do you all understand?" The group responded with silence which the Warrior of Darkness took as a yes. "Very good. The time has come for me to seize my destiny; for me to take what is mine." Montrox slowly shifted his gaze down to the single brilliant white gem in his dark armored hand and let his face soften, hungry with want. "Everything..." His eyes flared with malice then, biting at the Dégamar. "I want those shards. Find them."

It was a distant but piercing scream of anguish that rudely woke Tavinious Tieloc from his daydreaming outside of his and Ril's hollow in Keracon Valley moments earlier that night. He sat on a chair that Kira had brought him earlier in the day after they left the Grand Hall from their meeting with Zeroan, one leg slouched over its arm and his body sprawled into its comfortable back. After the scream had sounded through the otherwise quiet night air, however, his head shot up and his right arm flew to the hilt of the Sword of Granis resting by the side of the chair. Fully alert, he bounded up to the railing of the hollow's balcony, searching through the night air for where the cry had originated. Standing there waiting for another shout, it was not long before the sound of the hollow's opening door echoed into his ears, a worried Ril and Kira appearing out of it. They had been inside talking girl to girl while Tavin took some rest on his own. He looked back to them with concern in his face.

"What was that, Tavin?" Ril hurriedly asked scanning what she could see of the dark village for the source of the scream.

"I'm not sure," he shrugged, waiting for them to walk to his side. Tavin locked onto her bright eyes. "The only person that could have been would be-"

"Grandarian!" was the distant call that cut him off from the far side of the rope bridge to their hollow. All three wheeled around to face the dark opposite side of the bridge, finding a shadowy figure running straight toward them at full speed. Tavin and Ril didn't have to think twice to know who it was. "Grandarian!" he called again. "Grandarian, we leave now! We must leave now!" As Verix Montrox ran over the rope bridge toward them, the torchlight illuminated his hard face with pain embedded into it. Tavin's face morphed with anger, and he moved Ril and Kira back so he could make his way to the bridge.

"Are you trying to wake up the entire village, Montrox?" Tavin called out in an angry whisper. The Drakkaidian Prince remained beside himself with emotion, slowing to a halt as he reached Tavin.

"We must leave right now, Warrior of Light!" he bellowed again, impatience and frustration making him shake. Tavin's irritation grew as well, not sure what had provoked this sudden flurry of emotion in the junior Montrox.

"Calm down!" he almost yelled himself. "What's the matter with you? What just happened? Why did you scream?"

"The fool has torn it beyond repair this time!" Verix bellowed to no one in particular, turning and smashing his fist down into the railway.

"Verix, calm down-"

"Calm?" Verix interrupted him, moving into Tavin's face. "The cleave in the veil to the Netherworld has just been torn over twice what it was before! In a second it has doubled! My father has practically sent an invitation to every creature in hell to come out and destroy Drakkaidia, and you want me to be calm?" Verix raised his arms and took hold of Tavin's shirt, enmity in his eyes. "My home is teetering on the brink of destruction. Don't ever tell me to calm down." More to preclude Tavin from exploding himself than to back Verix down, Ril shot a wave of fervent red flame ripping between the two, forcing them both apart. They both turned to her angrily, but she met them with steady purpose holding her firm.

"Both of you are going to shut up right now," she whispered acidly, raising her flame covered fist. Verix stared at her for a moment breathing hard, but quickly grit his teeth and grunted, kicking the railway and cursing to himself. Taking advantage of her apparent control of the Drakkaidian Prince, she continued fiercely. "What do you mean the veil is torn?" He quickly brought his intense glare at her.

"What don't you understand about it?" he asked curtly. "Father has just summoned something of incredible power out of the Netherworld and it has ripped the tear in the veil over twice its previous length as it came. It is on the verge of shattering now. We must be off right now. We cannot delay." Tavin was the one to stop him this time.

"Hold on, Verix," he said, a little more controlled. "I'm sorry this happened, but don't let your emotions cloud your judgment. It's the middle of the night. Ril and I are tired and not the constantly moving travelers you are. We can't leave right now." Though Verix was about to challenge the Grandarian boy again, Ril chimed in to aid him.

"Verix, we can leave early tomorrow morning," she offered. "One more night is not going to make any difference in how fast we get to Torrentcia City." The Drakkaidian Prince stared at her with forceful eyes, leaving Tavin feeling the most uncomfortable as the seconds ticked by. Finally, Verix closed his eyes and nodded, his muscles loosening some.

"Dawn..." he murmured. "We will be leaving here at dawn, understand?" Ril nodded in acknowledgement.

"Fine," she agreed. "Now will you tell us what you... sensed?" she asked, uncertain how to word it. He held her gaze for a moment more before turning his back and walking away into the darkness of the night again.

"Dawn," he repeated striding away. Though he would have been content to let the Prince go, Tavin exhaled sharply and called out to him.

"Verix, don't you want to stay in a hollow for at least one night and get some sleep?" He merely walked on into the darkness not even acknowledging him. Tavin let a huff of breath out and turned his head back to the Warrior of Fire, already staring at him uncertainly. "This is going to be a long trip." Ril frowned in response, but silently agreed.

Chapter 55

<u>Company of Three</u>

The abrupt but insistent rapping of knuckles on his window the next morning was what rudely woke Tavin from his dreams. Slowly coming awake, he sluggishly let his eyes slide open and drift toward the source of the disturbance. The sun had yet to paint the skies with so much as a single ray of its warming light, so it was impossible to distinguish the form standing by his window, though he could guess without great difficulty who was there. Tavin's sleepy face managed to furnish a frown. Though he had expected the impatient Drakkaidian Prince to be at his door earlier than he would have liked, it was far before dawn judging from the thick darkness enveloping the world around him. He let his face cringe with exasperation. At least Verix was true to his word so far. The noise from fists on the walls of the hollow drifted from his window over to the other on Ril's side. Tavin grit his teeth at the boy's impatience and lifted his head off his pillow to yell out.

"We hear you, Montrox!" he shouted through the walls. As his words blasted to the exterior of the hollow the noise abruptly desisted. Tavin rolled his eyes and squirmed out of the sheets of his warm bed, the chill of the nipping morning air causing a mountain range of goose bumps to form over his bare upper body. He stood and threw the sheets he had disturbed back over the bed and proceeded to the doorway to appease the Prince's impatience until they were ready. He opened the door, ready for an argument, but was surprised to find no Drakkaidian Prince. Instead, peering over to his window, he found Kira Marcell's miniature frame staring back at him with an uncertain expression. He returned her gaze with a somewhat bewildered look of his own.

"Kira?" he mumbled sleepily.

"Good morning, Tavin," she whispered cautiously.

"Looks more like night to me, kiddo," he returned, easing his tight body realizing Verix was no where to be found. Kira could not help but smirk and giggle.

"Well, it's morning," she replied coyly. "Sorry to wake you again, but I think you had better get up. The other unfriendly person with you has been up for an hour waking the elders. They sent me to tell you and Ril that he wants to leave as soon as you're ready." Before Tavin even had a chance to think of a response her face drooped with depression. "Do you really have to go so soon, Tavin?" Though not quite sure how to reply, the Grandarian boy tried a quick smile that came out a little too quirky to be effective.

"I told him that we would leave early today, so I guess so..." he answered lamely, sensitive to the young girl's feelings. She sulked lower, letting her shoulders drop. "Oh, Kira, why don't you come inside out of the cold? I bet Ril's up so you can wait in her room while I get ready." Though she still harbored a defeated expression over her endearing face, she nodded and smiled. As she entered, Tavin told her she shouldn't be up so early in the morning and herded her into Ril's side of the hollow. The Warrior of Fire, having heard Kira herself, was already half dressed and prepared, currently fixing her flowing red hair behind her into a ponytail once again. Though she didn't particularly want the blonde haired girl for company at the moment any more than Tavin, she realized that she was in low spirits and let her in with a smile.

As Ril finished organizing herself with Kira, Tavin quickly dressed into his fresh clothes as quickly as he had the previous morning and strapped the Sword of Granis onto his side, illuminating the shadowy room with its golden light. Dressed and groomed minutes later, he exited the cozy cronom hollow for the final time and stepped out into the chilling forest air. Observing the illumination from the Sword of Granis outside her window, Ril gathered the last of her things and tucked them securely into her traveling pouch. She pulled her cronom cloak over her shivering body, its warm mass instantly dispelling the cold around her. With Kira following behind her like an afternoon shadow, the two walked out to meet the Warrior of Light waiting for them. Tavin and Ril greeted each other with confident smiles despite the uncertainty of their situation. After Kira took the lead and began guiding them through the intricate ropeways of the village toward the opposite side once again, the two exchanged their knowledge of what Kira had told them about what Verix was up to at the moment.

"Whatever he's doing and whatever he says, all I know is that I'm getting breakfast this morning," Tavin said with assurance, to which Ril only smiled and gently nudged his sarcastic figure. With the failing torchlight and the brilliant Granic Crystal on Tavin's weapon to illuminate their path, they reached the Grand Hall in a hurry. When Kira passed by the ramp leading up to it, however, Tavin and Ril questioningly caught up to the speeding girl and asked her where they were going.

"Oh, I'm sorry I didn't tell you," she began apologetically. "Like I said, the other one with you woke the elders early and got them to come out to the First Tree." Both the Elemental Warrior's remained confused.

"And that would be...?" Tavin continued for the two. Kira once again blushed with embarrassment.

"Oh! Sorry again. The First Tree is how the cronoms get in and out of the village. There is a pulley platform attached to the original tree they climbed up to get this high that lowers you down to the forest floor and then back up. It takes about half an hour to get up or down." Tavin's brow furrowed. All this time he had been in the cronom's valley, he hadn't even wondered how he got here in the first place. Though a little taken aback that a pulley had moved all this architecture up here, there wasn't much else that could pull off such daunting task.

Upon turning around a massive tree trunk, the light from the Sword of Granis spread to elucidate another colossal tree trunk with a group of cronoms standing around it. Walking closer, Tavin noticed a thick rope strung over a gigantic branch on the tree connecting a crank attached to the trunk and the platform that Kira had mentioned hanging at the end of the catwalk. Examining the platform more carefully however, Tavin quickly noticed the dark frame of Verix Montrox leaning against the railway with his arms crossed at the far end. An impassive but unfriendly look was on his face. As the Drakkaidian's eyes met with his, Tavin returned his inhospitable stare.

"Do you think you got us up early enough, Verix?" he asked with resentment intertwined in his voice. The Drakkaidian Prince remained indifferent.

"I said-"

"You said dawn," Tavin snapped, not giving him a chance to finish. Though Verix was most likely ready to fiercely retort back at the Grandarian boy, Ril once again stepped between the two to prelude any further hostilities.

"Well we're up now, so let's just get on with things, alright?" she said shooting Tavin a frustrated glance. Verix ignored the girl's advice as he opened his mouth to speak.

"I've been waiting for ages," he said dismayed.

"Well you're going to have to wait a little longer then, because we're not leaving without breakfast," Tavin decreed. This time it was Yerbacht who intervened in their quarrel.

"I believe we can help in that," he informed factually. "We have prepared a warm meal for you now, and have also packed you a healthy supply of rations and water." He turned to point to three packs stuffed with food and a plate of warm breakfast. The aroma found its way into Tavin's nostrils, making him weak at the knees with hunger. "It is quite a long trip down on the platform, so I trust you could eat this on the way if you wish."

"That will be fine," Verix agreed for them all, eager to be on his way. Though Tavin would have preferred to dine in the warmth of the Grand Hall one last time, he agreed that food was food and nodded his head in accord.

"Fine," he repeated. With that, Yerbacht instructed the few cronoms with him to load the packs of food onto the platform with Verix. Tavin and Ril thanked him heartily, for the food and their stay at the valley.

"I'm not really sure how we could ever thank you for everything you've done for us, Yerbacht," Tavin said grasping his miniature hand, to which the elder cronom just grinned and chuckled.

"Watching you eat the previous evenings has more than paid us back," he chortled. "You are quite the voracious young man! And besides, we are indebted to you for rescuing two of our people. If anything, consider us even my human friends. It was a pleasure to have you here with us." With that, Tavin shook the small creatures hand again and released it with a smile. Having concluded his business with the cronoms, he turned back to Ril and tilted his head. "Well, are we ready, Ril?" The Warrior of Fire shot him a look of deathly impatience, motioning with her fiery eyes to the dejected Kira standing beside her. Tavin had all but forgotten about the kind hearted girl with Verix drawing his attention and quickly knelt before her sulking form, gently taking hold of her chilled forearms. Her already moist eyes found their way to his.

"Why can't you and Ril stay for just a while longer?" she asked, her little voice quivering. Tavin shot Ril an empathetic glance to look for a suitable answer, which he could not find.

"I'm sorry, Kira," he began softly, "but you know we have important things to do and we have to be leaving as soon as possible." A swell of salty water rolled down her fragile white face at this.

"Then let me come with you," she begged suddenly, desperation pouring from her voice. Tavin breathed heavily, trying to formulate what he had to say in the easiest way possible.

"Kira, I think you also know that what we are doing is very dangerous. Too dangerous for someone still as young as you."

"I promise I won't get in the way!" she pleaded. Tavin tried an idiosyncratic smile but shook his head again.

"I like you too much to ever risk you getting hurt, kiddo," he told her tenderly. "I couldn't live with myself if you came with us and something happened to you. It will be hard enough to protect ourselves on our journey, and I couldn't properly take care of you. Neither of us could," he said, quickly pointing at Ril. The girl lowered her head then, another streaming tear flowing down her cheek. She tightly shut her eyes and pulled away from the Grandaria boy, running off behind the tree they had just emerged around. Tavin sighed deeply, slowly grinding his head to Ril, his expression begging for help. She quickly nodded and started off to the crying girl behind the massive tree trunk. Tavin rose then, Yerbacht trying to apologize for her behavior, which the Warrior of Light quickly dismissed. Though Kira was hidden behind the tree, he could make out Ril with her arms around the smaller girl gently whispering something to her. It was the rough grunt from behind him that drew Tavin's attention away. With a disgusted look of intolerance mounted on his face, he turned to find Verix Montrox staring at Ril with a similar expression making up his own visage.

Tavin turned and steadily strode onto the platform where the Drakkaidian Prince stood, his eyes shifting to meet him. Verix was the first to speak.

"Would you mind wrapping things up, Grandarian?" he asked cynically.

"Listen to me, Montrox," he fired sharply without missing a beat, a rush of thoughts bursting into his mouth waiting to be fired like shots out of a canon. "You always run off so quickly after you show up that I've never had a chance to lay out the ground rules. Not Zeroan's or Ril's- mine. Pay attention because I'm only going to say this once. First off, I'm not going to put up with this attitude of yours for another second. Drop it now, or I'll drop you. Second, you need to learn some patience. I know we've got to move, but rushing us faster than we can go is only going to slow us down in the long run, so back off." Verix broke his gaze with the Warrior of Light and placed it back on the red haired girl nestling Kira in her arms.

"If I were you," he said softly, "I would be a little less authoritative with your words, Tieloc. You may need more than your talk if the girl isn't paying attention to pull us apart." Tavin reeled forward, gritting his teeth with fury. Though he would have loved to hammer into the Prince, he contained his resentment, instead extending a single finger before his face.

"And last," he stated, struggling to control his anger, "keep your filthy Drakkaidian eyes off of that girl." Without moving his head, the Prince shifted his gaze back to the other, locking onto him. Tavin didn't flinch. "I may be trusting you to help us, why I still don't know, but that doesn't mean I'm an idiot. I know there is something you haven't told us; there's something else driving you here. Whether it's connected to why you saved Ril or not, I don't know, but you listen to me now." Tavin's eyes narrowed further as he quaked with quiet wrath. "If you touch a single hair on her head, I swear to Granis that you'll have three feet of cold steel down your throat the next second. Do you follow me, Drak?" His word's bit like a ravenous wolf and Verix's eyes flashed with an uneasy stillness for a moment, but soon regained their hard exterior.

"Afraid of a little competition, Tavin?" he mused mockingly. Though Tavin's taut body was ready to explode with rage and wrench forth the Sword of Granis, Verix quickly continued to prelude an outburst. "Relax, boy. You have nothing to fear from me on that front. I have little interest in an abrasive and annoying Southland girl when my home's fate hanging in the balance remains for me to worry about. I assure you that this is my sole 'drive.' You are aware of my motives; there is no sinister plot behind me." Tavin let his muscles loosen at this, but still stared at him hard and unblinking.

"...Then why did you save her?" he asked dubiously. Verix blinked and turned his head to the opposite side of the platform as Ril appeared with a tear soaked Kira beside her.

"It was the right thing, wasn't it?" he replied sarcastically, once again avoiding the question. Though Tavin was still unsatisfied with the Prince's mysterious actions, he let the subject go for the moment, turning his attention back to the two girls off the platform. Stepping forward, Ril gently smiled at Tavin.

"I told Kira here that though we can't take her with us now, we promise to come back after out journey is over," she said staring at him with a sense of helpless kindness about her searching eyes. Though he could tell that she wasn't entirely sure that was a promise they could keep, he nodded and redirected his smile to Kira.

"That's right," he agreed, to which Ril's taut frame eased. "You have my word that we'll be back, Kira." She smiled through what was left of her trickling tears then and nodded as well.

"I'll be waiting," she replied cheerful again.

With that, Tavin and Ril said their final goodbyes to Kira and the cronoms around them, stepping onto the pulley-powered platform to begin their long decent down to the forest floor. As the multiple cronoms manning the crank began to allow it to lurch down, so did the ground under the three humans' feet. With the still thick darkness of morning hovering around them, it was not long before they lost view of the group standing over the catwalk railing and soon even the torch-lit walkways altogether. After losing all contact with Keracon Valley above them, Tavin and Ril hastily dove into the warm food before them. As they delved into the abundance of exotic cooking, Verix remained stoic and aloof, making it a long and uneasy ride down through the thick growth of the massive trees. The only thing the Drakkaidian Prince ate was what Tavin threw to him.

Even with Verix's detached presence to elongate the decent, it was painfully slow and tedious on its own. Though they had left the cronom village well before dawn, by the time the forest floor came into view, the sun had begun to paint the skies in a heavy orange with the first rays of its fervent light. The platform made contact with the ground with an uneasy thud, making all three anxious to be off of it and onto the solid, constant earth again. Though Ril had loved the beautiful Keracon Valley, she told Tavin on the way down that she would be more than happy to be back on the ground after a week of being suspended hundreds of feet in the air with nothing but a thin wooden floor separating her from a very far earth. Tavin was all too eager to agree.

Upon stepping back onto the ground with their packs and belongs strapped back onto them, Verix quickly announced their plan of action. He informed them that it would most likely take a good week to make their way out of the Great Forests and into the eastern Grailen Plains above them if they moved at an enterprising pace. Having traveled with the grueling Mystic Sage Zeroan for as long as they had, Tavin and Ril felt more than up to the challenge. From there Verix would lead them back up to Torrentcia City and Zeroan. As they began their trek through the forests, he informed them that they had minimal latitude to use their powers with his to mask them, but he otherwise kept up the mandate that Zeroan had enforced to keep them sealed. Though not worried about Valcanor or Liradds, Verix remained disturbingly shaken up over whatever his father had summoned from the Netherworld the previous night. Tavin guessed that it was obviously a creature of enormous strength.

Despite this premonition of new danger, Tavin was confident in himself and his abilities. Now in control of his elemental powers like Ril and a new level of them revealed, he was certain that no creature could hope to stand up against him with the other two at his side. When the Dark Prince scouted ahead midday for lingering Golthrouts, Ril related the same to Tavin. Though they had lost Zeroan for the moment, she felt as safe as ever. At the mention of the Mystic Sage, Tavin remembered the last time they had met and asked Ril what he had wanted to be alone with her for. Though she did not want to lie to him ever again, Ril was too embarrassed to say, still unsure of her feelings in the matter herself. She merely told him that the sage had scolded her for being tricked by Seriol and to be wary of such people in the future.

As the sun set on that first day of travel, the group had already passed through the Selderien Woods, deep in the central western Great Forests. Now less than a week from the Grailen Plains, the company of three rested easy on the comforting earth that night.

Kohlin Marraea's eyes sharply narrowed as view of a familiar figure draped in tattered gray robes came into view entering the ravaged Miystirdal Village. He quickly turned back to Jaren, Parnox, and the cronom Yucono sitting around what was left of their fire outside a demolished inn, just finishing a quick snack. The group had been in the village for two nights now, one spent waiting for Zeroan to somehow communicate with Tavin and Ril, the next waiting for his return.

"He's back," the Windrun Warrior told them hurriedly, to which all three stood to look over the rubble of the inn. He strode toward them methodically, his massive shoulders shifting back and forth as he did. Before the sage could reach them, Jaren called out anxiously.

"Did you talk with Tavin? How is he? Are they all right over there?" he called out, his rushed words blending together. Zeroan threw up his hand, obviously vexed to the point where the insistent Grandarian boy's questions were not appreciated.

"Enough," he said stopping in front of them, breathing deeply. The sage shifted in his robes before further addressing them. "Listen carefully, for much has happened and there is not much time to explain it. First of all, both Tavinious and Arilia are perfectly fine." A wave of relief washed over Jaren and the others. "In fact, the Warrior of Light is stronger than ever, his powers now in his control. Because of this development, he is now strong enough to move on his own. He, Ril, and... another left or will soon be leaving Keracon Valley for Torrentcia City where they will meet you as they arrive." Zeroan had related so much to them so quickly that Jaren had to throw up his hands in confusion.

"Hold on for a minute, Zeroan," he interjected. "When you say 'you,' you mean all of us right?" The sage shook his head under his frayed gray hood.

"By 'you', I mean you three," he said passing his eyes over Jaren, Parnox, and Kohlin. "Yucono must be back to his outpost and responsibilities for his own people." Parnox's brow furrowed.

"What about you, Zeroan?" he asked uneasily. The sage shifted in his robes once again as he quietly responded.

"I must leave you now," he said soft but sharp, turning to bring his hands to his lips and whistle at an impossibly loud frequency. As the echoing waves of the whistle sounded through the air, Jaren's face froze with stunned incredulity.

"What do you mean you must leave!?!" he practically shouted. Zeroan remained coolly collected.

"As I said," he stated, turning to face a sudden noise on the horizon of the decimated village, "much has happened. My presence is needed elsewhere." Letting the matter rest for the moment, Zeroan waited for the now audible galloping hoof beats rapidly approaching their position increase until view of a speeding black horse came into view outside the forest borders. The others watched in amazement and disbelief as the steed pulled up to the cloaked figure and stopped, lowering its head. Zeroan outstretched his arm and patted the muscular creature's neck. "This is Nighcress. He is a mystical being from a time long passed. Because of his past affiliation with the Mystic Sage's of old, he has remained in the thin forests of the east for a great many years. This creature is able to run faster than otherwise physically possible because of its magic." Zeroan quickly took hold of the horse's frame and climbed up, riding it without a saddle or reins of any kind.

Jaren and the others stared at him with skeptic astonishment.

"What are you talking about, Zeroan?" Jaren continued with mass confusion mirrored in his flustered eyes. "What about the missing shards? What about us?" Zeroan turned the black steed around, preparing it for travel.

"There is no time for these questions, Jaren," he said calm but with urgency inside his voice. "Listen to me carefully, all of you. With Tavin and Ril separated from us, our situation grows more dire. Last night, Valif Montrox summoned something of great dark power from the Netherworld. It has already departed from Drakkaidia. If it, or they, are what I think they are, we have now entered very serious times. The shards at the Mystic Tower and even the one in Galantia could be at risk, and I must collect the two in the east before they are taken by force. Therefore, Parnox will lead you and Kohlin north to Torrentcia City now. You will most likely arrive before Tavin and Ril, and I will join you soon after that. Until then, try to prepare for whatever hostilities are sure to be moving toward the city. Parnox, I know it is beyond your power, but the Legion must be summoned. Try whatever you can to do so. Have you any questions?" All three gazed at him helplessly, not sure what to ask.

"What's going on, Zeroan?" Parnox asked nervously. "What has happened?"

"Now is not the time for me to explain in great detail, Southlander, for we have none to waste," the sage responded. "I will elucidate when we meet again at the capital. For now, just know that Montrox has accelerated his plans and is preparing to destroy the Southland. With his new demons at his side, we are in dark times. Be wary of foes in the plains and in the central Southland. That is all, my friends. Be away soon. I wish you luck." With that, the Mystic Sage commanded the mysterious dark horse onward and into the tree line around the village, speeding away into the shade. Though it was not difficult to realize something very big had happened, Jaren and the others could only imagine the evil occurring in Drakkaidia. The Grandarian boy frowned, feeling that things had finally begun to spin out of control beyond the point of recovery.

Part Four
Saving the Southland

Chapter 56

<u>Theft</u>

Her Royal Highness Princess Maréttiny Kolior sat in the upper library of the sage's Mystic Tower with a perplexed and captivated expression over her face. Her wide and mystified eyes were locked onto a detailed stone plaque elaborately edged with silver. At its center was a long cylindrical tube filled with a clear viscous liquid slowly circulating within. Mary blinked, wonder mirrored in her sparkling eyes. She sat hunched forward over a tabletop by the wall.

"How did you say this talisman works again, Master Sage?" the girl asked curiously, still staring at the slowly churning liquid. From the opposite side of the library, a sudden shifting of books on the shelves sounded through the large chamber, followed by a deep exhale of breath.

"To what are you referring, Princess?" was the response from the dark blue cloaked figure rising from behind a bookcase with several ancient texts in his arms. Mary turned her head back and pointed up to the magical icon hung on the wall between two bookcases.

"I think I forgot the name again," she confessed embarrassed. "The talisman on the wall, here." The other figure dumped the load of books in his arms over the top of the bookcase he stood by and collected his flowing robes about him. His eyes peered out from the confines of his concealing hood.

"Alberic's Guard," he began, once again reminding the forgetful Grandarian of its name, "displays the presence of all forms of magic, no matter how difficult to detect they may be. Even the mystic powers of old are revealed to us through it." Mary nodded quickly.

"Yes, I remember its purpose," she explained, "but how does it work?" The Master Sage shook his head, turning once again to the books beside him.

"For a Grandarian Princess taught to memorize every detail of your nation's history," he began piling books on top of one another, "you don't have the sharpest memory." Mary blushed, not quite sure how to respond. "The liquid. It... changes color depending on what sort of power it detects."

"How so?" the Grandarian girl pressed curious. The Master Sage froze once again and shot her a frustrated glance.

"You do realize that I'm very busy, Your Highness," he said. Mary blushed once again.

"Oh, I'm sorry," she stated apologetically, slightly bowing her head. "I'll leave you alone to your work."

"I didn't mean it like that," he said still holding her gaze. "I just wish you would remember what I tell you this time. Whatever kind of magic the talisman is detecting, it will display through the changing color of its liquid. If it is sensing an elemental power, it will turn color appropriately. Blue for water, red for fire, you know. A light power, it will shine with a golden radiance, and a dark power it will be shrouded by black. Anything else, well, you have to be a sage to see that." Deciding that the nature of the power fueling Alberic's Guard was simply beyond her, Mary let the matter drop, silently nodding. The Master Sage sensed her lingering confusion and added a little more as he sorted through what was left of his books in need reorganization. "It's complicated, I know, but that is the way it was constructed. Alberic, the first Master Sage of the first council ages ago, incorporated into that talisman his sixth sense to... feel the presence of magic and power. It is a process few understand, but know that it works quite well, Princess." Mary shot him a quick smile.

"I told you that you don't have to call me that," she reminded him friendlily. He shook his head.

"You are a Princess of Grandaria," he stated. "I will address you properly."

"Oh, come on," she said beaming. "I bet you don't like being called 'Master Sage' all of the time." A particular look swept across him before finally letting a smile appear on his short bearded face.

"*You* are more than welcome to call me Arius, Mary," he said, to which the girl smiled widely. The night Mary had volunteered to watch over the two shards of the Holy Emerald in the vaults of the Mystic Tower, Zeroan had warned her of the unreliability of the current group of sages. Though he imparted that their order was now nothing more than a social club for a collection of elderly men with a curiosity of ancient magics and that none of them could be trusted or accounted for, she had taken a liking to their leader almost immediately. This was the Master Sage Arius. The blue cloaked chief of the Mystic Sages was very different from Zeroan. While they were both deeply reserved, Zeroan rarely displayed his humanity at all. Arius, on the other hand, was a younger personable sage. Even in the brief time she had known him, Mary could easily detect a kind and concerning man behind his robes.

When she had arrived at the Mystic Tower with the Elemental Warrior of Wind weeks earlier, she met with him and the entire council to explain the purpose of her presence. Though she had expected to be thrown out or worse knowing the group's dislike for Zeroan and his business, Arius had allowed her to stay as long as she wished. The Master Sage did not agree with the urgency that Zeroan saw in current events, but he at least respected him enough to keep a close eye on the shards hidden in the massive Vault Room just down the hall from the library. In the two weeks that the Grandarian Princess had been stationed at the Mystic Tower, she had done a great deal with the Warrior of Wind and the Master Sage. Separately, for the most part. They seemed to be divided over the current situation with the Holy Emerald shards to the point where they did not desire each other's company. This night, the Warrior of Wind had ventured to Windrun City farther to the northwest when a band of farmers had requested assistance with a faction of the Purging Flame apparently in the area. She told Mary that she would be gone no longer than a few days, and that she would be safe with Arius in the meantime. She also reminded her of her purpose here, telling her to keep an eye on the sages and what they did concerning the shards. As she left with a party of Windrun Warriors, Mary followed the Master Sage to the primary libraries high in the tower. Though only sages were to be allowed entrance to the rooms where the accounts of history and legend from the dawn of history to present day were stored, he permitted her to enter if she stayed close to him.

As Arius lowered himself back to the ground to place the reorganized books back on the shelves around the room, Mary let her eyes wander out of the massive window next to him. It was dark outside, having been night for hours now, but she could still make out the landscape below her from the bright moonlight. The Mystic Tower rose from a small plateau in the center of a massive valley surrounded by hills of the Windrun territories. There was a small but dense forest around the plateau but nothing except the lofty tower stood upon its rocky base. Next to the Golden Castle with the Temple of Light at its center, the Mystic Tower itself was the most amazing structure Mary had ever seen. It was thick at its base, but as it soared into the sky its levels grew smaller and smaller until they reached the top, not even the size of the library she sat in now. It was a simplistic structure, though carefully crafted and detailed at the same time.

As the Grandarian Princess let the minutes pass staring out at the woods and hills far below her, a sudden change in the light of the room awakened her from her peaceful daydreaming. Blinking several times to see if her eyes were just playing tricks on her, she realized that the candlelit room had indeed grown substantially darker. She bent her head downward to gaze out the window and noticed that the moon had suddenly been completely obscured by an overcast sky of dark clouds. The girl's brow furrowed with puzzlement. It had been crystal clear not more than a moment ago. Where did those clouds just come from, she wondered to herself. Despite the sudden loss of light from the luminous white orb in the sky outside, the room still grew darker by the second.

She was about to call out to Arius to alert him of the bizarre weather outside when she caught sight of a strange light from the corner of her eye. Slowly turning her head back to the magical plaque on the wall, her eyes slowly but widely opened. Staring at the talisman, she watched as the once clear liquid churning within the cylinder at its center darkened to a pitch-black abyss. Mary froze for a moment, remembering what the Master Sage had just told her about its functions of changing color and what black meant.

"Arius," she called back with a shaking voice, her eyes still fixed on the ominous dark liquid slowly swirling in the cylinder. "Arius, why is it doing this?" The Master Sage exhaled sharply again, ready to once again explain Alberic's Guard. He stood from the lower shelves of the book cases, shuffling in his blue robes. As he turned his head toward the girl sitting on the other side of the room, his eyes fell onto the black liquid inside of the talisman mounted on the wall. He froze, his muscles tightening. Growing more than a little nervous, the Grandarian Princess managed to tear her gaze off of the dark plaque and back to Arius, still and silent. "Arius, what is going on?" He twitched, carefully walking across the room until beside Mary's chair, taking her out of it and backing her away. She once again asked him what was happening.

"I... don't know..." he murmured, trying to sort out what could be causing the sinister display. He at last shook his head, concluding that it was merely a mistake. "Three of the sages are currently locked up in various parts of the tower working with ancient magics. One of them must have... done something; unknowingly stumbled onto something dark in nature." Mary looked uncertain.

"Could it be because of that?" she said, nervously pointing out the circular window at the other side of the library. Arius quickly turned to find what she was pointing at and observed the suddenly clouded sky for himself. His brow furrowed as he took a single step forward.

"What...?" he asked to himself, scanning the rolling billows of black outside. "Where did that come from?" Mary looked up at him apprehensively. He shook his head again. "Something is wrong here. We need to go find whichever one of the sage's is responsible for this and..." Arius was interrupted by a sudden quake from outside the chamber in the halls. It wasn't strong enough to knock the two over, but several of the books fell from the shelves of the library. Both of them shot each other uneasy glances, and Mary took a step closer to the sage, uncomfortable. Arius breathed deep and began making his way for the door with Mary in tow. The girl once again asked what was happening, but he was too lost in thought to respond. He had no idea what was going on. One of the sages could not have triggered a presence of dark power as intensely as was portrayed in Alberic's Guard, and they could not have manifested a storm so large out of nowhere. Not even the Master Sage had that power anymore.

As he made his way for the door, it suddenly burst open, causing Mary to nearly jump out of her skin. As the twin doors swung open, it was another cloaked sage standing before them. Arius exhaled loudly, obviously nervous himself. The other was the first to speak, urgency in his voice.

"Master Sage, something has just appeared on the roofing and has crashed into the Vault Room. There is a beast of some kind in the-" The man was cut short by another loud crash of stone and a sudden collection of screaming from down the hallway. Arius nearly jumped himself, his face rigid with disbelief and terror, suddenly aware of what was happening. As the screaming and rumbling continued, he spun around and leaned down to Mary, terrified herself.

"Princess, I want you to wait here," he commanded, his voice shaking with turmoil. "Lock the door and barricade yourself in. Hide under the desk until Alberic's Guard returns to normal. Do not come out until the black liquid is gone. Do you understand?" Overcome with alarm and confusion, the girl could only nod as she fumbled to repeat the question she had asked before.

"Arius, what is happening?" she asked almost ready to cry. The Master Sage exhaled as he rose to gently push the girl back into the library and shut the doors.

"...I was wrong," he managed closing his eyes. "Zeroan was right." With that, he closed the doors and locked them from the outside, leaving Mary alone with the black light of the enchanted talisman on the wall enveloping the room. Scrambling to analyze the sage's response, she realized what was happening.

Demons.

The thing she was here to try and prevent had happened, and now they were all in danger. Mary closed her eyes and shook her head, not able to believe this was happening again. It was just like at Galantia, but now she didn't have Jaren to protect her. She loosened her tight face as thoughts of the brave hearted Grandarian boy came to her. Remembering his courage and strength on the wall that day, she tried to think what he would do. A sudden rush of footsteps and shouting of several men mobilizing and rushing past the locked door of the library brought her back to her senses. As the sounds of battle and death continued to vibrate down the hall into the library, her fear was finally overridden by her desire to help in any way she could and she decided to leave the library. Mary stepped forward to try and open the double doorway before her, though its lock from the outside was far too strong for her to budge. Not giving up, she scanned the room for another idea. Her eyes sweeping the shadowy chamber, she remembered the window and was filled with new resolve.

She quickly sprinted over to the massive glass pane and unlatched the heavy handle on the right side. She pushed the glass outward with a lurching shove and peered her head out of the window downward. Though it was no balcony, there was a fairly wide catwalk stretching out from the tower walls from this window to another far to the right. Though it was over fifty feet away, Mary knew the Vault Room was on the other side of this level and the window would have to lead to it. She swallowed hard and shifted her gaze back to the catwalk below. Though she was not the bravest person she knew, the Grandarian Princess dispelled her fear and lifted a leg from the library floor through the open window pane and onto the now much narrower catwalk. She slowly brought the other leg out, clutching the windowpane like a metal trap.

Completely outside the tower, Mary slowly peered downward to observe the seemingly endless darkness beneath her. The girl's delicate face turned pale, gulping once again. Letting her eyes turn back to the opposite window across the catwalk, however, she remembered her determination and began inching toward it, carefully strafing against the wall of the tower and groping for anything to hold onto. As she gradually passed along the wall, jets of wind whipped the ends of her casual pink dress back and forth. It was minutes later before the girl at last reached the window to the Vault Room, breathing heavily as she latched onto its edges. Pressed tightly against the wall, her curiosity finally returned to her and she forced herself to peer through, despite her fear of what she might find.

As the girl edged forward to make out what was happening, she was surprised to find the room completely devoid of battle. Examining the chamber more carefully, she quickly saw why. The bodies of cloaked sages and other defenders of the tower lay littered across the floor in a veritable lake of blood. Mary brought a shaking hand to her mouth as the carnage passed before her eyes and ripped into her mind. Nearly every sage she had seen upon arrival weeks ago was dead; mangled and dismembered. The chamber itself was equally ravaged, with craters in the floor and a gaping hole in the ceiling spreading rubble everywhere. She could not believe it. Someone had completely obliterated the most powerful group of men the world had ever known in less than a few minutes. As the horrified girl blinked her eyes with tears swelling, the movement of an enormous mass of blackness drew her attention back into the Vault Room. Though not wanting to look again, the Grandarian Princess could not help but open her eyes and gape through the window again. A familiar creature entered her field of vision.

It was one of the gargantuan flying monsters she had seen at Galantia nearly two months ago. As she stared horrified at the foreboding but motionless winged nightmare, the glowing light from its crimson red eyes reflected onto another much smaller figure beside the enormous vault. At first the girl took it for a sage, cloaked and hooded in what looked to be deep black robes. When she noticed another figure in his grip propelled off his feet and into the air, however, she knew he was an enemy. Mary shot forward to the window as she made out the tattered and beaten form of Arius hanging limply from the black figure's arms. She watched in dismay as the figure sharply drew Arius in front of his concealed face.

"*I will say it no more,*" a raspy and distant voice faintly spoke, barely audible to Mary pressed against the window. "*Only you can open the vault, sage. Do so, or suffer and die.*" Arius' bloody face tightened with what energy he had left.

"You will kill me in any case," he managed to breath through his blood and pain. "I will not open it. You will not have the shards." The black figure instantly thrust Arius back into the air and against the enchanted vault door. The broken Master Sage let out a scream of anguish, hearing his own bones break from the force. Mary cringed, wanting to leap into the room and save him. She tightly closed her eyes and shook her head, the tears falling over her soft cheeks. None of this could be real. She felt like she was trapped in the worst nightmare of her life and just wanted to wake up, but no matter how desperately she tried, she could not.

It was at this moment when the Princess was ready to break down and fall to her knees that her sorrow and pain were overridden by another emotion suddenly freezing her every nerve. Her eyes abruptly opened and she stood locked in place with her gaze fixed on the window and the enormous black mass reflecting off of it from behind her. The force of slow but steady flapping of colossal wings beating through the turbulent air sent the ends of Mary's dress flying toward the window. Her eyes shifted upward to the pair of crimson eyes staring at her with another black cloaked figure mounted behind its sunken head. A demon was behind her. She was about to try and run but the Valcanor's mighty gnarled fingers abruptly snatched her delicate form off the catwalk. All she could do was scream.

The girl's cry coupled with the shattering of glass as the Dégamar and his winged mount crashed through the window was what drew the attention of Arius and the other two of the Black Seven in the room, another standing guard by the doorway to the chamber. The Master Sage's already dejected heart sank to mesh with the bottom of his gut. The Valcanor touched down onto the bloodstained floor, its rider doing the same.

"Perhaps this will alter your decision," the demonic mage stated in a distant voice equal to the others, ripping the crying Grandarian girl from the Valcanor's grasp and into his own. Locked into the cold figure's hold, Mary shifted her tear soaked eyes to his face, only renewing her trepidation as she caught view of its scarred, rotting face. She tore her horrified eyes away and screamed with terror again, trying with no avail to squirm free. The Dégamar holding Arius was the next to speak.

"Open the vault, or she will suffer beyond your comprehension," the cloaked figure spoke with malice. Arius turned his head back and forth between the demon mage before him and the crying girl to his left. He remained rigid and still for a moment, as if torn between an impossible decision. Finally he coughed up a mass of blood and nodded, to which the Dégamar instantaneously threw him against the vault door. *"Quickly."* Though frightened out of her mind by the demonic figure pressing her against it, Mary violently shook her head and yelled out to the sage, struggling to rise.

"Arius!" she cried. "You can't let them have the shards! That's the whole reason that I'm here in the first place!"

"Silence, girl!" The Dégamar holding her maliciously lashed out. Though terrified, she continued.

"This is more important than you or me, Arius! You can't let them-" This time she was silenced by the iron grip of the demon mage's left arm painfully clamping around her mouth. The Master Sage stood and threw his arm out.

"Stop! I am opening the door! You must leave her be," he pleaded, to which the Dégamar eased his grip. The black figure closest to him instructed him to hurry. Though barely harboring the energy required to stand, Arius somehow nodded and turned to the vault door, summoning his age old mystic power. Though the vault appeared to be nothing more than a standard iron door built into the walls of the tower, it was comprised of ancient power that could not be deactivated unless distinctly ordered to by one with command of a specific power. No other power could damage it. Obviously from their previous attempts to break inside, the three Dégamar had discovered this. Though they would be able to overpower the ancient magic with the help of Valif Montrox, they were in too much of a hurry to go all the way back to Drakkaidia.

Ready to begin, Arius lifted his arms and spread his hands over the vault door. Letting a faint pulse of dim flashing energy emit from his palms, the entire metallic doorway followed in suit and flashed with faint energy. Not more than a few moments later, the entire door pulsed with light and disappeared. Mary watched in dismay as the inside of the vault was exposed, revealing a single pedestal in the center of the small space with two of the Holy Emerald shards resting upon it. As the last remnant of mystical power died, however, another light began to suddenly flare up before her. Arius had just consumed an entire vial of a strange glowing liquid from inside his robes, and she could hear it drop on the floor empty. Both she and the three Dégamar in the chamber abruptly shifted their gaze from the vault to the Master Sage, his body rapidly radiating a fierce white light. Just as the demonic mages realized what he was doing, Arius leapt forward into the vault and threw his hands around the two shards, bringing them tight against his body. Now practically bursting with the blinding white light around him, the sage locked his eyes onto Mary.

"They have to be destroyed. I'm so sorry, Mary," he stated just loud enough to be heard, all three Dégamar rushing toward him. "Tell Zeroan as well." Just as the dark mages reached him, Arius' very skin ruptured with white light and tore. Mary watched in disbelief and horror from the cold floor as his body exploded in a detonation of light, a wave of warmth rippling through her. Her eyes closing to block out the intense light, Mary remembered something the Master Sage had told her days ago about how a sage or a dark mage could 'self destruct' to release their life energy outward. Her eyes slowly opened, realizing what had just happened. He had sacrificed himself to destroy the shards with his energy. Tears began to form in the corners of her eyes. Arius was gone. They were all gone. All the sages in the tower were dead.

As the passionate light from the Master Sage's self destruction began to fade, Mary brought her head back to the opening of the vault once again. Though her eyes struggled to adjust back to the darkness of the chamber, she could make out three figures standing in the vault. The girl's eyes opened wide as the Dégamar picked up his blue robes; all that remained of the Master Sage. Her eyes trembled and streamed tears.

"*The sage is no more,*" one of the three black figures stated in its raspy voice.

"*What was the purpose of his suicide?*" another asked, reaching into the robes.

"*He must have been trying to destroy them,*" the third responded. "*Fool.*" The center demon mage dropped the blue robes then, revealing two shining objects in each of his rotting gloved hands. Mary froze and began trembling once again, realizing the figure held the two perfectly maintained shards in them. A new sense of sorrow and anguish enveloped her. Arius' sacrifice had been for nothing. As the three demons emerged from the vault, however, she could not help but be grateful that he would not have to endure the torture that she would. She silently cringed at the thought of the agony she was about to be subjected to. As she braced for the worst, she was stunned to find all three of the Dégamar walk straight past her to their winged mounts behind her without so much as a word. Still terrified out of her mind, she could not bring herself to move a muscle. It was the sound of the enormous flapping wings of the Valcanor taking flight that caused her to stir.

Slowly turning her head backward to the three dark mages and their demonic transportation now facing away from the tower and soaring off into the dense night, all of the various emotions and thoughts from the past fifteen minutes crept up on her and attacked, leaving her too overwhelmed to think. The only thing that could budge her was the collection of blue robes lying on the floor at the entrance of the vault ten feet away. Slowly crawling across the bloodied floor toward the soft cloak, she wrapped it in her arms and lay down upon it. Once nestled in its somehow lingering warmth, the beleaguered little Princess began to softly but steadily cry, letting her tears fall onto the comforting cloth. Besieged by her sorrow and incompressible grief, she could not hear the barely audible hoof beats on the earth so far below her.

Chapter 57

<u>Clash</u>

Tavin stood in a basin of massive rocks and boulders littering the ground like trees in the Great Forests he and his companions had emerged from days ago. Though they were still in the westernmost Grailen Plains, the earth around them had become exceedingly craggy and rough the farther north they progressed, signaling their approach to the rolling hills of rock leading up to the Coron Mountains of the west. From the day they appeared out of the dense woods, they had moved swiftly and silently across the western plains of the south with Verix leading them at a familiar taxing pace that a certain Mystic Sage had become infamous for. Having worked themselves into the veritable labyrinth of the rock basin, Verix had lost his bearings for a moment and called for a momentary halt in their journey. As rare as it was for the impatient Prince to allow for a lunch break, Tavin and Ril were both particularly happy to make use of it. As Verix left the two Elemental Warriors to regain his sense of direction, he informed them to take the time to eat. Ril, afraid to manifest a fire herself for fear of something sensing her magical power, set out to locate some wood to construct one the old fashion way.

Finding himself alone, the Warrior of Light quietly crept away from camp to a ridge above them to do something he had been dying to try for weeks. With his elemental power of light now under his control, his curiosity had been tempting to him to experiment with it to the point where the need to do so had all but consumed him. With Verix in their party to mask their presence from anything in close proximity that might wish them harm, he figured he had some freedom to test himself. Quietly drawing the Sword of Granis at his side, he made his way into a thick collection of boulders protruding from the earth to investigate the limits of his new strength.

The Grandarian boy looked around to be sure he was indeed alone, and positioned himself in the center of the rocky surroundings, raising the silver blade of the Sword of Grains in front of his face, preparing his battle stance. Tavin's now determined and excited eyes passed up and down along the shimmering steel, ready to begin. He slowly closed his eyes and let his conscience mind meld with his deep thoughts and feelings. In touch with his inner core, Tavin found his previously hidden power lying inside him bubbling with anticipation, ready to burst up on command.

Wrapping his thoughts around it, Tavin began to focus hard and summon it forth. It responded almost immediately with a sudden flare of golden energy swirling to life around him, causing his comfortable blue and white clothing to rustle over his body in the wake of its power. His cape flew backward whipping its tails as if caught in the grip of a gale. As he opened his deep blue eyes to find the fervent field of radiating power around him active and full, he could not help but grin. Despite all of his reservations and all the obstacles thus far, he had done it. The elemental power of light was his to command. Pleased with himself and his cooperating strength so far, the Grandarian continued to give in to his curiosity and realigned his body into his battle hardened fighting stance. With the shining Sword of Granis held firmly at his waist pointed upward, he raised it into the air with a wave of golden light following it. Gritting his teeth, Tavin slashed the blade downward straight through the colossal boulder in front of him. The blade sliced through its solid interior so quick and clean that he wondered if he had even come in contact with anything at all.

His doubts were dispelled as the top half of the once unyielding stone abruptly slid off of the bottom at a perfectly cut oblique angle. He let out a childlike giggle, unable to contain his exhilaration. Eager to continue his research, the Warrior of Light began slashing at the other boulders in close proximity in a similar fashion, perfectly slicing them to pieces. Upon destroying every boulder within the range of his blade, Tavin's pride and excitement boosted his stamina and power. The field of radiating golden light around him expanding to the point where its power began pushing the rubble of his handiwork away from him, he set his sights on the collection of boulders resting on the opposite side of the ridge some twenty yards away. Remembering how he had blasted his energy outward in his battle against the Golthrouts and their master, he planted the Sword of Granis into the earth at his side and began to focus once more.

His power surging inside him, Tavin tightened his body to flex it around him in a flurry of shining light, heightening his exhilaration until everything but his power was gone from his mind. He inhaled hard and shot his arm outward with a concrete fist radiating a sphere of golden energy at its end. Once fully extended, the Warrior of Light made a quick shout and released the sphere of light in a quick but forceful discharge of exploding energy, blasting away toward the rocks. The burst of shining light impacted the stone with a hard detonation of sound, shattering it into a cloud of falling ruble instantly. A broad grin overtook his astounded face. Impressed with himself, he once again built a quick charge of power around his fists and thrust them forward to blast out twin spurts of golden energy, once again demolishing a large boulder.

Feeling in total control, the Warrior of Light threw his right hand around the hilt of the Sword of Granis freeing its implanted blade from the earth and shot forward with a massive lunge to within a few feet of the remaining boulders. Sprinting forward with his blade in one hand and a concentrated ball of energy around the other, he leapt into the boulders slicing and blasting with indiscriminant power erupting outward. Maneuvering through the maze of rocks and rubble with speed and agility that he never thought he was capable of, Tavin interchanged his attacks of blasting energy and swinging steel between his hands, utilizing his years of training and finesse with the blade to the paramount of his ability. Mere minutes later, only a few boulders yards away remained intact. Caught up in the pleasure of his destructive rampage, Tavin tightly pressed his eyelids together and focused the most intense level of power yet into his arms, channeling his energy directly to them and firing them forward.

Because he did not open his eyes until the charge power exploded from his outstretched limbs, he did not notice Verix Montrox standing directly in his line of fire until it was too late. Tavin could only watch as his attack sped at the Drakkaidian Prince mere yards away. As the energy careened toward him, however, the dark figure's already unpleasant face tightened with anger, focusing his own power. His right arm suddenly engulfed in a deep crimson red aura, he threw it upward and deflected the incoming blast with a fierce yell, sending it careening off its path over his head to spiral into the earth far behind them with a distant explosion of power. Tavin, stunned that the Prince had reacted so quickly and efficiently, stood motionless in his aura of radiating golden light while the advancing Drakkaidian strode toward him with a look of twisted rage about his face.

When only feet away, Verix clenched his fist once more and threw it forward in a ball of potent power to punch Tavin straight across the jaw. The awestruck Warrior of Light flew off his feet backward to land in one of his piles of rubble. Though protected from the force of impact by his radiating power, his jaw still hurt like he had just ran into a brick wall. Not able to distinguish between his confusion and anger, Tavin brought his gaze up to the still advancing Drakkaidian, who, with enmity still in his eyes, reached down and heaved him upward by his shirt and into a rock wall.

"What in the name of Drakkan below do you think you're doing!?!" Verix bellowed. Tavin found himself speechless yet again. "What part of 'keep your power discrete' do you have a problem complying with? Are you trying to alert every demon in Iairia to our presence? For your sake especially, I suggest sealing it off *now*!" Tavin could not bear it. Despite his promised patience for the Drakkaidian Prince, Tavin's raw emotion corrupting his judgment ignited his anger. Allowing his resentment to trigger the depths of his power, he fed off of the building fury until the mounting energy forced Verix to release him and jump back.

"What is your problem, Montrox?" he roared back, throwing his arms upward. "You said that you could hide our power with yours!" Verix's exploded back at him.

"I meant if the girl wanted to light a quick fire or if you had to provide us with a little light from your glow stick sword! I can't do a damn thing when you summon your full elemental power and start blowing up everything in sight!"

"Then maybe you should have clarified that, Montrox!"

"I assumed you had enough of a brain to realize that when the paramount of your energy is revealed, the most powerful demon I have ever sensed can detect it!" Both of them were beside themselves with rage.

"I didn't know, alright?"

"Oh, well that makes everything alright then," the Prince yelled with sarcasm pouring from his voice. "I suppose because you're ignorant beyond comprehension I should forgive you, is that it? You really are the perfect Grandarian warrior. Undisciplined and indiscriminant power that is equaled only by your monumental lack of brainpower!" That was all Tavin could take. Already brimming with rage from the Prince's unnecessary hostility from the beginning, this gut wrenching insult completely pushed him over the edge. Now seeing only a loathsome enemy before him, he balled his fists and leapt forward with his power surging behind him. So quick was the boy's charge that the equally incensed Prince could barely dodge his soaring fist in time by spinning to the left. Tavin missed his face by a fraction of an inch, landing in a crouch on the rocks behind him.

A million thoughts and worries bounding back into Verix's head, his mind came back into focus as the Grandarian rose to his feet. Verix placed a hand in front of him defensively.

"Boy, this is not the time or place," he started again in a much more controlled tone. "I can't hide your power like this and-" He would not have time to finish with a sudden blast of golden energy sailing toward him from Tavin's radiating body. Verix peaked his strength to once again swat the shining projectile out of the way, though this time it nearly burnt his hand. Tavin lunged at him again with fists flying. Without enough time to dodge, Verix was forced to stand his ground and catch them in the palms of his hands, pushing back at him and summoning his own dark power outward to keep him steady. Verix's temper began to slip. "It's not worth you getting beat again, boy!" A poor thing to say when trying to back Tavin down, he only provoked the Grandarian further.

"Don't let that worry you, Drak!" he bellowed, pushing himself into the other. "You need to worry about yourself now!" With that, Tavin's field of radiating power rushed up again, expanding even further. Had Verix not summoned his own aura of dark crimson power about him, he would have been devoured by it. Though he knew that their feud was putting them and their quest at risk, Verix was suddenly curious himself. He was currently struggling a great deal to hold the pushing Warrior of Light back. The last time they had sparred, it was all Tavin could do to stay on his feet. Wanting to know just how powerful his opponent had become, he began to fight back instead of withdrawing, focusing and increasing his power level to better hold his ground and withstand Tavin's.

Their powers now equal, two brilliant fields of light could be seen from miles away; one vivid gold and the other electrified crimson. The two were deadlocked together by their hands, pushing against one another with arms stretched and feet embedded into the earth beneath them. So intense were their rising powers that the massive slabs of decimated rubble began to shift away from them and the earth around their feet began to smash and fracture. Tavin stood pushing with all his might into Verix's open hands, every muscle in his body taut with determination. He grit his teeth as beads of sweat passed down his face. He could feel that he was giving it his all now. His inner power was completely exposed, and his field of golden light was as big as he had ever seen it. Verix was equally stressed, finding himself pushing back with all of his might and his full power summoned forth to do so. Though the Warrior of Light had not surpassed him, he had somehow managed to match his royal Drakkaidian power that had been taught, developed, and passed down for generations in mere weeks.

Both determined to triumph over the other or die trying, it was not until the appearance of a strange light beneath them that the deadlock came to an end. Despite the intensity of the light from the their powers, Tavin could not help but notice the orange glow from under his feet between the two on the earth. It was a circle of burning energy, building in size as every moment passed by. By the time it stretched from Tavin's feet to Verix's, the Drakkaidian Prince had noticed it as well. Then, in a sudden explosion of heat, the orange circle erupted from the ground into a column of fire bellowing straight up at the two. Baffled, both of the two released each other and wheeled backward as the wall of flame rose past their faces, literally singing their eyebrows. Falling away from the towering inferno of circulating fire, they fell onto their backsides over the rock, their worked and tired powers dimming immediately.

The blazing column disappeared as quickly as it arrived, dissipating into the heated air like a wisp of wind. As its intense light vanished, Tavin noticed another fervent glow from his right and turned to find Ril, burning embers dissipating around her frame.

Letting the remaining blaze flowing from her body disperse, her taut face wrought with anger was revealed. Her crimson hair shown red from the fading aura of flame, as did her scarlet clothing waving back and forth from its force. She took a step toward Tavin, gritting her teeth.

"What is going on!?!" she bellowed louder than he had ever heard her. "Drakkaidia has a horde of demons out looking for us and you're out here blasting your powers up at full strength! Are you *trying* to get us killed?" Verix Montrox rose to his feet with a furious grunt, sealing off the remainder of his tested power.

"Don't presume to interfere with my business, girl," he lashed back with scorn. "I was trying to tell the Grandarian the same thing but I was attacked and-"

"Do I look that stupid to you, Verix?" she interrupted, unleashing her vehemence. "Tavin may have come at you but you were calling out every last bit of your power and you know it. You're just as guilty as he is." The Warrior of Light gave her a relieved look, glad that she was on his side. As he began to stand himself, however, the girl quickly wheeled to him pointing an accusing finger. "And you!" she shouted moving to his suddenly nervous face. "You're supposed to be a role model for integrity and doing the right thing! What are you doing attacking our guide?" Tavin stepped back but opened his mouth to speak defensively.

"He came at *me* first!" he fumbled, feeling a little intimidated by the Warrior of Fire.

"And that makes it okay to fight back?" she asked aghast. "What are you, Tavin? Nine? If I were him I would have slapped you around too! What were you thinking summoning your entire power when you know how sensitive those things out there are? Did you forget how they sensed my little spark back in Grandaria? And now we don't have Zeroan to hide us!" The Warrior of Light gave her a hurt look, wanting to give her some excuse but couldn't. Verix was quiet as well, letting the silence hang. "All right you two," she began acidly, shooting quick glances at them both, "shut up and listen up. I have had it up to here with your little feud, so it's going to end right here and right now. I don't want to hear the Grandaria vs Drakkaidia history speech of why you two have reason to hate each other because it's no excuse for any of this. We don't have time or room for it on this quest. So the both of you had better grow up and get over yourselves or so help me Granis I'm going to char you both to ashes. Do you understand me?"

Ril looked to Tavin first, who reluctantly gave a single nod as he deeply exhaled feeling as big as an insect. Next she spun her head around to Verix, ready to accept his apology as well. As she turned to face him, she found that the Drakkaidia Prince was no longer looking at her, but was turned around and staring over the ledge of the cliff they now stood over, his red hair and tattered gray goat flapping in the breeze.

"I'm not playing with you, Verix! Either you put this behind you and focus on our business at hand or-"

"Quiet," he practically whispered, raising a hand behind him. The strange aloofness of his response drew both Ril and Tavin's complete attention, worry suddenly enveloping them. After several moments passed with no one saying a word, the Prince at last dropped his hand with a hushed curse. He spun his body back to them motioning to drop down at once. There was an immediate urgency present in his eyes and body language that neither of the two Elemental Warriors had seen before.

"What is it, Verix?" Tavin asked hurriedly. The Drakkaidian's face went ridged with impatience and he repeated his motion for them to get down.

"Something is coming!" he whispered rapidly, a mix of fret and irritation in his voice. "Drop now and hide your faces. Try to seal your power as much as you can and don't move a muscle." Tavin and Ril shot each other panicky glances and began to slowly move down. "Do it now!" he whispered again, hastily moving toward them and materializing his savage broadsword from behind his back. Once Tavin was face down on the rubble strewn earth, Verix drove a foot down into his back.

"What are you doing?" the Warrior of Light bit at him. Verix motioned for silence with his dangerous eyes.

"Shut up and trust me!" With that, Tavin reluctantly obeyed, dropping his face to the ground and signaling for Verix to turn his attention back to the cliff. As he did, the already cloudy morning air was suddenly upgraded to dark rolling billows directly overhead, confirming Verix's fears. Feeling the inevitability of the incoming power now on top of them, he struggled to maintain his usual hard expression. As the agonizingly long seconds passed by, Tavin cast his hidden eyes over to Ril. Her face was buried underneath her arms and draping hair. He wondered why neither of them had sensed the apparent cause of Verix's concern, concluding that their senses were simply not as in sync as his.

The next moment, all three heard a sudden but an all too familiar noise from below them: the sound of air being savagely beaten by what sounded like a pair of gargantuan wings. Tavin raised his eyebrow. Though a demon had indeed found them, they had nothing to fear from a lone Valcanor. He remained quiet however, as the sound of massive wing beats appeared from over the cliff side. Verix Montrox deeply inhaled as the form of a Valcanor appeared from behind the cliff, rising steeply in the air to crash down before them. Analyzing the familiar creature, he knew that there was more to it than was evident. He knew what Tavin and Ril could not. Something else beyond what they could imagine had been summoned by his father and was divided amidst the world. Now he felt a part of it standing before him.

The answer was revealed as the Valcanor touched down and closed its massive wings, wrapping them around its oval body. Upon its back stood a figure draped in black. Verix knew immediately that it was a dark mage, but it was drastically different; its power was beyond anything he had ever sensed from a mere human before. Though frightened at what was sure to be revealed to him in the next few moments, he sustained his cold demeanor of Drakkaidian pride and malice.

"Can I help you?" he asked arrogantly to the black figure, shifting his foot on Tavin's back and tightening his grip over his sword hilt. The cloaked mage remained still for a moment, but swiftly jumped down from his winged steed a moment later to land but a few feet from him. As the figure rose, its face was exposed from behind the confines of his hood. Even the strong Drakkaidian Prince could not help but flinch. Its face was appalling. With rotting skin hanging off his bones by what appeared to be crusted blood alone and the corroded eye sockets missing the eyes, it was perhaps the most disturbing thing Verix had ever seen. Remembering his history and the legends of the Dark Mages, he realized what was standing before him.

A Dégamar. Verix gulped hard and grit his teeth, torn between his anger at his father for summoning such creatures of evil and his fear of what he would do now.

"*You battle erratically. What are you doing, Prince?*" was the hauntingly distant voice from behind the demon mage's hood. Verix pointed his broadsword down to the Warrior of Light and raised his brow.

"What does it look like, mage?" he asked insolently, surprising himself at how he could maintain his harsh image in the presence of such a fearsome other. "I am, or at least was before you interrupted me, disposing of the Warrior of Light and his party." The Dégamar shifted his eyeless gaze down to the fallen form of the Grandarian boy, searching.

"*He is not dead,*" the figure announced monotonously.

"He will be momentarily, if you would be so kind as to be on your way and let me finish my business." The Dégamar locked back onto Verix, staring him down. The Prince decided to press his luck and grill the creature. "What business is it of yours, anyway? Why are you not with the rest of the seven?" It paused again, but opened its mangled jaw to speak once more.

"*Three are at the Mystic Tower retrieving shards,*" it informed him flatly. "*Three others scour the west for another. I am to find you and bring you back if you had not completed your task. You have, so I will return.*"

"What do you mean, scour the west?"

"'*Tear apart every inch of countryside and village until you find it,*'" the mage said, repeating their exact orders word for word. Verix nodded, knowing they were his father's precise instructions.

"Have you?" he pressed. This time the Dégamar did not respond at all, though its silence was an obvious 'yes' to Verix. At last the mage spoke.

"*The Master grows impatient, Prince. Return soon,*" was the raspy command from the undead mage. With that it wheeled around, its black savage robes flying up behind it, and returned to the patiently waiting Valcanor's back. Upon landing over it, the winged demon rose back to its full length and spread its bat like wings again, turning back to the cliff side to coil its hydraulic legs and leap off. As the Dégamar and its steed soared away with the small but ominous clouds following it, Verix remained still, watching it depart, keeping his foot over Tavin. Once the demonic rider had all but disappeared from the horizon, Verix let out a deep breath, shaking his head in disbelief of what he had just successfully done. The Warrior of Fire was the first to speak after they were alone once again, raising her head from the ground and standing instantly.

"Verix what was that? And what did it mean by tear apart the west?" she asked with dread. The Drakkaidian Prince kept staring into space as he gradually lifted his foot from Tavin's cape and placed it back on the ground, lost in contemplation. As he stood silent piecing his thoughts together, Tavin rose from the gravely earth and proceeded to brush himself off. He reached over beside him and took hold of the Sword of Granis lying in rubble. "Verix?" Ril tried again, eager for an answer. He opened his mouth slowly, speaking in a hushed whisper.

"It was… a Dégamar," he stated, detached. His face slowly morphed from his expressionless state to a fit of rage, turning to kick a boulder fragment over the cliff side like a child's ball. Tavin and Ril watched still and silent as the Prince dropped to his knees and let out a blood curdling scream of anguish, maddening rage boiling in his veins. "He has summoned the Dégamar!" Verix plunged a fist into the rocky ground with such force that he split it into fragments. Allowing him time to cool down, Tavin at last spoke up.

"What are Dégamar, Verix?" he asked softly.

"A plague," he avowed coldly. "I can't believe I didn't see this before! Seven separate origins of the same power all over Iairia at once. It had to be them."

"You didn't answer my question," Tavin tried again, trying to evade the Prince's present anger with a gentle tone.

"Or mine," Ril chimed in, added urgency poured into her voice. The Drakkaidian wheeled his head around and locked his furious gaze onto them both.

"You want to know what they are?" he asked with violence in his shaking voice, standing up. "The Black Seven are the cursed spirits of ancient Drakkaidian Dark Mages that sold their souls to Drakkan for power beyond the others. They were destroyed during the first Holy War the same time as the first Warrior of Darkness, cast into the Netherworld. But my father," he said, his already furious tone escalating even further, "my brilliant father, has summoned them out once again. They are not alive, so they cannot die. Next to Drakkan himself, they are the most powerful demons in that accursed pit, and with their presence, the veil is most likely held together by a thread!" He screamed out in rage once again, cursing and stammering around like a raving madman.

"So what does this mean for us?" Tavin asked, trying to keep him on subject. Verix threw his hands in the air and dramatically shrugged with a fake smile over his sarcastic face.

"Hell on earth, I suppose!" he yelled back. Tavin's frown deepened.

"Look, Verix. I know this is the worst but we need you to stay with us here. We need to figure out what this means so we can adjust our plans accordingly."

"Well worry not, because we have quite a bit of that to do," he said, slouching in defeat. After cooling off in the silence that followed, the Drakkaidian collected himself enough to speak in a controlled tone once again. "Things just got complicated. That Dégamar will be going back to Dalastrak to report what just happened, but father will know that as long as you are still alive at this point that something is wrong. He's going to have all seven looking for us very soon. That makes our choices difficult."

"How so? Just how strong are these things, Verix?" Verix slowly shifted his gaze back to Tavin, narrowing his eyes.

"Together, we might be able to take one. Two, it would take a miracle, but maybe. Three or more, we'd be utterly destroyed." Tavin's brow furrowed at this.

"Even with my power to help?" he asked skeptically. Verix's frown deepened.

"Don't flatter yourself, Grandarian," he said icily. "These things are second only to Drakkan himself. It would take an army of us to stop all seven."

"Then what do we do now?" Tavin asked, swallowing his doubts for the moment.

"Well we sure as hell can't keep going like this," he stated. "They'll be specifically looking for us soon, so we can't be anywhere near the road to Torrentcia. The only thing we can do is wait and hide until my father calls them back to lead the army." Ril finally stepped forward then, a building dread in her deep eyes.

"Verix, that thing said that it was going to destroy the west looking for the shard there!" she exclaimed. "What are they going to do?" Verix broke his gaze from Tavin and placed it on the flushed red face to his left.

"You heard him," was the quiet response. "They have been given orders to find that shard by any means necessary. They will."

"So they're just going to destroy innocent towns and villages until they stumble onto it?" she cried, emotion building in her voice. Verix let out a huff.

"Nothing is innocent to them. Everything they find they will destroy." Ril's face went ridged with trepidation. Tavin could see the conflict in her eyes and tried to say something, though he was cut off before he could.

"Well we have to do something!" Verix raised an eyebrow at her.

"And what would you suggest we do, girl?" he asked cruelly. "Race to their rescue and stop an invincible group of undead Dark Mages from wiping out an entire doomed countryside?" Ril glared at him, anger flaring in her movements.

"That's my home you're talking about, Verix!" she cried, extraordinarily upset. She turned to Tavin and locked her eyes onto his. "Tavin, please. We have to do something!"

"Wake up, Arilia," Verix responded for him. "Even if we did go into the west, we are days away and the Dégamar are most likely already there. They are flying. They have enough time to annihilate every last person on the continent by then." Ril wheeled on him angrily.

"You just said that we can't go to Torrentcia City, Verix," she reminded him. "What would you have us do instead? Turn around and go back?" Verix remained silent.

"She has a point there, Verix," Tavin at last entered the conversation. "If we can't go to Torrentcia, we might as well go try to find the other shard before your father does. While we're there we can help what people we can." The Prince locked his frustrated eyes back onto him, obviously unhappy. Though he knew it was pointless, it was the only safe move they had. Moving forward or back in the Grailen was suicide if the Dégamar were looking for them, and traveling east was pointless. Verix breathed hard.

"Just so you're aware, I strongly advise against this," he said. "But if your minds are made up, I will go with you west. The Dégamar will be looking for us now, so we have to stay low until the time comes when they return to Dalastrak." With their guide's approval, Ril turned back to Tavin.

"Tavin?" she asked cautiously. He looked at her delicate form, knowing that she needed his approval as well. He nodded.

"To the west," he agreed.

Chapter 58

Storm on the Horizon

After the Mystic Sage Zeroan had mysteriously left them, Jaren, Parnox, and Kohlin quickly set off, promptly saying goodbye to their cronom friend Yucono and beginning their quick trek out of the Great Forests from Miystridal Village into the plains. Once back into open territory, they moved as fast as possible to reach Torrentcia City. Remembering Zeroan's final words to them, there was no time to lose with the Drakkaidians moving to somehow strike the Southland capital and cripple the Legion once and for all. To stop them and save the Southland, they had to somehow miraculously summon the entire Legion to the city in a matter of days with the Sarton most likely standing in their way. Though aware of the daunting task charged to them, they realized how desperate times had become and pressed onward knowing they had to try their best.

A little over a week since they exited the boundaries of the Great Forests, they found themselves in the wide open rolling plains with nothing but waving grass that seemed to stretch all the way up to the magnanimous silhouettes of the mountains far to the horizon. As the group strode through the beaten path in the grass around them, Jaren found himself in particularly low spirits. Though his goal was clear and focused, he felt as though something was missing. He didn't have to pick his brain too hard to realize what it was. He could freely admit that without his best friend he had felt incomplete for weeks. The two had been together in this adventure since their first encounter with Zeroan months ago, and separated, nothing felt right to him. It was like the entire quest had lost its original meaning.

The Grandarian boy lifted his head as he walked on behind Kohlin and Parnox, shaking off his negative thoughts. He had to force himself to accept that Tavin was on his own with his own problems to deal with, and now so was he. Though depressing, this thought gave Jaren a new sense of purpose. For the first time since they had begun this quest, he was doing something specifically assigned to him, not just backing up Tavin. He had a function apart from his friend. If nothing else, his presence on this journey was completely justified for the first time, and it gave him the strength to stay sharp.

As he trudged on down the path behind the burly Southlander before him, a sudden smell hanging in the air focused his attention out of his daydreaming. Slowing his pace to better analyze the dank odor, Jaren called out to the others.

"Hey, guys?" he called out taking a large sniff of the strange scent again, "do you smell that?" Parnox let out a small huff and turned his head back to the Grandarian.

"Smell what?" he asked perplexed.

"Yes, I can detect something in the air as well," replied Kohlin from the front of the line. "It is a foul stench." Jaren nodded, wincing the muscles in his face as more of the sickening aroma wafted their way.

"Granis on high, what is that?" he asked again, covering his face with his hand. Parnox inhaled deeply himself, at last catching the smell for himself as he took a step back in disgust.

"There must be something rotting not too far off," he commented appalled. As the three scanned their surroundings for the source of the odor, Kohlin at last stopped and let his face loosen.

"I know that smell," he said quietly, causing both Parnox and Jaren to stop and shift their gaze toward him. "That is the stench of death." Jaren nervously raised his brow and stared at him skeptically.

"That would have to be a whole lot of death," he remarked waving the air in his face away. "Where is it coming from?" Kohlin maintained his focused gaze at their environment and at last pointed over to their left.

"There is a depression of rock over there," he observed. "The smell is drifting from that direction. Perhaps we should take a closer look." Parnox rolled his eyes as he repositioned his colossal axe over his shoulder.

"We don't have much time for sightseeing, Kohlin," he reminded him.

"No, I think he's right, Parnox," Jaren chimed in from beside them. "Anything that god-awful out in the middle of nowhere deserves our attention. I say we at least take a look real quick. A couple of minutes aren't going to set us too far back." With an inaudible groan, the brawny woodsman gave in and nodded his head in accord. The three swiftly made their way off the beaten path and into the tall grass around them to the depression in the earth. As they progressed toward it, the smell grew worse, signaling they were indeed on the right track. After bridging the gap between the road and the source of the stench, they at last arrived to look over a small slope and into a little ravine of tall grass.

What they found lying inside, however, was anything but natural. Letting his eyes drift into the ravine, Jaren's jaw dropped and the air in his lungs withdrew. There was an entire Legion patrol lying dead and piled in a bloody heap. Between the overcoming reek of death and appalling view of the blood-soaked bodies strewn in the depression, it was all Jaren could do to suppress the contents of his stomach as he fiercely wheeled around to close off the image from his mind. With more age and stamina for such disturbing tragedies, Parnox and Kohlin stood still.

"What did that!?!" Jaren exclaimed, fighting to keep from vomiting. Parnox shook his head.

"There was a battle," he stated quietly. "They lost." Jaren looked up at him with equal disgust.

"Thanks for bringing some illumination to that question, Parnox," he retorted with angry sarcasm dripping from his voice.

"Look there!" Kohlin shouted, coming to life and leaping to run down the slope. He quickly ran across a few of the dead bodies and knelt down beside the form of a young man, his chest slashed and bleeding. "This one's alive!" Those words prompted even Jaren to conquer his disgust and leapt up to join him. As the trio converged around the dying man, Kohlin knelt to him and lifted his head upright. The figure began to cough up blood, and tried to pull away from him. "Young man, my name is Kohlin Marraea. My friends and I bear you no ill will. We are allies of the Southland and friends of the Legion. Do no be afraid." The man held his gaze for a long moment and at last settled down.

"W-Water," he stammered dripping blood as he spoke. Parnox reached into his satchel and pulled forth a flask of water. Kohlin took hold and brought it to the man's quivering lips. He took a long swallow but ended up spitting most of it up.

"Can you tell me what happened here?" Kohlin asked gently. The man let the flask fall from his mouth as he brought his fearful eyes back up.

"...Help me," he whispered, obviously teetering on the edge of life. Kohlin tried a comforting but weak smile.

"I will do what I can for you, but it is important that you tell me what happened here," he said tenderly. The man was quiet again, but at last nodded and spoke.

"Our patrol f-found a group of marauders m-mobilizing in the plains. We were... g-going to retreat to the capital but a scout f-found us. We were... annihilated."

"Are you sure that it was marauders?" Kohlin asked hurriedly. The man nodded.

"S-Some were dressed as Purging Flame," he confirmed.

"What of the others?" Kohlin pressed.

"There were those who wore... black s-strapped armor over their chests," he stated remembering. "Yes... They had wicked marks on them I have n-never seen..." Kohlin nodded.

"Stay with me, man," he said encouragingly. "Do you know where they are now?" The dying man opened his mouth to speak again, but coughed up more blood instead. Jaren felt horrible for him, knowing full well he had mere moments left.

"...They l-left to the north," he said in a painful whisper. "Hundreds and hundreds..." the man trailed off. Kohlin shot a troubled glace back to Parnox at this.

"Thank you, young man," he said turning back and pausing. "What is your name?" The man cringed again and struggled to respond.

"Kalas Morrol," he stated in a murmur, looking up with a faint smile. "I am going to die, aren't I?" Kohlin paused, at last giving him a faint smile and a single nod. Kalas let out a single laugh, closing his eyes. He slowly raised his hand and dropped it on his chest. "G-Give this to my brother... please..." The young man's grip over the object in his hand loosened and was gone then, along with his life. All three stood in silence for a moment, staring down at the lifeless man. Finally, Kohlin reached into his motionless hand and pulled out a locket of some sort, sealed shut.

"I promise you I will," Kohlin stated with quiet conviction. After another long moment, the Southlander tucked Kalas' arms to his side and rose, placing the object in his pocket. "You know what this means." Parnox nodded his head.

"Drakkaidians," he stated knowingly.

"Montrox must have smuggled some of his army through the border disguised as the Purging Flame and is moving them to strike the capital. We don't know how long they have been moving north, but it cannot have been long if Kalas here was still alive with wounds like those. They are half a day ahead- at most a whole." With that, Kohlin turned and started up the slope behind them. Jaren was filled with disbelief at what they had just learned.

"Wait a minute!" he called. "How could hundreds of Drak soldiers get this far south? And why? Wouldn't it make more sense to attack straight from the north?" Parnox turned to follow Kohlin as he responded.

"Montrox's moves may not make sense to us, but you can bet he's going to have the element of surprise when a couple battalions of Drak soldiers appear from the south," he stated. "This is what Zeroan warned us about. Drakkaidia is about to attack Torrentcia, and if we can't get the entire Legion together in time, they're going to take it. Come on, Grandarian, we've got to move." Though hesitant to just leave a mass grave like this without so much as marking it, Jaren decided that the burly Southlander was right and charged off after him. As he made his way up the slope, he wished more than anything that Tavin was here with him to tell him that everything was going to be fine. Right now, he wasn't so sure.

The Royal castle over Dalastrak shone with illumination as the lightning from the infuriated sky burst down to the ground around it, further scorching the already black countryside. High atop the savage peaks of the castle, six ghastly Valcanor were perched above the balcony outside of the throne room with their riders below. They stood facing the horizon to the south where another of the massive winged creatures materialized from the banks of thunderheads, quickly beating its massive bat-like wings violently to appease its malicious rider. As it came along the wall slowing and rearing back, the black robed figure on its back leapt off and plummeted down to the balcony. It landed mere feet away from the six Dégamar before him, splitting the tiled ground from the force of impact. It rose and brought its eyeless gaze to its kin. As if communicating telepathically, the lone Dégamar gave a silent nod and strode past them into the throne room. Quietly passing through the chamber, the few advisors, guards, and other Dark Mages shot nervous glances at it and each other, aware of what it was.

The King of Drakkaidia, however, was not present in his throne room. The Dégamar knew where he was, though, and moved to the massive doors at the other end of the chamber that lead to the Netherworld Portal. The black figure stopped and raised its hand before them. A subtle burst of force collided with the doors and blew them open, revealing the dark cylindrical chamber within. As the Dégamar stepped through, the doors closed shut behind him. He stopped, once sealed inside, and locked its gaze onto the savagely armor clad Drakkaidian ruler with his back to the door next to the portal. Montrox remained still as he opened his mouth to speak.

"After damaging my balcony and my door," he began with an impassive anger, "you had better have good news." The Dégamar responded in its usual distant and raspy tone of voice.

"*I looked for days without success but eventually found him, Master. He was engaged in a battle with the Warrior of Light*," it began directly. "*He informed me that he was about to destroy him so-*" Montrox immediately raised a fist from his side and opened it above his shoulder, signaling for silence.

"'About to?'" he repeated dramatically. "Why were they not already dead?"

"*He had just finished the battle-*"

"Silence!" Montrox blasted, wheeling around in rage. He paused for a moment, collecting his thoughts. After a long moment he continued. "Where did you find him?"

"*The southwest plains, Master. They moved northeast to the large city*," the demonic mage answered. Montrox remained still for a moment, but a quaking rage began building in his body movements. In the quiet that followed, the Dégamar spoke again. "*He said he would be returning soon.*" Montrox shifted his crimson eyes to the Dégamar and held his gaze for a long moment, before at last turning back to the position he had been in when the Dark Mage entered the chamber.

"No, creature," he said closing his eyes. "My son is not coming back." He exhaled deeply, obviously struggling to come to terms with something. He suddenly leapt across the gap in the floor between the ground and the hovering platform over the portal, then emotion entering his eyes. "If my son was going to kill the Warrior of Light, he would have done so weeks ago when he had the chance in the forests." Montrox rose to the pedestal resting on the platform that held his shard of the Holy Emerald. Reaching into his armor, he pulled forth two more, the ones he had gained from the Mystic Tower. Enmity and hatred were the elements that made up his speech. "My son is not coming back, and he is not going to kill the Warrior of Light. He has betrayed me and is aiding him on his quest to stop me." He stood still for a moment, shaking his head. "You must think I am an idiot, Verix. But you know what I would do now, don't you? So now I will have to do something different."

He piercingly locked his eyes onto the Dégamar, instructing it to get out and wait for its next orders.

"You think you are safe now, don't you, son? You think I'll send the seven to find you and bring you back to me. You think you can hide from them until they have to lead the attack on the Southland. Well you had best think again, because now," he said placing his hands around the two new shards of the Holy Emerald, "I have a way to harness the Warrior of Light's power for my own and bring you back to my way of thinking at the same time." He closed his eyes then and let his dark power flow out onto the three shards over the portal, the entire room coming to life with dark light once again. "You'll regret this, my son. How you'll regret this..."

Chapter 59

<u>Forbidden Feelings</u>

After their encounter with the Dégamar and their decision to move west, the trio gathered their things and began sprinting toward the volcanic mountains on the horizon. Though Tavin and Verix were eager to get clear of the Grailen with the Dégamar sure to be looking for them soon, Ril was the driving force of the party in the days that followed. During their marching in the day and their minimal down time at night, the normally fiery Southlander was as detached and distressed as she had been while still harboring her secret. She preferred to be alone in her worried state, but in the brief time that she permitted him to be with her, Tavin gathered that she was more worked up over the possible threat to her home and family than anything else could ever make her. He could tell that she would like to have talked and even cried whenever he walked with her, to spill her soul out to him once again, but something held her back each time. Though he would have listened and been there for her, he assumed that she just wasn't ready to break down and abandon her persona of independence to him.

In any case, the only thing that he could do was stay with her for when she did want him and hope she would eventually open up. This proved to be a distant wish with Verix constantly lingering by them one second and then completely disappearing the next, forcing Tavin to keep his attention on the Drakkaidian Prince. Walking through the rugged terrain into the basin of the Coron Mountains the day after their clash, however, Tavin realized that Verix had indeed been true to his word so far. If he was only deceiving them and trying to turn them over to his father, he would have done so when the powerful Dégamar had appeared. Instead he had saved them for certain. Though this lowered some of the tension between the two, Tavin and Verix were both still on

445

edge after such a high powered struggle. Ril, however, hardly had time to worry about the Prince and his true motives with her family and home to keep her attention.

After traveling northwest at a rigorous pace for the better part of two days, the trio entered the westland, a sprawling region full of humid green fields and active volcanoes, most notably, Mt. Coron. Coron Village at its foot was the largest and most commonly visited destination in the region. The home of everything from the provisional government of the region to bubbling hot springs from the Elemental Temple of Fire just a few miles up the mountain, it was literally a hotspot of attention. Naturally, this was also the mandatory home of the Warrior of Fire no matter who it was. Tavin remembered the day Ril told him she had been forced to move here after her induction as an Elemental Warrior as a child. She had learned to call the practically tropical village home right away however, as beautiful and rich with life as it was. There was nothing more devastating to her than its endangerment.

Though they could have passed by and checked on several smaller settlements and communities along the way, the Warrior of Fire marched straight past them through the green countryside and rocky patches of mountain to the largest peak on the horizon, Mt. Coron. So far, there appeared to be no damage or sign of hostilities anywhere around them, and Tavin let himself relax somewhat. Ril remained on edge, however, as her home would be the first target of interest for anyone wishing to inflict harm on the west. After they entered the westland, they spent another day moving upward toward the smoldering mountain of fire and the village at its base. Ril no longer needed Verix to guide her, close enough to home to know where she was. This kept them moving at a constant pace, never stopping even for a snack or an extra breath all day long. By that evening, Tavin felt like the muscles on his legs were going to ooze off his bones. Though Verix showed nothing but an impassive lack of concern for anything as usual, Tavin guessed he must have been at least winded no matter what level of stamina he possessed.

It was that evening when the sun began to sink into the clouds along the mountainous horizon casting deep auburn hues across the sky that they finally arrived at the ridge overlooking Coron Village. Though Tavin couldn't imagine taking another hill as steep as the one before was, Ril raced up it with anxiousness consuming her. By this time, the sun had all but disappeared over the ridge, so it was too dark to see much of anything. Thankfully, Ril knew this area like the back of her hand and could navigate them over it. The boys struggled to keep pace with her as she climbed up the steep hill plowing forward at least fifty feet ahead of them. As Tavin took hold of a nearby rock to bolster himself up and onward, he looked up to find that Ril had stopped. She was at the top of the ridge, still except for the soft breeze blowing her flowing red hair and the ends of her wavy skirt. Tavin breathed deeply with relief, guessing she had found her home perfectly safe as she had left it.

As Ril continued just standing still and silent, Tavin made his way up to her. Coming over the top of the ridge, he smiled through the darkness and walked toward her.

"See?" he chimed gladly. "I told you everything would be..." His words trailed off and the rest of his body suddenly froze. Looking down over the ridge was a dark, smoldering image, but it was not the colossal volcano in the background. The entirety of Coron Village from one side of the mountain basin to the other had been utterly destroyed. Charred and still burning in a few sparse areas, the devastation was apparently still fresh. Hardly anything remained intact; it had been torn to pieces. With the glow of orange light from the flame to illuminate what was left of the town, Tavin could only see a handful of structures still in one piece. Besides the slowly dancing fires, the village was devoid of movement. It truly looked dead. He felt his heart sink. Ril's home had been ravaged. Verix emerged from behind them then, slowly turning his head toward the devastation. He frowned and kicked a nearby rock over the ridge, murmuring some Drakkaidian curse under his breath. Tavin could barely bring himself to look at Ril, but forced himself to as the faint sound of her irregular breathing echoed through the night. He slowly turned to find her eyes tightly shut with tears streaming down her cheeks.

He deeply exhaled and took a step toward her, gently putting a hand on her shoulder. She remained still for a moment, but violently shook her head and jerked away from him.

"It can't... I don't... no!" she cried, unable to form the words to speak.

"Ril," Tavin tried to say something but was cut off by her sudden jolt down the ridge toward what was left of her home. As she ran she lit a brilliant flame around her arm to illuminate her way. "Ril!" Tavin called out to her again but she did not look back. He turned back to Verix behind him. "Can you hide that?" The Drakkaidian Prince silently nodded but advised him they should stay with her. He didn't need to be told that, already sprinting off after her into the village. The distraught Warrior of Fire ran into the town amidst the smoldering wreckage of buildings and homes, wild with grief and screaming out for someone to hear her. She ran into one of the few standing structures, but emerged when she found no one inside. She turned to a nearby home still ablaze and threw up her arms to quench the fire with her power, her face wrought with anguish. Tavin and Verix stopped behind her, both unsure of what to do or say. Verix was the first to try.

"Arilia, I can only mask so much of your power," he reminded her. "The building is destroyed; there is nothing more you can do. Let it go-" The girl spun around then, her face filled with fury.

"Let it go?" she repeated at the top of her lungs. "Let it go!?! My home, everyone I have ever loved, everything that ever mattered to me, they are all gone, Verix! My entire life has just disappeared in front of me! Don't tell me..." She couldn't finish, her sorrow far outweighing her anger. The strength keeping her standing gave out and she collapsed to her knees with anguish. She cried harder than Tavin had ever seen anyone cry, her emotion wildly out of control. After a long moment, the Warrior of Light bunched his cape up behind him and knelt down to her, once again putting his hand over her shoulder. She didn't pull away this time, too overcome with grief to do anything but cry. Verix turned and left to observe some of his surroundings for a few minutes, weaving in and out of the rubble and smoldering debris. After having a look around the central village, he came back with his tattered gray coat and fire red hair rustling in the dank breeze. Though aware she didn't care to hear him speak, he crossed his arms and prepared to do so.

"I am sorry this happened, Arilia," he began softly, "but I do not believe that your family and friends have been killed." They both looked up at the Drakkaidian then, confused. "If you calm down and take a good look around, you will notice there is not one body anywhere. When the Black Seven encounter any living creature, they tear it to pieces. This town would be littered with corpses if anyone was here. There is nothing but the remains of buildings- no bodies. They must have somehow known of the threat and left." Ril held his gaze through her tears, slowly letting the words digest. After a long pause, he continued. "Do you know where they may have taken shelter?" She slowly shook her head, still crying hard. Tavin gave her a gentle squeeze.

"Are you sure you don't know where they might be, Ril?" he pressed. The Warrior of Fire pulled away from him then, standing and taking a step back.

"I told you I don't know, Tavin!" she yelled hysterically. She looked him in the eyes, then, seeing his hurt when all he wanted to do was help. A fresh wave of tears streamed from her soaked eyes and she wheeled around to run further into the village, speeding into the darkness toward her home on the hill that she had told him about so long ago. Tavin remained on his knees over the ground, breathing deeply. He shook his head and looked up to Verix, unmoved with arms crossed.

"I don't believe any of this. How could this happen?" Verix shrugged.

"I told you," he said blankly, "my father is insane. He has become a monster that will do anything for power. We probably passed at least three or four other village either identical to this or worse on our way here." Tavin closed his eyes and slammed his fist into the ground, overwhelmed with anger.

"So what do we do now?" he asked annoyed. "Does this mean he has the missing shard?" Verix closed his eyes for a moment, searching. He opened them and nodded.

"It appears my father wants the Dégamar with him instead of looking for us. They are assembled in Drakkaidia already," he reported. "It would be safe to assume that, yes."

"So he's got two now?" Tavin asked with dread. Verix's face was grave.

"Four, I would guess," he corrected. "Remember the two shards in the Mystic Tower? Three of the seven were in that area but have returned as well. They would not have done so if their mission was incomplete. He also owns the shard in Galantia. When he is ready, he will acquire that as well." Tavin could feel his heart dropping again.

"So what does that mean for us?" he asked. Verix shook his head.

"Problems," he stated quietly. "With his power over the Netherworld quadrupled, the restrictions of how many demons he can summon to our world are all but gone and now he will begin building his army. One way or another, the end is coming." Tavin held his gaze, helplessness filling his body.

"So what do we do now?" he repeated. Verix turned and let his arms fall to his sides, turning to walk away.

"Rest," he said. "I'm going to the three villages I know we passed to see what the situation looks like there. I'll be back by morning. There are details I need to acquire." Tavin looked at him incredulously.

"And what am I supposed to do in the meantime?" he called out aggravated, rising back to his feet.

"I think you know what you should be doing, Grandarian," the Prince called back, disappearing in the night. Tavin stared out into the darkness after he was gone, once again not quite sure what the Drakkaidian Prince was about. Deciding that he was right, however, Tavin turned back to the hillside where Ril had disappeared. Though she was obviously too distraught to talk, he knew that he at least had to try. So tightening the belt holding the Sword of Granis at his side, the Warrior of Light pointed the light from the Granic Crystal at its hilt before him. He began walking though the ruin and destruction of Coron Village, remorseful such a beautiful, peaceful setting had met with such a dark fate. As he marched up the hillside, he was at least eased by the knowledge that the people of the village had somehow escaped. That was what really mattered, after all.

At the top of the hillside, what Tavin guessed to be Ril's home stood slightly charred and smashed up, but still intact. There were trees surrounding it, and in the daylight it would have surely been a beautiful sight. He slowly strode forward, nervous of what he was going to say when he found her. Ril was unpredictable when upset. She had emptied herself to him before, but now she didn't want him anywhere near her. He stepped onto an unsteady porch and moved to the splintered front door, but heard a sound to his left that drew his attention away. The faint muffle of crying could be heard, but not from inside. He moved from the front door to the left side of the house and peered around the corner to find Ril collapsed on the ground by a hulking tree in a small grassy meadow. It was compressed by the tree line around it, but with the warm orange light from the small fire that she had made in front of her he could see it was full of flowers and a diverse array of organic life.

Tavin took a deep breath and stepped off of the porch, moving toward the girl and her small fire at the end of yard. As he approached, he could hear she was still weeping but appeared to have calmed herself substantially. She sat with her back to him, hunched over her little flame with her teary eyes open. She could hear the Grandarian boy's footsteps and knew it was him, but didn't move. When only a few steps away, Tavin stopped and collected his thoughts one last time. At last he gave up trying to formulate some grand speech and placed his hands over his belt, sharply exhaling.

"I know it can't mean much from me," he started, staring into the ground between them, "but I'm sorry this happened. I won't tell you that I know how you feel because I don't, but I can guess what this place meant to you from hearing you talk about it and I know it's the worst." He paused for a moment, letting his conscience mind drift a little and his thoughts just come out how they were. "Sometimes, things like this happen and people are destroyed by them. Something you care for more than anything is taken from you and it's hard to forget or move on. I've seen people lose things important to them and never be the same again. But not you, Ril. I know you must not want to keep going on this stupid quest anymore, but I also know that you're too strong a person to give up. I've seen you cope with and overcome impossible odds that would toss most people up for life, but not you. Homes can be repaired, Ril. Entire villages can be rebuilt and be even better than before. But the most important thing is that your family and friends are safe somewhere. Verix is out looking for them right now, and we're going to find them."

The Warrior of Light stopped again, observing that the girl had gotten quiet. "I won't try and justify this for you, Ril; telling you that it was a necessary sacrifice for what we're doing. It wasn't. Montrox did this out of blind hatred and greed, and he isn't going to get away with it. I promise you he's going to pay. And after he's gone, the first thing I'm going to do is come back here and help you repair. I promise." Ril still remained motionless, giving Tavin the feeling this was not the time for what he was saying. He brought his eyes back to her and let his arms fall in sorrow and defeat. "I'm really sorry, Ril. I know this is hard and I understand that you don't want to talk. If you do, though, I'll be here." He slowly spun his head away then and shifted his feet, preparing to start back to the house. As he turned, he heard Ril's shaking voice emerge, weighed down with grief.

"I remember when I was a little girl," she murmured suddenly, catching him off guard. He turned his head back to her, patiently waiting. She remained at rest as she quietly continued. "My father and I moved into this house the summer I was anointed the Warrior of Fire. I remember spending nights out in this tree when it was warm enough to sleep in. I used to pretend I was a guardian on some grand mission to protect it." She ran her soft fingers up the bark on the trunk, seared and scarred with blackness from the fire she had just extinguished over it. "Then I did go on a quest to protect it; it and everything else. But look what's happened. It was destroyed anyway. What does that mean, Tavin?" He stared at her slender form a moment longer, watching her rest her hand over the tree. Finally he turned back and strode beside her, kneeling down to her level. He raised his hand and gently took hold of her shoulder. She slowly turned her head toward him, meeting his gaze.

"It means you're still human, Ril," he whispered with confidence. She tightened her eyes, unsure of what he meant. "You may be one of the most powerful people in the world, but even you can't be everywhere to protect everything at once. You're independence is the best thing about you, Ril, but sometimes, even though we'd like to, we just can't do everything. We're fighting a war here, and in war there are sacrifices. That's just the way it is. But as long as we stay true to what we believe and never give up, we won't ever lose." Ril was frozen, completely taken aback that the Grandarian boy could say something so grand so causally just to make her feel better. She held his gaze as he comfortingly passed his fingers along her cheek to wipe her tears. Losing herself in the emotions she had fought so viciously to suppress the past weeks, she began to lean in close to the boy. Tavin withdrew his hand from her face, now unsure of what to say. Ril started first.

"You know what the best thing about *you* is?" she asked. There was virtually no trace of sorrow or grief left in her voice, but she was still shaking all the same. Tavin was the one to be speechless now, curious what she was going to say as she continued to inch toward him. "That every time I feel like the world is going to cave in around me and that there is no reason to keep going, you're there to help me up and make everything worth fighting for again. ...I feel like I'm completely safe with you no matter what. There is no one on in all of Iairia that I would rather have with me than you." By this time she had come within a fraction of an inch of Tavin's face, but contrary to what he thought he should be feeling, he was strangely calm and secure with her. She took his hand from his side, covering it in hers.

"There is something that I've been wanting to tell you for weeks now, but I didn't think I could until now. I thought that I was in love with you for a long time, but I know that isn't true... I know I am." Another tear that had formed in the corner of her eye streamed down her cheek. "If I could only have one thing in the entire world after all this is over, it would be that you would love me too." She stared into his deep blue eyes, seeing them mirrored with wonder. He couldn't believe what he had just heard, but he was euphoric all the same. He couldn't help but smile as he brought his hand encased with Ril's back up to her face to wipe away one last tear.

"If it's alright with you, I don't want to wait until this is all over to do that," he said softly. Her eyes widened, taken aback by what he said. Tavin gulped and tried to organize the raw thoughts spinning around in his mind he so desperately wanted to say. "Since this started, you've given me the strength to be more than I thought I could be. Believe me when I say that I wouldn't have made it this far if it wasn't for you. And now- after all we've been through- every time I have to think about why I'm doing this and what it's is all for, the first thing that enters my mind is you." She held his gaze intensely, not sure if what he was saying could be real. "I love you too, Arilia Embrin." Ril's face was still at first, an overpowering rapture filling the emptiness left from her sorrow. Her breathing quickly became fast and heavy, new emotion rushing through every cell in her body. It was in this moment that the overcome girl pulled forward closing the small gap between them and gently put her lips onto his. She touched him soft and slow at first, but Tavin gradually closed his eyes and gently pulled her closer, kissing back. Ril ardently reached up and draped her arms around his neck.

After the passionate exchange was over, they both gingerly pulled back to a few inches away from each other and came together in a tight embrace over the organic earth beneath them. The two remained together silently staring at the small fire until they at last fell asleep in each other's arms. Before losing herself to her dreams, Ril remembered the warning Zeroan had given her about what she was now doing. Though she knew she was directly disobeying him, in the warmth of the Grandarian boy's arms, she didn't care.

Chapter 60

<u>Shadow of a Hero</u>

The sun rose with difficulty the next morning, clouds blotting half the sky to hide its radiant light. As the little warmth that did manage to make its way through the billowing obstacles in the sky fell onto Tavinious Tieloc's face, his eyes slowly came open, finding a mess of slurring images before him. The first one he identified was Ril, lying next to him with one arm over his chest and the other tucked into her side. Her flowing crimson hair was tangled in a mess around her, falling everywhere from Tavin's torso to the ground beneath them. As his eyes came into focus, he could see she was awake and had a quiet, modest smile on, staring intently at him.

"Good morning," she said softly, her coy little smile stretching wider. Tavin smiled back and silently chuckled.

"Good morning," he repeated, the lingering sleep still intertwined in his voice. "How long have you been awake?"

"A little while," she answered tenderly, tilting her head.

"What have you been doing?" he asked. Ril shrugged.

"Watching you sleep," she stated factually, her smile only growing. Tavin raised an eyebrow.

"What...?" he groaned dramatically, to which she giggled. Tavin propped himself up on his elbow, pulling free his other hand trapped underneath Ril to rub his drowsy eyes awake. After sleeping on the ground all night in his clothes and armor, he felt a little stiff. "I think I can say for certain that you have one of the most uncomfortable yards in Iairia." She giggled again, once more resting her head over his upper body.

"So what should we do now?" she asked peacefully. Tavin yawned and stopped to collect his thoughts, looking around the organic meadow they lay in. As thoughts of their current situation came flowing into his mind, the first thing he remembered was their third party member not with them.

"Well first off, I think we should go find Verix," he stated. "He said he would be back by morning, and he might have learned something about the villagers." As mention of her friends and family came up, Ril raised her head, nodding.

"Right," she agreed, looking suddenly hopeful but detached. Seeing the conflict still present in her eyes, Tavin reached over and brushed a lock of her fiery hair away from her face and behind her ear.

"Hey, they're going to be fine," he told her with assurance in his voice, to which she looked up at him with encouraged eyes.

"I'm so glad I have you with me," she said sincerely, leaning forward to gently kiss him. As she pulled back, he smiled again. After hurriedly stretching out his legs, he quickly jumped to his feet pulling Ril up behind him. She ran her fingers through her dense hair, untangling it as best she could while Tavin tried to straighten his now creased and wrinkled cape they had used as a blanket. Taking her hand, they began to walk back through the meadow toward the house. As they casually strolled, she told him that at least now she would be able to change her clothes and repair her mangled hair inside her house. Tavin shook his head and told her that her hair was always beautiful. She grinned but thoroughly rejected the compliment. Walking past the house and the porch, Tavin suggested they move back into the village to look for Verix. His idea was precluded by the rustling of cloth from behind them. He quickly spun around with his hand moving to the Sword of Granis, but eased it back as the source of the noise came into view.

"Catch you off guard, Grandarian?" asked Verix, impassive as always. Tavin frowned.

"Yes actually," he admitted grouchily. "I just don't take chances with the unknown anymore." Verix nodded as he thrust his body off the railing he leaned against, his frayed coattails chafing against it.

"A wise policy," he affirmed indifferently. His eyes drifted over to the Warrior of Fire and down to her hand in Tavin's. "Feeling better, Miss Embrin?" His question actually hinted a touch of concern. Ril silently nodded.

"That depends on what you have to tell me," she said, avoiding any conversation other than the whereabouts of her fellow villagers. Verix noiselessly chuckled, aware she didn't want him prying.

"Then I can lay the bulk of your concerns to rest," he reported getting back to the subject. "I backtracked to three villages we passed yesterday. Of them, only one had been attacked by the Dégamar; the rest were unharmed. All of them, however, were empty, leading me to believe some sort of evacuation warning was issued before the seven arrived. How, you could probably guess better than I, but they were completely empty. I did manage to find one stubborn old man in the southernmost village that remained behind. He informed me that the others of his village had fled into the mountain pass next to Coron leading to the village on the other side of the mountain."

"Fireite," Ril breathed, relief overcoming her. "I forgot that we have an evacuation plan in order if the volcano ever becomes too active." Verix nodded.

"Yes. In any case, I would guess that your family is perfectly safe," he inferred crossing his arms. Ril nodded as well, releasing Tavin's hand to step forward.

"Thank you, Verix. You didn't have to go out of your way like that. I really do appreciate it." Verix shrugged, turning his gaze out to the cloudy horizon.

"It was nothing," he replied with apathy. "I was primarily looking for information on the Dégamar. It was just a..."

He trailed off then, his brow furrowing.

Slowly letting his arms drop down to his sides, the Drakkaidian Prince sporadically spun his head around in every direction, wildly scanning the environment around him. Ril looked up in frightened confusion, unsure of what had so suddenly alarmed him.

"Verix, what's wrong?" she asked hastily. He didn't respond at first, dashing to the far side of the porch to look over its side.

"There's something here," he responded at last, quiet urgency in his voice.

"One of those Dégamar things?" she asked, suddenly afraid. Verix shook his head, bringing his body back toward Ril.

"No. I'm not sure, but..." Verix was cut off by a sudden jet of wind exploding out in all directions from behind Ril. She immediately wheeled around, ready to defend herself. Only Tavin was behind her, walking forward. She looked back at

Verix, puzzled. She was about to ask him what he was going to say, but Tavin suddenly placed his hand on her shoulder and harshly spun her around toward him. She looked up at him confused.

"Tavin, what are you doing?" she asked angrily. Verix's eyes exploded open then, realizing what was happening. As quickly as he could, the Drakkaidian ran forward and leapt off the porch toward the two, pulling back his fist. As he came flying over the railing, he threw it forward, ramming it across the Warrior of Light's face and sending him flying several feet back. Ril looked up at him horrified, but ran to Tavin's side before the Prince could grab her.

"Ril don't!" he yelled. Kneeling down to Tavin, she called back to Verix out of control.

"What do you think you're-" It was too late. Before Ril could so much as finish her sentence, Tavin's hand came flying up from his side to take hold of the girl's neck. Immediately after, he threw her back into Verix, causing them to both collide with the wall of her house, falling to the ground. Ril was confused out of her mind, watching Tavin leap back to his feet and draw the Sword of Granis. As its metallic ringing sliced through the air, she wildly turned to Verix already back on his feet. "Verix, what is going on!?! What's wrong with him?" Materializing his savage broadsword from behind him, Verix grit his teeth and shook his head.

"That isn't Tavin anymore," he breathed with contempt. "It's a Shadow."

"What are you talking about? What do you mean a shadow?" Verix pointed over to his face.

"Look at his eyes, Ril," he ordered. She did as she was told and quickly saw that something was indeed wrong. The Grandarian's eyes were completely layered in black. "He's been possessed." She rose to her feet frantically.

"What do you mean, possessed?" she pressed hysterically. "What is a Shadow?"

"It's a demon of the Netherworld," he answered icily. "It takes possession of a body and then relinquishes control over to its master." Verix looked back at her, enmity in his dark eyes. "My father has control of Tavin." Ril could feel her heart saturated with agony as it sank into the pit of her stomach. At last she was closer to Tavin than ever before, but they had been separated once again.

"What do we do, Verix?" she asked painfully. He clenched his fists around the hilt of his sword and let a burst of his dark power flare up around him.

"We have to stop him," he said purposefully. As the aura of black energy came to life around him, he turned his head back to Ril. "Listen carefully. He is still conscience in his mind but he can't physically control himself. He's going to be coming at us with everything he's got. We can't attack him, or we could kill the demon *and* Tavin. We have to go straight to the source." Before he could say another word, the possessed Warrior of Light lunged at him with his own field of radiating power bursting around him. Taking hold of Ril and leaping to the right, Verix barely managed to avoid a downward slash of the Sword of Granis, slicing through the side of the girl's porch like it was nothing but air. "You have to attack his shadow, Ril! I'll keep him busy and try to slow him down for you! Hurry!"

Touching back down to the earth, Verix quickly released her and shot to his side to meet the oncoming Grandarian. As their blades clashed, a wave of force exploded out almost knocking Ril to her feet. She kept her eyes on them as best she could, but they moved so fast back and forth across her yard that she could barely keep track of either of their bodies, much less their shadows. She grit her teeth with determination, flurries of passionate flame enveloping over her fists. As if losing Tavin was not bad enough, if Valif Montrox gained control of him there would be no one to stand up to him. She had to stop him and free the Warrior of Light. She charged forward, trying her best to keep up with the two giants of power. While Ril chased after them, Verix struggled to defend himself against the lightning quick slashes from the Sword of Granis. He parried as best he could but with Tavin's assault so quick and relentless, he didn't have the time to muster his energy.

Several minutes into the battle, Ril managed to let off a ball of fire between the two, forcing Tavin back. Utilizing this opportunity to charge his power, Verix kicked off the mound of earth he stood on and threw his elbow into Tavin's chest. This time the Warrior of Light was blasted back against the side of the house. Stunned, Ril threw an arm out to blast another fireball toward his shadow lying vulnerable in front of him. As it sped toward it target, however, the billowing masses above them finally moved in front of the sun, cutting off its light. The moment Ril's attack struck the ground, the shade disappeared. Verix cursed and readied himself for battle once again as the Warrior of Light's black eyes opened once more, still possessed by the demonic creature. Ril chaotically turned back to Verix.

"His shadow is gone! Now what?" she called desperately. Verix didn't have the time to respond as Tavin came blasting up to him savagely swinging the Sword of Granis. Verix was amazed at the brute force behind his attack, and barely managed to parry his attack away. With the Prince left in a vulnerable unbalanced state afterwards, Tavin threw his knee up into his gut, hammering the wind out of him. Dazed and incapacitated, it was all Verix could do to brace for the oncoming blow to his head, sending him careening backward into the trunk of a tree. The bark split from the force of his collision with its brittle surface. Verix fell to his knees in debilitation and leaned his weight on his sword, struggling to catch his breath. With the Drakkaidian Prince out of action, the Shadow turned Tavin back to face Ril, uncertainly standing behind him. With her target gone, she had no idea what to do. She might be able to at least slow him down enough for Verix to reenergize himself and begin the fight again, but it would mean hurting Tavin as well. Ril wanted to curse herself for even thinking that.

The possessed Warrior of Light began striding toward her with his power beginning to seal, obviously not viewing the frightened girl as any real threat. As he approached, Ril stood her ground, desperately groping for an idea. Only one came to mind, though she knew it would yield no results.

"Tavin," she started with fear in her voice, "Tavin you've got to come out of this. I know you can still hear me somewhere in there, and you can't do this. Please, Tavin, you have to fight it. Otherwise you're going to let Montrox win. You promised me you wouldn't let him, remember? Tavin, please, wake up!" Verix struggled to lift himself by the tree line, opening his mouth to speak.

"Ril, it will do you no good!" he managed, trying to rise. "No one can control themselves when a Shadow has possession of them. You have to fight him!" Ril violently shook her head no.

"I won't hurt him!" she yelled back, more frustrated with her situation than Verix. "There has to be a way to..." She stopped there, remembering her target and what it took to draw it out. As Tavin extended his arm out to grab her, Ril coiled back and summoned her elemental power at full strength. The quick layer of flame around her fists erupted outward around her entire frame to form a towering inferno in a matter of seconds, instantly igniting the surrounding vegetation and forcing the Warrior of Light back. "Verix! Get ready because it's coming!" she bellowed through the wall of flame between them. The Prince didn't understand at first, but as he watched Ril's firestorm intensify by the second, he realized what she was doing. With every moment that passed, the light from her fire became brighter and brighter until Tavin had to shield his eyes with his forearm and take a step back to avoid the heat. So brilliant was the fire's light that it cast a shadow of the Warrior of Light behind him, stretching back all the way to Verix.

As the passionate blaze reached the pinnacle of its power, the Drakkaidian Prince charged back up to his feet with his sword pointed downward in his hands and lunged forward. Raising the blade above his head, he soared above the shadow lying behind Tavin and plummeted it into its center. The moment he stabbed through, the demonic creature inside Tavin surged outward in pain. Verix's mighty broadsword kept it pinned to the earth beneath it, and in its struggle to free itself the demon retreated out of Tavin's body. As the evil spirit withdrew, Tavin's eyes closed shut and he collapsed to the earth, motionless. The moment he fell, Ril released her own power and quickly dissipated the enormous inferno around her to rush down to his side. With the fire gone, Verix let his arm previously guarding his eyes fall to his side. Below him the black pool of shade known as a Shadow violently fought to free itself from the object pinning it down.

Verix released his hold on his weapon and slowly turned his head to Ril, wiping a streaming trickle of blood from the corner of his mouth away. Sensing his eyes upon her, Ril shifted her gaze to meet his, then down to the demonic creature thrashing about on the earth.

"Why isn't it dead?" she asked perturbed. Verix merely extended his arm toward her, opening his hand.

"Give me his sword," he commanded quietly through his heavy breathing. Ril was still, but studied his weary face for a moment and nodded. She gingerly set Tavin's head in her lap and turned to pick up the enormously heavy Sword of Granis beside him on the ground. She passed it to Verix, summoning all her strength to lift it. He took it quickly, also struggling to lift the burden despite his incredible power. Somehow, only Tavin could wield it with any speed. He didn't hold on long, quickly forcing its sacred blade alongside his into the earth and the demon. As it made contact with the unholy being, the Granic Crystal burst awake with light and the Shadow seemed to shriek out like a Valcanor, erratically exploding with life. Its eerily black mass quickly cracked and seeped open with golden illumination, transforming into a pool of oozing light and evaporating. After a few moments of staring at it with wonder, both Verix and Ril watched as the last remnant of the Shadow's form dissipated into the air.

Once gone, the Drakkaidian Prince breathed deeply and quickly rubbed the hand he had used to pick up the Sword of Granis on his gray coat, leaving behind a trail of blood. Ril's brow furrowed, confused.

"Are you alright?" she asked worriedly. The Drakkaidian Prince shoved his hand into his pocket and used the other to wrench his broadsword from the earth, dematerializing it in its cloud of crimson mist a moment later. Once gone, he nodded with a grunt.

"I'll be fine," he replied deeply, still out of breath. "How is he?" Ril looked back down to the motionless Warrior of Light.

"I was hoping you would tell me," she responded worried. "He's not moving and he's hardly breathing." Verix nodded, shifting his feet toward them.

"That should be normal," he stated emotionless. "We successfully removed the demon, so he should just need some rest and he'll recover." As she nodded and tried to lift him up, Verix bent down and put a hand on her shoulder. "I'll take him. You get the sword." Ril gave him a peculiar look, searching his fatigued eyes.

"Why did it hurt you, Verix?" she asked looking at his bloody hand again. He leaned over and took hold of Tavin, standing and lifting him over his shoulder. As he turned for the house, he softly replied.

"I may be fighting with Grandarians for the moment," he began, "but that sword doesn't care. I'm just a Drakkaidian to it, and it responded accordingly." Verix took a slow step forward and made his way for the porch then, leaving Ril behind with the Grandarian talisman still embedded in the earth.

Chapter 61

<u>Besieged</u>

"What in the name of Granis is taking him so long?" Jaren asked with nervous impatience flaring in his hushed voice. He and Parnox were huddled together in the thick drooping branches of a willow tree in the central Torrentcia territories of the Southland, only a few miles away from the capital city itself. The burly Southlander uncomfortably shifted his crouched legs and rested his back against the thick trunk.

"He said he might be a good while," Parnox pointed out in a whispered tone of his own. Jaren narrowed his eyes and shook his head.

"It's been way past an hour now," he grilled. "Kohlin said he was just going for a peek. The Purging Flame... or Drak troops... or whoever's out there, probably found him out. He takes too many risks when he goes snooping around." It was Parnox's turn to shake his head, giving the easterner more credit than Jaren.

"You know he's better than that," he admonished, frustrated. "He's still out there somewhere." Kohlin had left almost two hours previous to scout out the area around Torrentcia City. The trio had followed the veritable army of marauders that massacred the patrol of Legionnaires they had found two days ago all the way to the city. With a fresh trail of death and destruction in their wake, they were never more than a day behind. They had arrived at the outskirts of the city that morning, taking shelter from enemy scouts in a thick willow behind a small ridge in the rolling wetland's hills. Though Jaren knew and was confident of his ally's skills and capabilities, two hours' wait for him to discover what he could have in ten minutes was too much to take. Something must have happened.

As the Grandarian archer was about to stand and demand they go looking for him, a sudden rustling of leaves from the edges of the massive willow drew their attention. They both spun their heads to find a figure cloaked in black entering the branches around them, his face hidden under a hood. When Parnox immediately reached for his gargantuan axe resting on the ground beside him, the figure threw up a hand defensively.

"Easy, friend," he spoke rapidly, "it's only me." He reached up with his opposite hand and hurriedly withdrew his hood to reveal his face. It was Kohlin. Parnox breathed deeply and dropped his weapon to the ground.

"What are you doing sneaking up on us in black robes?" he asked with annoyance. "I was about to spilt you down the middle." Kohlin only smiled, removing his dark attire and crouching down next to the two.

"Sorry, but I ran into some trouble back there and needed to be as discreet as possible," he stated exhaling. Jaren nodded.

"I knew it," he mumbled. "What happened? What does it look like out there?" Kohlin dramatically shook his head, an overwhelmed expression upon his face.

"It isn't very pretty," he began quietly. "Kalas was all too right. There are three battalions of Drakkaidian troops completely surrounding the city- just outside the range of the longbow. If they were dressed as the Purging Flame at one time, their need for secrecy is evidently over. All of them are boasting black armor covered in Drakkaidian glyphs. I managed to knock out a lone scout above this ridge and steal his apparel, so I made my way up to the soldiers to try and get some information. Believe it or not, they aren't going to do anything yet. They are just here to hold the city secure and make sure that no Legionnaires try to get in or out. A blockade." Jaren's brow furrowed, confused.

"You mean they aren't going to attack at all?" he asked bewildered.

"How do you think they would go about doing that, Jaren?" Parnox answered. "Remember, this city is made to repel invaders. There may not be many Legionnaires inside the city, but there are enough to shower the Draks with arrows if they get too close, and storming it is not an option when they have to circle the city to make their way to the gates." Though he admitted what the Southlander said made sense, Jaren still remained unconvinced. It wasn't like Montrox or any Drakkaidian to simply stand around outside an enemy fortress not doing anything. There must be some hidden purpose behind this action, he thought.

"If you'd be so good as to let me finish what I was saying, you two," Kohlin began again, "the Drakkaidians aren't here to take the city- only to secure it. Apparently, Montrox is marshalling another army even as we speak, and it's comprised of demons. They will be here in a matter of days to destroy the city. Then the soldiers will move in and kill anything not already dead." Jaren felt his heart sink. He remembered his encounters with just a few demons and how he had barely survived. What could they do against an army of them?

"Wait a minute," he thought. "I thought Zeroan said that Montrox couldn't summon more than a handful of those things at one time. Are you saying he's gotten his hands on more shards of the Holy Emerald?" Kohlin paused, not having thought of that. At last he swallowed and nodded.

"So it would appear," he managed. "I wonder if Montrox's son found the shard we missed in the south." Parnox put his foot down and shook his head.

"Worrying about the shards won't do us any good now, will it?" he asked them impatiently. "We have no control over the safety of the shards, so let's focus on our own business- like how we're going to get through three battalions of Drak soldiers and into the city." Kohlin looked at him uncertainly.

"That, I can't answer for you," he confessed. "The commander of this crowd has strict orders to not let anyone in or out. Getting by him will be no easy task. They caught onto me when I started asking too many questions and I was forced to retreat. I hid in another willow until I saw a passing wagon of fleeing merchants. That's where I got this cloak. Even if we do somehow manage to penetrate the blockade, however, there is still the matter of the long road to the gates with enemies at our backs. The Drakkaidians will not throw their lives away chasing us in a maelstrom of arrows from the walls, but they certainly won't let us by unchecked. I don't see a way through." In the silence that followed, Jaren silently brainstormed. There was no way that they would be able to fight through them. There were hundreds of troops surrounding the entire city, and these were sure to be Montrox's finest. The only other option was stealth. But with the entire perimeter surrounded, how could they slip by undetected? Chewing on this idea, the Grandarian's eyes fell upon the black cloak around Kohlin's feet. His eyes narrowed as sparks began to fly inside his head. After carefully studying the cloak for another minute and mulling over his thoughts, he at last nodded and spoke.

"I think I have an idea," he smirked.

Underneath the overcast sky above the besieged Torrentcia City, a single Drakkaidian soldier at the rear of the blockade slowly shifted his eyes from where they gazed at the walled capital on the plateau. Noticing a movement at a side-glance, he casually but curiously altered his view to better observe it. As he fully rotated his head around, however, the man's already frowning face was overcome with disgusted disbelief. Despite their sincerest efforts to frighten any and all Southlanders away from the proximity of the capital, three lone figures were steadily marching toward the Drakkaidian troops. The most noticeable was the gigantic man at the front, tightly wrapped in black robes. Striding behind him were two smaller bodies with hands behind their back. Though he could not be sure, it appeared to the soldier that their hands were bound.

Shaking his head incredulously he turned and slapped another soldier's arm. As he heatedly turned around, the first soldier pointed down the path where the three figures strode toward them. As the two Drakkaidians began alerting their comrades of the approaching trio, the first of the smaller figures behind the darkly robed form discreetly raised his eyes to briefly scan into the ranks of men.

"Here we go," he whispered to the larger form. "Remember to be brutal, Parnox. They will certainly do you the same. Are my swords still secure in there?"

"And Jaren's bow," he whispered back from under his draping hood, subtly patting a bulging area in the back of his robes. "I don't know how you talked us into this, Jaren." Marching behind Kohlin, Jaren couldn't help but smile.

"I think I'm going to enjoy this," he mumbled to himself. Kohlin's eyes narrowed.

"Keep focused," he admonished. "This isn't going to be easy." The Grandarian archer only chuckled to himself, trying to hide his smile. What they were about to do was dangerous beyond belief; suicidal. Marching straight through three battalions of Drakkaidian soldiers and trying to fool them all. It was clever to be sure, but it could hardly be called genius.

As the three moved up the hill within twenty feet of the first lines of Drakkaidians, the ominous sound of dozens of swords being drawn filled the air. Jaren swallowed hard, losing a bit of confidence. There was no turning back now. If the Draks didn't buy it, they couldn't run away. The first black clad soldier to speak was a filthy, obviously war torn man pointing his sword straight out at Parnox, not feet away. It was the moment of truth.

"Just who the hell do you think you-" The man wouldn't get the chance to finish. The burly figure in black slapped the flat side of his weapon aside and boomed him voice out at him.

"You dare to address your weapon to a Dark Mage!?!" he bellowed with rage. The befuddled soldier and the others around him ready to pounce abruptly froze, shocked at the figure's revelation. Jaren could see nervous conflict in all of their eyes, and rows of more soldiers from beyond and around them were turning to observe the cause of the apparent dilemma. They all remained on edge and armed, however. In the uncertainty that followed, Parnox seized on their hesitation. "What in the name of Drakkan are you fools doing? Are you going to stand there all day like a swarm of idiots or are you going to push your filthy corpses out of my way so I can pass?" The first soldier swallowed hard and nervously spoke up.

"We were told the mages would be arriving with the demons..." he trailed off indecisively, observing the impatience in the figure's body movements.

"Master Montrox sent me in advance," he explained intolerantly. "I am here to take command of this group. Clear a path." The soldiers slowly shot unsure glances at each other before hesitantly stepping aside. Parnox could feel the Drakkaidians scrutinizing him, obviously not convinced.

"Where is your demon creature, mage?" one of the men asked hesitantly. Parnox wheeled to where the voice came and threw a powerful punch to drop the man to the earth.

"Do you question me?" he asked indignantly. "The demons gather in Dalastrak. None can be spared for my transportation. I arrived by means of conventional beast."

"Wait, mage!" the first man to speak called. "We have been given strict orders to kill all Southlanders. Who are these two?" Parnox shifted his icy gaze to the man and took hold of Kohlin's bonds.

"They are captured Legionnaires that are going to help us prepare for the coming battle with their knowledge of the interior of this city. They stay with me. Now *make way*!" In the wake of the black figure's fury, no other soldier spoke. They quickly parted as the three figures passed through them, afraid, but obviously still doubtful. The further they passed into the ranks, the more skeptical and distrustful the faces of the Drakkaidians grew. Jaren knew them well enough to know they would rather kill both he and Kohlin for their mere existence than have to suffer their presence.

After a painfully long duration walking through hundreds of Drakkaidians brandishing scowls and sword points in their direction, Parnox at last pushed his way through to the front line, slowing to scan the area for the commanding officer. He found him with relative ease, standing by a small makeshift command tent with a collection of black armored horses around him. The fake mage pressed toward him at an enterprising pace, aware he was arousing more suspicion with every passing second. There was a man standing beside a tabletop map of the central Southland layered in thick black armor from head to toe. He was a large man, but Parnox was still larger and the commander looked up with surprise as he arrived before him. A look of loathsome anger overtook the commander's face as he stiffened and placed a hand on the hilt of his broadsword.

"And just who are you?" was his caustic question. From the tone of his voice alone, Parnox gathered this man was battle-hardened and fearless, and would not be so easily convinced to accept his authority.

"I am sent by Master Montrox himself," Parnox began equally heated, "so watch your tongue if you wish to keep it in your mouth. I am a Dark Mage, and I am here to take command of these battalions." The commander glared at him with hatred pouring from his eyes and moved around the table to face him.

"Well that's quite the order you have there, mage," he began sarcastically. "I'm glad to make your acquaintance. Now do you know who I am?" Parnox's frown deepened, feeling like his words had been ineffective on the man. "I am Battalion

Commander Nerkott, and I was personally placed in charge of this operation by Master Montrox. I was not informed of a Dark Mage arriving prematurely." Jaren and Kohlin could hear the soldiers around them whispering to each other.

"Perhaps that is because the decision was made after you left Dalastrak," Parnox continued, trying his best to remain furious. "You may not have been informed, but here I am. So stand down, Battalion Commander." The man's face was quiet with emotion for a moment, searching for some answer underneath Parnox's hood. After a long silence, the man smiled.

"Forgive me, but I do not recognize your voice, mage," he politely said. "This is embarrassing and strange to me, because I am familiar with every one of the current twenty-three mages. Can you explain this to me, mage?" Parnox's eyes rapidly shifted between the commander and the rows of Drakkaidians edging toward him. Their plan had failed. Parnox knew this man did not believe him. "I think I can. What if I was to say that you are not a Dark Mage? What if I was to say that you are a lying enemy spy? Because that is what I am saying." The rows of soldiers began drawing their weapons, slowly circling them. Kohlin and Jaren shot deathly worried glances at each other. The Battalion Commander smiled his twisted smile and took a step forward with his blade unfastened from his side. "Prove me wrong, mage! Use your magic to kill me if I am wrong. Go on, kill me, mage!"

So that's what Parnox did.

In one fluid motion, the burly Southlander clenched his fist, rotated it back, and threw it into the man's unprotected face with such power that his neck snapped in two with an audible cracking of bones. As soon as he hit the ground, Parnox reached for his robes and threw them off, exposing all the trio's weapons. While Kohlin and Jaren threw down their fake bonds to burst forward and take hold of their arms, Parnox took hold of his massive axe handle, screamed for his friends to duck, and proceeded to swing its gargantuan blade in a full circle around him, cutting down half a dozen men in one swift stroke. With hundreds of infuriated Drakkaidians now alerted to their presence and rushing forward to destroy them, Jaren and Kohlin had leapt for the horses standing beside the command post. Unsheathing his duel blades, Kohlin cut loose the ropes tying them down and bounded upward to mount them.

"Parnox, now!" he yelled at the top of his lungs. The bulking Southlander spun around from the waves of Drakkaidians dashing for him only mere feet away and threw himself up to the horse, already dashing after Jaren and Kohlin's. Realizing he was almost too heavy to move by himself, he dropped his beloved axe to lighten the load and crawled up to the saddle of the animal. Kohlin kicked the sides of his steed harshly, the need for haste paramount. The majority of the Drakkaidians were either in mass confusion or oblivious to what was happening, but there were dozens of troops wildly giving chase, beginning to assail them with arrows. Enraged and leaderless, scores of Drakkaidians pursued them. As the trio's steeds rapidly closed the gap between the advancing front line of their enemies and the city walls, Kohlin wildly scanned the rest of the Drakkaidian ranks coming to life with anger and purpose. Everywhere around the perimeter of the city the sound of iron blades being drawn and men shouting filled the air. Kohlin grit his teeth and silently cursed. They may have pulled away from the front line for the moment, but they would not survive the volleys of arrows that would be assailing them when they sped around the circling path up to the city gates. They wouldn't have time to enter the city before entering the Drakkaidian's bow range.

They weren't going to make it.

They couldn't. Even with support from the walls, there would still be more than enough Drakkaidian bows to pick them off as they sped around the plateau like sitting ducks. Knowing that Parnox was aware of this himself, Kohlin didn't bother to turn back. Instead, the Southlander turned his attention to the walls of the city now not more than fifty feet ahead. Scanning nearly a hundred feet upward, he observed the few Legionnaires atop the wall taking aim at them with longbows. Desperate, he threw up his right arm and bellowed out to them at the top of his lungs.

"Defenders of Torrentcia City!" he boomed louder than he was accustomed to, "we are friends! We are men of the Southland and allies to the Legion! Hold your fire!" With the incredible distance between them and the clamor of the Drakkaidians in the background, no more than a barely audible, incomprehensible blur of syllables reached the Legionnaires' ears. All three of the riders could see the men hesitantly turning to each other, but held their bowstrings firmly strung. As they continued to close the gap between them, Kohlin repeated himself with Parnox's commanding voice to bolster his own. At last the trio arrived at the wall. Making his way to the start of the road spiraling to the gates, Jaren observed his two friends halted at the wall. Seeing the hundreds of maddened Drakkaidians still surging toward them, he violently called back.

"What in the name of Granis are you doing!?!" he cried madly. Parnox spun to the hysterical Grandarian boy while Kohlin repeated himself one last time so the men atop the wall could hear.

"Jaren, there is no way we'll be able to get up to the city on the road!" he bellowed angrily. "We'll be cut down by archers on the way up!" Jaren fretfully pointed at the enemy troops to their rear.

"But-"

"No buts, boy!" Parnox cut him off savagely. "Now if you want to make it out of this, shut up and get the hell over here!" Though beside himself with worry, Jaren reluctantly put aside his complaints and moved his horse back along with the Southlanders'. By now, the Legionnaires had sent for their commanding officer already on the wall observing the Drakkaidians. As the image of another man appearing over the wall top came into view, Kohlin shouted up wildly.

"Please listen, Legionnaires!" he pleaded. "I say again we are friends of the Southland pursued by the Drakkaidians! Please help us now!" The newest man turned to speak to another. Kohlin nervously looked back to the black wave of Drakkaidians now halfway across the field they had just passed, still fiercely charging with bloodlust. Jaren's sweat beaded into bullets, his heart beating so fast he couldn't distinguish between one and the next. As Kohlin was about to call out again, the man on the wall turned his attention back to them.

"I am Captain Morrol, and I speak for the Sarton. What assurance can you give me you are who you say you are, and not Drakkaidian spies?" Kohlin's eyes lit up at the man's name.

"Morrol?" he repeated awestruck. The man nodded and replied yes. Kohlin hastily broke his gaze and threw his hands into his pockets, searching for something inside. After what seemed like an eternity for Jaren and Parnox with the charging Drakkaidians only yards out of bow range, he wrenched free his right hand tightly clasping something inside and thrust it up to the captain. "You are the brother of Kalas

Morrol?" he asked hurriedly. Even from the long distance between them, Jaren could see the man's face twist.

"How do you know of my brother?" he asked quickly. "Where did you get that?" Parnox was the one to respond, realizing they were out of time.

"There isn't time, Captain!" he bellowed, pointing back at the Drakkaidians. "Throw us ropes so we might escape into the city with our lives!" Though obviously bewildered and disturbed at how these three men he had never seen before had come to acquire his brother's locket, he at last shook off his uncertainty and nodded to the men beside him. After a few moments, three ropes over a hundred feet long came falling over the wall top toward them.

"Take hold!" the captain called. "We'll pull you up!" Virtually the instant after he finished his statement, the first wave of projectiles began landing behind them. Jaren spun his head around at the charge of Drakkaidians and raised his hand to his nearly depleted supply of arrows mounted to his back. They were still too far out of range for his bow, he thought, and wheeled around to the ropes. "Legionnaires return fire! Hurry!" The captain turned from the wall then and disappeared behind it. The moment Kohlin, Parnox, and Jaren had taken hold, the Legionnaires began heaving the ropes with such force that even the massive Parnox practically ran along the wall's rocky surface to keep up. Despite their speed, there was still nearly a hundred feet of vertical surface to scale and the Drakkaidians' missiles were growing closer behind them all the time. Looking down after a few moments, Jaren remembered how much he loathed heights.

After the trio had climbed up about half of the wall, their enemies finally caught up to them. Mountaineering up the moving rope as fast as his strained arms could carry him, Jaren was horrified to hear the sound of iron tipped arrow heads landing all around them, snapping and impaling the wall. The Grandarian wished more than anything that he could draw his bow and return fire, but every second he wasn't in the safety of the city walls increased the possibility of death. Trying his hardest to hasten his ascent and praying to Granis for the inaccuracy of their enemies, Jaren and the others pressed onward up the wall.

Only twenty some feet to the wall top, Jaren heard a scream of anguish from his left and shifted his view to his allies beside him. From behind the massive frame of Parnox, he could see an arrow shaft protruding from Kohlin's left shoulder. He had slowed, but still climbed on at a lesser pace. The Grandarian grimaced at his friend's pain but pressed onward with Parnox, aware the only way to save him was to get up the wall and help heave him up. The burly Southlander was the first to do so, clawing his way to the edge of the wall and, with the help of several men taking hold of his arms, pulled himself through the firing hole to safety. Jaren came next, pulled through by the Legionnaires. The next moment he was on his feet and leaning over the wall once again toward his wounded friend still besieged by the incoming iron tipped projectiles. Peering over the wall, Jaren was horrified. Kohlin had dropped the rope as a second arrow landed into his lower back and was clenching onto the thick bricks of the wall with only his right hand.

Not waiting another minute, Jaren drew his bow and leaned as far down as he could reach, extending its end to the wounded Southlander.

"Grab on, Kohlin!" he shouted desperately. He raised his head and met Jaren's gaze, a glassy expression over his face.

"I can't feel my arm, Jaren," he said strangely soft. "I can't..." His unstable grip weakened further as another arrow landed directly above his hand where Jaren's bow lay. The Grandarian's face twisted with pain and frustration and he wheeled back to Parnox.

"He won't last much longer! Lower me down!" he bellowed. A confused look overcame the Southlander's face, but Jaren cut off his question with a look of deadly impatience, dropping his bow. "Hold my legs, Parnox! *Now!*" Without another second of hesitation, he did as he was told and grabbed hold of the boy's legs and slowly draped him over the wall to Kohlin. Jaren stretched his body as far as he could and threw his hands over Kohlin's, locking his grip onto him like a vice. "You hold on, Kohlin!" He ordered with conviction. "Hold on!" Wheeling his head back to Parnox, he screamed for him to pull them up. The burly Southlander heaved, pulling so hard Jaren could feel his muscles ready to tear. He gripped his friend's hands firm, not letting go for anything.

At last Parnox and the Legionnaires hauled the two up back over the wall, carefully lifting them both free and inside its safety. Jaren landed in the arms of three men, breathing harder than he ever had in his life but still latched onto

Kohlin. Parnox came bolting to them, easing Jaren's grip and quickly lifting Kohlin. As he rose in the burly Southlander's arms, his left arm dropped the locket he had carried all the way up the wall to the ground. Rushing off to the medic waiting further down the wall, Parnox left the exhausted Grandarian struggling for breath behind the wall. As he sat dazed and overcome with feeling, one of the men in front of him leaned down and rested his hand over his shoulder. Slowly looking up to meet the man's gaze, he identified him as the captain they had spoken to minutes ago at the base of the wall. He had a stressed but friendly smile over his face as he complimentarily patted the Grandarian on his back.

"That was a brave thing you did, son," he stated. "Who are you?" Letting the man's question digest, Jaren extended his arm and picked up the object Kohlin had dropped. He presented it to the captain.

"We're friends," he breathed fatigued. "This was your brother's. If he makes it, you can thank my wounded friend for getting it to you." The man looked down and gingerly accepted the locket, examining it. He nodded, and brought his gaze back to Jaren.

"Kalas is dead then?" he asked quietly. Jaren nodded slowly. "Then I owe you and your friend a great deal for what you must have done for him before the end. Your friend will be alright, young man." With that, the captain turned and signaled for a man on the wall to come. He took hold of Jaren, helping him up, and slowly walked with Morrol to his friends.

Chapter 62

<u>Granis Bound</u>

Tavin opened his eyes to find a brilliant world of soft falling white, spanning for as far as he could see. He stood alone amidst a field of falling particles gently floating down from the endless white sky above him. Curiously reaching his arm upward and opening his hand, one of the specks gently drifted onto it and melted. Staring in dreamy wonder, he realized the flurries of white were snow. Lowering his arm he looked down at himself, feeling strangely comfortable. He was wearing nothing but a thin layer of loose white clothing gently swaying back and forth in the slight breeze. Despite the absence of his standard attire or shoes in the middle of the snowy field, he found himself warm and dry. His bare feet were not even touching the pallid earth but hovering directly above it. Confused and full of wonder, the Grandarian boy took a step forward, levitating over the ground.

Slowly sauntering forward, Tavin brought his gaze above him once more. Analyzing the surrounding environment, he observed that he ambled not through a field, but mountains. High up, as well. Around him was a dense blanket of ashen clouds, and below steep slopes and glaciers crested with the constantly falling snowfall. So beautiful and tranquil was the amazing view around him that questions like how, why, or where he was did not even enter his mind. Though the snowfall was constant, not a single flake would affect his body. Somehow he remained perfectly dry and warm no matter how far he walked. Passing along the mountain summit, Tavin's wandering eyes grazed over something ahead of him also untouched by the gently falling snow. Squinting through the flurries he couldn't make out what it was, but he could tell it was thin and flat. And big. The closer he got, the larger the object seemed to grow. By the time he was at its edge, he identified it as a colossal circle stretching hundreds of feet from one side to the other.

Moving forward with an intrigued gleam in his deep blue eyes, he identified the object as a stone platform rising from the snowfield. It was decorated with elaborate curving designs engraved into its massive surface, all beautiful works of art to behold. Coming up to its sides, his eyes widened further as he recognized the myriad engravings in the stone as Grandarian emblems like those found in the Temple of Light. Some were even on the hilt of the Sword of Granis. As thoughts of his mighty weapon came to mind, a sudden flash of golden light appeared in the center of the enormous platform hundreds of feet in front of him. With curiosity that knew no bounds, Tavin raised his bare foot onto the platform and stepped on, a strange sensation of warmth emitting from it as he did.

With both feet on the sprawling platform, the world around him seemed to abruptly accelerate, blurring together as if speeding forward at an incredible velocity. Without moving a muscle, Tavin stood frozen in awe as he suddenly jetted hundreds of feet over the intricate platform toward the golden glow at its center. Within mere moments, he found himself standing before it. After taking a good look around to be sure he had indeed just teleported halfway across the gargantuan platform, he settled his gaze back down onto the source of the steady golden glow before him: the Granic Crystal on the hilt of the Sword of Granis. It was embedded into a slab of ornately carved stone as it had been in the Temple of Light. Though he had no idea how the mighty weapon, or he, had come to be here, Tavin felt a rush of security and easiness enter his body upon seeing it. Reaching out, he wrapped his hands around its hilt.

As in the Tower of Granis, something incredible happened the moment his skin fell upon the talisman. The light, already pulsating from the sword, dramatically fled outward. From inside the intricate engravings and designs throughout the platform, the same soft but steadily intensifying golden glow weaved its way around him, forcing all other light in the environment to slowly fuse and blur together. Before he realized it, the entire immense platform had transformed into a colossal shaft of golden light beaming into the sky. Caught up in the righteous beam, Tavin felt the weight of gravity leaving him, slowly rising from the platform to gradually ascend upward. Though feet above the earth and rising by the second, he was unafraid and casually raised his head upward to find light brighter than the sun enveloping him. As it did, Tavin's eyes slowly slid shut to the soft, welcoming laughter of a familiar voice above him.

The Warrior of Light's eyes shot open the next moment in the Embrin household. He came awake with a start, thrusting his head up from the pillow it rest on to find himself in a cozy but dark bedroom, illuminated only by a single candle meekly burning on the bedside table to his left. The window above it was black, suggesting the presence of night. Tavin squinted his eyes, confused once again, and propped himself up from under the sheets of the comfortable bed. He was back in his normal attire, still wearing his white pants and blue undershirt, but looking over to the corner of the room by a single doorway he spotted his cape, chest and shoulder armor, and blue boots folded neatly on a wooden chair. The Sword of Granis stood leaning against his other belongings, sheathed and dark in the absence of its master's presence.

Staring at the talisman, thoughts of the strange dream and his encounter with the sword resting in the giant platform on the snowy mountain entered his mind. It had felt so real that he wasn't quite sure it was in fact a dream, but dismissed it for the moment as he gently raised the sheets on the bed and swung his legs out from underneath them. Right now, all he wanted to do was find Ril. He remembered all too well what he had done to her and Verix earlier that day. Though he was still conscience in the back of his mind and could see what he was doing, no matter how hard he tried, he hadn't been able to stop himself from attacking them. Something had taken hold of him. Though he was still unsure as to the cause of his dark loss of control, he knew it had to somehow lead back to Valif Montrox. Coming full circle with his thoughts, Tavin pushed everything aside except Ril.

He stood stiffly, feeling unusually sore but nevertheless intact after his heated battle with Verix that morning. Taking another more detailed look around the room, he decided that he must have been inside Ril's house. The rows of men's clothes at the opposite side of the room and the lack of anything feminine around him suggested that he was in her father's room. He wasn't going to find Ril standing there, however, so with a rigid lurch forward he started for the illuminated doorway. As he passed through, he took hold of the Sword of Granis, the Granic Crystal beaming to life as his fingers wrapped around the hilt. Responsible for his survival multiple times now, the boy felt insecure without it and strapped it over his back as he exited the bedroom, emerging into a larger living room decorated with fiery reds, oranges, and yellows in wild flowing designs that seemed to mimic the appearance of flame. Though foreign to him, he was not surprised to find such extravagant displays in the Elemental Warrior of Fire's home. There was a round table in the center of the room, and a cooking element on the far side, which, given the amount of dirtied plates strewn around it and the vast aromas of exotic flavors in the air, looked to have been in recent use.

There was another presence in the air of the house as well. Stepping into the living room, Tavin noticed the atmosphere was dense with humidity and moisture. Guessing someone had just taken a bath, he gradually walked around the table and spied another two doors in the walls. Steam poured out of one, and hesitantly peering in to confirm, appeared to be the bathroom where a massive steaming tub lay, still bubbling with soap and hot water. The room was devoid of any human presence, however, so he quickly took a step back and turned his interest to the door in the other wall. It was almost closed but for a small crack that barely allowed him to glimpse in. He did so, once again letting his curiosity get the better of him, and found another bedroom but littered with clothes in massive heaps all around the room. Gently pushing the door open to get a better view, he found a closet along the wall with clothes flying out. The boy couldn't help but silently laugh, realizing it was Ril.

She emerged from the compact closet a moment later with her back turned to the door. Her hair was still damp from the bath she had just taken and she was only wearing her scarlet locket and a thin white night gown that stretched from her slender shoulders to the tops of her knees. As she filtered through the various tunics, skirts, and other outfits thrown about her room, Tavin guessed she was obviously having a difficult time selecting the right thing to adorn herself with.

Trying to suppress his laughter as she scurried around her bed mumbling "she had nothing to wear," he silently pushed the door open all the way and bolstered himself against the door frame, folding his arms. As Ril lifted a casual red skirt in one hand and a dark green one in the other, he opened his mouth to speak.

"You always look best in red," he advised from the doorway with a playful smile. Ril jumped, quickly pulling the clothes over her half-revealed body as she wheeled around with a start. When her eyes fell upon the smiling Grandarian boy, the shocked expression on her frightened face only increased. Tavin guessed that maybe now wasn't the best time to be intruding. "I'll just wait-" His words were cut short when Ril dropped the clothes in her hands and ran straight for him, lunged, and wrapped her arms around him like vice, her wet hair sticking to his skin. As the oxygen began to withdraw from his lungs, thoughts of the night in Torrentcia City flooded his mind. Though happy to be loved, he lifted his arms to nudge her back a bit. "I've still got to breathe, Ril," he managed. She released her iron grip and pulled her head back. Though Tavin had expected to see joy in her face, irritation and concern were the only emotions present.

"Tavin Tieloc, what are you doing out of bed with that weight on your back?" she scorned harshly. Tavin raised an eyebrow but grinned widely.

"First of all," he began informatively, "this is like feather to me, and second, I've never felt better." Though obviously still concerned, the girl couldn't help but let out a smile and embrace him again.

"I'm so glad you're alright," she began, her voice taut with emotion. "Verix said you would be fine after you got some rest, but after that entire ordeal I wasn't sure." The smile from Tavin's face dissipated as thoughts of the demonic creature surfaced. He moved his head back in front of Ril's and stared into her eyes.

"I can't tell you enough how sorry I am about this morning," he stated somberly. "I could see and hear what was happening in front of me, even feel it, but I just couldn't stop myself. It was like sleeping awake; completely helpless." Ril pulled her head back and violently shook it.

"Don't you ever tell me that. It wasn't your fault- I know you had no control." Her face softened and inched closer. "I'm just glad you're okay." Tavin smiled again as he gently kissed her.

"When have I ever not been?" he asked teasingly. Though Ril could name more instances than she cared to remember, she only laughed.

After they released each other and Ril finished dressing, the two went back to the master room in the center of the house to eat. Ril had already prepared a mountain of nourishment, and the hungry Warrior of Light was only too happy to help her get rid of it with the lightning speed that she had notoriously come to admonish him for. She couldn't help but giggle as he shoveled the food into his mouth. She ate little, having already cooked something for Verix and herself that morning after they had put Tavin to bed and cleaned the Drakkaidian Prince's wounds. As Verix entered their conversation, Tavin noticed that he was nowhere to be found and inquired as to his whereabouts. Though Ril informed him he had taken a nap outside after bandaging himself up, she confessed that she didn't have a clue where he was now. Tavin was surprised to learn that he had given Verix such a difficult time containing him in their last conflict.

Ril proceeded to relate to him the fight from her perspective and how difficult it had been to combat him. After they dispelled the Shadow, she tended to Verix and fed the two, but while he left to rest, she remained with Tavin to keep an eye on him and reenergize herself. She had eaten breakfast and lunch, bathed, and as Tavin noticed, dressed in fresh clothes for the first time since Keracon Valley. She felt and looked like a new person- somehow even more beautiful than before. Once Tavin had finished his dinner, he began to tell Ril of his strange dream just before he woke. She listened attentively as he described the snowy mountain and the platform with the Sword of Granis at its center, but wasn't sure what she was supposed to say afterward.

"I don't know, Tavin," she began uncertainly. "It sounds like something important, but do you really think it was anything more than a dream?" Tavin nodded with confidence.

"I know it's hard to believe," he told her, "but you have to believe me when I say it wasn't just some dream. I could see everything around me with the clarity of the real world, and I could feel all of it like it was real." Ril shrugged and put down the last plate onto her stack, moving to sit next to him. She wrapped her legs underneath her and brushed a lock of her crimson hair out of her face.

"Sometimes I have dreams like those too," she offered. "They feel like you really are there. If it was supposed to mean something, what could it have been? Where would we find a giant Grandarian platform on the top of a mountain?" Tavin shook his head.

"It wasn't just the mountain or the platform that was real," he said, remembering. "When I was floating into the light above the platform, I could hear the voice of the sword." Ril raised an eyebrow at this.

"What do you mean the voice of the sword?" she asked skeptically. "Are you saying the Sword of Granis can talk now?"

"It has since the first time I saw it in Galantia," he stated right away, to which she stiffened with curiosity. Tavin saw the skepticism and disbelief in her eyes and tried to explain. "Not out loud, Ril. It pulls me into this... other world and puts its voice into my head. It happened when I took it in the Tower of Granis and when I unlocked my power in the caverns of the Golthrouts. It sounds weird, I know, but it's true. That was the voice of the sword in my dream. I know it." Ril loosened her body and put a hand over his on the table.

"I believe you," she smiled tenderly. "But what does it mean? What would a platform and the Sword of Granis be doing on the summit of a mountain so high there's snow everywhere around you?"

"He's talking about the Celestial Portal, of course," came the sharp voice from the shadows of the doorway to the house. Tavin and Ril both spun their heads toward the door. They had almost become accustomed to having their conversations interrupted by their third party member, however, and knew it was Verix before they even laid eyes on his dark form standing in the suddenly open doorway. As he tightly closed and locked the door, Tavin saw his hard body had been covered in cuts and bruises and thoroughly bandaged. Ril was right; he had indeed been more than a match for the Dark Prince that morning. His thoughts quickly focused back to the matter at hand and chewed on the Drakkaidian's words.

"The Celestial Portal?" he repeated confused. Verix rolled his eyes and shook his head, taking a seat on the opposite side of the table. His crimson hair was a tangled mess and judging from the condition of his already tattered gray coat and torn black attire, he had yet to bathe or refresh himself as Ril had.

"How you have made it this far in life on your own," he began cynically, "is beyond me, Tavin. Yes, the Celestial Portal. While it is more of a forgotten relic to your people, it is one of the most sacred of the Grandarian talismans and icons. I hope I don't have to explain its function." Tavin frowned, not appreciating his negativity.

"I had never even heard of a Celestial Portal before," he admitted defensively. "But I assume it works the same as the Netherworld Portal in Drakkaidia." Verix shifted in his seat and began to fidget with the thick collection of bandages around his right hand.

"In a general way, yes," he began staring into space. "But they are very different in nature and in their specific use. Being a Drakkaidian, I obviously don't know as much about the Celestial Portal as I do the Netherworld Portal, but I should know enough to enlighten the two of you." Though Tavin would have loved to recoil and tell him to shut up, Ril stepped in as arbiter once again.

"So you're saying that this place Tavin dreamt about is the Celestial Portal?" she asked perplexed. "How would you possibly know what it looks like?"

"I *know*," he snapped quietly. "I make it my business to know my enemy, as should you. My father and others have told me of it. The Grandarian religious authorities are aware of its existence, but they don't know its location. I know because my father found it years ago when he began preparing for his war. He wanted to make sure it could be of no use to him. It isn't of course. The Celestial Portal is a direct link to the Celestial world, as is the Netherworld Portal to the Netherworld. They are different, however, in that the Netherworld Portal acts more like a seal to keep the evil inside trapped. Your portal has no practical function other than to gain entrance to the Celestial World. Why someone would want to achieve that, I haven't the faintest idea. I don't know how to activate it, but I'm sure it has something to do with you and that piece of metal strapped to your back."

Tavin remembered the Sword of Granis and how he had found it at the center of the platform, just as it had been in the Tower of Granis.

"The Sword of Granis is a key," Tavin quietly repeated. "Zeroan told me that once. Maybe it unlocks more than just my inner power." Verix shrugged.

"Perhaps, but I don't think we're going to be able to find out," he stated. "If your little dream was in fact a signal from the sword, it isn't something we can achieve right now. The Celestial Portal is somewhere at the highest peaks of the Border Mountains far above your military base of the Battlemount. As far as I know, no one has ever seen it before. Not even my father knows its exact location. Just that it is somewhere in the mountains far to the north." Ril's face became curious.

"Verix, I thought the Netherworld Portal was in the heart of Drakkaidia," she began puzzled.

"It is," he nodded. "The Royal Castle of Dalastrak is built around it."

"Then why isn't the Celestial Portal in Galantia?" she inquired. "It's not even in Grandaria." Verix shrugged.

"The only person to ask about that is Granis. He placed it there when he disappeared after the Battle of the Gods. Why he separated it from the rest of Grandaria, I don't know. Either way," he finished, "it does us little good. It's on the other side of Iairia and we have nothing to gain from it. I think your little dream was a mere coincidence." Tavin raised an eyebrow and stared him down hard.

"A coincidence?" he repeated incredulously. "How could I have dreamed up a place that I have never even heard of before? And I am telling you, that *was* the Sword of Granis talking to me. I know that feeling all too well. It was the sword." Verix exhaled deeply and shook his head.

"Then what do you suggest we do?" he asked impatiently. Tavin shot a quick glace at Ril, already staring at him knowing what he was going to say. She nodded, behind him.

"We have to go there," he stated simply. There was a long pause after, but Verix finally shifted forward in his seat leaning over the table and cocking his dubious head.

"Say again?" he asked quickly. Tavin repeated himself, to which Verix closed his eyes and rubbed them with the knuckles along his hand. "What," he began agitated, "would we possibly have to gain by going to the Celestial Portal? Why?"

"I don't know," Tavin answered honestly, aware the Prince was not happy with what he was saying. "All I know is that I am supposed to go there, and I intend to." Verix fell back in his chair, impatience and anger flaring in his movements.

"Arilia," he pleaded to the Warrior of Fire by his side, "please tell him that he's lost his miniature Grandarian mind. Are you really ready to abandon everything we're trying to do right now because of one colorful dream?" It was Tavin's turn to be upset now.

"What do you mean everything we're trying to do?" he asked incredulously. "You said it yourself, Verix. Your father has four shards now, and one more waiting for him in Galantia. His army of demons is going to be set loose soon, and there is no one to stand up to them except you and me. But according to you, even we are outmatched by those Dégamar creatures. There isn't anything we can do now. We can't win anymore, Verix. I can't beat him." Hearing the eternally optimistic and determined Warrior of Light finish that painful statement was almost too much for Ril to bear. If Tavin knew they were at the end of their rope, what hope could be left?

As Verix mulled over his words, Tavin realized what he had said himself. It hurt, but he knew that they were outmatched in every way.

"Believe me when I say, Verix," he continued softly, "I don't like giving up or admitting that I'm outdone, but things are starting to spin out of control here. I promise that as long as there's breath inside me I will never give up or give in, but I don't think that we can beat the rest of Drakkaidia as things stand now. There is nothing we can do to be of any real help anymore, but I think that this dream was a signal. I don't know what we can gain from the Celestial Portal, but the sword has never lied to me before. It's a long shot, but maybe there's something there that can give us an edge. Right now, I don't think we have many more options."

Verix stared at him with hard eyes, an obvious struggle mirrored there. Though he didn't like balancing the fate of his home or the world on a hunch that Tavin had acquired in his sleep, he realized that his words were true. There was no way to beat his father and his legions of evil with only a handful of warriors to oppose them. He had known from the beginning that Tavin was his only chance, and now the Celestial Portal was his only chance of seeing that a reality. With quiet reluctance, Verix shifted his eyes to Ril.

"I don't have to ask to know where you stand," he said softly, to which she merely held his gaze. At last he nodded. "We still have one problem. As I mentioned before, the Celestial Portal is halfway across the continent in one of the most inaccessible places in the world, cut off by armies of Drakkaidian soldiers preparing for war. How in the name of Drakkan below do you suggest we get there?" A look of uncertain defeat overcame Tavin then, not sure how to answer. After a long pause, Ril suddenly came to new life and put a hand on his forearm.

"I can take care of that."

Chapter 63

<u>Red Source</u>

After taking the night to rest, Tavin, Ril, and Verix all woke the next morning revitalized. Verix had spent the night sleeping on the porch after their conversation, Tavin in Ril's father's room, and Ril in her own. In the morning, Tavin bathed and donned his slightly tattered blue and white attire once again. It had grown more than a little worn with its constant use and from his battles with Verix over the past few days, but it remained intact nevertheless. Though he had once hated the idea of wearing a cape everywhere he went, the Grandarian has become so accustomed to the blue material on his back he couldn't imagine himself without it. Strapping the shining Sword of Granis to his side, he exited his room and met Ril finishing her preparations for the next part of their journey. She was wrapped in similar attire to what Tavin had first met her in: thick white trousers and her fiery red over-tunic. Her hair was draped over her shoulders, flowing over them as she bustled from one task to another. She had arranged a pack for each of them with weeks of rations and water. Identifying the mistake she had made leaving Torrentcia City, she also took the liberty of packing herself a change of clothes.

They found Verix patiently waiting for them outside, resting his back against the wall with arms crossed. He had just placed the shard of the Holy Emerald in his pocket that Ril had entrusted him to look after while Tavin was incapacitated. Despite his usual dark demeanor, he appeared refreshed as well with his dilapidated gray coat washed and his wavy red hair neatly patted down. His impassive face was clear and crisp in the morning light. He informed them he had already eaten and that he was ready to set out once again if they were. Closing the door to her home once more, Ril stepped off her porch to make her way down the hill with

Tavin and Verix. They quietly proceeded down into the ruins of the village, both the Warrior of Light and the Drakkaidian Prince respecting Ril's moment to reflect. After they had passed out of the village into the hillside around it, Verix at last broke the silence.

"So how long will it take to reach this temple of yours, Arilia?" he asked as they walked through the refreshing morning air. She pointed up to the towering form of Mt. Coron before them.

"Do you see the path that runs up the side of those steep slopes?" she asked, to which he nodded yes. "It will take a few hours to get up to that, and it's an afternoon hike to the cavern. The Temple of Fire is inside there."

"All day," the Prince muttered to himself. Tavin smirked at him.

"Don't tell me you're not up for a little hike, Verix," he grinned. Verix looked back at him with a sneer.

"The mountain is nothing," he said flatly. "I'm just not partial to this kind of heat in the middle of the Drakkaidian black winter."

"Sorry, Verix," Ril smiled, "but it's only going to get worse the closer we get."

"I still don't know if this is even going to work," he continued to grumble. The previous night after Tavin had related his dream of the Celestial Portal to them and they had decided to go there in a desperate attempt to try and gain some new plan or power to wield against the senior Montrox, the question of how they would get there had been raised. Ril's idea was risky and experimental at best, but it was the only realistic option they had. She had explained that Elemental Warriors could use the six Sources in the various temples across Iairia to teleport themselves back to their temple of origin. Though she didn't know the exact specifics of the nature of her proposed transportation because it hadn't been attempted in centuries, she was confident that she could open the door to the Source of Fire with her power and then with Tavin's they could teleport toward Galantia and the Source of Light in the Tower of Granis.

Her plan was that while they were warping through the skies to Grandaria, they could somehow disengage the teleportation as they passed over the Border Mountains where the Celestial Portal lay, land, and find their way from there. While it was theoretically possible, Verix was quick to bring up several flaws with her plan. First off, Tavin had no idea how to begin the teleportation or how to control it. Though Ril strongly believed she could teach him, even she wasn't sure if he would be able to somehow stop it when they reached the mountains, or if it was even possible. Last, Verix hadn't actually been to the Celestial Portal before; he only knew of its general location atop the frozen peaks. They could be thrown anywhere in the mountains, miles away from the portal. If Verix lost his way or Tavin was unable to sense its location with the sword, they would be lost in the middle of nowhere in a perpetual blizzard.

Worst of all, it would take a great deal of detectable power to teleport across half of Iairia. Their location would be handed to Montrox and the Dégamar. Despite these possible risks, even Verix admitted that there was no other option and it was worth them. Tavin could not hope to defeat Valif Montrox as he was, and if he could indeed acquire some new power from the portal, it might be the edge they needed to win the war. So with new purpose, the diverse trio pressed onward to the Temple of Fire beneath the fiery crater of Mt. Coron.

As they moved through the last grassy region beneath the mountain and up the rocky paths toward the slopes, Tavin and Ril strolled hand in hand with Verix following quietly behind. Silently aware of the change in their relationship over the past few days, he felt uncomfortable talking. Tavin felt rude keeping him apart from their discussion, however, and quickly invited him up to them. Soon all three conversed freely. Tavin and Ril told their stories of the journey before Verix had "joined" them at the forest edge in the south, to which he listened intently, actually smirking and laughing when they remembered one of the many humorous instances they had shared. Tavin silently noticed that Verix had considerably changed over the time he had traveled with them, particularly over the past few days. Though he still harbored a nameless insecurity about the Prince, he truly had come to trust him. Verix had obtained multiple chances to betray them since they joined forces, but he had remained true to his word every time. He could have easily opted to kill Tavin to dispose of the demon that possessed him the previous day, but he fought valiantly to preserve its host instead. He could scarcely believe it, but Tavin realized that he now thought the Drakkaidian to be a friend. Though he wasn't sure what this meant, he knew that Verix had indeed proven himself to them and deserved their respect.

The group pressed on closing the gap between the village and the mountain base and found their way onto the steep paths to the caverns inside. Half the day went by slowly and cautiously climbing the narrow road, only stopping briefly at noon for a small snack. The higher they climbed the more they realized that Ril had been all too right about the increasing heat. One of the last active volcanoes in the known world, Mt. Coron was constantly bubbling thick molten rock to the surface of its gargantuan crater at the summit. Though far from the mouth of the lava, the trio could feel its heat emanating from the very rocks around them. Verix was quick to remove his thick coat made for the harsh biting winds of Drakkaidia, throwing it over his shoulder much like Tavin had with his cape when the heat become too unbearable for him. The view from the mountainside was marvelous from as high as they had climbed. Coron Village, the largest settlement in the west, lay beneath them like a collection of toy blocks scattered in a messy pile. Other villages came into view from beyond, almost too small to detect.

By mid-afternoon the three came to a sharp depression in the mountain hidden from view in the village. As they turned into it, Tavin and Verix were astounded to find that the steep road suddenly plummeted into a wide wedge in the mountainside that gradually came together some hundred feet away. At the point of intersection, a small opening in the rock was visible, emitting a haunting red glow generating from within. The path that led to the opening was decorated with scarlet clay torches burning with bright flames. Staring mystified at the scene before him, Tavin could feel Ril's eyes on him. Amazed, he turned to her. She stared back with a funny smile.

"This is the mountain's wedge," she informed them. "It was formed eons ago in the volcano's first great explosion, but while the rest of the mountain built itself back up, for some reason this area did not. It can't be seen from the grasslands, so it's the perfect entrance to the Temple of Fire inside the cavern." Tavin shot a nervous glace at the eerie glowing cave in the rock wall of the wedge, and then back to her, raising an eyebrow.

"The temple is *inside* the volcano?" he asked incredulously. "Isn't there lava in there?" Ril showed him a coy smile and nodded knowingly.

"Sort of," she teased. "You'll just have to trust me and see for yourself. Just make sure neither of you touch anything in there. The heat is going to be a little intense." Verix let out a sharp huff of breath as she began moving again.

"Wonderful," he smoldered, starting after her. As they moved down the path to the cavern entrance, Ril explained that because they were so close to the Source of Fire, the torches along the path never gave out, even in the rain. This was the reason Mt. Coron was always active as well. The Source was what provided the mountain with a steady supply of heat and magma, not the earth. The entrance to the cave was decorated in the same exotic designs of wildfire and smoldering images that Tavin had become accustomed to in the region. There were paintings and statues of columns of crimson flame on either side of the opening, and a mosaic of western emblems and symbols was engraved into the very wall of the rock. Though aware the Temple of Fire was not inherently evil, it remained a foreboding sight to behold nonetheless.

As they began to move into the entrance of the cavern, Ril turned back to the two boys with the utmost seriousness in her eyes.

"All right," she almost whispered, "we're entering the mountain. The temple isn't too far ahead, but it will take us a while to safely navigate through the fires inside. Both of you stay close to me and stay alert; this is the epicenter of the element of fire. Few people have ever or will ever see what you are about to, but remember that this element is dangerous in nature compared to most of the others, so act accordingly. The moment you don't respect this environment, it will eat you alive. All right?" Tavin stared at her captivated, remembering how commanding the Warrior of Fire could be when necessary. He trusted her completely, but admitted to himself he was more than a little nervous about this.

"How many times have you been in here, Ril?" he asked intently, sweat dripping from his chin. She finished tying her traveling cloak about her waist and wiped the perspiration from her own slender face.

"Since my anointment inside the temple as a child," she recalled, "twice." Verix shot a quiet glance in the young

Grandarian's direction, unsure what to think. Ril could see the unnerved expression in his eyes and placed her hands on her waist.

"Like I said, this isn't exactly the most welcoming place in the world. Don't get me wrong, I love it, but it's not like I come in here anytime a feel like it to report on my exploits as an Elemental Warrior or something. The only business I've ever had here is my anointment, the annual trip in to examine the Source, and once to reenergize myself. Otherwise I've never had reason to come here." This revelation only increased the nervous expressions over Tavin and Verix's faces. Ril rolled her eyes as she released her hands from her sides and slowly clenched them into fists, a slow wave of thin flame emerging around them. "Don't worry, boys, I may not be a regular here, but I know my way around. Stick with me and you'll be fine. Let's go." With that, the girl turned and slowly took a step into the red haze of the cavern's entrance. Tavin and Verix slowly followed, even the proud Drakkaidian Prince heeling like a dog. As the bright sunlight from outside dimmed, replaced by the dark red light from beyond, Verix tilted his head toward Tavin.

"Is she always like this?" he whispered just barely audible. Tavin kept his eyes forward and face still, but unhurriedly nodded.

"Basically," he responded. In the minutes that passed, the trio penetrated further and further from the entrance into an increasingly narrow tunnel illuminated by the faint crimson haze and Ril's burning fists. When it seemed to Tavin like the tunnel was going to cave in around them, the dim red light began increasing from ahead. Passing under the low ceiling and taking care not to touch anything, they emerged into a much wider portion of the tunnel with a truly incredible view at its end mere feet away. Tavin could feel the air in his lungs withdraw as the inside of the volcano appeared before his eyes. There was no floor in the cavern, only narrow pathways stretching from one end to the other over a veritable lake of molten lava. The ceiling was also unusually colored; it was redder than the rock around it as if lava hovered mere inches above. Remembering they were only halfway up the mountain, he guessed the crater was on top of them. Tavin gulped once again.

Stepping into the sprawling cavern, Ril slowed to a halt, closing her eyes. Tavin and Verix stopped behind her, puzzled.

In the moments that followed, the thin layer of flowing flame around her balled fists flared up rapidly, consuming her entire body.

"Don't move," she ordered quietly, focusing. Tavin and Verix looked at each other uncertainly, wondering what she was doing. At last, the flaring fire around her body spread wider and leapt from her body to wash over the boys behind her like a wave of the ocean. While Verix remained more or less impassive as always, Tavin's eyes burst open with anxiousness. Before he could so much as ask her what she was doing, both of them had been consumed in a radiating field of fire just like hers. His worries were dispelled quickly as a refreshing wave of coolness covering his sweating form. Taking a deep breath, Ril turned back to them lowering her fists. "It isn't fire," she started to explain. "It won't hurt you if you touch it. It's just a layer of elemental power to keep you from burning up in here, and especially in the temple." She raised her left arm then and extended a finger into the cavern, pointing. Following her gesture, Tavin caught sight of the massive structure sitting atop a rocky plateau inside the cavern. Previously masked to him by the distorting thermals of heat rising from around the cavern, the Elemental Temple of Fire stood basked in crimson red, pouring a river of lava into the lake around it.

Ril couldn't help but smile at the boy's amazement.

"Beautiful, isn't it?" she asked proudly. Tavin raised an eyebrow and looked at her.

"In a demonic way, yes..." he trailed off sarcastically. Ril gave him a frown, but Verix stepped past him toward the bridge.

"You know nothing of demons, Grandarian," he snapped curtly. "This is remarkable, though. Let's be on our way, Arilia." She took a step forward and snatched him by the arm.

"Remember what I said about this place, Verix," she admonished. "Stay with me and don't get ahead of yourself. If I lost focus of your shield while we were in here you'd... well, melt."

"That's a comforting thought," Tavin murmured to himself, knowing Jaren would have beaten him to that statement if he were here. With Ril in the lead, the trio pressed on into the molten cavern once more, carefully moving onto the single narrow bridge across the fiery lake to the temple. As they paced across the bridge, Tavin noticed the pillar of rock rising from the center of the temple.

"What is that column doing there, Ril?" he asked curiously. Her eyes drifted to the object of his interest.

"That's how the crater stays full with lava," she explained. "It's a tube forcing a river of it above us. The Temple of Fire is like a heart pumping magma into the mountains around us like blood through your veins." Tavin's mind reeled. He knew the Elemental Temples were responsible for generating their respective elements, but he never would have thought that the Temple of Fire directly created the molten rock under the ground for every volcano in Iairia. As they passed over the long bridge to the temple, its massive doorway came into view. It was a large slab of red rock mounted into the elaborately decorated archway. There were banks of long torches stretching from the front wall to an elaborate stone podium in the center of the bridge with a single white flame quietly dancing from the top. As they drew near, Ril lifted a hand signaling for them to stop. They both quickly obeyed.

The Warrior of Fire slowly walked up to the podium, raising her hands and gingerly wrapping them around the small white flame. Tavin watched with curiosity as she gently lifted the fire into her cupped hands and moved around the podium toward the doorway. She slowly approached and leaned down to place the fire in a small outlet in the door. As it entered, the burning red flame around the temple's gates abruptly flared up white. Moments later, a loud grinding noise filled the heated air as the colossal door began to slowly lift, revealing the interior of the temple. Ril turned and beckoned her companions to follow once more. They came after her swiftly, eager to see more of the temple.

Tavin broadly scanned his surroundings and noticed the interior of the temple was not so different from the Temple of Light back in Galantia. If anything, it was the exact same except for the fact everything was red instead of gold and the orbs of light had been replaced by thick torches of flame. Where he would have found a spiraling staircase leading to a tower like in the Temple of Light, however, Ril led them to a short bank of stairs leading to another large door blocking the way to the room beyond. This entrance was decorated with the design of a large beast on all fours emanating flame from its body. Its mouth hung open in three dimensions, as if waiting to be fed. Like at the door to the temple, Ril moved toward a small podium before it harboring another small white flame. She picked it up as gingerly she had the first and moved toward the door. This time she inserted the flame into the beast's open mouth. As she did, its stone eyes abruptly beamed white and the door gradually opened with a grinding noise similar to the first.

As it opened full length, a blinding wave of light met the trio's eyes. Hovering quietly in the next cubic room was a large orb of red light over a circular platform mounted to the floor. It was a perfect sphere; twice the height of any of them.

"This is the Source of Fire," Ril breathed. "It's the most magnificent thing I've ever seen." She stepped forward into the room, moving around the levitating orb. Tavin had never seen the Source of Light in his temple, but could imagine it would be something like the sphere before him. As he and Verix stepped through the doorway, both the door to the temple and to the Source began to slowly drop back down. Verix turned nervously.

"Don't worry," Ril started. "I closed them so we can leave." Verix nodded, folding his arms.

"And how are we going to go about doing that?" he asked focused. Ril broke her gaze with the Prince and set it upon Tavin, already staring at her.

"Tavin will take it from here," she stated with confidence. "Like I said, an Elemental Warrior can enter any Source to teleport back to their Source of origin. If Tavin summons his powers of light and enters the portal, we'll fly out of here in a beam of light toward the temple in Grandaria. When we pass over the Border Mountains, he should just have to seal his power and the teleportation will cease." Tavin gave her an uneasy glance.

"That's all there is to it?" he asked uncertainly. She nodded slowly.

"It should be…" she trailed off with a slight shrug. Verix breathed deeply, the doubt threatening to suffocate him.

"How many times have you done this before, again?" he asked. She frowned and ignored him.

"Just summon your power, Tavin," she urged him. "We can all step in because I'm here, and the Source will do the rest. Trust me." Tavin held her gaze steadily for another long moment, but at last nodded and placed his hand around the hilt of his weapon.

"All right," he agreed to himself. Quietly pulling forth the Sword of Granis to eliminate some of its metallic ringing, he tightened his grip around it and reached into the bottom of his soul to find his power shining with life, ready to emerge. Taking hold, the Warrior of Light closed his eyes and called it out, a steady aura of passionate golden energy enveloping around him. The force of his building power rustled the stagnant air of the small room, blowing their clothes and hair back and forth like the grass of the Grailen. The circulating field of energy flowing with strength, he opened his eyes and dropped the Sword of Granis to his side. "Ready?" Ril nodded and motioned for Verix to move to his side. Turning toward the hovering orb of elemental power beside her, Ril placed her hand upon it. The magical fire burning over all three spread onto the sphere, seeming to rouse it from some deep hibernation.

Closing her eyes, Ril let her arm slip into the light of the orb with her entire body following soon after. As the last fragment of her body disappeared inside, Tavin and Verix swallowed hard and stepped in after her. After all three had merged with the Source, the hue of its light began to swiftly alter. Changing from deep red to a brilliant golden, the hovering ball slowly rose from the floor and into the tube of stone above it. Accelerating at impossible velocities, the Source burst through the crater of the volcano and the molten lava bubbling inside. Once departed from the mountain, the sphere slowed and halted, leaving three blurring images beaming through the skies to the northeast. Once away, the orb's color slowly shifted back to its original hue and leisurely sank back into the molten lake in the crater of Mt. Coron.

Chapter 64

<u>Change of the Guard</u>

Amidst the confusion in the aftermath of Jaren and the others' dramatic entrance to Torrentcia City, the Grandarian boy was quickly whisked away after Parnox and Kohlin by Captain Morrol himself, who was eager to see to the heroic lad's health and find out what had happened to his apparently fallen brother. The wounded Windrun Warrior had been taken down to a small medical tent that had been erected next to the entrance of the lower city, housing a collection of injured Legionnaires in addition to Jaren's party of three. After the medics took a quick look at Jaren, patched up his few cuts and bruises and dismissed him to see to the critically wounded Kohlin, the weary Grandarian took Parnox's advice and left the stressful tent to rest his aching body.

He took a seat on a collection of wooden crates hurriedly stacked by the entrance to the lower city market, not wanting to be too far off from his friends still inside the tent across the courtyard he sat facing. Falling to his backside with an over-exaggerated grunt, Jaren remembered the last time he had been this bushed was his flight through the Hills of Eirinor with Tavin. As thoughts of his best friend snuck into his mind once again, he let out a soft huff of air. It had been almost two months since he had set out with Tavin to Galantia, and weeks since their separation in the Great Forests. Jaren shook his head, realizing that this was the longest that he had been away from his friend in his entire life. They had been together everyday since they were babies except on the rare occasion when Tavin went to Galantia with his father on military business. Having been separated so suddenly for so long, Jaren felt like a piece of himself had been lost. His mere existence didn't quite feel right without him. He could only pray to Granis that wherever he was and whatever he was doing, his friend and the girl with him were alright.

A sudden look of irritation overtook his face then, angry that he had made himself remember the Warrior of Fire. Though he had come to accept Ril's presence on the quest and appreciated her talents, he was still resentful of the fact that she had come to occupy Tavin's constant thoughts in his last days with him. In the time before their separation, the free spirited Southlander was all he talked about. Jaren knew that he and Tavin would always be best friends unto their final days, but he had to admit that he was had been filled with a sickening sensation of jealousy ever since her arrival. It was childish thinking and Jaren knew it, but it haunted his subconscious thoughts all the same.

As the Grandarian boy sat quietly recuperating and contemplating his feelings, a gradual increase in the activity in the gate yard garnered his attention. Since his departure from the wall top with Captain Morrol nearly a half an hour ago, the chaotic stress from the momentary hostilities had all but dissipated. Sulking in defeat, the blockade of Drakkaidians surrounding the city had retreated back to their previous formation, safely out of bow range. Judging from the sudden explosion of motion from the clusters of Legionnaires swarming into ranks and lines around him, however, Jaren wondered if their enemies had surged forward again. Rising from his seat in the corner of the gate yard with curiosity, the Grandarian noticed Captain Morrol emerge from the medical tent flanked by Legionnaires toward the lines of assembled men. As he took position in front of them, Jaren composed himself and approached. The captain noticed him coming and tightened his face nervously.

"Jaren," he shouted in a hushed tone, "go back where you were. You'll not want to be here for this." Jaren halted his advance but did not retreat.

"Why? What's happening?" he asked curiously. Before the captain could answer him, the rush of hoof beats on the rocky road of the lower city became audible, drawing both of their attentions. Staring at the road beyond him into the city, Jaren observed several horses emerge from around the first corner. There was a convoy of Legionnaires surrounding an elaborate looking man at the center, draped in regal attire and encased in the finest armor he had yet to see in the Southland. As the convoy entered the gate yard,

Jaren reeled back a step to avoid the rush of horses, almost mowing him down. He watched in annoyance as the rude man at the group's center quickly dismounted, immediately followed by the others. Captain Morrol stood attentively as did the other Legionnaires assembled. The ornately dressed man looked them over with a hard face, obviously angered by something.

"So where are they, Captain?" the man sounded ruthlessly at last. Morrol swallowed hard and formulated his answer.

"You refer to the men from the-"

"Don't jerk me around the subject, Captain," he interjected curtly. "Where are the men whom you allowed to penetrate the wall against my strict orders to admit no one entrance in the midst of this crisis?" Jaren watched as the man's relentless interrogation flustered Morrol, only adding to his growing disdain for him.

"Sarton, they offered me valid proof that they were friends of the Southland and were under attack so-" The man cut him off again, palpable dissatisfaction in his voice.

"So you disobeyed my direct orders put in place to protect the city from clever enemies who present seemingly valid proof only to prove themselves spies or assassins in the end. Is that what you are trying to tell me, Captain? I will ask only one more time. Where are these men?" The truculent man had tested Jaren's patience for the last time. Not willing to stand by and be called a Drakkaidian assassin by anyone or let the man that saved his life take a beating for him, he stepped toward the Legionnaires.

"I think you're looking for me," he stated in an equally churlish tone of voice. All eyes in the gate yard shifted to the boy behind them, including the ill-tempered man at the center. Captain Morrol gulped and gave Jaren an apprehensive face. The irritable man pushed his way through the two Legionnaires between them and stepped up to the boy. Overhearing the remark from a familiar cocky voice, the bulking form of Parnox emerged from the medical tent, eyes widening at what he saw. Finding Jaren facing down the ill-tempered man, his heart sank wondering how the boy had gotten himself into this.

"This is the Drakkaidian spy?" the man asked, addressing Jaren. "Do you know who I am, boy?" Jaren's eyes lit up with fire, vehemence tensing his body.

"Yeah," he informed him plainly, "the guy whose ass I'm about to kick if you call me a Drak one more time." Instantly, the Legionnaires flanking the man before him rushed forward to seize Grandarian boy. If Parnox hadn't stepped between them at the last minute to push them back, they would have.

"Please sir, the boy is a Grandarian," Parnox started apologetically. "He doesn't know of the Sarton and is very sensitive about being called a Drakkaidian. I'll remove him." The now irate Sarton locked his eyes onto the massive man.

"And just who are you, man?" he asked curtly. Captain Morrol again stepped in front of the man to wedge himself between them.

"These are two of the three men who we rescued, Sarton Othan," he informed him quickly. "The other is badly wounded in the medical tent. He speaks the truth, sir. The boy is Grandarian and the others are from the Southland. As I said, I have proof."

"Proof?" the unruly Sarton exclaimed incredulously. "The Drakkaidians could have made up anything to trick us into letting them in! I will not stand for your disobedience, Morrol! I..." This time it was the Sarton who was cut short, the sound of hundreds of men roaring to life from outside the city walls overpowering him. Immediately coming alert, Morrol spun around and yelled up to the wall top.

"Are the Drakkaidians attacking?" he bellowed anxiously. One of the many Legionnaires staring over the walls turned and shook his head.

"No sir! I'm not sure what's happening. You'd better come take a look for yourself!" Taking the man's advice, Morrol nodded and turned back to the Sarton, reluctantly nodding with quiet anger still present in his eyes. The captain quickly ordered Jaren and Parnox to follow him, which they did, all too happy to comply. As they ran for the stairs to the wall, Parnox locked his gaze onto Jaren with an annoyed look on his face.

"Do you try to get yourself into the most trouble you can everywhere you go, or are you just cursed with the worst luck in Iairia?" The Grandarian archer shot him a stern glance before shielding himself.

"Hey, I'm not the type that sits back and lets someone insult me in the most offensive possible way and let him get away with it," he stated defensively. Parnox shook his head as they turned up the staircase.

"It doesn't matter what he says to you, boy," Parnox continued exasperated, "you can't speak that way to the Sarton. If you'll be so good as to remember, he is the commander of the Legion." Searching his memory for the word Sarton, Jaren at last recalled the discussion he had once with Zeroan about the foolish leader of the Legion.

"I can see why Zeroan hates him," he stated zealously. "That man has the behavioral conduct of a donkey." While Parnox was not impressed with the boy's attitude, he silently admitted that it was an accurate metaphor.

Climbing the wall after Captain Morrol with the clamor outside the city only increasing, they at last reached the top once more. Wading through the staring Legionnaires behind Morrol, Jaren and Parnox looked out to the assembly of Drakkaidians disbelievingly. To their amazement, the thick ranks of enemy soldiers were being penetrated down the middle by something moving along the earth with incredible speed. As it drew nearer, Jaren could make out the Drakkaidians in its way not just falling before it but flying above and away from it, somehow being blasted. At last, the speeding force came blasting through the front line of soldiers, leaving behind a trail of incapacitated men littered in a straight line back to the far end of the blockade.

After carefully studying the rapidly moving figure, Jaren identified it as a black steed carrying someone draped in flying robes.

"Is it a horseman?" one of Legionnaires asked out loud. Parnox shook his head no.

"Impossible," he said. "It's moving too fast..." Though the physics of the situation seemed impossible, Jaren at last conceded to his eyes that it was indeed a horse and rider blasting toward them.

"It is a horseman," Morrol stated in disbelief. "Amazing. He penetrated three battalions of Drakkaidians so fast they still don't know what hit them." Then, as the rider closed the gap between the blockade and the city walls, Jaren's eyes slowly widened. He recognized the gray robes of the rocketing rider anywhere.

"It's Zeroan!" he exclaimed at the top of his lungs. Parnox and Morrol both shot him an incredulous look, then spun their heads back down to the advancing figure now racing up the circling road up to the gates. Though the captain had only seen him a few times before, Parnox quickly nodded with enthusiasm and threw his hand up to his forehead.

"You're right!" he confirmed. "Captain, we have to open the gates for him. That is the Mystic Sage Zeroan." Morrol shot him a look of anxiety, a torn look in his eyes.

"Surely you joke, Master Guilldon," he said slowly. "You heard the Sarton as upset as he was for letting the three of you in. There is no possible way what he would ever open the gates for the sage!" Jaren was beside himself.

"We have to let him in! He's the only one who will know what to do about all this. If anyone is going to save this city and the Southland all together, it's him." Parnox was quick to back him up.

"He's right, Captain. "There is more at stake here than you can possibly imagine. There is dark power growing in Drakkaidia that we have yet to tell you about. The battalions of Drakkaidians are not here to attack you. They are here to hold the city until Valif Montrox's army of demonic forces arrives to raze it to the ground. Without Zeroan's help, this city and nation are doomed. He must be allowed entrance." Morrol breathed hard, rubbing his neck with the butt of his hand.

"You're sure that is him?" he asked quietly. Parnox nodded.

"Who else but a Mystic Sage could move at speeds like that?" he asked. The captain exhaled sharply again and nodded.

"I will see what I can do," he said, moving back to the stairs. As the captain made his way down to the Sarton waiting for a report, Jaren and Parnox sprinted to the top of the gates. The horse arrived right behind them, slowing to a trot as it approached.

"Zeroan!" Jaren bellowed, waving wildly. "Zeroan, it's us! We made it!" The cloaked rider on the black steed shifted his gaze up to the wall top.

"There is little time for pleasantries, young Grandarian," was the rugged response from underneath the figure's hood. "Hurry now and open the gates before the Drakkaidians mobilize and start after me. Parnox nodded and called down to the men at the gates to open them. Jaren kept his gaze fixed upon Zeroan, however, noticing another figure tightly clutching to his gray robes. Before he could inquire who the hidden frame belonged to, the angry voice of the Sarton boomed through the air.

"How dare you tell me this, Morrol!?!" the furious man screamed. "I will not have my city besmirched by his presence. He will not enter!"

"My lord," Parnox called from the wall, "I know you have your differences with the sage but you must let him in or he will be killed by the Drakkaidians." Othan took a step toward the gate and the burly Southlander upon it, rage twisting his face.

"Then he should not have come here in the first place!" he retorted. "Do you hear me sage?" He called out beyond the gate to the man outside. "Turn around and go back from whence you came! These gates will not budge for you!" After a moment of silence from everyone, a voice echoed back from outside the gate.

"Sarton Othan, I have her Royal Highness Princess Maréttiny Kolior of Grandaria with me, and your hatred for me jeopardizes her safety. Open the gates for her sake at least." Jaren's eyes went wide at this revelation, and he quickly ran to the opposite side of the wall to get a better look. Peering down, he saw Zeroan spoke the truth. Mary was huddled behind him clutching onto him with an iron grip, the color gone from her beautiful face. She looked inches away from death. Jaren quickly wheeled around to where Parnox stood.

"He's telling you the truth, Sarton!" Jaren bellowed. "The Princess is with him, and she is not well! Open the gates!" Othan remained steady in his words.

"If there is anyone with him," he began scornfully, "it could be any girl he picked off the countryside. Why would he have the Princess of Grandaria with him?" Jaren was beside himself.

"I *know* her!" he bellowed indignantly. "It's her, now *open the gates you stupid son of-*" Parnox quickly took hold of the enraged Grandarian and clamped his hand over his mouth.

"You will not fool me with your lies, Zeroan!" the Sarton yelled back. The voice from beyond the wall came quick and powerful this time.

"There is no time for us to quarrel right now," the commanding voice boomed back. "I will make this simple; this gate is going to open one way or another, whether you order it or not. I suggest you do so I do not have to damage it." Though bursting with rage, the Sarton let out a laugh.

"You are most welcome to try, sage," he chuckled hatefully. "Do your worst!" It was no more than a moment later when the massive wooden gate began to abruptly shudder. The Sarton's face lost its emotion, hearing splintering cracks from the bars holding it in place. From the wall top, Jaren and Parnox watched in awe as the wave of distorted space surrounding the Zeroan's extended arm blasted forward to impact the gate with enough force to snap the multiple bars holding them down in two and splinter the exterior. The doors burst open, spewing massive chunks of damaged wood all about the gate yard before the Sarton, staring in horror as Zeroan strode through the open gates on his black steed hidden in his frayed gray robes. Jaren and Parnox rushed down from the wall top to meet them. The sage stopped feet away from Othan and dismounted with calm and collected movements. As he stepped down, Mary's besieged eyes met his, unsure what was happening.

Jaren was the first to meet them, rushing to the black steed to help Zeroan lower the Grandarian Princess to the ground.

"Be gentle, Jaren," Zeroan instructed softly. "She has been through more than you know and as you put it, she is not well. Hold her carefully." Jaren nodded and shifted his gaze onto her.

"What happened?" he asked horrified. "Where have you been Zeroan?" The sage rose and shifted in his ragged robes.

"The answers will come in due time," he said calmly. "See to her for now." As Jaren shifted his attention to Mary, Zeroan turned back to the Sarton still speechless before him. "I warned you, Othan. I warned you this would happen. Now the Drakkaidians are on your doorstep precluding your escape or aid from others. You must use the temple and summon the Legion, now." The Sarton's face twisted with rage once more and he pointed an accusing finger at him.

"What have you done!?!" he screamed with rage. "You have crossed me for the last time, sage! I tell you I do not want your advice! I am Sarton! I will deal with this as I see fit! I will not let you touch the Temple of Water! If you so much as go near it I will have your head! Do you hear me? I am the Sarton-" He would not have the chance to finish. With a sturdy thud from behind the man's head, he dropped to the ground unconscious. Standing behind him was Captain Morrol with the hilt of a dagger in his hand. Everyone in the gate yard, Legionnaire, Grandarian, and sage alike were quiet, waiting for Morrol to make the next move. At last he nodded and sheathed his weapon.

"Legionnaires, the Sarton is not well," he spoke to the men around him. "It is obvious to me that his mind is lost if he will not call for the Legion. We face the direst of circumstances the Southland has faced in over a century, and if we do not act we will not survive." He turned back to Othan's body and the sage before him. "Therefore, I, as secondary officer to the Sarton, suggest that the Mystic Sage Zeroan temporarily assume the position of Sarton until this crisis has been dealt with." Jaren's eyes widened, unsure if he had heard the man right. He shot a glance at Parnox, equally stunned.

"Can he do that?" he whispered, to which the man only shrugged. Zeroan remained hard.

"You offer me what is not yours to give," he responded quietly. Morrol instantly turned to the Legionnaires again.

"With the Warrior of Water still absent from the city, the Mystic Sage is the only one with the power to summon the Legion. We face invasion; we need the full Legion. What say you men?" After a quick moment of silent uncertainly, the Legionnaires in the gate yard and along the wall began to shout their approval until they began chanting yes. Morrol turned back to Zeroan. The sage remained immobile for a long moment, but eventually turned back to Jaren.

"Parnox, please take hold of the Princess and get her to a medic," he ordered softly. "You need to come with me, Jaren." He turned back then, striding to Morrol. "Very well, Captain. I will assume the charge of Sarton until this situation is resolved. I am going to summon the Legion. Mend the gates as best you can until my return." With that, Morrol nodded and announced to the men Zeroan's acceptance. They cheered out offering whatever plaudits they could as the sage marched through the gate yard, impassive and collected. After he had surrendered Mary to Parnox, Jaren bolted after him confused.

"What are we doing, Zeroan?" he asked baffled. The sage remained walking steadily forward as he responded.

"Summoning the Legion and getting rid of these Drakkaidians," he replied.

Chapter 65

<u>Overflow</u>

The quiet of the snow filled sky over the white peaks of the Border Mountains was shattered by a sudden beaming light soaring through it from the southwest, exploding through the flurries of snow with blinding speed and power. As the beam passed high above one of the tallest mountain summits, the massive power level emitting from it began to wane and steadily drop, dimming the once brilliant light with it. Right as the light passed directly over the mountain glacier, it imploded and vanished, spitting out three figures nearly a hundred feet over the towering peak. All three realized all too quickly what had happened. Tavin, Ril, and Verix had come out of their magical teleportation not safely on the ground like Ril had thought, but directly where Tavin ended it; in the middle of the sky. Even Verix could feel his heart pounding so hard it threatened to blast out of his chest. As they began to fall, the Drakkaidian Prince vehemently called out to the Elemental Warriors beside him.

"What have you done, Tavin!?!" he bellowed out of control. Though the Warrior of Light would have normally been quick to defend himself, he found that he had little interest in defending his honor when faced with the threat of falling to his death from a hundred feet in the air.

"What do we do now?" he barked at the top of his lungs.

"What can we do!?!" Verix roared back.

"Tavin!" was the scream from beside him. The Warrior of Light spun his head around to find Ril flailing about wilding, desperately trying to grip something that wasn't there. Reaching out to her with his stretched right arm, he managed to take hold of a finger and gradually pull her to him. As she drew nearer, Ril clung onto him pressing her shaking head against him. Throwing his head back to his left looking past his thrashing cape, Tavin could make out

Verix several feet below them. They were dangerously close to the earth now, and he knew full well they could do nothing. They had gambled with fate traveling this way, and now they had to face the consequences. Looking down, however, the Grandarian boy noticed that fate had given them a fighting chance after all, as they were going to land on a steep glacier that looked to level off further down. It was going to be a rough ride down, but they might be able to survive long enough to grip something and stop themselves. Just before Verix first hit the snowy mountainside, Tavin shouted for Ril to hold onto him no matter what. She didn't reply, but he could feel her head nodding up and down on his chest.

Verix slammed into the steep incline first, dropping like a rock from the top of the Tower of Granis. Tavin was blinded by the explosion of powdery snow surging up like smoke from a dropped bomb. His landing was more painful than he had anticipated, even though they rolled through feet of billowing powder softer than the clouds they had just left. All three rolled for the better part of a minute, Verix some ten feet ahead, Ril clutching onto Tavin, and Tavin clutching both her and the Sword of Granis. After what seemed like an eternity of painfully rolling down the steep mountainside, Tavin could feel the ground gradually beginning to level. Combined with the thick powder working against them, they had slowed just enough to take hold of something and not rip their arms out of their sockets doing so. Just as the Grandarian thought they were in the clear, he felt the sudden absence of ground beneath him. His eyes going wide, he looked down to find the mountainside nearly vertical again. As it curved out and they plummeted down, he landed on his back sliding down feet first.

Wilding searching past Ril crying out to Granis for help, Tavin spotted Verix ahead of them sliding down to a completely level cliff side. The only problem was there was a straight vertical drop off at the end of it that didn't look to have any end. They would not survive a drop off like that. Watching horrified as Verix slid toward his demise, a familiar surge of crimson mist suddenly appeared around his hands. A moment later he had his savage broadsword in hand. With a mighty scream of dark power surging to life around it, he thrust its blade into the ground, immediately slowing him to a crawl just before he would have disappeared over the cliff. Though it was the best idea he could think of, Tavin knew that the blade of the Sword of Granis wasn't broad enough to slow him, and he couldn't draw it and hold onto Ril at the same time. As the ground began to level onto the icy cliff, he shouted out to the girl in his arms.

"Hold onto me, Ril!" he shouted. "You're going to have to death-grip me! Don't let go!" Screaming back in acknowledgement, the girl's already tight grip increased to the point where Tavin could barely feel the blood moving in his veins. Releasing the hand over Ril, he dropped the Sword of Granis so it landed in the snow just before Verix, ready and waiting for him. As he passed the Drakkaidian, he gripped at his arm first, but as icy as it was and as numb as his hands had become, it slipped away from him. With both hands clamping down, he snagged Verix's frayed coattails. They ripped at the seams as he took hold, but, thanks to Verix's strenuous clutch on his weapon embedded into the icy mountain, it held firm and the two stopped with a bone stretching halt. Tavin could almost feel the muscles in his body tearing like tissue paper from the force. With half of he and Ril's bodies dangling over the cliffside, he summoned every inch of strength in his body and held firm. "Climb up, Ril! I can't hold much longer!" The girl did as she was told, quickly grabbing onto Verix's coat with one hand, then his leg with the other until she thrust her entire body back onto the level ground. She immediately turned back and took hold of one of Tavin's hands, pulling him up with every inch of strength in her freezing body.

Once both Elemental Warriors were safely on the cliff, Verix at last eased his strained body and rose, shaking the crested snow and ice off of his body.

"Are you both alright?" he asked taking hold of his weapon, vanishing into the cloud of red mist once more. They both nodded, shaking wildly from the cold.

"I'm a little more banged up than I wish I was and my arms feel like mush, but I'll live," Tavin managed to shiver. Verix let out a disgruntled huff.

"*Your* arms? I had to hold on for the three of us!" he reminded. "What about you, Arilia?" Her face was bright red, shivering violently.

"I'll be better when I'm dry," she said hurriedly. "Can you mask my power for a moment so I can warm us?" Verix nodded, raising his hand and pointing at her. A wave of small fire surrounded her arm and spread over her entire body in one massive flash. After doing the same to the boys, she let it dissipate. "Just like new." Tavin nodded, feeling much better dry and warm for the moment. As he strapped the Sword of Granis back to his side, he took a broad look around them. Like his dream, there was nothing but snow as far as the eye could see. The sky was densely clouded white, and snow fell quietly, gently rocked back and forth by the slight winds. They had made it, but now what?

"So do you have any clue where we are, Verix?" he asked hopefully. The Drakkaidian Prince met his gaze with a goaded look.

"I might have some idea where I was going if we entered from the western pass, but this?" he said looking around at the endless white. "I'd say we might as well have dropped out of the sky in the middle of nowhere, but analogies work better when they aren't literal, don't you think?"

"So we're lost," Ril breathed in a defeated tone. Tavin glanced at them both, then around at their surroundings again. Noticing a familiar feeling filling the back of his mind, the Warrior of Light slowly looked down to the mighty talisman at his side. As his eyes fell upon the hilt, he noticed the shining Granic Crystal was flashing. Lifting the weapon, he saw only one side was emanating the extra light. Following his eyes, Ril saw the sword's display as well. "What is it doing?" she asked perplexed. Shifting his eyes in the direction of the light, Tavin spotted a summit on the peak next to them, no more than half a day's march if they cut across the relatively flat glacier on the right side.

"It's pointing," he said at last. He did the same, motioning for the others to look up to the neighboring mountain summit. "We have to go there." Verix raised an eyebrow, noting the difficult road ahead.

"Well this is going to be fun," he breathed with dread. "We'd better hurry. Our position has been broadcasted to all of Iairia with that little display in the sky, and I had to draw from my own power to hold us on the cliff. Depending on how far ahead of schedule my father is, we may be having company very soon." With that, the group nodded and set off down from the cliff side to the bottom of the glacier that led to the mountain's summit across from them.

Jaren proceeded across the recently assembled bridge toward the towering Temple of Water, breathing heavy with nervousness coursing through his veins. From the first time he saw the mighty structure on his first visit to the city, he had been mesmerized by how the ancients could have built the equivalent of a lighthouse in the middle of the largest lake in Iairia, so tall it rivaled the Tower of Granis itself. When Zeroan had beckoned him to follow and help him "summon the Legion," he would never have guessed he would be doing what he was about to do. On their way to the Lake Torrent adjacent to the city on the plateau, the newly appointed Sarton had informed him that the only way to alert the entire Southland to immediate danger of invasion was to activate the Temple of Water. Jaren was confused at first, commenting that he thought the temples were always active. While this was true to a degree, the six temples only functioned at a very weak level on their own, so as not to upset the delicate balance between them.

Each temple was capable of much more. If the various Elemental Warriors were to "utilize" their respective Sources, they would unleash a colossal wave of whichever element they housed. If the Temple of Water was ever activated, it would abruptly begin to dump oceans of water into Lake Torrent, flooding the surrounding countryside and rivers connected to it all over the Southland. This was the warning signal that the Southland was under attack established by the first Sarton a century ago. Now the current Sarton was in need of the Legion, and the temple.

"There is one small hindrance to our plan," Zeroan had told Jaren as they arrived at the shores of Lake Torrent. "The only person who can enter the Temple of Water to activate it is the Warrior of Water, and he is currently not here. We don't have time to find him, so we are going to do this ourselves." Jaren gave him a skeptical look, attempting to brace himself for the impossible task being set up for him. "Remember that the sage's power is manipulation of all elements at a passive level. I am not the Warrior of Water, but I have enough sway over this element to temporarily open the temple." Along the shores, the sage pointed to a small azure pedestal rising from the rocky shore to his waist. "To do this, I must remain here and… influence the entrance with this. The Warrior of Water has but to pour a cup of the lake water in this to make the way to the doors, but I must remain to hold the way clear.

That means you will have to enter the temple and activate it yourself, Jaren." The boy stared at him incredulously.

"And how in the name of Granis am I going to go about doing that?" he asked throwing up his arms. "Maybe you've forgotten, but I don't have much elemental magic at my command like everyone else I seem to know nowadays." The sage patiently shook his head.

"You will need none for this," he informed him, moving to the pedestal. "As you can see, the Source of Water rests in the highest part of the temple in visible range. Your task will be to submerge it in the waters at its base. When it enters the lake, it will activate the temple." Jaren remained doubtful with his brow furrowed.

"How do I lower it?" he grilled. Taking position behind the pedestal and immersing his hands into the shallow water inside the bowl at its top, he shook his head once more.

"I have never had business in the Temple of Water before," he stated plainly. "It is only for the Elemental Warriors to know the insides of their temples, not for me. You will have to figure it out for yourself. I have confidence you can do it." Jaren stared at him hard for a moment before finally exhaling loudly and nodding his head.

"Fine," he agreed. "But how am I supposed to get out there? There's about two hundred feet of water between me and the entrance."

"Leave that to me..." Zeroan said quietly, closing his eyes and trailing off. In the silence that followed, the sage began focusing his energy into the pedestal, the water churning around his hands. From out under Lake Torrent, Jaren heard a deep mixing of water. The surface began to wave then, slowly coming alive with whitecaps. Crashing like massive ocean waves, Jaren watched in awe as a stone bridge rose from the depths saturated with dripping water pouring off its sides. "Go," Zeroan ordered quietly. Doing as he was bid, Jaren slowly make his way to the shoreline and stepped onto the emerged bridge, just wide enough to comfortably walk along without falling off. The structure was white but for the underwater plant life scarcely draped over the sides.

The Grandarian archer walked for several minutes until at last reaching the towering Temple of Water and its recently opened archway inside. Just like the thick stone visible from the exterior of the temple, Jaren's eyes found a diverse array of blue, azure, and cobalt hues waiting for him inside. Slowly stepping through the massive doorway, it closed shut behind him making the Grandarian more than a little claustrophobic. The temple truly took the appearance of a lighthouse; confined inside but tall. Around the circumference of the walls was a narrow catwalk of shining cerulean stone, branching out at the far end to the center of the temple which had no floor at all, only a surface of calm water. The walls were obscured by a thin but steady waterfall all around the boundary of the structure, noisily dumping onto the stone catwalk and draining into the pool of water at the center. The light from the few windows and the tower beamed inside casting a rainbow of colors over the mist from the falling liquid.

The most magnificent thing of all was the enormous sphere of levitating blue energy at the top of the tower. Jaren had seen the Source of Water from a distance before, but up close it was even more amazing- like a private blue sun illuminating the interior of the temple. Though captivated by its beauty, he was beset by the impossible task of submerging it into the center pool of water when it levitated so high from his reach. Observing the pedestal at the far side of the catwalk similar to the one Zeroan stood waiting by at the shores, he guessed that the Warrior of Water would only have but to drop a handful of water into its bowl to activate the temple. Without elemental power of his own, that would not a possibility for Jaren. Taking a sweeping look around for another idea, he was struck with a thought. What if he didn't have to drop the Source into the water; what if he could bring the water to it? There was a massive stone dais resting by the pedestal, just large enough to cover the pool, obviously intended for that purpose for some reason. Carefully making his way around the catwalk, Jaren knelt down beside the circular object trying to budge it. It was heavy, but teetering on the rim of the hole in the floor, it would not be hard to move.

Taking hold of the dais with both hands, Jaren summoned his full strength and lurched the massive stone over the water. To his surprise, it fell into place all by itself, instantly filling the hole in the floor. Satisfied that his idea might work, Jaren rose and turned his attention to the steadily falling waterfall around the perimeter of the walls. With no place to drain into, the water began to rapidly collect at Jaren's feet, instantly soaking him. As it began to rise up to his knees and then his waist, the Grandarian's contented smile quickly dispersed replaced by a fearful frown, realizing he had trapped himself. His heart pounding, Jaren was lifted off his feat as his buoyant body lifted with the speedily rising water level. Looking up for somewhere to go, he noticed the balcony surrounding the top of the lighthouse. If he could make his way out before the water level passed it, he could save himself from drowning with the Source. He rose with anxious dread for the next several minutes, struggling to keep his face out of the constantly pouring water and maneuvering to the side of the temple where he could see the small glass door.

As the water finally rose to the small catwalk around the Source, Jaren hurriedly took hold and climbed out, soaked. Frantically lifting himself out of the rising water, he noticed a door quickly opening in the glass around the temple's peak. Darting through it, he found himself outside with the door tightly closing behind him on its own. Fumbling over the narrow balcony in his drenched clothes, he quickly fell to his back and gazed up into the glass top of the temple. Somehow, the rising water from the ceiling did not follow him through the door, but stayed tightly sealed inside. The waterlogged boy stared with wide eyes as the steadily rising liquid began to flood the shining Source, submerging it underneath. The moment the water level completely immersed the blue sphere, it began to swell with radiating azure energy. Then, from far below him, the Jaren could hear the waters of the peaceful lake beginning to crash together. He turned and stood, slowly leaning over the thin railing to the most amazing view he had ever seen.

He could see for endless miles in every direction. The entire capital city below him looked like nothing more than a clustered little village on a hillside, and the Drakkaidian troops surrounding the plateau were nothing more than a black mass smaller than ants. In the distance Jaren could see the jagged peaks of the Iairian Mountain Chain to the east, the endless green of the Grailen in the south, and the smoldering volcanoes to the west. The most captivating sight of all, however, was directly below him. The once calm waters of Lake Torrent were crashing together and building with incredible speed. Like the interior of the temple, the lake's water level was rapidly rising. Within minutes, the surface was beginning to run over the plateau, streaming down the sides into the lands around. Before long the streams became rivers and waves crashing over the sides of the lake to pour down into the surrounding countryside. If the city had not been safely above the lake, it too would have drowned. Jaren watched with a depraved smile as the massive rush of crashing waves slammed into the Drakkaidians, washing them away like insects in a rainstorm.

The flood continued for several more minutes before the Source of Water behind him at last subsided, signaling the water below to follow suit. Jaren turned to find the water level draining away into the bottom of the temple once more. Realizing this was his ride down, the Grandarian quickly leapt through the now open doorway to dive into the dropping water. As he tread the falling water, Jaren smiled and silently laughed, reflecting on how, even though he had no magic power of his own, he had still done something amazingly magical. Now, he just hoped that the Legion would arrive before the demons did.

Chapter 66

<u>Ascension</u>

After half a day's march through the coldest environment any of them had ever thought possible, Tavin, Ril and Verix had ascended the icy glacier between them and the mountain summit holding the Celestial Portal. With the jagged ice flows, neck deep snow, and cold biting at them that human beings were not meant to be exposed to, it had proved to be one of the most arduous missions any of them had ever embarked upon. Though they managed to avoid freezing to death with Ril occasionally warming them with what power Verix could permit, the Warrior of Fire in particular was so cold she could feel the environment threatening to ice over the blood in her veins. Tavin kept her pressed against him for warmth when possible, but it proved a daunting task when navigating through the hazards obscured by the snow. Despite their long trek up the mountainside as miserable as it was, it would pale in comparison to what lay in store for them at the top.

After the trio had moved up the last leg of the glacier, Tavin squinted ahead through the snow flurries to find only a small hill between them and what looked to be the summit. Looking down to the Sword of Granis for confirmation, he saw the flashing crystal on his hilt beaming a solid ray of light straight ahead. He could not help but smile, looking at Ril clutching his right arm.

"We're almost there," he said through the light winds biting at their faces. She brushed a lock of frozen hair away from her face and met his gaze.

"That's the best news I've ever heard in my life," she violently shivered with a faint grin. Silently laughing, Tavin nodded and turned his head to the left toward his other companion.

"Did you hear that, Verix?" he asked. "We're practically there." The Drakkaidian Prince stood beside him slowly stepping forward with a deep scowl over his glacial face, not responding. Tavin tilted his head and repeated himself. Verix slowly panned his view around them, slow to answer.

"Good..." he offered mysteriously, trailing off. Tavin nodded, too cold to be curious of his absent behavior. They started forward again, gradually climbing up the final road to their destination. With his eyes on the shining talisman at his waist, Tavin was surprised to observe a radical change in the direction the Granic Crystal was showing. In the blink of an eye, it pivoted to the right, now pointing off to the west. He halted abruptly, a baffled frown over his face.

"What in the name of Granis..." he mumbled confused. Ril brought her gaze down to the sword.

"What is it?" she asked quickly. Tavin shrugged and turned his body in the direction of the beaming light.

"The sword is pointing over there all of a sudden," he said. "I can't figure out-"

"Something is wrong," Verix interjected suddenly, spinning around to face him with urgent eyes. "I can sense something, but...." His words were rushed and worried, and Tavin had never seen him so worked up. He paced back and forth from one side of the small ridge they stood on to the other, intently scanning around them. In the wake of his silence, Tavin's eyes fell back down to the golden crystal on his weapon. It was bursting with brilliant energy pointing like an arrow to the west. Slowly following the ray into the empty snowfield it pointed to, Tavin caught something moving in the skies. Squinting and leaning his head forward, he realized what the sword of doing.

It was trying to warn them.

"Verix," he called, "what is that?" The Drakkaidian Prince wheeled on him and looked to the western skies. Narrowing his own eyes, he saw what the Warrior of Light had and lowered his jaw.

"No..." he breathed, slowly shaking his head. Fixating his gaze on the approaching black masses in the sky, he swallowed hard and twisted his head to them in fury. "*Run!*" he blasted. Tavin and Ril stood frozen with dread for another moment, but started off with him the first second after. There were seven black winged figures in the sky rapidly closing the small gap between them, only a few hundred feet away from the summit. Tavin looked up to see another fifty from them to the portal, and after that there was at least another hundred to the pedestal at its center. Turning back to view the approaching threat, Ril shook her head and yelled out to Tavin.

"We aren't going to make it!" she exclaimed. The Warrior of Light wheeled his head back to hers with angry determination strapped to his face. He reached down and threw his hand over hers, pulling her after him.

"We have to!" he decreed. Speeding up the hillside, the group at last reached the top and the summit. Tavin found a familiar sight waiting for him. It was the exact image he had seen in his dream; a field of white harboring the clear Celestial Portal lying in all its glory. "Hurry!" he bellowed dashing forward with the southland girl in tow. As they closed the gap between them and the enormous platform, the Dégamar did the same, now only moments behind them. Tavin could hear the massive wing beats and the bloodcurdling shrieks of Valcanor rapidly trailing them, growing louder with each passing second. At last, the two Elemental Warriors stepped onto the gargantuan portal, taking off with new speed on the dry, solid ground.

As they pressed forward to the center of the platform and the pedestal lying there, however, Tavin noticed that he had lost the sound of the third pair of feet behind them. Wheeling around, he came to an immediate halt seeing Verix Montrox standing with his back to them and summoning his savage broadsword from the crimson mist around him. The Warrior of Light's face cringed with dread and dismay.

"Verix! What are you doing?" The Drakkaidian Prince did not turn, but allowed his dark aura of power to blaze up around his body.

"What I promised, Grandarian," he said powerfully. "I'll hold them for as long as I can so you can activate the portal. Go!" His words stabbed at Tavin like the point of his sword as the Dégamar grew closer still.

"No!" he returned straining his voice. "I won't let you do this alone!" It was Verix's turn to be angry now, spinning his head back to the two Elemental Warriors.

"This is your only chance, Tavin!" he bellowed irately. "You are the one who must live to fight my father and save our two lands, not me! I told you I would help you complete your quest, and that is what I am doing! Now go!" Tavin could not

516

move. Every nerve in his body told Tavin this was all wrong. Ril tugged on his arm violently.

"Tavin, he's right!" she pleaded with him. "He's our only chance! Don't let all we've been through be for nothing!" As her words stacked on top of Verix's, the Warrior of Light at last swallowed and turned, letting go of the Dark Prince. They ran as hard and as fast as their exhausted legs would carry them, speeding toward the center of the portal. Behind them, Verix Montrox flared his full power around him in a swirling vortex of crimson energy electrifying the space around his charged body. Responding to the explosion of power beneath them, the Dégamar came soaring in from the sky directly above to deal with him first. As the Valcanor plummeted at him, Verix grit his teeth and formed a rush of crimson light around his blade. In one fluid motion he swung it upward, releasing an arching wave of energy to slice the demonic creature in two. As its halves landed in front of him skidding to a halt over the snowy earth, the black rider atop its back tumbled down into the hillside apart from the others.

Watching the demon mage fall, Verix missed the other swooping Valcanor descending on him. Before he could so much as raise his sword in defense, the creature threw itself into him and sent him careening backward to land thirty feet away on his back. A swell of incapacitation overcoming his winded body, Verix struggled for breath and dropped his sword. Sensing the sudden disappearance of the mighty power behind him, Tavin spun his head around and found his friend lying on the hard platform motionless with the other six Dégamar swooping past him toward he and Ril. Gritting his teeth with righteous fury, the Warrior of Light stopped and released Ril's hand, instead placing it on the hilt of the Sword of Granis. He knew these creatures would be strong, but he would not let this happen without a fight.

"No," he breathed vehemently. Though Ril wanted to tell him to keep going, she knew as well as he did they would not make it to the pedestal still fifty feet away. Wrenching the Grandarian talisman from its sheath, Tavin sent its metallic ringing slicing through the air, threatening to tear a rift in the very matter around them. Gripping it with both hands, he reached inside himself and found his power, ready and waiting for him. Taking hold with unflagging resolve, the Warrior of Light summoned it all and let it explode outward. In one massive flash of righteous light, the six Valcanor speeding toward him shrieked out in terror as their flesh burned and crisped black. They all dropped to the platform and slid toward the radiating figure, smoldering crippled or dead. As their charred forms fell lifeless on the massive platform, Tavin brought his sword before his chest and flexed his surging golden power around him in a brilliant detonation of energy that tore through the air like hurricane wind.

Standing tall and at full strength, Tavin watched as the six black robed forms slowly stood to meet him. The one at the center was the first to move, slowly staring him down then ambling forward. Before it could leap forward, Tavin quickly threw his clenched fist behind him and formed a sphere of radiant golden energy around it. Punching it forward, the ball blasted forward impacting the demon with a cloud of smoke and shining energy. Tavin lowered his hand, unable to see through the light. Had he done it? Had he disposed of the supposedly all powerful creature so easily? He got his answer soon after, a bundle of black robes flying out of the smoke toward him. Before he could react, the Dégamar threw its rotting fist at him blasting him back by the chest. Tavin flew backward, but landed on his knees to stop himself.

The Dégamar quickly turned its attention to the girl now standing alone before him, a mix of horror and rage in her eyes. As it started toward her, Ril instinctively locked her arms perpendicular before her, building a cross of fire. Clenching her teeth, the Warrior of Fire threw them apart, releasing the wave of flame into the creature. It quickly threw up its robes in defense, catching the attack with its sage-like telekinetic power and deflected it back at her with a thrust of its forearm. So surprised at the creature's reaction, it was all Ril could do to raise her arms again and stop her own attack from throwing her off her feet. As she staggered back from the force of the blow, the Dégamar lunged forward and took hold of her neck, raising her off the ground. The demon mage would not hold onto her long, however, as Tavin charging forward thrust his blade down to pierce at the creature's robes. It reeled back defensively, not wishing to be slashed by a weapon so effective against its power.

The Dégamar quickly responded by motioning for its kin to begin assaulting him together. In unison, the six demon mages raised their hands in a triangular patter to form black balls of energy inside. Tavin moved in front of Ril as the energy began blasting for them in rapid succession. With his heightened strength and reflexes, Tavin was barely able to deflect their bombardment with quick movements of his blade. They impacted him with hammering force, but moving with his speed he repelled them every time. Ril, rising back from her knees on the ground, worriedly looked to Tavin struggling to avert the onslaught. Though he was giving it his all, it was obvious to her that the Dégamar were barely putting out any effort at all.

They were toying with them.

The demon mages apparently grew tired of the game quickly, as the frequency of their attacks suddenly rocketed. There was no way Tavin could deflect six blasts at once, and he was quickly showered by the dark energy losing his balance and toppling over Ril. The two Elemental Warriors struggled to rise, but the Dégamar in front once again thrust his grasping, rotting hand outward to magically take hold of their bodies, constricting their movement. Frozen in place by the Dégamar's power, Tavin and Ril watched with intensely beating hearts as it drew near, tightening its hold as it came.

Just when Tavin was sure his bones were going to break under the pressure the Dégamar held them with, he was surprised to be abruptly released. Looking back up to his foe in confusion, he found the reason why. There was a foot of bloody steel protruding from the demon's gut, with two more sticking inside and behind him. His mind racing, Tavin looked back behind the six mages to find Verix on his feet, breathing hard where he had fallen. The Dégamar wheeled around toward the Prince, taking his battle stance with a new wave of his temporarily downed power surging up around him again. The Dégamar impaled by his broadsword calmly and leisurely took hold of the blade stained with its tainted blood and effortlessly wrenched the rest of it through him. Ril watched horrified as it causally dropped it to his side.

Verix did not wait for his enemies to attack him first, quickly building his full power as fast and hard as he could muster it. As the electrified crimson energy raged around him blowing the air back in all directions, Tavin and Ril could both sense that he was holding back nothing. He was dipping into the very energy that sustained his life to focus into his duel clenched fists at his sides, bursting with volatile power waiting to be unleashed. Verix screamed out to the two Elemental Warriors.

"Hurry!" he ordered. "This will not hold them for long!" Then, in one massive motion, the Drakkaidian Prince threw his fists together and forward at the Dégamar, unleashing a beam of dark energy that tore through the atmosphere toward them, larger than the boy's body itself. Screaming with power, Verix let every ounce of his strength flow into the attack. Surprised the boy had summoned so much power so quickly, the Dégamar barely had time to prepare. In one perfectly coordinated movement, the six demonic mages leapt together, accepting the beam in the palms of their outstretched hands with an explosion of sound. Tavin could feel the force of Verix's attack blasting into the Dégamar and pounding through his body like thunder. "What are you waiting for?" Verix screamed again, shifting his heated gaze at them. "Go!"

Painfully wrenching his eyes off of the Elemental Warriors, the Drakkaidian locked them back onto the crimson beam of electrified energy blasting out of his outstretched fists toward the six black figures before him. Tightening his face with fortitude, he let out a scream that overpowered even the noise from his gargantuan attack. Realizing this was Verix's last stand for them- that he would have nothing left to give after this- Tavin struggled back up through his pain pulling Ril to her feet.

"Let's go!" he shouted, already dragging her after him toward the pedestal at the center of the portal. Though he knew Verix's diversion would not last for long, it was cut short prematurely as the seventh Dégamar at last reappeared at the end of the portal behind the Drakkaidian Prince, firing its own dark blast from the confines of its shredded robes. Striking Verix's back like a boulder, he immediately lost focus and control of his energy. The scarlet beam from his fists quickly dissipated along with the bulk of the dark aura of power around him. Seizing on his stall, the lone Dégamar behind him charged forward and gripped the stunned boy's arm, savagely picking him up and swinging him into the solid ground beneath with unnaturally prodigious strength. The fleeing Elemental Warriors could both sense Verix's power disappear behind them. Though Tavin wished more than anything that he could wheel around and charge to his aid, he realized they had been outmatched from the beginning and he would only let his friend's sacrifice be for nothing. After all the distrust and doubt about Verix's motives, he had indeed fulfilled his promise to help them and became a true friend.

The Dégamar quickly realized the purpose of the Prince's extravagant attack, however, spinning their rotted heads around to find Tavin and Ril sprinting toward the center of the portal. Letting out deep groans from the confines of their ragged hoods, all seven of the demon mages blasted forward levitating inches above the ground. With their foes trailing them twice as fast as they ran, Ril desperately looked ahead to find the pedestal meters away. As exhausted as she was, the only thing keeping her worn body in motion was the Warrior of Light's hand clamped tightly around hers. In his other, Tavin flipped the Sword of Granis downward and raised it above his head, ready to plunge it into the portal ahead of them. The Dégamar sped after them, reaching out with both hands extended to latch onto them before they could disappear.

Just as Ril could swear she could feel the tips of their rotting fingers along her neck, Tavin dove forward with every pocket of strength he could muster, throwing his blade into the open pedestal on the portal. A fierce radiant light flashed up instantaneously forcing them to shut their eyes. Though they were both falling toward the hard surface of the portal, neither of them ever felt the touch of the ground. Caught up in a wave of warmth suddenly wrapping itself around their bodies, Tavin and Ril were gently nestled into the air amidst the beaming golden light surging up around them. Like in Tavin's dream, the myriad designs and engravings cast across the portal lit up like the sun, forcing the seven black figures behind them to reel back in anguish. Retreating burned and smoldered, the Dégamar were forced to abandon Tavin and Ril softly floating into the colossal shaft of light that beamed into the clouds above them. The two Elemental Warriors fell into a comforting sleep.

Chapter 67

<u>Unleashed</u>

The new High Priest of the Black Church of Drakkan sped through the dark confined hallways of the royal castle with purpose in his step. Unfortunately, he was charged with conveying the unfavorable news regarding the fate of the Drakkaidian battalions holding Torrentcia City, just delivered by a scout who escaped the flood that had consumed the rest of them. Though he feared the temperamental king's reaction to such inauspicious information, he was not going to make the mistake of delaying the news to his ears. In the course of the past two months, two High Priests had been mercilessly murdered by the Drakkaidian ruler, and he was not about to become the third. Passing through the shadowy torch-lit hallways to the throne room, he quickly turned the final corner to his destination whipping the ends of his black robes about his feet. With a quick flick of his wrist, he motioned for the two armored sentries to open the doors, which they unanimously obeyed. Stepping through the arching doorway, he found the throne room full of Dark Mages and priests standing silent before the three empty thrones atop the rising stairs, obviously waiting for their absent ruler to emerge from the cylindrical chamber adjacent to them.

Aware that Valif Montrox could be found only in his throne room or the Netherworld Portal of late, he immediately stepped to the entrance of the latter along the right wall, momentarily pausing to collect the message he was about to impart and slowly exhale, audible to the entire room. After properly composing himself, the High Priest moved forward to push open the twin doors of the dark chamber and enter, finding the unmoving form of Valif Montrox standing beside the closest side of the portal with his darkly radiating shards of the Holy Emerald slowly levitating around his clenched fist. Making his way through the darkness, the High Priest bowed behind him and began.

"Your Highness," he began as poised as he could force himself, "I have an urgent message from a courier just returned from our battalions at Torrentcia City." Montrox remained still and silent, ominously inhaling. Before the High Priest could elaborate, however, he slowly shifted in his armor and slightly tilted his head back to him, barely revealing a sliver of his dark hidden face.

"Battalions?" he asked low and steady, his voice hauntingly deep. "Our battalions no longer remain." The foreboding figure's words surprised the nervous High Priest, unsure how he came to acquire this information already. Deciding not to grill him for the answer, he hastily gulped and continued.

"I am afraid so, Sire," he confirmed. "The messenger reported the lake on the plateau suddenly overflowed and flooded the proximity around the city. Our troops were drowned and washed away." Valif Montrox remained inert as a corpse for another long moment, but at last turned his thick armored form to face the uncertain man behind him. As the dark light from the four brilliantly white emerald shards around his fist illuminated the king's body, the High Priest felt a sickening sensation of trepidation rip through him. In the days since Montrox had obtained his new shards and spent more time around the Netherworld Portal, his physical appearance had drastically altered. The flesh along his right arm where he kept the shards hovering had swelled into thick brown muscles bulging from him, disproportionate to the rest of his body. His previously red hair had acquired streaks of black, and the pupils of his dead eyes had turned hellish red, pulsating with a low humming glow. Deep lines like tattoos and blood veins streaked across his face and his voice had grown distant and deep as if speaking from inside the Netherworld itself.

After steadily staring the High Priest down with his quietly menacing face, the Drakkaidian Ruler blinked once and began strolling past him toward the doors.

"It is of no concern," he breathed with malicious indifference pouring from his lips. "Let the Southland muster their little Legion. Their walls will crumble just as easily once we unleash our true soldiers." Slowly making his way across the chamber to his throne and unhurriedly taking a seat, he took an exaggerated heavy breath and shifted his gaze to the High Priest. "What is the status of the army?" The High Priest pointed over to the Dark Mages standing at attention at the left side of the room.

"The Dark Mages have assembled the entire force outside of Dalastrak," he reported. "Every last demon you have marshaled is ready to be let loose. They thirst for it. Give them rein to attack and they will be off as soon as you wish." Montrox held the man's gaze intently, but gently shook his head.

"In due time. The Dark Mages can assemble them into a makeshift rabble, but not control them in battle. We will send them before the sun sets, but we must wait for the Dégamar to return. Speaking of which," he said turning to the open balcony doors to his right, "it would appear they draw near. Leave me." Motioning for the entire assembly to exit, the High Priest bowed and withdrew, happy to yet draw breath. After the doors to the chamber sealed shut, Valif Montrox took a deep breath and set the hovering shards of the Holy Emerald beside him onto a tabletop beside his throne. As he set them down one by one, the thunderous dropping of two massive forms on the roof above drew his attention to the balcony once more. Locking his pulsating red eyes outside to the dark veranda, seven black robed figures dropped down to the ground one at a time. The last one fell with a particularly loud crash, towing something behind it. As the group passed through the balcony doors and into the throne room, Montrox saw what.

Hauled behind them in a near lifeless heap was his son, Verix, bloodied and broken. Though he waited on death's doorstep, the Drakkaidian ruler could sense life still lingering in him. Montrox remained motionless and impassive as the Black Seven assembled before his throne, throwing Verix's practically comatose form before him. He struggled for breath through the veritable lake of blood coughed up in his mouth, barely able to maintain the strength to remain conscience. After spitting out what blood he could, the defeated Prince slowly tilted his bruised face toward his father, still seated emotionless on his throne. New pain entered Verix as his father's altered appearance entered his eyes, almost too appalled to hold his gaze. After several long moments of silence staring his son down, Valif Montrox shifted his blood red eyes to the center Dégamar. It immediately produced the shard Verix had been carrying from its robes. Montrox quickly thrust his hand forward, gripping it with his power and levitating it toward him to hover in his armored palm for a moment. After setting it onto the table with the other four, he fixated his haunting eyes back on the Black Seven.

"I sent you to retrieve more than my treacherous son, creatures," he began reserved yet quietly malevolent, "yet only he is with you. Why is this?" The Dégamar was still as stone as always, its distant haunting voice sounding like death through the chamber.

"*They disappeared into light,*" it reported eventually.

"You mean the Celestial Portal," Montrox clarified for it. "They have escaped into the Celestial World. Why did you not stop this from happening?"

"*This one distracted us and they escaped,*" it stated as impassive as Montrox. The quiet malice in the Drakkaidian ruler's voice mounted as he leaned his head forward to respond.

"You're telling me that a boy outmatched all seven of you?" he asked. The demonic mages did not respond, cut off by the soft echoing laughter from the bloodstained body of Verix Montrox before them. The Warrior of Darkness shifted his gaze down to his son tilting his head to stare at him with a dark grin.

"Sad, isn't it father," Verix managed through his blood, "that your most powerful minions are defeated by three children?" Holding his gaze, Montrox rose from his throne and made his way to Verix, slowly kneeling before him. The smile over Verix's face dissipated as his father's radiating eyes locked onto him.

"You think you have won something today, don't you son," he breathed after a long pause. "You think that just because the Warrior of Light managed to flee into the heavens he will now be able to stop me. Well, Verix," he started with hateful cruelty dripping from his words, "I advise you to take a look out the window. In case you didn't notice on the way in, there is an infinite army of demons waiting to be unleashed onto the world. With the six shards of the Holy Emerald all but within the reach of my hand, I will be utterly invincible in a matter of days. Not even Granis himself will be able to stand up to me, much less your pitiful Warrior of Light. I have but to snap my fingers and the enemies of Drakkaidia will fall." Verix's eyes were hard and unafraid, his tenacity only bolstered by his father's words.

"The only enemy of Drakkaidia that I can see," he began weakly, "is you." Valif Montrox held his son's gaze with unmatched intensity for what seemed like an eternity before at last shaking his head.

"What a disappointment you have become, Verix," he breathed acidly. "To think what you could have- should have- become, and now look at you. Bloodied and broken; holding onto life by a thread. Why did you betray me, boy?" Verix coughed up another mouthful of blood before furrowing his brow and desperately summoning the strength to respond.

"I did not betray you, father," he struggled faintly. "You betrayed our country and people with your lust for power. How many innocent Drakkaidians have been murdered at the bloodthirsty claws of demons, and how many more do you put at risk by further summoning them?" Montrox only let out a disgusted huff as he rose back to his feet.

"How did a son of mine ever become so weak?" he asked mostly to himself. "The 'people' you speak of, Verix, are nothing but livestock. They are powerless, and those without power in this world are not worthy of my notice nor concern. Your absurd fear for them is your flaw." He paused there, looking down to his son mustering the power to respond.

"I may have my flaws, father," Verix began one last time, out of energy, "but at least I am not consumed by them." Valif Montrox stared down at him with contempt and confusion racing through his mind. Turning his back to him then, he opened his mouth to speak.

"We still agree on one thing, it seems," he commented slowly, summing his five shards on the table around his arm once more. "You are flawed, son. But worry not. I will bring you back to my way of thinking one way or another before this is over. You can rest assured of that." With that, the Warrior of Darkness raised his hand and motioned for the guards waiting by the door. "Take him away." They hurriedly made their way around the unmoving Dégamar and lifted the Prince on either side, carrying him out the doors of the throne room into the darkness of the long corridors beyond. Alone with the undead mages once more, Montrox deepened his frown and strode toward the arching doorway to his massive balcony with the Dégamar following him out in single file.

Waiting for them was Verix's worst nightmare come true. Passing over the length of the balcony and facing the railing, Valif Montrox looked down on over ten thousand demonic residents of the Netherworld that he had summoned forth with the aid of the Holy Emerald shards hovering around his swollen right hand. Ranging from sprinting runners like the Liradds to the flying monstrosities of the Valcanor, every creature that resided in the underworld had been called forth. Covering the land like a black plague from the lower city of Dalastrak out into the countryside beyond, they were everywhere, savage bloodlust coursing through their tainted veins.

Montrox quietly focused his dark power around the emerald shards in his possession and thrust them into the air before him, instantaneously drawing the attention of the diabolical horde.

"My creatures of the Netherworld!" he boomed in a voice that shattered the air about Dalastrak with its intensity. "You have been imprisoned in hell too long! Go forth now, and satisfy your appetite for death with the blood of the Southland! Follow your Dégamar to war!" Too barbaric to respond in any intelligent manner, the demonic host answered with a frenzied revitalization of their hatred toward all living beings, clawing and tearing at each other enraged. Satisfied with his army's power and resolve, Montrox turned back to the Dégamar, holding out the shards of the Holy Emerald that briefly pulsated with dark light once more. The flapping of Valcanor wings was soon audible and seven more appeared over the balcony, peering their blood red eyes onto the Drakkaidian ruler. "I trust you will hold onto these a little longer with the Warrior of Light indisposed at the moment." As the Black Seven mounted the demons' backs, Valif Montrox took a step forward, fixing his gaze onto them. "Take the army to the Southland capital. Destroy it, then turn for the Grandarian border and await my arrival. Do not fail me." The rotting demon mages unanimously nodded and commanded their winged steeds to take off.

The moment the Dégamar entered the air, the wildly howling legion of demons below them turned south and began marching toward the defenseless Torrentcia City. Montrox stood over his balcony for the next hour, watching until the black masses had emptied Dalastrak and disappeared from view. With a twisted smile, he at last turned and leisurely strolled back into his throne room and the Netherworld Portal inside.

Chapter 68

<u>Truth</u>

The next thing Tavin knew after slowly dissipating into the golden shaft of light beaming into the clouds over the Celestial Portal was that he was standing alone in a white emptiness that stretched for eternity in every direction. The Grandarian boy came to his senses with a start, nervously sweeping his eyes around the eerily empty space, completely devoid of anything but him and endless white. With no idea where he was or how he had come to be there, Tavin took an inquisitive step forward. As he racked his mind trying to figure out what this place could be or where Ril had gone, a familiar friendly voice sounded through the infinite emptiness.

"Hello again, Tavinious," the echoing voice greeted. It came from all around him, seeming to emanate from everywhere and nowhere at once. Seeing nothing before him but empty space, Tavin wheeled around to search for the source of the voice. Yet only the white infinity was there. His mind reeled with bewilderment. "What are you looking for?" Scanning the emptiness once again, Tavin realized that he knew the voice all too well. It was the Sword of Granis. He paused, waiting to see if it would speak again. It did, preceded by a gentle laughter bubbling throughout the blank environment. "I'm sorry to confuse you, Tavin. But don't look so lost. Sometimes what we first see is not what it seems. Turn around once more." Hesitantly soaking up the voice's words, Tavin did as he was bid and turned back to find a small, cozy garden billowing with lush organic hues laying not a few feet before him. He flinched in momentary shock to so suddenly be confronted with such an elaborate sight when seconds before there had been nothing but empty space.

His curiosity provoked beyond anything he had experience before, Tavin put aside his ambiguity and slowly stepped through the gate in the white picket fence stretching around the garden's small perimeter. Standing on grass amongst rows of diverse flowers in an otherwise empty space devoid of life, his eyes sparkled with amazement.

"Beautiful, isn't it," the voice of the sword echoed. Shifting his thoughts back to the illustrious weapon, Tavin looked down to his side to find that it was missing. His eyes going wide with panic, the voice uttered a soft laugh once more. This time however, it did not reverberate from all corners of the atmosphere, but directly behind him. Spinning his head around for the fourth time, Tavin was again surprised to find something added to the luscious scenery. An elderly man with white locks of hair stretching to his neck and dressed in humble gardening attire covered with soil stood before him. He had a tussled white beard grown thick off his disarming face with a deep smile resting behind it. Though the man was obviously well on in his years, he still maintained a strong, able looking figure and stood tall over Tavin.

Staring into the man's deep eyes even bluer than his own, Tavin tilted his head with curiosity, staying silent.

"Looking for this?" he asked, gently holding up his right arm. Shifting his gaze down, Tavin saw that he held the Sword of Granis, shimmering in its eternal radiance. To his surprise, however, the Grandarian boy noticed that the Granic Crystal embedded on its hilt was beaming with fervent light, something he thought it only did while in his grasp.

"...Who are you?" he asked slowly. The old man's smile only deepened.

"You know who I am, Tavin," he responded warmly, like an old friend. Tavin's face remained uncertain, a vague tentativeness swirling in his mind. Sensing the boy's doubt, the old man gave a quick nod and brought up the Sword of Granis to hold its blade before his face. Letting his eyes pass up and down its length, he began to speak once again.

"Did you know, Tavin, that this object is the crowning irony of the Grandarians?" His words were more of a statement than a question, but they remained pleasant and open nonetheless. "It's truly amazing if you think about it. This is their most treasured icon. The most powerful thing they have ever created, and arguably the most beautiful." He paused and gave Tavin a hard look. "Yet of all the monuments they have constructed over their long years, it is my least favorite. While I have imparted to the Grandarians to stand for the preservation of life, they place the most value on that which takes it. I have always been disappointed with them in this. I like to view this as a key, however. The key to something not dangerous that takes life, but protects it. That is what all talismans of magic are, Tavin. Even the Holy Emerald is merely a key that can only be activated at its shrine." In the wake of the old man's speech, Tavin could feel his mouth slip open; a profound majesty overcoming him. Realizing that the man's voice and the voice of the Sword of Granis were one in the same, he slowly shook his head. He couldn't believe it, but he did know who this man was.

"...Granis..." he murmured disbelievingly. The old man grinned and gently gave him a single nod of acknowledgment. Tavin was awestruck. Though every sensible logic in his body screamed at him that there was no way this man could be the God of Light, something deep in his soul where is power resided reached up to him and told him he truly was.

"Your insight serves you well, Tavin Tieloc," the man smiled, lowering the Sword of Granis to his side once more. "Very bright. A bit headstrong still, but very bright indeed. I am Granis." Letting the words digest, Tavin found himself speechless. Granis only smiled. "I am not quite how you would envision me, I see. Well, as you can imagine, I have no physical form of my own that you could comprehend, so I thought I would appear as something a little less intimidating. And what is friendlier than a garden?" He paused once more, allowing the Grandarian boy to let out the words formulating on the tip of his tongue.

"So, every time I heard the Sword of Granis speaking to me," he began slowly, "it was you? You were there, watching, when I took hold of it for the first time? Talking to me through it?" The God of Light beamed.

"Correct once again, Warrior of Light," he stated. "I have been with you from the beginning. I have always been with you. From the Temple of Light to here. From your birth to here. From before." Bringing up their strange surroundings, Tavin thought of what this must mean.

"So am I..." he trailed off, unsure of what to say or how to say it.

"In the Celestial World?" Granis finished for him. He slowly shook his head, letting out what looked to be a sad smile. "No, we are not. And while you are asking questions, allow me to save you the trouble and clear up the most pertinent ones. Ril is not with us, but I assure you she is safe and unharmed. I am the one who healed your wounds from your last battle, and I am sorry, but I do not know what has become of Verix." Tavin stared at him hard for another moment, then gave him a peculiar look.

"Lord Granis," he began quietly, his mouth ahead of his mind, "what do you mean you don't know?" The old man gave another quick nod and let out a deep breath.

"Why don't we sit down, Tavin," he beckoned, motioning for the boy toward the wooden bench suddenly resting behind him. Watching the god sit, Tavin took a deep gulp and gradually took a seat next to him, unsure of everything. Granis smiled again, planted the Sword of Granis into the soft earth before them. "There is no need to stand on ceremony for me, Tavin. I appear to you this way so we might have an equal human discussion. Speak to me as you would Jaren." The Warrior of Light let out a slow smile and shook his head.

"I wouldn't speak to anyone like I would Jaren if I had a shred of respect for them, much less you," he carefully grinned. Granis laughed. "Indeed. Well, your father then." He stopped for a moment, as if collecting his thoughts. "We have something to discuss, Tavin. Something not even your Zeroan is aware of. In fact, you are the only human being since the beginning of Iairia to hear this truth."

"Truth?" Tavin asked hesitantly. Granis nodded, resting a leg over his knee.

"That's right, Tavin," he began again, "truth." He paused once more, his smile dissipating to absolute seriousness. "History as you know it, how everyone knows it, is a lie. The prophesies I 'left behind' and the Battle of the Gods eons ago- all half truths at best. Are you ready to hear the truth, Tavin?" The Grandarian boy held the elderly man's gaze for a long moment, pondering what could be coming. He had been surprised before; had his world turned upside down by revelations from sages and friends, but was he prepared to discover something no one else knew from the God of Light himself? Though plagued by uncertainty, he pushed it aside and nodded firmly. "Very well then. I must start from long ago- long before Grandarian or Drakkaidia. By now you know all too well the legend of the Holy Emerald; the legacy of the Battle of the Gods; the prophesies left at the end of my time in your world. But there is more to these stories that you or anyone else could know.

"It begins in the great peace when I and my brother, Drakkan, lived together in Iairia harmoniously. We have always been stellar opposites, my brother and I, but we once coexisted peacefully. As what you would interpret as time rolled on, however, Drakkan somehow grew restless with his lands to the north and his dark power, and realized that there was more to be had. One day he appeared in the center of the world where I kept watch over the dormant Holy Emerald resting in its shrine, and told me he wished for it so he could activate its full power for himself. I told him what he already knew- that the Holy Emerald housed the power of all the six elements of the universe within, and it was not meant to be had by anyone. Impatient with this universal law, Drakkan moved to take the emerald for his own by whatever means necessary. This is the nature of light and darkness, Tavin; good and evil. It is the nature of evil to want, to have for itself. But good sees beyond itself to other life and works for it as well as itself. This act is what first defined the two ultimate forces. It is what first defined Drakkan and I.

"So as this nature we defined led us to conflict, and the Battle of the Gods commenced. The ancient Grandarians of old correctly painted it as the most massive struggle the world has ever seen, but that is the only accurate thing they know about it." Granis stopped for a moment, letting his eyes drift. Tavin could see an emptiness inside like nothing he had ever witnessed before, and felt insecure just looking at him. "History is a lie, Tavin. Though Drakkan was sealed inside of his Netherworld below Iairia, he was not driven there by me." The god shifted his eyes to Tavin, a knowing truth present. "It was I who was imprisoned, Tavin, not Drakkan. It was I who lost the Battle of the Gods." Tavin's face slowly tightened, scarcely able to believe he had just heard what he knew he had.

"What?" he asked incredulously. "Lord Granis, that can't be possible..." Granis shook his head with a faint smile quickly passing over his face.

"I'm afraid it is," he affirmed. "As you know, Drakkan did indeed steal the Holy Emerald before the end of the war, and he did summon its power. Though the legends say I defeated him before he could muster its true power, it is the exact opposite. With the activated emerald in hand straight from the shrine, Drakkan was all powerful. He quickly defeated me and sought to oust me from the world. So he tore a hole in space, time, and matter, and banished me here for eternity. To the void. He trapped me in the one place where I was completely helpless; in between Iairia and the Celestial World. And here I have been ever since. Condemned to eternal nothingness; separated from my people in life and afterlife." Tavin's brow furrowed and his mouth gaped open, struggling for a way to dispute what he was hearing.

"But that can't be," he protested. "If you lost the Battle of the Gods, how was Drakkan sealed back into the Netherworld? How did the Holy Emerald shatter?"

"As I said," he continued, "there are some half-truths to the legends. For instance, only I and my brother have the power to damage the emerald. The nature of our battle is beyond your comprehension, but as I was being locked into this prison, I managed to attack the emerald with my power as a last effort to stop Drakkan. His fatal mistake was forgetting to shield it from me when he knew I was capable of damaging it. I was successful in my desperation, and as I disappeared into the void it shattered into six shards, one for each element within, and spread to various regions of Iairia sculpting it as it is today. Without the power of the emerald to sustain the immense energy comprising his ultimate form, Drakkan was weakened to the point where he was forced to withdraw to his dark Netherworld to survive. What emissaries of mine that survived the battle left the prophesies behind for the ancients to find. The only truly accurate one is the Three Fates.

"Over the long ages, however, they have been contorted by the churches and politics between the two nations. This is how Drakkaidia emerged, Tavin. Drakkaidians were originally nothing more than disgruntled Grandarians seeking to free themselves from what they viewed as religious subversion, so they traveled north to the unknown lands Drakkan once occupied. Over the centuries they were tainted by the dark remains of my brother still infecting the area, and became the dark natured people they are today. So despite your longtime conflicts and hatred for the Drakkaidians, you now know that they are not as different from you as you thought." In the silence that followed, Tavin slowly broke his gaze from the deity, shaking his head bedazzled.

"I can't believe it," he murmured. "I mean, does anyone even know the truth about Drakkaidia?" Granis shrugged.

"I'm sure you wouldn't be surprised to know that Zeroan, now the last Mystic Sage, does, but apart from him, this information was lost over the eons of bitter war and hatred between these two nations. There are still records in places, but the disdain you have for each other precludes you from caring to look. They are both so bitter now that they wouldn't even care if they found the truth. In any case, Tavin, that is the truth that you needed to hear. I was defeated in the Battle of the Gods, and have been imprisoned ever since. I can see only a small amount of what happens in the mortal world, but most I am blind to. For example, I know of your battle before coming here, but I do not know what has become of Verix. Grandaria prays to a blind and deaf god. There is no greater torture for me than this."

"There must be some way for you to escape, Lord Granis," Tavin said hopefully. "If I could enter, why can't you leave?"

"Drakkan sealed me here with the power of the Holy Emerald," Granis reminded him. "Only it can set me free. If the emerald was complete when you opened the gate I could have escaped, but without its power present in the world you were summoned in and I remained." Tavin looked at him hard then, staring deeply into the God of Light's human eyes.

"Granis, why are you telling me this?" he asked suddenly. "Why did you beckon me here?" The God of Light smiled gently and laid his hand onto the hilt of the Sword of Granis.

"I care for my people," he said with utmost honesty, his godliness shining through. "All of them- Grandarian and Drakkaidian alike. Now, all of them are at risk of Drakkan's evil once more. They must be saved, but I cannot do this myself. So you, my young Warrior of Light, must fulfill your charge to save Iairia."

Ril came awake slowly, gradually letting her heavy eyelids slip halfway open and closed until she at last began to discern the soft, soothing voice from above her as one she recognized. She quietly lay in the center of an endless sea of soft flowers, unable to fully wake herself. Trying to figure out where she was, a sudden flood of memories bombarded her mind; images of Tavin and Verix battling the seven black demon mages in the snow crested Border Mountains.

As she lay contemplating where she was, the girl managed to open her eyes and focus them enough to find a boy sitting above her radiating a soft golden aura from his near transparent body. He wore simple white clothes and smiled warmly at her with a gentle look set into his face. Staring at him hard for a moment, she realized who the boy was.

"Tavin?" she asked hesitantly. The boy smiled but shook his head no. Looking at him more closely, she could see that while he did indeed look a great deal like her Grandarian love, it was not him.

"My name's Tieloc, if that's what you mean," he stated with a smile. "But not the one you know. You can call me Taurin." Ril looked at him peculiarly, unsure what this boy was.

"Is this a dream?" she asked at last, softly mustering the strength to speak. Taurin cocked his head peculiarly.

"More or less," he softly returned, running his fingers through her flowing crimson hair sprawled out around her. Her head rested on the boy's knees, gently propped up so she could see the beautiful world of pensive colors around her. Shifting her gaze to her own body, Ril could see the countless wounds from her previous clash with the Dégamar gradually shrouding with shimmering light. Soon, her entire body was wrapped in the soft glow, sending a warm sensation through her previously cold, aching flesh. Her skin was free of cuts, bruises, and blood; revitalized. As the light faded, her frayed and torn attire was replaced with a simple white dress, flowing down from its sleeveless top to the ends of her bare feet. She slowly shifted her gaze back up to the glowing boy holding her, feeling the light flow from him. She softly asked him where Tavin was, to which his smiled and nodded with assurance. "Tavin is elsewhere, but he is well, I promise you," he said.

"Who are you, Taurin?" she asked after. "What am I doing here?"

"You came here with Tavin, did you not?" he asked tenderly. "I am Tavin centuries ago. His ancestor, the first Warrior of Light. I come to you, even though I am not supposed to, because I know of the darkness he now faces. I defeated it in my time as he must do now. But he will face far greater evil than I ever did, Ril. He will not be able to defeat it by himself.

Time has no meaning for me, and I can see the time when he will need you. He will need your help before the end. You must be there for him, Ril. You are the only one who can choose to help him when he needs it the most. It will not be an easy choice. You will have to accept yourself as you really are to do so. Do you understand?" The radiating boy looked down to her with sincerity in his eyes, revealing to Ril strength inside her. She nodded, to which Taurin smiled. "Then go now, Arilia Embrin. Do not tell anyone of our discussion. Do what you must, for his sake and all of Iairia." With that, Ril's eyes slowly sealed shut once more, the warmth of the spirit's light fading.

In the wake of the God of Light's mighty wish for the young Grandarian boy, Tavin was momentarily speechless. He had known from the beginning, from the first time that he laid his fingers around the hilt of the Sword of Granis, that this was to be his charge, yet now, coming from a god, the impossibility of it seemed to impact him all over again. Staring at the ground, Tavin shifted his gaze to the Sword of Granis protruding from the earth. He had done so much with it that he had never though possible before, and now it had led him to Granis himself. With the God of Light imprisoned in a non-place, he was the only one who could stand up to Valif Montrox and Drakkan. His face morphing with determination, Tavin gave himself a single nod and locked his eyes back onto Granis.

"What would you have me do, Lord Granis?" he asked ready. The old man smiled at him once again.

"It is people like you, Tavin, that make me proud of man," he stated softly. "Despite his vast imperfections, his hope and will to achieve can make him truly great." After finishing his praise, he stood from the wooden bench and pulled the blade from its place in the ground. "I have seen the Warrior of Light defeat darkness before, Tavin, but not like this. The evil you face now is fueled by the unholy power of the Netherworld and its demonic ruler. Even trapped in this void, I can sense the emergence of his minions unto the world. Even the Warrior of Light cannot hope to defeat such creatures on his own, so

I must make you more." Stopping there, he bid Tavin to rise and stand before him. Gripping the Sword of Granis with both hands, a brilliant golden aura surrounded it. Closing his eyes, Granis' elderly face began to transform. The garden around them dissipated along with the god's sullied attire, replaced by regal flowing robes of gold.

As the brilliant field of light emanating from Granis grew large enough to engulf the entire void in passionate gold, he released his grip on the sword, allowing it to levitate over his outstretched hands. The Granic Crystal mounted to the blade burst alive with light that dwarfed even the sun, forcing Tavin to look away and shield his eyes. The light spread down the length of the blade, changing its perfectly crafted silver to gold. As the light from the crystal at last returned to its normal hum and Tavin could look back, he saw Granis' face changed, stronger and younger.

"Tavinious Tieloc, Grandarian Warrior of Light," he began with the same kindness in his voice as had always been, "I present to you this new Sword of Granis. Wield it and be bestowed with what power I have left to give. With it you will be able to stand up to any evil from the Netherworld, even if it is Drakkan himself. You will become me. Use this power to prevent Valif Montrox from assembling the Holy Emerald for himself, for if Drakkan seizes the Holy Emerald once again, he will not be defeated. You must preclude this from happening and save Iairia. Once you have, take the Holy Emerald and choose whichever of the Three Fates you wish. Do you accept this charge, Warrior of Light?" His words were regal, making Tavin sweat with anticipation. Swallowing hard, he nodded yes.

"I will," he stated with conviction, to which Granis nodded.

"Then take up the sword again and accept your charge." With that, Tavin stepped forward into the burning light and reached up to the hovering hilt of the golden blade, wrapping his fingers around it. At once, his elemental power of light exploded around him at full strength. Pulling the sword down, Tavin could feel power radiate from it like nothing he had ever thought possible. An entire new world suddenly opened itself to him, waiting for him to step in. His power waiting at the pit of his soul now filled every inch of his body, not willing to leave. After staring at the blade and exploring the strength surging forth, Tavin shifted his gaze back to Granis, standing before him in his aura of power smiling. "My power of light is now in the palm of your hands, Tavin. With it, you will have strength and wisdom beyond what any mortal ever had. Summon it, and you will be the Warrior of Light no more. You will be the Warrior of Granis, the most powerful being in Iairia. Should you fail to gather the emerald shards before Montrox, however, you will face an invincible Drakkan that even you will be no match against." The God of Light gave him a warm smile. "I give faith to you and mankind, Tavin. You know what you must do. Go do it."

With a single nod, Tavin wrapped his hands around the Sword of Granis. Closing his eyes, he took hold of the godly power coursing throughout his body waiting to be called forth. It came exploding out with a detonation of golden energy, and engulfed in the brilliant light, he disappeared from the empty void.

Chapter 69

The Warrior of Granis

After exiting the Temple of Water and making his way across the long bridge to shore, wringing out his soaked attire as he went, Jaren found Zeroan waiting for him by the pedestal controlling the door. As the Grandarian boy stepped off the narrow walkway across the expansive lake, the sage freed his submerged hands from the bowl of water they rested in and quickly pulled them inside his robes, releasing the bridge back into the now calm waters of the lake once more. Jaren approached him with proud incredulity.

"I've seen a lot of things on this quest that I had never thought possible, Zeroan," he started with a grin, "but that was the most amazing thing I could have ever dreamed of." The sage hurriedly collected himself in his robes and faintly smiled.

"You did very well, Jaren," he congratulated. "It is an amazing feat for the Warrior of Water to activate this temple, but for one with no power other than his mind and creativity, you have done something truly great." He stopped abruptly, making Jaren feel like he would have said something more but cut himself off. "We must hurry back to the city, though. Follow me quickly, Jaren." He turned then, the ends of his gray robes flying up behind him, and swiftly started up the long walkway back to the city walls. Noticing the sage's urgent voice and hurried movements, Jaren quickly concluded that something was wrong.

"No offense, Zeroan," he began catching up to him, "but I've been around you enough to know when something is bothering you. Something happened, while I was in there, didn't it?" Zeroan shifted his hooded head down to the boy, silently staring at him for a moment.

"Unfortunately, we may have activated this temple prematurely," he said unfavorably. "We haven't had a chance to speak since my arrival, so let me tell you what has happened since we last parted. The reason I left you, Parnox, and Kohlin in the first place was because I sensed the emergence of a new demon threat from Drakkaidia. They are called the Dégamar; seven dark mages that dwell in the Netherworld and serve Drakkan himself. They harbor extremely potent power, amplified by centuries in the Netherworld. I doubt if even Tavin can destroy them at his full power. In any case, I suspected it was them, but I could not be sure at the time. Whatever they were, I knew Montrox would be sending them to gather more shards for him, so I left for the Mystic Tower to try and save the two there before he could get to them first. Alas, I was too late. The tower had been attacked and every last sage was killed. The only survivor was the Princess who had volunteered to keep an eye on them. She told me that seven dark figures riding winged demons killed the Master Sage Arius in front of her and stole the shards.

"With more shards at his disposal, Montrox has been able to summon more demons from the Netherworld. Since gaining the shards to the east and the one he just found in the west, I have sensed him marshaling his demon army by the day. While you were in the temple, he unleashed it from Dalastrak. The Dégamar are leading them here, and they will arrive, at earliest, by tomorrow morning." At the finish of his speech, Zeroan shifted his gaze back down to Jaren, returning it with wide eyes and jaw dropped.

"What!?!" was all he could utter. "You have got to be kidding me! Why is Montrox sending his army here? Isn't the other shard in Grandaria?" Zeroan shook his head.

"That is another discussion," the sage stated knowingly. "Montrox believes that the shard in Grandaria is practically his, so he is not concerned with it at the moment. He is more concerned with the past. He remembers that it was the Legion that came to the Grandarians' aid in the Holy Wars and defeated his grandfather's armies then. He is driven now by revenge for their defeats long ago, and is exacting it in order of those who stood up to him to appease his vengeance. In addition to all this, Tavin and Ril have just disappeared from my sight. I don't know what he is up to, but the Warrior of Light will not be here to aid us."

"So what do we do now?" Jaren asked throwing his hands into the air. Zeroan let out a slow breath and looked to the citadel towering in front of them.

"The best we can..." he murmured. The two figures quickly made their way up to the city in the following minutes, moving toward the citadel of the Sarton. As they approached, Jaren noticed two riders waiting for them at the gates. It was Captain Morrol and Parnox.

"Zeroan!" Morrol called, coming into view. His face was enthralled, leaping down from his horse. "You have done it, Sarton! The Drakkaidians are gone! How did you activate the temple without the Warrior of Water?" Zeroan's face remained hard as he shook it.

"The Drakkaidians are gone for the moment, Captain," he began somberly, "but this city and this nation are far from safe. Did no one in this group inform you of the danger you still face?" The captain's face twisted with confusion, unsure what he was talking about.

"You mean the army of demons Valif Montrox is building?" he remembered gravely.

"I mean the army he has sent, Captain," Zeroan corrected coldly. "It departed from Dalastrak as we activated the temple. A force I would guess to be over ten thousand strong will take up the place of the Drakkaidians by tomorrow morning. How many will respond to the signal by then?" Morrol's face went pale before responding with a soft shrug.

"The Legion has not been called this way for over a century, Zeroan," he said. "I would not expect more than a few hundred by morning." Zeroan exhaled loudly again and nodded.

"A few hundred is better than nothing," he said trying to sound confident. "We must prepare for their arrival now." Morrol gave him an incredulous look.

"Zeroan, we cannot hope to defeat a force of ten thousand with only three hundred Legionnaires. Even if more arrive, they will do no good." Zeroan met his weak gaze with ferocity in his dark eyes.

"Captain, this army will not only outnumber us thirty to one, it will consist of bloodthirsty creatures of the Netherworld that cannot be stopped by arrows or swords. There is no way to defeat them. Our only hope is to hold them long enough for the entire Legion to gather. If they come, we will outnumber them two to one. It will be an arduous battle, but with my power to aid you, we may be able to stave them off just long enough. So I suggest, Captain Morrol, that you go see to the defenses of the city. Prepare the Legionnaires for battle. I will follow with these two shortly." Holding his gaze for another moment, Morrol nodded and mounted his steed once more to take off down the citadel road for the city.

As he disappeared from view, Parnox and Jaren both stared at the sage skeptically.

"Zeroan," Parnox began slowly, "we've encountered our fair share of demons on this quest and from what I've seen it's hard enough to take down one with six and magic to aid us. Do you really think that a few hundred scared and exhausted Legionnaires are going to be able to hold off an army of those things for even a few minutes?" The Sarton brought up his hand from the confines of his deep robes to slowly massage his forehead.

"Of course not," he managed at last, to which they both felt their hearts sink. Jaren frowned.

"Then why did you say that to Morrol?" he asked.

"What would you have said, Jaren?" the sage returned. "That he should tell the men they have no hope of victory and that they should just give up now? There may be virtually no hope here, but if the Southland falls without a fight, there will be no second chance for it later. We must stand, fight, and hope... something happens." He let his hand fall back into his robes, turning to his comrades. "You two, however, have a choice to make. You know the danger coming. You know that a victory is not possible as things stand now. So I leave whether you wish to stay or not up to you. You could fall back to Grandaria to try and prepare for the same threat in advance and deliver the Princess back to them safely. I will remain to stave off the demons as best I can." While Jaren just looked at him uncertainly, Parnox let out a huff of air in disgust.

"That is one hell of a thing for you to say to us," he stated acidly taking a step forward. "I haven't come all this way and gone through all I have to turn tail and run now. If this is to be the last stand of the Southland, I will be here for it."

"You should know by now you can't get rid of me that easily," Jaren smiled. The sage nodded.

"Very well, then. Let us make our way to the gate yard and make what preparations we can." With that, the three turned back for the citadel to gather another two horses for Jaren and Zeroan. As they walked, however, Zeroan suddenly froze. After a long moment of just standing there not moving a muscle, Jaren and Parnox looked back to him worriedly. They asked him what was wrong, but the sage's mind blocked everything except the phenomenon he had just sensed. Focusing hard, he wheeled around facing the south. Somewhere beyond even the Great Forests, the most massive power he had ever sensed detonated to life with such power and force he could feel it tear through his heart even here. The sage's jaw dropped as the power only grew, blasting higher and more potent than should be possible. He could tell it was not dark in nature, but it was so great and intimidating that he found himself trembling. Silently murmuring to himself that what he was sensing was not feasible, the incredible energy bursting awake and echoing into every cell in his body told him otherwise. Whatever this new strength was, Zeroan knew that it was the greatest power to ever emerge.

Ril stood over a beach with her white dress wildly flapping in the wind blowing out to the endless blue ocean waters before her, befuddled. She had come sharply awake from her dreamlike state a moment ago, appearing in a brilliant flash of light and gently touching down with the earth below her, the gritty sand meshing with her bare feet assuring her she was not dreaming. Realizing she had somehow been returned to the physical world once more, the Warrior of Fire was bombarded by the same explosion of power Zeroan had felt moments ago. Unlike the awestruck sage half a continent away from its source, however, Ril found herself standing right behind it. Though the sheer force emitted from the radiating power tore through every cell in her body with intimidating potency, there was a familiar warmth buried deep at its core. She slowly began to rotate her head with her crimson hair flying back into her soft face.

Struggling to look on the shining light with squinted eyes, she fully turned her body to face it. Though the righteous light burned her eyes, they quickly opened wide as view of a perfect golden sphere of shimmering energy entered them. The raw power and force emanating from the sphere threw the sand at its base away like spray from the ocean behind her and the tropical growth behind it. Staring into the anomaly of power, Ril's sensation of familiarity grew and her mouth opened wide as she observed the silhouette of something inside the glowing sphere. With her fear overridden by curiosity, the mesmerized girl took a small step toward it. The sphere began to gradually dissipate into the growing field of rising golden light around the frame inside over the next few moments, but the power level from within only grew.

After staring in awe as the last remnant of the golden sphere was caught up in the steady aura of golden power circulating around the form, Ril brought her hand to her mouth in shock. The form inside the sphere was a person, dropping down from where he hovered inches over the sand to gently touch down. As he did, the power around him blasted to life again, now constantly emanating from his body. He stood in regal white garb, ornately decorated with aureate designs of curving, sweeping gold. A flowing white cape draped from his back, attached by the gold plates of thin but powerful looking armor mounted to his shoulders and chest. The figure's face was quiet; emotionless. His hair blew to and fro along with his cape from the force of his power, but his eyes and mouth were closed as if asleep. Ril let a half smile spread from the corner of her mouth.

It was Tavin.

He had been transformed, but she knew it was him. She knew his warm power anywhere, even if it had been multiplied by what felt like infinity. She stood in awe of his kinglike appearance and godly power for several long moments, overwhelmed by the rush of various emotions flooding her mind. At last, the girl flinched with surprise as his eyes burst open and his body came awake. As his muscles tensed, so did the commanding field of power around him, quickening and expanding. Ril didn't concern herself with the power, as his eyes were far more intriguing. His pupils and irises were no longer black and blue, but both gold. They seemed to stare at nothing and everything at once, making him all the more foreboding and gentle at the same time. At last Ril could stand it no longer, and took a sweeping step toward him, lowering her hand from her amazed face. Tavin's eyes shifted toward her instantaneously. Their pure intensity penetrated, stopping her in her tracks. She stood with her bare arms dangling at her sides and her flowing hair and dress flying behind her toward the ocean.

After what seemed like an eternity for the Warrior of Fire, Tavin's eyes at last softened and his tense body rigid with purpose and power eased. Humanity rushing to his face once more, he allowed a slow smile to spread across it.

"Ril..." he stated, as if announcing it was her. She slowly lit up as the sound of her name escaped from his mouth, beaming. With newfound energy electrifying her, she bounded toward him. Tavin opened his arms and eased his incredible power to let her in, catching her as she leapt into him. Throwing her own arms around his neck, Ril immediately brought her head in and kissed him hard. Tavin gently wrapped one hand around her back and pushed the other into her flowing hair, holding her tight. After the long embrace, Ril slowly pulled back her lips and opened her eyes, letting out a heavenly smile. Tavin did the same, holding her tight.

"It's you," Ril whispered blissfully, to which Tavin nodded and grinned.

"It's me," he repeated, leaning in to kiss her again. "We made it back." Ril nodded as well, but eased her grip over him to examine his transformed body again.

"...What happened to you?" she asked still astounded. "Is this power for real? How did this happen?" Tavin held his beaming smile and shrugged.

"We were right to go the Celestial Portal," was all he could think to say after all that had befallen him since they separated in the void. Noticing her own change in appearance, he began again. "But what about you? Are you alright?"

"I'm fine," she assured him. Remembering Taurin Tieloc's words, she kept her experience in the void to herself. "All I remember is dreaming that my wounds were healed and getting this." She tugged on the simple white dress stretching from her shoulders to her feet.

"I like it," Tavin complement her with a grin. "I've never seen the great tomboy Ril Embrin in a dress before." Ril cocked her head at his words but couldn't hide her smile.

"Where did all this power come from, Tavin?" she asked looking him over again and feeling the warmth of his radiating energy encompassing her. Tavin thought back over his experience with Granis and shook his head, remembering his task at hand.

"It will have to wait, Ril," he said with meaning filling his voice. Tavin wrenched his eyes off of her and shot them around to the north, sensing the mass of dark power slowly spreading down from Drakkaidia. It was bigger than he thought. Ril stared at him curiously.

"What is it?" she asked gravely. Tavin breathed hard, resolve morphing his body tense again.

"I'll explain on the way, but we have to get to Torrentcia City *now*," he told her quickly. "Montrox has his demon army marching there as we speak, and I'm the only one who can stop it." Ril's eyes reflected her sudden confusion.

"What? How do you know, Tavin? All I can sense is you!" she told him incredulously. "And where are we now? Shouldn't we be surrounded by snow?" Tavin shook his head no, pinpointing where they needed to go in his mind.

"It's a *very* long story, Ril," he told her strenuously. "I'll tell you on the way, but if you look down, this is the Celestial Portal." Her brow furrowing, Ril shifted her eyes toward the sandy beach beneath them, noticing something she hadn't before. A platform began where they stood, stretching out in a massive circular arch toward the ocean. She turned to find what looked to be an exact replica of the Celestial Portal hovering just over the water's surface. Her face twisted with confusion, but before she could ask what was going on, Tavin heaved her off the ground, lifting her back with one arm and her legs with the other. Pulling her against him and summoning his incredible power outward once more, Ril shot her head up to him.

"What are you doing, Tavin?" she asked. "What is this?"

"This is the real Celestial Portal," he said concentrating his power around them, "and we are going to the Southland. Hold on to me tight." Just as she was going to ask them how they were going to get to Torrentcia City from wherever they were before the Drakkaidian army when they had no transportation, Tavin's power blasted up around them with greater potency than before. Bending his knees and charging his energy, the Warrior of Granis leapt off the earth and into the skies, blasting off to the north with incredible speed. As the two jetted across the sky in a beam of light, Tavin smiled down to the girl in his arms clenching onto him like death.

"Tell me before you do something like that!" she shouted with crazed emotion. "I leave you for a measly hour and you go and transform into Granis himself!" Tavin couldn't help but smile. She had no idea how right she was.

Chapter 70

<u>Power</u>

Jaren stood on the north wall of Torrentcia City with an empty expression over his face. It had been night for hours now and was particularly dark with the massive storm from the north looming over them, but he had seen only a few patrols of the Legion arrive so far. Nearly an hour ago, men from the border arrived scared out of their minds, reporting they had seen the massive black swarm of creatures advancing on their position. They gave up the border without so much as the drawing of a sword. It was the right thing to do, however, as fighting the demons on open ground was nothing more than foolish suicide. The Warrior of Water who volunteered to guard the border against the Drakkaidian army arrived with them, quickly asking how the temple had been activated without him there. Upon hearing of the newly appointed Sarton, he got his answer. Jaren let out a quiet breath of disappointment. Otherwise, the only aid they had received so far were loose militiamen from villages in close proximity to the capital; their rivers and creeks flooding with warning. It would not be enough to give them any better odds against the incoming horde of the demonic adversaries.

Jaren was alone on his portion of the wall. The few hundred Legionnaires in the city were busy preparing weapons and supplies in the gate yard below him and rushing up and down the stairs by the repaired gates to distribute them along the wall top. Parnox had been with Kohlin for the past hour trying to convince him to stay at the citadel during the battle, still being so gravely wounded. The Windrun Warrior would have no part in that, however, not willing to sit out of things any more than Parnox or Jaren had when they had the opportunity to leave. Zeroan had been in the gate yard informing the Legionnaires what to expect from the demons and making the city as battle ready as he could. He had been particularly distant and quiet since he apparently sensed something earlier in the day. Instructed to let the Legionnaires worry about the fortification of the city, he had retired to the wall top for time of his own.

Reflecting over the previous action filled day, the Grandarian archer was surprised to find Captain Morrol steadily making his way toward him. Jaren gave him a forced smile as he stood next to him, leaning over the wall.

"Are you holding up alright?" the captain asked. Jaren gave him a single nod.

"Well enough under the circumstances," he answered briskly.

"So you're ready for this, are you?" Jaren raised an eyebrow and gave him an almost insulted look.

"Captain, this will not be the first time I have fought off demons from high up on the wall of a city," he informed him. "All I can say is, they'd better be ready for me." Morrol laughed, nodding apologetically.

"I'm glad at least one of us is that confident," he said, his voice turning somber. Jaren could see the strain in the man's eyes. "Tell me the truth, Jaren. Do we have any chance at all?" The Grandarian slowly shrugged, not really sure what to say.

"Zeroan said we did, didn't he?" he offered. Morrol shot him a knowing glace.

"I hope you give me enough credit to know that I am aware when I am being lied to," he said. "The sage was merely trying to make me feel like there was some hope." Morrol broke his gaze from Jaren and sunk his head below his shoulders. Jaren swallowed hard, his thoughts shifting back to Tavin like before.

"If there is one thing I've learned in this life," he began quietly, "it's that willpower is power. Pure and simple. I've seen people fall under impossible circumstance with *no* chance of success; they were doomed from the beginning. But somehow, someway, they still managed to come out on top." Jaren turned his head back to face Morrol. "We've got the willpower, I know that. So we've got the power." The Southlander held Jaren's gaze for a long moment, then rose and placed his hand on the boy's shoulder.

"I've never been too fond of most Grandarians that I've know, Jaren," he admitted sincerely, "but if there are more like you up there, I'll never have another sore word about them again." Jaren smiled and looked out into the darkness again.

"There's at least one," he said softly.

The remaining hours of that night yielded no more reinforcements than what they had already received. The gates opened one final time at dawn to let in a patrol from the eastern mountains, but were sealed closed after. Jaren remained at the wall for the rest of the night, joined by Parnox and Kohlin after the last patrol entered. They could tell the sun had risen and morning had come, but the darkness of night remained. The fierce storm that followed the packs of Valcanor had completely overtaken the sky above the city. Black billowing clouds rolled about the space above them, covering the sky as far as the eye could see in any direction. So dark was the surrounding environment that Zeroan had ordered the torches around the city remain lit. The Mystic Sage joined the trio on the wall with Captain Morrol at the sound of the bell being gonged; the city's warning for enemies within visual range. Though it was nearly impossible to see anything through the thick darkness defiling the morning air, Jaren could indeed detect a think mass of moving black over the hills to the north not more than three miles away. Zeroan told Captain Morrol to spread the word to be ready in the ranks. What Legionnaires there were quickly lined the city walls with bows ready.

"Is that them?" Jaren asked quietly. The Sarton nodded in his thick robes.

"The Dégamar are waiting on the ridge to the left," he confirmed gravely. "They will hold there as the demons attack." Straining his eyes to peer out into the darkness, Jaren could barely detect seven small forms resting quietly ahead of the army on the ridge. Though he could only make out their frames sitting in the shadows, he could guess they were staring them down the same as they were. In the long silence that followed with the Legionnaires' anxiety only growing, the Black Seven at last turned their winged mounts to the army and gave an ear piercing shriek through the gloom, loud even to the men miles away. Immediately after, the dim morning air was shattered by the eruption of howling and crazed groans of hatred from the swarming black masses, brimming with erratic movement. Zeroan narrowed his eyes.

"Here they come..." he thought aloud. The next moment, the entire horde cried out one unison battle cry and charged forward with burning vitality. Jaren quickly drew an arrow from his overflowing quiver and brought it to his bow string, remembering how fast the unholy creatures could move when they wanted to. From the heart of the army came the Liradds sprinting forward ahead of the rest in groups of five or six with packs of Valcanor soaring overhead, the red light from their glowing eyes ominously illuminating the otherwise dark sky. As the first wave of the charging swarm rapidly closed the gap between them and the city, the Southland's Sarton turned his head to his right to boom his voice over the hushed murmurs of the men.

"Legionnaires!" His voice charged through them like electricity; all of them turning to face him. "You face the greatest challenge of your lives now: an army of unholy creatures vying to destroy you for no reason but their blind hatred for life. They have no conscience and will show you no mercy, so be sure you return the favor! This is your capital city: stand firm on its walls!" As he continued, the first hundreds of the approaching Valcanor began to descend, screeching through the darkness. Zeroan raised his arm and a coursing white light appeared, shifting from a sphere of electricity to a burning flame. Thrusting his arm outward, it sailed forth into the sky and impacted one of their sunken heads, dropping it to the ground. Jaren eyed him peculiarly, having never seen him do that before. "Do not give into fear! Your courage is the most potent weapon you have! Use it, and we will repel them! Stand tall, men of the Southland!" Turning to watch the faces of the Legionnaires, he saw Zeroan's words mirrored in their faces, nodding powerfully with bravery. He knew better than most that hope was slim, but seeing courage in the eyes of his allies revitalized the Grandarian boy as well. He was going to give it his all.

With that, the Legionnaires strung their bows and pulled them taut, waiting for Morrol to order a volley. With scores of Valcanor swooping downward to the wall, he bellowed to fire at will. A streaking barrage of missiles flew from the walls, tearing into the flying demons. While most Valcanor picked the arrows off or simply charged forward regardless, six were impaled so many times they dropped from the sky with a distant thud from the cold earth below. The bulk of the Valcanor assailed the wall with sweeping attacks from their gnarled disproportionate limbs, powerfully wiping three to five men off the wall at a time. Zeroan stood at one side of the wall casting his mystic telekinesis into the Valcanor overhead and pushing them over the wall with the flick of his wrist. The Warrior of Water had taken position at the other. He stood at the base of the wall using the creek flowing down the side of the city as his weapon to launch blocks of razor sharp ice missiles and jets of speeding liquid so powerful it wore through the very skin of the creatures.

While the city's defenders concentrated on the flight of Valcanor striking from above, few remembered the groups of Liradds dashing forward. Turning to launch an arrow at a sweeping Valcanor, Jaren noticed three pairs of the mighty runners making their way around the spiraling city road, nimbly evading the pitfalls and blockades put in place the previous night. He wheeled around to Parnox and Kohlin on the stairs struggling to finish off the downed Valcanor, screaming to be ready for the ground based foes. Zeroan spun around as well, shouting for Jaren to follow him to the wall above the gate. The two jostled their way across the wall to find the Liradds already clawing their way up the wooden doors. Jaren quickly released a salvo of arrows toward their heads while Zeroan threw out his hands to grip one of the charging Liradds midair and stop it cold. Tightening his grip on the squirming creature, the sage grit his teeth and thrust his opposite hand outward as well. A throbbing wave of invisible force came forth, blasting the demon back into its kin from the massive force of collision.

More Liradds quickly arrived to take up the place of the few the pair managed to down, however, also aided by three Valcanor dropping to ground level outside the gates. Preoccupied with the Liradds, neither of them could take a clear shot at the massive creatures below, pounding on the gates with supernatural force. Hearing the already damaged wood splinter, Zeroan spun his head around as he took hold of a passing Valcanor's wings and crippled them, sending it plummeting toward the earth. Screaming at the top of his lungs, he ordered Legionnaires to draw swords. Parnox and Kohlin both quickly leapt down from staircases and into the gate yard, ready for whatever was about to enter. Despite the volleys of missiles from Jaren and the Legionnaires, the sturdy Valcanor managed to penetrate and crash through the gates with their last breath, allowing dozens of Liradds passage into the city.

Jaren turned and watched in horror as the crimson skinned creatures poured through the gates and scores more rounded up the path to the gates. The few Legionnaires still alive in the yard fought valiantly, but were quickly cut down by the agile Arnosmn clawing through the Liradds. Jaren turned back to the fields outside the city, watching the entire army charge on. Within a matter of minutes, they would all be on the city's doorstep. It was already over. Jaren swallowed hard and cursed under his breath as he fired another arrow into the waves of dark writhing bodies. This was not how or where he wanted to go; away from Tavin and Grandaria.

As Jaren prepared for the worst, Zeroan suddenly ceased his wave of mystic attacks and slowly turned to the southern sky, a familiar awestruck look about his face. Jaren stared at him for a moment, then turned himself to find what the sage could be so engrossed with that he had stopped fighting. He saw it at once. There was a sudden light streaking toward them through the dense clouds far to the south. It looked to be dozens of miles away, but he could definitely make out a burning bright light charging through the clouds. Though surprised enough at first, Jaren's amazement only grew as he watched it tear through the black storm clouds like a bolt of lightning. Despite being so thick, the light parted the clouds as it jetted toward them, revealing bright sunlight shining down through the storm as it approached. Before anyone knew it, the light had charged directly overhead and stopped right over the city. By now most of the Legionnaires had noticed it, and even a few of the demons had halted their movements, obviously sensing the incredible power it was emitting.

As the light grew in the clouds above them burning the darkness away, a streaking bolt of golden energy blasted down, sailing through the sky to land directly in the center of the courtyard. All eyes, human and demon alike, shifted to the brilliant luminosity embedded into the earth. As the light slowly dissipated, they could see it was a golden sword. Zeroan's jaw slowly dropped, and the energy built in his hands disappeared.

"The Sword of Granis..." he murmured. The next moment, the Granic Crystal burst alive, sending an explosion of righteous light burning through the gate yard. Screams of terror sounded through the air as every last demon in the city was instantly incinerated. As the flash of light faded, the only thing left of the unholy creatures were collections of ash scaring the earth where they had once stood. Every Legionnaire stood in awe, slowly peering up to the sky toward the golden light dispelling the clouds around it. After it had driven them back, the light abruptly plummeted from the air driving toward the city. As it fell inside, Jaren, Zeroan, Parnox, and Kohlin all froze, feeling the air from their lungs withdraw.

Hovering above the earth draped in white and emanating a field of golden power unlike anything they had seen before was Tavin, with Ril in his arms. Everyone was so stunned that no one dared to speak. The golden figure quickly lowered Ril to the gate yard and plucked his blade from the ground.

"I want to stay with you!" Ril cried not letting go of his hand. He looked down to her and gently shook his head.

"I can't fight them while protecting you at the same time," he told her quickly. "I promise I'll be back. You know I won't lose." She held his grip firm for a painfully long moment for them both, but at last released him. Tavin turned his head and blasted back into the sky with his power flaring up even brighter than before. As he rose, he met eyes with Zeroan and gave him a quick nod, then shot upward with a detonation of power and force that knocked most of the Legionnaires over. As he flew skyward, Jaren threw up his hands, launching his bow into the air.

"*That was Tavin!*" he bellowed at the top of his lungs. The Grandarian's words brought the rest of the men to their senses, and the entire populace of the city seemed to roar out battle cries on the Warrior of Granis' behalf. Charging upward with the Sword of Granis tight in his right hand, Tavin's golden eyes burned with fortitude. With an army of thousands still before him, purpose filled his adrenaline pumped body. Shooting forward, the rest of the Valcanor and other flying beasts came soaring toward him with bloodlust in their crimson eyes. Focusing his power in front of his chest, the Warrior of Granis let it charge into a steady circle and beam forward, tearing into the advancing Valcanor. It blasted through the sky all the way to the end of the army, incinerating anything in its path.

As the rest of the Valcanor charged ahead with boiling hatred in their tainted veins, Tavin took hold of the Sword of Granis with both hands and shot forward at speeds so fast the onlookers from the city could barely keep an eye on him. Darting in and out of the bulking figures' paths, he relentlessly slashed his golden blade like lightning. As it sliced through the demons' flesh, they exploded in flurries of light spraying into the constantly brightening sky like golden fireworks. Within a matter of minutes, every last Valcanor from the once thousand strong flight had been obliterated.

With the sky clear of adversaries once more, the golden warrior set his sights on the army still charging at the city on the ground. Taking the Sword of Granis and flipping its blade downward, Tavin closed his eyes and focused his swelling energy into the blade. It pulsated with shimmering light, drawing the attention of the writhing black masses beneath him. Immediately opening his eyes, the Warrior of Granis let out a scream that could be heard for miles and blasted downward with the blade of his sword pointed to the earth. Leaving a trail of golden energy in his wake, he landed in the center of the demon army with an earth shattering thud that shook the very foundations of Torrentcia City. The moment the energy charged blade drove into the earth, fissures of light forced their way open around him, shining golden radiance outward and exploding his field of emanating power to consume the army for hundreds of meters in every direction. Brighter than the sun, the massive half sphere of energy rose higher than the tower of the citadel itself.

Zeroan and the others who quickly rushed to the walls watched in awe as the boy brimming with incredible power covered hundreds of square feet of land with his burning field of power.

"How is this possible..." the sage trailed off in awe. As the energy from the attack began to dissipate and the light fade, the Legionnaires atop the city walls found most of the demon army no longer there; they had been eradicated in one massive attack. The steaming power evaporating into the morning air, all that was left on the field were the lucky few hundred demons that had escaped the blast radius, wildly retreating with fear in the direction they came from, and Tavin rising from the ground where he knelt latched onto the Sword of Granis. Leaving the simmering blade at rest in the earth, he stood radiating his aura of power around him, unmoving.

"What's he doing?" Jaren asked, watching his friend just standing there.

"Waiting," Zeroan answered, sensing the seven dark powers approaching the boy's position. As Tavin stood with patient resolve in his golden eyes, seven last Valcanor touched down, surrounding him. The Dégamar on their backs dismounted slowly, waiting for their leader to move. After staring the shining Warrior of Granis down for well over a minute, the Dégamar at last drove forward as they had done at the portal to the void, levitating inches off the ground toward him. Closing the twenty foot gap between them in a split second, the Dégamar were surprised to be stopped in their tracks by the field of golden light instantaneously exploding outward yet again. The force sent all seven flying back and vaporized the Valcanor. Zeroan shook his head from the wall, unable to believe what he was seeing.

Rebounding back to their feet, the Dégamar shot forward once again, this time grouping together in front of him. Instead of charging forward once more, they put their hands together in front of them and began chanting in a low menacing tone, their raspy voices sounding even as far as the city. As their mantra continued, the crimson glowing outline of an ancient Drakkaidian glyph appeared before them. As it grew larger than even Tavin, they threw their rotting hands forward, releasing a beam of dark energy from the glyph's circular core, large enough to blow a hole through their target's chest. As the attack rocketed toward him, Tavin threw up his hand and braced for impact, accepting the beam in the palm of his hand with the colliding sound of energy on energy. Though surprised the boy had stopped their attack without so much as breaking a sweat in the process, the Dégamar held firm and kept their beam flowing toward him.

As they maintained their attack, however, Tavin collected it in his hand and let it grow as the moments passed. Once the ball of crimson energy pulsating larger than his own body grew to the point where he could no longer hold it on the ground, the Warrior of Granis launched skywards with his sword, released the ball of power, and with a swing of the blade swatted it toward the seven mages who just realized he had moved. The Dégamar were devastated by their own attack; sent flying back in a massive explosion of power. Rising to their feet, the defeated demons turned and beckoned seven of the fleeing Liradds to them, mounted, and ran with the rest of the decimated army shrieking out with hatred as they did.

Holding the Sword of Granis firmly in his grasp, Tavin hung in the air with his golden power still passionately flaring around him. He watched the remaining demons retreat into the receding stormy horizon, hovering alone in the center of the blackened battlefield with the clear morning sky letting rays of brilliant sunlight shine down onto him. He had done it. He had single-handedly destroyed over ten thousand demonic creatures from the Netherworld itself and rescued the Southland. Tavin smiled and shifted his gaze upward to the blue sky, hoping Granis had been able to watch him. From behind him, Tavin heard the ferocious plaudits of the Legionnaires atop the walls of Torrentcia City cheering out for him. Turning in midair to face them, he grinned, finding Ril, Zeroan, Jaren, and his other friends at the gate.

Jaren laughed insanely, dancing around the wall with Parnox and Kohlin.

"Did you see that!?!" he shouted. "That was the most amazing thing I've ever seen!" He turned to find Ril over the balcony as well, tears in her eyes. Calling her name, the Warrior of Fire turned to him with a smile and gave him a tumultuous hug. He greeted her with a beaming smile.

Tavin couldn't help but laugh watching his friend parade around the wall, and decided it time to venture back to the city. As he went to sheath his golden blade in its ornate scabbard, however, a strange sensation crept into the Warrior of Granis' body. He felt a sudden wave of dimness wash over him, pulling a blurring blanket over his senses. Struggling to fit the sword in its sheath, he lost his grip on it altogether and dropped it to the earth several feet beneath him. Watching the Warrior of Granis drop his sword, Ril and Jaren both guessed something was wrong. Moving to the wall, they gazed uncertainly as he slowly lowered from the sky, his golden power beginning to flicker and fade around him. By the time he touched down again, it had all but disappeared and his regal white and gold attire had softly morphed into his traditional blue and white garb. Even his golden eyes turned blue once more. Struggling just to stand, the Grandarian boy at last lost control over even his balance and dropped to his knees, then down on his chest.

Ril's eyes went wide, her face going pale. Jaren twisted with worry.

"What happened to him?" he yelled at Zeroan.

"His power level is almost completely diminished," Ril answered for him. The baffled Mystic Sage at last returned to his senses, wheeling around with his gray robes flying up behind him.

"We need to gather him now," he stated quickly. "He should be fine, but let's move with a purpose." With that, the three rapidly tore off the wall down the stairs to the gate yard, barking for horses. One of the Legionnaires opened the makeshift pen they had erected the night before to house the two horses left in the city. Zeroan mounted one, with Jaren and Ril on the other. They raced out of the smashed gates around the circling road to the bottom of the plateau, carefully avoiding the hazards and dead Valcanor corpses not incinerated by Tavin. Upon reaching the base of the plateau, the trio raced across the field some hundred feet out where the boy lay on his front. Leaping off their steeds, Ril and Jaren were the first to his side, working together to pull him up and lay him on his back. All three were relieved to find Tavin awake and smiling as his face came into view.

"Hi guys," he managed to murmur. Jaren and Zeroan smiled relieved, but Ril pulled in close slid her hand over his face.

"Are you alright?" she asked hurriedly. Tavin's tired blue eyes shifted toward her.

"I promised you I would be, didn't I?" he said with a soft chuckle. Ril grinned back at him, gradually calming down with Jaren and Zeroan, nodding.

"What happened to your fancy new power, Warrior of Granis?" she beamed, overcome with joy. Tavin weakly shrugged.

"I think I just used a little more than I should have on my first time," he guessed. "Right now I'm just the Warrior of Light again." Ril remembered how he had told her his new powers from Granis weren't really his, and they would only be with him when he called them forth from the sword.

"Hey buddy. Do you remember me?" Jaren asked sarcastically, holding him by the shoulders and back, to which Tavin weakly laughed and nodded.

"Well I'm not sure," he murmured with a sly grin. "I don't remember knowing anyone so ugly." Jaren only laughed out loud again,

"Same old Tavin," he said. "This is the longest we've ever been apart, and now when we're finally reunited you can't be serious." Tavin laughed again, his attention shifting to the massive gray form of Zeroan towering over them. Peering up into his hood, the Grandarian could detect a soft smile.

"I don't know how this happened and right now I don't care," he said, "but it is good to see you again, my young friend. You have saved an entire nation today. I could not be more proud of you." Tavin smiled again and nodded.

"I missed you too, Zeroan," he said slowly. The sage's smile broadened.

"We need to get you some rest, Tavin," he said motioning for Jaren to lift him. "I've never dealt with this kind of power before, but I would guess that your body is merely exhausted from such an awesome display for, what I assume, is you first time. We have much to discuss, but it can wait for this evening after you have regained enough stamina to do so." He turned back to the horses, gathering them so Jaren could rest the boy on its back. Mounting up, the group rode back to the city together again.

Chapter 71

<u>Reunited</u>

As soon as the four arrived back inside the city gates, Tavin was met with wild applause from the remaining hundred Legionnaires. Zeroan was eager to keep his contact with them limited, however, immediately ordering Jaren and Ril to get him to a bed. Captain Morrol suggested they retire to the citadel now that it unofficially belonged to Zeroan, but the Sarton instructed them to go to the inn in the lower city courtyard instead, not wanting them to get lost in the middle of the giant citadel. The sage was obviously desperate to hear what had befallen the two Elemental Warriors since their last parting, but he realized that Tavin wouldn't be able to get past his first word if he didn't rest and regain his strength. With the gate yard of the city also in shambles, his new responsibilities as Sarton were sure to hold him there for hours as well. So with a reluctant parting, the sage ordered the trio to get moving into to the lower city courtyard.

As they left the chaos and confusion of the gate yard, Jaren and Ril proceeded into the empty city market with Tavin hoisted over their shoulders. The Warrior of Light struggled to keep his eyes open as they carried him, but managed to stay awake with a smile on his face all the way up to the central courtyard. There was no one on the streets or in the buildings, ordered by Zeroan to group inside the citadel should the battle go ill. As they reached the familiar cozy inn nestled on the right side of the courtyard, Ril moved to the door to gently force it open, remembering the lock had been damaged from their last stay. Entering the brightly lit room with the morning sunlight pouring through the windows, Ril couldn't help but giggle from the memories of their last visit here. It had been over a month, but looking around the familiar setting, it felt as if it had only been yesterday.

Lugging Tavin up the stairs, the three proceeded to the room the Grandarian boys occupied during their previous stay. They laid the Warrior of Light over the first bed and quickly started unfastening his chipped, dented armor. Though he was only moments away from sleep, Tavin was awake enough to slap them away with a smile.

"I don't need you to change my diapers for me," he smirked, getting another giggle from the girl at the end of the bed.

"Well at least you can admit you still wear them in front of her," Jaren stated, sarcasm laced in his voice. Tavin chuckled one last time and told them he thought he would try to catch up a little rest before Zeroan and the others arrived for what he knew would be a very long discussion. Jaren and Ril both wished him a peaceful sleep as he fell into his dreams, and suddenly found themselves alone with each other. Though Ril was eager to treat herself to a long bath and to find some more substantial clothing than the thin white dress she had been wearing since her experience with Taurin, Jaren immediately insisted that she tell him everything from their parting in the Great Forests to how they had arrived at the city that morning. Ril breathed hard and pushed her flowing hair behind her slender face. Though she knew his insistently stubborn personality would annoy her to no end if she didn't appease him, she calmly explained that she needed to hear the most important parts from Tavin. Even she was still greatly confused over his encounter with Granis, and didn't dare tell a Grandarian as rambunctious as he that the basis of his country's entire history was false.

"Sorry, Jaren," she said one final time, "but you need to hear it from him." After a long pause, the Grandarian archer sank back in the chair beside Tavin's slumbering form and nodded.

"It's that big, huh," he murmured seriously. Ril nodded yes.

"You saw him for yourself this morning," she reminded him, shifting her leg over the end of the bed. "Yes, it's big..." She let her deep eyes wander onto Tavin's body and slowly exhaled, her face soft with longing. Jaren stared at her for a long moment with his arms crossed, searching her expression to confirm what he had noticed earlier. Finally breaking the silence, Jaren abruptly spoke.

"You love him," he said flatly, more of a statement than an inquiry or guess. The Warrior of Fire's eyes awoke with a start and swiftly shifted over to him. Her face flushed with color, unsure what he was trying to say. As he opened his mouth to continue, however, the words that came were not biting or resentful as she thought they might be, but sympathetic and understanding. "Don't you?" Ril shifted uneasily, letting her eyes drift back to Tavin and slowly acquiring their gentle yearning again.

"Yes," she managed at last, letting the truth in her soul craving to be released surface. Jaren remained still and emotionless for another moment but let a faint smile appear soon after.

"I thought so. You know for yourself I'm not the most intelligent or observant guy in Iairia, but it's never been too hard to tell." He leaned back on the back legs of his chair, looking at Tavin. "And he loves you. I could have told you that from the first time I saw you together in the Golden Castle. I might have had my objections at first," he said, his grin increasing, "but I'm glad he found you." Ril held his gaze and smiled coyly, flattered that her once bitter rival spoke so kindly. The two talked a brief time more about her and Tavin, but at last Ril declared she must get a little sleep and take her bath, which she suggested the battle-dirtied Grandarian do as well. Leaving for the room she had occupied in their previous stay and instructing Jaren to keep a carefully observant eye on Tavin in her absence, Ril dropped onto her bed, falling to sleep the moment her head hit the pillow. With her circumstances finally permitting her to rest easy for at least the moment, she slept for the better part of the day, waking in the afternoon to gather some water and draw herself a warm bath. She removed her simple yet elegant dress to carefully fold and lay on her bed, wanting to take care of something given to her by a spirit of another world. Stepping into her steaming bath, the Warrior of Fire let the warm contentment wash over her skin and slipped her head beneath the water.

While Ril relaxed by herself for the next hour, Jaren woke from his nap shortly after, following her advice and enjoying a bath of his own. Quickly dunking himself in and out of the tub, he set aside his worn, battle weary, green Grandarian hunting attire and dawned a simple brown set of clothes from the shelves of the room across the hall. Refreshed, Jaren entered the room to find Tavin awake, already making his way to the tubs in their bathroom. Though the Warrior of Light was still hard pressed to move about on his own, his strength had increased enough for him to do so. After finishing, Tavin dressed himself in similar clothes to what Jaren had found and sat back down on his bed. They began to talk, but the gradual resonance of voices from outside the inn drew their attention. Leaning out the open window to face the setting sun, Jaren spotted Parnox and Kohlin strolling through the courtyard toward them.

Jaren made his way down the stairs to greet them, leaving Tavin waiting in their room. As he flew down the hallway, Ril opened her door, dried and dressed in a red tunic with her pristine white dress underneath. Informed her of their friends' arrival, Ril turned back for the boys' room and entered to see Tavin first. Resting against the wall adjacent to the bed, he beamed as she entered and flopped down next to him. Running her fingers through the boy's damp brown hair, she leaned in and quickly kissed him on his lips.

"Are you alright?" she asked looking him over.

"I am now," he responded quietly, passing a finger along her cheek, garnering another ravishing smile. They both stood as the clamor of footsteps racing down the hall echoed into the room, followed by a beaming Parnox blasting into the room with arms spread. Ril and Tavin stepped forward to be swept up in them, held tight.

"I missed you children so much!" he chortled merrily. Tavin and Ril giggled to each other, amused how such a brawny giant could be nothing more than an overgrown toddler. After the massive woodsman released them, Jaren and Kohlin entered. Ril frowned at the bandages around Kohlin's arm and along his back, but quickly rushed to embrace him as well. Tavin shook his hand and gently hugged his able side, asking him what happened. As the five friends greeted each other, the sun disappeared behind the mountains to the west. Not long after Parnox and Kohlin's arrival, another convoy of horses came racing into the courtyard from the lower city. Peering out the open window, Kohlin reported five horses outside, one of the riders dismounting. His vision as precise as ever, he made out the figure of Captain Morrol entering the inn through the darkness. As he entered their room, Jaren quickly introduced him to the savior of the day and Ril. Impressed enough to meet two Elemental Warriors, the captain was ready to bow for Tavin.

"That display today was the single greatest thing I have ever seen," he repeated over and over throughout their discussion about the battle. "I don't care if you're a resident of the Southland or not; I will personally see too it that you are given our highest award for your heroics today." Tavin shrugged and shook his head almost embarrassed.

"I appreciate your words, Captain," he interrupted, "but it really isn't necessary. It was my charge; I was just fulfilling it."

"Fulfilling your charge?" Morrol repeated incredulously. "My boy, you just eradicated a legion of demonic beasts and saved an entire nation! I mean, how did you do that?"

"A question we all are eager to have answered, Captain," came the deep voice from the doorway, "and you will have it soon enough. For now, however, why don't you give Tavin a little room to breathe?" All heads turned to the door to find the greyly robed Mystic Sage towering there, slowly entering. Tavin smiled as the lofty figure drew near. "Is your strength recovered some, Tavin?"

"For the most part," he answered with a nod. "After tonight I should be fine."

"With what you must have to tell us," the sage started again, "I would be surprised if anyone gets any sleep tonight. Are you prepared to talk?" He addressed both he and Ril, who shot anxious glances at each other. Tavin could see a worried hesitancy in her eyes, obviously wondering if he was going to tell them the entire story. He turned from Zeroan and leaned in close to her, holding her nervous gaze.

"Are you ready?" he asked quietly, remembering some of the potentially upsetting spots in the narrative that she might not want some of them to hear. She slowly nodded, reaching for his hand and gently squeezing it. Tavin tried a tender smile. "If I start to say something you don't want everyone to hear, stop me, okay?"

"They need to hear it all, Tavin," she told him seriously. "I only care what you think." He let a pause hang between them before gripping her hand back and nodding. Turning back, he asked his friends to sit down. Parnox, Kohlin, and Jaren took a seat on the far bed, Morrol on the chair along the wall, and Zeroan by the windowsill, leaving the second bed for Tavin and Ril. Taking a seat, Tavin began. He started from the night their group was separated in the caverns of the Golthrouts and how he had gained control over his power, and let Ril take over from when she awakened in Keracon Valley for the first time.

They proceeded to tell them how the village's inhabitants had brought the Drakkaidian Prince Verix Montrox with them, and the harrowing experience they had when Tavin discovered his presence. After that came their meeting with the elders the first night they were both awake. Ril went silent as Tavin began to tell the group about their walk back to the hollow later on.

Only Zeroan was aware of what was coming, and when Tavin informed the group about Seriol's betrayal and how he had tricked Ril into almost killing him, Jaren was on his feet with rage.

"That son of dirty..." he ranted with fury. "I *knew* there was something off about him!" Parnox quickly yanked the Grandarian to his posterior once again, sensitively motioning toward Ril with his eyes. After Zeroan confirmed what he said was true, Tavin blew them all away once again with their encounter with Verix and his wish for defection. On his feet again, Jaren leaned forward with a disgusted look on his face.

"You mean to tell me you've been traveling with a Drak for the past month?" he asked incredulously. Both Tavin and Ril's faces went hard.

"Jaren, you're my best friend," Tavin began coldly, "but if you ever disrespect Verix Montrox again I'll come at you harder than I did those demons today. That 'Drak' has more character and honor than most Grandarians put together. He saved my life and Ril's on more occasions than I can remember, so watch what you say around me." By the end of Tavin's speech, Jaren had withdrawn back to his seat on the bed, painfully holding his friend's heated gaze. He nodded apologetically.

"I am familiar with all of this, Tavin," Zeroan interceded, keeping him on topic. "Please continue." The Warrior of Light shifted his gaze to the sage and nodded, beginning again. After telling them of their departure from Keracon Valley with Verix, he skipped ahead to his and the Prince's conflict in the western Grailen and their encounter with one of the Dégamar. He told them how they learned of the senior Montrox's search for the shards to the east and the one in the west, and their decision to head to Coron Village until the road to Torrentcia City was safe. As he related the carnage of

564

Coron to them, Ril went quiet yet again, carefully listening as Tavin avoided the other major event that transpired that night, obviously trying to keep their relationship as discrete as possible. Next Ril took over to retell her and Verix's battle with the possessed Warrior of Light and how they ousted the demon from his body.

After Ril finished with the battle, Tavin took a deep breath and prepared for the part they were all waiting for. He began to tell them about his dream from the Sword of Granis where he found the Celestial Portal in the Border Mountains and how he interpreted it as a signal to go there. Zeroan above all seemed skeptical, but Tavin continued and told him of their perilous arrival and how the sword reacted to the proximity of the portal. Both he and Ril related their struggle against the Black Seven, how they were mercilessly overpowered, and barely managed to escape into the portal thanks to Verix's selflessness. Ril shifted from speaker to listener as Tavin began to tell them of his experience in the void, for she had barely understood anything the first time he had told her. After he had related everything, carefully taking his time so as not to surprise anyone more than absolutely necessary, he drew the newly empowered Sword of Granis from its sheath beside him. The blade was golden now, just as he said.

Though Jaren sat with jaw agape and eyes wide, not able to utter a single word, Zeroan was by far hit hardest by the revelation. Tavin stopped after he showed them the sword, searching the sage's hooded face for his reaction. After a solid minute of silence, he at last rose from his seat on the windowsill and slowly paced forward.

"You are sure of this beyond any doubt, Tavin?" the sage whispered, delving his voice to the lowest level Tavin had ever heard. The Warrior of Light nodded firmly, assurance in his eyes.

"It was hard for me to swallow, too, Zeroan," he said meaningfully, "but it is the truth. Granis has been trapped in a non-place for eons, sealed away in defeat. And that's where he will stay if I don't stop Montrox." Zeroan remained distant, but peered down at him with an expression that hurt Tavin to see. He knew that Zeroan was perhaps the wisest sage in the history of Iairia, and to find out now that the one great truth that he believed above all else was merely fiction probably caused him more anguish than any other pain could. The sage paced back to the doorway, aloof once more. Realizing he was too lost in thought to say anything else, Tavin sheathed the Sword of Granis and continued. "In any case, you all know the rest. After I summoned my borrowed power from Lord Granis, Ril and I arrived back in the deep south where the true Celestial Portal is. Even though this power was new and beyond anything the world has ever seen before, I felt like I had it mastered already and knew exactly what I was capable of from then on, so I took Ril and flew off."

Tavin set his golden weapon down against the wall again, letting his eyes pass over the illustrious hilt one last time. "I will say this much, though. My entire... being is changed now. Now that I've felt this power; now that I know it exists, it feels like the life I've been living up to now has been lived in ignorance. Then again, it might be bliss because even though this is good... righteous power I'm using, it scares me how strong it is. I mean, if I wanted to I could do something..." he scanned over the faces of everyone staring at him, "godly." There was a long silence afterwards, everyone confused at what Tavin was trying to say.

"The power you wield is nothing for you to fear, Tavin," was the soft response from Zeroan, turning to face him. "You will do right with it, nothing else. For now, however, we must put all this aside and focus on the present. We must act, and we must do so immediately." Tavin looked at him hard, purpose and readiness in his eyes.

"Am I going to Drakkaidia tomorrow?" he asked. Zeroan shook his head no.

"No, you will not," he stated, to which the Warrior of Light gave him a peculiar look.

"Wait a minute," Jaren said, rising once again. "You just said time is of the essence here. I'm not eager to send my friend into the battle of his life, but don't you think he should take care of Montrox now before he gets more powerful and we can't stop him anymore?"

"That is exactly why we must go to Galantia tomorrow at first light once Tavin's strength is fully recuperated" the sage continued. "As we have just learned, the Dégamar have recovered the second missing shard that Verix was carrying when they attacked Tavin's party. This means Montrox now has five of the six shards. And as we all now know, the last shard in our possession in Galantia is at risk of falling into his hands. In fact, it is practically in his lap already. Montrox may have suffered a defeat here today, but it will only increase his need and urgency to collect the last shard of the emerald so he can grow more powerful than Tavin and destroy him before Tavin can do the same to him. We must intercept the last shard in Grandaria before it falls into Montrox's hands. Everything depends on this. If he reunites all the shards, it will not matter how powerful Tavin has become. Nothing can stand up to the universal might of the Holy Emerald."

Zeroan's voice was urgent but quiet at the same time, and by the end of his speech he had moved out of the door frame into the hallway.

"You will ride with the Princess and I to Galantia tomorrow, Tavin," the sage decreed.

"Hold on, Zeroan," Tavin stopped him. "I can get to Galantia on my own now. Why don't you take the Princess and someone else with you, and I can fly." The Sarton turned back to stare at him through his hood.

"There is one code of magic that must be followed at all times, Tavin," he began almost menacingly. "It is not to be used as a convenience, only as a necessity."

"With all due respect, Zeroan, I'd say it is a necessity. I can get there hours before you, even if you're on Nighcress. That may be all the time it takes for Seriol to evacuate with the last shard. You must let me go." The sage held his gaze, eventually nodding.

"Very well, your point is made," he conceded. "The Princess will go with me while Tavin flies to Galantia ahead of us. It is settled." Zeroan took a long sweeping look around the room, into the faces of his comrades. "I suggest we get some sleep then. While most of you will remain, you will still have a pressing day ahead of you as the Legion assembles in its entirety. You will take command in my absence, Captain Morrol. Parnox and Kohlin will advise you well. Let us retire." With that, the sage turned and disappeared into the blackness of the nighttime hall, leaving the rest alone. Morrol was the first to rise, once again praising Tavin and Ril for their bravery and bid them goodnight, following after the sage. Parnox and Kohlin went next, and gave them both fierce hugs but told them not to leave in the morning without saying goodbye. As they left, only the Grandarians and Ril remained.

"Tavin," Jaren started, gripping his friend by the shoulders, "you don't have any idea how glad I am to have you back. Nothing seemed quite right without you there with me, buddy." Tavin smiled and embraced him heartily for a long moment. As he pulled away, Jaren took a deep breath and bowed to Ril. "Miss Embrin, thanks for taking such good care of him. I know how much of pain in your backside he can be." Ril smiled and concurred.

"It's a full time job, but somebody has to do it," she smiled. Tavin chuckled, rolling his eyes at both of them. He was surprised, however, to see his friend turn then and make for the door.

"Where are you going?" he asked baffled. Jaren tilted his head and shrugged.

"Like I told Ril," he began, gripping the doorway. "I may not be the brightest guy on earth, but I can see what's going on here." Tavin eyed Ril, already staring at him with a knowing look. He silently laughed and shot a glance at his fiend.

"Don't be jealous, Jaren," he teased, to which Jaren raised an eyebrow.

"Jealous?" he repeated with a smile, cocking his head. "Mine's a Princess, so shove it in your scabbard." Jaren disappeared from the door, gently pushing it halfway closed behind him. Giggling at his witty rejoinder, Ril shook her head at the two boys' friendly banter and turned back to Tavin embarrassingly shaking his head. She took hold of his left hand and began tugging him toward his bed.

"Do you Grandarian boys always get the important girls?" she teased playfully, taking hold of the ends of her dress and sitting on edge of the bed. Tavin shown red again and shrugged, weakly taking a place beside her. He raised a hand to her silky hair and ran his fingers through it.

"We're just lucky, I guess," he replied with growing fatigue in his voice once more. Ril smiled, sitting up and placing her hands on his shoulders to easily push him back onto the sheets.

"You sound tired again," she told him concerned. "Maybe I should go. You're going to want all your strength for tomorrow." Resting his head back on the feathery pillow behind him, he reached up and around her back, gently pulled her down to him. Ril permit herself to loosen, letting him pull her close to him.

"The only thing I want is you," he spoke tenderly, brushing her cascading hair behind her back. "We haven't had a calm moment since Coron. Stay with me." Ril slowly let her warm smile spread across her face as she leisurely picked her feet up from the floor and brought them up behind her on the bed.

"I'm here," she whispered lightly, her arms moving up his chest and tucking around it. As she closed her eyes to lean forward and kiss him, however, a menacing voice from the doorway shocked them both.

"I might have known," it rumbled. Ril flinched with surprise and quickly turned over from Tavin, staring back to find Zeroan's dark outline towering in the doorway. He stared with accusing eyes, unmoving and brooding with quiet antagonism. "I would ask you if you forgot our discussion in Keracon, Arilia, but it is obvious to me that you simply chose to ignore my warning." He stepped through the doorway into the faintly lit room, impatience flaring in his movements. "I hope I am not interrupting." Tavin held his gaze with equal frustration mirrored in his eyes.

"Actually, with all due respect, you are," he said challengingly, not appreciating the sage's words.

"What part of our discussion was unclear to you, Arilia," Zeroan started again, not letting Tavin continue. "I forbid this." Despite his lack of strength, the Warrior of Light quickly roes to his feet.

"Excuse me?" he asked questioningly. "I don't think I'm hearing this right. What exactly is it that you forbid-"

"This relationship that you have become entangled in, boy," Zeroan ripped acidly, cutting him off.

"This entanglement," Tavin repeated scornfully, "*should be* and *is* none of your concern. What business is it of yours to try and regulate others' personal lives?"

"My business, Tavinious, is the survival of Iairia. I do not want to see you fail in your coming battle because of a potential liability like this clouding your judgment should you have to make a choice between fulfilling your obligation and your 'personal life.'" Tavin's face reeled with angry confusion.

"What are you talking about, Zeroan? What do mean, choice?" Zeroan flared once more, ready to explode on the challenging boy, but instead stayed his tongue and slowly backed down, turning his back on them.

"As always," he began quietly, "there is more at work in the grand scheme of things than it would appear. You may have discovered a great truth today, Tavin, but there is still much you do not and cannot know. This relationship is... dangerous for more reasons than you could imagine. You are both too young and shortsighted to be aware of such causes for reluctance as I must be." He turned his head back to them, Ril now standing by Tavin's side with his perpetual determination now reflecting from her eyes as well.

He knew they had indeed fallen for each other; their behavior since their dramatic arrival that morning had made this fact more than clear. The sage shook his head and breathed hard.

"Yet now, it is too late for my intervention. You feel as you feel, and there is no way I can change that. I only hope this will not come back to disturb us later. Get some sleep, you two. You have a trying day ahead of you tomorrow." With that, the sage left the room for the final time, striding into the darkness of the hallway leaving Tavin and Ril standing behind in the faintly illuminated room, hurt by the confusion of why he so hated the idea of their love.

Part Five
Elemental Endgame

Chapter 72

<u>On Wings of Light</u>

"Master Tieloc, sir," was the muffled call that roused Tavin from his dreams the next morning. The Warrior of Light's blue eyes struggled to pry themselves open, slowly letting the bright light from the gaping cracks in the wooden window shutters around the room. "Master Tieloc, I have an urgent message from the Sarton. Are you awake, sir?" By the time the man's second call sounded into the room, Tavin had managed to lift his heavy head from his pillow, raising a hand to wipe the drowsiness away from his face.

"Yes, I'm coming," he replied as loudly as his sluggish voice would allow. Throwing the sheets from his bed, he rotated his legs perpendicular to the mattress and leveled them with the chilly wooden floor, quickly bolstering himself upright to walk to the door. The nippy morning air leaking in from the windows bit at the bare skin along his arms, only covered by a simple brown shirt and pants from the inn. Moving to the door, he quickly unlocked it and opened it halfway to reveal an apprehensive man in makeshift Legionnaire uniform. His eyes quickly shifted downward from where they had been aiming feet higher before the door opened. Tavin could tell he was amazed to find a mere boy as the mighty Warrior of Granis he had heard about. Sensing the man's hesitation and surprise, Tavin tried a quick smile and continued. "If you're looking for Tavin Tieloc, here I am." The man came to his senses at once, quickly swallowing and giving a quick nod.

"Of course," he began again. "My apologies, sir. The Sarton is currently in the gate yard preparing for your arrival, sir. He wishes your presence as soon as possible." Tavin inhaled with longevity, nodding slowly and deliberately.

"Very well," he acknowledged. "I will join the Sarton as soon as my companions and I are prepared."

573

"The Sarton also asked me to inform you that Master Garrinal and her Royal Highness the Princess of Grandaria arrived moments ago, so you should not wait for them." Tavin raised an eyebrow at this, scarcely able to believe that Jaren had beaten him up and was already moving without him. With a curious smile, he nodded again and thanked the man for the message. After he departed and Tavin closed the door once more, he turned back and leaned against it. Breathing deeply, he thought over the difficult day that lay before him. Contemplating, his eyes drifted down to the fiery Southland girl still silently nestled beneath the sheets of the opposite bed in the room. Half of her face from the top of her nose down was hidden by white blankets bunched up in her clasped fingers, while the top was partially obscured by locks of her crimson hair cascading over it. Though the majority of her soft skin was concealed, the mere sight of her slender form embossed in the sheets was enough to ease his wheeling mind and allow him the peace to focus.

Deciding it best to let Ril have what time he could give her to rest a bit more, he thrust himself off of the door and strode into the bathroom adjacent to their room to begin preparing himself for the day. Quickly brushing his hair and washing his face with what was left of the cold water Ril had collected before going to bed the previous evening, he removed his borrowed brown clothing and neatly folded it for the innkeeper's wife to tend to when she and the rest of the city's populace were allowed to return to their homes from the citadel. Gathering his battle weary Grandarian attire once more, Tavin dawned each article of clothing while locating and remembering where he earned each and every rip, tear, and scratch present. Though Kira had repaired and refreshed the garments less than a month ago in Keracon Valley, they were devastated once again. Despite the disrepair running rampant throughout the fabric and armor, they somehow felt more comfortable and fitting than ever. Tavin could not bear the thought of parting with them after all this was over.

As he began fastening his dented and faded blue armor around his chest and shoulders, he stepped back into the bedroom and took a seat on Ril's mattress beside her. She remained still at first, but as he shifted back and forth between his boots and his cape, her tired eyes at last began to slide open behind her tumbling coils of hair. Feeling the sheets budge behind him, Tavin looked back from his boots with a quiet smile. Only her eyes were visible from behind the bedding, but he could tell from the way they squinted she was grinning behind them.

"Well good morning, sleepy," he greeted softly, his smile only building. Pivoting his torso toward her, he reached down and brushed a lock of her hair out of her face to lean down and gently kiss her forehead.

"I think this is a record for you," was the muffled response from beneath the sheets.

"Oh yeah? What's that?"

"This is the first time you've *ever* been up before me," she beamed, her smile obviously stretching from ear to ear. Tavin silently laughed and shot his right hand into her tummy buried under the sheets to tickle her awake. She giggled and rolled over pulling the blankets over her head in defense.

"Oh no you don't," Tavin decreed, standing to lift the girl off the bed holding her back and legs still wrapped in the sheets like sheathed steel. She laughed rowdily and wrestled back and forth in his arms. After holding her into submission, she at last raised her hands and pulled the sheets over from her face, revealing her ravishing smile once more with her laughter subsiding.

"I always wondered what it would be like if you woke me up for a change," she said soothingly, raising a hand to his hair to ruffle it back.

"Don't be too proud of me," he said setting her back down to the bed. "It sounds like Jaren beat both of us this morning."

"As in *our* Jaren?" she asked incredulously. Tavin chuckled again, telling her it was one in the same and how the messenger had told him he and the others were waiting for them in the gate yard. Ril was quick to rise after, conquering the bathroom as her own to dress into the simple clothing she found alongside the nightdress she had borrowed while she slept. While she changed and rinsed her face with the cool water, Tavin fixed up the room and finished dressing himself by strapping the aureate Sword of Granis to his side once again. As always, the brilliant Granic Crystal on its hilt burst alive with golden light, so bright at first Tavin was forced to squint. Upon laying his fingers around the mighty talisman, he could feel the vast well of power dwelling inside both the blade and his own body, ready.

Ril emerged from the bathroom several minutes later dressed in a simple flowing skirt and much lighter yellow tunic with deep red seams sown through. Though she had merely found it in a closet somewhere in the inn, it looked like something she would wear. She ran her fingers through her long flowing hair and smiled, telling him she was ready when he was. With that, the Warrior of Light nodded and bid her to follow him out the door. Passing down the hallway and the staircase to the primary chamber of the cozy little inn, Ril sidetracked to compose a quick note for the innkeeper and his wife for their generosity and the clothes they borrowed.

They exited the building soon after and emerged into the sun-drenched streets of the courtyard, still devoid of anyone but them. As they entered the morning sunlight hand in hand, Ril voiced her concern about what Zeroan might say to them; how he was most likely going to tell her she had to remain behind. Though they had delved through all possible motives, neither of them could figure out why he so vehemently opposed their relationship. Despite her persistent worries, Tavin was confident he could persuade the inflexible Mystic Sage that he wasn't going anywhere without her.

As they rehearsed what they would say to the sage, the Elemental Warriors leisurely traversed the colorful yet empty city streets winding through the market. Approaching the city gates, busy noises of construction and mass troop mobilization echoed into the morning air. Rounding the final corner of the lower city, they found a gate yard bursting with Legionnaires jostling their way back and forth, rapidly repairing the damage still lingering from the previous day's battle. Tavin immediately noticed the gates themselves had already been nearly reconstructed and hoisted back inside the stone archway they protected.

"Look's like your popularity has increased overnight," Ril suddenly leaned into his ear and whispered. Tavin gave her a quirky look before realizing what she meant. As they passed into the gate yard, the men around them quickly fell quiet, whispering and pointing in his direction, some even applauding as he walked by. Not sure whether to be more flattered or uneasy, he pressed forward toward the gate where Captain Morrol stood attentively beside a small makeshift tent. He saw them coming and met them with a warm smile.

"Good morning, Elemental Warriors," he greeted, extending his arm. Tavin took it first, firmly shaking it.

"And to you, Captain," he returned. After Ril greeted him as well, Morrol motioned into the tent.

"Sage Zeroan, or rather, the Sarton," the Captain corrected himself, "awaits inside. Her Royal Highness of Grandaria and the rest of your party is with him. I was instructed to wait for you and accompany you in. Are you ready?" Tavin shot a quick glance at Ril, already staring at him.

"As we'll ever be, I suppose," he murmured at last. With a nod, Morrol turned and pushed the opening to the tent. Tucking his head in, Tavin entered first with Ril in tow followed by Morrol. Parnox, Kohlin, and Jaren sat along the right side of the tent with Mary at the far end, immediately rising as they entered.

"It's about time," Jaren smirked from his chair with a widespread grin. "You think just because you're half-Granis now you come and go any time you please?"

"If I recall correctly," Tavin replied quickly, "this is the first time in the history of history that you've *ever* been up before *anyone*." The seated Grandarian boy only shrugged and silently laughed as they took a step closer.

"While I do wish they would have seen fit to rise earlier," the brooding voice from the end of the tent began, "they are here, so perhaps we can begin, Jaren." Tavin and Ril both turned to find Zeroan standing in the background of the assembly, draped in fresh gray robes.

"We're ready," Tavin spoke in an organized tone of voice.

"Good," the sage nodded, taking a step forward. "Then let us make this quick. As we decided last night, we must make our way to Galantia today with all speed. Because of its considerable distance from our current position and our lack of transportation, however, our band must separate once again." The sage turned to the two Southlanders sitting beside Jaren. "The finale of our quest is one that you cannot aid us in, my friends. Your part in this adventure has come to an end. You will remain here to aid Captain Morrol in the mobilization of the Legion should the need for it resurface before the end. Keep them strong and finish the repairs to the city." Both Parnox and Kohlin nodded with a hint of sorrow mirrored in their eyes.

"The Southland will be safe with us, sage," Parnox smiled. Zeroan nodded with a faint smile of his own.

"I have no doubt. As for you, Captain," he said turning to Morrol, "I lay my title of temporary Sarton of the Legion to you in my absence. The men have come to respect you, and you will lead them far better than I ever could. Look after them until you elect a new Sarton." Morrol stood flabbergasted for a moment, but at last bowed in acceptance and thanked him. Zeroan then turned in the direction of Tavin, Ril, and Jaren at the end of the tent. "As for our younger comrades and I," he began, "we have more to do. As you know, I can take two other bodies with me on Nighcress to Grandaria. I have decided that in addition to the Princess, Jaren will accompany me." Jaren's eyes lit up with glee, looking up to Tavin. "Don't get excited, boy. I want you with me because you have proven yourself a valuable asset and may prove useful before the end. Besides, I'm sure you wish to see your home again."

"More than you know, Zeroan," the Grandarian boy confirmed. Zeroan nodded.

"Yes, well, in the meantime, Tavin will be on his own. Because of his convenient ability to fly, he can make his own way to the golden land. I am reluctant to let him do this, yet no demon would dare come near the Warrior of Granis after yesterday, and Montrox will have them at Dalastrak now for reorganization anyway. After his last defeat, the Drakkaidian ruler has surely lost his patience and is summoning the final shard to him. If Tavin can arrive earlier on his own to stop Seriol, it is that much more reason for him to go." Zeroan paused for a moment, shifting in his robes. "And I want you to take Ril with you." Both Tavin and Ril went dead still, shocked beyond belief at the sage's order. "I would have her stay behind to aid the Warrior of Water in whatever he may need her for, but there may be reason for her presence in Galantia. I trust you can provide her a means of transportation, Tavin?" Still almost too stunned to respond, it was all he could do to nod in compliance and mouth yes.

Zeroan let out a small huff of air and shifted in his robes again.

"Very well. Every second that escapes us is one more than Montrox may be using to steal the final shard of the emerald, so we must be off now. Sarton Morrol, please send for my horse immediately." Morrol hesitated for a moment, a strange smile quickly passing across his face then fading, obviously from the shock of being called Sarton. He quickly bowed and exited the tent, leaving the party of six and the Princess to themselves. Zeroan slowly turned back to them from the entrance of the tent, sweeping his gaze over them all. Though his face was hidden as always, they could all see the rare gentleness hovering over it. "Well, I'm afraid that this will be the last time our party is together before the end. I..." he trailed off for a moment, as if trying to say something that had difficulty forming. "I... suppose I just wanted to say that I'm very proud of you. All of you. You have all demonstrated your outstanding skills and values on this quest, and all of you were vital to getting us this far." He stopped there, exiting the tent a moment later bidding them to say their farewells then meet him outside.

After he departed, it was Mary who at last stood and spoke.

"He may be hard on the exterior," she began, "but he is truly a great man at heart." Kohlin nodded, rising alongside Parnox.

"That he is," the Southlander confirmed. "I have no doubt that with his help, you will be able to stop Montrox, Tavin." Moving over to the Warrior of Light, Kohlin wrapped his free arm around his back to firmly embrace him. "It has been an honor to travel with you, Tavin. You are an extraordinary young man." Tavin was quick to return his friend's hug, telling him the honor was his. After the two separated, Kohlin turned to Ril, her eyes moistening as well. "Until we next meet, my lady. Keep an eye on him for us." Ril beamed as a single tear fell down her cheek, fiercely pulling forward to hug him as well.

"You take care of yourself. Thank you for being there for me." As Ril and Kohlin bid goodbye, Jaren had risen to leap into Parnox.

"I'm going to miss you, big guy," he said merrily. Parnox chuckled and patted him on the back.

"As will I, little guy," he returned merrily. "Stay safe 'til we meet again. There'll be one hell of a party when this is over." Kohlin and Parnox quickly switched comrades to bid farewell, including the Princess, who exited with Jaren after they had all said their goodbyes. Outside, Zeroan sat waiting on the back of the midnight black Nighcress, beating its hooves with anticipation.

"Are you all ready?" he asked collected once again. They all nodded, and Parnox carefully lifted both the Princess and

Jaren to the massive horse behind its first rider. "Very well," he inhaled loudly, turning to Tavin. "We will arrive by late afternoon, Tavin. I'm not sure how fast you can travel, but I will be pushing Nighcress hard to try and keep pace with you. Proceed at full speed. I imagine you will arrive a good hour before us at least. We take our leave now, so godspeed my young friend."

"See you at home, buddy," Jaren smiled down to Tavin, taking hold of Mary and Zeroan in front of him. Tavin nodded with a proud smile as Zeroan turned Nighcress for the open gate, and began speeding out commanding his passengers to hold onto him. As they disappeared, Tavin turned back to Ril.

"Can you believe this?" he asked.

"You mean Zeroan all of the sudden *wanting* me to go? No." Tavin let a confused smile spread across his face.

"Well, I've given up trying to figure him out or guess ahead of him. What do you say we go?" Ril took a deep breath and nodded. "Okay, then, everybody stand back." With that, Tavin wrapped his grip around the hilt of the Sword of Granis, pulling it free with its metallic ringing catching the attention of the entire courtyard. With both hands on the talisman, he sealed his eyes and took hold of his power, immediately blasting it outward in a surge of golden light. His own power now swirling around him, he focused on the sword and the enormous strength lying within. With the Granic Crystal burning with life, the golden blade of the sword beamed a sudden flash of blinding light around its holder. With a mammoth display of righteous power blasting to life in the entire gate yard, the power of Granis enveloped Tavin again. Though shielding her eyes from the potency of the light, Ril could still feel the incredible explosion of power soaring out of control.

After several long moments of exponentially building his energy, Tavin let it begin to settle. As the light began to gradually soften, Ril looked back to find Tavin transformed into the Warrior of Granis once more. Dressed in regal while and golden attire, eyes shining yellow, and surrounded by a sphere of energy giving off more power than she could comprehend, she was again overwhelmed by the seemingly limitless strength her love once more exuded. Breathing deep and sheathing the Sword of Granis, Tavin locked his eyes onto Ril and opened his arms. With a warm smile, she took a step toward him passing into his field of radiating power. Tavin swept forward and gathered her in his arms once again, gently lifting off the ground. Grinning as she put her arms around his neck, the Warrior of Granis slowly rose into the sky above Torrentcia City and shot off to the northeast.

Hours later that day, two bolts of careening light streaked across the skies over the Hills of Eirinor in central Grandaria drawing sharp golden contrails after them. After spending so much time in the skies in the Warrior of Granis' arms, Ril had finally gotten used to soaring over Iairia and conquered her fear of heights. So much in fact that she had allowed Tavin to experiment his power with her. Remembering that he could do practically anything he wanted, he tried to form a wave of energy around Ril, wrapping her in a protective sphere of golden light that he could manipulate any way he saw fit. After getting the hang of how to transfer his energy, Tavin released Ril altogether and let her trail after him in her own sphere of power. Though petrified at first, it was not long before she began wildly laughing and flapping her arms like wings, effortlessly following Tavin wherever he went.

After playing follow the leader with her for miles across the deep blue skies, Tavin at last slowed himself alongside her and gradually took her back into his arms. Ril shook her head in thrilled amazement, giggling with glee.

"Is there anything you can't do anymore?" she asked brushing a lock of her streaming hair out of her face. "You do realize what you are now, right? You're the most powerful living thing I have- no the world- has ever seen." Tavin just shrugged and grinned.

"Maybe, but I don't think even the Holy Emerald could give me enough power to stand up to my mother when she finds out I've been out battling demons for the past two months." Ril giggled and eyed him peculiarly.

"Why would you say that?" she asked. Tavin flipped upside-down so the girl could look down on the land beneath them.

"See that village down there nestled in the little patch of trees?" Ril's eyes went wide, a new growing smile overtaking her face.

"Is that your home, Tavin?" she asked hopefully, fixing her gaze back on him. Tavin nodded with a proud little smile.

"Eirinor Village," he announced. "I've missed the old place."

"Tavin, if it's sitting right underneath us why don't you touch down for a moment to let your parents know you're alright?" Tavin turned right side up again, raising an awestruck eyebrow at her.

"Oh that's a good idea. Hi, mom. Hi, dad. Oh, what's that radiating light swirling around me? Well, it's the power of Granis himself that he personally gave to me in the void where he's been trapped for eons. This is the Sword of Granis, the sacred icon you used to tell me stories about, and now it's mine. I'm going to go use it to save the world now. Well, I have to go. See you." Tavin stared at her hopelessly. "Are you crazy?" Ril huffed in defeat before acquiring a knowing little smirk and leaning in close to his face.

"I know what's really going on," she stated with a sarcastic grin. "You just don't want to tell them you've fallen for a non-Grandarian girl, do you? I bet they'd flip. Or maybe you just don't think they'd like me. Is that it, Tavin?" He silently laughed for a moment before opening his eyes and locking them onto her.

"They'll love you whether you're Grandarian or not," he stated softly. "Just like me." The Warrior of Fire let her sarcastic expression dissipate, replaced by one full of tenderness.

"How did I ever survive without you, Tavin?" she asked with sincerity. The boy just smiled back, gently kissing her and pulling back to blast off with renewed speed toward the Grandarian capital.

Chapter 73

<u>Shadowy Corruption</u>

They arrived a few hours later as the sun began to drift toward the western sky, hinting it was ready to being its descent for the day. Speeding into the Valley of Galantia, Tavin quickly spotted the shining Grandarian capital and charged forward with renewed vitality, eager to arrive and do what he came to do. Blasting across the sky with the golden contrails from his radiating body streaking behind him, the Warrior of Granis quickly closed the gap between him and the city, watching as the populace below gazed up with wonder at his display. Within moments they reached the upper city and the Golden Castle reflecting the auburn sky's failing light in beautiful hues of yellow and orange. Peering down to find the courtyard of the mighty citadel devoid of life, Tavin began to slow and flip his body perpendicular to the ground. Gradually levitating downward with this golden aura of circulating power beginning to slowly fade, the Warrior of Granis touched down to the stone courtyard to meet with gravity once more.

After safely landing, Tavin began focusing deep within to slowly will his godly power away to a state of dormancy in his body once more. Still in his arms, Ril watched with amazement as the swirling golden field of warmth around the two slowly faded into the evening breeze while his regal clothing transformed back into his worn blue and white garbs. When the last remnant of his power had sealed, Tavin's eyes remained closed. Staring at him in wait, Ril's concern at last compelled her to speak.

"Are you alright?" she asked softly, obvious worry in her voice. A long moment passed, but eventually the Warrior of Light opened his eyes to reveal their standard blue hue once again. Though he was fully awake, a temporary fatigue was present behind them.

"Fine," he smiled in return, yet remained otherwise motionless. Ril's eyes widened curiously.

"Do you think you should let me down now?" she asked with a hint of sarcasm. Tavin's eyes shot wide open, an embarrassed smile sweeping across his face. He quickly rotated her slender form to the ground, gently setting her down beside him.

"Sorry," he started. "I just seem to feel a little weird when I transform between the Warrior of Light and Granis." Looking around, Tavin's brow furrowed. "So what do you make of this?" Ril turned to observe the rest of the castle's courtyard, completely empty.

"Make of *what*?" she returned quietly. "Is it normal for the Grandarian royal castle to be this quiet?" Tavin shook his head, peering at the massive entrance to the structure.

"I can't ever remember... wait, there's someone coming out of the hallway." Shifting her gaze back to the entrance, Ril saw the lone figure adorned with elite Grandarian attire swiftly approaching them from the massive Grand Vestibule. Looking back to Tavin uncertainly, she found a distrustful expression on his face.

Motioning for Ril to walk with him, the two started forward until face to face with the figure, looking to be a royal servant.

"Greetings, Warrior of Light," the man said rapidly with a quick bow. "The Supreme Granisian has been expecting you. I have been instructed by His Eminence to summon you to the throne room at once. Please follow me." Shooting a quick glace at Ril, Tavin's already estranged eyes grew skeptical.

"We're expected?" he asked curiously. The man nodded, already turning back toward the entrance to the castle.

"Yes," the man confirmed. "The Supreme Granisian has been waiting for you for some time. Please hurry." Once again letting his gaze pass to Ril, he shrugged uncertainly and motioned for her to continue with him. As they passed into the Golden Castle and moved through its ornate hallways, Tavin noticed that veritably no one could be found. Even the sentries perpetually on guard were absent. He was quick to inquire as to their whereabouts, to which the servant informed them the Supreme Granisian had ordered the entire castle to be evacuated to the city earlier in the day. Why, he did not know. Pressing on through the intricate hallways of the citadel, the trio finally reached its upper levels and the entrance to the throne room. Pushing one of its massive double doors open, the servant turned back and bade the two Elemental Warriors to enter.

Tavin went first, followed by Ril grasping for his hand. The chamber was uncharacteristically dark, even as the evening sunset poured through the massive arching windows. Once they had stepped several feet inside, the door hastily closed shut behind them, causing them both to jump and spin their heads around.

"Why is it so dark in here?" Ril asked, suddenly fearful.

"I'm more concerned with where the Supreme Granisian is," he spoke uncertainly, motioning for her to look up to the empty throne at the end of the chamber. "Didn't he say he's been waiting for us?" Ril didn't respond, yet tightened her grip on his hand as they began to slowly inch forward, carefully examining their quiet environment. As they reached within a few feet of the stairs leading up to the Supreme Granisian's throne, a sudden movement from behind them finally broke the silence. Reeling his hand to the Sword of Granis, Tavin found a figure emerging before him accompanied by a tranquil voice.

"You have no need for that, my young friend," the man spoke. Hearing the voice and eyeing the figure, Tavin realized that he was the Supreme Granisian. Easing his hand away from his weapon, he slightly bowed and tugged on Ril's hand to signal her to do the same. "Rise, Elemental Warriors. I am glad to see you both in good health after your arduous journey across Iairia. But to business. I'm afraid we have much to discuss and not much time to do it in." Tavin's eyes were focused yet questioning as they searched for his, hidden by the room's darkness.

"Yes, Your Eminence, but I must confess my curiosity to how you knew we were coming," he spoke civilly. Corinicus Kolior smiled quickly while he shifted his footing.

"I could not easily miss a power such as yours, Warrior of Light," was the oblique answer. "But do not dwell on this when more important matters deserve our attention." Tavin nodded, taking a step forward.

"Yes, Your Highness. Ril and I bring news from the Southland and the Mystic Sage Zeroan. Much has happened since our departure from Galantia, and we have discovered a sleeping danger lurking here." Before Tavin could elaborate further, the Supreme Granisian raised his hands motioning for him to stop.

"I know you carry important news, young Tieloc, but before we discuss anything further you must come with me. I have something to show you of the utmost importance." Turning suddenly with his elaborately decorated robes swirling after him, Kolior disappeared behind his throne. Caught off guard by the Supreme Granisian's odd behavior, Tavin's brow furrowed once more.

"I don't like this, Tavin," Ril whispered distrustfully. "For the regal, noble leader he's supposed to be, he's acting more than a little strange."

"He's the Supreme Granisian, Ril," Tavin reminded her sharply, more to reassure himself than her everything was all right. "Whatever's going on around here, he must have a reason for it. Come on." Despite his own lingering doubts, he obediently pushed forward up the stairs toward the throne with Ril hovering behind. As they passed the opulent chair, Tavin found Kolior below the opposite side of the stairs placing his hand over a small dais embedded into the golden stone wall. Descending the stairs after him, they watched with incredulity as an arching golden outline of light suddenly flashed inside of the wall, quickly spreading to encompass the entire area within. In the next moment, the light abruptly dissolved, revealing an arching passage in the once immovable stone wall and another room beyond.

"Please follow me," Kolior bid them without turning, stepping through the new entryway. Entering after him, Tavin's face was overcome with wonder.

"Supreme Granisian, what is this place?" he asked inquisitively.

"The means for my escape, young Grandarian," was the direct response from inside the room. Spinning his head into the small chamber, Tavin immediately found the white robed figure of the Supreme Granisian's trusted advisor, Seriol, standing next to a massive dark beam of slowly radiating energy rising from a black dais in the floor. Instantly on the offensive, Tavin's hands flew to the hilt of the Sword of Granis, wrenching it free to send its piercing metallic ring ripping through the atmosphere around them. Though surprised by the intensity of the Sword of Granis, Ril immediately tensed her body with a detestable glare forming in Seriol's direction.

The Supreme Granisian reeled back from the Warrior of Light, afraid of the weapon.

"Tavinious, what are you doing?" he called. Tavin's gaze remained hard, fixated on the coolly collected figure before him.

"This is what we had to tell you, Your Highness. I'm afraid we have bad news about your advisor Seriol," he began coldly. "Your most trusted consultant has betrayed you and all of Grandaria. He has been working for Drakkaidia for Granis knows how long; Valif Montrox's personal spy and an assassin on the inside." Kolior was still, keeping his gaze intently locked on Tavin but saying nothing. In the face of the accusations, Seriol too remained passive. "Somehow he managed to fool us all- even Zeroan. He used his position of power to enter the Temple of Light and place Drakkaidian crystals of dark magic onto the Sword of Granis itself in an attempt to sabotage my power and kill me." Seriol's previously emotionless face acquired a dark grin.

"Seeing as you still stand alive to accuse me, apparently my plan failed," he smirked. "Oh well, I suppose I should have guessed not to trust a little girl to see to my affairs." Ril's already irate face tightened with enmity.

"You heard it from his own mouth," she breathed icily. "This piece of garbage is a double-crossing traitor. He's trying to deliver the final shard of the Holy Emerald to Montrox." As Ril finished her vehement outburst, Tavin shot a glace toward the silent Supreme Granisian. There was a peculiar look about him; he had just been told that his most trusted advisor had betrayed him yet he remained still as stone with his eyes hidden.

"Your Eminence, you must believe us," Tavin tried, unsure what Kolior was making of all this. At last, his mouth opened to slowly form the words to speak.

"I do, young Tieloc," he stated softly. "I knew all this some time ago." Both Tavin and Ril's eyes widened as their mouths slipped open, bombarded by uncertainly and throbbing bewilderment.

"...You mean you've known this was happening?" Ril asked painfully. "You've known he was working for Montrox?" Kolior took a careful step toward the girl, his eyes sealed shut.

"Of course," he stated simply. "I have been as well." Frozen in shock by the Supreme Granisian's words, neither of the Elemental Warriors could react in time to stop him from suddenly lunging toward Ril, locking his right arm around her and pressing the dagger previously hidden in the confines of his layers of robes against her neck. Awestruck by agonizing confusion and rage, Tavin found himself unsure of what to do.

"Make so much as one move, boy, and he'll open her throat," Seriol shouted from beside them. Tavin's expression was wild as he carefully threw up his free hand defensively.

"Your Eminence, what are you doing!?! Let her go!" he pleaded commandingly. The only response was Seriol's mocking laughter echoing from his right.

"Please, boy," he started cynically. "Your heroic little words will have no effect on him. Take a look at his eyes." Shooting a quick glance at Seriol, Tavin set his gaze onto Kolior's eyes, for the first time illuminated. Instantly, he knew what was wrong.

They were pitch black.

"A Shadow..." he murmured in horror. Seriol chuckled again.

"Intelligent boy," he applauded. "Now if you're truly smart, you'll listen to what I'm about to say. There is a demon in possession of your beloved Supreme Granisian, and if you so much as flinch the wrong way or summon a fraction of your power, it will have him slice her from ear to ear. That goes for you and your little power as well, my dear." On the verge of igniting into a towering inferno, the panic stricken Ril decided to control herself and not take the risk with the sharp blade on the verge of penetrating her skin. "Very good, Tavin. Now pay close attention, because I'm only going to say this once. You're going to place that little poker of yours onto the floor and slide it out the door into the next room. I suggest you do it now." Though hesitant to relinquish the Sword of Granis, the sight of the possessed Supreme Grandarian pressing his blade ever closer against Ril's neck forced him to do as he was told.

"Fine," he agreed slowly, turning to set the mighty talisman on the floor and kick it through the doorway back into the throne room. He turned back to face the white robed figure immediately. "Now let her go," he commanded, to which Seriol only laughed.

"You are in no position to give orders, boy," he scoffed. "Kolior, bring her here." Tavin's face twisted with alarm and fury.

"Why are you doing this, Seriol?" he asked incredulously. "If you help Montrox win, all you're going to do is release Drakkan from the Netherworld so he can destroy Iairia! What do you have to gain from that?"

"You haven't the faintest idea of what you speak," he returned spitefully. "Once Valif Montrox assembles the Holy Emerald, he will have total control of the world. After his armies have conquered it, he will give me rule of the new Grandaria that will emerge. Only a fool would challenge the might of Drakkaidia. You may have acquired an impressive new power, but it is nothing compared to this." Reaching into his robes, he pulled free Tavin's old lucky charm; the sixth shard of the Holy Emerald. "And now, we're going to step into this portal and deliver it to him."

"If you give that shard to Montrox, no one will live to see a new Grandaria. The world will be consumed by Drakkan!"

"Well you are entitled to your delusions, but we are leaving regardless," he stated. "And you're going to stay right where you are or this girl's blood will stain the entire room." Tavin's face tightened with rage.

"Let her go, Seriol," Tavin commanded. "You don't need her."

"On the contrary, I do," he stated informatively. "Lord Montrox has ordered me to bring her with me. Apparently he has some use for her." Tavin watched in anguish as horror filled the Warrior of Fire's eyes.

"*Tavin!*" she screamed violently. Inching forward with utter disdain for the man before him, Tavin could feel the blood in his veins boiling.

"If a single hair on her head is harmed, I'm going to blast you to ashes," he threatened hatefully. The tension was suddenly interrupted by the sound of massive doors bursting open from behind them in the throne room.

"Tavin!" was the distant cry from Zeroan speeding toward them. Turning back to Seriol, Tavin found them already moving toward the dark beam in the floor.

"It would appear the time for us to take our leave has arrived," he grinned darkly. "Give my regards to the sage." Seriol quickly pulled the Supreme Granisian still savagely gripping Ril into the portal after him. As Ril began to rise in the darkening shaft of black light, Tavin could see her screaming one last time though her voice was silenced by the energy swallowing her. Charging forward after them,

Tavin lunged at the fading portal shrinking by the second. Bellowing her name, he landed on the Drakkaidian dais as the last remnant of energy dissolved into the air, far too late. Gritting his teeth with fury, a wave of profound failure and helplessness overcame him. He possessed the greatest power the world had ever seen, yet he wasn't even able to save one person when she needed him the most. A single tear swelling in the corner of his eye fell to the ground. Now she was in Montrox's clutches.

Moments later, Zeroan burst into the chamber with his gray robes soaring behind him. As his eyes fell upon the Warrior of Light lying on the ground distraught with emotion, his face was grave.

"Tavin, what happened?" he inquired immediately. "Are you hurt?" Tavin remained silent for a moment, too choked up to speak.

"He has Ril," he murmured through his raging emotion. Zeroan quickly drew closer and dropped to his side.

"Who has Ril?" he pressed urgently. Tavin threw his fist into the ground, a small surge of his power flaring up on impact.

"Seriol took her!" he bellowed indignantly. "He's got her *and* the last shard, and now both of them are in Drakkaidia! I let them go!" Though sensitive to the boy's emotions, Zeroan lacked the patience to decipher his half pieced together thoughts.

"Tavin, slow down," he commanded vigorously. "Gain control of your feelings and tell me what happened. I sensed a demon in the castle. Was it here?" Tavin raised his red face to Zeroan's.

"It was Kolior," he said darkly. "Seriol infected the *Supreme Granisian* with a Shadow. I was so surprised I couldn't stop him from taking Ril. He had a knife to her neck the entire time. They escaped into a portal of energy rising out of this spot on the floor just before you got here."

"He has the shard?" Zeroan asked dreadfully. Tavin nodded.

"And Ril..." trailing off for a moment, Tavin's eyes suddenly burst open and locked back onto Zeroan's. "He said Montrox wanted Ril, Zeroan. Why would he want her?" Zeroan's face remained horrified from what he had just heard and didn't speak. When Tavin asked again fiercely taking hold of the sage's robes, Zeroan's impatience flared as well.

"Tavin calm down," he ordered loudly. "You need to focus and think clearly-"

"Tell me what he wants with her, Zeroan!" Tavin grilled, overcome with rage. The sage's face was hard, but did not reveal the answer.

"I don't know, Tavin," he said gently. Maintaining his hold on the sage for a long moment, Tavin's face at last lost the edge of its wrath and concentrated with passionate resolve. Releasing Zeroan and rising to his feet, he marched past him for the doorway. Zeroan was instantly on his feet following him, aware the Warrior of Light had something in mind. "Tavin, you must collect yourself before we act. I want to save Ril as much as you, but we have to organize ourselves and make a plan. Tavin!" The Warrior of Light continued walking and picked up the Sword of Granis from where it lay on the floor in the throne room, the Granic Crystal bursting to life. As he sheathed the weapon, he could see Jaren rushing into the room winded. Spotting his friend in his distressed state, Jaren slowed.

"Tavin, what's wrong?" he asked, getting no more response than he gave to Zeroan. Making his way to the massive arching windows alongside the wall, Tavin at last halted and balled up his fists.

"I'm ending this now," he decreed resolutely, a faint golden aura beginning to shine to life around him. In the next moment, it quickly exploded to life, forming a sphere of vibrant radiance swirling around him. With one massive detonation, Tavin opened the power in the sword and transformed. As the light faded enough to look at him again, Jaren and Zeroan found him standing engulfed in yellow energy and wearing his regal white and gold attire.

"Tavin, you must not rush to battle before we are ready!" Zeroan roared to him furiously. "We aren't prepared..." He was cut off by the explosion of charged power as Tavin lifted off and blasted into the skies through the window, soaring off to the northwest nearly ten times faster than he had on his way to Galantia.

As the waning flurries of light left over from Tavin's ascent wafted into the evening air, Jaren looked to Zeroan in astonishment. Too stunned to speak, he left the silence hang between them until the sage at last lowered his head and shifted in his robes as always. Though he expected the sage to go on tirade on how Tavin risked the lives of everyone in

Iairia with his rash charge into battle, he was instead calm and collected as he turned from the window and gradually began walking past him.

"I need time," the sage stated, barely audible. "Go to the Princess and distract her from thoughts of her father. Do not disturb me for any reason." As Zeroan strode out of the room, Jaren was left in a world of painful confusion of which he had never felt the likes before.

Chapter 74

<u>The Red Pennant</u>

Ril's eyes began to drift open slowly as the chilling breeze blowing in from outside her dark surroundings gently brushed across her sweaty face. Quickly forcing herself awake, a wave of confusion overcame her, unable to remember where she was or how she came to be there. As her mind gradually retraced her memories to piece together her location, she felt a strange coldness around both of her wrists. Looking down, she observed she was bound in chains by the hands and feet to a massive chair in which she sat. Alarmingly scanning her environment, Ril found herself sitting in a dark stone chamber savagely decorated with angular, twisting glyphs and decorations embedded and hanging from the walls only faintly illuminated by torchlight. Quickly identifying the dark décor as Drakkaidian, Ril's face went pale with remembrance. She had been kidnapped by the possessed Supreme Granisian and Seriol. A portal identical to the one in Galantia rested on the floor not more than a few feet from her chair.

"Arilia," was the soft voice from beside her. The frantic Warrior of Fire wheeled to her left in surprise, her eyes falling onto a familiar figure also chained to another chair to the left an even more massive throne between them.

It was Verix.

The frenzy in Ril's face abruptly faded, replaced by a stunned horror. The Drakkaidian Prince lay in a broken heap, his life force hanging by a thread. Crusted blood and open wounds were strewn across his bruised face with gashes and rips in his battle-weary clothing. His usually bright crimson eyes were dark and faded, on the verge of death.

"...Verix?" Ril replied almost inaudibly. "What happened to you?" He remained still for a moment, his eyes searching. A flash of lightning ripped across the sky outside, causing an

593

already unnerved Ril to jump. "Where are we, Verix? What is this place?" He was quiet again, but at last opened his mouth to speak, obviously struggling for the energy to do so.

"Drakkaidia," he breathed, mustering the strength to bolster himself in his seat. Ril let out a heavy breath, dread in her eyes.

"But where?" she pressed anxiously. Verix was slow to respond, obviously trying to say something that he could not quiet formulate.

"Home," came a low rumbling response from the other side of the room. Ril's head jerked away from Verix toward the source of the reply on the opposite side of the chamber as two massive double doors along the wall unhurriedly began to slide open. Verix painfully shook his head and spoke again.

"Ril, you... have to... be strong for this," he managed to utter. Her eyes quickly shifted back to him, confusion and fear running rampant in them.

"For what?" she asked hastily.

"For me," the menacing voice from the wall interjected once again, this time much closer. Fixing her gaze back on the wall, Ril found both doors now open with a lone figure standing in between them, a dark grin on his mutated face. Ril went pale. All three were silent for a long moment, the dead silence of the dark Drakkaidian atmosphere broken only by the sporadic rumbling of thunder outside. At last, the black armored figure in the door took a slow step forward and started toward the three thrones atop the staircase at the end of the chamber. As he closed the gap between them and began leisurely ascending the stairs toward her, Ril tightened and swallowed hard, her rhythmic breathing heavy. The man was a horror to behold. His body was twisted and contorted, the pupils of his eyes had turned blood red as a Valcanor, and deep red streaks were strewn across his face. Most disturbing was his swollen right arm, bulging with savage brown muscle over twice the size of his opposite arm. After what seemed like an eternity, the monstrous figure climbed the final stair and stopped before her, his smile renewed.

Staring each other down for another long moment, the man spoke once more.

"You look tense," he observed quietly, strange kindness in his voice. "Let me bid you to calm yourself. You have nothing to fear from me." Ril remained silent but for her strong breathing. The figure tilted his head at a slight angle. "Oh, forgive me. I've failed to introduce myself."

"I know who you are, Montrox," the girl at last managed, her voice shaking with emotion. "You don't scare me." The figure's dark grin only widened at this, his head slowly beginning to shake back and forth.

"Ah, such spirit," he purred. "No doubt from your ill treatment on the way here. I apologize for that. My servant Seriol is prone to volatility in his methods, but they are effective nonetheless. You won't have to worry about him again, though, as he and the Supreme Granisian have... outlived their uses." Outstretching his arm to the massive throne between Ril and Verix, a dark pulse of light flashed around his six shards of the Holy Emerald resting there and flew to levitate around his hand. "Beautiful, aren't they? Thanks to my treacherous agent in Galantia, I now have the final shard of the emerald. I have but to piece them together and the power to control the universe will be mine." Ril remained firm, not giving into her fear.

"Tavin is going to stop you," she decreed as if already set in stone. Montrox silently chuckled.

"The Warrior of Light has somehow gained new power to be sure," he granted, "yet no power can stand up to the ultimate might of the Holy Emerald. And once I am all-powerful, I will crush Grandaria and your precious Warrior of Light. I advise you to accept things for the way they are and quit deluding yourself with false hopes. I have already won." The Warrior of Fire clenched her fists and shot forward in her chair, fury flaring in her face.

"Then why did you kidnap me?" she shouted irately. "What do you want with me?" The Drakkaidian ruler slowed for a moment, letting the shards of the Holy Emerald drift back to the table beside his throne. Carefully turning, he placed his hands behind his back and began to pace.

"I've been watching you for some time, Arilia," he began coolly, causing Ril to cringe hearing him call her by name. "Your friend the Mystic Sage has done a brilliant job keeping you hidden from me in your early years, yet as you began to mature I found you. Though I wanted to summon you to me years ago, I have been biding my time, waiting for the right moment. Then, something happened I did not expect. Verix found you first, that night in the forests to the south. Oh yes, I know all about that. I'm sure this was the trigger that sparked his betrayal. Yet he's never told you how he knew you or why he saved you that night, has he?" Verix shifted in his seat, desperately summoning the strength to speak.

"Don't father," he managed to plead. Montrox turned his head to the boy beside him. Staring at him for a quick moment, he suddenly plunged his fist into the boy's stomach. Though he exerted no effort, the blow was enough to ensure Verix's silence for the rest of the conversation, his eyes widening and mouth leaking fresh blood once more.

"Now, son, it's rude to interrupt," the senior Montrox informed him turning back to Ril, returning his gaze with a scowl of deathly hate.

"Leave him alone!" she commanded ardently. The Warrior of Darkness ignored her, pacing back in her direction quietly.

"It will be almost a shame to destroy your home in the west, you know," he stated again in a factual tone of voice. "I've always loved that region of Iairia. In my time before assuming control of Drakkaidia, I traveled there every year. My last visit was years ago when not much older than you. As I was returning home, I encountered a beautiful young female in a small village behind Mt. Coron. Fireite, I think it was. For some reason, I found myself taken with her, and even more strangely, her with me. I decided to linger a bit longer, and the night before I left for home, I let her enjoy the pleasure of my company in her bed. Then, almost a year later, I felt a presence appear in the world like I have never felt before. It was me; my power, but originating from the Southland. Intrigued, I decided to make one last trip to the west. Following the strange power, I found myself back in Fireite Village.

"Upon my arrival, I learned the woman I had once known had recently died in the process of giving birth to a child, which was now in the care of its grandparents because the father could not be found. Further intrigued, I ventured into the village to find the child. After I killed the grandparents, I picked up the child and realized it was the source of the strange power. He was my son, with my power in his veins. Deciding I would someday need an heir to my throne, I took him with me back to Drakkaidia to become a Prince." Montrox's eyes shifted back to Verix's weakened form, shaking his head. "Perhaps his impure blood is the reason for his inability to appreciate my plans.

"In any case, once I returned to Drakkaidia, I realized something was wrong. Verix was with me, yet I still sensed the same power lingering in the Southland. The only explanation was there had been another child, one that I missed in my excitement to have found Verix. As I was about to venture back to the Southland yet again, however, the power suddenly disappeared. Into thin air. Confused, I sent one of my servants to Fireite to inquire further. He arrived several months later with disturbing news. The woman had birthed twins. After one of them was taken and the grandparents killed, the other was left alone in the world. It was apparently taken by a Mystic Sage. I could only guess that it was Zeroan, who somehow masked the child's presence from me so I could not find it. Even the clever sage could not hide it forever, though, for as the child matured I was able to ferret out its presence once more." Ril's eyes were soft now, a frightened glaze giving away her vulnerability.

"Why are you telling me all this?" she asked perplexed. Montrox remained silent and still, finally raising his hand to Ril's face, gently letting it fall down to her neck to grasp the red chain around it. Pulling it free, he revealed Ril's scarlet locket, gently laying it on her chest. He stared at it for a long moment, then sharply turned to unhurriedly stride back to Verix.

"Before I left the woman in the west, I left her a gift to remember me," he stated quietly. Beside Verix, he placed a hand on his son's chest, feeling around for the lump inside his shirt. Reaching down, he pulled forth an object that stole the air from Ril's lungs. It was a scarlet locket. Montrox slowly tilted his now serious face back to Ril. "This is called a Red Pennant. It is a unique one; made for me by my mother. All Drakkaidian men give pennants to the woman they love. They are supposed to be divided in two pieces and worn by both, but I left the entire thing with her when I left. When I found Verix, half of it was around his neck. I didn't bother to look for the other half at the time, yet now," he paused for a moment, ripping Verix's locket off his neck and moving back to Ril. Picking up Ril's, he gently placed the two halves together with a tight click of metal. "I have finally found the other half." Her eyes locked onto the complete locket around her neck, Ril could feel a tear stream down her face. Trembling with the utmost fear and dread in her shaking eyes, she shifted her gaze to the man before her.

"What are you doing...? What do you want?" she managed through her trepidation. Montrox released the locket to hang back around Ril's neck.

"I want what any man wants, Arilia," he spoke softly. "I want to be with my family. I want my children with me. My son," he said, pointing at Verix, "and my daughter." Watching in horror as the Warrior of Darkness extended his finger at her, Ril felt her heart sink, meshing with her lower insides. Her eyes frozen to his, she slowly began to shake her head back and forth, emotion lodged in her throat.

"No..." she breathed. "...No..." Valif Montrox kept his solemn stare upon her.

"You never knew your mother," he began again, "and you already knew the man that raised you was not your true father. Zeroan stole you and hid you from me by transforming your inherited powers of darkness to fire when you were a baby. You have your mother in you, but your Drakkaidian side as well. You can see it. Surely you have noticed your hair, your eyes; they are the same as Verix's. The same as mine. Your Drakkaidian side is what gives you your strength. You are my daughter conceived with blood from the House of Montrox; a Princess of Drakkaidia." Tears were now streaming down Ril's ghostly pale face, her head violently shaking no.

"You're lying!" she shouted. "I am not a Drakkaidian! I can't be..." she trailed off, emotion choking her words. Valif Montrox extended his normal arm to her face, opening his hand. With a faintly glowing surge of dark light, Ril's body was suddenly encompassed with a thin aura of the same. Staring at him horrified trying to tell him to stop, she sat helplessly and the Warrior of Darkness reached inside the deepest level of her soul and took hold of her elemental power. Wrapping his grip around her, Ril could feel the darkness spreading through her body; invading every last cell. After a long moment, Montrox at last eased his hand to his side and let the dark light around the crying girl fade.

"I have dispelled the false power given to you by the sage," he spoke callously. "Your true strength is restored. Now you will be able to join Verix and I in ruling the world. Live your life a lie no more. You are Arilia Montrox, Princess of Drakkaidia." Words could not formulate in the girl's mouth. Her distraught eyes falling everywhere, she noticed her crest of fire was no longer present on the back of her hand. Tears streaming once more, it was all Ril could do to sit and cry.

She felt sick just lying inside her own body; the offspring of evil. She felt unworthy to draw breath.

As his daughter wildly wept, Valif Montrox shifted his blood-red eyes to Verix, only staring at him with a dejected expression on his bloodied face.

"Well," the Drakkaidian ruler started slowly, "I believe our family reunion is over for the moment." Turning then, the Warrior of Darkness beckoned for the seven robed figures waiting on the balcony outside the throne room to enter. The Dégamar stood at attention before him, filing in one by one. "The Warrior of Light is on his way here. He is powerful, but you can still stop him. Do so." Digesting their command, the Black Seven unanimously turned and wordlessly exited the room to make their way to the Valcanor outside.

Once again left with his two children, Montrox turned to make his way to his own throne and slowly took a seat. Folding his hands in his lap, he breathed deeply. Despite all of the hindrances to his plans, everything had worked out perfectly. His family was complete at last, and soon so would be the Holy Emerald. He would have his vengeance on Grandaria, the Warrior of Light, and the world. The Warrior of Darkness smiled, his glowing eyes brightening. He had done it. He had won.

Chapter 75

<u>Revival</u>

Tavin blasted through the tempestuous Drakkaidian skies with such velocity his streaking golden form moved faster than the lightning erupting from the dark billows around him. His godly power now fueled by the uncontrolled anger, the black earth beneath him appeared as only a blur of darkness. He drove through the banks of storm clouds, the wake of his radiant energy parting them to leave a temporary trail of light pouring through the otherwise constantly sinister sky. Since he had transformed and departed from Galantia, he had been able to faintly detect Ril's energy signature as it appeared in Drakkaidia and soared through the Iairian skies after it through the night. Though it had taken him the entire day to reach Galantia from the Southland, with his desperate resolve to save Ril and stop Montrox once and for all now driving him, he had flown all the way from the Grandarian capital into the black Drakkaidian skies in no more than an hour.

In the last few minutes, however, Tavin had sensed Ril's power suddenly change, as if it had become something else entirely. Though he could still feel the girl's life force, the nature of it had altered. Plagued by the uncertainty of what this newest occurrence meant, the only thing he knew for certain was that if Montrox had harmed her in the slightest way, his life would end painfully slow. As his need for haste and power heightened, a revitalized burst of it came flaring up around him. Though Tavin was too preoccupied with Ril to concern himself with it, his strength had now reached heights beyond what even Granis had intended him to use. The power radiating from his body was truly supreme.

Drawing nearer to Ril's changed power, he charged into the Drakkaidian skies with even more speed, coming up on what looked to be a city. Scanning every detail of his environment with his senses perfectly in tune, it was not long before the Warrior of Granis detected seven dark images in the sky ahead flying to meet him straight on. Remembering all too well the creatures that gave off such a unique dark power, Tavin grit his teeth with determination and boomed forward. Moving as fast as he was, it was only seconds after sensing them that the Dégamar and their winged steeds were before him. Only concerned with the creatures' master, Tavin immediately wrenched the Sword of Granis from his side to send its metallic ringing and a wave of arching golden energy flinging from its aureate blade to catch three of the demonic riders, instantly slicing them in two. Summoning a surge of righteous power around his free balled fist, his thrust it out to squarely pepper another swooping down to him.

As for the final three, Tavin charged forward in an explosion of energy, driving straight between them. Before the undead mages could so much as raise their hands to form a counter spell, the sonic boom from the detonation of power caught up to them, throwing them into the skies leaving their steeds to be incinerated. They would be back, he knew, but not to pose a threat to him again. With the Dégamar neutralized once more, the Warrior of Granis soared into the black Drakkaidian city. Focusing, he felt Ril inside the towering citadel on a mountaintop before him. Within visible range of her position, Tavin shot up toward the foreboding structure. As he drew closer, he could sense three energy signatures lingering close together beyond the uppermost wall of the tower. Throwing the Sword of Granis back into its sheath, Tavin clenched his fists forward and set himself on a collation course for the stone barrier.

Valif Montrox swiftly rose from his savage throne as the enormous power booming into the city approached.

"It appears I will have to deal with the Warrior of Light after all-" Montrox was cut off by an explosion from the wall in front of him. With power that could easily punch through mountainsides, Tavin blasted into the castle sending dust, rubble, and righteous energy in all directions.

Instantly halting his lightning fast flight, he hovered over the decimated wall to peer through the fading debris in the air. Tavin immediately found what he was looking for. Ril and Verix sat before him on either side of a monstrous looking figure nervously rising from a savage black throne between them, unexpected shock in his contorted face. Instantly recognizing his enemy, all other thoughts and emotions were immediately overridden by what he was here to do. Vehement fortitude strapped onto his face, the Warrior of Granis blasted across the throne room to throw his burning fist into the Warrior of Darkness' jaw. The massive Drakkaidian was instantly sent careening backward through his throne and beyond to puncture the opposite wall in the room with another cloud of dust and debris.

As the Warrior of Darkness lay momentarily stunned and out of his sight, Tavin let his immediate anger subside enough to drop to his feet where the throne once sat. Calming his fiercely radiating aura of power to touch Ril, he bent down to her and took hold of the chains around her wrists, effortlessly pulling them apart with his bare hands. As he freed her from the shackles around her legs and quickly gathered her in his arms, the disillusioned girl managed to turn her crying face up to him, tears still pouring down.

"What happened, Ril?" he pressed immediately. "What did he do to you?" The girl's eyes slowly found their way up to his but did not linger there long. She twisted away from him to start crying hysterically again. Confusion and anger at his uncertainty besieging his mind, Tavin wheeled around to Verix staring at him in a broken heap. While keeping a tight hold of Ril, he leaned down and with one hand broke the chains over him. "Verix, what happened to you two? What did he do to her?" Verix returned his gaze intently, struggling to respond.

"Something he shouldn't have," he managed as Tavin wrapped his body in a protective sphere of golden energy. The Dark Prince was quick to shake his head with tired frustration. "Don't... worry about us," he continued. "You have to stop him before-" Verix was cut short by an earth shattering explosion of another power from the confines of the second pile of rubble. Before Tavin could fully turn his head to face the source of the eruption of dark power, its raw force sent even the Warrior of Granis off his feat flailing backward. As he fell back through the air, he hurriedly grabbed out at Verix with his free hand to protect him from the rough landing he sustained on the stone floor. Staring with amazement through his own field of radiating energy, Tavin watched as an expansive blast of potent black power exploded around them, ripping through the thick stone walls and ceiling. Flexing his power and tightly pressing Ril and

Verix against him, Tavin held firm until the dark explosion at last faded.

As it did, Tavin opened his eyes to find new darkness above him. To his shock and amazement, the ceiling of the once towering castle was no longer present. Every last stone above them had been blasted away to nothing from the eruption of power. Turning his head to Ril and Verix to make sure his energy had protected them as well, he noticed the walls of the chamber were also missing. All that was left of the once foreboding throne room was the debris strewn floor and what remained of another smaller chamber to their right. It had been leveled. Carefully nestling both Verix and Ril against him, he rose to his feet and gently let them down beside him. Shifting his attention to the source of the explosion, his golden eyes observed a levitating figure rising from the dissipating dust where the wall on the opposite side of the throne room once stood. It was engulfed in a slowly burning aura of black and violet energy, menacingly dancing over his body like flame.

When the last of the dust cleared, Tavin found himself staring at the Warrior of Darkness, a hateful expression embedded into his blood red eyes. Though Tavin was undaunted by the ominous figure, the sight of the six shards of the Holy Emerald hovering around his disfigured right arm in a black orb of electrified energy unnerved him.

"So we meet at last," the Drakkaidian ruler breathed almost inaudibly. Tavin remained hard.

"What did you do to Ril and Verix?" he grilled immediately.

"As long as they do not resist me," he returned icily, "they will live. Which is more than I can say for you, boy." Tavin remained impervious to the figure's threats.

"Wake up, Montrox," he stated scornfully. "You won't scare me with your little tantrum. I am empowered by Granis himself, and we all know you're no match for me." Though Verix expected his father to grin darkly and return with another threat, Montrox's hatful expression remained set in stone.

"Don't be so sure!" he shouted back heatedly. "I'm not sure how you managed to acquire so much power, but it pales in comparison to what I am about to have. Bear witness, Warrior of Light, to the ultimate power of the Holy Emerald!" Knowing they had no time to risk letting each other remain unchallenged, both Tavin and Montrox acted. Despite his son's final plea to leave the emerald as it was, the Warrior of Darkness thrust the black orb of energy containing the shards between the palms of his hands, summoning all his energy to draw them together. Realizing the moment of fate was upon him, Tavin reluctantly released Ril and Verix to flare his power around him and drive forward wrenching the Sword of Granis free. Though he advanced with godly speed, even he was not quick enough. When only inches away from the shards, Tavin watched in horror as the six pieces suddenly flashed alive with white light and instantaneously fused as one.

The next moment, Tavin felt a penetrating wave of force pass through him. Though not painful, it felt as though it touched the innermost core of his soul and forced him to stop where he was, releasing control of his power. Falling back to the floor, Tavin threw his head up to Montrox, also struggling to maintain his dark energy. Tavin's eyes went wide and his face pale. The complete, restored, Holy Emerald sat in Valif Montrox's outstretched hands, a twisted smile over his dark face. The Drakkaidian air was suddenly so quiet the only thing Tavin could hear was their breathing.

"I have... done it..." Montrox at last whispered to himself, his voice rising. "The emerald is mine. The power is mine. I have the infinite power of the Holy Emerald! It is *mine*!" Staring up at him from the ground, Tavin couldn't find the strength to move, too terrified he had just let what happened happen. Clutching the emerald tighter in his armored hands, Valif Montrox raised it above his head and screamed out to the black sky. "I summon the power of Holy Emerald! Come to me now! Let its power flow to me!" The following moments were the longest of Tavin's life. The utmost dread filling his heart, Tavin waited for the Holy Emerald to burst alive with brilliant white energy and cover Montrox, making him unstoppable. But as the painfully long seconds slipped by, something happened that Tavin did not expect.

Nothing.

Nothing happened whatsoever.

Not a thing.

Not so much as a spark of light shown from the emerald; not so much as a fraction of power was granted to Montrox. The dreadful anticipation in Tavin, Verix, and Ril's eyes subsided, replaced by absolute bewilderment. Valif Montrox let his own eyes shift up to the white stone in his grasp, a nervous expression slowly transforming his face.

"I summon the power of the emerald!" he shouted again, a hint of desperation in his voice. When another long moment passed with no reaction whatsoever, Montrox let the emerald fall back in front of his face, torn with annoyance and desperation. "What is wrong?" His voice was quiet and shaking with fear. "Why is nothing happening?" Staring at the brilliant yet passive emerald, a flash of remembrance echoed into Tavin's mind. A bitter smile of relief faintly spread across his face, remembering what Granis had told him.

"What's the matter, Montrox?" he called up to him suddenly, to which the Warrior of Darkness cast his nervous eyes upon him. "Did you forget the legend? When Granis shattered the emerald, it became dormant again. Now it's just a key. If you want its power, you have to activate it at its shrine like Drakkan did in the Battle of the Gods." Montrox's already deformed and mutated face paled, his eyes spreading wide while Tavin only smiled, gathering the Sword of Granis in his hands. "But I promise you, you won't get that chance while I'm here. You've lost Montrox. All the pain and death you've caused has finally caught up with you, and it's about to visit you back tenfold. It's over." Tavin's golden aura of power flared up once again, circulating around him like hurricane winds.

Valif Montrox looked down at the powerful Grandaria boy before him with fear and fury tearing through his glowing eyes. This didn't make any sense. How could he have overlooked a minute detail like this? How could such a menial nuance bring down his entire plan? The confusion and rage filtering through his mind caused his dark power to explode out once more, but Tavin stood firm before it, unwavering.

"This is not possible!" be boomed through the black Drakkaidian sky. "I was supposed to become a god! I was supposed to become..." Valif Montrox stopped suddenly, his apparent rage subsiding. Slowly turning his head back toward what was left of the adjacent chamber to the throne room, Tavin sensed what had caught his attention. There was another power rising from somewhere below; one that felt almost as large as his own. Turning his head to Verix and Ril leaning against one another to his right, Tavin could see a look of supreme fear over the Drakkaidian Prince's face.

"The veil is torn," Tavin could see him murmur, "it is gone." Then, it came. Rising with such velocity and power that Tavin's mind could not even grasp its limits, a horrible dark energy blasted alive from the Netherworld Portal. Arching waves of electrified black, purple, and bleeding red energy exploded out of the portal, careening into the swirling sky in the form of a colossal beam. The demonic power cut through the raging storm clouds, charging them with surging energy. Unsure if this was the work of Montrox or if the Holy Emerald was indeed activated after all, Tavin watched in awe as power that rivaled his own poured into the atmosphere around them.

The most shocked of all, however, was Valif Montrox, as a massive dark purple mass of solidified energy drove its way out of the portal, breaking the stone floor and rock around it from its immense size. As the massive form fully emerged leaving waves of burning black light behind it, Tavin could tell it was a hand and arm made up of demonic energy. Opening its dark fingers, the arm suddenly shot forth at Montrox to seize both he and the emerald still in his hands with such force Tavin could hear the bones in the powerful Warrior of Darkness's body snapping to pieces. As he let out a horrifying scream of anguish, Tavin realized what was happening and came back to his senses. With the Sword of Granis in hand, he mustered his fiercely radiating power around him and shot into the sky after the withdrawing hand. As he charged toward it, the arm seemed to sense him coming and wound back to forcefully send its knuckles sailing into the Warrior of Granis, swatting him back to the stone platform below.

Smashing into the ground through the rubble, Tavin quickly flexed his power around him pushed his way free. By the time he was back on his feet, however, the arm was already sinking back into the Netherworld Portal with Valif Montrox and the Holy Emerald in tow, disappearing into the blackness below. The moment they were gone, the beam of black demonic energy surged up once more tearing through the Drakkaidian sky and earth. Tavin could hear the jagged mountain their quaking flooring stood on crumbling and falling apart, as was the rest of the ground around the city. Determined not to let the emerald escape, he charged his power once more. He stopped, however, as he felt a hand take hold of his ankle. Looking to his right, Verix lay beside him with Ril, shaking his bloodied and bruised head.

"The veil between this world and the Netherworld has finally torn!" he shouted as loud as he could to be heard over the quaking ground and fierce storm in the sky above them. "Drakkan has my father and the emerald!"

"That's why I have to go in after them!" Tavin returned back. Verix only shook his head once more, desperate.

"You must listen to me, Tavin!" he begged. "You cannot go into the Netherworld. Even with your power, you would not survive there! We will have another chance to stop Drakkan, but we can't do it now! Hell is breaking loose here, and we're going to be consumed by it if we don't retreat now!" Tavin's golden eyes were hard and adamant. He did not want to give up now after he just let Drakkan himself take the emerald. The ground around them spilt then as the entire mountain began to crumble. "Tavin! You must trust me! There is nothing we can do here now! Think of Ril! Will you let her and I die while you chase after Drakkan in his own unholy terrain? We must leave!" Shifting his troubled eyes over to Ril, still crying beside him and Verix, he took a deep breath and nodded.

"Fine," he reluctantly agreed, anger about the situation in his voice. "Be still and I'll get us out of here-"

"No!" Verix cut him off, fighting for the strength to continue. "The sky will... destroy us if we fly out! Use that!" Pointing over to where Montrox's throne once stood, Tavin spun around to find a portal identical to the one Seriol had used to escape from Galantia. Guessing it must work both ways, Tavin reached down and took hold of Verix and Ril once more. Shooting off from the shattering floor, he soared across the throne room to the portal. Standing on it, he waited as Verix closed his eyes and mentally activated the portal with his dark power. A familiar beam of slowly rising energy wrapped itself around the three, and they disappeared into the sky with it just as the final stable section of the towering castle gave way, sending the entire structure plummeting into Dalastrak in a gargantuan rain of rubble. As the earthquakes and the supernatural storm ripped the city apart, waves of demons began to pour forth from the portal, once more loose upon the doomed lands of Drakkaidia.

Chapter 76

<u>Love</u>

Jaren sat blankly in the chair below the staircase of the Supreme Granisian's throne; the chair where his traitorous Chief Advisor once sat. His left leg was asymmetrically folded over the left arm while his tilted head rested on his balled fist bolstered off of the right. He had been sitting there in the dark throne room since Zeroan had left him an hour and a half ago. Mary had been with him most of the time, confused and fearful of where her parents and all of the people in the Golden Castle had gone to. After she helped him illuminate the ornate torches in the otherwise dark chamber, Jaren had suggested she get some sleep after such an arduous day of riding. She did so with reluctance, not wanting to leave her friend to wait for Tavin and the others alone, but as tired as she was, finally agreed.

Jaren had fallen into a state of confusion himself; far worse than Mary's. From the moment he entered the throne room after Zeroan, all he knew was that something had gone wrong when Tavin and Ril confronted Seriol because he had prematurely blasted off to confront Valif Montrox. Jaren recognized the unstoppable determination in his eyes as he departed; he was going to stop Montrox or die trying. Jaren shook his head with annoyance at himself for even thinking the latter.

As he sat trying to guess what happened to spark Tavin's furious charge into battle, a sudden flicker of light filled the torch-lit chamber from behind him. Curiously turning his head toward the anomaly, Jaren witnessed a faint dark glow emerging from the small chamber Tavin and Zeroan had emerged from upon his arrival. Slowly rising and making his way around the chair, he watched in shock as the faint illumination was replaced by a sudden burst of brilliant golden energy. Recognizing the radiating light anywhere,

Jaren tore out of his chair and into the adjacent room to find a heavily breathing Tavin kneeling on one knee over the strange platform in the center of the room, his godly power burning around him. In either arm he held Ril, red with emotion, and Verix, red with blood. Though hesitant of why Tavin had the Drakkaidian Prince with him, he remembered how he had helped and saved them countless times after their parting and his mind eased.

Watching as Tavin's awesome power began to slowly fade and his clothes returned to normal, Jaren's senses returned to him and he charged forward to help his obviously fatigued friend.

"Tavin, are you alright?" he asked quickly. "What happened?" The Warrior of Light slowly opened his normal blue eyes to meet his, gradually shaking his head.

"It'll have to wait, Jaren," he breathed slowly, struggling to hoist Verix in his direction. "This is Verix. Hold him for a minute, alright? He's been beaten to the edge of his life, so be careful." Jaren eyed them both for a moment, but quickly nodded and gently wrapped his arms around the Prince, struggling for breath. Tavin instantly turned to Ril, still faintly crying in his arms. "Ril," he tried to communicate with her. "Ril, please, calm down. It's alright now. We're back in Galantia. You're safe now." The girl's eyes shifted up to his with anguish inside, as if his words stabbed at her. Shaking her head she violently strengthened and pulled away from him, rising to her feet and rushing out of the room crying hysterically once more.

Mass confusion and hurt locked into Tavin's face, he rose to start after her but quickly dropped back to his knees with his energy failing him. Jaren hurriedly grabbed hold of his arm.

"Slow down, buddy," he advised quickly. "I don't know what just happened to you guys, but even I can guess that after all the power you've been using today you've got to be out of *normal* energy by now. Let her go for a minute." Struggling through his irregular breathing, Tavin wheeled down to Verix, staring back at him in Jaren's arms.

"What did he do to her, Verix?" Tavin pressed once more. "What?" Verix kept his gaze fixated on him for another long moment before heavily blinking and opening his bloodied mouth to speak.

"Help me... up first," he ordered weakly. Pushing himself to his feet, Tavin motioned for Jaren to do the same and they both took hold of Verix by the arms to bolster him upright. They moved him into the throne room to the chair Jaren previously rested on, but as they were about to set him down something caught Verix's attention from the corner of his eye. Freezing in place, he motioned for the two Grandarians to release him. Confused, they watched as he hobbled a few feet in front of him to lean down and pick up a scarlet locket lying on the floor. Tavin instantly recognized it as Ril's, but it looked larger than usual. Upright again, Verix held the object in his open hand with his back to the others. He stood there a long moment before letting a single tear drip from his face onto the locket. Both Tavin and Jaren stared uncertainly, surprised to see the usually emotionless Drakkaidian Prince speak through forming tears.

"All my life I've dreamed of meeting my mother," he said with a shaking voice. "My father gave me a painting of her when I was a child. About that same time he told me I had a sister. When I asked him where she was, he told me she had been stolen away from us when she was a baby, but I would see her again someday. I have always looked forward to that day, but when it came I wasn't expecting it..." He paused for a moment, clenching his eyes together. "She looked just like mother..." Though Tavin was about to ask him what he was talking about, Verix slowly turned his head back to him, a tear streaming down his face. "That's why I hesitated in the forest, Tavin. That's why I saved her in the cave. It was even the first reason I came to you that night in the cronom village. I... I did it for my sister."

Tavin stared at him hard for a moment, letting the Prince's words digest. At last, staring into Verix's moist eyes, it hit him.

"...No," he thought out loud, rejecting the idea as soon as it entered his mind. Verix kept his gaze fixed on the Warrior of Light, nodding once.

"Ril is my blood, Tavin," he said softly. "My twin. My sister." Tavin's eyes were locked onto his, disbelief engulfing them. Jaren slowly looked at his friend with uncertainty.

"Why are you saying that?" Tavin asked incredulously. "That isn't even possible..." He trailed off.

"It is, Tavin-"

"Stop it, Verix!" Tavin abruptly shouted, cutting him off. When Verix refused to break his gaze, Tavin started toward him and took hold of him by his shirt. "You're wrong, Verix! You don't know what you're talking about!"

"Yes he does, Tavin," another voice came from the doors of the chamber. Spinning his flushed head toward the voice, Tavin found Zeroan standing in the half open door. Slowly releasing Verix, Tavin's face filled with pain.

"...What?" he asked. Zeroan breathed heavily from beneath his gray hood and slowly approached, stopping feet before him. His words came slow and deliberate.

"There was a time when Valif Montrox frequently visited the western regions of the Southland. Almost twenty years ago now, he impregnated a young woman in Fireite Village who later gave birth to twins. As did I, Montrox sensed their presence and came for them. He only thought there was Verix, however, and left behind the other, a girl. I sought her out when I sensed her presence and found her alone, but I knew Montrox would be back for her when he realized there was another child. To protect her I took her to the Temple of Fire to erase, or rather, replace her dark power with that of fire. Safe from Montrox for the moment, I entrusted an old friend to raise her in Coron Village; the man that would become her adopted father. Over the years Montrox must have somehow figured out the Warrior of Fire was his daughter. I know it is difficult to accept, Tavin, but that is why Montrox wanted Ril. He is her true father, making Verix her brother." Tavin stared at him in disbelief, his own eyes growing moist.

"This is why you didn't want us to fall in love. It's why you wanted me to take her with me today. You knew she was in danger. You knew the entire time," he whispered with quiet anger in his voice. He turned back to Verix. "So did you. How could you keep this from her?" Verix could not find the words to reply, leaving Zeroan to continue speaking.

"What would you have done, Tavin?" he asked curiously. "Would you have told a girl raised to view Drakkaidians as enemies she was their Princess?" Tavin was beside himself with rage, leaping at the sage.

"I wouldn't have let her find out from the most evil human in the world!" he bellowed indignantly. "Can you even imagine how horrible it must have been for her, Zeroan? Can you imagine how she must be feeling to have found out that way?" Zeroan remained calm and collected as always.

"Your words carry conviction, Tavin, but they lack sense," he informed him. "It would have been nearly as detrimental to her to hear the truth from me as Montrox. I did what I had to do for her sake. If you were I, you would have made the same decision." Tavin was silent for a moment, taking a step back. As he prepared to respond, his eyes were hateful.

"If I were you, I wouldn't go around playing with people's lives in my hands," he breathed icily. "After all we've been through, you still keep secrets from us, Zeroan. How can you expect anyone to trust you when we always think you're withholding something from us? You play us like we're some game, sage. I'm through with it." With that, Tavin stepped around him and marched out of the chamber. Though Jaren called after him, Zeroan motioned for him to be quiet.

"Let him go, Jaren," he spoke softly. "He is just upset at this revelation. Give him time to sort it out, and he will return." Jaren nodded slowly, casting his head at the floor in disbelief so much had occurred without his knowledge. As the Grandarian boy turned to pace back to the chair, Zeroan turned to Verix, still loosely holding the Red Pennant in his hand. "You must tell me what happened in Dalastrak, Verix. Everything." The Drakkaidian Prince let his eyes fall back down to the locket, and slowly nodded.

The soft white moonlight was all that illuminated Ril's delicate face in the open gardens outside the Golden Castle. She had been sitting on her knees before the railway she damaged nearly two months ago for several long moments, weeping silently. Her very soul felt dirty, as if it might as well have been tainted by Drakkan himself. Everything she knew had been thrown in her face and replaced by a dark truth she could not even imagine in her worst nightmares. She had become what she was fighting against. Though she wished she could run to Tavin and pour herself out to him, she was too afraid he would push her away as the filthy Drakkaidian she was.

As her thoughts drifted to the Warrior of Light, she heard the faint footsteps of someone striding down the bridge toward her. Afraid to look up, she kept her head down letting the tears continue to drip from her face. After what seemed like forever, the footsteps stopped next to her. Listening as the figure dropped down to crouch on his knees and place his hand on her shoulder, she shook her head and opened her mouth to speak.

"I just want to be alone," she managed to murmur through her tears. The hand on her shoulder gently flew down to her arm to pull her around to face him.

"I don't care," he said tenderly. Ril found herself staring at Tavin, an unyielding power in his deep blue eyes. "You need to hear this."

"I suppose you know who I am now," she finally muttered shamefully. Tavin stared at her hard, moving down to join her on his knees. After a long pause to collect his thoughts, he replied.

"Yes I do," he stated strongly. "You are Ril Embrin, a proud Southlander with more spirit than the entire Legion. You're a strong, independent, loving girl that makes the world better everywhere she goes. You're the girl who's been with me since the beginning of this thing, always there for me when I needed you and always there to help. You're the sweetest girl I've ever known and my favorite person in Iairia. The last thing I care about is who your family or people are. I love you for you, Ril, not for where you come from." Ril's eyes were soft and vulnerable, struggling to accept what he was telling her.

"You're a Grandarian, Tavin. You hate Drakkaidians. How can you say that you love me knowing I'm...?" Tavin shook his head and held firm.

"You of all people should know how stupid I was to think that way about all Drakkaidians," he said. "You and I know first hand that there are Drakkaidians out there better than most people. What about Verix? Hasn't he proven himself to be one of the best people you know? One of the best friends you have? I know he's one of mine. I have different eyes now, Ril. Remember?" Ril still harbored uncertainty in her expression. Tavin pulled in close, bringing a hand to her face. "Do you remember what I told you today when we were flying to Galantia? I said I'd love you whether you were a Grandarian or not, and I meant it. I know it must be hard Ril, but it doesn't change anything. You are who you are, and I love you for it. I love you as much as ever, and I want you to realize that. I love you now, and I always will."

Ril sat silent for a moment, letting the warmth of his hand seep over her cheek. At last, the tears swelling in her eyes began to stream once more. This time, however, she leaned forward against him, wrapping her arms around his body.

"Tavin..." she whispered. Though she continued weeping, Tavin could tell her tears were of release, not grief. For several long minutes they sat holding each other before Ril at last pulled back to wipe her tears away with the sleeves of her shirt and smile. Contagious, it quickly spread to Tavin as well as he rose and helped her to her feet. Taking her hand, the pair turned back for the entrance to the castle. As they walked, they noticed Zeroan standing in the doorway, still and silent. Slowing to a stop before him, Tavin took a deep breath and spoke.

"I'm sorry for what I said to you before, Zeroan," he apologized. "I was just angry at what happened, not you. I know you have to make difficult decisions as a sage but you always try to do the right thing. If anything I should be thanking you."

"I need to apologize as well, Zeroan," Ril quickly followed. "For so many years I treated you like an adversary when it was you that saved me from Montrox as a baby. For all the trouble I've caused you with Montrox, the Sarton, and the other sages because of my anointment, I thank you." The sage remained quiet as he nodded his head to reply.

"I appreciate your words; both of you," he returned serenely, "but you have just reason to be angry. I have kept much hidden from you for a great time. And even though I had to, it was still wrong. I hope you can forgive me for that. But I assure you now, that there are no more secrets. We all know everything about each other and who we truly are, so I hope I still have your trust." Both Tavin and Ril nodded with a smile.

"No more secrets, huh?" Tavin grinned. "And here I half expected to find out Jaren has been a Mystic Sage all these years." Ril giggled for the first time in several long hours, as did Zeroan with a quiet chuckle.

"Very clever, young Tieloc," Zeroan smiled. "But now I suggest we all get some sleep. Verix told me everything that happened in Dalastrak, and we are sure to be in store for a... full day tomorrow." The smile disappearing from Tavin's face, he began to explain what had gone wrong and how he had failed but the sage quickly cut him off. "Do not apologize for what happened, Tavin. If you hadn't been there, Verix and Ril would be dead now and Montrox may have escaped to activate the emerald on his own. Do not dwell on it. We will make our plans tomorrow." With that, the sage motioned for the two youths to move past him and enter the castle. He followed behind them with the silhouette of his massive shoulders swaying back and forth fading into the dark.

Chapter 77

<u>Three Plus One Makes Four</u>

Tavin woke the next morning with Ril in his room tugging on his shoulders, concerned at his irregular breathing and sweaty face. In the night he had slept poorly, having frequent nightmares of the enormous dark power he could subconsciously sense erupting in Drakkaidia. He came to his senses slowly after his eyes burst open in surprise, not sure where he was at first. Scanning the room, he remembered he and Ril had retired for the night in the two rooms he and Jaren had rested in their last time in Galantia. When Tavin told Ril of his troubled sleep, she responded she had a difficult time of her own and had crept over to his room in the early hours of the morning. Though Tavin had helped her come to terms with her new identity, her body was having trouble accepting her new dark energy that had unnaturally resurfaced. She felt tired and weak no matter how much she tried to sleep, and parts of her body felt numb at times.

Realizing they had little time to cope with such trivial problems as these compared to what lay in store for them, they both decided to venture forth into the castle to find Zeroan and the others. Ril departed for a moment to find a new set of bright yellow Grandarian casual wear while Tavin refreshed his own attire with a new blue over shirt and a set of simple white trousers identical to his old ones, now so ripped and frayed they would not stay put on his body. Deciding his cape and armor had become meaningless with power such as his to protect him, Tavin left them behind for the first time in months and strapped the Sword of Granis over his back. On his way out he picked up a new set of dark blue boots and cutoff gloves to better grip his sword hilt.

As he shut the door to his room and stepped into the castle hall, Tavin noticed the virtual absence of any light passing through the windows above him. Though he knew it was morning from the birds chirping outside and the faint activity from the city below him, the sun was concealed by rolling black clouds polluting the sky. Ril had noticed the uncharacteristically bleak Grandarian atmosphere as well as she came from of the opposite room to meet with him, her crimson hair falling behind her in a ponytail. Starting down the hallway, they were quick to guess it had something to do with the massive unholy power they could both sense pouring into Drakkaidia.

They swiftly passed through the faintly illuminated castle halls hand in hand, eager to locate the others. Breaking the silence that hung in the empty structure, they heard voices echoing from a small doorway near the stairwell to the throne room. Peering inside, they found Mary sitting on a wooden chair before a table, casually eating a modest breakfast. Jaren stood behind a counter behind her cutting up a plate of bread and cheeses to munch on. He grinned as he spotted the Warrior of Light in the doorway.

"Bring out the food and in he comes," he stated jokingly, causing Mary to drop her fork and wheel around to politely smile.

"Good morning," she greeted softly. "Did you both sleep well?" Stepping through the doorway, Ril tilted her head and shrugged.

"We slept, at least," she replied vaguely for both of them.

"What about you?" Tavin returned, remembering she must be going through an ordeal as painful as Ril's own with the death of her father. Mary's cheery smile slowly weakened.

"It's difficult," she stated quietly, "but I have to be strong in my parents' absence." As Ril took a seat beside her, Tavin walked around to the counter to stand next to Jaren, leaning his elbow over the surface.

"Nice to see you again, buddy," Jaren began as the two girls started a conversation of their own. "I swear to Granis I almost don't recognize you anymore you've changed so much." Tavin let a silent chuckle escape from his blank face.

"I can imagine," he returned, "but the same goes for you. It's been... weird not being with you for so long. The last time we were apart this much was... never." Jaren smiled and popped a slice of cheese into his mouth.

"Yeah, well, things are almost back to normal, right?" he grinned, throwing a hand on his friend's shoulder. Tavin shook his head and drug his free hand through his longer hair.

"I'm not sure things are ever going to be 'normal' again, Jaren," he said honestly. Jaren's smile dissipated, nodding.

"Yeah," he replied quiet. "Speaking of which, I'm supposed to tell you we're on with Zeroan in about an hour." Tavin frowned, confused.

"What do you mean?"

"I mean we're having our last 'get-together' before this is over," he explained seriously. "We're supposed to meet him and Verix in the audience chamber when we're done with breakfast to decide, well, what to do." Tavin nodded slowly, realizing the end was coming. One way or another, he thought, it would be over soon. Driving such thoughts from his mind, Tavin took a seat beside the two Princesses and gorged himself with a hearty meal of assorted foods. The group conversed about the least grave things they could think of for an hour, wishing to enjoy this last time together before splitting for the battle to come.

They left the kitchen after finishing the last of the food, gradually making their way to the audience chamber adjacent to the throne room. Passing through the colossal double doorway, Tavin immediately spotted Verix Montrox standing to the side of one of the massive arching windows, peering out at the dark morning sky. His face was covered with bandages and scars that were already forming, and his left arm hung in a makeshift sling. As the group entered, Tavin motioned for Jaren and Mary to linger at the table while they approached the Drakkaidian Prince. As they did, Tavin could feel Ril's grip tighten on his hand, obviously nervous to meet the boy as her brother for the first time. Though Verix's face remained traditionally impassive when they stopped before him, he turned to face then with a deep breath, swallowing hard. His eyes were full of color and his body looked to be filled with energy once more.

"You're looking better," Tavin smiled softly, to which the Prince nodded once.

"The sage is quite the healer, it would appear," he almost whispered. Past that, Verix was silent, obviously not sure what would be appropriate to say. Mustering her courage, Ril at last cleared the knot in her throat and took a step forward, seizing the boy's free hand in hers. Verix was still, his eyes meeting with hers uncertainly.

"...I'm sorry for the way I acted yesterday," she spoke with a shaking voice. "I know this is hard for you too, having known from the beginning. I just want to tell you..." She paused for a moment, trying to fight the tears building in her eyes. "You're a good person, Verix. Tavin was right. You are one of my best friends now, and I... I'm proud to have you as my brother." Verix's didn't react at first, a single tear falling from his own moist eyes. Fighting past the emotion covering his face, he nodded once more, taking hold of her hand as well. Feeling him respond, Ril smiled and uncertainly inched forward. "Can I...?" she trailed off, raising her arms. Verix opened his mouth to speak, but when nothing came out he drew closer to her opening to her embrace. They came together slowly, but eventually hugged tightly. As Ril softly wept with happiness, Verix at last found his voice.

"Thank you, sister," he managed quietly. Watching contentedly as Ril embraced her brother with love, Tavin turned and smiled back to Jaren and Mary at the table. After the siblings pulled apart, Verix was quick to wipe the tears from his face. As the three moved back to the table to join the others, the final member of their party at last entered from the doorway.

"Impeccable timing as usual," Jaren grinned at the sage, leaning back in his chair. Zeroan replied in an easy but serious voice.

"You should know by now that sages have a way of owning the clock, Jaren," he stated. "Are you all ready to proceed then?" The group of youths all nodded wordlessly. "Very well, then. As I'm sure you have noticed, morning has come yet the darkness of night has remained over Iairia. Our worst fears have come to pass, and if we are to stop them from laying waste to the world we must act quickly. Pay very close attention to this, for this will be our last council before the endgame commences." Zeroan took a deep breath and shifted in his robes, collecting his thoughts.

"Yesterday, Tavin and Ril arrived here to stop the traitorous spy of Valif Montrox, Seriol, from stealing the final shard of the emerald. Unfortunately, he used a demonic Shadow to possess the Supreme Granisian and make their escape with Arilia in tow. Despite my wishes against it, Tavin immediately transformed into the Warrior of Granis and took off for Dalastrak to attempt to stop Montrox on his own. While his power was far greater than anything the Drakkaidian ruler could have matched him with, he was able to complete the Holy Emerald before Tavin could stop him. Fortunately for us, all of us including Montrox forgot one important detail in the legend of the Holy Emerald. The talisman was left dormant after Granis shattered it, and even though it was reconstructed, it will remain that way until activated at its shrine. This is what our enemy will seek to do now.

"Unfortunately for us, our enemy has changed. Even though the emerald is still inactive, its mere completion created enough of a tear in the veil in the Netherworld to shatter it for good. That was what you three felt that disturbed your power when Montrox completed the emerald. I felt it even here. With the barrier trapping him in the underworld gone, Drakkan himself rose from the unholy portal and seized Montrox and the emerald, pulling them back into his dark realm. You wisely chose to retreat, Tavin, as hell itself has now emerged to engulf Drakkaidia." Verix harbored an anguished look in his red eyes, knowing what he had defected from his father to prevent had happened anyway. "While hope now seems faint, we still have a chance to stop Drakkan.

"The Holy Emerald is not yet activated, so Drakkan has not and cannot emerge in his true form in this world. Like Granis in Tavin, he will place what power he can in Valif Montrox's body and send it back into our world to activate the emerald. He will seek out the Holy Shrine to do this. What is left of it lies in ruins inside the scarred lands where the gods once battled. If Drakkan enters the shrine and places the emerald in the altar, he will have its power and he will be unstoppable. Tavin must stop him to preclude this from happening.

"While Tavin's power once overpowered Montrox's, both of these warriors now have the strength of gods. When they clash, it will be an even match. If Tavin is unable to defeat Drakkan, he will have to do as Granis once did and shatter the emerald again. If this happens, it will be sure to weaken Drakkan enough for Tavin to drive him back to his underworld. We can then search out the shards again and gather them for ourselves to seal the Netherworld and complete the Three Fates." This possibility was met with a dreadful group of faces in the party before him, all of them realizing the time and risk that would bring. "Hopefully, Tavin will be able to stop Drakkan without doing this, but if it comes down to it, that is what he will be forced to do.

"I'm sure Verix can sense this happening because his senses are so in tune with the Netherworld, but Tavin and Ril most likely cannot. Drakkan and his power are steadily rising. The Netherworld is pouring itself out into Drakkaidia, and when it is completely emptied, Drakkan will be free to emerge in Montrox's body. When this happens, he will most likely go straight for the Holy Shrine. We must be there before him. If his power continues rising as it is, he will be free in a matter of hours. It will take him at most one more to get to the shrine. Therefore, Tavin and those going with him must depart as soon as we are done here."

The room was quiet afterward, everyone wondering who Zeroan had in mind.

"As you can see," the sage began again, "our number is back to six as it was when we left Galantia to search out the shards, and while the roster of our party has changed since then, we must now divide once again. I will be going with Tavin to help him in any way I can. He will most likely need my power and guidance. The rest of you however, will be staying here." Ril's face instantly transformed with incredulity, ready to stand and tell the sage he was dead wrong if he thought he could keep her here at the end. Before she could object, however, her brother was on his feet.

"Zeroan," he began, his authoritative voice returned to him, "this is not acceptable. I have done too much, come too far, and sacrificed too much to sit by at the end of this while Tavin faces off against my father alone."

"You are brave and true, Drakkaidian Prince," Zeroan told him, "but you are out of your league now. You are still weak from your battle with the Dégamar and even if you were at full strength, it could not help Tavin." Verix held firm before the sage, his eyes determined.

"I know all that, sage," he said potently, "and I don't care. I may not be of any help to the Warrior of Light, but this is the battle for my people; for my home. If we lose my life no longer has meaning. I am the next strongest of anyone here, and whether I can aid you or not, this is my fight. I must be there." Zeroan stared him down for a long moment, but at last nodded.

"I knew you would feel this way, Verix," he gave in. "I warn you one last time that you could very well be going to your death, but this is your fight. I will not stop you from going." Ril was the next to rise.

"And I'm going as well," she decreed. Zeroan was slow to shift his eyes to her, but when he did he could see they were hard and unmoving.

"I also anticipated this," he acknowledged, "but this time, it is not something that is open for debate. Ril, it is far too dangerous for me to allow you to go. You must remain." Ril's face with filled with disbelief, unable to comprehend his logic.

"I can't believe I'm hearing this, Zeroan!" she almost shouted. "You'll let Verix go even though he's still on the brink of death, but not me? I've been with Tavin twice as long- I've stood by him through this entire quest- and now you won't let me see it through?" Though Zeroan was about to justify himself, he stopped short as he saw Tavin's hand take hold of the girl's wrist. Ril looked down to Tavin as he slowly pulled her back down to her chair and turned it toward him. Staring her in the eyes, Tavin took hold of her hand again.

"Ril," he started quietly, "Zeroan is right this time." She looked at him hard, not believing what he just said. He could see the hurt and confusion in her eyes and shook his head. "It's not that I don't want you with me, Ril, it's just that... Zeroan knows what he's talking about. Verix may not have all his strength, but he's a warrior born that knows how to take care of himself and this is the fight for his life. You may be his sister, but you told me yourself: you can't control your new power at all right now. You're more tired than he is, and I can tell your body is still struggling to deal with it. I wish you could be there, Ril, but this battle is going to be too huge for you. If it were up to me, I'd tell Zeroan and Verix to stay behind too because it's too big for them as well. I'm going to be trying hard enough to protect myself without having to worry about protecting you. The only way I can win this one is if I know you're here, safe. You have to stay."

Tavin could tell she was crushed; even though she knew she might not survive she wanted to be there with him. Ril was torn with anxiety. She knew she had to be with him at the end because of Taurin Tieloc's warning, but she had been forbidden to tell anyone.

"In addition to that," Zeroan returned, "your power is still raw and uncontrolled. The blood in your veins connects you to Montrox and him to you; Drakkan could seize control of you as if you were being controlled by a Shadow. There are simply too many risks. Listen to Tavin, Ril." She looked over to him, then back to Tavin. She kept her composure, but let her head drop in defeat. Tavin moved closer to wrap his arm around her and gently rub her back. Shifting in his robes, Zeroan gave them a single nod and began again. "Very well. Tavin and Verix, say your goodbyes and meet me on the balcony outside the window. We must be off to be sure we arrive before Drakkan." With that, the sage turned from the table and strode past them out of the doors to the left of the room toward the balcony. With a deep breath, Tavin rose, pulling Ril up beside him. Running his fingers through her thick hair, he asked her to wait as he said his goodbyes to Jaren.

"I wish I could be there with you, but it looks like we've got to split one more time," Jaren said tilting his head. Tavin put a hand on his shoulder and nodded.

"And just like before, I'll be back," he told him with assurance. Jaren laughed quietly.

"I know," he said. "Just promise me you'll be careful out there. If you've got to break the emerald, that's what you've got to do. I've got all the time in the world to find the shards again."

"What does that mean?" Tavin asked him baffled. Jaren raised an eyebrow knowingly.

"You think I want to go home anytime soon? I was still in trouble for shooting that arrow into our house when we left. We've been gone for over *two months*. My dad's probably already dug my grave for when he sees me next." Tavin chuckled silently, pulling in to embrace his best friend.

"Hold down the castle while I'm gone, okay?" Tavin smiled.

"You got it, buddy," Jaren returned. As the two friends parted, Tavin bowed to Mary who hugged him in return, wishing him luck and safety. As he turned back to say goodbye to Ril, however, she was nowhere to be seen. Slouching with pain, he realized she had left.

"She walked out a moment ago, Tavin," Verix told him softly. "She didn't say anything."

"Tavin," was the muffled call from outside. "We don't have time. We must leave now." Looking to the balcony, Tavin peered back to the empty doorway of the audience chamber to look for Ril one last time. His heart weighed down with disappointment, Tavin slowly nodded and turned for the balcony with Verix. Jaren and Mary followed them out, waiting side-by-side in the doorway. Tavin stopped in the center of the balcony and nodded to Zeroan.

"I'm ready," he announced with purpose.

"I know, Tavin," the sage responded placing a hand on his shoulder. "Let's go." Nodding again, Tavin slowly closed his eyes and clenched his fists at his sides. Reaching inside himself and the Sword of Granis, he took hold of his power to summon it out. A slow radiating aura of gold shimmered to life around him, building until his body was engulfed in blinding light. Then in a massive detonation of righteous energy, the power of Granis exploded out sending burning light careening into the dark morning air to illuminate Galantia like midday.

As the initial blast of power calmed, Zeroan and the others looked on him to find the Warrior of Granis standing before them, even more transformed than usual. His simple Grandarian clothes had morphed into brilliantly white armor with streaking golden curves and emblems stretching over the ornate surface. The Sword of Granis stood upright along his back, floating there without its sheath as if Tavin's body produced enough gravity to keep it hovering behind him. His hair had lightened from its usual waving brown to shining blonde, and both the irises and pupils of his eyes were gilded over. The circulating field of energy around his body shown intensely bright but as beautiful as ever.

Tavin outstretched his hands at both Verix and Zeroan and both of them slowly levitated inches off the ground covered in spheres of golden power. As they rose into the sky, Tavin turned back to the doorway to nod once to Jaren and Mary. They did the same, silently wishing him good luck. With that, Tavin bent his knees and pushed off from the ground into the air, quickly accelerating into the dark skies to leave a trail of golden light in his wake. As the three bolts of light charged through the Grandarian sky, neither they or Jaren and Mary noticed the impossibly fast blur of black exiting the Golden Castle below them with a lone rider on its back.

Chapter 78

<u>Sacrifice</u>

Tavin blasted through the dark Iairian skies for the rest of the morning, determined to get to the Holy Shrine before Drakkan. With purpose and resolve driving him once more, he soared across Grandaria, the Border Mountains, the Wall of Light, and the war zones in a matter of hours. Zeroan and Verix followed tightly after him encased in orbs of shimmering light. Nearly halfway through their flight, Tavin sensed the final immense eruption of power from Drakkaidia. Immediately after, an unfathomable source of dark energy began streaking away from it to the south. Tavin knew it had to be Drakkan.

Scanning the ground for what Zeroan described the ruins of the Holy Shrine would look like, the boy at last spotted a collection of rocks and rubble scattered around a massive stone platform sunken into the scarred earth around it, overgrown with vegetation and decay. Looking back to Zeroan, he saw the sage pointing down and nodding his head. Giving a quick nod back in confirmation, the Warrior of Granis swooped downward in a new flash of brilliant light, his two companions closely trailing behind. Closing the gap between them and the shrine, Tavin gradually decelerated and flipped himself upright in the air to prepare for his brutish landing, splitting the earth around his feet from the powerful impact. Zeroan and Verix touched down considerably softer, gently laying their feet on the grassy earth as the spheres of light around them gradually faded into the brisk air.

Tavin turned back to them, scanning the ancient remains of the shrine skeptically.

"This is the Holy Shrine?" he asked doubtfully. Zeroan carefully swept his eyes across the quiet structure as well, nodding.

"What is left of it after eons of lifelessness without the emerald," he explained. "The alter was the enormous rock platform we saw from the air. In the center is a pedestal where the Holy Emerald must be inserted to activate the shrine, and in turn its dormant powers. As we can all sense, Drakkan is on his way here as we speak so we should make our way there immediately to be ready to confront him." Tavin acknowledged and turned to Verix, summoning his broadsword from a cloud of red mist appearing beside him. The group turned then and started making their way into the ruins. The platform before them was sunken into the earth, but rested on top of something else obviously buried beneath, woven in between felled columns of elaborately carved stone.

As the group ascended the small leaning staircase leading up to the platform, however, they encountered something that caused them to freeze in their tracks. Standing in a perfect line before the end of the stairs were all seven of the Dégamar, still as stone. Verix raised his sword defensively with deathly hate in his crimson eyes.

"It appears Drakkan has sent an advance party to meet us," he said with disdain. "How come we didn't sense them? They seem... different." Tavin frowned and shook his head, reaching behind his back to take hold of the Sword of Granis hovering there.

"They don't seem to take a hint, do they?" he asked threateningly. "How many times do I have to kill you things before you figure it out?" As he took a step forward with his golden power flaring up, Zeroan's eyes suddenly burst open with realization and he threw his arm up defensively.

"Tavin, *wait!*" he bellowed. Both Verix and the Warrior of Granis spun to him with their guards going up. *"Get away from them!"* But it was already too late. Before Tavin could turn back to the seven demonic mages, they simultaneously lunged at him, clawing onto his body with their rotting, clenching, hands. Wheeling around, Tavin prepared to ignite his energy into an inferno of righteous light to burn them away. As he reached into the depths of his power, however, a strange sensation of immobilization came over him. Something was wrong. Sweeping his eyes across the faces of the seven figures viciously latching onto him, he instantly realized what. The faces of the usually putrid, decayed Dégamar were covered in a layer of dense black matter, loosely swirling about like liquid. At once, it rapidly began flowing from the skin of the Dégamar to his and seeping inside like poison. A wave of dark remembrance entered his mind. He recognized this feeling of penetration all too well.

It was the feeling of a Shadow taking hold of him.

This time, however, there were seven invading him at once. The last free breath of air in his lungs swiftly escaped him. Unable to summon his power in the grip of the dark presence, Tavin stood helpless as the last of the demonic parasites changed hosts and the Black Seven dropped lifeless around him. The Sword of Granis falling out of his suddenly numb hands, Tavin soon dropped to his knees incapacitated. A horrified Verix and Zeroan rushed up to him as he fell to his hands to support his body exploding with pain. Every cell in his being felt like it was being ripped apart from the inside, and instantly he knew the Shadows were not merely taking hold of him: they were killing him.

"Blasted creatures!" Verix screamed, summoning a quick burst of dark power to fire from his clenched fist to blast the motionless Dégamar away. "What happened?" Zeroan hurriedly tried to turn Tavin over, but was forced away by the dark energy squirming inside him.

"He's been possessed by Shadows, but there are so many fighting for control of his body they are killing him!" he explained wildly.

"What are you going to do?" Verix grilled. "Can we-"

"There are too many to attack the shadows on the ground, and there is no light," Zeroan precluded.

"Then what!?!" Verix was beside himself with worry. Before the sage could even reply, the two froze sensing the greatest power in existence soaring toward them from the north. Rocketing forward, it was on top of them the next instant, coming to a complete halt. Verix's mouth dropped open with disbelief. Just as Tavin had become the strongest light based power in the world, the most intense and frightening dark energy was now hovering over their heads. It slowly descended for the next painfully long moments until a menacing figure engulfed in slowly burning black and red energy touched down at the center of the alter before them. It resembled Valif Montrox, but his body had become so swollen with mutated bulging muscles protruding great spikes of black bone from their ends and the ominous stains of blood red tattooed over what was left of his dark armored body, it looked like an entire different person. Verix swallowed hard, realizing the God of Darkness stood before him.

"Granis..." was the low rumbling that escaped Drakkan's mouth. "I see you have fallen for my trap like the fool you are. I was hoping you would die by my hand, but as long as you are dead, I am satisfied." The god reached inside his stretched black armor with his bulging hand to pull free the brilliant white Holy Emerald. Verix instantly stepped forward, dispelling his fear.

"Father!" he called desperately. "Father, I know you are still in there somewhere. You must listen to me! You have made mistakes in your life that have led to your fate now, but you must fight now to gain control back! Do not let him activate the emerald or all of us will die! Please father, you must-" Verix stopped short as the echo of a charge of energy sounded through the air. Spinning his head around to the suddenly silent Drakkaidian Prince, Zeroan's eyes went wide to find a bloody puncture in his chest from where Drakkan had blasted a beam of black power clean through him. Stunned by the strange sensation of numbness inside his chest, Verix slowly peered down to notice the wound as well. As he raised a hand to press his fingers against the running blood, the strength in his legs gave way, and the Drakkaidian Prince dropped to the hard ground where he stood, dead. Zeroan stared at his lifeless form for a long moment before turning back to Drakkan, his right index finger still outstretched where he had fired a beam of energy from it to murder Verix.

Dropping the limb to his side, the God of Darkness turned back to the pedestal at the center of the alter and raised the Holy Emerald above it.

"Goodbye to you, Granis. Your time is finished. It is my time now," he spoke in the coldest voice imaginable. With that, Zeroan watched in horror as Drakkan plunged the emerald into the pedestal to tightly lock in the stone around it. The gem gradually came to life with blinding white light pouring out, spreading between the cracks of stone in the pedestal and the entire platform. When fully illuminated with the shining light, the pedestal itself began to rumble and quake. Smiling, Drakkan turned back to Zeroan to wave goodbye as the entire structure began to rise into the air, grinding stone against stone and revealing the true towering form of the Holy Shrine, hundreds of feet high.

As the soaring platform slowly ascended into the dark Iairian sky, Zeroan quickly turned back to Tavin, the life draining from his body by the second. Realizing it would be over if the demonic parasites choking the energy from him were allowed to remain much longer, Zeroan took a deep breath and rolled back his hood to reveal his determined face. Reaching inside his gray robes, he quickly pulled free his vial of the enchanted Sage's Draught. Eyeing it up and down one last time, he quickly braced himself and tipped his head back to swallow every drop of the vial's contents. Immediately dropping the glass container, Zeroan brought the peaks of his mystic power to bear and threw his arms around Tavin's weakening body. It burned alive with the seven demonic creatures swimming inside, but he held tight with the mystic grip he had mastered over the long years of his life.

Reaching inside Tavin with his telekinetic power, Zeroan sought out the dark energy buried within and took hold with every ounce of his concentration to begin pulling it out. The Shadows instantly resisted, savagely gripping Tavin's spirit to remain. Zeroan's unnaturally strengthened power was too much for them to oppose, however, and with reluctance, the parasites angrily made the jump from Tavin's body into the new host drawing them out. One by one the black fluidic beings surfaced from Tavin's skin and dove into Zeroan's, blasting him back each time. As the final Shadow transferred to the sage, he released his grip on the boy and fell back to the ground helplessly. With the dark spirits out of him, Tavin quickly came back to his senses, struggling to dispel the lingering pain left from their attack on his body. Though still transformed as the Warrior of Granis, his radiant field of golden power had disappeared. Not understanding what had made them retreat, it was not until he turned to find the Mystic Sage faintly convulsing on the ground next to him that he realized what had happened.

Tavin's heart plummeted with dread and dismay, but he quickly rushed to the sage's side.

"Zeroan!" he cried uncontrollably, noticing the empty Sage's Draught to his right. "What did you do?" The sage looked up at him with night in his eyes, struggling to respond.

"I have... purged the demons from you, Tavin," he told him quietly. "I used my power to take hold of the darkness in you and pull it out. Unfortunately, the Shadows still had to have a host so they moved into me." Tavin's eyes quickly moistened as he shook his head with angry misunderstanding.

"Why would you do that, Zeroan? You told me more than a drop of that draught could kill you. Why did you let them attack you?" he asked with a high shaking voice. Zeroan cringed as he spoke.

"Because you are the only one who can stop Drakkan," he managed through his pain. "He has placed the emerald in the alter. You must stop him before it is activated. You are the world's last hope... Tavin."

"Zeroan, don't leave me," Tavin whispered with emotion choking his voice. "I can't do this without you..." Zeroan paused for a moment, his face placid. He smiled up to him.

"You are like a son to me, Tavin. I know you; I know you can do this. Now go." With that, Zeroan pushed Tavin away by his chest. The Grandarian boy's tears were streaming now.

"Zeroan, please," he tried, inching forward. Zeroan violently shook his head.

"Do not let all we have done be in vain, Tavin!" he struggled, his body slowly brightening with white light. "You can do it. Stop Drakkan..." Trailing off, Tavin watched in anguish as the sage's very skin tore with lines of brilliant light and his body quietly exploded, obliterating the demons inside him as well. As the flurries of light disappeared, all that remained of the Mystic Sage Zeroan were his flat and empty gray robes strewn across the stone. Tavin felt a swell of pain and hurt overcome him like nothing ever had before. The driving force behind all that he had done from the beginning of this quest to the end was gone. The sage had given his life for him, and it felt as if he had lost a father. As Tavin crawled toward the loose gray robes to gather them in his hands, his exposed skin suddenly felt cold and wet. Peering down, he saw he was kneeling in a pool of blood.

Spinning to his left, Tavin's already distraught soul was torn further as he found Verix Montrox lying on the ground motionless beside him, a massive gap in his bloody chest. The Grandarian's face twisted with pain. Two of his best friends had just died because of his foolishness. If he had possessed the clairvoyance to open his mind and realize the danger lurking behind the Dégamar, both of them would still be alive. As he allotted blame to himself, he sensed the incredible power above him on the now motionless platform. Though the Holy Emerald's power was rising to life, he could sense his polar opposite standing beside it as if seeing it with his own eyes. The pain and sorrow in his heart rapidly transforming into ultimate rage, the Warrior of Granis' power unconsciously flared into being around him. His tightly closed eyes bursting open with righteous anger, he realized there was only one person to blame. Only one thing that mattered now.

Drakkan.

Standing and clenching his fists with the blood of Verix and the robes of Zeroan in either hand, Tavin began summoning back every last ounce of his godly power. Opening his hands to lean down and pick up the Sword of Granis at his feet, Tavin strapped the ultimate fortitude and purpose to his soul and let his power explode around him with a vengeful scream. So awesome was the display and the potency of his power that the very stones in the tower beside him began to crush and shrink back away from him. Wrapping both hands around the hilt of his mighty talisman, the Warrior of Granis crouched down to push himself off and shoot skyward in a flash of detonating golden light.

Careening upward with impossible speed, it was mere seconds before he soared up over a hundred feet in the air to the top of the towering shrine. Blasting over the top, he let himself drop to the platform's surface crumbling the stone upon landing. As he rose to his feet, Tavin laid eyes upon the shining Holy Emerald lying in the center pedestal of the platform, and his mortal enemy beside it. The dark mutated face of Drakkan smiled as his eyes met with his opposite.

"Well, it would seem you aren't ready to die yet after all, brother," he spoke menacingly. Tavin stood firm, raising the gilded blade of the Sword of Granis to point it at his foe's face.

"You've just done your last evil, Drakkan," he declared vehemently. When all the God of Darkness did was return his stare with a twisted smile, Tavin's face was wrought with fury. "Do you hear me!?! You are *done*, Drakkan! *I am going to finish you!*"

"Those are bold words for a child, Granis," Drakkan responded with a mocking tone of voice. "But if you really think you can best me after all theses centuries, I shall make you a wager. If you can defeat me as we are now, I will yield and the emerald will be yours. What say you, brother?" Tavin held the foreboding figure's gaze for a long moment before finally nodding.

"Very well," he agreed. "I suggest you prepare yourself." Drakkan smiled and motioned with the flick of his misshapen wrist for him them to begin. Assuming his perfected battle stance and tightly wrapping his fingers around his sword, Tavin flexed his circulating aura of radiating energy around him, the pinnacle of his godly strength brought to bear. Every cell in his body was brimming with unimaginable might; with the slightest swing of his sword he felt he could bring down mountains. Staring down his enemy engulfed in a slow blaze of black and purple energy radiating like fire, the Warrior of Granis at last kicked off the stone surface beneath him and charged forward to begin the Final Battle of Destiny; the second Battle of the Gods.

Chapter 79

<u>War</u>

As Tavin charged forward at Drakkan with speed beyond what he could even comprehend and the Sword of Granis arching downward toward him, the God of Darkness at last reacted. When only an arms length away, Drakkan opened his misshapen armored hand to materialize a crimson blade of malevolent power and forcefully swing it upward at the perfect angle to parry his oncoming assailant. Deflected in the blink of an eye, Tavin was redirected to brutishly land feet beyond, his boots sinking into the stone crumbling beneath his power. By the time Tavin came to a halt, Drakkan was already charging with his blade careening downward toward him. Aware he had left himself open, Tavin wheeled around to defensively raise the Sword of Granis. Though he blocked the attack, the godly force behind it knocked him backward with the stone tiling on the platform snapping and crushing further.

Staggering backward off balance, it was all Tavin could do to brace himself as Drakkan renewed his charge, raising his free fist ahead of him to rush into Tavin's face. Shielded from the raw force of the blow by his radiating field of power, the boy was launched off his feet careening back through the air so fast the next second he was over a hundred feet from the Holy Shrine. His senses returning to him quickly, Tavin remembered he was warring with one as fast and powerful as he, and he had to fight accordingly. Gritting his teeth with determination the Warrior of Granis let his waning aura of circulating energy explode to life once more, shooting upward into the sky to raise his sword in preparation for the God of Darkness racing toward him.

Drakkan hurriedly closed the gap, summoning his own power to bear and crafting a swarm of spherical electrified bursts around him. As they orbited his massive frame, he

633

began savagely throwing his arms forward. The orbs of dark power followed one at a time, lunging at the boy. They came so hard and fast, and it was all Tavin could do, still adjusting to the insane speed of battle, to deflect them with his blade. Redirecting their trajectory, Drakkan's attacks wildly spun down to the earth leaving explosions and craters the size of Lake Torrent behind. Feeling out the pattern of his enemy's attack, Tavin at last swung the Sword of Granis at a different angle to bat the final ball of energy back at him. Not ready to be hindered by his own attack, however, Drakkan took his own weapon in both hands and savagely made a vertical slash downward to sever the incoming blast in two, narrowly plummeting on either sides of the Holy Shrine to explode below.

Abandoning his long ranged attack, Drakkan blasted forward once more to meet blades with Tavin. Though he had difficulty battling apart from solid earth, Tavin's supernatural reflexes only enhanced his prowess with the blade and kept him equally pitted against the dark god, savagely batting him around the skies until eventually their blades locked. Now matched in a battle of raw power, Tavin let his strength feed off his anger and determination, giving it the fuel to expand even further. Drakkan's burning field of black energy rose on par with the Grandarian boy's, encompassing the sky behind him with storm clouds surging with lightning while Tavin's side grew clear and bright. Holding the God of Darkness at bay was the most physically demanding task of his life, and every second that passed by with him still holding firm seemed like hours.

Eventually, Tavin's constantly escalating power at last triumphed. With all his strength pressing into Drakkan's crimson blade, the Warrior of Granis finally wrenched it from his grip to hurl it away into the air. Drakkan hovered there stunned, and Tavin instantly reacted. The Sword of Granis plunged forward through the air and into the dark god's gut to impale him clean through. Drakkan's face froze with emotionless shock. Realizing this was his moment, Tavin pressed his attack. He released his grip on the sword and leapt back to summon the most intense collection of power around his fists that his body would allow. Drawing from his very life-force, Tavin threw his fists forward together to fire a colossal blast of beaming energy over ten times his height straight into Drakkan to illuminate the entire sky in blinding light. Holding the godly barrage for as long as he could draw into his peaked energy, Tavin at last released his grip on his power and cut off the attack.

Breathing heavily from pouring out so much power at once, Tavin watched as the lingering luminosity from his blast began to slowly fade. For several long moments, the sky was perfectly quiet; only the sound of Tavin's labored breathing could be heard. As the final flurries of gold dissipated from the skies however, Tavin watched in trepidation as the black form of Drakkan emerged from the light sailing forward with his right fist clenched in a dark sphere of power. Having not even dropped his hands from his bombardment, Tavin was helplessly swatted downward to plummet through the skies and land on the platform of the Holy Shrine with the stone floor breaking around him.

In the dust and rubble of the broken stone loosed from his impact, Tavin lay propping himself up by his arms. Struggling to rise, Tavin observed Drakkan slowly descending through the air with his dark power burning off his mutated body and the Sword of Granis still embedded in his middle. It didn't make any sense, he thought dreadfully. Tavin had plunged the bane of darkness into his core and blasted him with everything he had and more; the full power of the God of Light himself. How could he still be at full power and physically unscathed in every way? As Drakkan gently touched down to the platform, he reached up and wrenched the Sword of Granis free from his gut and threw it back on the ground before Tavin with a dark grin. The Warrior of Granis was silent, a desperate helplessness growing over his face.

Tavin turned to face the Holy Emerald, shining with brilliant white light in its pedestal. He had to shatter it. He couldn't do this on his own. He had given it everything, but somehow it wasn't enough to even slow the dark god. He was out of options; the emerald had to be destroyed to give him an edge and make sure Drakkan didn't become more powerful. Shifting his eyes to Drakkan still standing before him with a twisted smile, Tavin took a deep breath and lunged forward to take hold of the Sword of Granis. Quickly summoning a wave of power over its gilded blade, he pointed it at the emerald and screamed, simultaneously firing a thin but powerful beam of golden power from the tip. It rushed to the emerald and pierced it through the middle, shattering it instantly. Struggling for breath, Tavin slowly turned his head back to Drakkan. Staring him down for a long moment, he squinted uncertainly. Drakkan was still smiling. And he had done nothing to prevent the emerald's destruction; he hadn't even tried.

"It's a little late for that, Granis," Drakkan at last spoke in his low, menacing tone. He then reached up into the plating of his midnight black armor and pulled free a brilliant white light. Tavin's eyes went wide; his heart dropped. Sitting safely in the dark figure's hand was the Holy Emerald, radiating with power. Drakkan nodded satisfied and smiled back to Tavin. "I'm afraid I've been cheating the whole time, brother. I have the complete, activated stone in my hand. I brought the fake to toy with you." Drakkan's smile faded and he placed the emerald back in his armor. "But now I'm tired of playing this game," he said clenching his fists. "It's time for you to die." Even with his godly power to aid his reflexes, Tavin could not see Drakkan at the speed that he next moved. Skimming across the stone floor of the platform, the dark god thrust his fist into Tavin's armor plated middle to once again force him sailing back. Without his guard up to brace himself, however, Tavin soared helplessly like a rag doll. Once more seizing upon his adversary's shock, Drakkan shot past him and stopped as he passed over the edge of the shrine to raise his fists above his head and plunge them down into Tavin as he sailed forth to meet him.

The next thing Tavin knew was that he was plummeting downward to blast into the grassy earth beneath him, forming a veritable crater from the collision. Stunned and fatigued even in his transformed state, the once fiercely radiating field of power around his body began to wane to a slight aura of weak luminosity shimmering across his skin. Tavin lay immobile in the depression he had made, his regal armor soiled with dirt. Feeling his godly power failing him, Tavin struggled to rise back to his feet. Drakkan softly fell before him, placing one of his armored feet on his chest to force him back down. He created another blade of crimson energy that materialized from his hand and slowly took hold of it with both hands.

"Now, brother," he began in a deathly rumble, "I will finish what I started eons ago. Your time was the past, Granis. The future is mine." Caught under the menacing being's massive weight, Tavin lay powerless as the dark god raised his sword above his head, the blade pointed downward. The boy's hearted pounded so hard he was sure Drakkan could feel it through the armor.

Just as the Drakkan was about to plunge his blade downward and Tavin knew it was over, the powerful God of Darkness suddenly froze, the burning black energy around his body relinquishing. Confused, Tavin's once emotionally blurred senses suddenly felt another presence next to them. Peering up through the crater and the hulking form of the frozen god, Tavin found its source. His eyes widened, disbelief mirrored inside. Standing in front of the midnight black horse Nighcress was Ril, her hands outstretched at Drakkan with spheres of electrified dark energy hovering about them. Her face was sweaty and rigid with turmoil. Though confused at what she was doing at first, Tavin at last sensed what was happening. Remembering what Zeroan had said earlier in the day about how Ril's blood was connected to Montrox, he knew she had somehow taken hold of the dark power of her father still lingering inside Drakkan's physical form and was holding him back. Her desperate eyes quickly shifted to Tavin.

"*Hurry!*" she screamed urgently. Realizing she was giving him a chance to save his life, Tavin grit his teeth and wrapped his fingers around the Sword of Granis sitting loosely in his hand. Raising its tip up to Drakkan, he summoned what energy he could from his beaten body and channeled it into the blade. Exploding with power, a blast of potent light fired free peppering the dark god's body and blasting him back into the stone wall of the Holy Shrine behind him. Free once more, Tavin breathed deeply and let the sword fall back to the ground in his hand. Remembering his savior, he conquered his fatigue and strenuously rose to his feet to find Ril collapsed on the ground to his right. Hurriedly placing the Sword of Granis behind his back and dashed over to her, leaning down to gather her depleted form in his arms. She looked up to him with an exhausted face. Though he wasn't sure how she had just done what she did, Tavin could sense holding the God of Darkness back had taken every ounce of her still new and weak power.

"I had to come," she whispered out of energy. Tavin smiled and nodded.

"I know," he replied with emotion, pulling his voice taut. Before he could ask her how she had stopped Drakkan, the dark god's power exploded to life again, devastating the

Holy Shrine to rubble. As the dust and debris cleared, Tavin found Drakkan engulfed in a field of power larger than he had ever thought possible; the entire sky was swallowed by it. Drakkan had the emerald in his hands now, obviously charging himself with its power. Realizing he could not stop Drakkan by himself, much less with the ultimate supremacy of the Holy Emerald empowering him, he desperately looked back to the Sword of Granis for help. "I can't do it, Granis," he whispered overwhelmed. "Help me. Give me strength. What should I do?" Nothing happened. No voice echoed into his mind, the world remained as it was. "Please, Granis. I don't know what to do..." He was desperate, plagued by defeat. This time, it seemed, Granis would not be there to aid him.

As his thoughts drifted to the imprisoned God of Light, however, Tavin was slowly struck with a thought. An idea. It was a long shot to be sure, but it seemed possible. There was still a way to rid Iairia of Drakkan. His desperate expression morphing into one of hope, he stood straight and spoke out to the girl in his arms.

"Hold on, Ril," he told her quietly, his field of circulating energy slowly coming to life once again. "We're not giving up." Reaching into the innermost energy of his soul, Tavin summoned every last bit of power in his body and more. He was going to use everything he had. After this there would not be another chance; he would have nothing left, and he knew it. With the righteous power of the God of Light exploding around him one last time, the Warrior of Granis blasted into the dark sky with Ril in his arms, sailing into the northeast.

Sensing his opposite's power ignite yet again, the God of Darkness at last let his charging power relax. Noticing Tavin was no longer present, Drakkan focused his radiating red eyes into the horizon to find him blasting away into the sky. His mutated frown only deepening, Drakkan placed the Holy Emerald in his right hand, crouched his body to build potential energy, and shot off in a detonation of electrified dark energy after him.

Chapter 80

Fate's Irony

Tavin tore through the dark Iairian skies faster than he had ever moved before, desperate to reach his destination before the already trailing God of Darkness could catch up to them. The ultimate need for speed and power driving his every thought, Tavin pressed on to the northeast through the darkness with the utmost fortitude set into his face. Moving as fast as they were, it took only minutes for them to exit the war zones and pass the Grandarian Wall of Light. Making their way into the Border Mountains, however, Tavin realized that no matter how fast he traveled, it would never be fast enough to prove any challenge for Drakkan. With the ultimate power of the Holy Emerald coursing through his tainted veins, he caught up to them in the blink of an eye.

Before Tavin knew it, the dark god was soaring beside them, a dark grin set into his face.

"What are you doing now, brother?" he bellowed forebodingly. "Are you afraid to stand and fight so you retreat? You have never dishonored yourself this way before. Perhaps you wish to play more before you die. Very well, then. We shall play." Desperately trying to accelerate further, Tavin helplessly watched as Drakkan began circling around them leaving a spiraling black wake behind. As he circled, he began firing burst after burst of electrified dark energy careening at Tavin. Though the Warrior of Granis valiantly struggled to evade what he could, the constant barrage proved too intense for him and he was pelted from every side with torturous bursts of pain seeping into his body. Still jetting through the air at top speed, however, Tavin felt the freezing touch of snowflakes cascading into his face and knew he was almost to his destination.

Escalating his power, Drakkan swooped underneath Tavin and fired one last burst of black power into his face.

His body shocked and blasted with pain, Tavin lost his grip on Ril and reeled upward losing his momentum. Realizing what he had just done, Tavin quickly regained his balance and peered down to find Ril plummeting to the snowy earth. Mustering all his strength, he shot downward to leap over Drakkan's hulking form and snatch her from the air. Instantly charging forward again, Tavin found himself facing a familiar mountain glacier. Blasting upward inches from the surface, a wall of powdery snow flew up in his wake. Within seconds of the summit, however, Drakkan once again appeared beside him.

"I am already tired of the chase, brother," he spoke darkly. "It is time for you to give up." When Tavin did not even acknowledge him as he blasted clear of the summit, Drakkan's twisted face morphed angrily. Letting his surging black power explode to life, he threw himself into Tavin and took hold of his neck. Raising the Warrior of Granis above his head like a rag doll, the dark god threw him downward before the massive platform resting in the mountaintop. As he met the ground, Ril fell from his grasp once more, skidding onto the stone dais. Tavin collided into the ground to make another deep crater, snow exploding around him. As it slowly dissipated from the frigid breeze blowing through the suddenly quiet mountain air, Tavin lay in a broken heap. He could feel his power fading; the last remnant of his gifted strength from Granis lost to him. It was all he could do to hold onto his transformed self, much less summon the power to rise.

Knowing he was only feet away from what he had so desperately fought to reach, Tavin's grit took hold of him again. Refusing to lose now after all the sacrifice he and his friends had made to stop this from happening, the near lifeless Warrior of Granis found the strength to crawl free from the crater he was lodged in. Taking the Sword of Granis in his right hand from where it lay, he struggled his way onto the dry stone platform before him. As he inched his way forward, however, he was stopped by the pair of black armored boots gently falling in his path, shrouded with burning dark energy.

"I don't understand, Granis," Drakkan spoke, strangely calm though still dark and powerfully. "Why have you led me to the entrance of your void? Do you wish me to place you inside once again?" Staring at the boy by his feet, Drakkan's curious eyes noticed the mighty weapon still tightly clutched in his hand. A slow, knowing smile crept onto his face. "I know what you are trying to do. You thought you could use my own work against me, didn't you? You were going to try and seal me into the void I created for you." The dark god let a slow menacing laugh echo from his sinister throat, leaning down to effortlessly wrench the sword out of Tavin's hand. "What kind of plan was this? Even if you had opened the gate, we would both have been sucked into the void. You would not have escaped your death, Granis." Drakkan threw the sword of behind his back, landing on the other side of the platform with a metallic crash. "A creative idea, brother, but I'm afraid it is too late now."

Tavin's head slowly fell to the ground, his heart sinking after it. His last attempt to seal Drakkan's evil had failed as well. A painful tear swelling in his eye, Tavin peered over to the pedestal in the center of the portal. After all he and his friends had endured and given up, he had been too weak to fulfill his part of the quest. Now, all of Iairia would pay the price for his failing. As he stared out at the pedestal, however, a movement from behind it caught his attention. The pain in his eyes slowly dissolved. Drakkan watched curiously as his hurt was replaced by amazement.

"I always hated this about you, Granis. You would never give up, even when your destruction stands before you as surely as I do now. You cannot win, brother. You can't defeat me." Tavin remained still for a moment. Though every last cell in his body was drained of power, a final burst of strength appeared in the center of his heart to bring a faint golden aura of power around his body one last time. Slowly raising his head to find Drakkan's deathly crimson eyes, a flash of light and hope shimmered across his.

"I can't," he replied in agreement, his voice masking hidden knowledge. "But she can." Drakkan's face confused and abruptly nervous, he followed Tavin's shifting eyes to what he stared at behind him. Rotating his head, the dark god's eyes fell upon the fiery haired girl fallen from his brother's grip, weakly standing above the pedestal in the center of the platform. So weak was her power that he had not even sensed her moving. Drakkan's jaw dropped in horror as he found the Sword of Granis in her hands, burning them with its righteous power. Before he could so much as blink in reaction, the girl tightened her face and summoned all her strength to plunge the golden blade home into the platform.

"*NNNOOOOOOOO!!!*" Drakkan bellowed, his dark voice ripping through the air with anguish and torment threatening to steal the very life out of Tavin and Ril. In the next instant, the elaborate lines throughout the portal ignited with golden light shimmering forth, a shaft of celestial power beaming up from its center into the sky. Engulfing the entire platform, all three figures began to slowly rise with it. Realizing he had to escape with Ril before they disappeared inside the void, Tavin seized on the dark figure's fear and shock. Summoning power he no longer had, his aura of golden light exploded around him. Shooting himself past Drakkan in one last charge, he hurled toward Ril's flaccid body gently ascending into the air to catch her in his arms. Soaring out of the warm call of the rising celestial beam, they burst forth from its perimeter to land on their backs in the snow. With Ril tightly nestled in his arms and his last measure of power escaping with his panting breath, Tavin's golden eyes watched as the black form of Drakkan helplessly rose into the sky and past the clouds, his power fading from this world to the void.

The moment his black mass disappeared from view, another form appeared from the clouds where he had been. Squinting from the heightened intensity of the golden light, Tavin could barely make out the righteous form of a being comprised of light staring down at him with a warm smile over his face. Tavin knew immediately it was Granis, finally freed. Staring upward at the beautiful display, he watched amazed as the golden figure spread two massive wings of light behind him and soared upward to disappear into the sky.

After several long moments of witnessing the massive shaft of golden energy shrink and fade into the sky after Granis, the world was returned placid and white once more. Separated for so long from the Sword of Granis and having just enough strength left to breathe, Tavin finally felt his godly powers slip away and he transformed back into himself. Peering at the once again quiet portal with his returned blue eyes, Tavin noticed two objects had remained. In the center of the platform, the golden Sword of Granis rested peacefully in its pedestal. Though it was still, Tavin noticed the Granic Crystal on its hilt was still glowing. Focusing his mind, he sensed that it was active on its own; now somehow part of the portal itself. To the right of the Grandarian talisman, however, was an icon of far greater importance. With a tired smile, Tavin let his eyes pass to the still brilliantly shining Holy Emerald lying on the ground. Once again, Drakkan had possessed the ultimate might of the talisman but was still defeated by the ingenuity of his opponent.

Tavin slowly turned his head down to the girl in his arms, already staring up at him with exhausted eyes.

"I'm glad you don't listen to me," Tavin whispered with only the energy to speak and breathe. "You did it. You saved me. You saved Iairia." Ril gradually nodded and faintly smiled.

"We did it," she responded even more distantly. "I'm glad I don't listen to you too. I told you I had to be here." As she finished her words, Tavin's face lost its smile. Her power level was nearly gone, and the cold environment was not helping to sustain it. Ril's smile was steady however. She raised a hand to Tavin's face and rested it against his cheek. "I'm glad I could see you one more time." Tavin went rigid, now knowing something was wrong.

"What are you talking about?" he pressed quickly. Ril kept her hand on his face, gently rubbing it back and forth.

"You were wrong about my power, too," she said weakly. "I knew how to use it. I don't know how, but... I could. And I used it all." Her body was going pale and limp; Tavin couldn't even sense her heart beating anymore. He shook his head violently.

"Ril, stop talking," he ordered quickly. "You don't have enough energy. Just hold on. I'm going to get us out of here..." He stopped short watching the girl shake her head.

"You don't have enough either, Tavin," she stated quietly. The boy's face tightened with emotion, tears swelling in the corners of his blue eyes. He knew as well as she did the life in her body was slipping away. "Thank you for being who you are, Tavin. For everything you did for me. I... would have loved you... forever..." With that, her hand slowly fell back to the icy earth and her dim red eyes gradually closed. Tavin stared down at her with the utmost dread in his tear-filled eyes.

"Ril," he whispered, his voice shaking with emotion. He gently shook her lifeless body, desperately willing her to open her eyes. "Ril..." They didn't open, however, and Tavin could feel his heart crumbling to pieces inside his chest. Lowering himself to her motionless form, the devastated Grandarian boy rested his head over her, tears streaming down his face. He cried out loud in anguish, his sobs echoing through the peaks of the snowcapped mountains. Though he had defeated Drakkan and saved the world, he felt like he had lost everything. It was a meaningless, empty victory.

As the grief-stricken Warrior of Granis lay weeping beside his lifeless love, a slowly growing warmth from behind him drew his attention. Gradually turning his broken eyes to search for the strange feeling, Tavin found the Holy Emerald shining like a star on the platform, its power reaching out to him as if asking to be taken up. Pausing to realize for the fist time the untold, limitless, power that lay inside, his distraught eyes slowly focused. The emerald was his now, and its universal power to do- anything, with it. His grief immediately overridden by new hope, Tavin reached out to the talisman with his right hand. Obeying, the emerald rose from the platform and soared into his grasp. Laying his fingers around it, Tavin was filled with total awe. The incredible power inside was beyond comprehension; with the talisman in hand, anything and everything was possible. With a mere thought, he suddenly felt his body completely revitalized and his power restored.

With the ultimate power of the Holy Emerald in hand, Tavin turned back to Ril's lifeless body beneath him. Holding the white stone over her, he closed his eyes and focused his entire being into his thoughts. *Granis*, he silently prayed, *please let this work. Let me have her back. Please...* In the excruciating moments that followed, Tavin gradually let his eyes lids slip open to stare down at Ril. She was still for a long moment, but with a single flash from deep within the emerald, her head suddenly shook. Tavin's heart began to beat wildly as he felt her body gradually tighten and shift like waking from a deep sleep. Her eyes slowly opened, full of color and life. She met his gaze immediately, a tired confusion in her rejuvenated face.

"Tavin?" she spoke meekly. With an almost painful sigh of relief, the Grandarian boy dropped the emerald and threw his arms around her. They embraced tightly for what felt like an eternity before he at last loosened his grip. Remembering the last thing she had said to him before slipping away, he smiled with a blissful tear rolling down his face.

"Now you can..." he whispered with emotion. With tears of her own building in her eyes, Ril instantly knew what he meant and pressed forward to kiss him hard. As she pulled back, she nodded and smiled through her own tears of joy.

"I will," she managed. Their bodies illuminated by the sacred power of the Holy Emerald, Tavin and Ril came together again to passionately kiss, a soft layer of snow gently falling around them. The world and its saviors were finally safe.

Chapter 81

<u>Homecoming</u>

Healed and rejuvenated by the Holy Emerald, Tavin and Ril were quick to rise and prepare for departure. With their quest finally complete, however, neither were sure what to do next. At last, Tavin remembered he had two friends back at the ruins of the Holy Shrine that needed the resurrecting power of the emerald. Telling Ril what happened to Zeroan and Verix, she quickly agreed they should depart immediately. As Tavin prepared to utilize the Holy Emerald and leave, Ril's eye caught the Sword of Granis still embedded in the platform before them. Perplexed, she asked him what he was going to do with it. Tavin explained to her that when she planted the sword in the pedestal she opened the gate to the void both ways; Granis was now free and Drakkan had been sucked inside. The sword, as Granis had put it, was now a key; the key that would keep things this way. He had to leave it as it was.

Not quite sure she understood, Ril decided all that mattered was that they had won and it was over. Moving close to Tavin, the Warrior of Light opened his mind to the Holy Emerald and wished it to take them to Verix. Obeying, a deep burst of light flashed from the emerald encompassing them both. Though Tavin had expected it to lift them off the ground and fly them to the Holy Shrine, the light merely passed over their bodies and the ground beneath their feet seemed to shift, and they suddenly found themselves standing before a massive pile of ruble where the ruins of the activated Holy Shrine once stood. So abrupt was the speed of their travel both Tavin and Ril jumped nervously at the immediate change in their surroundings.

After their senses returned to them, Tavin took hold of Ril's hand and quickly led her to where he had left the dead Drakkaidian Prince and Zeroan's empty robes. They found them both quickly, buried under a collection of dust and debris. Rushing to Verix's side, Tavin quickly leaned down to lift a stone slab off of his motionless legs while Ril fell to her knees to examine the bloody opening in his chest. Tavin quickly dropped to her side with the emerald in hand.

"You can bring him back?" Ril asked anxiously. Tavin looked at her uncertainly and lifted the glowing emerald above Verix.

"We're about to find out," he told her shifting his gaze to the emerald. Focusing on what he wanted once more, Tavin lowered the Holy Emerald to Verix's wound and willed it to close. After the flash from inside its core, the white stone passed its power down to the lifeless Drakkaidian boy and spread over the fissure in his chest. Tavin and Ril watched in amazement as the blood stains over his dark shirt began to dissipate and the opening slowly sealed shut. With is wound healed, the emerald's brilliant light shimmered once around his entire body, breathing new life inside. In the next instant, Verix's rich cherry eyes slid open and his body shifted on the ground. Coming awake, Verix swept his gaze up to Tavin and Ril above him staring down with wonder, then to the shining talisman in Tavin's grip. Realizing what it was, the Drakkaidian Prince smiled.

"You did it, then," he spoke slowly, the most content look either of them had ever before seen on his face. Tavin looked to the boy's sister beaming down at him with joyful tears, then back to Verix.

"No, we did it," he said satisfied, to which Ril smiled over to him. Helping Verix to his feet, Tavin explained to them both what had happened from before he was infected by the Shadows, how Zeroan had saved his life, how Drakkan had killed both the sage and Verix, and how he and Ril worked together to defeat him. Verix could only smile with happiness at the end, thanking them both for saving them all. Tavin quickly remembered his other lost comrade, however, and shot down to gather the soiled gray robes lying at their feet. Producing the emerald and its power one more time, Tavin willed the Mystic Sage to return. After a long moment, the emerald flashed but something other than what he had anticipated was the result. Instead of summing Zeroan's lost spirit back to the living world, the emerald created a wave of swirling colors before them. Staring into the sloshing hues of blue and brown with curiosity, the group watched as they took form.

Projected before them was a painting of light picturing the Sapphire Pool they had once talked with the lost sage through in the treetop village of the cronoms. Puzzled, Tavin tried to wish for Zeroan again but the image of light before them only grew brighter each time. Hurt and confused at his failure, he turned to Ril and Verix uncertainly.

"I don't understand," he thought out loud. "It can do anything. It brought back Ril and Verix, why won't it for Zeroan?" The siblings remained quiet, not sure if they should try and respond or not. At last, Verix opened his mouth to speak.

"I'm not sure if this is right or not, Tavin," he began doubtfully, "but I may have a theory. There were dark arts that ancient Drakkaidians once practiced that resurrected the dead. The catch was, they returned to our world only if the deceased spirit so chose. Perhaps Zeroan does not want to be revived..." He trailed off there, sensing the obvious frustration in Tavin's eyes.

"Why wouldn't he want us to bring him back?" he asked incredulously. Verix only shrugged.

"Perhaps he is telling you to ask him there," he guessed, eyeing the image of light before them. Shifting his gaze back to the picture of the Sapphire Pool, Tavin remembered how they had once communicated with the sage's spirit using its power. He couldn't think of any reason why this would be happening, and decided Verix must be right. So with a heavy heart, Tavin nodded and told his two friends they should be off. Taking hold of the sage's robes to bring with them, Tavin wrapped the power of the Holy Emerald around them and they disappeared into the air once more, leaving the ruins of their battle basking in the clear afternoon light.

They arrived in Galantia a moment later in a flash of gleaming light, frightening Jaren nearly to death. He had been standing alone on the balcony adjacent to the throne room in the Golden Castle since they departed hours ago, desperately praying for Tavin and the others to appear back in the skies covered in streaking golden light. This, however, he wasn't expecting and leapt into the air in surprise. As the light dissipated and he found himself staring at Tavin, Verix, and Ril, a tearful incredulous smile spread across his mouth. Wishing them away from the Holy Shrine, Tavin had focused on Jaren, wherever he was, and now he was standing before him with his own smile building.

As Tavin began to merrily laugh at his friend's supremely confused but joyful face, Jaren realized it was not an illusion or dream and bounded forward to strongly embrace his friend.

"I knew you'd do it," he spoke a little choked up. Tavin returned his hearty hug and nodded.

"Never any doubt," he confirmed laughing. They stood laughing in each others arms for a long moment before Jaren at last noticed the friendly warmth behind his back and turned to find a radiating stone in his friends hand. His eyes went wide, pulling away.

"Is that what I think it is...?" he trailed off with amazement. Tavin didn't have to look at the emerald to know what he was talking about.

"Well if you're thinking this is the complete, active, Holy Emerald, you wouldn't be wrong," Tavin beamed holding it up to him. Jaren marveled at it for a long moment, smiling and shaking his head with wonder.

"You never cease to amaze me, buddy," he grinned giddy. After Jaren got over the ultimate power in his friend's hand, he turned to Ril and Verix standing beside him, a look of abhorrence on his face.

"You had us scared to death, Ril," he said accusingly. "But when Mary went looking for you and said Nighcress was gone, I knew instantly. The next time you want to give me a heart attack, why don't you just lay down in front of the city gates and wait for them to crush you." Ril couldn't help but smile apologetically, moving in to offer him a tender hug.

"Sorry, Jaren," she told him sincerely. "I just did what I had to do."

"What does that mean?" he asked questioningly. "And where's Zeroan? And how did you guys get the emerald? What happened out there?" Tavin's smile faded.

"It's a long story, Jaren," he said with fatigue already filling his voice. "We need to sit first." Jaren nodded, but raised an eyebrow nervously.

"I hear you, but that may be a problem," he said, motioning to look in through the windows of the balcony. Turning his head, Tavin noticed the throne room was once again full of Grandarians all staring out at them. "Mary went to fetch the Queen and the rest of the castle's occupants this morning after you left. They've been back for an hour, and I think they're going to want some answers pretty quick."

"I'll take care of that," a voice sounded from the doorway. Everyone turning, they found Mary walking toward them with a grateful smile. Walking to Tavin, she bowed before him. "From your amazing return, I can only assume you defeated Drakkan. On behalf of Grandaria let me be the first to thank you, Tavin." The Warrior of Light looked at her uncertainly, then to Ril and Verix.

"Thank you for your gratitude, Mary," he began, "but these two deserve as much credit as me, and there's a lot we need to talk about before you can really thank us." The Grandarian Princess nodded with an understanding smile.

"I'm sure," she said agreeably. "For now, I will see to it you three get the rest you need. When you feel up to it, you can tell me what happened and I can tell my mother and mob inside." Tavin smiled and silently laughed at her good humor.

"That sounds great, Your Highness," he slightly bowed in response. With that, Mary went back inside and announced Tavin, Ril and Verix's presence and for a clear path so they could move through freely. Though the Queen was eager to hear an explanation of what had happened, Mary respectfully informed her that they were in no condition to speak at the moment, having just returned from battle. Understanding, the Queen ordered the finest rooms in the castle be prepared for them. Passing through the throne room, Tavin and the others bowed to her for her hospitality. Mary and a host of servants quickly led them to rooms only under that of the royal family themselves and let them alone. Though rejuvenated by the limitless energy of the Holy Emerald, Tavin, Ril, and Verix were exhausted of their natural strength from the emotional strain they had been so pressured by throughout the day, and quickly took their seats with Jaren and Mary on another small balcony outside their room.

After taking their moments to just sit and breathe easy, Tavin, Ril, and Verix began to retell what had happened for Jaren and Mary. From their encounter with the Dégamar to the appearance of Drakkan to Verix's murder and Zeroan's sacrifice, Tavin retold every detail. Jaren in particular felt a piece of his heart die as he heard of the sage's heroic death for Tavin, knowing it was something he would have done for any of them. Tavin then began his battle with Drakkan and the power they both used during it. Neither Ril nor Verix had heard this before, so they listened as intently as Jaren and Mary to how the dark god had tricked and cheated Tavin, using the Holy Emerald in their battle the entire time. At this point, both Tavin and Ril were able to tell the story of how she had saved him with her new dark power. It had done little to Drakkan in the end, however, except fuel his rage. Tavin painfully explained how he knew he could not defeat the God of Darkness, but remembered the words of Granis and tired to seal him in the void.

Tavin told them it was Ril that opened the gate to the void and stopped Drakkan, to which Jaren and Mary were glad she had disobeyed Zeroan and followed them. After that, Tavin watched Drakkan fall into the void and Granis rise out, free at last. He told them how Ril had died in his arms but he had used the active Holy Emerald to resurrect both her and Verix. When Jaren asked why he hadn't done the same for Zeroan, Tavin looked down to the frayed gray robes still in his free hand and told him he didn't know. Sensing the lingering pain still consuming Tavin about the subject, Ril stepped in and told them how the emerald had showed them the Sapphire Pool.

After they finished with their long story, it was already late evening. With tears in her eyes, Mary once again thanked all of them for their bravery and excused herself to go to her mother and retell the story. Verix was the next to leave, hugging his sister and bowing to Tavin and Jaren. Though all of them insisted him to stay, he told them he was less than comfortable staying in the Grandarian castle as it was and that they would see him soon enough. Slipping away with a happy smile, Tavin, Ril, and Jaren were left to peacefully reflect over everything they had done in the past months: the obstacles they had overcome, the good times they had enjoyed, the dangers they had defeated, and the friendships they had made. With a painful goodbye, Jaren at last took his leave at nightfall to his own room.

Tavin and Ril stayed out on the balcony wrapped together in thick blankets for the rest of the night. They silently stared up at the crystal clear moonlit sky until Ril peacefully fell asleep in Tavin's arms. The Warrior of Light stared down at her beautiful face overwhelmed with all the thoughts and images of their adventures swirling in his. He head could barely believe this life he found himself in was his. Tucking the blankets up to her neck, he looked back up to the starry sky with a smile.

Chapter 82

<u>Fulfilling Destiny</u>

Tavin, Ril, Jaren, Verix, and Mary spent the next three days casually talking with each other in the castle, not quite sure what else they could do. After such an abrupt finale to their grand quest, none of them really knew what was next. It was the first time in months they didn't have the wise voice of Zeroan behind them, instructing them what to do. The only thing Tavin knew for certain, was that Mary needed her father back. With the power of the Holy Emerald, he granted her wish. A dazed and confused Supreme Granisian appeared before them the next day in his personal chambers, to which Mary and the Queen were overjoyed. After he learned of all that had befallen him and of Tavin's struggle to defeat Drakkan, he immediately ordered a grand celebration to honor all of them. It was to be held three days after their return, and invitations to attend would be sent all over Grandaria and even to Torrentcia City in the Southland to call for the members of their party that still lingered there.

As they waited for Kohlin, Parnox, and whoever else would be coming from the Southland, the group spent well deserved time relaxing. In the three days before the ceremony, there were two things that Tavin never let out of his sight: Ril and the Holy Emerald. Both of them were constantly within his touch. Jaren could be found with them most of the time, but often accompanied Mary on her various tasks around the castle like her shadow. Verix, though transformed compared to when they first met, maintained his predictably distant demeanor. It was no secret he felt estranged and uncomfortable in the Grandarian capital, and he appeared only when he chose. When he did, however, he was warm and open with Tavin, Ril and even Jaren, whom he still considered somewhat of a friendly idiot. When he confessed this to Tavin in private, the Warrior of Light only laughed and told him he understood.

They all woke on the third morning to the sound of people frantically running back and forth through the halls outside their rooms in preparation for the massive celebration that crowds of Grandarians were already gathering for in the courtyard of the Golden Castle. A messenger was sent to each of their rooms to rouse them for the festivities, but Tavin was already up preparing himself. He quickly bathed and came back outside into his room to find the most extravagant attire he had ever seen. A familiar set of feather-light golden armor set out for him with an ornate white and blue shirt, pants, and cape. Though he was comfortable with a cape behind him again, he felt like only half of himself without the Sword of Granis by his side. Every morning when he woke he wished he could teleport out to his old weapon and take it up once more. He missed everything from its familiar weight tugging at his side to the brilliant little Granic Crystal illuminating every step he took. Now, however, he had the gleaming Holy Emerald to look after. He carefully tucked it behind his cape in a small pouch that he had found to wrap it in.

Tavin left his bedroom and stepped out of the hall to find Mary waiting for him, once again adorned in her golden, royal garments with a soft pink dress beneath them. Though he half expected Jaren to be standing with her, his best friend emerged from the room adjacent to him nearly a moment after. Mary smiled at both of them.

"What perfect timing, boys," she laughed. "I'm glad you're both prepared. The men from the Southland arrived about a half of an hour ago and are getting ready after their long ride here. They are in the Grade Vestibule waiting for you." Tavin and Jaren's faces both lit up, turning to each other excitedly.

"How many are there, Mary?" Jaren questioned.

"Did you recognize them as the men from the first council?" Tavin added. Mary only smiled knowingly.

"I guess you'd better come see for yourselves," she teased, turning. The two boys quickly followed after her, realizing she wanted to surprise them. As they left the bedroom hall, Tavin looked uncertainly to the Princess.

"Where's Ril this morning?" he asked, to which she smiled coyly again.

"I was wondering when you would ask," she replied with a giggle. "She woke ahead of you this morning and left her room to prepare for the ceremony. She wanted me to tell you not to look for her; she will find you when it begins." Tavin peered at her curiously, then to Jaren staring at him with an eyebrow raised.

"Calm down, boy," he commanded jokingly. "Half an hour out of two months of being together isn't going to kill you. And if it does, well, you deserve to die, you lovesick animal." Tavin grinned and slightly blushed, shaking his head.

"Well, Ril's accounted for, now what about her brother?" he asked, changing the subject. Mary gave a slight shrug.

"I haven't seen him since yesterday, but Ril assured me this morning that he would be present," she informed them. "He just doesn't want to be mentioned by name in the proceedings." Tavin frowned at that, upset the obviously still proud Drakkaidian Prince would not accept accommodation after all he had done to help them.

The trio pressed on down the levels of the Golden Castle until finally arriving at the Grand Vestibule to find a mass of busy servants bustling about to prepare for the impending ceremony. As the boys parted with Mary, Tavin and Jaren spotted a band of familiar faces attentively standing to the side of the hallway. Sprinting over to them, Kohlin Marraea, Parnox Guilldon, Captain Morrol, and Garoll Nelpia with a host of Legionnaires beside them, turned with beaming smiles. Jaren practically leapt at Parnox, wildly laughing in the jolly woodsman's arms. Tavin maintained himself in a more civilized manner, realizing Kohlin was still weak from his injuries at the battle in the Southland capital. They all greeted warmly, happy to see each other after everything was over at last. Though the Southlanders were eager to hear how Tavin had stopped Valif Montrox, they understood when he told them it was too long a story to begin now.

"I'm just happy you were able to make it with such short notice," Tavin smiled shaking Morrol's hand.

"Well, the new Sarton of the Legion is going to be a friend to Grandaria, I give you my word on that," he promised. "It was the least I could do after all you've done for us."

"And besides," Parnox interjected with a grin, "we Southlanders never miss a good party!" Jaren laughed and slapped the burly man's hand in agreement. As the group laughed, Tavin caught the dark figure of Verix Montrox leaning against the wall of the hallway away from them, his arms crossed. He stared with an unmoving smile but a passive look glistening over his crimson eyes. Tavin quickly excused himself from his friends for a moment, leisurely walking over to him.

"I thought you'd at least go out of your way to dress a little nicer for a ceremony like this," he said with a faint smile. Verix remained unaffected in his standard black clothes and his mended gray battle coat, shrugging his arms.

"What would you have me wear, Tavin?" he began sarcastically, "royal Grandarian battle armor like you?" He paused for a moment, searching Tavin's deep blue eyes. "Things are different now, friend, but I not going to forget who I am and where I come from. I am a Drakkaidian Prince, raised in center of our culture and traditions. Don't take offense, but this is all the fine dressing you'll get from me." Tavin looked at him for a long moment before finally nodding with understanding. As he convinced the Prince to join him and his friends, however, a servant rushed from the stage outside the exit of the Grand Vestibule and bowed before Tavin.

"The Supreme Granisian asked me to inform you that we are ready to begin, sir," he said quickly. "He will introduce you, then please come forward with your party on the stage below him." Tavin acknowledged him and bowed, releasing the man back to his duties. Moving to the side of the stage, Tavin and the others watched as the Kolior, his wife, and Mary rose from their thrones to call the massive crowds of Grandarians filling the courtyard to attention. They applauded rowdily for a moment, then quickly fell silent.

"Grandarians and friends, thank you for accepting our invitation to this most significant of assemblies today," the Supreme Granisian began in an authoritative yet majestic voice. "We gather today under the greatest of circumstances. We must celebrate a group of individuals who fought to destroy the evil that threatened to ensnare the world. As most of you know by now, the fabled Warrior of Light was reborn some time ago, and has been on a quest of epic proportions to stop Valif Montrox of Drakkaidia from subjugating the whole of Iairia under his tyrannical rule. He fought with the aid of Grandarians, Southlanders, and even helpful Drakkaidians, all contributing to this cause."

After Kolior's noble introduction, he briefly retold all that had come to pass from Montrox first finding the shard of darkness to the second Battle of the Gods days ago. At its end, he began honoring each of the individuals before him with Grandarian medals of honor. As Tavin watched his friends one by one move up to the Supreme Granisian's throne, he realized that Ril was still no where to be found. Sadness and confusion were tormenting his mind, and he almost didn't hear the Supreme Granisian announce his name to come forward. Gently nudging his arm, Jaren motioned for the Warrior of Light to get moving. Bringing his mind back to the task at hand, Tavin walked up to the throne and knelt. Kolior smiled warmly and motioned for Mary to come forward. Tavin was surprised to hear the Princess speak next.

"Tavinious Tieloc of Eirinor Village," she began proudly, "you have done our Grandaria and all of Iairia proud. Thanks to your true spirit and unflagging will, you have conquered the ultimate evil and saved us all. We owe you more than we can ever repay." She then leaned down and gently placed a gilded medal with the seal of Granis embossed inside around his neck. "Rise, Tavin." Before he could turn to face the crowds, the Supreme Granisian spoke once more.

"Tavinious, do you have the emerald?" he asked warmly. Tavin reached behind his back and pulled free the brilliantly shining form of the Holy Emerald. He nodded. "Proceed whenever you are ready, Tavin." He took a deep breath, then turned to face the crowd. With the emerald in hand, he closed his eyes and reached inside. With a flash of brilliant light, the Warrior of Light felt the world blur before him and his spirit drift out of his body.

Tavin opened his eyes to find his wish had come true once again. He stood in the center of a sprawling garden that stretched to infinity in every direction; luscious vegetation rich with color all around him. Above was a deep blue sky with puffy white billowing clouds gently floating by. Slowly turning his eyes back to the garden with a smile, Tavin heard the faint humming of someone crouched behind a row of shrubbery. Unhurriedly making his way around them, Tavin

657

spotted a familiar old man digging in the earth to make room for a golden flower beside him.

"I've been waiting for you," he chortled merrily. Tavin softly smiled.

"I wasn't sure what I'd find when I asked the emerald to take me to the Celestial World, but I can't say I'm surprised," he spoke calmly. The elderly man chuckled again and placed the golden flower inside the hole.

"Like I said," he began, filling the hole with fertile soil, "there's nothing friendlier than a garden." He smiled warmly at the boy, his deep blue eyes welcoming and kind. "Thank you for giving me mine back. I'm very proud of you, Tavin." Tavin didn't know what to do except smile back and slightly bow in response.

"So this is what the Celestial World looks like?" Tavin mused. Granis smiled and tilted his head.

"This is how it appears to you now, if that's what you mean," he answered obliquely, patting down the loose soil in the hole. "Just like me, Tavin, there is no physical form of the Celestial World you could comprehend as you are." Tavin gave him an honestly confused look, but smiled a quirky smile deciding to just accept what he was saying. Granis laughed as he reached for a wooden watering can resting beside him and poured a shower of pure water over the golden flower. "But I'm sure you didn't travel all the way here just to say hello. Why don't we get the little questions out of the way so we can get to the big one?" Tavin kept his gaze on the god, aware he could hide nothing from him.

"You don't even need to hear me ask the questions to be able to answer them, do you?" he began, shifting the weight on his feet and moving his white cape back over his shoulder. "You already know what I'm going to ask." Granis nodded, setting back down the watering can.

"I do," he acknowledged, "but you should know by now it is not my nature to hand mankind his answers. So ask me your questions, Tavin." The Warrior of Light nodded, a little taken aback at the response.

"Very well," he started. "Lord Granis, why didn't the emerald bring back Zeroan when I called for him?"

"You already know why," the god replied beginning to dig once more. Tavin frowned at him sadly, remembering what Verix had told him.

"He doesn't want to come back?" he asked hurt. "Why not?" Granis shot him a knowing glance and grabbed a handful of soil from beside him.

"That is something you should ask him, not me," he replied. Tavin remembered the image the Holy Emerald had shown him and nodded, realizing there was no point in furthering this particular inquiry.

"All right. I think I can guess the answer to this, but I want to know for sure. Why weren't the Sword of Granis and the Holy Emerald pulled into the void with Drakkan?" Granis tilted his head and smiled.

"Well, you would be somewhat right if you guessed, Tavin. You have the right idea, but it's a little more complex than what you're thinking. When Ril opened the gate to the void, it was under difference circumstances than the last time you opened it."

"The Holy Emerald was complete this time," Tavin continued for him. Granis nodded.

"That's right. With its power active and free in the world once more, it was able to flow to me as the void opened and I was given the strength to escape. Drakkan however, was still pulled in by the power of his void. The power of the emerald cannot leave the world, so it remained behind. The Sword of Granis remained for different reasons. First of all, its master did not enter the void this time. You remained in your world, so the sword did as well. Because it remained outside after the void sealed, it became connected to the portal itself. It is now the lock that will hold it closed and the key that can open it up. And only the Warrior of Light can pry it free." Tavin looked at him strangely, a dumb look in his eyes.

"I had no idea all of that would happen," he confessed. "I was just trying to seal Drakkan inside. I didn't mean for the sword to get stuck there." Granis shook his head.

"Don't worry, Tavin. I once told you I thought of the talisman as a key. It is an appropriate fate- it will be used to lock evil away for the rest of time." With that, the God of Light rose and removed his dirty gloves. "But why don't we put that aside for the moment. I know you don't have much time. There's an anxious crowd of Grandarians waiting for their Warrior of Light to come back to his senses, isn't there?" With a friendly smile, Granis raised his hand and, with the snap of his fingers, the world around them suddenly began to swirl together; all of the rich colors mixing into a white blanket below them. Peering down, Tavin saw they were now standing on a bank of transparent clouds. Below them was a green land mass so huge Tavin could feel his heart levitating with amazement.

"Is that..." he trailed off.

"Iairia," Granis answered softly. He slowly turned to face Tavin. "And now you have to decide what to do with it." The Grandarian boy's amazed expression slowly turned into one of painful dilemma. He brought up the shimmering Holy Emerald in his right hand and stared down at it.

"Granis, I shouldn't be the person making this decision," he confessed slowly. "What gives me the right to decide the fate of the entire world? I'm not even legally an adult yet..." The God of Light grinned and chuckled for a moment, then let his smile weaken.

"I know you are beleaguered with indecision, Tavin," he started friendly, "but this is the reason I left the prophesy of the Three Fates. Everything goes back to that first act by Drakkan that defined the nature of good and evil. Ever since that day these two forces have been on a collation force for this moment, vying to decide the destiny of the world. Drakkan and I are biased; beings completely comprised of one side or the other. We cannot make the choice, so mankind must do it. When I left the prophesy, I knew all of humanity could not make the decision because everyone wants different things. This is why the victor of the Final Battle of Destiny would choose. You may shine the light of the Celestial World downward to make heaven on earth, engulf the land in the darkness from below, or..." Tavin looked up to him uncertainly.

"Or what?"

"Or leave things as they are," Granis finished. Tavin started at him hard, trying to ferret out what the God of Light was attempting to say to him.

"Well I'm obviously not going to turn the world into hell, Lord Granis," he began, "but I don't have the first clue what to do with the other two choices. I mean, wouldn't it be best to make the world a paradise? If I chose to let your power return to the world, it would be perfect. There would never be pain, suffering, hunger, or sickness. Everyone would become equal." Granis nodded.

"That would be true, Tavin," he confirmed. "Everyone would become exactly the same. Forever happy and the same.

The question is, is that what you want for humanity?" Tavin's eyes fixated on the god's, unsure what he was saying.

"This is what Zeroan once told me," he said, remembering their conversation in the edge of the Great Forests. "I know I'd be nullifying the future of what we could become, but isn't it worth it? I have a chance to eliminate pain and suffering for the rest of time. How could I live with myself the next time I see someone lose a loved one, knowing I could have stopped it from happening by the decision I make today?" Granis held the flustered boy's gaze seriously.

"Everything you're saying is true, Tavin," he agreed, to which Tavin felt only more lost. "You have the opportunity to give the world paradise without end. The only thing you need to remember is, they will find that on their own one day. I created man with the knowledge that their lives in a world without my full power would not be perfect. There would be pain, suffering, and death. But after all of that, they have the chance to find their own paradise here in this world depending on their actions in life. The question before you now is, do you give humanity that life as they are born or do you give them the chance to work for it on their own? Do you give them the chance to build, create, evolve, and ascend by their own hands? Or do you simply wish to provide it for them?"

Tavin stared at the God of Light hard for the long pause that followed, his mind reeling with thoughts. Silencing them, he moved his gaze down to the brilliant stone in his hand. He still couldn't believe it; the power to do anything and everything in the palm of his hand. And it was all on him. He had been chosen to decide for everyone what should become of existence, and in that moment it was suddenly clear. There was only one choice he could make.

"Granis," he almost whispered, his eyes still glued to the emerald, "you've told me more than once that you didn't make mankind for yourself. You didn't make them to be subjects under your rule. It's no one's place to give them a new world, and that includes me." Tavin raised his stare back to Granis. "Humanity has done too much and come too far for me to simply erase all we have endured and accomplished on our own and give them a new destiny. It is up to them, to us, to shape our own world. Lord Granis, please take back the power that you granted me." He placed both hands on the Holy Emerald and raised it to his chest. "I choose the neutral fate. We will write our own density." With that, the Holy Emerald came alive with shimmering white light and began to slowly levitate out of his grasp. As it rose, the light spread to encompass the entire world around them until it gradually dematerialized, its energy fading back into all matter of the mortal world forevermore. Tavin felt his spirit drifting once again.

"You have chosen well, Tavinious Tieloc," the warm voice of Granis sounded one last time. "Go now to your world, Tavin, and live your life. Goodbye, my son."

Chapter 83

<u>Partings</u>

Tavin opened his eyes to find the last remnant of the gleaming white light from the Holy Emerald dissipating around him, revealing him to the massive crowd of mesmerized Grandarians before him. They were all quiet, unsure what had just taken place. Even the Supreme Granisian and Mary behind him stood silently, waiting. Sensing the hundreds waiting for him to say something, Tavin swallowed hard. There was so much he could tell them all, but he wasn't sure if they were ready to hear it. Deciding what to say and what not to, he nervously opened his mouth to loudly project his voice to the courtyard.

"The prophesies left behind by Lord Granis are fulfilled," he boomed as loud as he could. "The Holy Emerald is now one with the world, and we are free from the demonic power of Drakkan to live our lives in peace." Tavin stopped there, letting his voice drop. The crowd remained silent for another long moment, then exploded with wild applause and cheering. Tavin smiled with relief, just happy that they had accepted his vague explanation. As he began to turn to make his way back to Jaren and the others lined up next to the Supreme Granisian's throne, Kolior rose and called to him one last time.

"Tavinious," he beckoned cordially, "please remain a moment longer. There is one last matter of business to attend to." As the Warrior of Light froze and turned back to face him, the Kolior turned back to the cheering crowd to quiet them again. "After consulting with the Granisians in the church and as the acting ruler of Grandaria," he announced, "I am a making the Warrior of Light an official title of power in the Grandarian government. It will carry the same weight and responsibilities of the Supreme Granisian's Chief Advisor, but has special authority in times of peril." He turned back

663

to Tavin, his eyes wide and mouth open. "Should you choose to accept this title, Tavin, it would not be a full time position. You may still live your life as you wish outside of Galantia, but I hope that you will return periodically to advise us. What do you say, Warrior of Light?" Tavin stared at him with disbelief, then back to Jaren beaming at him from behind. Turing back, he smiled weakly and shrugged.

"Why not?" he actually laughed, to which Mary giggled with glee. "I mean, I'd be honored to accept this title, Your Highness. Thank you." Kolior smiled his regale smile once more and bowed to him.

"Thank you, Tavin," he expressed gratefully. Once again, the crowed flared up with applause. Mary then stepped forward and stopped before Tavin, motioning for quiet once more.

"No medal we can bestow upon you can ever express our gratitude, Tavin," she spoke softly, "but there is one last thing we have to present to you." Staring at the knowing little smile building on her face, Tavin curiously watched as she stepped away and motioned for two armored sentries on either side of a doorway in the Grand Vestibule draped with white cloth to take hold and spread them open. A slender figure tightly covered in an ornate white dress sown with deep red lining stepped forward, the tails it flowing back in the cool breeze with the long red hair cascading around her shoulders. Tavin felt the rest of the world fall away into insignificance, his sole attention focused on the beautiful girl slowly striding toward him. Stopping before him, Tavin felt a mist of tears cloud his eyes. Ril stood before him the most beautiful he had ever seen her, her ravishing smile deeply set into her joyful face.

"You said you liked seeing me in a dress," she smiled, inching forward coyly. "I thought this occasion might call for one." Tavin's mouth was open, but he could not speak the words he desperately wanted to say.

"Though Ril may not be Grandarian born," Mary said from the side, just loud enough for those on stage to hear, "she is a welcome member to our home. We want you to be together." Tavin shot her a quick glace of mixed emotion, before laying his eyes back on Ril, beaming.

"What do you think, Warrior of Light?" she asked alluringly. Tavin continued staring at her for a long moment before rushing forward and wrapping his arms around her waist, pulling her tightly against him to kiss her hard on her delicate lips. Though Ril had hoped Tavin would react positively to the surprise, he embraced her so quickly she was still astonished halfway through his kiss. Bliss coursing through her, Ril closed her amazed eyes and returned his kiss, letting him wrap his arms around her tighter still. From the moment they came together, the crowd once again burst alive, cheering wildly. As Tavin at last withdrew his head and opened his eyes, he saw Ril slowly open hers after him and beam with a tear of her own in her eyes. "I love you, Tavin," she whispered, her voice shaking with happiness.

"I think this is the best day of my life," he told her, his own voice pouring out with emotion. "I love you too, Ril." With that, they kissed again and the grand celebration began. Children sitting along the top halls of the castle above them gleefully began dropping blue, white, and gold confetti into the air to gently float down to the enthralled crowd. The regal trumpets burst to life around them. The group standing on the stage applauded the hardest, even Jaren's eyes going moist. As Tavin and Ril finally broke to turn and walk back to their friends, Tavin waved to the crowd one last time boosting their applause. The festivity that ensued lasted for the remainder of the day. Tavin and the others retreated back into the Grand Vestibule to sit and talk about what had happened since their last parting and to feast on the finest food and drink that the Golden Castle could provide. All the while Tavin and Ril remained inseparable with gleaming smiles on their faces.

The next day came all too soon for anyone. Tavin and Ril rose the earliest they had in days. Tavin dressed in his traditional blue and white casuals while Ril had found some of her own clothes that she was forced to leave behind when their adventure had began. Their friends from the Southland unfortunately had to be off immediately to the slightly chaotic Torrentcia City with the Legion assembled but no Sarton to deal with it. Rushing outside their room, Tavin and Ril went to Jaren's door and kicked it open. As Tavin had suspected, his friend lay snoring in his bed. Ril giggled as Tavin literally leapt onto his slumbering friend and wrestled him awake, pulling him free of his sheets.

After Jaren quickly dressed and vented his playful frustrations at the Warrior of Light, the trio set off for the courtyard to find a ride to the massive Gate Yard at the front of the city. When they arrived, the party of Southlanders,

Mary, and a host of servants, stood by the open gate, horses around them. Tavin and the others quickly walked up with sad smiles. The Windrun Warrior extended his hand to him, shaking it heartily.

"It appears this is it," he began softly," "I won't say goodbye because we're bound to see you sooner or later, Warrior of Light." Tavin grinned and nodded.

"You can bet on it," he confirmed. "Thank you for all your help, Kohlin. Take good care of yourself."

"Ah, don't worry, lad," came the burly voice from beside them. Parnox released his hands with Jaren and walked over to them. "I'll be there to watch over him." Tavin beamed once more.

"I feel better already, Parnox. You stay safe too." As Tavin and Jaren said their goodbyes to Sarton Morrol, Garoll, and the other Legionnaires that had come, Ril hugged Kohlin and Parnox goodbye.

"I couldn't have made it through this without you two," she smiled. "I think I might be spending a little more time up here from now on, but you can be sure I'll see you soon." Parnox laughed and gently patted her on the back.

"I look forward to it, young lady," he smiled.

"You take care of him, now," Kohlin told her looking to Tavin. "He's an incredible man. You deserve each other." Ril smiled with a deep breath, emotion in her voice again.

"Thank you for everything, Kohlin." They embraced quickly, the others already mounting their horses. Kohlin and Parnox rose to their steeds and waved goodbye a final time, Morrol leading them out of the golden city. As the group waved the Southlanders goodbye, Verix Montrox stepped out from behind the horse where he had been hiding and gradually made his way up to them. His crimson hair was combed back revealing the whole of his serene face.

"Well," he started slowly to Tavin and Ril, "I think I should be on my way as well." Both of them instantly frowned.

"Verix," Tavin began with concerned impatience in his voice, "I was hoping you would stay with us from now on." The Drakkaidian Prince quietly laughed, a tired smile on his face.

"I appreciate the gesture, Tavin," he stated, "but I've already overstayed my welcome. I told you before- I'm a raised Drakkaidian Prince. My place is in my home with my people. The Southlanders may have a city in chaos to return to, but

I have a nation in chaos waiting for me. With my father dead and our High Priest the weak fool he is, there is no leadership. It is up to me to bring Drakkaidia back together." The Dark Prince could see the pain and frustration with his decision in Tavin's eyes particularly. His face tightened with seriousness. "Tavin, I may be going back, but it doesn't mean things are going back to the way they were. Like you, I see the world with new eyes. Grandaria is no longer my enemy. I promise you that as long as I draw breath, you will not see aggression from Drakkaidia. I have a nation to rebuild, and hopefully I can build a new sense of fellowship with Grandaria in the hearts of my people. It won't be easy to change eons of hatred, but I am going to try."

He stopped there, looking to Ril with hurt in her face as well. Verix slowly softened and took her hand in his.

"I'm glad I was finally able to find you, my sister," he spoke looking down to their hands. "It did me good." Pausing for a moment, he used his free hand to reach into his gray coat and pull free something that caught Ril's eye. It was her half of the Red Pennant. "I wanted to offer this back to you. Not to remember the family you come from, but... the brother that loves you." Ril pulled her eyes off the locket to meet his gaze, soft and pure. With streaming tears, she rushed forward to embrace him. Her hand fell onto the scarlet object and tightly gripped it.

"I won't ever forget you, Verix," she promised. "I love you too." They were together for a long moment, but eventually Verix leaned back and nodded, his fiery eyes once again moist. Blinking rapidly and wiping the tears away, he nodded and turned to mount his horse. Turning it toward the people at his feet, he locked his eyes back onto Tavin.

"Thank you for what you have done, Tavin," he said, honesty and benevolence the elements in his voice. "Thank you for trusting me when you did, and thank you for giving me back my home. I am forever in your debt." Tavin smiled up to him.

"I couldn't have done anything without you, Verix. And if you ever need help for anything, we'll be here." Verix nodded, and gently bowed.

"Until we next meet then, Tavin Tieloc," he said. With that, the proud Drakkaidian Prince Verix Montrox turned for the gateway and trotted out of Galantia toward home.

Tavin, Ril, and the others watched Verix ride into the west until he was completely out of view, then returned to the Golden Castle, eating breakfast as a group and retiring back to their rooms to prepare for the day. Nearly an hour later, Tavin and Ril made their way back to find Jaren and Mary walking into the Grand Vestibule from an errand in the courtyard. A cool breeze blew through the ornate golden hallway, gently pushing them on. As his best friend came into view, Jaren's brow furrowed. He and Ril were both wearing heavy clothing and packs of supplies over their backs.

"Just what is going on here?" he asked curiously. Tavin smiled as he closed the gap between them, putting a hand on his friend's shoulder.

"Ril and I have one last thing to do before this is completely over, buddy," he told him with a smile. Jaren's eyes went wide with disbelief.

"What in the name of Granis on high are you talking about?" he asked incredulously. "We won! It's over! I know its going to be tough going home after all this adventure- you know, with no demons or anything trying to kill us- but come on man! What do you still have to do?"

"We're just going to tie up some loose ends from when you weren't with us," he said. "We have to go back to the Southland, so it may be a while." Jaren stared at him for a long moment, then let out a dramatic huff of air and opened his arms.

"Okay," he gave in hopelessly, "come here, you." Tavin laughed and hugged his friend goodbye. "You be careful down there. The bad guys are gone, but you don't have your Granis power any more, so-"

"We'll be fine, mom," Tavin joked as they pulled apart. Jaren grinned.

"Speaking of which, I think I'll be going home pretty soon too," he announced, to which Mary looked at him with a hurt frown.

"You're leaving, Jaren?" she asked quickly. The Grandarian boy turned to her with a smile and wrapped an arm around her neck.

"Well, I was thinking of taking you with me, actually," he told her with a grin. "I figure my parents can't punish me too bad if I have the Princess with me." Mary giggled and said she would love it. All of them laughed and said their final goodbyes. "I'll see you when you get home, buddy."

"I can't wait," Tavin smiled back, turning to take Ril's hand and start down the hallway into the courtyard. Jaren and Mary waved goodbye until they were gone, then turned back for the castle.

Chapter 84

<u>Not Goodbye</u>

Nearly a month later, Tavin and Ril arrived at the First Tree beneath Keracon Valley. They had traveled south on Nighcress at a leisurely pace, just happy to enjoy the pleasure of each other's company. Though they had been together for over two months prior, it was the first time they had ever traveled together without someone driving them forward like mules, the worries of the world on their shoulders, or the constant threat of demonic forces after them. Both of them found they enjoyed each other even more without these elements in their life. As they moved south, they made a few brief stops along the way including a visit to Eirinor Village at Ril's request. Though Tavin didn't want to be stuck there explaining where he had been for the past two months and what he had been doing, he discovered his parents already knew. Apparently, they had received an invitation to the award ceremony the previous day and had been told everything by the Supreme Granisian himself.

While they were nothing short of awestruck and astounded at their son's exploits, both of Tavin's parents, particularly his mother, were more interested in the fiery haired young lady he had kissed in front of the entire Grandarian capital when he arrived with her in tow. Though they were tentative at first, Ril quickly found that Tavin had been right the day they flew over the cozy village: they both loved her. Informing them they had one last errand to run to complete their grand adventure, the Tielocs reluctantly said their goodbyes once more and saw them off.

After Tavin and Ril passed through the Great Rift and entered the Southland, they decided they would retrace the steps they had taken on their quest for the shards. From finding the creek outside Agealin Town where Tavin's mysterious sickness had struck the hardest, to passing by Torrentcia

City and Greenwall themselves, they covered every inch of the land they had seen. As they found themselves at the end of the Grailen and the edge of the western Great Forests where they had emerged with Verix, the duo dismounted Nighcress and let the mystical steed run free. Zeroan had told them he was an ancient ally of the sages and his place was not in a stable.

Moving into the forest, they had little difficulty retracing their steps to the entrance of Keracon Valley. Looking up into the infinite heights of the trees around them, they remembered the signs the cronoms had taught them to look for if they ever needed to find the First Tree. Arriving at the base of the massive trunk, they were both surprised to find the pulley platform that connected the treetop village to the earth was resting at the forest floor. Exchanging curious glances at each other, Tavin and Ril carefully stepped onto the platform. Though it remained still for a moment, they were both surprised to feel it jerk up and slowly ascend into the trees. Just like on the way down, it was a beautiful ride up through the branches of the massive forest.

As the intricate rope bridges of the village came into view, both Tavin and Ril could hear their names being called from above. With warm smiles they looked up to find a familiar blonde haired girl waving wildly and literally leaping up and down with excitement. Rising alongside the sturdy wooden catwalk, Kira Marcell leaped at them both with open arms. As he returned the little girl's embrace, Tavin looked up to find Yerbacht and the rest of the cronom elders waiting for them with broad smiles. Apparently word had been passed up through the trees by the cronoms watching the forest floor that they were moving toward the First Tree and the platform had been lowered for them.

After greeting Kira and the cronoms, Tavin respectfully informed them that they needed to use the Sapphire Pool one last time. The gracious Yerbacht was only too happy to oblige, leading them back to the Grand Hall and the Chamber of Elders. Asking the enthralled Kira to wait with the cronoms while they finished their business, the two ascended the stairs and stepped onto the balcony holding the enchanted pool. Moving forward to dump a handful of the azure powder Yerbacht had given him into the still liquid in the hollowed tree stump, the pool instantly began to swirl to life again. Stepping back to take Ril's hand, they watched anxiously as the cobalt fluid came alive with deep blue light and formed a column of liquid sculpting itself into a familiar robed figure.

As the pool at last settled, Tavin and Ril found themselves looking at the liquid spirit of the Mystic Sage Zeroan. The hood usually concealing his haggard bearded face was pulled down, revealing a soft smile over his lips.

"Hello again, my young friends," he softly spoke in a tired but contented tone of voice neither of the two had ever heard from him before. "I was hoping you would arrive soon." Both Tavin and Ril beamed.

"Why am I not surprised you knew we were coming?" Tavin asked with a smile. Zeroan shrugged.

"I am a sage after all," he replied. "And now I can see more than you can imagine, Tavin. Though I could not be there physically, I also saw your battle with Drakkan. Despite all that was against you; all the power he had that you did not, you still defeated him. There are no words in this world or the next to describe the pride I have for you. For both of you." Both Tavin and Ril thanked him modestly. Though Tavin was happy to see his friend once more, the pain of his loss was renewed by his appearance.

"Zeroan, Granis told me I couldn't revive you with the emerald because you didn't want to return," he said uncertainly. "Why?" The sage's smile softened, and he shifted in his fluidic robes as if standing before them like always.

"Tavin," he began slowly, "do you know how old I am?" The Warrior of Light stared at him perplexed, but finally shook his head no. "I once told you I sensed a shard of the Holy Emerald in the hands of a Tieloc before. That was your ancestor, the first Warrior of Light. I was a Mystic Sage even back in the time of Taurin Tieloc. I have lingered in the mortal world far after my time to leave it, waiting for this time of prophesy that was just fulfilled. Now it is over. I have lived a long life, my friends. It is time for me to at last rest." An obvious hurt was in both Tavin and Ril's eyes, growing with each word he spoke.

"But Zeroan," Ril pleaded, "if it wasn't for you neither of us would be standing here right now. I'd be a Drakkaidian Princess and Tavin would have been murdered by demons I could have sent to kill him. If it wasn't for you we couldn't have succeeded in our quest to stop Montrox. The world needs you, Zeroan." The sage silently chuckled at the girl's words.

"Thank you for the vote of confidence, Arilia," he smiled, "but my time in Iairia is complete. I have taken it upon myself to look after the world for long enough. Now it is someone else's turn."

"You mean us?" Tavin asked uncertainly, to which the sage laughed once more.

"You two have enough to worry about in your new life with each other and your responsibilities as the Warrior of Light. I would not lay such a charge down to you." Ril gave him a confused look.

"Then who?" she pressed.

"That will be revealed in time, Ril," he stated, his form beginning to wane in the pool. "Listen to me now, my friends. I am grateful for your friendship, but our time together has come to an end. It is my time to rest now. But you two must remain on the alert. The Mystic Sages are all but gone from the lands now, and will not return until they are ready. Without them, the Elemental Warriors will disappear as well. In their absence, you two and your future family will be one of the last bearers of the powerful magics left in the world. Remember that the evil of Drakkan has been sealed away, but it is not destroyed. It is your responsibility and that of those who come after you to make sure it is never allowed to return. There are other dangers in the world besides that of Drakkan, and eventually they will surface. It may not be in your lifetime, it may not be in that of your children or your grandchildren, but someday it will happen. When it does, you must be ready. You must pass on the legacy of your family, Tavin."

As the sage's charge fell upon them, Tavin and Ril kept his gaze with determination and strength. Zeroan smiled at the courage he could see in their eyes.

"In the meantime, enjoy your new life together, young ones," he continued. "Though I will be very happy to be free of his voice for the rest of eternity, tell Jaren I will miss him." Tavin grinned and silently laughed, looking down to the floor and nodding his head. As he brought his eyes back to the sage, they were torn with happiness and mourning.

"We're never going to see you again, are we?" he asked softly. Zeroan smiled gently again.

"Not even I can answer that for sure, Tavinious," he stated. "For now, however, my spirit will remain over Iairia in the winds. Perhaps someday we may meet again." Tavin and Ril smiled up to him, holding each other close. As Zeroan spoke again, his words were quiet. "I am so proud of you both. Arilia, your valor to do the right thing and be there for Tavin when he could have otherwise lost the will to keep going was invaluable, and I hope you can forgive me for keeping the truth about your past hidden for so many years. I know you have never thought much of me, but I have always respected you for the amazing young woman you have become." As the sage's voice destabilized, Ril in particular softened to him like never before.

"I can never thank you enough for all you've done for me, Zeroan," she said back, shaking. "I love you like a father." Zeroan smiled and nodded, at last turning to Tavin.

"There is nothing I even need to say about you, my young Grandarian," he said calmly. "Everyone knows as well as I do the incredible young man you are. I could speak of your unstoppable determination to do what is right and your self-sacrificing nature to help everyone around you before yourself, but we already know all those things. I just hope you yourself realize the admiration we have for you, Tavinious. You have already done more in your life for the good of the world than anyone ever before you. Let me speak for Iairia when I say... thank you." With that, the sage's liquid form began to slosh back and forth ready to fall back into the pool. Tavin's emotional face looked one him as he began to fade. His voice was distant as he spoke on last time. "Now, it is time for me to take my leave, but do not let your hearts be troubled. Anytime the wind blows around you I will be in it, looking in on you. Take care of each other, my friends. Goodbye..."

His final words echoing into the branches of the Great Forests, the liquid form of the Mystic Sage Zeroan did not fall back into the Sapphire Pool, but rose and evaporated into the air, the faint breeze catching it and lifting it into the sky. Tavin and Ril stood watching as the last remnant of his spirit dissipated into the atmosphere, then turned to each other with emotion in their eyes. Ril leaned against him, mixed tears of joy and sorrow falling down her delicate cheeks. As the Warrior of Light raised his hand to her cascading crimson hair, he breathed deeply, the last of his lament for the sage emptying itself out. They stood in each other's arms for several long minutes before Tavin at last forced a smile, realizing Zeroan would want him to be happy now. He looked down to Ril and gently raised her head up to meet his with a finger under her chin. Her warm eyes fell to his, instantly generating a smile.

"I'm so glad I have you, Ril," he told her gingerly, wiping the last tear in her eyes away.

"Me too," she whispered back, pulling in to gently kiss him on his lips. "I love you, Tavin." A warm smile spread over his face, a shaft of golden light shining down on them from the tops of the trees. For the first time for as far back as he could remember, everything in the world felt right. Reaching down to take Ril's hand in his, the two turned to walk back into the cronom village together.

Tales of Iairia

Shards of Destiny

The End

Special Thanks from the Author to the following people for their support in making the publication of this book possible:

1) Mom, Dad, and Jenna
2) Grandma and Grandpa Tullis
3) Grandma and Grandpa Thomas
4) Grandma and Grandpa White
5) Mike Blanchard
6) Kyle Pearson
7) Tanner Meloy
8) Cody Skipton
9) Megan Cyr
10) Mary LaBissoniere
11) Brigitte Miller
12) Amy Heinze
13) Rachael Glaspie
14) Meggie Graf
15) McKenzie Headly
16) Jake Hanson
17) Alex Kaluza
18) Mike Smith
19) Glynnis O'Connell
20) Eddie Jenkins
21) Samantha Door
22) Rowan Ringer
23) Morgen Anyan
24) Ashlee Piper
25) Nick Hater
26) Ariel Berube
27) Sue Ford
28) Michelle McCartney
29) Kristen Harris
30) Angie Ozanich

Printed in the United States
44456LVS00001BA/46-510

9 781425 900427